Millennium's Dawn

MILLENNIUM'S DAWN

Ed Stewart

VICTOR BOOKS

A DIVISION OF SCRIPTURE PRESS PUBLICATIONS INC.
USA CANADA ENGLAND

More fiction by Ed Stewart
Millennium's Eve
The Pancake Memos and Other Stories for Growing Christians
A Window to Eternity: Twelve Short Stories Based on the Sayings of Christ

Copyediting: Carole Streeter; Barbara Williams
Cover Design: Paul Higdon
Cover Illustration: Gary Meyer

1 2 3 4 5 6 7 8 9 10 Printing / Year 98 97 96 95 94

Millennium's Dawn

DEDICATION

To my family,
Carol, Kenneth, Kristine, Jim, and Olivia.
This achievement would be hollow if I couldn't enjoy it with you!

To the "Pinochle Club"
and to our Care Group at Sunset Church.
Thanks for asking, "How's the writing going this week, Ed?"
and for reminding me, "We're praying for you."
I couldn't have done it without you!

FRIDAY
June 22, 2001

One

The forest-green 1999 Mercedes 850 SEL kept pace with three lanes of heavy Stadium Way traffic speeding through Elysian Park. The expensive sedan was only two years old, but several layers of road film and numerous fender dings allowed it to blend in with the cheaper Buicks, Fords, Bolt 770s, and Zap Runabouts surrounding it. The image and anonymity of slovenly wealth had been carefully planned by the Mercedes' driver and those he worked with.

The endless stream of cars coursing into Elysian Park was an offshoot of the raging river of traffic on the Golden State Freeway at 6:30 P.M. this June evening. As the work force in Los Angeles escaped the city for the suburbs, a small fraction of L.A.'s nine million residents—a paltry 30,000 or so—peeled off the freeways onto arterial roads like this one which emptied into Chavez Ravine. Nearly fifty years earlier the O'Malleys of Brooklyn, New York selected the sprawling, brush-choked Ravine as the new site for their thriving family business. Walter O'Malley's Brooklyn Dodgers moved west to become the Los Angeles Dodgers, and Chavez Ravine, overlooking L.A.'s bustling Civic Center, was transformed into the Dodger Stadium complex.

The surging traffic slowed as it neared the Stadium entrance. Sweeping around the bend from Stadium Way onto Academy Road, the stream of cars and vans expanded to a broad tide ebbing toward six automated ticket dispensers. The row of four-foot metal sentries stood against the flow of cars like a dam holding back a reservoir. At the dispenser, an inserted bank card was debited $5 in nanoseconds and the driver received a parking pass. Lines of ticketed cars then dribbled like rivulets over a spillway from the elevated stadium entrance into the massive parking lot surrounding the ball park.

The dirty green Mercedes crawled behind a line of cars toward a distant ticket dispenser. The man at the wheel and his passenger had not spoken since they left downtown for their purposely circuitous route to the Stadium. They were neither friends nor business associates. And even though they were dressed like baseball fans—one of them wearing a monogrammed Dodger cap and the other a black windbreaker sporting the logo of the Colorado Rockies—they had not come to the Stadium on this warm summer evening to enjoy major league baseball.

"I don't think I'm ready for this, Donatelli," the passenger said soberly. He stared straight ahead and nervously fingered the zipper on his windbreaker.

Donatelli snorted with disdain and flicked a cold glance across the seat. He was husky, well over six feet, with a large head and exaggerated brows and jaw. A mass of unruly black and silver hair cascaded from beneath his baseball cap. His cheeks and chin were pockmarked with acne scars and shaded with black stubble. His nose appeared to have been broken several times.

Donatelli was too ugly to be a cop—which made him perfect for undercover work.

"I guess that's just tough, isn't it, Jakes?" Donatelli said, chewing on a cigarette which flooded the cabin with acrid smoke and sprinkled ashes on the man's shirt as he spoke. "You had your choice, man: this operation or the penitentiary," he continued, easing the Mercedes forward in line. "I still think we should lock you up, whether you work with us or not. You broke the law; you should pay the price. Clemency for informants . . . " He broke off as the words turned sour in his mouth. Then he swore.

"Clemency *and protection*," Jakes corrected. "The Feds promised that if I take you to the guy you want, they will—"

"I know what they promised you, Jakes," Donatelli snapped, "and I couldn't care less. You just play the game tonight until you convince your partners to mention the big man's name for the DEA's ears, or the whole deal's off. And if you blow my cover, man, I swear I'll see to it that you get a one-way ticket to the federal pen for felony trafficking— if I don't shoot you first."

Jakes considered Donatelli's veiled threat to be more than just an attempt to scare him into compliance. He had watched the burly undercover Los Angeles policeman stuff a loaded Colt Anaconda .44 Magnum with stainless-steel finish into the waistband of his corduroy pants before they left Parker Center downtown. It wasn't a police-issue weapon; it was the kind of street gun any up-and-coming dealer might carry, which was precisely the image Donatelli hoped to sell to Jakes' co-conspirators after the baseball game.

"Won't they pat you down and find the gun and call off the deal?" Jakes had asked Donatelli during the briefing at Parker Center.

"They expect me to be packing," the cop had answered smugly. "If they want to see my weapon, I'll pull out my old .44, nice and easy. If they want to hold it while we talk, I'll hand it over butt first. By showing them my steel cannon so willingly, they probably won't notice my little Panda."

Donatelli had patted the lower pant leg of his cords as he spoke. A lightweight, polymer automatic pistol of Chinese manufacture, dubbed the Panda because of its innocent appearance and deadly punch, was strapped to the inside of his calf. Donatelli's compact plastic Panda couldn't blow a hole in a target like the Colt .44. But it could deliver its ten rounds in less than three seconds, turning its target into a sieve.

The Mercedes crept slowly toward the automated dispenser. Jakes thought about Donatelli's ample firepower in the light of his own defenselessness. "Shouldn't I be carrying some . . . protection . . . in case something goes wrong?" he asked. "After all, I'm the one wearing the body wire." Jakes touched the shoulder of his black nylon windbreaker where a thread-thin mike and transmitter had been sewn into the seam. It was undetectable to the human eye.

Donatelli blew a derisive laugh. "You seem to forget, Jakes—you're one of the bad guys. We don't give guns to bad guys. Besides, these scumbags trust you. You're one of them, and you're just bringing me in to make a big buy. The only protection you need is your act. If you sell me to your friends tonight, you're home free. But if you screw up, you deserve to be wasted by these hoods. And if it comes to a firefight and I have to drop you to get to them, I'll do it, Jakes. I swear I will."

Jakes believed him.

Donatelli crushed his smoldering butt on the floor mat with the heel of his boot and immediately lit another, exhaling a billow of smoke. The air conditioning couldn't draw away the polluted air as fast as Donatelli produced it. Jakes noticed a steady twitch in the driver's hand as he fingered the smoldering cigarette. Donatelli's chain-smoking, coarse, defensive demeanor, and nervous twitch made Jakes uneasy.

As the car pulled within three lengths of the dispenser, Jakes gazed past Donatelli to a driveway leading away from the Stadium entrance. The sign beside the road read LOS ANGELES POLICE ACADEMY. *That's where the backup team will be concealed tonight,* Jakes remembered with relief. The proximity of the Academy on the hillside to the north of Dodger Stadium is precisely why Jakes' superiors had selected the south rim of the parking lot for the post-game rendezvous with a new "dealer."

If something goes haywire, Jakes assured himself, *I can make it to the Academy for protection.* Then a cloud quickly darkened his optimism. *But nothing better go wrong, or the cops won't let me off like they promised. I have to deliver them a drug kingpin or I spend the next ten to fifteen years in the penitentiary.*

They finally reached the ticket dispenser and Donatelli zipped down the power window and secured a parking pass with a bank card from his wallet. The card was a fake, of course, as was Donatelli's complete ID package. He had been sold to and checked out by Jakes' superiors as Teddy Brukow, a former Teamster goon and ex-convict from Chicago. The real Teddy Brukow had been strangled by a fellow prisoner in Joliet Prison two weeks earlier and his ID marketed to LAPD for undercover purposes.

Donatelli's Mercedes had been selected from a vast fleet of confiscated vehicles in the LAPD impound garage to sweeten the con act. The grimy green sedan had once belonged to a high-living pimp who was busted during a vice raid along the Sunset Strip.

"Let's go over this again, Jakes, to make sure you've got it straight," Donatelli said, as he maneuvered the Mercedes through the traffic flowing counterclockwise around the Stadium.

Jakes groaned inwardly as the reality of what would happen in a few hours twisted a knot in his stomach. He knew the plan thoroughly, but he reluctantly recited it again to placate the on-edge cop who held his life in his hands. "We park on the south side of the lot overlooking the city, away from the crowds. We watch the game from the right-field pavilion, sitting in the open where Chance and Fernandez can see us through the binoculars."

Donatelli grunted agreement and blew another cloud of smoke. "Try to look like you're enjoying the game, Jakes," he said curtly. "If your goons see that you're uptight, they won't talk. And if I don't get my bad guy, you don't walk."

Jakes nodded servilely and continued. "After the game we hang out at the car, drinking beer as the crowd thins. When Chance and Fernandez drive up, we offer them a beer and talk loudly about the game. When most of the cars around us are gone, they will check you for weapons and wires."

"This is critical, Jakes," Donatelli interrupted, adding a curse and coughing a smoker's cough. "Don't turn on your wire until those hoods put away their wand."

Jakes nodded again. The cop had drummed the command into him countless times. Jakes brushed his fingers over the remote on-off switch secreted in the watchband on his left wrist. He had only to touch the band while ostensibly checking the time and the body wire in his jacket would be activated, opening a channel to the backup team of undercover LAPD officers and federal DEA agents waiting on the Academy grounds.

"If they detect that transmitter on you, man," Donatelli continued threateningly, pointing at Jakes, "your life is over."

Yours too, jerk, Jakes retorted silently, fear mounting at the vision of guns being drawn and fired in a life-and-death confrontation. *I may catch the first bullet, but the second one will surely drop you.*

Jakes tried to calm himself by continuing with the ideal scenario, the plan to which both the law and his "employers" had independently agreed. "Once Chance and Fernandez see that you're clean, they'll bring out bags containing sixty kilos and exchange it for our bag containing $620,000. I will get them to speak Fryman's name as the kingpin of the operation. The whole deal will be filmed and recorded from the Academy for evidence.

"When the deal is done, we leave the way we came in. Before Fryman's people know what hit them, the drug team at the Academy will swoop in to 'take them off,' as you guys say."

Jakes decided not to verbalize the final scene of the drama—the one most important to him—thinking it would irritate Donatelli further. Once clear of the Stadium, Jakes was to be spirited into protective custody to await the arrest and trial of the primary target of this operation: Jakes' boss, G. Billy Fryman. Jakes would testify in federal court against Fryman and his lieutenants, and they would be convicted. After the verdict Jakes would collect his reward: his freedom and two plane tickets to anywhere in the world he wanted to go. He had calculated that by Christmas, he and Margo would be so far from his past and the police and the claws of G. Billy Fryman that they could live the rest of their lives in peace. He wasn't sure where they would go, but he hoped it would be a place where there was no Los Angeles on a map.

Donatelli didn't speak again until after he had backed the Mercedes up to the guardrail, at the southern perimeter of the Stadium parking lot. Beyond the guardrail the terrain fell off to a steep, brushy slope that cascaded 100 feet into an old residential district. In the distance the skyline of downtown Los Angeles faded to a silhouette against a twilight horizon that showed pale blue, pink, orange, and rust, all dulled by the ubiquitous L.A. haze. In front of the two men were acres of asphalt teeming with cars jockeying for parking spaces and eager baseball fans hurrying to their seats. In the middle of the parking lot stood the Stadium.

For a few seconds after Donatelli shut off the engine, all was silent. The city behind them and the crowds before them were muted in the distance. The scene suddenly appeared surreal to Jakes, as if he were trapped in an undersea capsule surrounded by a dangerous world he wasn't equipped to inhabit. The world outside the Mercedes' doors tonight was swimming with fearsome sea monsters: kilos of deadly drugs, unconscionable criminals, undercover police, and lethal weapons. This wasn't his world, at least it hadn't been up until the last few years, when a seemingly harmless tide had pulled him under and dragged him to the depths.

The real world—Jakes' world—was at the surface: freedom from fear and days of leisure and love with a magnificent woman. But the only way to reach his world was to swim through the murky, beast-infested world which would encompass him for the next three hours. His unlikely partner in his dash to freedom was the swarthy, trigger-happy, would-be drug buyer sitting beside him. Jakes realized he would be swimming for his life, and the thought of depending on Donatelli for his success brought a new wave of panic.

The momentary tranquility was abruptly terminated by a loud, metallic *clack-clack* that caused Jakes to flinch. He snapped his head left to see Donatelli checking his .44. The cop rubbed his fingers reverently over the barrel where the model name, Anaconda, was engraved, as if calling on the spirit of the deadly snake for good luck. Then he returned the gun to his waistband where an oversized, zipped-up, blue sweat jacket would conceal the bulge on his hip.

Donatelli pointed to the paper grocery sack at Jakes' feet, and his look communicated, "Get with it." Jakes pulled the contents out of the bag and laid them on his lap: a man's wig, medium length, light brown; a well-worn Panama straw hat with a narrow brim and a black band advertising a Mexican beer; a pair of aviator sunglasses; and a fake mustache the color of the wig.

It was agreed by all parties that Jakes would enter the Stadium in this simple disguise, not to conceal his identity from the cops or the criminals—they knew who he was and what he was doing—but from the fans. Nolan Jakes wasn't exactly famous, but he was still a recognizable personality in Los Angeles. And no one, especially Jakes, wanted an already dicey drug deal complicated by the intrusion of unknowing citizens wanting to shake hands with the "Zap Man."

Jakes pulled the wig over his half-inch, blonde crew cut and topped it with the hat. He peeled the adhesive away from the mustache and pressed it onto his upper lip, checking his reflection in the visor mirror to get it straight.

"Okay, Jakes, you know what to do," Donatelli said at last, lighting up a fresh smoke. "Let's go watch a ball game and then make it happen." He seemed as matter-of-fact about the deal as if he were ordering a hot dog, Jakes thought, except for the nervous twitch in his fingers.

The two men stepped out of the car, slipped their shades into place, and started toward the Stadium. As he walked, Jakes found himself trembling with fear. His stomach boiled acid into the back of his throat. He hoped he wouldn't be sick in public.

Jakes could only hope that the ploy in which he was a less than willing participant was working. But his churning gut screamed at him that it couldn't possibly work against an elusive drug baron like G. Billy Fryman. Jakes writhed inside at the unbidden words that drummed ever louder in his brain: *Nolan Jakes, tonight your life is over!*

Two

Dr. Evan Rider hurried toward the elevator as fast as he could without breaking into a trot. Still, his lab coat flapped at his sides, keys and instruments jingled in his pockets, and his dark, wavy hair, sparsely flecked with gray, bounced with every long stride. Evan hoped he didn't appear to be scrambling to a red-blanket or straight-line crisis. Such frantic activity alarmed people and provoked questions, and Dr. Rider didn't have time for unnecessary questions. So he kept walking quickly while smiling and nodding to hospital staff and patients as if on a casual stroll.

Evan had a squared, chiseled but pleasant face, with large, alert hazel eyes. He despised facial hair, which was unfortunate considering the dark, heavy growth he had inherited from his father. Five o'clock shadow on Evan appeared closer to midnight, so he often shaved twice a day, especially when his appointments or social engagements kept him in the public eye beyond office hours. The doctor had shaved for the second time today only moments earlier in his office across the street. And he would have been appalled to learn that, in his haste, he had left a tiny dab of shave cream behind his left ear.

Evan reached the elevators and noted from the digital wall display that the nearest car was three floors away. He glanced at his watch and sighed impatiently: 7:07 P.M. Pushing open the door marked STAIRS, he bounded up four flights—three stairs at a time—from the second to the fourth floor. The trim, six-foot, 170-pound, forty-year-old physician was in excellent condition. He barely exerted himself during the rapid climb.

Dr. Rider didn't usually race through his rounds at Ventura's Community Memorial Hospital. He was a detail-conscious, caring internist in private practice who took no shortcuts in the care of his patients. As a result, a normal day in his office at the Community Medical Plaza across the street often continued into the evening—*late* evening on many days—as he managed the care of his patients. And he never begrudged the long hours. Caregiving was his calling—and his livelihood.

But Dr. Rider couldn't stay late tonight. He had to be out the hospital door by 7:20 at the latest. Even now his home was filling with guests on one of the most important nights of his life—and he was the host! As much as he despised quantifying his ministrations by the clock, he had to do it tonight, especially on this last call.

Hustling through the stairway door and onto the fourth floor, Evan resumed his hurried pace along the carpeted hallway, smoothing his hair as he went. He stopped at the busy nurse's station long enough to scan the computerized chart of his only patient on this floor: Larry Kaiser, age fifty-three, in room 441. Evan Rider had been Larry's general practitioner in the beach community of Ventura for almost nine years.

Two days earlier, Larry's off-road motorcycle ride in the hills above Ojai had ended with an ambulance ride to the emergency room. An ugly fall had resulted in a compound fracture of the left femur and numerous abrasions and contusions. Assured by the emergency room trauma team that Larry was free of serious internal injury, Evan had turned his patient over to Dr. Robert Finnegan, Ventura County's leading orthopedic surgeon, who expertly repaired the leg. Thanks to the wonders of medical technology, Larry would be back on his trail bike before summer was over.

On Evan's previous rounds Larry had checked out fine: vital signs strong, no evidence of internal bleeding or damaged organs. Evan didn't have time to see Larry again, and he really didn't *need* to see him. Dr. Finnegan was handling follow-up visits on the surgery, and he would doubtless be sending Larry home tomorrow. But Evan's personal follow-up schedule required him to pay one more visit—a mere formality in light of how well Larry was progressing. So Evan had saved it till last, hoping to be in and out in five minutes or less.

Evan breezed into room 441. Committed to presenting a professional appearance when so many physicians in Ventura had opted for casual summer wear, he was dressed in dark slacks and leather oxfords. He wore a long-sleeve dress shirt in a subdued print and solid tie under his white lab coat. Evan's year-round tan was a by-product of his love for gardening around his hillside home and for surfing Ventura's beaches.

Larry Kaiser was flat on his back, watching baseball on television with his left leg—in a cast—displayed on two pillows like a prize albacore on ice. His deeply tanned face and arms were splotched crimson and blue with scrapes and bruises, looking like he had been caught in no-man's-land during a free-for-all between two warring groups of painters.

A skinny teenaged girl sat in a chair on the far side of the bed, playing chess on her pocket computer.

"Hello, Larry," Evan said pleasantly, walking directly to the bedside. "How are you feeling today?" It was the standard question Evan asked patients all day every day. Evan's friends often chided him for greeting them at parties with the same generic question.

Larry smiled broadly. "Great, doc," he said, reaching for the bed controls to sit himself up a little, "except for a bad case of cabin fever. When can I get out of here?" Larry muted the ball game.

"That's Dr. Finnegan's call, Larry." Evan pulled a stethoscope out of his coat pocket and adjusted it in his ears as he spoke. "But it looks like you'll be out of here tomorrow." He placed the scope on Larry's chest and said, "How about a few deep breaths." Larry complied, taking a fresh breath with each movement of the instrument. Then the doctor repeated the process with the scope on Larry's back.

"Lungs sound clear," Evan reported.

"No rales or rhonchi during inspiration or expiration, doctor?" said the girl in the chair. Her interest had shifted from the chess game to the doctor's cursory examination.

Evan risked a quick glance at the precocious teen. "To be technically correct, yes, no rales or rhonchi. And the heartbeat is good."

"No arrhythmia or murmurs?" the girl said.

"Beating as steady as a grandfather clock," Evan assured as he curled up his stethoscope and returned it to his pocket.

"This is my daughter, Callie, doc," Larry said. "She lives with her mother in San Luis Obispo. Had to come down for a couple days and see how badly her old man had banged himself up."

Then Larry added proudly, "Callie wants to be a doctor herself someday, right, Callie?" The girl nodded eagerly.

Evan responded with a noncommittal, "Hm," as he reclined Larry's bed to a horizontal position again. Inside he was groaning, *Oh no, not another young genius who wants to know how to get into medical school. I don't have time for this tonight.*

"Any soreness here?" Evan asked, as he pressed his fingertips into Larry's upper abdomen, examining the spleen. He avoided making eye contact with young Callie Kaiser who was watching his moves keenly.

"Nope, feels fine," Larry reported.

Evan probed around the liver and kidneys. "Here?"

"Nope."

"Any soreness in your chest or abdomen since I saw you yesterday?"

Larry shook his head. "The only thing that hurts is the leg and a few spots on my arm and shoulder. But the hurt-no-more pills take care of it."

Evan retreated to the foot of the bed, preparing for a quick getaway. "Have you been voiding today, Larry?" he asked matter-of-factly.

"You mean am I peeing and pooping okay?"

The doctor nodded.

"Yep, no problem there, doc," Larry answered smugly. Evan had done his job. From the perspective of internal medicine, Larry was ready for discharge. Ordinarily he would have closed the bedside exam with, "Any questions, Larry?" But he didn't want to give the nerdy-looking kid with the pocket computer a chance. It was time to race for his car to begin two glorious weeks away from the office and the hospital with the woman he loved. Evan casually backed two more steps toward the door. "Well, Larry, your engine parts are working fine. Dr. Finnegan will keep track of you while your leg heals. I don't need to see you again, but be careful when you get back on that motorcycle."

"Thanks, doc, I will."

Evan added a small wave to the girl. "Nice to meet you, Callie. Have a nice—"

It was all the encouragement she needed. "Excuse me, Dr. Rider," Callie interrupted, rising. She was tall and pale, as if she was allergic to the sun. "May I ask you a question?"

Evan looked at his watch and grimaced inside. *What are the chances she can confine herself to only one question?* "Okay, I have time for a quick question," he said, allowing a contrived kindness to momentarily overrule his urgency to get away.

"You're an internist, right?" Callie began.

"Yes, officially I'm a licensed, board certified physician of internal medicine in the state of California."

"Just what kind of a doctor is an internist, anyway?" Callie continued.

Evan swallowed a sigh of impatience. "An internist is to adults what a pediatrician is to children. We diagnose and treat adult diseases."

"Does that mean you don't deliver babies?"

Evan took one small step toward the door, confirming his need to get away as soon as possible. "As a rule, we don't do obstetrics, but we can deliver babies if we have to. I've delivered a couple."

Interpreting the doctor's answers as a green light for more questions, Callie moved on. "I'm planning my pre-med education, sir. Would you tell me where you completed your undergraduate studies?"

"University of Denver. I recommend it highly. It's a great school." Evan hoped the short answer would suffice. It didn't.

"I know," Callie answered confidently. "Denver is one of the most highly rated pre-med programs in the country."

Evan looked at his watch again to emphasize his need to leave. "Hey, it's been nice visiting with you, Callie, but—"

"Did you major in science and biology at Denver, doctor?" the kid pressed on determinedly.

"Yes. That's a typical major for pre-med. I earned a B.S. in biology from Denver. I was also a teaching assistant in the biology department the last two years of my studies."

"Not too many people make it through pre-med, right, doctor?"

Evan looked at Larry Kaiser, begging with his gaze to be rescued. But Larry simply returned a wink and a delighted that's-my-girl! grin.

"In my pre-med class at Denver, 161 began and 34 graduated—and only 25 of us actually went on to medical school. It's a tough course, Callie."

"Why did you choose Denver over Stanford?" Callie continued. "Weren't your grades good enough?"

"My grades were *very* good," Evan said, deciding not to pile it on by admitting that he had been a four-point student in high school. "I chose Denver for the academic scholarship and the skiing, two things Stanford couldn't offer me."

Evan decided that his best chance to get away was to flood the kid with information in order to preempt her next question. "After graduation I spent a year as a research assistant at the University of Colorado Medical School in the Department of Clinical Pharmacology. Then I was accepted at USC's med school where I specialized in internal medicine. That was a four-year hitch followed by three years of medical internship and residency at Los Angeles County General Hospital.

"At the ripe age of thirty, I joined the practice of two internists in the Medical Plaza across the street. Four years ago they both retired, and another doctor and I took over the practice. That's it, Callie: my life story in a nutshell. Now if you will excuse me—"

"Why are you in such a hurry, Dr. Rider?" Callie interrupted again. Her clouded expression mirrored the slight she perceived from a new hero figure. "I want to be a doctor too, and Dad says you're the best one he's ever had. I just thought you could help me a little. Aren't you interested in giving me some advice?"

"Doc Rider has other patients to see, Callie," Larry interjected. "Maybe he can talk with you another time."

A dagger of guilt slashed through Evan's conscience, short-circuiting his hasty retreat. *The old, self-centered Evan Rider rears his ugly head again*, he remonstrated himself. He recognized that he was standing at the crossroads of a decision. He could either blow the kid off and leave, or sacrifice a few more minutes of his schedule for kindness. *The odds against this kid surviving the blood, sweat, and tears to become a doctor are formidable*, he assessed. *Regardless, my need to get home isn't as great as her need for a little encouragement. Lord, forgive me.*

Evan moved back to the foot of the bed. "No, I don't have other patients to see tonight, Larry," he said with chagrin. "I'm afraid I let my impatience get the best of me." Turning to Callie, he said, *"I am* under a bit of a time crunch, Callie, but that's no excuse for being so short with you. I'm sorry. Please forgive me."

Unaccustomed to apologies from adults, Callie shrugged and said with a wan smile, "Yeah, whatever."

"So what's the big hurry, doc?" Larry chimed in with a mischievous grin. "Are you late for a hot date?" The patient had razzed his doctor good-naturedly from time to time about being single.

Over the years Evan had persevered in his determination to keep his private and professional lives separate. Patients weren't invited to dinner, and friends weren't treated for free. But he quickly decided that, under the circumstances, a little transparency might help to authenticate his apology. Besides, he had suppressed his anticipation for the events of the next two weeks long enough. It was time to share the good news with someone who would doubtless enjoy it.

Evan pulled a chair alongside the bed and sat down on the edge of it. "Can you two keep a secret?" he said with a hint of boyish excitement.

Larry's and Callie's eyes widened with interest.

"I'm getting married tomorrow."

"Married? Way to go, doc!" Larry whooped.

Evan shushed his patient overdramatically, then continued. "I'm on my way home for my fiancée's birthday party—today's her birthday—and for the rehearsal for our wedding. The ceremony will be in my garden tomorrow afternoon. Now do you understand why I'm in a hurry?"

Both listeners nodded. "So the doc is taking the plunge," Larry chuckled with delight. "I can't believe it. I'm happy for you. Callie's mother's marriage didn't last five years, but that's probably because she was married to me. I wish you the best, doc, I really do." Larry stretched out a congratulatory hand and pumped Evan's arm enthusiastically.

"Do doctors get to take time off for honeymoons?" Callie asked with a playful smirk.

Evan was pleased that the girl had momentarily abandoned her previous line of questioning. "This doctor does, Callie," he said, smiling. "We're taking a couple of weeks to drive to the Grand Canyon; she's never seen it." Then, turning to his patient, he added, "Dr. Weintraub will be covering for me at the office. So if you need anything, Larry, don't hesitate to call him."

"Hey, doc, don't worry about me," Larry said. "Now get out of here. Don't keep the little lady waiting or she might change her mind about marrying a doctor."

Evan welcomed the invitation to be on his way. He stood, pulled a business card from the breast pocket of his lab coat, and stretched it across the bed to the younger Kaiser. "Here's my office number. Give me a call in a few weeks and I'll be happy to answer all your questions about the healing profession."

Callie eyed the card as if the doctor had just handed her a $100 bill. "Thanks, Dr. Rider," she said. "I *will* call you."

"And now, I'm out of here." With a final, friendly wave, the doctor left the room.

"Congratulations, doctor," Larry called after him, causing two nurses in the hallway to look up from their duties and eye him curiously.

Something began to pick at Evan's insides as he hurried toward the stairway. It was the uneasy sense that something was wrong, a familiar prick of guilt over an unidentified offense. He tried to brush it away, reminding himself that he had repented of his lack of kindness toward Larry and Callie and made it right. What else could it be?

Then a word burned onto the screen of his consciousness—*Denver*—and a kangaroo court of accusing and defending thoughts was suddenly in session in Evan Rider's mind. The scenario had recurred frequently over the last year, the most gratifying yet challenging year of his life.

You led Callie and Larry to believe that you attended the University of Denver all four years, the prosecution lectured him. *You conveniently forgot to mention that you began your education at California State University, Northridge, spending a year and a half there before transferring to Denver on a scholarship for your final three years of pre-med.*

Not important, the defense objected. *The issue of the conversation was my pre-med education—which for all intents and purposes was completed at Denver.*

That's not why you avoided bringing up CSUN, the prosecution pressed, as Evan scampered down the stairs to the first floor. *You don't mention CSUN to anyone because after all these years you're still ashamed of what happened there in the middle of your second year. And the shame continues to resurface because your guilt has never been expunged.*

Evan's defense moved in strongly. *But it* has *been expunged. I am a man of the faith now, adolescent though my faith may be. And faith and forgiveness are inseparable. All offenses—harmless or heinous, secret or sensational—have been dealt with by faith, even the events of that horrible night almost twenty-two years ago. I won't let false guilt rub my nose in it again.*

The impromptu session was abruptly recessed by the soft chiming of the personal phone in Evan's shirt pocket. Evan owned the popular fold-over model trimmed in calfskin, about half the size of a man's wallet.

"This is Dr. Rider," he answered, walking briskly through the main lobby. He expected it to be his answering service, confirming that his calls were to be routed to Dr. Weintraub's service for the next two weeks. Evan had already confirmed the switch with three different operators.

"Where are you, Evan?" The feminine voice was warm and pleasant with a molasses-sweet drawl and just a tinge of mild panic. "Our friends are arriving."

Evan smiled at the voice of the woman who in less than twenty-four hours would be Mrs. Evan Rider. "I'm walking out of the hospital right now, angel," he assured. "I'll be there in five minutes tops."

The disbelieving laugh coming through the receiver was free of scorn. "I've heard *that* before, Dr. Rider. Then I don't see you for two hours."

"I am *literally* walking out of the hospital as we speak, Mrs. Rider-to-be." Evan passed through the automatic doors of Community Memorial Hospital into the hazy twilight. The fragrance on the breeze announced that the heavy marine air was creeping up the hill from the beach like a tide. "The car is in sight in the parking lot across the street sitting next to our 'honeymoon coach.' I'm pulling the keys out of my pocket—"

"Okay, Evan, I believe you," the voice interrupted with a light laugh. "Just get up here as soon as you can. It's a little comical explaining that I'm the honored guest, but that the host isn't here yet."

"You found the sparkling punch and the hors d'oeuvres?"

"Yes, darling. As always, your lists of instructions were crystal clear. I put everything out just as you asked. The flowers you picked from the garden are lovely. Handel's 'Water Music' on the sound system is perfect. Everyone is raving about your salmon paté. The only thing missing is you."

Evan stopped beside his "beach buggy"—a well-preserved, brightly polished twenty-year-old Datsun station wagon with a roof rack for his surfboard—to locate the door key.

The voice on his phone dropped lower. "I don't mean to sound ungrateful, Evan. I love our families and friends, and the party you have planned will be a lot of fun. But a quiet dinner for two at the Ranch House and a romantic stroll on the beach suddenly sounds like a beautiful way to spend our last evening as an engaged couple."

Evan unlocked the door and slipped behind the wheel, smiling at the prospect. "Very tempting, angel. But I think we would be conspicuous by our absence, especially during the rehearsal. As I recall, you and I play major roles in that scene."

A soft hum of pleasure wafted through the receiver.

Evan continued, "So dinner at the Ranch House is out. But I think we can fit in that stroll on the beach when everybody leaves, if it's not too damp down there."

"The sooner you arrive, the sooner the festivities will begin—and end," she said.

Evan turned the key and the noisy four-cylinder engine revved up. "Hear that, angel?" he said. "I'm almost there."

She laughed her lovely laugh again as she said, "I'll believe it when I see it." She was still laughing as she hung up.

Evan pocketed his phone and eased the Datsun into first gear. He would have released the parking brake and been on his way had he not glanced casually to his right. There stood the "honeymoon coach"—the used RV Evan and his bride-to-be had purchased and refurbished for their two-week trip to the Grand Canyon and subsequent trips they were planning for their life together. The Fleetwood Flair, vintage middle '90s, had been parked in the lot behind the Medical Plaza for the last two days while Evan, in between patients, tended to final preparations. The coach had been previously stored at an RV lot on Telephone Road. Evan's home, perched on a steep hillside at the end of a narrow, dead-end street, afforded little room for visiting cars, let alone a thirty-foot recreational vehicle.

It was another last-minute detail, remembered at the sight of the RV, that caused Evan to shut down the engine, loosen his tie, and step out of the car. He had left the new smoke alarm disassembled and dangling from the cabin ceiling that afternoon, when he was summoned to his office for an appointment. Evan loathed leaving a task undone. It would take less than two minutes to insert the battery and snap the alarm together.

He glanced far up the hill to the area near his home, as if to say, "Just a second, angel. I have one more thing to finish in the RV." Evan's angel was already quite familiar with his penchant for tardiness, due to a seemingly endless string of just-one-more-thing items vying for his time and attention at the office, at the hospital, in his garden, in his workshop, and now in their RV.

Evan unlocked the only entrance to the coach, a right-side door a third of the way back from the RV's European-styled bus front. Stepping up into the dark cabin, he switched on a battery-powered light. He stood in the middle of the mini-living room, which consisted of a plush, swivel chair immediately to the right of the entrance and a six-foot sofa bed on the wall directly opposite it.

Forward from the living room was the open cab—two more swivel chairs facing a sweeping instrument panel and dashboard. A television monitor was mounted in an oak panel above the windshield. Aft of the living room was the kitchen, featuring a dinette directly behind the entry door, and a sink, range, microwave, and refrigerator against the opposite wall. Beyond the kitchen was the bathroom, complete with a tub/shower. The bedroom, furnished with a queen bed and two small closets, was at the rear of the coach.

Evan stood in the soft light for a few seconds appreciating his handiwork. They had purchased the well-traveled Flair from a dealer in Thousand Oaks only a few hours after a retired couple, full-time RVers, had traded it in on a newer, larger model. The dealer had discounted the purchase price significantly when Evan agreed to take it "as is" and detail it himself—something he would have done anyway.

With his fiancée's occasional help and full-time encouragement, Evan spent several weekends replacing the carpet and vinyl floor covering, refinishing the kitchen cabinets, and thoroughly cleaning every remaining square inch of wood, plastic, metal, and fabric. A local mechanic, one of Evan's patients, gave the Flair's Chevy 454 engine and transmission a thorough going-over, assuring the doctor of thousands of miles of trouble-free traveling.

Evan's diligent scouring of RV newsletters had turned up a used auto carrier in Santa Barbara for a great price. Evan would be dragging his beach buggy behind the coach by the front wheels to use for nosing around Grand Canyon, Sedona, and Flagstaff while the Flair stayed in the campground. The empty auto carrier was hitched to the rear of the coach.

The happy couple had spent one evening shopping for new linens, disposable paper goods, staples, and other supplies, and another evening stocking the RV for their trip. The rig was ready for a Sunday morning departure—except for topping off the seventy-five-gallon fuel tank, which Evan would do as they drove out of town.

As he assembled the device on the kitchen ceiling in the silent coach, Evan's debating thoughts took up where they left off.

If you're guiltless of that incident twenty-two years ago, why haven't you told your bride about it? Why haven't you told anyone about it? The innocent have nothing to hide.

Defense scrambled for a response. *I will tell her about it some day. It just hasn't been appropriate, and it certainly isn't so on the eve of our wedding. It would be selfish and unkind of me to burden her with those details now, even though I'm sure she will agree that my sin is buried in the past. She was the one who encouraged me to let go of the past and to live by faith in the present.*

The prosecution went for the jugular. *Married couples share everything with each other. There are no secrets. When will you tell her? You are so fastidious about everything else in your life. Why are you so careless on this issue? Doesn't it prove that you are hiding something?*

The battery installed, Evan concentrated on setting the final screw in place and quickly twisting it down. The dark questions swirled through his mind like the mist that swirled around the outside of his coach. He had no answers. Some day he would settle the issue once and for all. But not tonight, not this weekend, not until the honeymoon was over and they were back in Ventura. Until then he would run for higher ground and leave the nagging questions behind him.

After a quick test of the smoke detector, Evan turned out the light, locked the coach, and headed for home.

Three

Evan Rider had occupied his eighty-year-old, Spanish-style home on the Ventura hillside for nearly four years. It was in a quaint but rather exclusive section of the city, popular for its ocean view, narrow, winding streets, and classic homes from the '20s, '30s, and '40s. Residents on this old west side of town generally disdained the housing developments from the '70s, '80s, and '90s which stretched for miles east of Victoria Avenue. To westsiders, quintessential Ventura was "on the hill above the high school."

When young Dr. Rider first joined Dr. Earl Wiggins and Dr. Wyatt Hornsby in their Ventura practice in 1991, he opted for a small, rented, two-bedroom house in the Pierpont area within walking distance of the beach. Fresh from three years of residency at L.A. County General and a childless, two-year marriage that he wished had never happened, Evan absorbed himself in two major pursuits: building his practice and paying off his medical school bills. The former was the unavoidable prerequisite for the latter.

Evan's parents, divorced and both remarried, had been very proud of their son's choice for the medical profession. But they were unable to fund his education. An academic scholarship got Evan through pre-med. But four years at USC med school, even with a partial scholarship and a couple of minor grants, left him with a financial obligation bordering on six figures. An expensive home on the hill where other professionals in the city resided was little more than a distant dream during the early years of the young doctor's career.

Evan's "beach pad" wasn't cheap, but it was the least he felt an up-and-coming—albeit indebted—internist should settle for. Besides, with limited discretionary income, Evan's house just off Seaward Avenue near California Street afforded him unlimited access to his favorite diversion: the surf, sand, and sun of Ventura Beach. He had traded his immaculate '84 Volkswagen Jetta two-door straight across for a low-mileage '81 Datsun wagon which better accommodated his surfboard. In contrast to most of the other beach buggies on the Ventura beach, Evan's wagon was always spotless and highly polished, an extension of his fastidious nature. Evan was a confirmed neat freak.

Except for early-morning surfing at the Point or the South Jetty and a rare day off soaking in the rays on the beach near his home, Evan was thoroughly immersed in his profession. He instructed the receptionist to double-book most of his time slots in the appointment calendar during office hours. He hopped between examination rooms at a frantic pace, performing physicals, burning off warts, and diagnosing and treating innumerable varieties of colds, coughs, headaches, viruses, and bacteria.

Several evenings a week had found Evan at local nursing homes removing ingrown toenails and treating bedsores for the reluctant, terminal tenants. On weekend nights he worked the emergency room at Community Memorial, often serving as "pit boss" during the midnight-to-seven shift. His multifaceted practice was rewarding, but more important to Evan, every month he was able to chip $1,000 to $3,000 off his school bill, and put another grand or two away toward buying out his senior partners and owning a house on the hill.

Evan's exhausting schedule had left little room for socializing. Yet the attractive physician still found time for a few stolen nights a month with an alluring ER nurse who was equally desperate to quench heated, frustrated drives apart from a lifetime commitment. And occasionally a bikini-clad, sun-bronzed acquaintance from the beach charmed her way into Evan's bed for a night or a week or a month. Evan knew enough to take steps to "protect himself" during these liaisons, but he was also smart enough to know that he couldn't protect himself completely. In the quiet corners of his heart, which he visited only in his infrequent moments of solitude, he wondered if his promiscuity in the face of such a lethal risk was some kind of death wish.

Most of the time Evan welcomed the nonstop pace of his practice and the dizzying roulette-wheel spin of his relationships. His lifestyle served to divert him from the dark, jagged memories which stalked him when inactivity left his mind unguarded.

In the spring of 1997, Dr. Evan Rider made his bold financial move. Drs. Wiggins and Hornsby retired as planned and sold their practice to Evan and Dr. Aaron Weintraub, who had joined the office in 1995. Evan used much of his savings as a down payment on the practice. Modest monthly payments for the next ten years would keep Wiggins and Hornsby well-stocked with fishing equipment.

And though Evan had planned to reinflate his bank account before buying a home, he couldn't pass up the opportunity of a lifetime when it landed in his lap that summer. He had learned through the grapevine that Dr. Marshall Winstadt, an oncologist and long-time resident on the hill, was moving to Bend, Oregon, where he could ski Mount Bachelor year round. Evan had approached Winstadt with a fair offer before the departing physician put the house on the market. Then Evan scraped together what money he could and borrowed back from Dr. Hornsby enough for a down payment on the old, charming house at the end of Foster Road on the hill above the high school.

Built in 1926, the house was originally a simple two-bedroom, one-bath dwelling. It had been owned for a time by eccentric mystery writer Erle Stanley Gardner, who was rumored to have often slept on the patio roof under the stars. Over the decades, subsequent owners had remodeled and redecorated the house to suit their fashion. Additional rooms, porches, patios, and a garage were added, and the wiring, plumbing, and insulation were modernized.

When Evan Rider bought the house for $660,000 in the summer of 1997, it was still "cozy" by modern standards—only four bedrooms and three baths with a relatively small living area. But to Evan and his envious colleagues, the spectacular view was worth it all. Stretched out behind the house was a gently terraced lawn lushly bordered with bougainvillea, miniature palm, and sculpted gardens. Flower beds were walled with thousands of eggshell-smooth rocks the size of inflated pancakes, which a previous owner had carted up from the Santa Clarita riverbed, load by load, in the trunk of his Cadillac.

And beyond the gardens, a magnificent panorama: the city of Ventura cascading down the hill to the water's edge, the Pacific Ocean shimmering away to the horizon, the Channel Islands heaving up from the depths like a pod of frolicking sea creatures, and 365 one-of-a-kind sunsets a year. For Evan, retreating to his hillside home after a hectic day, to sip Cognac on the patio overlooking the garden, was more cathartic than a week at Vail.

Though his transition from the beach to the hill rewarded him personally and bolstered his status among Ventura's professionals, Evan's lifestyle changed little. He still drove his Datsun wagon to the South Jetty below the marina in the early mornings to surf the southerly swells, or to the Point near the Holiday Inn to catch the swells rolling in from the north. And he still crammed his days, evenings, and weekends with patient services for which he billed substantial fees. After all, he had a mortgage and medical practice to pay off and a hillside home to keep up.

And Evan still welcomed the emotional and sexual diversion of an occasional girlfriend, someone to warm his bed and brighten his elegant home, just as Cognac on the patio warmed and soothed his soul. But the same qualities that drew women to Evan—his independence, his energy, his passion for his work and play—also drove them away. He bullishly refused to compromise his schedule to accommodate a friend's desire for more time with him. Nor did he comply when a partner expected physical intimacy to blossom into emotional intimacy, least of all reveal to her the source of the dark guilt that continued to fuel his frenetic schedule.

Eventually every one of his special friends tired of waiting for him and walked away.

As the months ticked down toward the new millennium, Evan Rider had become increasingly intense in his work and withdrawn in his relationships. He had never claimed to be a religious person; yet, like much of the population in the late '90s, he feared the end of the twentieth century to be a kind of spiritual precipice, a thundering eschatological waterfall over which the world would tumble into utter and final blackness. He had always laughed at cartoon caricatures of the doomsday prophet proclaiming, "The end of the world is at hand!" But as 1998 drew to a close, Evan had the premonition that millennium's end only a year away would surely be marked by cataclysm—if not global, certainly personal.

God was out to get him for that horrible deed twenty-two years ago, he reasoned in his moments of nighttime solitude on the patio—for *all* his misdeeds, to be sure, but especially for that one. He had spent most of his adult life scrambling headlong into the future, in hopes of outrunning the darkness of his past, which seemed always at his heels. But as he stood on the threshold of the last year of the millennium, he had somberly realized that his flight, no matter how fast or how far, would only end with a plunge into the very darkness he was so desperately trying to escape.

Darkness behind him and darkness ahead of him. Of what use, then, was his life, a mere, fleeting spark in an incomprehensible void? He had studied hard and long and spent tens of thousands of dollars to become a doctor. What did it matter? He had used his skills to alleviate pain and save lives. What was the point? And now he had his castle on the hill and a stable full of well-insured patients who winked at his above-average fees and paid their deductibles on time. Who cared? If nothing counted before and nothing counts afterward, how could anything in the present, even his admirable accomplishments, be meaningful at all?

Evan Rider's ongoing soliloquy on the meaningless of his life reached its climax on Wednesday, January 6, 1999—his thirty-eighth birthday. He spent the entire day alone at the house, canceling a full day of appointments at the office and forgoing evening rounds and a trip to the nursing home. He left his personal phone in the drawer, allowing the calls of a few well-wishers and inquiries from his office nurse to stack up on his machine unanswered. He refused to go to the mailbox or answer the door when UPS attempted to deliver a gift from his parents. He ate nothing.

It was a damp, cold day, yet he sat on the patio in a sweat suit, tennis shoes, and a golf hat, staring at the ocean—or at least *toward* the ocean, which was obscured from his view by low-hanging clouds. A bottle of Cognac and a small snifter sat on the table beside him. He went inside only three times—just long enough to urinate.

After ten hours and half a bottle of Grand Marnier, Evan Rider reached a crossroads of reason. *If life is meaningless,* he thought, *I may as well check out now and end the mental anguish.* Evan had steadfastly refused to join many of his colleagues who had been certified to perform euthanasia, which was legal in California under certain circumstances. But he often amused himself by devising new combinations of drugs that quickly and painlessly ended life. He knew he could brew up a quick, effective suicide cocktail from drug samples in his office if he wanted to.

But if there is meaning to all this beyond my perception, and relief from the misery of who I am and what I have done, he countered during his moment of truth, *I had better find it and get in sync with it.* Once the two alternatives were clearly in his view, it hadn't taken long for Evan to choose the acceptable path. He had seen too much of the wonders of human anatomy and physiology, too much of the delicate intricacies of the plant life in his garden, and too much of the majesty of the sea spread out beneath his hillside home to attribute life to random, meaningless chance. *There is design and purpose to all this somewhere—there must be,* he concluded. *I have nearly a year to find it. If I fail, I will assume that the gods have excluded me from their plans. If and when that becomes clear, I will step out of their way before the new millennium dawns.*

Having verbalized his declaration, Evan went into the house with a guarded sense of peace. He concluded his thirty-eighth birthday by showering, preparing and eating a simple supper, and going to bed by 9 o'clock. It was the first time he had been in bed—alone—before 11 P.M. since high school.

The next morning he surfed the beach break off the South Jetty and returned to the office. But he had a new resolve, a resolve which would eventuate quite unexpectedly in a previously unimaginable faith.

The driveway and street in front of Evan's house at the end of Foster Road were jammed with the cars of guests who had arrived before him. So Evan had to park his beach buggy several houses away. It was 7:50 P.M., and the coastal overcast had blotted out the last rays of a sunset which the community of Ventura had not witnessed on this June day.

Evan stepped out of the car, hurriedly removed his lab coat, and laid it neatly on the backseat. He tightened his tie, retucked his shirt, and grabbed his lightweight sports jacket from the hanger inside the back door. As he locked the door, another car pulled up behind his, flashed its high beams in greeting, and parked. Evan recognized the new, cream-colored Lexus to be that of his associate in the practice, Dr. Aaron Weintraub. Evan smiled and nodded to return the greeting.

"Hey, I thought we were going to be late, darling," Aaron said to his wife, Sheila, with a chuckle as they approached Evan. "But if the host is just arriving, we must be right on time. Just like a Gentile to say a party starts at 7:30 when he really means 8."

Aaron was in his mid-thirties, tall, thin, and prematurely balding. He wore a beige silk suit with no lapels—the summer style for the fashion-conscious gentleman, which Aaron definitely was—and a shirt and tie of compatible colors and cut. Sheila, short, round, and eight months along with their second child, was dressed in a flattering rose-colored maternity dress with matching jacket.

Evan groaned overdramatically. "This Gentile is going to be left standing at the altar tomorrow if he doesn't get into the house post-haste," he said, slipping on his jacket and urging the couple to hurry along with him.

"Not so fast," Sheila complained good-naturedly, "or this bloated woman may deliver a baby at the altar in the middle of your beautiful garden ceremony tomorrow."

Evan laughed, then slowed his pace to match Sheila's labored gait.

"This is a treat for us to be included in your special weekend," Aaron said. "It can't be much fun for your little lady, though," he added, tongue in cheek. "She's getting hit with the double whammy: today she turns forty, and tomorrow she marries you. That's grounds for clinical depression, if I've ever heard them."

"Don't listen to him, Evan," Sheila cut in, tossing a comic scowl at her husband. "She's a very lucky lady, and I can't wait to meet her."

Evan stopped dead in the street and turned to Sheila with his mouth agape. "What? You haven't met my angel? Where have you been? Why, I thought . . . "

Sheila shook her head while patting the basketball-sized mound protruding from her abdomen. "This little gremlin has kept me out of a lot of fun things this year. I was barely pregnant and sick as a dog when you had your engagement party at the office. I couldn't come, remember? And the few other times your fiancée has been up from L.A. since then, we haven't connected. Aaron tells me she's a wonderful woman and that she's . . . well . . . that she's been through a lot in the last couple of years. She was quite the celebrity at one time; I remember seeing her on TV. And now she's marrying our own Evan. Meeting her in person will be a real treat."

"I apologize, Sheila," Evan said, as they resumed their progress toward the house. "If I had realized you two hadn't met, I would have brought her over and introduced her to you. I guess I really blew it."

"Nonsense," Sheila said, waving her hand to dismiss the unintentional slight. Then she laughed and added with an affected Yiddish accent, "Not inviting us to the party or to the wedding—*that's* when you would have blown it!"

Evan chuckled at her humor. "I couldn't have pulled this wedding off without you two, Sheila," he said as they mounted the brick porch and approached the oak door. "After all, your husband will be on call for two weeks straight, while we're soaking in the sun at the Grand Canyon. I figure that must be worth at least a few hors d'oeuvres and some wedding cake."

The chatter coming from inside the house assured Evan that his guests were having a good time, despite his late arrival. Opting on the spur of the moment for a grand entrance, he winked at the Weintraubs and rang the doorbell instead of walking in. The electronic chimes inside the door played the first four bars of the wedding march, which he had programmed into the unit two weeks earlier.

After several seconds the door opened, and the vision before Evan caused him to draw a long, slow breath of delight and appreciation. She was five feet, seven inches tall with the figure of a twenty-five-year-old. Her naturally blonde hair was fashionably short and gently curled.

She wore a festive cotton dress, belted at the waist and swirled with the colors of a spring garden. Evan had bought it for her because "the colorful print and the flowing style reminds me of the joy you have brought into my life." The dress neither flaunted nor denied the woman's trim and shapely body. It wasn't too formal for her low heels or too casual for her gold earrings, necklace, bracelet, and engagement ring.

The woman's stunning powder-blue eyes locked onto Evan's and her small mouth opened into a radiant smile. "Welcome home, darling," she sang affectionately, as if the Weintraubs were invisible. Then she stepped across the threshold and walked into Evan's arms. Any displeasure she may have harbored about having to start the party without her fiancé was absent from her greeting.

Evan embraced her warmly and held her close, daring not to let her go for fear that this angel, this miracle in his life, would somehow be lost to him. It had been her friendship that had plucked him from the dark river rushing to the precipice and had guided his feet to the solid ground of faith and truth and meaning. It had been her love that had melted his stony, cynical, self-absorbed heart and molded it into a vessel of caring like her own. And it had been her promise of marriage that had commissioned him to be the man he always wanted to be: caring, protecting, sharing, nurturing.

This was no mere gift in Evan's arms; this was an incalculable treasure. He was unworthy of what he had found; yet she had been brought to him, as surely as the tide brings the waves to the shore. She had taught him so much, and he yearned to learn more. She had welcomed him and accepted him so freely, and he hoped that her heart was deep enough to accept all of him, even the dark corners he yet struggled to accept in himself. *Don't let this woman get away, Evan,* he remonstrated himself, *or you have lost everything.*

The beautiful blonde released him with a loving kiss on the cheek, then turned to Aaron and Sheila Weintraub who had been waiting patiently, enjoying the brief reunion. "Please excuse me," she said. "I didn't mean to ignore you." Then she extended her hand to Aaron. "Welcome, Aaron. It's so good to see you again." The greeting was warm and genuine.

Aaron shook her hand and smiled, appreciating that she had remembered his name. "Thank you," he said. "Happy birthday — and happy wedding. This is one big happy weekend for you two."

They all enjoyed a comfortable laugh.

Evan spoke up as his fiancée reached out to shake hands with Sheila. "Angel, this is Aaron's wife, Sheila. I thought you two had met months ago, but Sheila just informed me — and I had no idea — that you *haven't* met." The two women clasped hands and exchanged pleasant smiles. "And Sheila, I am pleased to introduce the love of my life. I know her as Shelby Tuggle from Los Angeles, California. But you probably remember her as Shelby Hornecker from Dallas, Texas."

Four

The retreating sun was still dazzling low in the sky northwest of Seattle at 8:30 P.M. on the second longest day of 2001. On the 700-plus acre main campus of the University of Washington, less than ten miles from downtown Seattle, the buildings seemed to plow toward the glowing horizon like a fleet of huge barges laboring across Puget Sound, leaving long, boxy shadows in their wake. Around the state, the University of Washington was affectionately referred to as U Dub, short for UW. In Seattle it was simply called the U.

Few classes were being conducted at the U on this Friday evening. But it was not unusual to find a number of students and local residents crisscrossing the beautiful grounds on the shore of Lake Washington. It was precisely why the young man striding purposely along Stevens Way, wearing a purple Huskies cap and toting a nylon book bag over his shoulder, had chosen evening for his mission instead of after dark when his presence would have been more conspicuous to security personnel. The girl walking with him was along for the adventure.

Brett Carroll, a lanky twenty-year-old African-American with handsome features, and his eighteen-year-old white girlfriend, Andie, looked every bit the parts they were playing: that of UW students on their way to a summer school class or to Allen Library. In reality, Brett had just completed his sophomore year, and Andie her freshman year, at rival Washington State University in Pullman, on the eastern side of the state.

They walked past Guthrie Hall, home of the Psychology Department, and Architecture Hall, and fell in behind—at a comfortable distance—a cluster of alums revisiting their alma mater on vacation. As the gray-hairs passed the administration building, Brett and Andie peeled away and followed a walkway down the side of the long building. Brett appeared to be looking at Andie as they walked, talked, and laughed. But he looked past her to scan the building's windows. They revealed what he had expected and hoped for: lights off, cleaning staff finished and gone, offices locked up tight for the weekend.

The couple walked past the end of the building, then angled through Central Plaza Garage and returned to casually reconnoiter the north side of the administration building. Assured that the path was clear to his target, Brett took Andie's hand and circled the building once more for good measure, then approached a secondary entrance in the shade of Meany Hall for the Performing Arts, where traffic on the nearby walkways was sparse and distant.

The main entrance to the building was more convenient to Brett's purposes. But using the shadowy back entrance and taking a long walk through the building was necessary to reduce the risk of detection.

Once in the shadows beside the door, Andie put herself in Brett's face. "Will you *please* tell me what this is all about?" she insisted, wide-eyed and grinning with anticipation. "I can't stand the suspense." Andie had a freckly pixie face framed by shocks of frizzy auburn hair.

"Be patient," Brett said, smiling, as if trying to quiet a child hounding a parent for a promised piece of candy. He relished the attention he was receiving from Andie by stringing her along on his "secret mission." He quietly pushed away the taunts of conscience which begged him to consider the trouble he might be getting her into.

Producing a plastic key card from the back pocket of his jeans and sliding it through the lock slot, the young man admitted himself and his girlfriend to the building.

Once inside Brett disarmed the alarm with another swipe of the magic card through an electronic sentry. After processing the entry in less than a second, the sentry flashed a message on its small display screen, a standard message that someone in the administration had programmed into the unit to amuse its employees: GOOD EVENING, DR. CARROLL. WORKING LATE TONIGHT?

"*Doctor* Carroll?" Andie giggled, eyebrows raised.

"That's my mother," he whispered, as he tapped in a memorized security code on the sentry's keypad with the eraser of his pencil. "If we run into anyone tonight—which we won't—I'll tell them I came to pick up some books for my mom, and you came along for the ride."

"I still don't understand why you chose Wazzoo over Washington when your mother works here."

"That's precisely *why* I chose Wazzoo over Washington, because my mother works here. Besides, if I hadn't enrolled at State, I might not have met you. It was fate, precipitated by my urgent desire to get out from under my mother's heel."

"So what are we doing here at U Dub? What's this secret mission you keep talking about?" Andie was almost ecstatic with curiosity. She clung to Brett's arm excitedly, and he loved it.

"I told you. I'm conducting a little business for a couple of clients of mine. Then I'm going to leave a calling card from good old Wazzoo that'll really freak out the Husky brass this fall."

"What kind of business would bring you here after hours? Is it illegal?" Andie's giddiness was tempered only slightly by the seriousness of her question.

"If it is, do you want out?"

Andie searched Brett's clear, dark eyes, looking for a clue to the secret, weighing the possible dangers. Then she beamed another impish smile. "Not yet, not until I find out what's driving that high-tech brain of yours."

The sentry received Brett's numeric code and responded: THANKS,

DR. CARROLL. PLEASE STOP BY ON YOUR WAY OUT TO SAY GOOD-BYE. Brett and Andie didn't stay around to read it. Brett had seen it before.

The halls of the administration building were a maze of deepening shadows and shafts of orange sunlight intruding though a few windows on the west side. Brett led Andie stealthily through a half mile of hallways and up two flights of broad marble stairs. He approached every turn in the hall with caution, acknowledging the remote possibility that a university official might be in the building. He had his very plausible alibi ready for that eventuality. But they saw and heard no one.

Brett led Andie to a suite of offices at the east end of the third floor marked only by a brass doorplate announcing: DR. LIBBY CARROLL, PROVOST AND VICE-PRESIDENT FOR ACADEMIC AFFAIRS. The same key card which admitted them to the building opened the main office door. Andie stopped at the threshold. "This is the Provost's office!" she whispered reverently, as if they were about to trespass a sacred burial ground. "You're breaking into the office of the Provost of the University of Washington!"

"This is my *mother's* office," Brett corrected. "Don't worry about it. I've been visiting mom's office—with and without her permission or knowledge—since I was seven years old. It's no big deal."

Brett ushered Andie inside the door and locked it behind them. He led her to a spacious corner office with a view of Drumheller Fountain in the center of Frosh Pond, Lake Washington, and Mount Ranier in the distance. Andie gripped his hand with both of hers and couldn't keep from tiptoeing on the plush carpet in fearful anticipation. The private office was much darker because it faced the southeast side of the building. But Brett didn't turn on any lights.

Andie surveyed the spacious office as Brett dropped his book bag on the mahogany desk and plopped into his mother's leather chair. The walls of the office were lined with bookshelves laden with hundreds of substantial volumes interspersed with plants, knickknacks, and decorative bookends. A contemporary, floral-print sofa, flanked by a white wicker side chair and lamp table, faced the desk.

"I'll bet your mother doesn't know you're here tonight," Andie whispered excitedly.

Brett rocked back in the chair like a fat cat executive. "No, she doesn't, and I'm not telling her," he said cockily, beaming. "And after a few critical keystrokes, even the sentry downstairs will conveniently 'forget' that we were here."

"Maybe *I'll* tell her," Andie taunted playfully. "I know where you live." Brett wagged his finger at her. "You will swear to secrecy or—"

"Or what?" Andie giggled deviously.

"Or I'll have to find a way to shut you up."

Andie threw herself into her boyfriend's lap. "How are you going to do that, hm?" she cooed. "Bribe me with dinner on the way home? Ply me with a night of passion? That's what it's going to cost to keep me from squealing, you know. A good dinner—no, make that a *great* dinner on the pier. And then I want to do it with you tonight, Brett, somewhere new, somewhere exciting. Deal?" Andie signed her offer by kissing Brett longingly on the forehead, cheeks, and mouth.

"You cut a hard deal," Brett said with a pleased sigh, inwardly rejoicing at his good fortune. "But you have me at your mercy, so I must agree to your terms." He wrapped his arms around her and kissed her on the face and neck, warming with desire. It took great restraint for him to break away.

"But first," he said, catching his breath, "I have a little work to do. Business before pleasure, you know."

Andie uncoiled to sit on Brett's knee. "Just remember, a deal's a deal," she reminded him.

"Right, a deal's a deal," he agreed eagerly. "Now hand me my 'brain.' It's in the bag."

Andie reached into the nylon bag, found the tiny computer—about the size of a short paperback book—and laid it on the desk in front of Brett. He tapped the machine on and accessed a short list of names and numbers which glowed faintly on the flip-up monitor.

Then Brett slid out the center drawer of the desk, revealing a full-function, built-in computer keyboard. "Watch the picture." He nodded toward a professional videograph glowing in an 11 by 16 inch pewter frame on the corner of the spacious desk. The videograph, in still mode, pictured Libby Carroll and her son, Brett, at age twelve, sitting in a Land Rover parked in a game park outside Nairobi. Mother and son were both tall and slender. Libby's skin was dark mocha. Brett's was mocha and cream.

Switched to album mode, the videograph would dissolve between a dozen or more family video snapshots. In action mode, the videograph was programmed to display a number of clips: Brett's first steps, his mother's graduation from Central Washington State University, Brett's high school graduation, and footage from memorable vacation trips the two had taken together during Brett's childhood.

"I'll bet you've never seen one of these before," Brett said.

"Brett, I'm a college sophomore, not a bumpkin from Ritzville," Andie snorted defensively. "I know what a videograph is."

"Just wait," Brett said. Keeping Andie on his knee, he wrapped his arms around her and entered a command on the keyboard. The videograph portrait dissolved to paper-white, casting a pasty glow onto the faces of the watching couple. Then no fewer than twenty colorful menu-option icons exploded into neat rows on the background.

"The videograph is a computer monitor!" Andie gasped in amazement.

"Impressive, isn't it?" Brett said as he spun the keyboard roller, shooting the on-screen directional arrow toward a cartoon icon of an old-time coin-operated parking meter. "Mom always could squeeze the university for the latest in office toys."

Brett clicked on the parking meter icon, and it expanded to fill the screen. A row of American coins appeared beneath the meter: penny, nickel, dime, quarter, half-dollar, silver dollar. "Mom's computer security system," Brett informed. "It's a little time-consuming, but she thinks it's cute."

He moved the arrow to the row of coins, dragged a dollar to the slot in the meter, and dropped it in. He repeated the process with another dollar, two dimes, and four pennies. With each "deposit" the *clink-clink-clonk* of a coin settling into the meter emanated from the speaker in the computer's CPU mounted under the desk top.

When Brett dropped in the final coin, a green flag flipped up on the meter. Then the screen dissolved back to the original menu—to the accompaniment of a little tune from the CPU.

"You're right back where you started from," Andie said.

"But if I hadn't fed the meter the correct amount of change—$2.24, the computer wouldn't have granted me access to any other pro-grams—either mom's or the university's."

Andie sucked a noisy, astonished breath. "University programs. Geez, Brett, you can't snoop through U Dub's files."

"Of course, I can," Brett chuckled. "My mom is the vice president of academic affairs. Mommy always lets me do what I want."

"If she finds out, she'll kill you on the spot," Andie countered, squirming on Brett's knee. "And she'll have me arrested."

"Simple solution: she won't find out." As Brett spoke, he clicked through several levels of access. The levels were pictured on the screen by a variety of doors, desks, drawers, filing cabinets, and file drawers, all in full color. At each level the computer asked Brett to enter an authorization code—a word or phrase or a series of digits—which he quickly supplied.

"How do you know all the right codes?" Andie asked, reveling in Brett's skill.

Brett smiled smugly in the glow of the screen. "A combination of two vital qualities: my sneaky resourcefulness and my mother's naive trust. She didn't give me the university's codes, but she didn't hide them from me either. You just have to know where to look."

"Are you sure you can snoop around like this and not get caught?" Andie pressed, torn between excitement and nagging worry.

"I've done it lots of times and never even raised a suspicion."

"Yeah, but I've never been with you. It'll be just my luck that the U Dub police do a building-by-building security sweep tonight." She squirmed nervously on his knee.

Brett's hands left the keyboard and enveloped Andie, nuzzling the back of her neck with his nose. "Easy, baby. They don't do security sweeps here like they do at State. Just relax and let me do my business. Then we'll get on to . . . something a little more user friendly."

Andie sighed her compliance.

Brett entered a final command and the front of a large file drawer filled the screen. The drawer was labeled: ACADEMIC RECORDS. Below the label was a nameplate marked: STUDENT, with a flashing cursor ready to receive name and number.

"What's the first name on my list?" Brett asked, fingers poised to type.

Andie leaned over to study the list on the screen of Brett's hand-held computer. "Goodwine, Ryan D."

Brett tapped in the letters. "Student ID number?"

"Six-five-five-five-nine-zero-dash-four-one-four."

In response to the name and number, the drawer on the screen opened to reveal a row of folders, each with a visible tab. Brett clicked on the tab labeled BS310, and the folder slid out of the drawer and spread open. The complete record of Mr. Ryan D. Goodwine's encounter with upper division biochemistry filled the screen.

Andie leaned in to look. "Is this some kind of kinky thrill for you, peeking into grade files like some guys peek into dorm windows?"

"The only thrill I get out of peeking into these files is when Ryan Goodwine and Megan Thoms and Isaac Merton and a few other of my clients at U Dub cross my palm with $100 for helping them pass their classes."

Andie breathed an expletive mirroring her shock and disbelief, then added, "You're doctoring grades!"

"Please, Andie, that sounds so . . . criminal," Brett said, as he scrolled through lines of data. "My clients and I think of it as adjusting grades to reflect best intentions. Goodwine here *intended* to study for the biochem final in order to pull his course grade up into the two-point range. And he needs to maintain a two-point or his parents will cut off his college money and make him move back to Puyallup to work in the family's pet store." Brett underscored the unpleasantness of the scenario with a gagging sound.

Then he continued. "It's just that, as Goodwine tells it, a weekend sailing the San Juans with his girlfriend was more important to his emotional health than a weekend cramming for the biochem final. And he didn't trust himself running loose in Seattle under a cloud of emotional deprivation. People wouldn't be safe on the streets.

"Had Goodwine studied up to his potential, he would have pulled an 85 or better on the final, assuring him a GPA of 2.3 for the year and another term of fun and frolic at U Dub. Dr. Fudgebottom—or whoever teaches biochem at this institution—is too narrow-minded to factor

Goodwine's potential into his grading system. I'm just helping the prof lighten up and grade a tad more charitably."

"But the professor will know the grade has been changed," Andie objected. "Faculty members keep their own records, don't they?"

"Fudgebottom will never know. Spring term biochem and Ryan Goodwine are history as far as he's concerned. The prof submitted his grades and left town for the summer. By now he's probably somewhere in Central Africa dissecting algae or cross-breeding tsetse flies."

"Then someone in this office—your mother or one of her staff—will know the grades have been doctored." She was watching in awe as Brett changed the final score of Goodwine's biochem final from 54 to 85.

"Wrong again, Andie," Brett said, kissing the back of her neck softly, then returning to his task. "We are in the golden period between the submission of grades by the faculty and the permanent recording of grades. The grades that I 'adjust' tonight will be accepted by the administration as the grades that Fudgebottom submitted, because they will be entered under Fudgie's code—which, thanks to my trusting mom, I happen to have access to."

Andie seemed transfixed by the activity on the screen as Brett pried open the files of Megan Thoms, Isaac Merton, Gordon McAllister, and three other students, and adjusted the grades. "Geez, Brett," she said, leaning back into his chest as he worked, "this is so illegal, so dangerous, so . . . exciting."

Brett smiled, pausing in his work to caress Andie's cheek and ear with his lips. "I thought you would enjoy it once you got past the initial shock."

"Enjoy it! This is an utter rush! My heart is beating like I'm running a marathon."

"Mm, let's see." He slipped his hand inside her oversized sweatshirt and nibbled at her ear. "I hope the rush isn't all from the danger."

Andie squealed and jumped and jerked his hand away. "Brett, not now!" she said, unable to fully mask her enjoyment of his advances. "Do your adjusting, then let's get out of here. I can only take so much danger in one night."

"One more little job, then I'm done," Brett said, reluctantly returning his attention to the computer.

His agile fingers flew across the keyboard, closing the student files and returning to the main menu. He created a new file and on the blank screen called up a bright red background. Across the background in large, bold, gray letters he typed: GO WAZZOO!—the colloquial pronunciation by Washington State University students of the initials W-S-U.

"Okay, what's the deal with Go Wazzoo?" Andie probed.

Brett kept tapping as he talked. "I'm injecting a little time-released virus in the menu batch file for the university's mainframe. On November 19, the Monday before the UW–WSU game, every computer on the university's system will boot up to this screen. They won't be able to clear it without a software tech. It'll drive them crazy."

Andie squealed at the clever prank, and the two of them burst into a giggling, hugging fit on the leather chair. Trying to muffle their laughter only provoked them to greater hysterics.

Finally, Brett returned his mother's computer to videograph mode. The sudden dimming of the screen plunged the room into romantic near-darkness. The couple took advantage of the moment, enjoying prolonged embraces, tender caresses, then deep, passionate kisses.

"You'd better get me out of here," Andie panted near Brett's ear. "I'm getting hungry—hungry for you."

"I know a place that's new and exciting where we can do it," Brett whispered seductively. Then he lifted her up and carried her to the office sofa. His kisses quickly doused Andie's resistance.

Five

Nolan Jakes kept his eyes on the field and cheered whenever the Colorado Rockies scored a run against the Dodgers—which they seemed able to do at will. He felt strange whooping it up for the visiting team; Jakes had been a Dodgers fan all his life. But the body wire had been secreted on the Rockies jacket he was given to wear by the LAPD drug unit, so he had to play out his cover by appearing to be a fan of the two-time National League Champions from Denver.

By the top of the eighth inning, Colorado was up 10-3, and Jakes had tried to act appropriately elated about the team's success. In reality, his thoughts were far from the game. Veiled by his simple disguise, he sat with Donatelli in a corner of the right-field pavilion, several rows from the nearest occupied seats, acting out his hollow charade and churning with apprehension as the game neared its end. He had left his seat only twice: to get a hot dog and a beer which he couldn't finish, and to regurgitate what his nervous stomach wouldn't keep down. Donatelli and his deadly Colt Anaconda .44 Magnum were with him constantly, even in the restroom.

Every time Jakes thought about Victor Chance and Reynoso Fernandez scoping him out from somewhere in the loge seats across the field, his stomach took another sour turn. Could his fellow employees for drug kingpin G. Billy Fryman read the terror in his eyes with their powerful glasses? Did they smell a setup? Could they see through

Donatelli's scruffy appearance and detect the LAPD blue in his veins? Had they phoned Fryman to call the deal off? Had they already received orders to blow Jakes and his cop friend away behind the green Mercedes and dump their bodies over the guardrail into the brush? Every new possibility made Jakes shudder.

During the bottom of the eighth inning Jakes had to hurry to the restroom under the pavilion again. His nerves were shot and he dry-heaved for five minutes, almost losing his fake mustache in the toilet.

He had hoped that Sergeant Donatelli would allow him to go to the restroom alone. If he had, Jakes might have taken a chance on slipping out of the Stadium and disappearing into the city. But his police shadow never left him for a moment. Donatelli and his .44 Magnum waited for him outside the stall as he retched.

"I'm too sick to do this, Donatelli," Jakes moaned at the sink, as he wiped his mouth and chin with a wet paper towel. "I'm puking my guts out, and I can't stop shaking." He held up his trembling hands as evidence. "Those guys out there are killers, man. They're going to see right through me and—"

Donatelli grabbed Jakes by the front of the jacket and slammed him against a metal stall with a bitter curse. Two other men in the restroom, startled at the sudden scuffle, quickly exited without drying their hands.

"Listen to me, you scummy excuse for a human being," Donatelli hissed three inches from Jakes' nose, pummeling him with the stench of rancid cigarette smoke. "We've been waiting three years for a break on Fryman, some way to get our hands around his fat, greasy neck and pull him out of his insulated ivory tower. We needed someone on the inside, someone desperate, someone a little careless.

"Then you came along, the fair-haired football hero returning to L.A. from Canada. And you came home poor and hungry, whipped and needing a job bad. You were an easy mark for Billy Fryman. He reels in washed-up ex-jocks around L.A. who are crazy for his bait: the promise of fast, easy money for fast, shady business deals. We kept watching you, and eventually you screwed up big-time. You took me for a customer just like I knew you would, and you sold me ice, Jakes. We have you dead to rights on a felony drug rap in quantities that will book you a room in the federal pen until your teeth fall out." Donatelli punctuated his accusation with a vile, demeaning expletive.

Something inside Jakes—a remnant of the fierce, competitive spirit that once ruled his life—taunted him to fight back, to crash the cop's ugly face with his fists. But Jakes was no longer the fighter he once was. The last few humiliating years had quenched much of his fighting spirit. Besides, Donatelli's free hand was resting on the bulge at his waist: the loaded .44. Jakes feared that any retaliation on his part might spur the cop to postpone the Fryman operation just for the pleasure of pistol-whipping a reluctant informant who didn't deserve the charity he had been promised by the Feds.

"I don't care what kind of a hero you were in this city, man," Donatelli continued, shaking Jakes by the shirt. "You're a worthless has-been now. And you're dirty, Jakes—drug dirty. Even worse, the Feds are letting you slime out of the punishment you deserve. But you're not free yet." The cop added another searing curse. "You *are* going to help us first, Jakes, and it's going to happen tonight, whether you're ready or not."

Donatelli released his grip on Jakes and stepped back, forcing himself to calm down. Then he reached inside his sweat jacket to a shirt pocket and pulled out a small, flat packet of paper. "Stick this on your butt," the cop said in a deliberately subdued tone. "It'll calm you down and keep you thinking straight." Donatelli tore open the packet and thrust an tiny adhesive patch into Jakes' hand.

Jakes stared at the patch. He recognized it to be an illegal transdermal tranquilizer designed to dull his nerve endings and quiet his emotions without affecting his mind. He had used drugs like this during his career to take his mind off his pain after a game, in order to give a lady friend the attention she deserved.

"Do it, Jakes—now!" Donatelli snapped just above a whisper. "Then do the job you came to do and get out of my life." The burly cop lit another cigarette and with a nod urged Jakes to comply.

Aware of the futility of resisting or trying to escape, Jakes stepped back into the stall, dropped his pants, and applied the patch with trembling hands near the top of his right buttock. The calming effects of the transdermal drug began to overtake him before the two men left the restroom. By the time they returned to their seats in the pavilion, Jakes' trembling had stopped and the raging inferno in his stomach had been temporarily doused.

Jakes settled in to watch the last inning and mentally rehearse his role in the drama that would be played out in the parking lot afterward. But his thoughts kept being distracted by two words Donatelli had spit at him in the restroom, words which cued a library full of memories.

Donatelli's spiteful use of "hero" and "has-been" burned into Nolan Jakes' soul more painfully than the cop's physical threats. Nolan Jakes had been a hero in Los Angeles, beginning as an All-City quarterback and safety at Chatsworth High School in the affluent West San Fernando Valley. He had been small for a high school football player—only five feet, ten inches tall. But he more than made up for his lack of size with exceptional speed, physical and mental toughness, and an uncanny instinct for the game. Young Jakes maximized his natural traits with tireless, year-round weight training and physical conditioning. He was the fastest, most naturally skilled player in the San Fernando Valley.

As an athlete Jakes was talented, toned, tough, afraid of no one. And as a person he was self-confident bordering on cocky, but good-natured and fun-loving, always with a ready smile. As a student he struggled, prompting his high school coaches to employ a corps of peer tutors to help him keep his grades up.

In the months before his graduation in 1977, the high school phe-nom had been offered football scholarships by over thirty major colleges, including perennial national powers like Penn State, Notre Dame, Nebraska, Oklahoma, and his personal choice, USC. But none of them wanted him as a quarterback. "You aren't tall enough to be a college quarterback, and you don't have a college-level arm," they said. "You're a natural-born, supremely gifted, future All-America tailback, cornerback, or kick returner. You don't need to call the plays. Just take the ball and run or lead the NCAA in pass interceptions and return yardage."

But Nolan Jakes' bulging self-confidence, overfed by his momentous success, had developed a malignancy: a serious attitude. "I don't want to be a college tailback," he announced coolly to each eager coach who contacted him. "I will play quarterback or I won't play at all."

"But you have a chance to make it as a pro if you play tailback or defensive back," they argued. "You have zero chance to make the NFL as a five-foot, ten-inch quarterback."

"I *will* play quarterback in college," Jakes insisted arrogantly, "if not for you, for some other school. I'll make All-America, and I'll probably win the Heisman Trophy by my junior year. And I will make it to the pros—you can bet on it." And so the battle raged between Nolan Jakes and more than two dozen major college coaches from across the country.

Enter Leland Dandridge, head coach at California State University, Northridge, a Division II school less than ten miles from Jakes' home in Chatsworth. Having caught wind of Jakes' dilemma, Dandridge huddled with the school's administration to propose a cure for the school's flagging football program, which the bigwigs eagerly endorsed. Then Coach Dandridge made a personal visit to the Jakes residence.

CSUN would award Nolan Jakes a full football scholarship to play starting quarterback for the Matadors all four years of his eligibility, Dandridge had announced proudly to Jakes and his parents. What could be better than being a star college quarterback in front of your hometown fans?

Several things would be better, Jakes had determined, as he considered the offer. He would prefer playing quarterback for Joe Paterno at Penn State or John Robinson at USC where Heisman candidates were more prominently showcased. He would prefer being a big fish in a big pond and eventually getting his picture on the cover of *Sports Illustrated*.

He would prefer moving away from home to experience the wild side of college life in a major college town free from his parents' scrutiny.

But nothing was going to deter him from his haughty goal of being a college quarterback, and no one else seemed to want him at that position. So, contrary to the advice of practically everyone who knew him, Nolan Jakes signed a letter of intent to matriculate to Cal State Northridge.

In his freshman year at CSUN, Jakes struggled to learn the offensive system, to read complex college defenses, and to perfect his passing and running. He played well for a freshman, but many in the university's sports program feared that CSUN football was in for a long, depressing four years under Jakes' leadership.

But as a fired-up, superbly trained and prepared sophomore quarterback, Nolan Jakes began to make things happen. He was no disappointment to his coach, the administration, his team, or any of the thousands of fans who flocked to the stadium to watch him play. The sophomore sensation rushed and passed for more yards than any quarterback in school history.

As a junior, Jakes led the Cal State Matadors to second place in their conference, missing the championship by the slim margin of three points to Portland State the last game of the season. He was voted to the All-Conference first team and made second team All American. And he even got his picture in *Sports Illustrated* — not on the cover, but on one of the back pages. There he was in uniform — pads but no helmet — sporting that wild-eyed, cocky grin and his trademark half-inch crew cut.

Then something happened. Nolan Jakes returned to school after Christmas break sullen and noncommunicative, as if his family had suddenly died or all his friends had abandoned him, neither of which had happened. He stopped partying and moved out of the frat house into a single apartment. He ignored his tutors and his grades plummeted.

Well-meaning friends and teammates probed him with questions to uncover the problem, to which his stock reply was, "It's no big deal; I just need some space." Rumors abounded behind Jakes' back, the most popular of which were that he had impregnated the professor's daughter he had been dating or had contracted a sexually transmitted disease. Jakes wasn't talking, so his fellow students continued to wonder and eventually stopped asking.

Then, in the spring, he was suddenly gone. Without so much as a "Thanks and good-bye," Jakes left school before finals, bailed on his scholarship and final year of eligibility at CSUN, and signed a contract to play professional football for the British Columbia Lions of the Canadian Football League. A few NFL teams had scouted Jakes during his first two years at CSUN, but the CFL Lions had actively solicited the rising star to turn pro, assuring him that he could complete his college education during the off-season, at the Lions' expense, if he so chose. And the Lions wanted him at quarterback, not defensive back, which is what most of the scouts were predicting he would play in the NFL.

Jakes had steadfastly refused their repeated offers in the fall, citing his desire to finish school at CSUN and play pro football in the States. But when the Lions' tenacious scout pitched Jakes again during spring workouts, not really expecting a change in his disposition, Jakes surprised him with a keen interest and, eventually, a signature.

Jakes seemed to pull out of his funk during his rookie season in B.C., making new friends and establishing himself as a major league party animal. He went on to play thirteen seasons in the CFL. He was a reliable, steady player, but he wasn't a great player by NFL standards. A few NFL teams scouted him in his early years in Canada, then gave up. The consensus was that Nolan Jakes had reached the pinnacle of his ability in the CFL and would never make it in the States as a pro.

Life in the Canadian Football League didn't quite match up to Jakes' dream of playing quarterback in the NFL. But the money was good, and he spent it in large quantities. Available women were plentiful, so he used them and discarded them like suits. And the modicum of fame he achieved gratified him, especially when he appeared on the cover of *Sports Illustrated*—with four other teammates—when his B.C. Lions captured the Grey Cup. He wore the same boyish grin and half-inch buzz-job haircut that had marked his first appearance in *SI*.

Once his knees gave out, Nolan Jakes' fall from grace was fast and sure. After ten years with the Lions, surgery forced him to the sidelines. Following rehabilitation he was still fast, but not fast enough for the Lions. So they unceremoniously traded him to Toronto where he sat on the bench for most of the year. The next year he went to the Blue Bombers with the same results.

Finally, in response to Jakes' immense popularity with the fans in British Columbia, the Lions took him back for one last year at a severe cut in pay. Jakes played sparingly, but his presence in Vancouver, especially as the television spokesperson for B.C. Tire and Brake Stores, was good for the team's box office and the city's economy.

When Nolan Jakes left the Lions after his sentimental retirement year, 1992, he quickly slipped into oblivion in Canada. The team did well without him, his groupies dropped him for more popular athletes, and B.C. Tire and Brake opted for an active Lions player as its television spokesperson. Within a year of cleaning out his locker, Jakes was out of work and far out of the limelight.

He still had money and friends, and he lived off both for a few more years, but eventually his lifestyle caught up with him. He was forced to liquidate much of his personal property to pay outstanding debts. Humiliated and defeated, he sought financial help from many who had borrowed from him during his first ten years in Canada. All but a few turned him down cold, and those who did help him couldn't help enough.

In the fall of 1997, Jakes decided to return to L.A. where he hoped his past successes and familiar name would help him slime his way into a job—any job. The dark specter which had urged him to leave college early for the CFL still leered at him from a distant, shadowy corner of his mind. But with each intervening year its threat had diminished to the point where Jakes' desperate hope for a job in L.A. overpowered his need to stay away.

Shortly after arriving in L.A., an old teammate from the Lions introduced Nolan Jakes to G. Billy Fryman, the flamboyant auto baron of the San Fernando Valley. The portly, loud-mouthed, hard-nosed entrepreneur owned a string of high-volume auto dealerships along Van Nuys Boulevard between Burbank Boulevard and the Ventura Freeway. He was famous for his hard-sell TV commercials blitzing local stations during all-night movies and professional wrestling broadcasts.

Fryman, the patron saint of has-been jocks in L.A., had remembered Jakes and was immediately impressed with his experience pitching front-end alignments and brake jobs in Vancouver. Two weeks later Nolan Jakes was taping commercials from one of Fryman's used-car lots. Within three months he had claimed the position of Fryman's "Zap Man," the celebrity spokesperson for his electric Zap Runabout dealership on Van Nuys Boulevard.

It didn't take long for Jakes to detect that the success of Fryman's auto empire was rooted in shady dealings. Jakes knew that odometers were often rolled back on trade-ins before resale, that noisy transmissions on used cars were packed with oatmeal to quiet them, and that new-car customers were overcharged for some options, with the scam veiled behind double-talk in the sales contract.

These injustices bothered Jakes only a little, because he couldn't afford to be bothered a lot. He wasn't about to let minor qualms of conscience jeopardize his very fortunate circumstances. And his conscience adapted and numbed quickly, priming him for future compromises.

The money Jakes earned from Fryman wasn't anything like he had enjoyed as a professional athlete, but it was surprisingly good—far better than he could earn selling sneakers in the mall. And Fryman had generously offered him a substantial low-interest loan to clear his outstanding debts and to bankroll a wardrobe and residence befitting a television spokesperson. He was still a has-been, Jakes acknowledged, but he was one of the lucky has-beens, with a comfortable apartment in Encino, nice clothes, a company car, and a little spending money at the end of the month. He quietly decided that he would do anything

Fryman wanted—tell lies on TV, cheat customers, anything—to hold onto the piece of security the shady auto man had offered him.

And, after two years in Billy Fryman's employ, Nolan Jakes had a new girlfriend. Margo Sharpe, the office manager for a small talent agency in Studio City, came into the dealership to test-drive a Runabout one day when Jakes was taping a commercial. She kept coming back until he invited her to lunch. She wasn't glamor-magazine stunning or girlie-magazine tantalizing, like many of the women who had thrown themselves at Jakes during his football career. Instead, Margo was petite, pretty, practical, and smart—smarter than he was, Jakes admitted. She was ten years younger than Jakes and divorced.

Jakes was unaccustomed to seeing the same woman for more than six months. Most others quickly bored him with their demands for things and trips. Margo was different. Jakes offered to take her to fancy restaurants, but she preferred a breezy drive to Malibu in his company convertible and a picnic dinner on the beach at sunset. Once he surprised her with a necklace which had cost him his monthly bonus. She thanked him graciously, then made him return it for a refund and use the money to pay off his apartment furniture.

Margo had never heard of Nolan Jakes the football player. He was blown away by the fact that she liked him for who he was, not for how many touchdowns he had scored or how much money he had made as a football star. And she eagerly displayed her affection for Jakes by welcoming him into her bed. They had celebrated the arrival of the new millennium together with a brief but romantic trip to the Grenadines. Jakes couldn't remember being happier with any woman.

Jakes felt a deep love for Margo Sharpe, a love he had not felt for any of a myriad of women he had been with. Margo may even be the one, he had pondered cautiously, to whom I will finally unburden my soul about that frightful night in December twenty-two years ago.

It was eight months later when G. Billy Fryman called Jakes into his office for a startling revelation. As two associates, Victor Chance and Reynoso Fernandez, stood by, he announced to Jakes that his most lucrative business wasn't automobiles, but "ice": base methamphetamine, the purest and most addictive form of a plethora of methamphetamines marketed through L.A.'s extensive drug network. Jakes learned—without really wanting to know—that the roly-poly auto dealer had clandestinely bankrolled the manufacturing, smuggling, warehousing, and sale of ice in the Valley in a big way, moving as many as 60,000 kilos a month through his "ice house" in Sylmar.

"You have exceeded all my hopes for you in the dealership, Nolan," Fryman had said with a syrupy smile. The man's fat head made his vague gray eyes, small nose, narrow mustache, and thin-lipped mouth appear bunched in the middle of his face like holes in a bowling ball. "You're still a winner with me."

Jakes decided to ignore the backhanded reference to the fact that his days as a star were far behind him. In his younger days he might have jumped over the desk and smashed Fryman's face and taken on both goons for such a snide remark. But defeat and self-doubt since the disappointing end of his football career had drained much of the fight from him.

"To show my gratitude for a job well done," Fryman continued with plastic beneficence, "I offer you a position in our 'subsidiary' at a substantial raise in pay. This is the chance of a lifetime, Nolan; I generally do not staff my chemical company with people working on the automotive side. But you have excellent people skills and some contacts we can use. What do you say?"

It was an offer Jakes knew he couldn't refuse, even though he wanted to. He was in hock to Fryman up to his biceps. To say no would doubtless mean his job, not to mention, he realized with a sobering chill, the possibility of unthinkable misfortune at the hands of men like Chance and Fernandez, whom Fryman retained as "security staff."

Fryman never said anything to Jakes about an alternative to his offer, at least not with words. But there was a tone in his voice and a threatening snap in his steel gray eyes that communicated, "If you don't accept my offer, you will have no use for a job or a company car or an apartment or a girlfriend." Jakes saw his options clearly. He could ride up the company elevator or step into an empty shaft and plunge to the bottom.

Victor Chance, a cold-eyed, hairless man whose face and disposition both appeared to be hewn out of granite, confirmed Jakes' fears during the first months of "management training." Chance stayed with Jakes day and night, curtly instructing him where to go, who to meet, when to speak, what to say, and how to keep the cops away. And whenever he wasn't instructing Jakes on the finer points of transporting and selling kilos of ice, Chance was disassembling and reassembling, loading and unloading his compact nine-millimeter Rourk polymer semi-automatic where Jakes could see it and hear it. Occasionally, a cold glance from the gunman, as he deftly snapped the Rourk together, telegraphed his eagerness to use the weapon if Jakes stepped out of line.

And Reynoso Fernandez's black, menacing eyes conveyed the same threat. Fernandez was short and thick with a bushy mustache and goatee and wavy black hair. His hands were large enough to engulf a Rourk nine-millimeter, so he preferred an old, substantial .357 Magnum which he carried in a shoulder holster under his leather jacket.

Fernandez often drove Chance and Jakes to their appointments with clients. Perhaps under instructions from Fryman, Fernandez occasionally waved the massive Magnum under Jakes' nose while saying to Chance in his heavy Latino accent, "This will put the brakes on Señor

Jakes, Victor, if he starts rolling away." Then Fernandez would laugh. Jakes never saw so much as a smile crack Chance's stone face.

The substantial "raise" Jakes received in his new position had helped ease his discomfort about being in the drug business and his fear about working under the scrutiny of two killers. And Jakes' compliant conscience eventually adjusted. *People are free to buy or not buy Fryman's ice; nobody's forcing them,* he rationalized. *I'm merely providing a service to those who make that choice.*

Furthermore, the large wad of bills in his pocket was a reassuring tie to his glorious distant past. He never wanted to be poor again. He hoped to get out of Fryman's organization some day, but he planned to grab as much cash as he could before he left.

Jakes saw little of Margo Sharpe for the first several months of his indoctrination into the subsidiary. Fryman had strictly forbidden him, in a clearly threatening tone, from telling anyone about his "promotion." When Jakes talked to Margo on the phone and she asked about his sudden preoccupation with work, he made up stories about shooting commercials away from L.A. and visiting the Zap factory in Michigan. He didn't like stringing her along, but he liked even less the reality of the danger they would both be in if Fryman found out he had told her. So he allowed his head to overrule his heart and kept quiet.

In the spring of 2001 Nolan Jakes met "Teddy Brukow" – Sergeant Angelo Donatelli, undercover cop with the Metro drug unit – through a "mutual friend." Brukow wanted to buy. Jakes told Chance, and Chance did a background check, finding Brukow to be the Teamster strong-arm he claimed to be. So Jakes sold him a kilo, then two, then a dozen. Brukow seemed happy, and Jakes couldn't see past the stacks of $100 bills Brukow handed him and the healthy cut he would take away for his part.

On their fourth secret rendezvous, Donatelli-alias-Brukow slammed the surprised Jakes against the wall, cuffed him, and read him his rights. During the subsequent midnight interrogation at Parker Center in downtown L.A., Jakes explained that Fryman had forced him into dealing. The cops laughed unsympathetically. Then the Drug Enforcement Agency officers present offered Jakes the choice between being a federal prisoner or an informant and witness to help them nab Fryman. In exchange for his testimony, Jakes would go free and be anonymously relocated.

The shaken suspect realized he had no more of a choice than he had when Fryman conscripted him for his drug organization. Sick with panic, Jakes nodded submissively. The cops sneaked him back home to Encino with instructions to set up a major buy with Fryman's stooges, Chance and Fernandez, during which Jakes would prompt his coworkers unwittingly to recite for the hidden microphone that Fryman was the head of the organization. In the meantime, the cops said, just shut up and keep doing what you're doing—selling kilos, keeping Fryman happy.

The greedy Fryman quickly agreed to the buy, with Chance's assurance that Brukow was a legitimate major customer. Dodger Stadium was selected as the site for the June 22 rendezvous. Jakes informed Brukow-alias-Donatelli. The sting was co-planned by the LAPD and the DEA under tight security.

The night before the big meeting, Jakes had told Margo everything: his involvement with Fryman's subsidiary, falling into the hands of the law, and the meeting which would topple one of the southland's major drug kingpins. He explained that he would be held in protective custody until after Fryman's trial. "Then I'll be going far away for a long time," he concluded, "and I want you to come with me. It won't be easy, I know that. But we will be together. I love you, Margo. Will you please come with me?"

Margo's face had registered shock as she listened to Jakes' bizarre story. She sat speechless for several moments after his proposal. "I want to be with you, Nolan; you know I do," she answered at last. "But this is so sudden. Leaving my job, leaving the Valley . . . I don't know what to say."

"You don't have to answer me now," he had assured her. "It will be weeks, maybe even months, before I testify. I'll call you. We'll talk about it. We can go wherever you want—Europe, Tahiti, Africa. Think about it, please."

"I will, Nolan," she had promised with a brave smile. Then she embraced him longingly. "I love you too, Nolan," she whispered.

I love you too, Nolan. Jakes fondled the words in his mind as he watched the Colorado right fielder make a nice running catch for the second out in the bottom of the ninth. The pavilion was nearly deserted except for him, Donatelli, and about twenty diehard fans who would stay until the last out, even though their team was losing 12-4.

Margo's hesitancy to accept his invitation last night had sobered him to the gravity of what he was asking her to do. But those words, "I love you too, Nolan," brought hope. It was the first time she had told him that she loved him. *She will decide to go away with me*, he assured himself. *I know she will.*

The batter at the plate struck out swinging and the Dodger faithful sprinkled around the Stadium groaned a final groan as they rose to leave. Donatelli poked Jakes' arm. "C'mon, Jakes, let's get it over with," he said. A stab of fear pierced Jakes' heart as he stood and followed the cop toward the exit. The last place he wanted to be tonight was in a remote corner of the Stadium parking lot with Donatelli, Chance, and Fernandez. But there was no way out, and the fear of death gripped Jakes like a vise.

Six

Reginald Martin Luther King T. Burris was too large for a standard issue uniform. So the officer for the University of Washington Police Department made do with whatever he could find at the big-and-tall shop that came close to the uniform's colors: a pale-blue, short-sleeve shirt and navy slacks. Divorced and living alone, Reginald had sewn on the shoulder patches himself. Other campus officers wore dark-blue caps sporting the UWPD patch. But Reginald's nearly bald head was too large for even an adjustable cap. So he wore a roomy black beret complete with the patch he had sewn on, which kept his head warm on the chilly nights around Puget Sound.

No one at the university complained about Reginald's minor departure from the dress code. For one thing, a man six feet, seven inches tall, and tipping the scale at 280 pounds, tends to provoke more respect than criticism—even if that man is almost fifty. For another, Reginald was good at his job. As a twelve-year veteran, Officer Burris was thoroughly professional and courteous in his dealings with students, staff, and visitors within the 700-acre "city" of over 50,000 daily residents served by the fully accredited U Dub police force.

Reginald overwhelmed his chair, devouring two sub sandwiches he had picked up off campus during an abbreviated dinner hour. The UWPD office, which occupied the Bryant Building on Boat Street along Portage Bay, reeked of jalepeño peppers, onions, and vinegar. A bank of monitors on one wall provided half a dozen live camera-eye views of the grounds, with another assortment of shots available on command from the control panel. The clock on the wall read 9:25 P.M.

Two computer monitors on the old metal desk supplied additional security information. One showed a simple aerial sketch of the entire campus and located four on-duty officers and their vehicles with pulsing dots of light. The other monitor reported the minute-by-minute status of campus buildings. At the moment, a few classroom buildings were reported still open and occupied as the limited schedule of Friday night classes drew to a close. The readout on the administration building showed it to be vacant and secure with one exception. The simple message glowed green, signifying an acceptable condition: DR. LIBBY CARROLL IS WORKING LATE TONIGHT.

As he ate his second sandwich, a pastrami, salami, and provolone on sourdough, Reginald watched the security monitors out of the corner of his eye. But he was more interested in a TV/VCR unit which sat on the corner of the desk. The machine was playing a tape of a UW football game against Stanford which had taken place in Husky Stadium in October 1973.

Reginald used the zoom feature on the remote control to focus on a hulking defensive tackle wearing number 96 on his purple Husky jersey. When Stanford running backs tried to get through his side of the line, number 96 engulfed them and flattened them like a purple tidal wave. When the quarterback dropped back to throw, 96 thundered into the pass protection like a bowling ball through ten-pins, repeatedly thwarting the attempted pass.

Reginald replayed each crushing tackle two or three times, sometimes grunting his delight through mouthfuls of sandwich. And whenever the screen offered a good rear view of number 96, Reginald freeze-framed it and zoomed in on the name stitched in block letters across the back of the shoulder pads: BURRIS.

Life had never been sweeter for Reginald Burris than during his football days at the University of Washington. He had been a star—as much as linemen can be stars when so much of the limelight in football is soaked up by quarterbacks, halfbacks, and wide receivers. He was voted best defensive player on the Husky team three of his four years. He was second runner-up for the Outland Trophy in his senior year, a national award presented to the best college lineman.

Reginald refused to let anything dim the glory of his four years as a Husky star, even though many disappointments over the first six years might have done so, except for his firm resolve. His failure to last a full year in the NFL (bad shoulder, slow feet), an unfaithful wife and subsequently dissolved marriage, and eventually an adequate but uninspiring job as a longshoreman at the Port of Tacoma, had been less than what Reginald had hoped for after college.

After six years on the docks, an old friend from the U talked Reginald into applying for the Tacoma Police Department. To the longshoreman's surprise, he was accepted, and he worked patrol in Tacoma for ten years. It was hard work, but it was good work. Reginald's background as a former Husky great made him a natural for community and school PR.

When a position at UWPD came open, Reginald jumped at the chance to return to his alma mater. He applied and was warmly welcomed. He had no desire to climb the political ladder in the department, content to remain a patrol officer until retirement. Rather, it was his vivid, larger-than-life memories of four years as a monster tackle on the Husky line—and miles of tape in his videocassette library which kept those memories alive—which bolstered Reginald's self-esteem through an exciting but rather lonely existence.

The videotape ended with the victorious Huskies trotting off the artificial stadium turf to strains of the fight song played by the marching band. Number 96 was being handed a game ball by the defensive coordinator. Reginald still had a closet full of such awards in his apartment. The big man eased back in the little steno chair and licked his fingers, relishing the two subs in his gut and the pride in his heart at being number 96.

It was at times like this that his thoughts turned to Libby Carroll. To Officer Reginald Burris she was *Dr.* Carroll, the strong, intelligent, ambitious woman occupying the office of university provost, and he respected her position. But to old number 96, she was Libby, a beautiful forty-two-year-old single mother—tall, lithe, outgoing, desirable, an unattached woman who probably yearned for the company, protection, and affection of a strong unattached man.

Reginald's interest in Libby had caused him to ask about her and read about her in *University Week* and *The Daily*. He knew that she had grown up in Seattle, the youngest of six children. Her father had been an assembly worker at Boeing who worked up to shift supervisor before he retired.

Reginald had read that Libby ran track—sprints and relays—in high school and college. She had even run in the Olympic trials and qualified as an alternate on the 4-by-100 relay team for the 1984 games in Los Angeles, but did not compete.

Libby's past success in athletics became another point of attraction for Reginald. Athletes of both sexes shared a common bond that excluded lesser mortals: the consuming passion to compete and win at great cost in physical pain and deprivation. Reginald had never enjoyed the acclaim and respect of the university's intelligentsia as Dr. Carroll had, nor had he ever expected to. The two were leagues apart in that sense. But he knew that Libby had once pumped iron, just as he had, until she groaned in agony and quivered with exhaustion, only to press the bar again and again. And the graceful, completely feminine administrator who walked the UW campus, powdered, perfumed, neatly combed, and swathed in professional attire, had once sweat the sweat of a gladiator, caring little about how she looked or smelled as she hurled her fleet frame toward the tape.

Yes, Reginald knew that he and Libby shared a small but meaningful parcel of common ground, though he doubted that she knew it yet.

He also knew that Libby Carroll had a son—a student at Washington State—but no husband. The scuttlebutt was that she never had a husband, that her only kid was illegitimate. The fact that a relatively young black unwed mother had risen to such a position of importance in the university's hierarchy had convinced Reginald that times had definitely changed since he was a college student. He thought it likely that Dr. Libby Carroll would someday be the president of the University of Washington—a position, he had heard, to which she heartily aspired. Reginald had assured himself repeatedly over the last couple of years that even an upwardly mobile college president-to-be needs the comfort and affection of a gentleman friend.

Reginald Burris was not naive. He readily acknowledged that Libby

Carroll outranked him in intelligence, station, and social grace. But she had spoken to him a few times in her office regarding security issues, and she had been cordial, approachable. He had joked with her—respectfully, of course—as he assured her that the security of her office was his top priority.

There would surely come a time when he could tell her that his interest ran deeper than her safety on campus. But he was not about to rush the issue and lose the fragile platform of friendship he had constructed. If he played his cards right, perhaps she would even consent to have dinner with him some evening. A woman of her beauty and stature might enjoy a mature and imposing escort who could accompany her anywhere she wanted to go in Seattle in complete safety.

Reginald found himself staring at the words on the computer monitor: DR. CARROLL IS WORKING LATE TONIGHT. He first thought it sad that such a talented, attractive woman was spending a gorgeous summer Friday night in her office, something she rarely did. She should be at the theater or at one of those posh parties the university brass are always throwing in their elegant homes in Bellevue or on trendy Queen Anne hill.

Then he considered his good fortune as he rolled up the sandwich wrappers, tossed them in the can, and wiped off the remote control and the desk top with a napkin. *The fact that Libby is here tonight instead of out partying may mean that she has no one to be out partying with. Perhaps a visit to her office in conjunction with an unofficial security check of the building will give us a chance for a few minutes of friendly conversation.*

Reginald hailed one of his fellow officers on the radio. "Hey, Taggart, come in here and take the con for a few minutes, will you?"

"What's up?" Taggart probed.

"Nothing, really, I just need to get outside for a while."

"Okay, Reg, I'll be right there."

By the time Taggart arrived, Reginald had been to the restroom to wash the vinegar off his hands and face, slick back the few wisps of black and silver hair left on his head, and tuck in his shirt. "I'll be over in the administration building," he said to Taggart, who had taken over the steno chair. Reginald grabbed his beret and opened the door to leave. Then, after a moment of thought, he tossed the beret back on the desk. An old girlfriend once told him he looked sexier without it.

The sun had dropped behind the Olympic range, turning the sky deep orange and drenching the campus in shadow. Reginald drove slowly from the Bryant Building up Brooklyn Avenue to Fortieth Street to the administration building, thinking about what he would say to Dr. Carroll when he "happened onto her" during his security sweep. It was dark enough between buildings that Reginald had to turn on the headlights of his electric Zap Toteabout pickup. Foot traffic was down to a few scattered students leaving campus for home.

Reginald parked his truck in front of the main entrance to the building where Dr. Carroll worked. He had purposely avoided driving along the south side of the building, because he didn't want Libby to see his truck from her window and anticipate his visit. Had he passed by that side and looked at her window, he would have been concerned and suspicious that the lights were out.

Admitting himself through the main entrance with his security key card, Reginald cleared the electronic sentry without pausing to read the message: Welcome, MR. BURRIS. ALL IS SECURE. DR. CARROLL IS WORKING LATE TONIGHT. He would not need to keep in radio contact with Taggart while inside the building. The homing signal on his radio would pinpoint his position minute by minute on the office monitor.

The halls and stairwells inside the building were dimly lit by recessed security lamps. Reginald ascended the marble stairs to the third floor as soundlessly as possible and turned down the broad carpeted hallway toward the office of the provost. He paused at the door to retrieve a compact atomizer of breath freshener from his pants pocket and dispel the smell of peppers and onions with two quick sprays. Then he slid the key card through the lock and slipped quietly into the suite.

Reginald stood motionless in the near darkness inside the door contemplating why no light was visible from Dr. Carroll's private office in the back corner of the suite. *I just missed her,* was his first thought. *She must have gone down the back stairs while I was coming up the front.* But he quickly dismissed that conclusion. He could see that her office door was slightly open, which was a security no-no. All private offices were to be securely locked by their occupants before leaving. The electronic sentries at the building's exits were programmed to scold forgetful personnel and send them scurrying back to secure their unlocked doors. Reginald knew Dr. Carroll would never leave the office for the night with her door standing ajar.

There was another reason why Reginald was concerned that Dr. Carroll's door was ajar with the lights off. There were sounds coming from the corner office: not the soft clack of a computer keyboard or hum of a printer or copier, but the faint rustle of fabric, hushed whispers, and an occasional subdued giggle. Reginald crept closer to the open door, then stopped and listened again.

The big officer suddenly flushed warm with embarrassment and envy as the realization dawned on him: *Libby Carroll is partying tonight after all, except it appears to be a very private, very intimate party with . . .* Reginald stiffened with suspicion and drew his pistol. *That's not Libby Carroll's laugh; it's from a much younger woman, a girl. And there's a man in there too, not a man Libby's age, but a young buck.*

Reginald didn't stop to think if he was moved to action more by curiosity or duty. He simply pushed the office door fully open, hit the switch on the overhead light, and called out in his most intimidating voice, "Hey, what's going on in here?"

The response was a series of terrified yelps followed by a frantic flurry of activity, a blur of arms and legs, brown skin and white, flying up from the sofa like frightened doves at the sound of a shotgun blast. The white blur raced toward Reginald shrieking, aiming for a small space between him and the doorway. Old number 96 threw out his left arm and tackled the blur which turned out to be a teenage girl in her underwear. She had frizzy hair and a pixy face which was contorted into a look of utter humiliation.

Reginald held the girl fast in his left arm with ease, lifting her off the floor for good measure. She squirmed and cried but had sense enough not to strike the officer. In the meantime, the brown blur had disappeared behind the sofa.

"Be still," the big man barked to the girl, and she quickly stifled her crying and became a statue in his arm.

Then he leveled his pistol at the sofa. "You, behind the couch. I have a gun, and I *will* use it if I have to. Now stand up, hands first."

A pair of long brown hands, fingers outstretched and palms facing the officer, slowly appeared above the back of the sofa. The hands were followed by bare arms, head, and chest, as the young African-American stood. He was wearing only a pair of baggy blue boxer shorts. He looked barely in his twenties. The expression on his face reflected no sorrow for what he had done, only sorrow for getting caught.

Reginald kept his pistol aimed at the young man as he carried the girl to the sofa and ordered her to sit down and not move. Then he waved the boy around the sofa to sit down beside his girlfriend.

The girl, clearly mortified at sitting before a stranger dressed only in her panties and bra, reached for a sweatshirt on the floor. "I said don't move!" the officer shouted sternly, turning his gun on her. The girl jumped with fright. Then she covered as much of herself as she could with her arms and began to cry again.

"You don't have to be so rough on her," the young man snapped angrily. "She's no criminal."

Reginald's eyes bored into him. "Look, kid, anybody who's clever enough to get in here without setting off the alarm is clever enough to hide a gun under a sweatshirt." Then, keeping his pistol trained on the couple, the officer dragged the sweatshirt toward himself with the toe of his shoe.

Inspecting the garment and finding no weapons, he tossed it to the girl, who quickly slipped into it. "Thank you," she whimpered.

Reginald tapped his radio to life. "Hey, McConaghy, meet me at Dr.

Carroll's office. I have a couple of trespassers to transport." Reginald's coworker responded affirmatively.

As they waited, the girl buried her face in her hands, sniffling. Reginald stared at the young man, who tried to avert his gaze. There was something familiar in that handsome, creamy mocha face: the angle of the brow, the jut of the chin. Perhaps the boy was a student he had seen around campus before—or even arrested before. It was hard to tell in a university hosting 38,000 students.

The officer glanced away from his prisoners occasionally to inspect the office for possible vandalism or burglary. He guessed that the computer had been tampered with, from the presence of the nylon bag and the hand-held device lying on the desk. *Another hacker dissatisfied with the grades he earned,* Reginald surmised, *so he brings his girlfriend in for a new report card and a stolen thrill in the provost's office.*

Reginald's eyes fell on the framed videograph. There was Dr. Libby Carroll sitting in the Land Rover. She was several years younger, but just as beautiful as ever in her khaki safari jacket and wide-brimmed straw hat. And sitting beside her, beaming with excitement at an African vacation, was a handsome young man of about thirteen. Reginald realized the boy must be Libby's son.

Nice looking kid, Reginald thought, studying the picture. *He has his mother's eyes, mouth, chin—*

The officer's eyes snapped to the young man on the sofa, then back to the videograph, and finally back to the young man. The means for the undetected break-in was suddenly apparent to him. He breathed an expletive, then said, "You're Dr. Carroll's son. You got into this building and this office using your mother's key card. You've been digging around in the computer with her codes. Geez, man, this is no small thing, even for the provost's kid. This is breaking and entering. You and your girlfriend are in deep pucky."

The boy gave the big man a sideward glance, then dropped his head, saying nothing. The girl whined in despair and broke into tears again.

Reginald shook his head slowly, both in disgust at the underhandedness of young Mr. Carroll and in sadness for his mother. The officer realized he would be talking to Libby Carroll tonight, all right, but it wouldn't be the pleasant encounter he had hoped for.

Seven

Shelby's fortieth birthday party was a raging success. Decorations were simple but elegant, limited to several arrangements of fresh flowers from the garden. Evan's tastefully furnished hillside home conveyed more warmth and welcome than balloons or streamers ever could, so there were none. Sparkling punch, Evan's homemade hors d'oeuvres, and birthday cake were available throughout the house and eagerly consumed.

Entertainment was also at a minimum, confined to a stack of classical CD's—music from the late Baroque period, Evan and Shelby's favorite—playing on the integrated entertainment unit and piped throughout the house. In reality, the music was little more than background for the spontaneous chatter filling the living room, dining room, and kitchen where knots of guests huddled.

The party was even more successful than Evan had hoped, considering that the guest list was comprised of two groups of people who didn't know each other: Shelby's family, friends, and coworkers—clearly the larger group, and his own small circle of acquaintances. At first the two groups were politely standoffish toward one another: smiling, nodding, saying hello, but engaging in small talk and more meaningful interaction only among themselves. But as the evening wore on, Evan and Shelby flitted between clusters like shuttles on a loom, making introductions, initiating conversations, refilling punch glasses, slowly drawing the warp and woof of the two groups together.

It was his awareness of the two distinct groups that prompted Evan to call their nearly thirty guests to crowd into the living room and dining room at close to 10 P.M. for more formal introductions. Aaron Weintraub pulled two stools into the living room from the kitchen bar for the hosts to sit on. The rest of the furniture was full to capacity, with half of the guests standing.

Evan had another purpose for bringing everyone together. He planned to hasten the obligatory singing of "Happy Birthday" to Shelby, then formally thank everyone for coming and remind them that the wedding started at 1 P.M. sharp tomorrow. He hoped that the majority of the crowd would take the hint and leave, so the small wedding party could rehearse their cues. Evan was mindful that his bride had to return to Los Angeles for their last night apart, and he wanted to get her on her way at a decent hour.

It took Evan less than three minutes to introduce his guests: associates from the office, Aaron and Sheila Weintraub, the office manager, the receptionist, and two of the nurses; a couple of colleagues from the ER at Community Memorial Hospital; Ben Heath, Evan's CPA and longtime surfing buddy who was the best man; and his mother and her husband, Terry and Sid Conrad, whom Evan had flown in from Yakima, Washington, where Sid was an apple and prune grower. Evan mentioned that his father and his wife, who lived two hours northeast in the desert community of Acton, would be down for the wedding tomorrow.

"Where do I start?" Shelby said, nearly speechless at the sight of so many loved ones spread before her and beaming at her good fortune.

A jokester from the dining room called out, "A lady preacher at a loss for words—I can't believe it." Laughter was abundant.

"Shelby's forty now," another friend piped up. "She still has plenty to say, but she's forgotten all our names." A chorus of belly laughs echoed through the house. Shelby and Evan laughed too.

"I haven't forgotten any of your names," Shelby countered in a tone of mock pride. Then she added with a hint of nostalgia softening her voice, "And I never will. I don't know where I'd be without people like you." Several faces nodded, conveying a similar feeling about the lovely, poised woman speaking to them.

Shelby gestured to a distinguished-looking couple in their early sixties, respectfully afforded a seat on the couch by younger guests. "This is Stan and Eleanor Welbourn, dear friends and spiritual mentors who have been so supportive and helpful to me, especially in the last three years. Stan has been lead pastor at Victory Life Ministries in Dallas since I formally resigned a little more than a year ago.

"Stan and his staff have done a marvelous job implementing the resolutions which came out of Unity 2000 in Los Angeles. Victory Life has taken quite a turn under Stan's leadership, clearly a turn for the better. They're feeding Christ's sheep in Texas and—"

Shelby interrupted herself, smiling self-consciously. "Here I go, wanting to tell everyone's life story in glowing detail. We could be here all night." Shelby's audience laughed politely at her transparency. "Anyway, Stan and Eleanor are very special. Stan will be officiating at the ceremony tomorrow." A few soft hums of satisfaction were heard around the room.

Shelby shifted her gaze to the elegantly dressed woman in her mid-forties sitting beside the Welbourns on the sofa. "Theresa Bordeaux has been like a loving big sister to me for a number of years," Shelby said, affection glowing on her face. "Theresa was my personal assistant and housemate until I resigned and sold the ranch in Austin. At my encouragement, she has remained with Stan and Eleanor in the ministry, but we are yet the closest of friends. She will be my maid of honor tomorrow." Theresa flashed a warm smile and wink.

Next Shelby gestured toward an Oriental family standing under the arch between the dining room and living room. "I am also so pleased to have you meet Thanh Hai Ngo—or Dr. No as he is known to so many of us, his wife Mai, and their delightful children, Wendy and David. Dr. No is the director of King's House in Los Angeles.

"At the turn of the millennium I took a three-month sabbatical from Victory Life Ministries to volunteer at King's House." Shelby chuckled lightly at the memory. "At first I thought of God as the ultimate killjoy for asking me to leave the Dallas ministry and my beautiful home in

Austin for three months—which stretched into eighteen—in downtown L.A. But He knew what He was doing. I learned more about serving God and serving people during those months than in the previous ten years in Dallas' most influential church."

An image-filled breeze from the past fluttered into Shelby's consciousness as she spoke, like a sudden draft bringing an instant chill. Ten years of experiences, victories, and heartaches were compressed into the tiny memory-chip of a moment. Yet the entire sum of those ten years was indelibly tainted by the last eight, heartwrenching days of 1999: Shelby's own moral failure and attempt to run from God; the shocking revelation concerning her "late" husband, Adrian Hornecker; the humiliation of a call to the back streets of Los Angeles to a shelter for the homeless and the hurting, as if God were demoting her to a remote and inconsequential post.

But, as often had been the case in the last eighteen months, Shelby's discomfiting memory was mercifully fleeting, quickly overpowered by the warmth of acceptance and new direction discovered under the leadership of an unassuming Vietnamese-American engineer-turned-missionary to L.A.'s discarded thousands. Millennium's dawn in Los Angeles had unpredictably turned as bright and promising for Shelby Hornecker as Millennium's Eve had been dark and defeating.

"For those of you who don't know," Shelby continued, glancing toward Evan's acquaintances, "Dr. No leads a staff of more than fifty full-time caregivers and a volunteer roster approaching 400. Mai, his wife, used to be assistant religion editor at the *Los Angeles Times*, but is now fully involved with us at King's House. Wendy, their daughter, just graduated from high school. She is entering nurses' training in the fall. And David will be a high school junior next fall, following an accelerated track in math and science."

The other guests saluted the family with a polite ripple of applause.

Shelby introduced several more staff members from King's House whom she had asked Evan to invite to the party. Most of them were her associates in overseeing the spiritual life of the staff and residents of King's House, a responsibility Dr. No had turned over to her at the first of the year.

"I've saved the best for last," Shelby said, beaming toward a couple in their late sixties sitting in the loveseat. The gentleman wore western-cut slacks, a dressy western shirt, and boots that had never been soiled with the muck of a horse stall. The lady's silver hair was still laced with strands of gold from her youth. Her powder-blue eyes gazed at Shelby with pride. "I'd like you all to meet my parents, Jimmy and Evelyn Tuggle from Waco, Texas. I reclaimed their name eighteen months ago. I guess I needed to do that to return some stability to my life after the events of Millennium's Eve.

"But now," Shelby said, smiling to the couple on the loveseat, "I'm giving up your name again. Thank you for the strength you have always provided. No one can ever take your place, but God has given me someone to take some of your responsibilities." Without breaking her gaze from her parents, Shelby reached out to grasp the willing hand of her fiancé.

"Finally," Shelby said, sitting upright on the stool to shake off the misty-eyed sentimentality that her parents' presence induced, "I want you all to meet a young lady who has literally changed my life over the last eighteen months." She made eye contact with a tiny seven-year-old black girl sitting between the Tuggles on the loveseat. Her tightly braided hair and fashionable, pastel dress clashed with the scars on her ebony face, scars which evidenced that she had not lived long in the safe, comfortable, privileged environment enjoyed by the other guests in the room.

The girl's eyes were wide and darting, as if constantly looking for a stalking enemy. Those in the room who *had* noticed her during the evening, and the few who had attempted to speak to her, found her to be unsmiling and unresponsive.

"I met Malika the day I moved into King's House. She was a resident of our women's shelter, and I assumed that her mother was one of the women living on that floor. I later found out that Malika's parents were . . . out of the picture." Shelby strategically avoided mentioning the details for the girl's sake. Malika had never known her father. She had lived in a squalid L.A. flophouse with her prostitute, drug-addicted mother. From infancy the girl had been the object of unspeakable abuse at the hands of her mother and her clients. One of these men eventually beat the woman to death with his fists, while the terrified child hid in a cabinet under the bathroom sink.

King's House volunteers had found Malika wandering the downtown streets, half-starved and sick from infected wounds which had never been treated. She appeared to be retarded, possibly brain-damaged from beatings and malnutrition. Malika hardly ever spoke, and when she did it was in barely intelligible clumps of words, not sentences. If she had a name when she arrived at the King's House shelter, she was unable to communicate it. A volunteer staff member found "Malika" written in ink on the label of the child's shirt.

Despite the unsightly scars on Malika's slight body, the fear and suspicion in her mood, the total disregard for cleanliness in her appearance, and the lack of awareness and respect for others in her behavior, Shelby was attracted to her. It wasn't just sympathy for a pathetically disadvantaged child that drew her close. Shelby noticed something in Malika's eyes, a flickering candle of life which cowered in fear of being extinguished, to be sure, but which also yearned to burn brightly.

This child is not a piece of spoiled meat ready for the garbage heap,

Shelby had acknowledged after watching Malika for several days. *There is a person inside, a person of worth and dignity, just waiting to be coaxed into the light and loved to health.*

There were many other abandoned children at King's House about whom Shelby felt deeply, and for whose health and family placement she tirelessly worked. But the light in Malika's eyes was special, as if God had placed a tiny homing beacon within the girl and tuned it to Shelby's heart alone. Shelby could no more explain or deny the call to focus her energies on Malika than she could explain or deny the call to leave Dallas for Los Angeles and King's House.

During the first four months of their interaction, a love for Malika welled up in Shelby that she had known for no other person outside her own family. Malika seemed to trust Shelby and blossom under her care more than for any other caregiver at King's House. The phenomenon confirmed to Shelby that Malika wasn't just a child she was to care for, but someone she was to belong to.

Shelby continued, "Malika and I became good friends during my three month 'sabbatical' at King's House, and we did lots of things together." Shelby's unspoken translation: *Malika came with no understanding of basic cleanliness, grooming, manners, personal discipline, or modesty. Dr. No assigned me to be Malika's "Annie Sullivan," teaching her what it means to be a young lady.* "We became such good friends, in fact, that when my three months were up, I couldn't leave. I had so much more love to give to Malika and others at King's House. That's when I knew God wanted me to make an indefinite commitment to Dr. No and the ministry here."

Shelby extended a hand and a warm smile inviting Malika to join her. The girl stood and walked to Shelby's side obediently, although her expression communicated self-consciousness and hesitance. The guests watched her silently.

As Malika came, Shelby said, "After six months together, it became obvious to me that Malika was the answer to a prayer I had been praying for more than ten years, a prayer which I thought had gone up in flames along with the rest of my life on Millennium's Eve. But God has a way of making beauty out of ashes, and He did that for me in this beautiful little girl."

Shelby lifted Malika into her arms, like a mother hen comforting a frightened chick. The girl's face was stiff with the discomfort of being the center of attention. "The child my late husband was unable to give me came into my life in a most unusual and serendipitous fashion." Shelby paused as a swell of emotion and maternal pride momentarily choked back her words. Evan reached out a comforting hand that touched both Shelby and Malika.

After a silent moment Shelby added a final, tearful sentence. "I'm so happy to introduce to you all my dear adopted daughter, Malika Tuggle."

Little Malika had no defense against the affirming applause and warm smiles beamed at her. Her eyes, drinking in the sight before her, telegraphed recognition that the loving gestures were for her, and a subtle, unbidden smile brightened her usually clouded face.

"Okay, you two, let's hear a love story." The request came from the affable Aaron Weintraub, just as Evan was about to strike up a rousing chorus of "Happy Birthday" and officially close the party.

"Yes, tell us how you two met," someone else chimed in.

"We want to hear it all, especially the romantic parts," called out another guest, provoking a ripple of good-natured laughter.

With their guests prodding them to speak, Evan and Shelby found each other's eyes. They acknowledged with a brief, smiling gaze, "We don't have time for this. But our friends are so insistent, and it really is a wonderful story. Why not?"

Finally, Evan nodded and quieted the crowd with an upraised hand. Then he looked to Shelby and said with a grin, "Unaccustomed to public speaking as I am, I'll let my bride-to-be begin."

Shelby coaxed Malika back to her grandparents and answered him loudly enough for everyone to hear, "But if it hadn't been for King's House, darling, we wouldn't have a story. They all know how I got involved. Maybe you'd better start by telling our friends how you ended up there."

Caught up in the festive mood, Evan couldn't pass up the opportunity for a little fun. Turning to the guests, he began with a put-on plaintive expression, "Well, I was destitute. I had no food or money, and I was living in a cardboard box under a freeway overpass when this nice lady came along and—"

"O Evan!" Shelby interrupted, playfully punching him on the arm. The room exploded with laughter, everyone enjoying the entertainment.

"Okay, I'll be good," Evan said, hugging Shelby and playing to the crowd.

The laughter died down, and the couple returned to their stools. Evan began again in a more serious tone. "Actually, I really *was* destitute. Back in January of '99 I experienced—what shall I call it?—a kind of personal identity crisis. I should have been the happiest man in Ventura County. I had a great practice, plenty of money, a beautiful house, good friends. But sitting out there on the patio on the day I turned thirty-eight, it was suddenly all meaningless.

"I added up everything I had accomplished and accumulated, and I still came up with zero. My life was kind of like a jigsaw puzzle. I had most of it put together, but the most important pieces in the middle were missing, so I couldn't tell what the picture was supposed to be."

Evan avoided eye contact with his associate, Aaron Weintraub, and others of his friends in the room whom he knew didn't share his perspective on success and failure. He welcomed the opportunity to verbalize the change which had occurred in his life. But he determined not to alienate those in the room whom he knew were still clinging to the hollow, earthly values he had discarded and replaced with faith nearly two years earlier.

"So I set out on what you might call a quest for meaning. I wanted to find something to do that would fill in the big hole in the middle of my puzzle. Luckily—or I guess I should say providentially—I heard about King's House down in L.A." Evan turned an affectionate gaze toward Dr. No and Mai. "An old friend from County General told me that King's House needed volunteer physicians to care for a variety of destitute patients, including AIDS victims.

"I thought, 'Now that's about as far from what I'm doing as anything: urban L.A. versus suburban Ventura; an old hospital versus a modern office; impoverished patients versus wealthy clients; no fees versus substantial fees. Maybe the missing pieces can be found in the inner city.' So I cleared one day a week on my appointment book and became a King's House volunteer."

Evan paused, ordering his thoughts, weighing his words.

"But I didn't find *missing pieces* to my picture at King's House; instead I found a *whole new picture*. These people weren't running a shelter for the homeless and dying in order to find meaning in life; they did what they did because they already understood their purpose, and they were free to give themselves to others who were still lost.

"Dr. No used to tell us at staff meetings, 'We reach out to these people with tenderness and treat them with respect and dignity, not because they deserve it but because that's how God reaches out to us and treats us. You'll never be able to take care of these people with compassion until you let God fill your need for love and acceptance.'

"At first, I didn't know what he meant. But after a few months of watching the King's House staff work and sitting in on several of Dr. No's talks, I realized that I had never let God reach me and care for me at the deepest levels of my life. When I finally let Him do that, my quest was over. This may sound trite, but I allowed God to come into my life through His Son Jesus Christ, and the whole picture changed. I found that success isn't measured by what I accomplish or accumulate in life, but by how I respond to what God has done for me."

Evan ventured a gaze across his rapt audience. Facial expressions reflected a range of personal responses from wholehearted approval to mild but tolerant skepticism. He continued, "As the new millennium dawned, my whole view of life changed. I saw my God-given abilities in new light: not as something with which to indulge myself, but as tools for serving people who, for whatever reason, were not as fortunate in life as I.

"So I continued to work at King's House one day a week and learn the real meaning of the ministry of caregiving. In the process, one February day I met the most attractive and fascinating new volunteer on the fifth floor."

Evan turned to Shelby and invited her with a smile and a nod to pick up the story. She leaned slightly forward in her stool, taking the cue.

"At Dr. No's direction, I had been spending a week or two on each floor of the House learning the ropes. The fifth floor was my last stop. I was certain by then that I wanted to invest the remainder of my sabbatical working with homeless and battered women and children. But Dr. No still thought I should spend a week with AIDS patients to complete my well-rounded education before settling in on the second floor with the women and children. To tell you the truth, I wasn't looking forward to spending a week in the AIDS ward."

She smiled respectfully toward Dr. No across the room and said, "I want to thank you for insisting that I go through with my tour of duty on the fifth floor. I had no idea what an impact that week would make on my life."

Dr. No telegraphed his, "You're welcome," with a warm smile.

Shelby continued, "My first day on the floor, this rather good-looking doctor approached me and—"

"*Rather* good-looking?" Evan's tongue-in-cheek question, accompanied by an exaggerated sadsack look, provoked another shower of laughter.

"All right, *very* good-looking," Shelby corrected, giggling at her fiancé's repartee.

"That's better."

"Anyway, this very good-looking doctor approached me at the nurses station and said, 'Mr. Carpenter in 502 pulled out his catheter. Will you go in there and reinsert it for me, please?' I was a little flustered at the thought, so I said, 'I'm sorry, but I don't know how to do that.'

"Then the doctor said, 'Oh, a little rusty in our nursing skills, are we?' Then he began describing to me in great anatomical detail how to insert a catheter into a male patient. I'm sure I turned five shades of crimson before I cut him off by saying, 'Doctor, I can't put in Mr. Carpenter's catheter because I'm a helper, not a nurse.' "

Evan and Shelby's party guests laughed louder and longer with every colorfully descriptive line.

Shelby continued, "Evan just stared at me for a moment with those captivating dark eyes. Then he said, 'Well, you're certainly pretty enough to be a nurse.' "

The overdramatic oohs and ahs of the crowd brought a sudden blush to Shelby's cheeks. Evan turned his head away trying to cover his giddy grin. "What a lady-killer!" Aaron Weintraub called out with a laugh, giving voice to everyone's thoughts.

Shelby moved on quickly. "To be perfectly honest, my first reaction was that this very good-looking doctor had made a very sexist remark." Another chorus of exaggerated oohs rose from the audience, mostly from the men.

Evan threw up his hands in surrender, saying, "I was just trying to give the lady a nice compliment." The men in the room cheered in his defense.

Shelby continued, "But then I had to consider the source and exercise mercy. The poor guy didn't know what he was doing." This time the ladies cheered. The laughter was ongoing, proving that the sparring was all in fun.

"Seriously," Shelby said, "Evan and I saw each other every Friday at King's House. Either he would come down to the second floor on some trumped-up errand, or I would wander up to the fifth to see if anyone—especially the handsome doctor with the dark wavy hair—needed any help. Before long we were eating lunch together every Friday in the cafeteria—first with a group of colleagues, then at a table alone."

Evan interjected with a thoughtful expression, "Those lunchtime discussions with Shelby were very meaningful to me. I was very green in the faith and ignorant about the Bible at that time. I thought the Book of Judges was probably an indictment of the Supreme Court. The Acts of the Apostles sounded like a book of religious plays." The chuckles at Evan's prior ignorance were polite and forgiving.

"Shelby tutored me in the ABCs of the faith during our lunches together, and the pages of my Bible are still spotted with split-pea soup, salad dressing, and coffee to prove it."

"Come on, you two," called one of Evan's colleagues from the hospital, "get to the good stuff: first date, first kiss." The woman was obviously not taken with the recitation of his religious pilgrimage.

Shelby responded, ready to bring the story to a close. "In May, Evan took me to Sea World in San Diego for our first official date—Malika went along too. In July, I took him to the Chandler Pavilion for a concert of choral works by Saint-Saëns, Mendelssohn, Gounod, Handel, and Bach—Malika stayed home for that one. I believe our first kiss was in September at sunset on our way in to dinner at the Ranch House Restaurant in Ojai. Malika missed that milestone event too. And the rest, as they say, is history."

Evan wrapped his arm around Shelby's waist. "Not being very clever, I proposed to Shelby on Valentine's Day at the Ranch House during dessert. Actually, I only asked her to pray about my offer. But over coffee ten minutes later, she admitted that she had already prayed about it, and her answer was yes." A warm, triumphant cheer echoed around the room.

Evan gave Shelby another loving squeeze. Then to his guests he said, "What can I say? I'm the most fortunate man in the world to have found this woman. I covet your prayers for our marriage, even though I can't see anything but a wonderful life ahead for us. I couldn't be happier."

Then Evan hastened to lead the small throng in singing "Happy Birthday" to Shelby. He hoped the boisterous chorus would drown the somber drumbeat sounding from the dark periphery of his consciousness. It was a persistent, accusatory rhythm daring Evan to hope for a happy future, in light of his shadowy, unresolved past. Could the rhythm be translated into language, the same word would sound repeatedly: *Unworthy, unworthy, unworthy.*

Eight

Nolan Jakes and undercover officer Donatelli stood beside the dirty Mercedes as other cars left the Stadium parking lot to clog the exits and drain slowly out of the Ravine. Jakes leaned against the front door on the passenger's side holding an open bottle of beer which he had not tasted. He was grateful for the transdermal tranquilizer that kept his hands from shaking and spilling the brew all over himself.

When they had first reached the car, Jakes casually touched his watchband and switched on the secret transmitter for a moment at Donatelli's command. "In position," Jakes reported. He spoke the words as if in conversation with Donatelli, in case Chance or Fernandez had the glasses trained on them from some distant vantage point. As soon as he delivered the message, he switched the wire off again.

There was no response to the message because Jakes had not been equipped with a receiver and miniature earbud. Wearing the transmitter wire, though it was virtually invisible, was risky enough.

Donatelli slouched on the car's front fender a few feet away, with a bottle of beer in one hand and a cigarette in the other. Jakes watched the cop's hawkish eyes nonchalantly sweep the lot around them like a surveillance camera. Occasionally, he would lift his bottle to a nearby car heading for the exit and yell, "Go Dodgers!"

Jakes flicked a glance toward the dark tower across the parking lot on the elevated Police Academy grounds, which was over a mile from where the Mercedes was parked. He knew there was a powerful TV camera trained on them "which can zoom in tight enough for us to count the hairs hanging out of your nose," the cops had said. Jakes blinked at the irony. He had been on TV many times, playing football in Canada and doing Fryman's commercials in L.A. Would this be his last appearance? He hoped his command performance tonight wouldn't end with him getting shot by Fryman's men or the police or both.

Every couple of minutes Jakes saw Donatelli's left elbow intentionally brush against the bulge on his left hip. *Yeah, you've got your security tucked into your belt,* Jakes complained silently, *but what about me?* He wished that the tranquilizer numbing his nerves would somehow quiet the alarms of imminent danger clanging in his brain.

Once Jakes' eyes met Donatelli's for a few seconds. The cop locked Jakes into a gaze, then casually lifted his beer bottle to touch the shoulder of his sweat jacket, clearly referring to the body wire sewn into Jakes' jacket. Then he lifted his index finger away from the bottle and waggled it slightly to communicate, "No, no."

Lecturing me up to the last moment, aren't you, sergeant? Jakes thought wryly. *Relax, jerk,* he assured with an annoyed nod, *I won't turn on the wire until they've scanned us.*

After forty-five minutes the parking lot on the south side of the Stadium was empty, except for a few scattered tailgate parties and a couple of cars with dead batteries. Donatelli seemed unaffected, as if used to people showing up late for appointments. Jakes began to fear that something had gone wrong and that Chance and Fernandez might not show at all. *Perhaps they're waiting inside my apartment to finish me off in private when I go home,* he thought.

Jakes smiled to himself at the small victory. He wouldn't be going back to his apartment tonight—or for many nights to come. Following the bust he would be taken to a safehouse and provided everything he needed until after the trial. All the same, he had left his apartment intact—food in the fridge, clothes in the dryer, toothpaste on the bathroom sink—in case Chance and Fernandez showed up there on the way to the game. An obviously deserted apartment would have immediately alerted Fryman's henchmen to a plot.

Jakes stiffened as he recognized a lone car sweeping slowly around the west side of the Stadium and heading in their direction. It was Reynoso Fernandez's black Continental Mark XII coupe.

Donatelli saw the car at the same time and knew who it was without looking to Jakes for confirmation. He casually took another sip of beer and brushed his elbow over his concealed .44 again. Jakes shifted from foot to foot, feeling suddenly chilled even though the temperature was still in the high sixties.

The Mark XII angled off the beltway encircling the Stadium and aimed its high beams straight at the Mercedes. As it approached, Donatelli dropped his smoke and disintegrated it with the toe of his boot. Jakes set his untouched bottle of beer on the roof of the car.

The Mark XII nosed into the guardrail on the passenger's side of the Mercedes. Fernandez stepped out first and bellowed across the roof with a laugh, "Those Dodgers!" He walked with an easy gait around the back of his car and onto the twelve-foot square of asphalt between the two cars. The husky Latino wore loose-fitting jeans, a black T-shirt, and a tan leather jacket. Jakes pursed his lips slightly as he thought about the cannon holstered under Fernandez's left armpit.

"Yeah, those Dodgers!" Donatelli echoed boisterously, inserting an expletive. "They can't win at home; they can't win on the road. What can I say?"

It was all show, of course, to assure the nearest tailgaters that these four "buddies" were meeting to drain a couple of brews and swap baseball stories before heading home.

Chance stepped out of the car and closed his door, saying nothing. His uneven bald head glistened under the parking lot lights. He wore tan slacks and an open-collared shirt under a lightweight jacket with a nautical insignia on the front. Jakes imagined that Chance's small plastic pistol was resting in his right jacket pocket—precisely where he had stuffed his right hand.

"Get our friends a beer," Donatelli said loudly in Jakes' direction. Jakes moved to the open trunk of the Mercedes and pulled two cold bottles out of the cooler. He eyed with envy the bulky sport bag full of $620,000 in large unmarked bills behind the cooler. For security reasons, the money had been hidden and locked in a specially prepared compartment in the trunk until Donatelli pulled it out after the game. In keeping with Fryman's directive, the money was "clean": There were no transmitters or exploding die-packs in the sport bag.

Jakes held out the beers to his two coworkers, but Fernandez motioned him to put them on the hood of the Mercedes.

Chance and Fernandez stood about five feet apart, with their backs to the Mark XII. Donatelli had told Jakes that the two men would keep some ground between them, to make it harder for both of them to be shot by the same person. All the bad guys worked that way, he had said. The cop had instructed Jakes to stay several steps away from him for the same reason. So Fernandez faced Donatelli on one end of the patch of asphalt and Chance faced Jakes on the other end, like the four corners of a twelve-foot square.

In an awkward moment of silence, Jakes knew it was time to speak, not in a boisterous parking lot voice but in a quieter, private tone. "Mr. Brukow, I'd like to introduce Mr. Fernandez and Mr. Chance." Jakes marveled at how calm he sounded. *That patch on your rear end may just help save your rear end!* he told himself.

The two men acknowledged Donatelli-alias-Brukow with a nod. None of the men showed the slightest interest in shaking hands.

"Are you carrying?" Fernandez asked Donatelli in a low voice. There was the hint of a threat in his tone.

"I never leave home without it," Donatelli replied confidently.

"Let's see it," Fernandez said, then quickly added, "with your left hand, safety on, butt first."

"No problem, Mr. Fernandez," Donatelli assured him. Then he slowly reached his left hand beneath his sweat jacket and removed his huge Colt .44, holding it toward Fernandez by the barrel.

"On the ground," Fernandez instructed.

Chance, standing statue still, watched Donatelli carefully while flicking an occasional appraising glance at Jakes.

Donatelli placed his weapon on the asphalt in front of him in exaggerated slow motion. Fernandez crossed the twelve feet between him and the undercover cop and scooted the pistol to his side of the square with his toe. He never looked away from Donatelli's eyes.

"What about you gentlemen?" Donatelli said. "Do you have some hardware you'd like to show me?"

Chance sneered. "We're higher on the food chain than you are, Brukow," he said contemptuously. "We don't have to show you anything."

Donatelli acquiesced with a shrug. "Whatever you say," he said. "All I'm interested in is trading a serious bundle of money for a serious stash of ice. Your boy here has been real good to me"—he motioned toward Jakes—"and I'm looking forward to an even better relationship with management. I can bring some major dollars to your organization, gentlemen. My end of Orange County is crying for good product. I just need to cut a deal with your boss and the money will roll in like a flood. Mr. Jakes thinks I can handle it, don't you, Jakes?"

Jakes recognized Donatelli's prearranged cue for him to get into the conversation and bring up Fryman's name. According to plan, Fryman's goons would feel safe enough to implicate their boss for the ears of the law listening from the Academy.

But they haven't scanned us for a wire yet! Jakes thought in mild panic. *I can't turn on the transmitter until they check us with that high-tech wand that picks up radio waves.*

"Yeah, Mr. Brukow can handle it," Jakes agreed, trying to buy time. "He's a good customer; he'll be a good middleman." Fernandez and Chance barely gave Jakes their attention; their eyes were glued to Donatelli.

The cop seemed poised to press on with the interview, whether Jakes was or not. "Tell me about the big man," the cop asked in Chance's direction. "What kind of volume discount can I expect in order to service eastern Orange County for him?"

"Mr. Fryman will determine the percentages," Chance replied crisply, "and you, if we decide to deal with you, will have nothing to say about it."

Jakes' mind was suddenly a battleground of conflicting orders. *They're already talking about Fryman; I have to turn on the wire! Donatelli wouldn't have steered the conversation to Fryman if he didn't think it was safe to flip the switch.*

But a corner of his brain that was keenly aware of the weapons tucked inside Chance's and Fernandez's jackets shouted conflicting warnings: *They may be monitoring you right now! Don't touch that switch on your watchband!*

"Mr. Fryman is a reasonable businessman," Donatelli pressed. "I'm sure he'll want to work with me when he sees what I can produce." Then he glanced at his partner as if to say, "This is the stuff we came for, Jakes. We'd better be on the air!"

Jakes feared that a failure on his part would jeopardize the freedom the Feds had promised him. So against his better judgment, he sucked a slow breath and casually pressed the watchband against his hip to activate the transmitter.

"You will show us what you can produce first, then—" Chance stopped abruptly, raising his left hand to his ear. Then he snapped a fiery look directly at Jakes. "There it is, Rey," he growled, pointing to Jakes. "Let's take them and get out of here!"

In an instant of terror, Jakes realized that Chance had been listening for radio transmissions all along, probably with a wand inside his coat and a tiny earbud in his left ear.

The next ten seconds were a blur of deadly confusion. Had a remote camera not recorded it, it would have taken the LAPD several days to reconstruct the action from the bloody aftermath.

At the first utterance of Chance's warning, all four men reacted with a mixture of fear, rage, and self-preservation as if spring-loaded. Donatelli dived to his left and rolled on the pavement, retrieving the plastic Panda from his ankle strap in one well-practiced motion. Fernandez simultaneously ripped his .357 Magnum from its holster and swung it to the right, to follow Donatelli's roll.

While he was still speaking, Chance drew the plastic Rourk from his jacket pocket, leveled it at Jakes with a demonic glare, and fired. But Jakes, anticipating Chance's pistol, lunged frantically to his left just as three rounds crashed through the side window of the Mercedes, precisely where he had been standing. The plastic pistol rang with a characteristic *ping-ping-ping.*

Another *ping-ping-ping-ping-ping* sounded to Jakes' left, as Donatelli's Panda automatic launched five slugs at Fernandez from the cop's prone position. Four of the shots missed, and the last barely ripped open the sleeve on Fernandez's leather jacket. Donatelli's inaccuracy would prove fatal. The Latino quickly squeezed off three thunderous rounds from the .357, two of them finding their mark.

Jakes' evasive leap had propelled him along the side of the Mercedes. In a split second he saw the open beer bottle on the roof, grabbed it, and hurled it at Chance, who was poised to fire again. The flying brown bottle, leaving behind a wild trail of foam in the air, ricocheted hard off the gunman's cheek and shattered against the doorpost on the Mark XII.

Fernandez continued to fire at Donatelli, who was already mortally wounded, until he had emptied the Magnum. Then he grabbed the cop's .44 from the asphalt, flicked off the safety, and took aim again.

Before all the glass from the broken bottle had fallen to the pavement, Jakes charged the stunned Chance, whose gun hand had dropped limply to his side. Jakes drove his right shoulder hard into Chance's chest, throwing him into the Mark XII with such force that it cleared the gunman's lungs of air. Jakes' panama hat and wig flew off on impact. Chance gasped frantically, his arms flailing.

Jakes threw his right fist into the side of Chance's face, where the beer bottle had opened a one-inch gash, and grabbed for the gun with his left. Chance buckled from the blow but held onto his gun.

Convinced that Donatelli had been neutralized, Fernandez swung the cop's Colt .44 toward the struggling Jakes and Chance. Seeing the movement out of the corner of his eye, Jakes bear-hugged his opponent and swung him between himself and the .44 just as Fernandez fired.

The force of the slug, which went clear through Chance but miraculously missed Jakes, toppled the two men to the glass-strewn pavement where Jakes landed hard under the weight. Fernandez cursed in Spanish, then stepped forward for a clear, finishing shot at Jakes who was imprisoned under the dead weight of Chance's profusely bleeding body.

Fernandez didn't see the small Rourk pistol in the tangle of bodies. Chance's limp right hand had released the pistol into Jakes' left as they fell. Jakes raised the weapon blindly in the Latino's direction and closed his eyes, expecting to die. Then he squeezed the trigger and held it there. *Ping-ping-ping-ping!*

It was a full five seconds after the Rourk had emptied before Jakes opened his eyes, surprised that he wasn't full of bullet holes. His weapon was pointed at the sky. Fernandez was gone. Victor Chance's lifeless body was spread-eagled over him, with the bald man's face nuzzled into his neck like he was a sleeping baby. Warm blood seeped from the hole in Chance's back and down his side into Jakes' jacket and shirt.

Jakes lowered the gun and lifted his head to see Fernandez's crumpled form at his feet. Several yards away Donatelli was lying facedown and motionless in a pool of blood, with the Panda pistol in front of him.

Jakes squirmed to push Chance's body off of him, then stopped abruptly, groaning in pain as shards of bottle glass dug into him. His back was already cut and bleeding from his fall. But he had been distracted from his injury by the terror of the moment and partially numbed to the pain by the drugs still in his system. Trying to move under Chance's weight brought him fully in touch with his injury. *At least I'm alive,* he thought, wincing.

A chorus of wailing sirens in the distance urged him to ignore the pain, get to his feet, and gather his wits quickly. He gritted his teeth, rolled Chance's body off him with another painful groan, and stood up to survey the parking lot. The nearest tailgaters, having heard the pistol shots, had hit the deck behind the cover of their vehicles. And about a mile away, four unmarked police units were racing down Academy Road toward the entrance to the Stadium parking lot.

It had been barely thirty seconds since Jakes switched on the body wire, provoking a deadly explosion of gunfire. But the LAPD and DEA had witnessed everything from their blind in the Police Academy, and they were already rolling to pick up the pieces. They would be on the scene in a minute or less.

The reality of what the cops would do to him when they arrived rocked Jakes like a shotgun blast at point-blank range. *I have failed as an informant,* he thought. *One cop and two drug dealers are dead—at least they look very dead to me, and the LAPD and DEA are no nearer apprehending Billy Fryman. In fact, Fryman will probably be harder to catch than ever. And without Fryman the Feds will console themselves by sending me away for ten to fifteen years. I can't expect Margo to wait that long for me. I won't go!*

Then a second shotgun blast exploded into his consciousness. *The police aren't the only ones who are after me.* Jakes held his breath as the paralyzing scenario formed in his head. *As soon as Fryman finds out that I rolled over on him, I'm a dead man. Maybe he already knows. Didn't Chance say,"There it is, Rey," as if he expected to find a wire on me? Somehow Chance and Fernandez knew about the setup! Fryman sent them to kill me tonight, and he won't quit trying until he gets me!*

The wail of the police cruisers grew louder. Jakes could also hear tires squealing as the units raced along the curved beltway, red and blue lights flashing from each grille, toward the south end of the lot.

Mounting fear pounded in Jakes' brain like a jackhammer. He wanted out. He wanted to go away with Margo. He wanted to get lost, never to be found by the police or G. Billy Fryman or his haunting past. He had to run—he had to run *now*—but where?

Suddenly a football axiom from Jakes' high school coach flashed into his brain: *When you get the ball, don't look for the goal; look for the hole. If you don't find the hole in the defense you'll never cross the goal line. But once you see the hole and blow through it, you can run forever.*

Jakes instantly knew what to do. He ripped off his body-wire-equipped jacket, which was now torn from broken glass and wet with his blood and Chance's, and tossed it aside. He quickly assessed that Donatelli's .44, still in the hand of the fallen Reynoso Fernandez, had more rounds in the cylinder than the other three guns used in the melee. He pried the big Colt .44 out of the dead Latino's grip, flipped on the safety, and stuck it in his belt.

The first cop car left the beltway and screamed straight at him, followed by the other three. He had ten seconds to make it through the hole.

Jakes leaped to the open trunk of the Mercedes and grabbed the big bag of money. Then he stepped over the guardrail and gazed down the steep slope of brush tumbling to the dark street somewhere below. This was the hole—his only way out. Jakes didn't know how far he could run from the cops or from Fryman, but he knew he had to go through the hole first to find out.

Jakes glanced over his shoulder. The cops were five seconds from the scene. He slung the strap of the money bag over his arm, threw himself over the side, and tumbled into the darkness.

Nine

Nolan Jakes rolled helter-skelter down the steep hillside until a clump of oleander bushes abruptly broke his fall. Numerous cuts searing his back with pain begged him to abort his flight, but he didn't stop for a second. Scrambling to his feet, he thrashed past the oleanders and started blindly down the hill again at a run.

The cops in the parking lot would be charging down the hill after him in seconds. A police helicopter with its brilliant searchlight would doubtless be overhead in minutes. In all probability, commands had already been given to throw a dragnet around the area near the Stadium. Jakes knew that he had to get outside that perimeter before they could trap him within it. So he ran wildly, stumbled and fell again, sprang to his feet and kept running.

In his muddled brain, Jakes found no option to running. His choice had been made at the top of the hill. Though he had no idea where he would go, the terror he perceived at his heels propelled him onward. The LAPD would blame him for the death of Donatelli, and Jakes knew they would throw the book at a cop killer—if they let him live so long. And vengeful Fryman was well connected to a network of cold, unscrupulous men who would jump at the chance to track down and neutralize a deviant and disloyal employee.

Jakes could no more turn around and give up than, as a ball carrier in his younger days, he could stop running in the middle of a play. He had hated it when some of his teammates would run out of bounds or dive to the turf to avoid a tackle. Even during a busted play, when his blockers went the wrong way and he was about to get smeared for a loss, Jakes didn't give up. He would improvise and look for a way out, something he had been very good at on the football field. He had a sense for finding creases in the defense and making yardage where others ate dirt.

Yes, the cops might catch him, even gun him down during the chase. And if they didn't, Fryman's goons might find him and kill him wherever he tried to hide. But until then he would run hard to daylight, use every trick in the book, and punish anyone who tried to take him down. It was the only way he knew how to play the game.

Bounding nearly out of control through the brush toward the bottom of the hill, Jakes barely saw the eight-foot chain-link fence before his momentum carried him into it. The fence, topped with strands of rusty barbed wire, surrounded the entire perimeter of the Stadium. A quiet, dimly lit street lined with old, ramshackle houses lay just beyond it.

Jakes threw his shoulder into the fence and bounced off it, scraping the side of his face on the heavy wire mesh. Maintaining his balance after the rebound, he tossed the sport bag over the fence to the street and in one continuing motion leaped against it, dug in the toes of his shoes, and climbed. With the sound of police officers tumbling through the brush in pursuit above him, Jakes didn't have time to be careful going over the barbed wire. The rusty spikes punctured his palms and slashed across his forearms as he pulled himself over the top of the fence and dropped to the street.

Miraculously the Colt .44 was still wedged into his belt. Jakes quickly abandoned a momentary thought of firing blindly up the hill to delay the pursuit. The action would only confirm his location and provoke a hail of return fire from the officers charging down the dark hill. No, his best chance for escape was to run fast and far. Even for a has-been athlete, he was still in excellent condition, despite the wounds he had accumulated since the firefight in the parking lot. He had always been able to run, think on his feet, and make yardage where there was none. He would stay with his strength and run.

Scooping up the bag of money with his bleeding hands, Jakes paused only a second to consider his route. Turning left or right and staying on the pavement along the fence would leave him exposed to the cops behind him and to the wailing patrol cars and the thundering helicopter which would soon invade the neighborhood. So he darted across the street and plunged into the deep shadows between two run-down stucco houses.

Neighborhood dogs barked and porch lights blinked on as Jakes raced through weed-infested yards and vaulted cement-block fences. A yappy little dog charged him as he ran through one yard, but one swipe of the money bag caught the mutt in the ribs and sent him away yelping, and Jakes never broke stride.

Jakes hopped a gate between houses and ran out into another dark, narrow street. Sounds in the distance urged him to keep moving fast. The jangle of the chain-link fence behind him told him that at least one officer was scaling it—no doubt more carefully than Jakes had—to continue foot pursuit. The sirens of several black-and-whites converging on the neighborhood grew louder. Jakes didn't yet detect the muffled rumble of the approaching LAPD air unit, but he expected it at any moment. And louder than any of the sounds of pursuit was the constant roar of blood in his ears.

He veered to the right, sprinted about 100 feet on the pavement, then cut between houses again. Stumbling over toys, sprinkler heads, and small dogs, he almost fell a couple of times. But he maintained his balance, clambered over fences, and knifed between darkened houses until he found himself at the curb of four-lane Stadium Way, which circles around the Stadium from the north where Jakes and Donatelli had entered.

With the post-game rush dissipated, traffic on the four-lane street was light. Jakes knew that crossing Stadium Way undetected would be a major accomplishment. But he had to do it in order to get out of the neighborhood which in minutes would be cordoned off by uniformed officers and subject to a yard-by-yard search under the powerful searchlight of the police helicopter.

Jakes dropped into the shadows of a curbside bush until a black-and-white sped by with lights ablaze and siren screaming. The patrol car skidded around the corner and accelerated up the hillside toward the fence Jakes had scaled only a minute ago. This was the first unit to reach the area, but more were on the way; he could hear them coming. And the chopper's motor was now audible from the north, beyond the Stadium. Jakes had to move.

He quickly drew the gun from his belt, unzipped the money bag, and threw it inside. There was no way to avoid being seen by a few motorists as he crossed Stadium Way, he reasoned, but he *could* avoid looking blatantly suspicious. A quick but panic-free trot across the street would better serve his escape than a mad dash with a pistol flashing from his belt.

Assured from the sound of the siren that the next black-and-white was still seconds away, Jakes sucked a deep breath and stepped into the street behind a passing car and jogged to the center yellow lines. He paused to let another car pass, keeping his face away from the glare of the headlights, then trotted to the far curb. A brushy hill sloped gently upward before him to another neighborhood of shanties.

Safe from the view of passing drivers, Jakes dropped into the brush. He slung the money bag over one arm again and began crawling rapidly up the slope as two more police cars appeared around the bend on Stadium Way, spraying the hillside with red and blue light.

Jakes reached the top of the rise, which was separated from the old housing development by a six-foot chain-link fence. He crept along the base of the fence, with a cover of brush obscuring any view from the street below—but not from the air. Jakes prostrated himself and pulled brush over him as the LAPD air unit swooped around the opposite hill and hovered over the spot where he had scaled the barbed-wire fence. A brilliant cone of light from the chopper swept the little neighborhood he had recently passed through.

Jakes knew the chopper was also performing an infrared heat scan as well as a visual scan to locate any warm bodies hiding in the neighborhood. Soon they would broaden the scan to his hillside. As soon as the tail of the chopper was turned toward him across the ravine, he would continue his flight. But for the moment he was pinned down. He could hear nothing but the roar of the jet engine.

Being unable to move, Jakes was assaulted by the throbbing discomfort of his wounds. Even the slightest twist of his back reminded him that he had fallen hard on a bed of broken glass. Jakes was sure there were slivers of glass still embedded in his skin.

The left side of Jakes' face seemed on fire from his abrupt encounter with the chain-link fence. But he felt no oozing blood, so he figured it was more of a scrape that a cut. His hands and arms burned with pain where the barbed wire had ripped open his skin. The bleeding had slowed, however, because the wounds were caked with dirt from his crawl up the hill.

Jakes also had a fleeting moment to consider where he would try to go. First, he had to get through the fence above him and put more yardage between him and the cops across the ravine. But he wasn't going to run all night. He had to find somewhere to hide, a place where he could think and come up with a plan. He had to get out of L.A. Even better, he had to get out of the States. And for that he needed clean clothes, transportation, and maybe even another disguise. And if he didn't get his wounds treated, he might successfully escape the pursuit only to rot away from infection.

In the jumble of thoughts and emotions addling his brain, one directive sounded repeatedly with ever-increasing clarity: *Get clear of the area, then call Margo. She's in big trouble. As soon as Fryman hears about my escape, he'll go looking for her. I have to warn her.*

Jakes heard excited voices nearby over the roar of the helicopter. From under his blanket of brush, he turned to see a cluster of Latino children gathered at the chain-link fence about twelve feet away. They were pointing at the police activity across the ravine and chattering excitedly. Had they turned their heads slightly to look in Jakes' direction, they would have seen him. But they were captivated by the hovering chopper and flashing lights. After a few minutes they retreated to a nearby house.

With the sightseers gone and the chopper and ground units temporarily preoccupied with the yard search across the way, Jakes resumed his crawl along the fence. After a few dozen feet he found an opening between the bottom of the fence and the earth, where a pet had no doubt dug his way to freedom. Jakes pushed the bag of money under the fence, then slithered through the tight opening on his back. It was all he could do to stifle a cry of pain as the fence dug into his palms and the cuts on his back scraped over the rough soil.

Once inside the yard he ran at a crouch between two houses to the sidewalk. Then he zig-zagged through a run-down neighborhood of narrow streets made even narrower by the numbers of cars—half of them old beaters ready for the wrecking yard—parked at the curb. He kept his distance from homes where lights glimmered or Latino music could be heard. And he slipped into the bushes when an infrequent car passed.

He stayed with streets that sloped down the hill away from the ravine he had just escaped. He knew that Sunset Boulevard was only a few blocks away. If he could cross busy Sunset, he would be one more neighborhood removed from his pursuers. Jakes' self-imposed order kept drumming in his brain: *Get clear of the area; then warn Margo.*

Suddenly Jakes stopped dead in his tracks, frozen with fear by a chilling new sound piercing the roar of the helicopter in the distance. Dogs. Not yappy neighborhood dogs but large dogs, tracking dogs. The LAPD K-9 unit had been called in. The dogs sounded to be far behind him, perhaps still on the north side of Stadium Way. But they were on his trail.

Jakes swore under his breath to keep a wail of panic from swelling in his throat. He knew he couldn't hide from the dogs. Nor could he outrun them. *Think, Nolan, think. Find the hole. Exploit the weakness of the defense. They will narrow the gap and eventually catch you unless . . .*

An old Dodge station wagon with a hole in the muffler lumbered noisily around the corner. Jakes bolted behind parked cars before the headlights hit him and prostrated himself in the street between the curb and the flat rear tire of a rusty sedan. The bag of money was under his chest.

The station wagon rattled halfway up the street, then turned into a driveway three houses ahead of where Jakes lay. Parking next to the house and shutting down the engine, the driver and one passenger—an older couple, Jakes surmised, from their plump forms and slow movements—got out and entered the house. On this pleasant summer evening in Los Angeles, the occupants had left the windows of the station wagon down.

Maybe they left the keys inside, Jakes thought hopefully. With the bark of police dogs persisting in the distance, he didn't dare wonder too long. He pulled himself out of the street and crept quickly down the uneven cement sidewalk to the driveway where the station wagon stood creaking from its journey. He reached into the driver's window to the steering column, feeling for the ignition. He found it, but there were no keys. He quietly opened the driver's door and patted around the front seat and the floor. No keys. He silently cursed his misfortune.

Jakes thought about kicking in the front door of the house and demanding the keys to the station wagon at gunpoint. But the couple would surely dial 911 as soon as he left and give the cops a license number and description of the vehicle. And with the armada of black-and-whites pouring into the area, he wouldn't get six blocks in the stolen station wagon.

Jakes left the door of the wagon ajar and returned to the street. *There must be a vehicle in this neighborhood with the keys in it,* he reasoned, *if only a junker that the owner is inviting someone to steal so he can collect on the insurance.*

Jakes raced from car to car searching for a set of keys left in the ignition, on the floor, or on the seat. Working on Fryman's car lot, he had learned from one of the juvenile delinquent lot boys how to hot-wire some of the older, less complicated ignitions. But he couldn't do it without any tools. And even if he *had* the right tools, he probably couldn't get a car started before one of the K-9 German shepherds caught up with him and tore him apart. If he didn't find car keys in the next few minutes, he could kiss his short-lived freedom good-bye.

Jakes worked his way down the narrow street, moving away from the barks of the K-9 unit which, he judged, had crossed Stadium Way by now and found the place in the fence he had slid under. By the sound of it, the chopper was also getting nearer.

Jakes almost passed by a corroded '62 Chevy pickup with the hood, bed, and driver's side door all missing and the windshield caked with several months worth of undisturbed grime. But the truck was pointed downhill with enough space at the curb for him to coast away from the owner's house before firing it up—if he could find a key. His hope waning, Jakes reached into the open cab and touched the ignition. There it was—a single key stuck in place!

With his options draining to zero, he threw the money bag on the seat and jumped in. *This junker may or may not start,* he assessed. *But I can at least coast to the bottom of the hill or farther and get another head start on the law.*

He cranked the wheel to the left, pushed in the clutch, and released the safety brake. The truck began to inch away from the curb, squeaking and scraping as if it hadn't been on the road in months.

The slope of the residential street was moderate, so the truck gathered momentum slowly. Jakes kept the headlights off, using moonlight and an occasional flickering streetlight to help him stay in the narrow channel of pavement between parked cars. He glanced at the rearview mirror repeatedly—the side mirror had gone with the door—looking for signs of the pursuing K-9s and their masters, but he saw none.

After rolling two short blocks, the truck was up to 10 MPH Jakes reached down and turned the ignition. Nothing, not so much as a click or a groan. He muttered a curse as he turned the key again and again fruitlessly.

Then, remembering a trick from his early days of driving a stick shift, he eased into second gear, turned the key on, and popped the clutch. The engine made a noisy cough, tried to turn over, then died. The compression slowed the truck to under 5 MPH, but sounds of life in the engine compartment encouraged Jakes to try again.

The street was approaching a forced left turn. Jakes guessed that the turn would aim him at Sunset Boulevard. He had to get the truck started to cross Sunset and get lost in Echo Park before the police expanded their search to that area. He calculated that he had enough straightaway for the truck to get up to speed for him to pop the clutch once more before hitting the turn. He double-clutched into first gear, then pumped the accelerator several times to prime the carburetor with fuel.

One block before the hard left turn, Jakes popped the clutch. The engine coughed and spat and groaned, then sprang to life. Pushing the clutch in again, he gunned the engine several times to keep it alive, even though it sounded like it was firing on only half of its eight cylinders. Jakes pulled on the headlights—only one of which worked—and braked for the turn. The brake pedal plunged nearly to the floor, barely slowing the truck as he swung a hard, tire-squealing turn to the left. He narrowly missed two parked cars on the right curb.

Back on the straightaway, Jakes saw the lights of Sunset Boulevard ahead of him at the base of the hill where the residential street dead-ended. He accelerated through the forward gears and found them all working, though the engine continued to sputter. Luckily, the signal at the intersection was green, so Jakes downshifted and turned right, relieved to find no black-and-whites in sight. Unwilling to push his luck by staying on a major thoroughfare, he took the first left to get off the main drag onto a less-traveled parallel street.

Ignoring the faulty brakes, Jakes pushed the sputtering truck up to near 40 MPH on a quiet side street. The wind rushed in through the open door, swirling leaves and dust throughout the cabin. Jakes didn't care. He wasn't free yet, but he had crashed through an improbable hole in the line and he was now in the open field. He had a long way to go before he would be safely outside the reach of the police and G. Billy Fryman. But for a brief moment, at least, he felt free. And for the first time in days he smiled.

Ten

Libby Carroll had been looking forward to a quiet Friday evening alone all week. Her son, Brett, and his college friend, Andie, who was staying with them for a week, had left three hours earlier for a city bus tour of several jazz clubs in downtown Seattle. They would likely be out until the wee hours, which suited Libby's plans for peace and quiet just fine.

She lounged luxuriantly on the sofa in her silk pajamas, engrossed in a fascinating biography of Pablo Casals. A steaming cup of cappuccino was within reach on the end table, and a collection of Motown "golden oldies" purred from the Sony entertainment unit. The magnificent view from the large bay window on Queen Anne hill soothed her after a hectic week at the university. Brightly lit ferries and pleasure craft glided across Puget Sound below, with the lights of the city and distant islands providing a sparkling frame.

The call came at just past 10:30. Libby's "hello" was cheerful. She expected to hear the voice of one of a number of friends who knew she was a night owl and frequently called her after 10.

But instead she heard, "Good evening, Dr. Carroll, this is Officer Reginald Burris, with the University of Washington Police Department." The man's introduction ended with a questioning lilt, as if asking, "Do you remember me from our previous visits on campus?"

Libby remembered. The image of a pleasant but ponderous, bald black man in uniform came to mind. For months she had suspected that Reginald Burris' occasional visits to her office and friendly demeanor might eventuate in his asking her out, a prospect she did not welcome. As a high-ranking member of the university's administration, she could not afford to mix socially with such a man, affable and competent though he might be. He was only a policeman. And the fact that he was calling her at home—and calling so late at that—assured her that Burris didn't understand the protocol of dealing with university administrators.

"Yes, Reginald," Libby responded, barely congenial. Then she quickly added in a businesslike tone, "What can I do for you?"

"I'm sorry to bother you so late, Dr. Carroll, but we have a security concern here that needs your attention."

"Do you mean my office?" Libby asked, suddenly anxious. "Has my office been broken into?"

"Yes, as a matter of fact, it has. But—"

"Oh, my God," Libby groaned, her beautiful evening suddenly squelched by the news. "I was there until past 6 tonight. When did it happen?"

"About an hour ago. And I need to tell you that—"

"Is anything broken? Was anything taken?"

"No, Dr. Carroll, your office is fine, but—"

Libby interrupted again, now irritated that the guard had called when the office was intact. "If my office is fine, Reginald, couldn't this wait until—"

"It's your son, Dr. Carroll," Reginald cut in forcefully, his voice equally sharp with irritation at Libby's unwillingness to listen.

"I beg your pardon."

"I caught your son in your office tonight tampering with your computer. He won't tell me exactly what he was doing. He had your key card."

"Brett? In my office?"

"Yes, with his girlfriend. They were . . . fooling around . . . on your couch when I caught them."

Libby dropped her head in her hand and mouthed a silent expletive. Reginald continued in a softer tone, "I can arrest them and process them through the system, like I would with other suspected burglars. Or, if you like, you can pick them up at our office tonight and deal with them yourself. It's your choice."

Libby was so angry and humiliated that she couldn't answer for several seconds. The feeling was all too familiar. As an adolescent with a clever mind and quick wit, Brett had embarrassed his mother before with his antics. Some of his pranks were merely foolish; others bordered on being hurtful and destructive. Libby was convinced that he was acting out his brazen disregard for her desire that he play the role of the up-and-coming administrator's gentlemanly son. To date he had avoided getting into trouble with the law—or at least getting caught.

Libby acknowledged that Brett's two years away at WSU had been good for both of them. He was clearly ecstatic about being out from under his mother's thumb, and Libby was equally pleased that Brett's fraternity brothers had to worry about where he was at 3:00 A.M. instead of her. Moreover, his scholastic achievements had been worth boasting about to her colleagues and friends, while his mischief was directed at rival fraternities and sororities on the other side of the state, with no reflection on her or her career.

Libby Carroll had hoped that Brett's summer with her in Seattle would be free of incidents that might further contaminate their strained relationship or in some way cast her in a bad light before her peers. She had even hoped they might have some fun together, as in summers past when Brett was less independent and she was less protective of her image at the university. But as she pondered the depressing alternatives presented by Officer Burris, she suddenly despaired that she and her son would even survive their summer together.

"Dr. Carroll?" Reginald prodded gently.

Libby gripped the phone and bit her lip. She had to make a difficult choice. She quickly assessed that being arrested by UWPD might put a healthy scare into Brett. But she would be disgraced when his arrest got back to her coworkers. And how would she explain the incident to Andie's parents? No, for her own sake she had to get out of this with the least amount of negative publicity.

"I'm sorry, Reginald," Libby said finally, "but I'm dealing with quite a shock here."

"That's okay, Dr. Carroll. Take your time." Libby found the officer's voice steadying, affirming, like a strong but gentle arm supporting her.

She said, "Are you saying, Reginald, that if I decide to handle this incident myself there will be no police charges?"

"That's right. We will be happy to skip the paperwork and get on with business."

"And we can avoid mentioning this to the university?" Libby groaned inside as she heard herself begging for mercy.

Reginald's reply implied no condescension. "Since it's you, Dr. Carroll, I'll be happy to leave the matter in your hands and keep the whole thing under my hat—providing your son undoes anything wrong he did on the computer."

Libby released a deep, silent, relieved sigh. "Thank you, Reginald. You're very kind. I'll be there as soon as I can."

By the time Libby tapped off the phone, she was steaming, cursing, crying mad. It took her almost an hour to get dressed and drive to the University of Washington Police Department, and she needed every minute of it to get a grip on her emotions.

As she changed out of her pajamas into a long-sleeve, kelly-green jumpsuit, she lectured Brett in her thoughts: *How dare you sleep in my house and eat my groceries, then sneak into my office to entertain your girlfriend! How dare you take advantage of my trust and jeopardize my career to advance your own ends! I know what you were doing on my computer: hacking. For whom were you doctoring grades? No doubt for your old friends from high school who chose the U instead of defecting to WSU like you did. And I'll bet you demanded plenty for your services. Whatever you were paid, it's pocket change compared to what you almost cost me tonight.*

Libby combed her shoulder-length black hair into a ponytail and secured it with a clasp. Then she dabbed a little makeup on her face, highlighted her dark eyes with liner, and applied a thin layer of gloss to her lips. She had leisurely bathed, cleansed her face of makeup, and brushed out her hair earlier in the evening. It would have been faster for her to slip into sweats and tennies and cover her hair with a scarf. But she wouldn't think of appearing in public—particularly at the university—without makeup and so shabbily attired. Having to make herself presentable again in the middle of the night because of Brett further fueled Libby's displeasure with him.

As Libby guided her midnight-blue Seville down the narrow streets of Queen Anne hill on her way to the university, her anger at Brett was overcome by chilling fear, as she contemplated what his deed had almost cost her.

She saw herself walking a tightrope from one platform—her moderately successful but clouded past, to another—a dream-fulfilling future as the first black woman president of a PAC-10 school. In her hands was a long balancing pole. One end of the pole represented her credibility in higher education achieved through her rigorous scholastic endeavors: a bachelor's degree from Central Washington State, with honors, a double master's from Washington, with high honors, an administrative position at the university, and finally, during an extended sabbatical, a Harvard doctorate in public administration, also with high honors.

The other end of the pole was weighted with Libby's significant accomplishments since joining the UW faculty in 1989. She was a full professor of anthropology with adjunct appointments in linguistics and women's studies. She had chaired the African Studies program, the Faculty Senate, and the Faculty Council on Academic Standards. She had served on the University Committee on Foreign Study and the Fullbright-Hays Dissertation Research Review Committee. In 1995 she became the youngest dean of the graduate school and vice-provost in the university's history.

Libby's professional affiliations were equally impressive. She had served on the Board of Directors of the African Studies Association. She had chaired the Committee on Scientific Communication of the American Anthropogical Association and was an elected member of the association's executive board. She had also served on the policy board for the Northwest Center for Research on Women.

Then, in 1998, came the big break. The board of regents appointed her provost and vice-president of academic affairs. It was this secretly coveted and lofty rung from which Libby expected to step to the top of the ladder before age fifty: a university presidency.

Only Libby Carroll understood how tenuous was her foothold on the wire. Her colleagues saw her as an intelligent, confident, tireless, financially successful university administrator—the image she had carefully cultivated throughout her career. They didn't perceive her as inching along a tightrope; they saw her sprinting a clear lane to her career goal, much like she had sprinted to national fame with the 1984 U.S. Olympic track team. Only this time Libby's fans expected her to grab the gold—the president's chair—instead of hanging up her spikes after the heartbreak of not competing in the Olympiad.

But while enjoying continuing progress toward her life goal, Libby was well aware of forces capable of toppling her from her precarious perch into the dark net below. The tightrope trembled constantly with the ominous threat of prejudice. She was a *woman*. She was a *black woman*. She was an *unmarried black woman* with an illegitimate son. At one time those credentials amounted to strike one, strike two, and strike three to significant career aspirations.

Even at the dawn of the new millennium, with widespread acceptance and vigorous promotion of women and minorities at all strata of society, Libby's sights were set extremely high for a single black mother. She feared that a throwback, a bigoted influence, might spring out of the darkness and land heavily on her wire, catapulting her into a fall.

There was another unnerving vibration on the wire from Libby's deep past. The appalling incident, and the faces of the two men involved with her in it, were shrouded in the cobwebs of more than two decades of secrecy, avoidance, and denial. And with no repercussions from her criminal actions, Libby tended to regard the deed and the cover-up as no more real than vivid memories of a horror film. Yet occasional stabs of real guilt reminded her that the long-buried episode, like a slumbering ogre, might yet awaken and rip the wire from beneath her feet.

Now, on top of Libby's other silent concerns, there was Brett. He had a way of slamming into her on the wire from the blind side, like a spiteful trapeze acrobat intent on stealing the spotlight. Libby had viewed the snowballing mother-son rivalry as Brett's rather juvenile but necessary means of punishing her for not giving him a father, and of removing himself from her imposing shadow. So far his antics had been arrogant, and at times disrespectful, but not devious, conniving, or illegal. Nor had his pranks endangered Libby's position at the university.

But tonight Brett had stepped over that line in a way that greatly disturbed her. He had proved himself capable of harming her, even jeopardizing her career if he so chose. Libby was not really sure why he might want to injure her so, but she was sure it was time to start asking those questions.

While Brett and Andie sat sullenly in another room with Taggart, Reginald Burris and Libby Carroll conferred in the UWPD communications center. Sitting on the corner of the desk with his large bald head gleaming under the fluorescent lights, the towering officer still looked down on the standing administrator, who had politely refused the steno chair he offered.

"I found this on your desk beside the boy's bag," Reginald explained, holding the tiny computer in his massive hand. The data for Brett's "clients" was still displayed on the small screen. "He won't tell me what he was doing, and the girl isn't saying anything. All I have to do is look at her and she starts bawling. But I think your son may have been tampering with some of the university's files. These are student names, ID numbers, and course numbers on this screen."

Libby nodded, fully aware of what her son had been doing on her computer. At least now she knew which files Brett had invaded. She would be able to restore them without drawing attention to the incident.

"And if it's any comfort to you, Dr. Carroll, I think I arrived before they . . . well . . . they were still in their underwear when I turned on the lights." Reginald cleared his throat self-consciously. "What I mean is that I don't think they really did anything on your couch."

Libby shrugged away what Reginald considered a minor victory. She already knew that Brett was sexually active; he had told her as much during his first year at WSU. The news, which Brett delivered in a haughty, what-are-you-going-to-do-about-it tone, had disappointed Libby. She had hoped against reasonable hope that Brett would master his college male hormones at least until he met a girl he intended to marry. But she had never asked him to swear to abstinence. How could she when the evidence of her own promiscuity as a college sophomore was irrefutable in the person of her son?

Reginald continued, "As I mentioned on the phone, Dr. Carroll, since this is basically a family problem, I won't write up a report or anything. You just take care of it the way you want to, and the university won't even know it happened."

Libby sensed that the officer was overdoing it a little by restating his generosity. As an attractive, available woman, she was used to being favored and fawned over by men, single and married. But whenever she responded in kind to an admirer, she often scared him away with her take-charge personality and high-energy lifestyle. Perhaps due to his size, Libby mused, Reginald Burris wasn't intimidated by her. To the contrary, *she* felt overshadowed by *his* strength and kindness at a time when she found herself uncharacteristically helpless.

"Thank you, Reginald," she said sincerely. "I can't tell you how grateful I am that you found Brett and Andie when you did. How did you know to check my office? Had an alarm sounded?"

Reginald casually slid a large hand over the top of his bald head hoping to mask his mild embarrassment. "Well, no, there was no alarm. Since the boy was using your key card, the electronic sentry thought that you were working late. I actually came to your office to say hello . . . and to make sure you were all right, since you were in the building all alone. That's when I found the kids."

Libby forced a warm smile. "I'm grateful for your . . . concern, Reginald. Thank you." Ready to leave, she offered him a polite hand, expecting him to assert his masculine superiority, as most men did, with a commanding grip.

Instead, Reginald's baseball glove of a hand enveloped hers gently and respectfully. Had he been wearing a cap, Libby judged, he might have tipped it. "It's my pleasure, Dr. Carroll. I'm glad this turned out okay for you. You deserve it. I have a couple of kids myself, so I know how hard this is for you."

Libby was suddenly curious about Reginald being a father. It had never occurred to her that he would have a family.

"You have children?" she asked.

"Yeah, two girls," Reginald answered, clearly pleased at her interest. "Lucille is married, and Sandra is a junior at Pacific Lutheran." Then he quickly added, "Sandra lives with her mother. I'm not a married man myself."

Libby nodded, not to approve his marital status but to acknowledge the information.

Reginald said, "If there's anything else I can do to help, please let me know." Then he stood and ushered her out of the office.

Brett and Andie slid into the backseat of the Seville without looking at or speaking to Libby, Taggart, or Reginald. Libby thanked both officers again, then drove off.

She did not speak to the somber couple in the backseat for several minutes. She was thankful that her initial anger had begun to cool, allowing her to choose her words carefully. "We will talk about this tomorrow morning, Brett," she stated firmly. Brett and Andie said nothing.

Libby drove the rest of the way home, marveling at the good fortune of Reginald Burris' timely intervention in Brett's misconduct and his disarming courtesy to her.

Eleven

Nolan Jakes angled through the dark side streets of Hollywood until he felt it wasn't safe to be seen in the battered '62 Chevy pickup any longer. He judged that nearly an hour had passed since he plunged over the side of the hill at the Stadium, beginning his flight from the police. By now the K-9 unit had likely tracked his scent to the curb where he had commandeered the pickup. The vehicle was probably hot. It was time to abandon it.

Furthermore, Jakes could no longer put off warning Margo. He feared for her immediate safety, knowing that Billy Fryman would soon send someone for her in an attempt to find him. And whoever Fryman sent would be no more kind and forgiving of Margo's involvement with Jakes than Chance and Fernandez had been with him. Sweet, innocent, loving Margo was in mortal danger. He had to tell her to run.

Driving along residential Rosewood Avenue in southwest Hollywood, Jakes doused the lights and cut the engine, allowing the truck to coast for two short blocks in dark silence. Once stopped at the curb, he grabbed the bag full of money and headed for the well-lit thoroughfare directly ahead: Fairfax Avenue. He had two immediate needs. First, he had to contact Margo Sharpe and convince her to get out of her apartment as soon as possible. Second, he had to do something to keep himself from being recognized on the street until he devised a long-range plan for escape. That meant not only keeping his face out of the light as much as possible, but covering up the telltale signs of the chase: the wounds on his face, hands, and arms and his dirty, blood-stained clothing.

Approaching Fairfax, Jakes found a pay phone and tapped in Margo Sharpe's personal number. "Nolan, where are you? I've been worried sick," she said, as soon as she recognized his voice.

"Listen carefully, Margo. I'm in trouble—*big* trouble, and you may be in danger too."

"Why? What's wrong?"

"I can't explain everything right now, but all hell broke loose at the Stadium tonight," Jakes said, keeping a wary eye on the traffic around the phone booth. "The cops are after me. Even worse, so is Billy Fryman, and he's a killer. You have to get out of your apartment right away. It won't take long for Billy to remember that you've been with me. He'll come for you, Margo. He'll hurt you trying to get to me. Go to the police and let them protect you from Fryman."

"What about you, Nolan?" Margo's voice seemed strained with shock and concern.

"I have to disappear. I have to find a hole to crawl in where the police and Billy Fryman will never find me. Maybe some day I'll be able to see you again, but for now I—"

"I want to go with you, Nolan," Margo interrupted. "I've thought about what you said last night, and I want to be with you. Let me come get you and we'll disappear together."

"Margo, this is a completely different scenario from what we talked about last night. I'm not a government-protected star witness; I'm a fugitive from both sides of the law. If you run with me, you will never—"

"I need you, Nolan; I realized that last night after we talked. My life, my career—it doesn't mean anything if I can't be with you. I love you, Nolan. I don't care what you've done. We can find a new life together somewhere. Please let me go with you."

I need you, Nolan. I love you, Nolan. Please let me go with you. The words stunned Jakes. She was too smart to make such a hasty, foolish choice. He didn't deserve this level of commitment from a woman, and for her sake he dared not give in to it. But he desperately *wanted* to deserve it, he *wanted* to yield to it. Yet the cost to Margo seemed excessive.

"Margo, you don't realize what you're giving up by coming with me," he argued weakly.

"I *know* what I'm doing, Nolan," Margo said forcefully but without animosity, "and I do it willingly. More important, I know what I'm giving up if I let you go." She began to cry softly. "I can't do it, Nolan; I can't just let you leave without me."

Jakes agonized in silence as his desire for Margo and his desire for what was best for her warred within him.

Sensing his hesitance, Margo added, "At least let's be together tonight. If I have to hide, let me hide with you. Tell me where you are, and I'll come pick you up."

Jakes had no defense against the proposed compromise. Everything within him yearned to allow Margo to convince him that she was ready to leave everything for him.

"All right," he said at last with a sigh. "I'm in Hollywood. Come over the hill on Laurel Canyon and wait for me where it meets Hollywood Boulevard. Bring me some clothes; I think there's a shirt and pants in your closet. But hurry, and make sure no one follows you."

"I will, Nolan," Margo said in a quavering voice. "I'll be there as soon as I can."

Stepping cautiously out of the phone booth, Jakes spied an all-night Unocal service station and minimart a block away. Having achieved his first goal, he hurriedly moved to accomplish the second: making his appearance less noticeable in order to travel by foot to the corner of Laurel Canyon and Hollywood Boulevard, several blocks away.

Staying at the perimeter of the street lights, he found his way behind the store and into the men's restroom. He locked himself inside the filthy, foul-smelling cubicle and gingerly cleansed his scraped and torn hands, arms, and face in cold water, drying himself with the only towels available: used ones from the trash can.

Jakes' clothes looked a mess, but he flicked off the burrs and foxtails as best he could and tucked in his shirttail. His back still burned with pain. He suspected that the dried blood had glued his shirt to his torn flesh. With nothing else to put on, he decided to leave the shirt in place until he could soak it off.

Studying himself in the grimy mirror after washing, Jakes thought he looked like he had been a scratching post in a cage full of tigers. But at least he was clean enough to walk into the store and look for something to keep him from being so obvious on the street.

Leaving the restroom, Jakes walked around to the front of the store.

In the window was a partial answer to his need for a cover-up: a blue plastic Unocal windbreaker with an orange 76 logo on the front, on sale for $1.99 with a $10.00 purchase. And he could see a rack of cheaply made caps inside advertised for the outrageous price of $8.95.

Purchasing a cap and something to quench his prickly, dry throat would easily put him over the $10.00 limit and qualify him for the gaudy plastic jacket. It wasn't much of a disguise, but he hoped it would keep him from being spotted until he could find a dark place to wait for Margo.

But what if someone saw him before he covered up? What if the clerk or a customer inside the store recognized him from a TV bulletin and called the police? Jakes hesitated only briefly at the questions. It was just a matter of time before the stolen pickup was discovered on Rosewood Avenue, alerting the cops that he was—or recently had been—in the vicinity. Every moment he spent second-guessing his instincts in the midst of his flight was a moment forfeited to those pursuing him, police and criminals, both of whom intended to slam the door forever on his newfound freedom.

Jakes thought it ironic that, even though there were enough $100 bills crammed in his sport bag to buy the entire inventory of the little store, he couldn't spend a dime of it. Convenience stores in L.A. often weren't very convenient at all when it came to money; they never accepted bills larger than a $20 during the graveyard shift. Besides, flashing a Ben Franklin here could tempt a suspicious clerk to call the police.

Also, he carried Donatelli's loaded .44 Magnum, which would quickly persuade a clerk in most stores to let Jakes take anything he wanted. But in this convenience store, as with many in L.A., the night clerk was locked into a bullet-proof plexiglass cage. A cash drawer, controlled from inside, faced the self-serve gas pumps outside, and another drawer opened to the minimart inside. At the threat of an armed robbery, the protected clerk needed only to tap 911 on the phone and then sit back and make faces at the robber in safety until the police arrived.

No, if Jakes was going to get what he needed here, he would have to pay for it with his own money. He had brought along his last $300 for spending money while in hiding during Fryman's trial. Jakes usually carried more money, but he had made an especially large payment to Fryman against his loan balance of several thousand dollars, just to keep his employer happy. Jakes easily had enough for a cap, a liter of juice, and a jacket. So he slung the money bag over his shoulder and walked inside the tiny store.

A gray-bearded clerk occupying the cage—a Sikh, Jakes judged by his turban—gave him only a glance before returning to a book spread on the counter before him. Racks lining the clerk's cage were stacked with packages of cigarettes, bottles of hard liquor, and other expensive items kept inside for obvious reasons. Scratchy rock'n'roll music played over the speakers. There were no other customers in the store.

Doing his best to stay out of the clerk's direct line of sight, Jakes approached the aisle where the Unocal jackets, folded flat and wrapped in clear plastic envelopes, were displayed. Unwrapping one labeled L for large, he tried it on. Like most large shirts and jackets Jakes bought off the rack, the cheap Unocal jacket was longer in the arms and the waist than he preferred. But it accommodated his broad shoulders comfortably, and he needed the extra room for mobility.

Jakes kept the jacket on as he moved to a rack of baseball caps near the back of the store. Aware of the video system tracing his moves from the corners of the room, he kept his head subtly turned away from the nearest camera. He selected a black cap bearing the silver and blue logo of the most popular full-sized electric sedans on the road in 2001: the Bolt 770. He adjusted the sizing strap and donned the cap, further shading his face from the store's prying electronic eyes.

Moving to the refrigerated cases on the back wall, Jakes grabbed a liter of juice—he didn't look to see what flavor—and started toward the front to pay and leave. He was halfway up the center aisle when the glass door at the front of the store swung open and a husky, curly-headed LAPD officer strolled inside.

Jakes froze in the aisle. The sight of the traditional navy-blue uniform and silver badge instantly flooded his system with adrenaline for flight. But the casual stroll quickly assured Jakes that the officer had not entered the store in pursuit. Fighting the temptation to panic, Jakes forced himself to turn nonchalantly to the shelf of freeze-dried meals next to him and begin flipping through several packages as if making a selection.

The cop nodded to the clerk behind the glass, only barely aware of the store's other customer. "Got any Tums?" he called out, as if there was no speaker in the cage. He patted his slightly protruding gut to emphasize his problem. The Sikh pointed to the rack of stomach remedies near the end of the cage, then returned to his reading. The cop found the rack and studied the brands and flavors.

Watching out of the corner of his eye from thirty feet away, Jakes contemplated his next move. The dragnet for the alleged cop-killing fugitive from Chavez Ravine apparently had not yet expanded to Hollywood. Jakes concluded that his best option was to stay cool, keep "shopping" until the cop left with his Tums, then leave the store as quickly as possible to rendezvous with Margo.

Then a sudden innocuous crackle on the cop's remote radio alerted Jakes that a backup plan may be needed. *At any moment the pickup may be located and my description broadcast over that cop's radio*, he thought, barely breathing. *He's between me and the door. He'll have me pinned down in here! What will I do then?*

The image that filled his mind in response to the question so surprised Jakes that he fumbled the package of instant stroganoff he was holding. The cello-wrapped box hit the terrazzo floor with a noisy *slap* that made both the clerk and the cop glance at him. He quickly picked up the package and returned it to the shelf.

He was thinking about the Colt .44 secreted in the nylon sport bag presently slung over his shoulder. Yes, if the radio gave him away, he would have to go for the gun and shoot his way out of the store before the pudgy cop could draw down on him.

The thought of trying to kill the cop at the counter—and others who might try to apprehend him—bothered Jakes, yet he wondered why it should. The LAPD already regarded him as a cop killer; what chance did he have to prove himself otherwise? He had already made the choice to run instead of go to prison for trafficking. Neither would he go to prison for a homicide he didn't commit, but to which he would surely be judged an accessory. Taking out another cop in his attempt to get free shouldn't seem any worse, but it did.

It's a simple matter of self-defense, Jakes argued with himself, *just as it was when I blew away Reynoso Fernandez with Victor Chance sprawled over me like a blanket.* Jakes felt no compunction at the flashback of killing Fernandez. In fact, at this very moment the memory brought a rush of confidence, a sense of destiny. Unarmed, he had survived a firefight against three experienced killers. For whatever reason, it had been his fate to escape the trap set for him. And the loaded .44 Magnum in his bag was an omen to Jakes that his luck would hold, even if he had to fight his way through half of LAPD's Hollywood division.

Jakes' sudden sense of invincibility buoyed him with confidence bordering on cockiness. He hadn't felt this bold since his last 100-yard game with the Lions. Then it had been his ability to juke and spin and dart that spurred him fearlessly to run straight at tacklers the size of gorillas. But at this moment it was his sense of uncanny luck, his awareness of Margo's feelings for him, and a hunk of cold steel in his nylon bag that swelled his ego and prompted his next move.

Before the cop had decided on a flavor of Tums, Jakes walked straight to the counter with his purchases. Showing the jacket, cap, and juice to the clerk on the other side of the glass, he shoved $15 into the cash drawer. The Sikh recorded the purchase on his register and retrieved the customer's money from the drawer.

"Hey, buddy, you look like you tried to stop a cat fight." The cop was standing beside Jakes, peeling away the wrapper on a roll of cherry Tums, waiting his turn to pay.

Jakes retorted with his head down as he received his change from the drawer, "If you think *I* look bad, officer, you should see the *cats.*"

The cop was still laughing as Jakes walked past him and out the door.

Twelve

G. Billy Fryman hated being called away from a party, especially one of his lavish parties for his auto dealership managers and their dates, in his sprawling, hillside home in Sherman Oaks. The round and jovial entrepreneur prided himself in keeping his top-level staff happy and productive by feeding them at his table, quenching their thirst at his bar, and allowing them to splash in his custom backyard pool and spa until well past midnight.

But the unobtrusive appearance of Braxton Mooney at the wrought-iron side gate signaled that something important was transpiring in a much darker corner of Fryman's financial empire. Braxton Mooney was the master strategist and financial genius behind the success of G. Billy Fryman's drug enterprise. The kingpin had insisted that his executive lieutenant communicate with him only through intermediaries or coded faxes unless a security-critical issue demanded a personal meeting. Seeing Mooney at the gate, Fryman cursed under his breath, aware that such an issue must be at hand.

Fryman turned the party over to his middle-aged Japanese housekeeper with a few whispered words. Then, without looking toward the gate where Mooney stood in the shadows pulling on a cigarette, the fat man plodded heavily through the house to the front door. His tentlike Hawaiian shirt and baggy linen slacks rippled around his jiggling flesh as he walked.

Braxton Mooney met his employer in the circular driveway between two luxury cars owned by Fryman's employees. Mooney's shiny BMW sport coupe sat at the curb of the dark residential street.

As always, Mooney was fashionably and expensively dressed. Dark, trim, and in his mid-forties, Mooney had the appearance and bearing of a high-level financial executive, which he had been in Atlanta until six years ago when his penchant for embezzled funds was discovered. Mooney was acquitted of the charges on a legal technicality, but his name and track record in the South were too well known to land him a decent job. So he moved to L.A., fell in with G. Billy Fryman's budding drug operation, and made them both very wealthy. Fryman and Mooney were within months of retiring to separate, anonymous lives in Mexico and the South Pacific respectively.

"It was a setup, just as we were informed, Mr. Fryman," Mooney said in a subdued and deadly serious tone. His accent revealed that he had been born and educated in the deep South. "But, I'm sorry to report, it went badly for us."

"Badly? How badly?" Fryman was equally serious.

"Chance and Fernandez are dead, sir. So is the cop. From what I heard on the scanner, it was a firefight at point-blank range in the Stadium parking lot."

Fryman muttered an acid curse. Then, "What about Jakes?"

Mooney blew a stream of cigarette smoke over his shoulder, delaying the worst of the bad news he had come to deliver. "He got away, sir."

"What?" Fryman snapped.

"Somehow Jakes survived the gun battle. The cops say he ran down the hill from the parking lot, jumped a fence, and disappeared into the neighborhood. The dogs tracked him for a while, then lost him. They're doing a house-to-house search now."

Fryman cursed again, primarily at himself for allowing the relatively unproven Nolan Jakes such a long tether. Then he said, "Did he talk?"

Mooney shook his head confidently. "No, sir, the cops didn't get anything. As soon as Jakes' body wire was activated, Chance must have heard it and started shooting." Then, more to himself, he added, "I don't know why Chance and Fernandez didn't get him. And I can't believe that a wounded cop could take them both out."

Fryman turned away, spitting oaths. Then he turned quickly back. "What about the stuff, Braxton?"

Mooney shrugged and released a smoke-filled sigh. "It was still in the trunk of Rey's car, so I assume the cops got it." Then raising a hand as if to swear the truth, he added, "But it's clean, Mr. Fryman. It can't be traced to us. And the cops still can't tie us to Chance and Fernandez—at least, they can't make it stick."

"And the money?" Fryman was thinking about the $620,000 in large bills he expected Victor Chance and Reynoso Fernandez to bring back with the large stash of ice after dealing with Jakes for his disloyalty.

Mooney screwed his face into a scowl. "Apparently Jakes got it, sir."

Fryman bored into Mooney with a look of skepticism, so the well-dressed man explained, "I heard the cops say over the scanner that Jakes grabbed the money—stuffed in some kind of a big bag—and ran with it."

Fryman fumed aloud, "Are you telling me that a washed-up, over-the-hill football player eluded our two best triggers and a parking lot full of cops, and he's hiding out somewhere in L.A. with over half a million dollars of our money?"

The question didn't require an answer, but Mooney gave one anyway, "Yes, sir."

Fryman dropped his head in thought as Mooney stood by for instructions. The fat man wasn't so sure that Victor Chance and Reynoso Fernandez and the bundle of white powder in their car couldn't be traced to him. Nor was he certain that the police wouldn't try to use Jakes' testimony and the incriminating debacle in the Stadium parking lot to begin tightening the noose around his neck, greatly delaying his "retirement."

In a matter of seconds, G. Billy Fryman decided on a strategic response to Mooney's news that would require three specific actions. He looked up at his lieutenant to initiate the first stage. "Well, Braxton," he said in a defeated tone that was artificial but convincing, "it's apparent to me that we have worn out our welcome in L.A. I believe we need to implement our evasive maneuvers sooner than we had planned—starting tonight. I suggest that you drive straight to LAX and book passage on the next flight to that South Seas island you've set your heart on. I'll be on my way to the Yucatan before morning."

"Yes, sir, I understand," Mooney replied.

Fryman waved his subordinate toward the BMW waiting on the dark residential street, and they walked there together. Once Mooney was seated with the motor purring, Fryman motioned for him to pull the window down. "You have plenty of money, don't you, Braxton?" he said.

"Yes, sir, you've been very good to me. I'll be comfortable."

"Fine, fine," Fryman said. "You've worked hard, you deserve a good rest where it's safe and—"

Fryman didn't need to finish his statement because Braxton Mooney could no longer hear him. While speaking, the fat man had surreptitiously slipped the small, quiet Panda automatic from under his flowing Hawaiian shirt. Then with one motion he pressed the barrel to Mooney's temple and squeezed off a quick round. The slug killed Mooney instantly and propelled his head and torso sideways into the passenger's seat. The shot from the polymer pistol was no louder than a quick pull of a zipper on a canvas bag, and the idling engine and the party noise drifting from the backyard covered even that subtle sound.

"Sorry, Braxton," Fryman said without sympathy, "but I must cover as many tracks as possible."

The fat man opened the door, electronically raised the window, and shut off the engine. Then he reclined the passenger's bucket with the touch of a button and muscled Mooney's lifeless body into a prone position, folding his hands in front of him. Except for the dark rivulet coursing from the head wound, Mooney looked like a man sleeping off too many martinis.

Locking the car door, Fryman hurried up the front steps and entered the house through the ornate oak door. His well-oiled guests were raucously partying beside the pool and did not see him enter. He waddled down the hall and into his private office, locking the door behind him.

Having efficiently silenced Mooney, Fryman quickly moved to launch stage two of his hastily devised plan. He could not retire in peace to his own personal paradise on a remote beach in the Yucatan Peninsula, knowing that Nolan Jakes was still roaming free. Jakes had to be found and fully paid for his deceit and disloyalty.

There was also the matter of $620,000 which Jakes didn't deserve and which Fryman now voraciously coveted for himself. It was imperative that he leave the country tonight, but not before he was assured that Jakes would be hunted down, relieved of his ill-gotten gain, and neutralized before the police found him.

Fryman pulled the phone from his shirt pocket, flipped it open, and tapped in the number of his most loyal and trusted associate, a player in his organization known only to himself and the unfortunate Braxton Mooney. This strategic employee, who preferred to be called by the alias Bishop, had uncovered Jakes' defection and the fake drug buy he had planned with the LAPD and DEA. Bishop had notified Fryman, who in turn had ordered Chance and Fernandez to play the game long enough to get the money and terminate Jakes' employment.

Holding the phone to his ear, Fryman stepped to the floor safe in the corner of the office and knelt beside it with a grunt. He disarmed the alarm, spun the combination, and opened the small steel door.

"Yes," came the familiar voice through the phone's tiny speaker.

"Bishop, we have a problem," Fryman began, pulling bundles of bills out of the safe and tossing them into a soft-sided leather briefcase.

"Say, Billy, you're up pretty late tonight, aren't you?" Bishop said pleasantly, as if not hearing the word "problem."

"I said we have a problem," Fryman repeated, adding intensity to his tone to underscore the seriousness of his message.

Unfazed by Fryman's attempt at intimidation, Bishop said, "I know, Billy. Chance and Fernandez are dead, Jakes is on the loose with all that money, the cops are closing in on you . . . yes, I'd say you have a *big* problem."

Fryman suddenly stopped moving his money. "You already know?" he said in disbelief.

"Billy, I'm disappointed that you're so surprised," Bishop said teasingly. "I'm *supposed* to know these things. I have a reliable network. That's why you pay me the big bucks."

"Do you know where Jakes is now?" Fryman pressed.

"I have a good idea," Bishop answered, with purposeful vagueness.

Fryman wanted to ask more questions about Jakes' location and Bishop's mysterious contacts, but he didn't have time. He resumed stuffing the leather bag with money as he tersely issued his orders. "Listen, Bishop. Use your network to find Jakes before the cops do. Terminate him and get the money. Leave no tracks."

"No problem, Billy," Bishop answered confidently.

Fryman continued, "Bring the money to my villa in Mexico as soon as you can. I'm leaving tonight. We'll settle up accounts, and you can stay with me for a few weeks if you like, before beginning your 'retirement.' "

Fryman had a much different scenario in mind, of course. After completing this final assignment, Bishop would also be terminated in Mexico and fed to the sharks in the Gulf, thus eliminating another set of tracks to the exiled kingpin.

"I should be there no later than Wednesday," Bishop asserted confidently. "Thanks for the invitation."

"But don't leave for Mexico until Jakes is out of the picture," Fryman insisted.

"Not to worry, Billy. I'll put a man on his trail tonight—a professional. Jakes will be taken care of."

Fryman hung up without saying good-bye. Stage two was under way, and he was confident that Bishop would get the job done and then walk blindly into his trap in Mexico.

It was time for stage three: immediate departure. As Fryman finished cleaning out his safe, a quick phone call alerted the hanger crew at Van Nuys Airport to prepare his Cessna for a 1:00 A.M. departure. He snapped the briefcase shut, then carried it out of the office, locking the door behind him.

Fryman did not delay to pack clothes. He walked directly out the front door—unseen by his guests—to Braxton Mooney's BMW. Speed was of the essence. Besides, his villa was already well supplied with everything he needed. Nor did he pause to excuse himself from his guests. He would be at Van Nuys Airport in less than ten minutes. He would park the BMW on a dark side street, wipe it clean of his prints, and disappear from California forever in his Cessna. Bishop would finish off Jakes and deliver the money to Mexico, and Fryman would finish off Bishop. Everything would be neat and tidy.

G. Billy Fryman eased his ample frame behind the wheel of the BMW, leaning the briefcase against Mooney's body in the other seat. Then he fired up the engine, said good-bye to his expensive home with a quick glance, and roared away into the night.

Several miles away, Fryman's trusted employee Bishop placed a series of telephone calls before reaching the desired party. The ensuing conversation was crisp and professional. A verbal agreement was quickly reached regarding the termination and disposal of Nolan Jakes. A substantial fee was approved without contest and a cash down-payment drop was arranged. A precise communication strategy was outlined by which Bishop would supply specific directions regarding the target within the next twenty-four hours. The entire conversation took less than three minutes.

Had G. Billy Fryman been listening in on Bishop's conversation, he would have found good reason to doubt the loyalty of his valued employee. It was clear from the dialogue on the phone that Bishop's agenda for the disposal of Nolan Jakes was markedly different from that of the fleeing fat man.

Thirteen

It was nearly midnight before Evan and Shelby finally said good-bye to their last guest. Evan's colleague, Dr. Ari Benari, a trauma surgeon from the ER at Community Hospital, missed every clue that the birthday party had ended almost two hours earlier. He stood around during the walk-through of the wedding ceremony in the garden, chatting with Shelby's parents and offering suggestions on where the bride, groom, matron of honor, and best man should stand. Then as the Welbourns, the Tuggles, and Theresa Bordeaux departed for the Hilton in nearby Oxnard, Ari stood at the door pumping their hands and bidding them all good-night like the maitre d'hotel.

Aware that Ari, a bachelor, preferred the company of friends to his lonely condo on the beach, Evan and Shelby graciously allowed him to stay and help them pick up glasses and plates while listening to him talk. Had he not received a call on his personal phone summoning him to the ER, Ari might have stayed all night.

After waving to Ari as he roared off in his classic TR7, Evan and Shelby stood on the front porch holding each other for a full minute, exhausted and content at finally being alone. "So much for our romantic walk on the beach," Evan said, after kissing Shelby softly on the forehead.

"Ari needed company tonight," she said. "There will be many more nights to walk on the beach together."

Evan ushered her back into the house. "But for now, you and Malika had better get on the road."

"Evan, the house is still a mess," Shelby contested. "If we work together it won't take long to—"

"No way, angel," Evan interrupted. "You need to hurry home and get to sleep. You have a big day tomorrow."

"I hope it's just as big a day for you," Shelby said, pecking him on the cheek.

"It will be the most wonderful day in my life," he assured her, smiling. "But I don't have to drive into L.A. and back between now and then like you do. So you need to get going. I'll load the dishwasher and turn it on before I go to bed. Then I'll finish everything else in the morning. I've lived alone for a long time. I can handle it."

Shelby threw her arms around his neck and smothered his mouth with a long kiss. Then she whispered close to his ear, "Starting tomorrow, my darling, you can forget everything you ever learned about living alone, because you won't need it. I'm moving in for good."

"Mm, I can't wait," Evan whispered back.

After another moment of kissing, the couple broke off their embrace. Shelby collected her jacket and purse while Evan headed upstairs to carry Malika to the car.

Evan crept into the master bedroom, which was barely illuminated by a sliver of light seeping in from the adjoining bathroom. He found Malika asleep under the comforter on his large oak four-poster bed. A rush of emotion swept over him as he stood in the near darkness watching the still form and listening to the rhythmic, unhurried breathing. He was not only taking to himself a wife tomorrow, he was inheriting a seven-year-old daughter, a battered waif of a child who looked barely five.

Had Evan's first wife conceived during their stormy two years together, he might have had a son or daughter now. Despite their difficulties, he had wanted to produce a child by Katrina. As a physician enthralled by the miracle of life, he had yearned to initiate that miracle himself.

But now Evan was grateful that Katrina had not conceived because of all the grief their breakup would have caused their offspring. Yet Evan's desire to be a father had never left him. Ever since Shelby and Malika had come into his life, he had been amazed at how his paternal aspirations were being fulfilled in the skinny black child lying before him. He couldn't wait to formalize the adoption and give her the name he was about to give his bride. Tomorrow, Shelby Tuggle would become Shelby Rider. And shortly after the honeymoon, her daughter, Malika, would become his daughter too—Malika Rider.

Shelby slipped into the bedroom unnoticed and drank in the scene before her in the dim light: Evan standing over the bed adoring sleeping Malika. Shelby had been amazed at how easily Evan had accepted Malika. She had made it plain to him from the earliest days of their acquaintance that Malika would be part of the package a man would receive, if and when she ever married again. Evan had been so taken with the girl that, at their engagement party, Shelby had joked that he was marrying her only so he could gain Malika as his daughter.

Evan and Shelby had talked about children often during the latter stages of their courtship. Malika was a godsend, Shelby had admitted, but she still longed to bear a child of her own. She told Evan that she understood the risks of becoming pregnant at forty, but she insisted that she was not convinced enough by them to abandon her dream of becoming a biological mother.

When they first began to talk about marriage and possible children, Evan had been less than enthusiastic about their becoming parents in their forties, especially since they already had Malika. But Shelby's passion for motherhood soon infected him. He immersed himself in the latest research on middle-age pregnancies, and they discussed the necessary medical precautions they would observe. He suggested that they give themselves a year to learn how to be a family of three before trying to become a family of four. Shelby had quipped, "I've waited forty years to become a mother; I can certainly wait one more year."

Warmed by the love she felt for the man God had brought to her, Shelby moved in behind Evan, slipped her arms around his waist tightly, and pressed herself against him. Then she whispered words she knew would please him, "Tomorrow night at this time, Malika will be at the Hilton with my parents, and we will be in this house alone and in that bed together as husband and wife. Then we will spend two weeks in our RV getting even better acquainted."

Evan gripped her hands with his and leaned his head back until it touched hers. He said softly, "I hope you're not offended, like I'm some kind of an animal, but I've been looking forward to tomorrow night with great anticipation."

Shelby laughed at a whisper. "I would be offended if you *weren't* anticipating it, because I certainly am."

Evan turned within the circle of Shelby's loving grasp and enveloped her in his arms. Their prolonged kiss was ardent, eager, expectant.

The stirring of the child on the bed startled them, but Malika did not wake. For another minute Evan just held Shelby.

"I don't deserve you, angel," he said at last through a sigh. "You should be marrying a gleaming saint, someone who hasn't been so tarnished by the world."

Shelby pulled back to face Evan in the dim light. "Evan, we have already discussed this many times," she said sternly, still speaking at a whisper. "That's all behind us. God has forgiven you for your past just as He has forgiven me for mine. I accept you as pure because God does."

"But you still don't understand my past. You still don't know—"

Shelby stopped the words at his mouth with the gentle touch of her fingers. "Darling, it doesn't matter. God has taken care of your past. That's what grace is all about. You can't buy it. You can't earn it. You can only—"

"Yes, I know, 'you can only receive it,' " Evan interjected with a soft laugh. "You've lectured that to me a thousand times. You won't give up, will you?"

Shelby returned to his embrace. "No, I won't give up on what God says, because it's true. And I won't give up on you, because I love you."

"You may have to keep reminding me about what God says," Evan said.

Shelby smiled, resting her head on his chest. "I promise I will. But let's try to get through tomorrow night without a theological discussion, okay?"

Evan had to cover his mouth to keep from laughing out loud. "I thank God for you, Shelby," he said finally with a squeeze.

Evan buckled a half-awake Malika into the front seat of Shelby's white Lincoln Tour de Grace. The car had been a Christmas present from her adoring congregation in Dallas a year and a half earlier. When she resigned her position as pastor at Victory Life, she had tried to give the car back to the church, but the people wouldn't hear of it. Instead they presented her with a $10,000 love offering and sent her off to King's House in Los Angeles with their blessing. Shelby had used the gift to purchase furniture, linens, and clothes for the women's shelter in the House.

After a final, lingering kiss in Evan's arms, Shelby backed the Lincoln out of the garage and headed down the hill toward U.S. 101 and the sixty-minute drive into Los Angeles. Malika was asleep again—leaning on a pillow Evan had propped between her and the doorpost—before Shelby reached the freeway. She accelerated up the on-ramp and merged into light traffic. With a touch of her finger she turned the wipers to INTERMITTENT to keep the windshield clear in the heavy marine air, and then set the cruise button for freeway speed. Programming the sound system for soft instrumental praise tunes, Shelby settled into the plush leather seat to savor the memories of a hectic but pleasant evening.

Face after face came before her, each one prompting a smile. She thought at length about her father, Jimmy Tuggle. She felt again his surprisingly tender embrace during a lull in the rehearsal. "You deserve this new beginning, sugar," he had whispered for her ears only, as tears filled his eyes. "I pray that God will wash away the sorrows of the past with a deluge of happiness." Shelby had wept too, and her throat swelled with emotion now as she clung to her father's words. What a rock of support he had been to her over her forty years.

As the Lincoln swept past the city of Camarillo and up the Conejo grade, Shelby thought about Theresa Bordeaux' timely "interruption" during the party. It was a strategy Theresa had employed numerous times as Shelby's personal assistant, whenever she thought Shelby needed a short break from the people crowded around her. Theresa understood how prolonged social interaction tended to drain Shelby's batteries.

"Excuse me, Shelby," Theresa had said in a pleasant but businesslike tone during the party, "but may I see you for a moment please?" At the time, Shelby was cornered in the dining room by Aaron and Sheila Weintraub and the ER nurse.

Theresa had whisked Shelby out to the patio, which was deserted. "I just thought you might need a quick breather 'far from the madding crowd,'" she announced.

"Thank you," Shelby responded with an exaggerated sigh and a smile, as they sat down facing the lights of Ventura. "I'm really having a wonderful time. But you're right: I need a moment to recharge." They sat in silence for several uninterrupted moments.

"I know that we won't have much time together this weekend,"

Theresa added, "so I want to give you your birthday gift now." She produced a beautifully wrapped box the size of a large hardback book. "I know that you and Evan insisted on no gifts. But fortieth birthdays are too special. And besides, you're not my boss any longer, so you'll just have to take it and enjoy it."

It was a beautifully framed, 8 by 10 holograph of the two of them standing in front of the Olympic stadium in Sydney during the summer games of 2000. It was the vacation they had put off for years because of Shelby's feverish schedule at Victory Life Ministries in Dallas. But with the turn of the millennium and Shelby's new call to King's House in Los Angeles, the two friends were able to carve out three weeks in July for their special trip.

I will *enjoy the gift, Theresa, for the rest of my life,* Shelby thought as she drove.

Shelby pictured Dr. No and his petite wife, Mai, the most gracious, humble Christians she had ever known. How appropriate it would be for Dr. No to offer the dedicatory prayer over her and Evan during the ceremony.

She thought of Stan and Eleanor Welbourn, her former co-workers from Dallas. Shelby did not miss the daily stresses of being the head of a national ministry, but she did miss the daily love and nurture of her spiritual uncle and aunt.

Shelby tapped off the wipers as the Lincoln raced past the community of Thousand Oaks. According to the digital readout on the console, the drier inland air outside the car was fifteen degrees warmer than in Ventura, which was often overcast and damp in June. Shelby breathed a silent prayer that tomorrow's weather would be suitable for her 1 P.M. wedding in Evan's garden.

There had been a few invited guests missing from her party tonight that Shelby wished had been there. She was most disappointed that Grace Ellen Holloway and her husband were not able to be present for the big weekend. Simon Holloway had scheduled a preaching campaign in Great Britain months before Evan and Shelby's wedding date was set. Upon receiving the invitation, Grace Ellen had called with her sincere regrets, explaining that she felt constrained to stay with her husband through the trip, especially in light of the tragedy that had befallen the Holloways in the winter.

Shelby hoped that she might receive a video-call from Grace Ellen in Scotland tomorrow to congratulate her and Evan. She wanted to hear firsthand how Simon, Grace Ellen, and their surviving son, Mark, were dealing with the devastating loss.

Shelby's feelings for her friend and mentor ran deep and strong. After the humiliation of a moral lapse and the trauma of Millennium's Eve, Shelby needed a confidante and a counselor, someone to help her take personal inventory and to hold her accountable for changes she needed to make. God had sent Grace Ellen Holloway to her.

Shelby had met with Grace Ellen monthly through most of the millennium's dawning year—either in Los Angeles, Orlando, or somewhere in between—for two or three days of intensive conversation, Bible study, and prayer. When apart, they spoke by phone or fax at least once a week, usually for Shelby to report on reading and study assignments Grace Ellen had given her.

Under Grace Ellen's mentoring, Shelby's faith in God and confidence in herself as His servant had soared. As they sought God's guidance together, it became clear to Shelby that her future was not in Dallas as the pastor of a continent-wide television ministry, but in Los Angeles as a caregiver and Bible teacher alongside Dr. No in a renovated old hospital in Echo Park called King's House.

By late summer, a new topic had begun to monopolize much of their time together: a dark-haired, strikingly attractive, unmarried physician named Evan Rider. Dr. Rider volunteered at King's House—one day a week, caring for AIDS patients on the fifth floor. Grace Ellen was the first to hear of Shelby's romantic interest in Evan, which escalated over seven months to an intense mutual interest, a dating relationship, and finally an engagement. During that time Shelby held herself strictly accountable to Grace Ellen for her behavior when she and Evan were together. Shelby had shared more of her thoughts and feelings with Grace Ellen than with any woman in her life, including Theresa Bordeaux.

Then in November came the crushing blow that made Shelby's new ministry and romantic interest seem suddenly unimportant. Simon and Grace Ellen's younger son, nineteen-year-old Tim, had returned to King's House for a second stint as a volunteer. Late one night he was walking in downtown L.A. with two other volunteers, looking for homeless men in need of shelter. Tim and his friends came upon a street fight between two winos and tried to break it up. One of the combatants pulled a small caliber pistol during the argument and fired wildly, missing his antagonist but striking Tim Holloway in the head.

Deeply comatose, the young volunteer hung between life and death long enough for his grief-stricken parents and older brother to fly in from Orlando. They hovered over him, crying out anguished prayers and saying their last good-byes. Tim died less than twenty-four hours after the attack.

For a month, the roles of the Shelby and Grace Ellen were reversed. Grace Ellen was the deeply wounded, distraught counselee, and Shelby was the compassionate counselor and caregiver, not only for Grace Ellen but also for Simon and twenty-two-year-old Mark.

The awful experience brought the two women even closer than before. How Shelby wished her dear friend could be with her this weekend.

Also missing from the crowd in Evan's home tonight were two faces Shelby had hoped to see but hadn't really expected at the party. Journalist Beth Scibelli and LAPD Sergeant Reagan Cole had saved her life on Millennium's Eve in the Los Angeles Memorial Coliseum. Shelby owed much to these two people whom, it seemed, God had brought together to effect her rescue.

Shelby had asked Evan to include Beth and Reagan on the guest list for her party, just as she had included them among a small group of friends invited to the wedding. Sergeant Cole—now *Detective* Sergeant Cole—had responded to the invitations in person, since he saw Shelby about once a week on his regular visits to King's House as a volunteer. Unfortunately, he had explained to her, he would be unable to attend the Friday night party in Ventura because his current assignment was keeping him busy most nights, especially as he was trying to clear his desk for vacation. But he hoped to get there for the wedding on Saturday, after which he would be driving to Lake Tahoe to spend several days with his mother and his four sisters and their families.

Shelby had heard nothing from Beth Scibelli, nor had she seen the journalist in almost a year. For a few months after Millennium's Eve, Beth had flown in and out of L.A. several times from her home on Whidbey Island across Puget Sound from Seattle, principally to strengthen her relationship with her parents and to foster the romance with Reagan Cole which had budded during the last eight days of 1999. Beth was frequently with Reagan when he came to King's House to volunteer in the prisoner rehabilitation and release program.

But by June of 2000, the romance had apparently cooled, and Beth didn't come to King's House with Reagan any longer. Sergeant Cole had not confided to Shelby the reasons for the breakup, but she had her ideas.

Dr. No and King's House and the effectiveness of prayer had obviously made an impact on both Beth and Reagan during the harrowing days before Millennium's Eve. And after it was all over, both of them were interested in getting better acquainted with Dr. No and Mai and investigating their very practical, demonstrable faith.

But other strong forces were vying for Beth's attention. When the story of the foiled assassination plot in the L.A. Coliseum became public, people wanted to read more. Beth's paperback news story on Unity 2000, which she had contracted to write for a modest flat fee of $10,000, sold 400,000 copies the first week it was out, and kept selling well for two months.

She followed the book with a dramatic first-person account of her capture, her escape, and her race against time to avert the deadly disaster. This popular book, which several publishers had bid for, sold even better than her first one, and she had wisely signed for a healthy royalty instead of a flat fee.

Beth's unforeseen literary success seemed to turn her head away from the unspectacular ministry at King's House in run-down Echo Park. Coincidentally, her path and Reagan's, which had been closely parallel for several months, began to diverge.

Reagan Cole spent more and more of his free time at King's House meeting with Dr. No, learning about the prison ministry from its director, big Bill Fawcett, and taking an active part as his work schedule allowed. But Beth, from the little Reagan had told Shelby, became increasingly absorbed with her writing opportunities, which flourished following the success of her two books about Unity 2000. She had been courted by several publishers who offered her intriguing writing assignments around the world at enticingly substantial fees. She obviously savored the recognition among her peers, welcomed the opportunity to choose her assignments, and craved the financial rewards she felt she deserved. And since King's House couldn't compete with the allure and excitement of her newfound niche, she drifted away from it and from Reagan Cole, who had opted for the quieter, less glamorous life.

At least that's how it appeared to Shelby. She hoped to be able to talk to Sergeant Cole during the reception and ask him about his former love interest. But Shelby was sure that Beth Scibelli had many more exciting offers around the world for this June weekend than to be in Ventura for a wedding.

Shelby reduced her speed 5 MPH as Highway 101, known in the L.A. area as the Ventura Freeway, descended gradually into the densely populated West San Fernando Valley. Traffic on the Ventura Freeway was rarely light, even in the middle of the night. King's House was only twenty minutes away, providing that a jackknifed truck or multiple-car accident hadn't jammed the freeway up ahead. No such alert had been posted on the computerized freeway reader boards, but that was no guarantee.

Another face from the party filled Shelby's mind as she drove: Evan's. And words that accompanied his image were discomforting to her. She heard again Evan's recently repeated insistence that he was unworthy of her. *If anyone is unworthy, darling,* she argued with him silently, *it's me. Your moral failures, and whatever other past sins are troubling you, occurred while you were an unbeliever. Sinners sin; you couldn't help but be guided by your sinful nature. But that was all washed away when you became a believer. You were given a clean slate. It's still clean, and you have remained pure throughout our courtship, a model of propriety and restraint, for which I will be forever grateful. But I failed in the presence of great light—as a believer, as a minister of the Gospel.*

Shelby winced as the memory of Christmas Eve 1999 crested the banks of her will against it and flooded her consciousness. It had happened exactly one week before the diabolical, murderous plot against the Unity 2000 leaders was discovered by Beth Scibelli and disarmed by Sergeant Reagan Cole. It had been the most distressing week of Shelby's life.

On that dispiriting Christmas Eve, the party for Shelby's top ministry staff at the Austin ranch had ended, and her guests had been air-shuttled back to Dallas—everyone except her good friend in ministry, Jeremy Cannon. Then, in a moment of personal weakness and blinding deception, she had offered herself to him. The mental image still made Shelby cringe nearly eighteen months after confessing the foolish, sinful act to God and embracing His forgiveness.

But thankfully, like Joseph under the seduction of Potiphar's wife, Jeremy had found the strength of character to flee. Faced with the full reality of what she had done, Shelby ran too, trying to flee the God she had failed, reckoning herself to be of no further use to Him. Dramatically arrested, humbled, and affirmed by His grace in the remote desert of south Texas, she returned to Austin, then went on to Los Angeles to survive the unimaginable horror of an assassination attempt.

It had taken Shelby several months of counseling and prayer under her godly mentor, Grace Ellen Holloway, to mend the deep wounds incurred during the last week of 1999. In the meantime, God brought her to the sanctuary of King's House. There her attention was diverted from her needs and painful healing to the blatant physical and emotional indigence of hundreds of souls who passed through its doors each month. It was at King's House that she received a new call, found beautiful and fragile Malika, and met the man who was to become her husband.

The steadily rising tide of Shelby's good fortune over the past eighteen months tended to dim the memory of her failure, but never fully obscured it. She affirmed that God had forgiven her and restored her, and she knew the affirmation was solidly based on truth. But her usually clear thinking on the matter was sometimes clouded by troubling emotions prompted by still-painful memories. In God's eyes she was no longer a failure. But occasionally she still *felt* like a failure.

Curiously, Shelby's times of greatest confusion came when she was with Evan, especially during their moments of physical closeness and affection. She had never told him how unworthy *she* felt in *his* arms— the same feelings he had expressed to her again tonight and for which she often scolded him. Evan was so marvelous, so perfect for her. He was the answer to the deep yearning for partnership she had known since her late husband had emotionally abandoned her nearly seven years ago, the yearning which had betrayed her in that careless, ugly moment with Jeremy Cannon.

The warmth of Evan's arms, the amazing strength of his character as a new believer, the sincerity of his commitment to her, the promise of their idyllic life together—it was all too good. Shelby wanted to accept him for what she knew he was: God's gift to her. But she couldn't shake the notion—though she resisted it with all her mind—that there was a price to be paid for her blessings. Nothing could be this perfect for someone who had failed as she had. Shelby only hoped the price wouldn't be exacted from the two people she loved most in all the world: Evan Rider and Malika Tuggle.

Unwilling to allow her disparaging thoughts to spoil the rest of her drive and pollute her last night to sleep alone, Shelby tapped the memory button for Evan's number on the phone mounted in the Lincoln's visor. She was just passing the Hollywood Bowl less than ten minutes from home as the tone indicated that his phone was beeping. Malika slept on undisturbed.

"Yes?" Evan answered, sounding like a doctor on call.

"Were you asleep, darling?" Shelby said.

"No, angel, I'm not even upstairs yet. I'm doing a little mopping and vacuuming while waiting to hear that you're home safely. Are you?"

"We're in Hollywood, just a few minutes away," Shelby said.

"Good. I'll stay on until you're parked and one of the night butlers comes to escort you in."

"Thank you, Evan. You're so thoughtful. It's one of your many fine qualities."

They reviewed the highlights of the evening and admitted their excitement about tomorrow, which Shelby reminded Evan was already here: It was 1 A.M. Shelby wanted to confess her feelings of unworthiness to Evan and hear him chide her and absolve her as she had done to him an hour ago. But she couldn't bring herself to spoil the magic of the moment or to quench the obvious elation she sensed in his voice.

Shelby exited the freeway at Alvarado and climbed the little hill into Echo Park, winding through the quiet streets to King's House. Parking in her accustomed spot near the back entrance, she put Evan on hold long enough to phone into the building for an escort. Within a minute, a burly college student in denim shorts and a UCLA sweatshirt stepped out the back door, hopped off the loading dock, and headed in her direction.

"Rudy is on his way out to get us, darling. I'd better sign off. I'll see you at about 11."

"I'll be waiting for you. Sleep well."

Shelby searched for a final, hope-filled comment. "I trust that our wedding day will meet all your expectations, Evan."

"Shelby, my angel, nothing in the world could spoil the day I take you as my wife."

As she tapped off the phone, Shelby so desperately hoped that Evan was right that she turned her desire to an urgent silent prayer.

Fourteen

Nolan Jakes soaked in a tub full of warm water while Margo Sharpe sponged his back and gently peeled the shirt away from the scabs forming over countless cuts on his back. The transdermal tranquilizer and painkiller had long since lost its punch, and Jakes felt like a thousand yellow jackets had used his back for target practice.

Jakes and Margo had rendezvoused without incident at Laurel Canyon and Hollywood Boulevard. She then drove them back over the hill and out to the West San Fernando Valley. After waking the night clerk at a small Days Inn on Roscoe Boulevard, Margo took a single room under the name of Jackie Taylor. Parking in the underground garage, she used the elevator to smuggle Jakes into her room.

After soaking and removing his shirt in the tub, Margo used tweezers from her cosmetic bag to pluck fragments of brown glass from his back, reopening several wounds in the process. Then she applied antiseptic cream as Jakes winced. As she did so, he scrubbed the barbed-wire cuts on his hands, trying to dislodge the dirt which had worked into them.

All through her ministrations Margo pressed her wish to leave with Jakes. She would never love anyone like she loved him, she said. She reminded him that her life in L.A. was also at an end. She expected the police to pester her relentlessly for information, and she feared that G. Billy Fryman's thugs might stalk her, torture her, or even kill her in their attempt to learn Jakes' whereabouts. She would go anywhere with him. She would live the rest of her life in anonymity for him. Together they could protect each other and comfort each other. "Please, Nolan," she begged repeatedly, "don't leave me here alone. Take me with you."

It had been Jakes' deepest wish that Margo go with him. The thought of living in exile without her had lurked painfully in the shadows of his mind ever since he escaped the Stadium parking lot. But he knew he could never expect her to go with him—and certainly not demand it of her—now that he was a marked man.

A much lesser but still persistent concern was that Margo might be a detriment to his successful escape. As difficult as it would be for him to elude the police and a powerful drug lord by himself, it would be even more difficult for the two of them. He did not know Margo very well. Well-meaning though she seemed, she might get in his way and slow his flight. She might even be the inadvertent or unwitting cause of his capture or death. The risk was a small but real factor in his contention that she go her own way.

Yet Margo seemed undaunted by his objections or concern for her safety. Rather, Jakes was touched by her desire to leave everything for him. Despite the danger to Margo and possible hazard to himself, he could not deny a growing love for this woman, even though his love would require that he exercise even greater caution to allow her to go with him. So he allowed her passionate importunity to gradually wear him down as they sat on the bed, and he finally assented.

Margo was so overjoyed at Jakes' decision that she disregarded the many abrasions on his body and smothered him with kisses. Aroused by her affection and euphoric at being safe, clean, and cared for, Jakes temporarily forgot about his pain, and they made love.

Later, as Margo slept, Jakes lay awake in the darkness. Still smarting at the beating he had taken from the bed of broken glass, the hillside, and the barbed wire, he was unable to find a comfortable position for sleeping. So he gingerly shifted from side to belly to side, but without relief.

His thoughts were as obstinate to his falling asleep as were his wounds. Questions, like tree branches banging at the bedroom window during a midnight wind storm, kept him wide awake.

Where will we go? Jakes knew that he and Margo could hide out in L.A. for only a few more hours, and he doubted that they would feel safe anywhere in California for more than a day or two. They had to find a place where the police and Fryman's goons would not find them.

He assessed that their ultimate destination need not be excessively distant as long as it was remote. *There's no reason for Margo and me to run to the deep jungles of Borneo when we can find as much seclusion and privacy, say, in the Canadian Rockies.*

Jakes warmed to the memory of trips he had taken into the wilderness of Western Canada with a couple of his B.C. Lion teammates during the off-season. There were remote towns he and Margo could go to, where the neighbors were miles away and nobody from the outside would think to look for them. They could change their identities, buy some land with the money he had stolen, and enjoy life unmolested in the pristine Rockies.

After half an hour of silent, personal deliberations, Jakes had decided on heading for a place somewhere between the Cariboo Mountains and Spectacle Lakes; close enough to Quesnel or Prince George to visit them when it was safe, but far from the prying eyes of the RCMP or Billy Fryman's hired killers.

The next question was more difficult: *How will we get there?* Public transportation was definitely out; the police would be monitoring airports, train stations, and bus depots. They could try driving north, but Margo's car would soon be on a nationwide hot sheet, as would any cars they stole or bought along the way. They'd be lucky to get as far as Fresno on their own.

They needed an accomplice. But this simple deduction introduced yet another knotty question: *Who will want to help us?* Jakes had some law-abiding friends who owed him favors. But none of them would go so far as to harbor or transport an at-large criminal. He also knew a few shady characters who might do the deed for a price. But they would just as likely turn on him if they were offered more money from Fryman's organization.

It was during a mental inventory of people who owed him that Jakes struck upon the idea. It was so startling that it drove him from the bed, and he began pacing the dark hotel room as Margo slept on. There *was* someone who could take him and Margo out of the country—and who could probably get him more money for their exile. Although they had not seen or talked to each other in over twenty years, Jakes recalled that the man was somewhere in Southern California. Jakes had seen something in the papers about him a couple of years back. All he had to do was find him.

Jakes was confident that the man he was thinking about *wouldn't* want to help him. Not that they were enemies; far from it. They had been college teammates, buddies. But one dark, thoughtless, terrifying night had changed everything. The two friends—and a third, who by design had also disappeared from Jakes life—had perpetrated a grievous moral wrong. Though not intentional, their crime was so grave that, had it been traced to them, a conviction would doubtless have sent the three bewildered and terrified collegians to prison.

But it didn't happen. The deed was discovered within hours, but by some stroke of blind luck, the perpetrators were not. Being as inexperienced in avoiding the consequences of a crime as they had been at committing one, the trio of friends somehow escaped the scene and were never implicated. The crime had remained on the books as unsolved.

Realizing their extraordinary good fortune, within minutes of their escape the three friends rationalized their ugly misdeed into an unfortunate accident and swore themselves to eternal secrecy. Dissolving the friendship was not a conscious part of the bargain. But the seeds of guilt buried in their hearts soon flowered into avoidance. Within days they were no longer meeting for lunch, and within weeks each had become a nonentity to the others. Geographic separation soon followed.

No, Jakes' old friend would not be happy to hear from him. And he would be even less eager to help him out of his serious jam. *But he can be persuaded,* Jakes figured. *Blackmail—I believe that's what it's called. If he helps me get safely out of the country and contributes to my "retirement fund," I keep our deep, dark past a secret. But if he refuses and the police take me in, I tell the whole story, and he goes down the toilet with me. It's an offer a successful, established professional can't refuse.*

Jakes moved silently to the desk and searched the drawers in the darkness for the telephone book. Finding it, he went into the bathroom, closed the door, and turned on the light. A search of the West Valley directory proved futile; the name of Jakes' unsuspecting angel of mercy did not appear in the listings. He would have to find other directories for the Southern California area. In an instant, he knew where to look.

Turning off the light, Jakes left the bathroom. He fumbled in the darkness for the short-sleeve cotton shirt and summer-weight slacks Margo had brought him from her apartment and slipped into them. He tucked the Colt .44 into his waistband and left his shirttail out to cover it. Then he left the room barefooted.

As he made his way down the carpeted hall and three flights of stairs toward the lobby, Jakes thought of the third member of the disbursed secret society. Where was she now? What was she doing? How might she be able to help him flee hell and find paradise, once he threatened to turn her world upside down by uncovering their common past? He would search the directories for her name too, although it might be changed by marriage. And she could be anywhere in the world by now. The chances of finding her seemed more remote than finding his old football buddy.

The lobby was vacant and semidark, with the door to the outside locked. The orange neon NO VACANCY sign glowed outside the door, even though half the motel was unoccupied.

Jakes walked soundlessly past the counter to a short hall where two pay phones were attached to the wall. A shelf was mounted above the phones, and on that shelf stood a library of dog-eared telephone directories for the counties and communities of Southern California.

Jakes searched book after book for two people from his past who, had they known of Jakes' endeavor, would have fallen to their knees praying that he fail. The woman's name never appeared. But in the directory for Ventura County, Jakes traced his finger down a list of names near the back of the book until—"Yes!" he exclaimed barely at a whisper. "I *knew* you were around here somewhere. You don't know it yet, but you are about to be visited by a ghost from your past."

Jakes' finger was tapping just below a name: RIDER, EVAN, M.D.

SATURDAY
June 23, 2001

Fifteen

The twenty-five first-class seats on American's Saturday morning flight from Miami to Dallas were filling fast. The young woman in seat 3-A next to the window furtively eyed each new passenger entering the cabin from the rear, willing them to sit anywhere but in seat 3-B, which was still vacant. She hoped to ride to Dallas and then on to Seattle in solitude, without a seat partner annoying her with small talk. She was in no mood to visit with anyone.

She was tall and beautiful, an early thirty-something. She wore belted white shorts, a sleeveless navy top, and white sandals, allowing plenty of the rich tan on her long arms and legs to be displayed. Accents of gold jewelry and the subtle fragrance of her expensive cologne confirmed that, despite her casual attire, she was at home in the first-class cabin.

Her dark hair had recently been cut short for style and easy care during the summer. Dark glasses shielded her eyes, which were puffy and red from two days of crying.

A large, graying man in a rumpled business suit approached the third row. Glancing at the leggy, good-looking woman in the window seat, he secretly hoped that the aisle seat was his. He compared the seat assignment on his boarding pass with the seat number displayed on the overhead bin. Delighted with the match, he dropped himself heavily into the plush leather seat identified as 3-B.

Sliding his briefcase under seat 2-B, he flashed a salesman's eager grin toward the passenger in the window seat and extended his hand. "Howdy, ma'am," he drawled. "Frank Fagan, southeastern representative for Lone Star Life and Casualty, Dallas, Texas."

The young woman reluctantly took his meaty hand. Mr. Fagan worked her arm like he was drilling for oil, but all the gushing came from him. "I don't usually ride up front—the company always sends me coach. It saves money for our policyholders, if you know what I mean. But I got one of those upgrade coupons for all the miles I fly to Atlanta, Charlotte, Baton Rouge, and Miami month after month. I've been looking forward to the free booze you folks get up here. And it's a real pleasure to sit next to a lovely lady like you. And your name is. . . ?"

The woman in 3-A didn't want to tell Frank Fagan her name, but she did anyway, hoping her simple response would satisfy the old guy so he would leave her alone for the rest of the trip. "Beth Scibelli, Seattle, Washington."

"See-attle! My stars, ain't that a coincidence! My ex-brother-in-law lives in See-attle. Actually, he lives in Pasco, which is closer to Idaho.

But from where I live, all those cities up in the rain country run together, if you know what I mean."

Mercifully for Beth, the flight attendant arrived to offer Frank a pre-takeoff drink and to hang his cheap suit coat in the closet. When he stood to remove his coat, Beth excused herself to use the lavatory before takeoff and to secretly scout out another empty seat in the cabin. But when she emerged from the lavatory, first class was full. She silently cursed the airline for being so liberal with first-class upgrades for people who paid with miles instead of money. Then she returned to her assigned seat.

To her relief, Frank Fagan was preoccupied with a trade journal and intent on downing his double Dewars and soda before the flight attendant came to take his glass for takeoff. Beth squeezed past him and sat down, quickly pulling the complimentary headset over her ears and selecting a music channel from the control panel in front of her.

Within minutes, the recorded spiel on the plane's audio-video system interrupted her music. Ignoring the boring details about seat belts, window exits, and emergency oxygen masks, Beth watched out the window as the Boeing 767 pushed back from the gate and began taxiing toward the end of the runway. When the music returned, she increased the volume, as if a flood of vintage Moody Blues oldies from the oldies channel would wash away the pain of the last few days. She couldn't get home fast enough.

It all started in Hartford, Connecticut four months earlier. Beth had been contracted by Havercroft and Wendt Publishing to write a series of books on the three most influential women in politics, one of whom, Senator Nell Champion of Tennessee, was jockeying to become the Democratic presidential nominee in November 2004. The lucrative writing project promised to supply another ego-building boost to Beth's rocketing career. Her credibility as a writer had been abruptly propelled to warp speed with the success of her two volumes on Unity 2000 in the Los Angeles Memorial Coliseum on Millennium's Eve.

Released shortly after the foiled assassination plot, Beth's supermarket paperback, *Faith under Fire: The Unity 2000 Story*, was an immediate bestseller. Written as a third-person news story, the book described the central characters and recounted the horrifying events leading up to the near tragic megagathering in the Coliseum. The assassination plot was reported, but it was subordinate to the overall account of the event.

The second book, *Race against the Devil*, was Beth's dramatic, first-person account of how she discovered and tracked the assassin and helped disarm his evil plan. It sold even better than the first book and brought a flood of writing opportunities. Beth Scibelli was far from a household name, but she had gained sufficient respect in her industry to attract the attention of the prestigious Havercroft and Wendt.

The most alluring element of Beth's contract with the Hartford publishing firm had turned out to be the publisher himself. Colin Randolph Wendt, an urbane forty-eight-year-old bachelor with piles of old New England money, had a penchant for leisurely, intimate yachting voyages with beautiful, articulate young women. Unaware of his history as a pirate of hearts, Beth was smitten with Colin's sophistication, intelligence, worldly wisdom, and striking good looks. Within weeks of their first encounter in the Hartford office, business between publisher and writer was being conducted aboard Colin's 55-foot private yacht in the waters of Nantucket Sound and Cape Cod Bay. And eventually, business gave way to pleasure in their relationship.

Beth's reverie was briefly interrupted by the mounting thunder of the 767's engines, as flight 414 for Dallas charged down the runway and lifted off from Miami International Airport. She watched below as the ascending plane cleared Florida's east coast then banked left to assume its west by northwest trajectory toward DFW. She was glad they weren't banking right to afford her one last view of the Caribbean. It was all over down there. In fact, her life on the east coast was over. She wanted to go home.

What had begun so promisingly in Hartford in February ended bitterly off the shores of quaint Antigua on Thursday. Actually, storm warnings had been raised days earlier as Colin and Beth, pampered by a small, efficient crew, sailed from Long Island Sound to the Bahamas, Puerto Rico, and the islands of the Eastern Caribbean for a three-week working vacation.

During the voyage they had maintained a protracted, spirited discussion about the Nell Champion book. Beth held that to be honest and comprehensive in her writing, she had to dig up and report the truth about a consistently denied allegation clouding Nell Champion's past: namely that the never-married senator had maintained a lesbian relationship during her term as a Memphis congresswoman. But Colin insisted that the book focus on Champion's career successes and future in politics and leave her warts in the shadows.

On Thursday evening they were anchored off the powdery beaches of Antigua, the quietly sophisticated former British colony. During a dinner of pasta and local fruit which they barely touched, the simmering issue mushroomed into a fiery impasse.

"We are doing our readers a great disservice if we purposely withhold from them vital details about a viable presidential candidate," Beth asserted. "We must get to the bottom of these allegations and tell the truth."

"We are doing a greater disservice by bringing up insignificant dirty laundry which may negatively impact Nell Champion's electability," Colin countered.

Beth steamed at Colin's stubbornness. "If dear Nellie's dirty laundry becomes public and the electorate denies her the White House, then she's clearly not the right person for the job."

"No, Beth," Colin pronounced firmly, waving an authoritative finger in her face. "Nell Champion *is* the right person for the job, and I'm not about to let long-buried weaknesses block her chances for the presidency."

Beth hated to be told no when she knew she was right. She sat staring at Colin in the twilight, processing his comments, and hoping she was wrong about where the discussion was heading. Colin averted his eyes, preferring a visual sweep of the uncomplicated aquamarine horizon.

Beth regarded her position as a conviction, and she quickly decided not to back down. Finally she spoke, unable to completely curb the harsh edge to her voice. "Which is it, Colin? Does Havercroft and Wendt want me to write a truthful, unbiased book about Nell Champion or a fairy-tale biography about a candidate who doesn't stand a chance against the truth?"

It was Colin's turn to stare, as the meaning of Beth's words fully registered. But she did not flinch against his hard gaze.

Colin's words were even and cold. "*I* alone decide what Havercroft and Wendt publishes. And I can find a dozen women as smart as you, as pretty as you, and as . . . easy . . . as you to write my books. The only question here tonight is, do you want the job or should I start looking at resumés again?"

The bitter words pierced Beth like a rapier through the heart, shocking her to mouth-agape silence. In an instant she knew she had been deceived. Her vision of Colin Wendt had been a naive fantasy. He wasn't interested in her as a person. He was using her, and entertaining himself in the process at the expense of her emotions, to get the book he wanted. The lavish yacht was suddenly a slave ship and her handsome captain an inhuman ogre.

A dozen vile retorts flooded Beth's mind, but none of them were nearly hurtful enough to repay Colin for the words with which he had thrust her through. She wanted to scream, and she felt a gut-wrenching cry coming on, but she wasn't about to give Colin the satisfaction. To cover her pain, she growled a bitter curse. Standing, she said with a deliberate arctic chill in her voice, "I think I'll spend the night on the island." Then she went below to hurriedly pack an overnight bag.

Colin, who was used to women wilting under his authority, called after her, "Don't be a fool, Beth." Beth did not respond. Within ten minutes she was climbing over the side into the yacht's small, motorized launch. Colin clambered after her, realizing that she would take the boat without him if he didn't, leaving him at her mercy for getting to the island in the morning.

At Beth's insistence, Colin dropped her at the marina. His curt questions about where she would spend the night and when he should come back for her were answered with silence. She strode quickly away from the launch, slipped into a taxi, and drove off.

Beth held herself together until she checked into a small resort hotel, using the Havercroft and Wendt credit card. Then the dam burst. She paced the room for half the night, bawling and berating herself for being so gullible, so stupid. She thought about punishing herself by ordering half a dozen Mai Tai's up from the bar and getting thoroughly snockered. But she resisted the temptation. She had no intention of returning to New England aboard Colin's yacht or honoring her contract to write for him. She would leave for home in the morning, and Colin would pay for it. She needed a clear head and a calm stomach for her flights.

As it turned out, the Friday morning flight from Antigua to Miami was full, and Beth watched it leave without her. She had to wait for the afternoon hop, then take a room at the Airport Hilton because all Friday night westbound flights out of Miami were overbooked with business people heading home.

She was grateful that Colin had the decency not to interfere with her plans. *He probably spent the day shopping Antigua for another bimbo he can talk into riding home with him,* she thought wryly, disgusted again at her foolish blindness. *And if by some chance she's literate, he might even sign her to write his books.*

Beth also appreciated that Colin had not yet acted to cancel the company credit card he had given her. She had used it to purchase her first-class ticket to Seattle without incident, then destroyed it. Colin had always insisted that she travel first class on Havercroft and Wendt business. It was the last time she would do anything he wanted her to do.

Beth picked at her gourmet breakfast of tropical fruit, sweet breads, and vegetable quiche. Chummy Frank Fagan tried a few more times to hit on her, but she staved him off by hiding under her headset and busying herself with her electronic appointment calendar. Shortly after his second double Scotch, the nuisance beside her drifted off to sleep.

Scrolling backward from December 2001, Beth realized that her schedule was suddenly wide open. Havercroft and Wendt had reserved the next two years of her life with a substantial advance, most of which she would return with the voided contract as soon as she got home. So she methodically deleted from her calendar every appointment and deadline associated with the tyrannical Colin Wendt and his publishing firm.

Beth was quite comfortable financially, thanks to a steady stream of royalties from *Race against the Devil*. But she wasn't comfortable enough to quit working, nor did she want to. She had to work to keep her sanity in the midst of the damnable craziness of her relationships—like the last four months with Colin Wendt. Beth cursed at herself again for allowing him to beguile her.

She had other potentially rewarding projects on the back burner, of course. She would have to reestablish some contacts and make her availability known. It might take a few weeks to put something together, then she would be off to China, Tel Aviv, or Mexico City to—

Beth's thoughts were abruptly derailed by an entry staring up at her from the screen of her calendar. She had scrolled back to the present month—June 2001—when two words leaped out at her from the square identified as Saturday, June 23: TUGGLE WEDDING. With one keystroke she opened the file for the twenty-third and read the full message: 1 P.M.: SHELBY TUGGLE (USED TO BE HORNECKER) IS GETTING MARRIED TO SOME GUY NAMED EVAN RIDER (NEVER HEARD OF HIM). The entry continued with an address in Ventura, California—a church or a hall or a residence, Beth didn't remember which—and closed with the words: SEND CARD/GIFT WITH REGRETS.

When Beth received the invitation in the mail over a month ago, it had provoked instant mixed feelings because of the memories it revived. The same clashing feelings flooded her as she stared at the words on the screen. She was stung again by the sensation of danger, despair, and hopelessness which had gripped her as the minutes ticked down to midnight on Millennium's Eve.

But that harsh memory was quickly displaced by another, as a refreshing breeze clears away the stale air in a room when the window is opened. It was a flashback to a number of people who had helped take her mind off her frightful Millennium's Eve experience in Los Angeles.

There was the warm, quiet Vietnamese-American couple, Thanh and Mai Ngo. What a contrast between Dr. No's humble caregiving ministry, King's House, and the ostentatious trappings of some of the other Unity 2000 participants.

Then there was the brash, handsome, heroic cop, Reagan Cole, who had disarmed the madman at the Coliseum and averted a horrific disaster. Yes, Beth and Cole had had something going for several weeks after Millennium's Eve, something very special and very good. *And we would be together today, if Reagan had been more interested in me and my career than in becoming a disciple of Dr. No*, Beth thought with a tinge of sadness.

Curiously, with Beth still smarting from her sudden falling out with Colin, she found the warm memories of her time with Reagan to be a comfort. She pushed away the nagging notion that she had walked away from the best thing she'd ever had, when she turned her back on Reagan and his newfound faith.

And there was the spirited televangelist Shelby Hornecker, now

Shelby Tuggle and soon to be Shelby Rider, who had also survived the trauma of Millennium's Eve. Shelby's character, fortitude, and resilience had surprised Beth and attracted her to the lady preacher. Beth wondered what kind of man Shelby was getting involved with this time.

Beth considered the last words of her calendar entry: SEND CARD/GIFT WITH REGRETS. From day one she knew she couldn't attend Shelby's wedding even if she wanted to, and she hadn't been sure whether she wanted to. The sailing trip to the Caribbean with Colin was already on her calendar. At the time, spending three weeks on a yacht with Colin was a much better offer. Beth shook her head in disgust. *What a jerk you are, Beth*, she thought sourly. *You should have gone to the wedding. You would have had a better time.*

Then it hit her. Beth focused on the date in her electronic calendar to make sure. *It's the twenty-third—the wedding is today at 1. I could still make it!* She envisioned many of those she had met in Los Angeles eighteen months earlier, gathering in Ventura for the happy occasion. Going home to an empty house on Whidbey Island suddenly sounded dismal. But the idea of being with people who knew and appreciated her came to Beth with a revitalizing, healing rush. Seeing Dr. No and Mai and Shelby and her associates again—yes, and even Reagan Cole—was the therapy she needed. What kind of man had Shelby chosen? Beth had to know firsthand.

But could she get there? Beth checked her watch and did some quick calculating. *It's 9:30 on the east coast; 6:30 in L.A. If I can get a flight out of Dallas that will get me to LAX by about 11 and rent a car . . .* Suddenly invigorated, Beth reached for the phone in the service panel in front of her, activated it with the swipe of her credit card, and contacted American Airlines reservations.

Yes, the agent informed, there was a flight Beth could catch that was scheduled to touch down in Los Angeles at 11:28. Since she was exchanging a full-fare, first-class ticket purchased with Colin's card, Beth booked another first-class seat to L.A. With a follow-up call to Galaxy Rent-a-Car, Beth reserved a new Buick Barego sport coupe at LAX.

Beth snapped the phone into the service panel, reclined her leather seat, and gazed out the window. Below her was the Louisiana coast with the Gulf of Mexico spreading south to the horizon. She thought about the treasure lying on the sandy bottom off the coast of Antigua. She had dumped overboard a four-month emotional investment and a contract worth several hundred thousand dollars when she walked out on her publisher boyfriend.

Good riddance, she thought with a sigh, turning away from the window and closing her eyes. Then, anticipating a surprise reunion with several people who were more important to her than she had wanted to admit, she assured herself, *There is life after Colin Wendt*. In two minutes she was asleep.

Sixteen

The Pasadena Rose Bowl was jammed with 80,000 eager spectators bathed in the brilliance of the stadium lights. A lone rider sat astride his rumbling, custom jump bike at the top of a ramp on the north rim of the Bowl. The narrow wooden highway before him dropped sharply down the face of the huge stadium to the floor. The course continued straight to the upward sloping launch ramp which ended abruptly where a row of twenty-five city buses were parked side by side, with only inches of clearance between them.

Another wooden ramp just beyond the buses stood ready to welcome the rider—if still united with his bike—on his descent. The track continued up the distant south rim where, with any luck, the rider would brake to a stop before his momentum propelled him into the eucalyptus trees outside the stadium.

The rider was sheathed in skintight, electric-blue leathers with helmet, gloves, and boots of luminous yellow. A circling helicopter trained a cone of brilliant light on him. A dozen television cameras zoomed in from every side as he eagerly gunned the engine and awaited the momentous jump.

The crowd began the countdown: 10, 9, 8, 7. The rider gave one last tug on his helmet, then gripped the controls. The 80,000-voice human clock thundered the last seconds: 4, 3, 2, 1. The zero was overcome by a deafening cheer mingled with the throaty roar of the machine's powerful engine.

Motorcycle and rider plummeted down the ramp—60, 70, 80 MPH. By the time he reached field level the bike was nearing 100, but he held the throttle wide open and continued to gain speed as he streaked up the launch platform. Then he was airborne over the buses.

The beeping began immediately. The rider recognized it as an altimeter warning on his bike: he was too high. He flipped the front wheel sideways to create more wind resistance, but he continued to climb. He cleared the twenty-five buses as well as the landing ramp, and was still ascending, up, up, and away toward the south rim of the Rose Bowl on the fly. The bike was out of control.

The panicked rider cut the engine in a vain attempt to abort his trajectory. The crowd was stunned to silence. Man and machine sailed over the rim of the huge bowl into the blackness of night. All the rider could hear was an insistent *beep-beep, beep-beep, beep-beep* until he realized . . .

Reagan Cole reached an arm out from under the sheet to the bedside table and fumbled for his beeping phone. His dream had suddenly dissolved into reality, but the sensation of flight and the anticipation of a horrible crash left his heart beating wildly and his stomach doing flips.

Cole found the phone and pulled it into bed with him. "Yes," he answered in a gravely voice, eyes still closed against the morning light filtering into his bedroom.

"Did I get you up?"

It took a couple of seconds for Cole's brain to process the voice. The scene from the Rose Bowl was still vivid in his mind. Then he answered, "Not completely, mom."

"Oh, I'm sorry I woke you, Reagan," Jacqueline Cole said with true remorse. "I thought you would be up packing for your trip."

Cole ran his free hand through his sparse sandy hair and yawned. "What time is it?"

"It's almost 9."

Cole groaned. "You're right. I should be up." He threw the sheet off with his leg and struggled into a sitting position.

"When do you plan to leave there?" his mother asked.

"Tomorrow. I can't leave until tomorrow."

"I thought your vacation started today, Reagan." The disappointment in her voice was evident.

"It does—officially, but there are a few things I need to get squared away before I can leave. I have to go into the office this morning and get Sergeant Chavez caught up on my work so he can cover for me."

As he talked, Cole rose and shuffled into the kitchen where a pot of hot coffee had been waiting for him in the automatic coffee maker for an hour. "And I have a wedding to attend in Ventura this afternoon. I'll leave home tomorrow morning and be at your place sometime in the late afternoon."

He poured a mug of coffee and took it and the phone to his favorite chair by the living room window of his Santa Monica condo. The view across Ocean Avenue and the promenade of Santa Monica beach was dominated by gray. It was overcast at the beach today, as it was many mornings in the early summer. But the soup was scheduled to burn off by noon. Cole hoped it would be warm in Ventura for Shelby's early-afternoon wedding.

"I wish you were coming today, son," Jacqueline lamented. "Mom, I'm sorry," he answered, cautiously sipping coffee. "But I really need to be at this wedding. The bride is a good friend of mine."

"When is one of these lady friends of yours going to be *your* bride, Reagan? You're thirty-three years old, your sisters are all married. . . . " Jacqueline's voice trailed off plaintively.

"Don't worry, mom," Cole assured, smiling at her maternal concern. "When I find her, you'll be one of the first to know."

"What about that girl from last year—Beth what's-her-name? Are you still dating her?"

The mention of Beth's name weakened the smile on Cole's lips and brought a twinge of melancholy to his heart. How long had it been since he had seen her? Eight months? Ten? Whatever it was, it was too long. But then the distance between them hadn't been his idea.

"No, mom," Cole said without tipping his feelings. "I haven't seen her in a while." Without giving her a chance to probe further, he asked her about the weather at Lake Tahoe and told her that he was looking forward to his week visiting her. He assured her that he was prepared to complete some big chores for her, and she sounded pleased. They finished the conversation without talking about Beth again.

Cole sat staring out the window at the battleship-gray sea beyond the sand and palms of Santa Monica beach for several minutes. Cruising up to Lake Tahoe on his Kawasaki 1200 promised to be fun. And getting away from the office to spend a week at his mother's place would be a relaxing break from the routine. But thinking about Beth suddenly made his week of vacation seem as dull and uninviting as the gray sea. He revived the fragile hope he had harbored since receiving the wedding invitation from Shelby: *Maybe she will come. Maybe I will see Beth at the wedding.*

Theirs had not been a hostile relationship or a bitter parting. Beth just drifted away, and Cole was sure he knew why. After the terrifying events of Millennium's Eve were miraculously resolved, Cole became fascinated with King's House and the faith and love and prayer that drove its founder, Dr. No. But Beth, while clearly the beneficiary of the prayers and support of the godly people of Unity 2000, was lured in another direction. The sudden fame and fortune resulting from her two books about her Millennium's Eve experiences apparently made the daily routine of caregiving at King's House seem unexciting by comparison.

In the early months of 2000, Beth had traveled to Los Angeles frequently from her island home in Puget Sound to visit Reagan. But with every visit, he spent more time talking about his new faith than about her flourishing career. She wanted to spend time alone with him fostering intimacy. But he couldn't wait to show her the latest development at King's House and include her in his friendships there.

Cole wondered if he had pushed his new lifestyle too hard, but he didn't think so. His fresh excitement about God was important to him, and he wanted to share it with Beth, whom he thought was just as impressed by the miracle on Millennium's Eve as he was. But for some reason King's House, faith, and prayer didn't "take" for her. Cole could no more sway her to his perspective than he had been able to keep the motorcycle in his minutes-old dream from sailing out into oblivion.

As the year wore on, Beth cut back on her visits to L.A. and was less punctual in returning Cole's calls. There was never a harsh word, a confrontation, an explanation, or a good-bye. She just pulled away and stayed away. It hurt Cole deeply, but he could not bring himself to compromise the truth he had found to try to hold her, though he was sorely tempted to do so.

Cole drained his first mug of coffee and went to the kitchen for a refill. The deliberate physical movement helped him set his thoughts about Beth aside and turn toward the day's agenda. He returned to his chair with the steaming mug for an activity which in little more than a year had become as important to his daily routine as his three cups of home-ground Kona blend.

He lifted a hardback, modern-speech version of the Bible from the coffee table to his lap and flipped it open to a place kept by a slim ballpoint pen and a spiral bound steno pad. Picking up where he left off yesterday, Cole read from Paul's letter to the Colossians, pausing occasionally to ponder or underline a passage or to jot a note on the pad. Then, after a sip of coffee, he read on.

After several minutes of reading, Cole set the book aside and knelt beside his chair to pray. As he did most mornings, he thanked God for His blessings and verbalized his needs in an earnest but conversational tone. His petition was simple, direct, and free of religious clichés. It was the style of praying he had learned from Dr. No and other King's House workers during weekly Bible studies at the old hospital in the shadow of the Los Angeles skyline.

Prime among his concerns today was Beth Scibelli. As in countless numbers of his prayers over the last year, Cole asked God to protect her and help her find inner peace. Then he concluded by praying something for Beth he had never prayed before, "God, I'm kind of worried about how Beth is doing. If You can arrange it, would You please bring her to Shelby's wedding today so I can just see her? I'd really like for us to be friends again, but that's something only You can do. Well, God, that's about all for now. I've got to get going. Amen."

He rose from his knees to shower and dress, whistling a tune he had learned during a recent chapel service at King's House.

Cole found Sergeant Frank Chavez on a coffee break with several other detectives in the commissary at Parker Center in downtown Los Angeles. The topic of conversation was last night's shootout in the parking lot at Dodger Stadium, that left an undercover officer and two drug dealers dead and an informant at large with over half a million dollars and the officer's gun. One sober-faced detective advanced a graphic description of what he would do to the cop killer if he found him alone in a dark alley. Others nodded while cursing the fugitive under their breath.

"Do you always dress up like this when you go on vacation?" Frank Chavez joked with Cole, as they walked back to Cole's office with coffee cups in hand. Chavez was eyeing Cole's dark-gray suit, white shirt, mottled gray, white, and burgundy tie, and Brazilian loafers. It was an outfit Beth had helped him select over a year ago. He had worn it only twice, to receive awards for his heroic actions on Millennium's Eve. Beth had been by his side during both ceremonies.

Sergeant Chavez, a stumpy Latino with perpetually bulging eyes and a narrow mustache, was dressed in the standard "uniform" for LAPD detectives: dark slacks, sport jacket, shirt, and tie—all of indeterminate style—with rubber-soled oxfords.

"I'm going to a wedding today, Frank," Cole explained, smiling. Then he added before Chavez could insert his wisecrack, "No, not *my* wedding. The bride is a good friend from King's House."

Chavez acknowledged with a hum which communicated little interest. "And then what? Lake Tahoe to see your mom?"

"Right. I leave tomorrow sometime. I'll be back next Sunday. Hopefully, my pigeon will sit tight this week and you won't have to worry about him. I have a couple of guys monitoring his movements, but they won't bother you unless it looks like he's up to something. I just need you to be aware."

They reached Cole's crowded cubicle, and he retrieved a diskette from a file beside his computer and tossed it to Chavez over the desk. "We're tailing this guy in cooperation with the FBI—which means that the Feds don't want to get involved unless something big goes down."

"I don't have time to read this, Reagan," Chavez complained, holding up the diskette. "Give me the Cliff Notes version."

Both men sat down across a relatively organized desktop of papers, pens, books, and data files. "The FBI calls him Rennie Barbosa," Cole began, "but who knows if that's his real name. He's used three other aliases since we've been watching him. According to the dope we were given, Barbosa grew up in the Shining Path, the son of a guerilla leader. He learned how to assemble and use a variety of lethal weapons, while other kids his age were still playing with blocks. By the time he was a teenager, he could kill a grown man in five seconds, using any one of a dozen different methods."

"I know several guys like that living in South Central L.A.," Chavez quipped wryly. "Must be his cousins."

Cole continued. "Barbosa rose quickly through the ranks by proving himself to be a brilliant, clever leader and a ruthless killer. He took great pride in his assassinations. Killing was an art form to him, almost a religious experience.

"Then the Path collapsed. But Barbosa didn't. Killing is in his blood. The dissolution of the Path simply provided him the opportunity to rise to a new level in his expertise. He can't stop killing any more than an off-duty cop can stop watching his back. So he went free-lance, marketing himself to the international drug underworld as a hired gun.

"According to the Feds he's not a big-time assassin who attracts a lot of attention. He slips in and out of major cities around the world, taking jobs where he can find them. He doesn't need the money. To him finding, stalking, and killing someone is a sport. If he had a business card, it would probably read, 'Have gun, will travel; no job too small.' "

"And nobody's nailed him," Chavez advanced, sipping coffee.

Cole shook his head. "The FBI has been watching him in the States for several months. They suspect him in a few hits, but the guy is a professional. He's sharp, quiet, unspectacular. Blends in like a chameleon wherever he goes. Speaks several languages without an accent, including English. Can pass for a light-colored Latino or an Anglo with a nice tan."

"So what's he doing in L.A?"

"So far, nothing. It's like he's on vacation. Has a room at the Sheraton Universal. Goes to Disneyland, the movies, out to dinner. Usually has a nice-looking woman with him—we've counted three different ones in the month he's been here."

"But he's not . . . working?" Chavez said.

"Under contract, on somebody's trail? Not that we can tell. We've had him under twenty-four-hour surveillance since he came into town. If he's doing business on the side, he's left no clues. He doesn't sneak out at night or disappear in a crowd. He uses his hotel phone to order room service and to charm his ladies into going out with him. He's about as exciting as watching mold grow. No wonder the Feds don't want to bother with him."

Cole looked at his watch. "I've got to go, Frank," he said, standing. "All I'm asking is that you keep in touch with my field officers. If Barbosa does something out of the ordinary, call in the FBI. But be sure and let me know if something goes down—day or night. You have my number."

Chavez stood and tossed his empty cup into the trash can. "This is why we became detectives, Reagan," he said, tongue in cheek, "to watch mold grow at taxpayers' expense."

Cole blew a disgusted sigh. "I sure expected more action than this, man. But maybe I'll get lucky this week and Rennie Barbosa will move on. I could use a bigger challenge."

Chavez wished him a happy vacation and assured him that his project would be covered. Cole straightened a few piles on his desk and left for the garage, saying good-bye to several coworkers on the way.

Pulling his electric-blue nylon flight suit over his dress clothes, Cole admitted to himself that he might have given Chavez less than a complete picture of his interest in Rennie Barbosa. Cole didn't really expect anything to happen while he was gone—he certainly hoped nothing would. If Barbosa was up to something, he wanted to be here when the killer made his move. Had he not promised his mother a week of his time, Cole wouldn't leave the city until Barbosa did.

This is *why I left the streets and became a detective, Frank,* he thought, pulling on his helmet and gloves. *To get inside the skin of the professional criminal, to anticipate his crime, and to be waiting for him when he strikes. Don't do anything until I get back, Barbosa. Nobody else is as interested in you as I am.*

It was bright and warm when Cole pulled out of the Parker Center garage and aimed his Kawasaki 1200 toward the Harbor Freeway and a one-hour ride to Ventura. His thoughts were soon redirected to a topic even more captivating than a Peruvian assassin lurking in Los Angeles: the possibility of seeing Beth Scibelli. Before he reached the Ventura Freeway, he was praying for her again.

Seventeen

Libby Carroll had been up for over four hours waiting for her son, Brett, to emerge from his room and face the music for breaking into her office and tampering with her computer. She had puttered around the house in her robe and slippers, tidying the living room, emptying the dishwasher, and halfheartedly reading the Saturday morning edition of the *Post-Intelligencer* over two cups of herb tea.

It had occurred to Libby around midmorning that Brett might have skipped out of the house during the night to avoid the stern lecture he no doubt anticipated from her. But a quiet peek into his room found him to be dead asleep and breathing noisily, with his head screwed into a large pillow and his muscular brown limbs hanging out from under the wrinkled sheet. Libby was relieved not to find Andie in bed with him—something she had strictly forbidden in her house. She thought about peeking in on Andie too, but couldn't justify a breach of the girl's privacy.

In order to pass the time and keep her simmering anger from mounting into an unproductive boil, Libby changed into her tights and spent an hour working out in her mini-gym in the basement. Over the years she and her son had spent many grueling and rewarding hours together lifting weights in the basement. Libby had stressed fitness throughout Brett's upbringing. Her disciplined workouts had kept her within one dress size of her figure as a track star at Central Washington. Brett's routine had produced a trim and toned physique that had buoyed his self-esteem during his high school years.

The workout gave Libby time to gain needed perspective on Brett's misdeed. *Basically, he's a good kid*, she acknowledged, grimacing through two dozen leg lifts on the apparatus. *Thank God he's not an addict or a drunk or gay. He's always been above average academically, even though his intelligence and wit—lacking the wisdom and common sense of maturity—have often lured him into trouble. And his fierce independence has moved him out of the house before being asked to leave. He is certainly not a spineless mamma's boy.*

But somewhere along the line, Libby, you failed to get through to him on the issue of respect, she lectured herself. *Respect for me, respect for himself, respect for institutions, respect for the law. Don't jeopardize the whole relationship with Brett just because of one incident. Deal with the offense justly and kindly. Try to equip him with a measure of respect for his own good. But keep him close in the process. He's all you have.*

Libby showered and dressed and busied herself in the kitchen as she continued to wait for Brett to appear from his room. She rearranged files on her countertop computer and baked a batch of peanut butter and oatmeal cookies, Brett's favorite. *He's probably lying in there awake, summoning the courage to face me,* she pondered wishfully. Libby hoped the incident was weighing as heavily on him as it was her. She assessed that her attitude was as positive as it could be for their impending confrontation.

At noon she heard Brett shuffle from his bedroom to the bathroom. The shower ran for twenty minutes. Then, from her vantage point at the kitchen counter, Libby caught a glimpse of him in the hall on his way back to the bedroom. He was wearing a pair of denim shorts, and his black hair, which was more wavy than curly, was uncombed. She continued to busy herself by arranging the cookies on a platter and rehearsing her lecture.

By the time Brett finally came out, he had put on a T-shirt and sandals and combed his hair. Libby was wiping down the inside of the convection oven with a sponge as he sat down at the kitchen counter and grabbed a cookie. When she finally looked up, impertinence sheathed Brett's face like a mask, and defiance made his large, dark-brown eyes seem to glow red. His narrow nose was flared and his thin lips were taut. The expression turned Libby's blood cold and instantly soured her hopes for a quick resolution of their conflict.

"Well?" Brett said, slinging the word at her as he wolfed down a cookie. Libby noted that he had purposely spoken with his mouth full and allowed cookie crumbs to litter the counter.

Libby felt herself stiffen as she turned to face him. She put the sponge on the counter and weighed her words. Hoping for a conversation instead of a fight, she knew she could not back down. Brett's misbehavior and disregard for her could not go unchallenged.

"Brett, your actions last night—"

" 'I' messages, not 'you' messages, mom," Brett shot back disdainfully. "A confrontation should begin with 'I' messages. That's what you taught me."

Libby felt her knees weaken as if the blow had been physical instead of verbal. Brett's interjection was valid, she knew, but the way he had bludgeoned her with it hurt. She stood tall and continued. "All right, I feel grossly violated by what took place in my office last night. I feel—"

"Embarrassed, mom?" Brett spat. "Did I embarrass you last night? Did you feel your career and your hopes and dreams slipping through your fingers as you drove over to get us?"

The words pierced Libby like a lance. Brett had never spoken to her with such venom in his tone. His words burned into her soul. She steeled herself to hold it together emotionally until she set her son straight. But she didn't know how many direct hits she could take.

"Yes, Brett, I am very embarrassed."

Brett glared at her. "How about humiliated? How about hurt? How about downright torqued, mom? Is that how you feel about what I did in your office last night?"

Libby winced from another verbal harpooning. "Yes, I feel humiliated and angry and wounded and—" Against her will, Libby's facade of strength cracked. A swell of emotion choked off the words in her throat, but she forced one more, "Disrespected."

Brett took a big bite out of another cookie and watched the tears fill his mother's eyes, seemingly with pleasure. "Respect—now there's a concept. I suppose you think that an intelligent, twenty-year-old young adult would have more respect for his mother than to violate her office and threaten her precious career with criminal misconduct."

Libby reached for a tissue. "I had hoped for as much," she said. She realized with some embarrassment that Andie, Brett's petite, gullible girlfriend, was awake by now and hearing the argument from the guest room. Libby expected the girl to stay holed up at a safe distance until the mother-son storm blew over.

Brett leaned forward on the counter and bored into Libby with his eyes. "Well, what I did doesn't seem any more disrespectful to me than for an intelligent, forty-two-year-old university administrator to withhold the identity of the father of her bastard child."

Libby's eyes widened in disbelief and squeezed fresh tears onto her cheeks. She gripped a tissue over her mouth and held her breath, searching her son's dark, fiery eyes. "Is that what this is all about?" she said at last. "Are you trying to punish me because I can't tell you about your father?" Her voiced was strained but controlled.

"Punish you? By using your computer last night? Not at all," Brett said, still with an insolent edge to his voice. *That* was about money— easy money—for doing something I don't think is wrong. And if that big clod of a cop hadn't come along, you wouldn't have even found out.

"But getting caught and feeling no remorse about what this is doing to you? Yeah, I guess *that's* what it's all about. I didn't plan it this way, although some shrink may say I did without realizing it. But what I did to you last night is exactly what you have done to me since I was born.

"Do you have any idea how violated I feel because you won't tell me who my father is? Do you know how embarrassing it is to write 'unknown' in the space marked 'Father's Name' on my college registration and job applications? Do you realize how humiliating it was to explain to Andie and the rest of my friends in Pullman that I was the product of a one-night stand involving my mother and a man she won't even acknowledge existed?"

Libby began weakly, "Brett, that was a very—"

Brett cut her off and finished the familiar sentence for her, " '—a very difficult time in my life.' I know, mom. You were away from home, and you were under a lot of pressure. A couple of bad choices almost ruined your life, and you don't want to ruin the life of the man who conceived me by revealing his identity."

He stood up and paced a short path behind the kitchen counter. His voice grew louder and more insistent with each turn. "Well, what about *my* life? You left my father behind over twenty years ago and chose to keep me. You say you've never talked to him or seen him since, and that you care nothing about him. Yet you're protecting him and forcing me to go through life knowing him only as the 'black phantom.' "

Libby interjected in a quavering voice, "I've tried to tell you, Brett, but it's not that simple. We were not lovers, just friends who got into trouble. He's out of my life. I don't know where he is—"

Brett slammed his fist on the counter. "Damn it, mom, I have a right to know who my father is, whether you care about him or know where he is or not. And he has a right to know who I am." Brett hit the counter hard with each use of the word *right.* "You know his name— you're lying if you say you don't. I need to know his name. I want you to describe him to me and tell me what you remember about him. And I want you to show me where to start looking for him. You've got to understand, mom. I can't go through life without knowing about him, and you're standing in my way by not telling me."

Brett was clearly angry, but there was a plaintive nuance in his voice as he ended his plea.

Libby saw through the anger and bitterness to the hurt, and it touched her and provoked fresh tears. She had not talked with Brett about his father until he broached the subject as a precocious four-year-old. She responded simply, "Yes, honey, you have a daddy, but he lives far, far away. But I'm sure he loves you very much." This satisfied the boy for several years. Further explanations included, "Your daddy and mommy didn't get married, so your daddy doesn't live with us"; "I knew your daddy many years ago, but I forgot his name and where he lives"; "Daddy left all his love for you with me, so I can love you twice as much."

As a late preteen, Brett grasped that he was the product of a brief, illicit relationship, and that his mother had kept him instead of aborting him or giving him up for adoption. He was mature enough to sympathize with his mother over her admitted "mistake" and appreciate her for choosing to keep him. But he was also clever enough to suspect that her story about "forgetting" his father's name was fiction. He regarded the explanation with as much credence as he did the rapidly dematerializing myths of Santa Claus and the Easter Bunny.

Yet long after his mother had admitted responsibility for the presents Brett found under the tree on Christmas morning, she persisted in propagating the myth of the unknown daddy. Brett didn't buy it, and he occasionally probed his mother about it during his high school years. The result was much personal affirmation for him but no new information, as Libby held fast to her feeble story. Brett had never made it an issue until now.

He had stopped pacing and was waiting for a response. Libby wiped the tears from her eyes and blew her nose. Then she said, "I know this is important to you, Brett. But you also need to see it from my perspective and from your father's perspective. I think you deserve to know about your father, but the timing isn't right. I can't afford to have a skeleton pop out of the closet right now. And who knows what your appearance would do to him, his career, and his family, wherever he is. If you could just wait—"

Brett leaned across the counter to interrupt. "You're not going to tell me his name, are you?" he summarized, teeth clenched.

"Honey, please understand, I just can't. Someday, but not yet."

Brett whipped his right arm across the counter to the platter of cookies and sent it sailing across the kitchen. The platter smashed against the wall, showering the ceramic range top and the floor with shards of china and crumbled cookies. Libby jumped back, stunned.

Brett waved a finger at his mother and hissed, "Then don't you ever talk to me about respect again, because this is the most disrespectful thing you could ever do to me." Then he stomped off to his room, cursing. Libby wanted to call after him and try to comfort him, but she didn't know what to say.

In ten minutes Brett had packed his belongings and hustled Andie out the door without another word. Libby could do nothing but watch in distraught silence. She felt as gray as the fog that was draped over the Sound.

Twenty minutes later her phone sounded. Libby answered eagerly in hopes that Brett was calling to make amends or tell her where he and Andie were going.

"Good morning, Dr. Carroll. This is Reginald Burris again."

"Oh . . . Reginald," Libby replied, unable to disguise her disappointment.

"I hope I'm not interrupting something?"

"No, nothing."

"I'm sorry to bother you, Dr. Carroll, but I just wanted to see if you're okay after last night."

Libby's first response—that Reginald's call at this moment was an intrusion—was quickly tempered by the winsome kindness she perceived in his gentle tone. Yet he was still a virtual stranger to her. She could not bring herself to include him in the disappointment and shock which hovered over her like a personal black cloud. So she perked up her voice and lied, "I'm fine, Reginald. Everything went just fine. Thank you for asking."

Reginald responded with a long hum. Libby could almost hear the gears in his brain as he tested her optimistic words against his expectations. Then he said, "I also wanted to inform you that Security has authorized a new electronic lock and security code for your office—a standard precaution after a break-in. You can bring your key card in to be reprogrammed any time this weekend or first thing Monday morning."

"I won't be on campus until Monday, Reginald, so I'll have my card redone then."

"Yes, that will be fine. Bring your card to the UWPD office and someone will take care of it for you. It'll only take a minute."

"Thank you, Reginald."

There was a moment of uncomfortable silence before the officer spoke again. "Is there anything else I can do to help you, Dr. Carroll?"

Again she opted to foist a fabricated optimism on the kind man speaking to her, "You have been very kind, Reginald, but I have everything under control now. Thank you again for your concern."

"If you think of something I can do to make things easier for you—anything at all—please give me a call."

"I will, Reginald. Thanks again."

Libby tapped off the phone, wishing that just one of the men she dated showed her as much kindness as Reginald Burris.

Eighteen

"Good morning, Billy. How's life in balmy Mexico this morning?"

G. Billy Fryman had been awake all night and was in no mood for

Bishop's glib chitchat. He took the phone and waddled out to the veranda beyond the housekeeper's earshot, even though he knew she didn't understand English. The tranquil, turquoise water of the Gulf of Mexico stretching out below his secluded villa brought him little comfort today. He was weary and frazzled after his hasty retreat from the States. And he was anxious to have Jakes and Bishop out of the picture for good, so he could commence a life of leisure and luxury far beyond the reach of the law.

"What about Jakes and the money, Bishop?" Fryman grumbled.

"Relax, Billy," Bishop said. "You're letting your worries spoil your vacation. Jakes will be found and neutralized, and the money will be—"

"What do you mean 'found'?" Fryman growled. "I thought you knew where he was."

"I said I had an *idea* where he was. But my idea didn't pan out. Jakes has apparently found a real good hiding place. I appreciate that kind of initiative and creativity. It makes the hunt so much more entertaining, don't you think, Billy?"

"I'm not interested in being entertained, Bishop," Fryman steamed, his massive jowls fluttering with every angry word. "I want him found and finished. And I want that money here in Mexico. Quit screwing around and get it done."

"You're working yourself into a stroke over nothing, Billy," Bishop said, almost laughing. "The job will get done; my man is on top of it. And you'll get your money—except for the ten percent 'service charge' he requires. It just may take us a few days."

Fryman paced the length of the veranda. The wooden floorboards groaned under each step. "Ten percent? That's a little steep, Bishop." There was an icy threat in his tone.

Bishop blew it off with a laugh. "Quality service costs money, Billy. I'd hate to see your retirement ruined as a result of poor workmanship."

"What about the cops? What if they find Jakes first?" Fryman pressed.

Bishop laughed again. "Billy, the LAPD can't find their own butts with a bloodhound. They won't find Jakes. In fact, they'll never turn over a trace of him; we'll make sure of that. I'll keep you posted about our progress."

"And the money? When do I get my money?"

"You're hurting my feelings, Billy," Bishop said in a sarcastic whine. "You're so paranoid about getting your money that I wonder if you want really to see *me* at all."

"Nonsense," Fryman answered, suddenly sounding chummy. "When you finish up in L.A. and get down here with the money, I'll show you a real good time." As he spoke he smiled and patted the lightweight plastic Panda in the back pocket of his baggy linen trousers. "You'll love it."

"That's more like it, Billy. I could use a couple of weeks of sipping margaritas with you on the beach. I should be down there with the cash in five days."

The parting comments of both parties were carefully veiled lies, of course. But only the latter was believed. Bishop had no intention of ever seeing Billy Fryman again.

Nolan Jakes paced the motel room anxiously. His joints and muscles throbbed with a dull ache, and his eyes were grainy from insufficient sleep. The scuffle on a bed of broken glass, the tumble down the hillside, the painful encounter with a barbed-wire-topped fence, and the frantic run through the dark neighborhoods of L.A. had left him with more scrapes, cuts, and bruises than he had ever received in a football game. He knew it would take his body several days to recover.

Margo had been gone for over two hours, completing critical preliminary details of the escape plan. Jakes had outlined the plan to her as they lay in bed together after she awoke just before 7. Jakes had been awake most of the night piecing together a strategy that would get them across the Canadian border with enough money to survive in hiding for years. The $620,000 of unmarked drug money stolen from the cops was a great start, but it wasn't enough, he had asserted. Margo quickly agreed. His plan could possibly double that amount as well as assure their safe passage to Canada.

He had continued by explaining to Margo his decision to immediately look up one of two old college friends, Evan Rider in Ventura, and ask him to assist in their escape with money and transportation. He also expressed his hope of locating the other friend and getting more money from her.

Jakes' explanation had provoked from Margo a flurry of questions. The discussion lasted over an hour.

"How can your old friend Evan Rider help us?" Margo began. She lay on her stomach, propped up on her elbows so she could gaze down at Jakes who was on his side facing her. "He's a doctor; he has money. Besides, he can drive us straight to Canada. No one will suspect his car."

"Why would he want to help us? He will certainly know that we are running from the law."

"He probably *won't* want to help us. I'll have to convince him."

"Why don't we just take his car and his money? Why drag him along with us?"

"Because he would report the car stolen, and the Highway Patrol would nail us before we went 100 miles."

"So how are you going to convince him to give us money and drive us out of the country?"

Evan stroked Margo's black hair and relished the warmth of her body next to his. He loved Margo and felt he could trust her with anything. But he had not planned to open the dark, inner chambers of his past to her so soon. However, Margo's willing involvement in his desperate flight from the police and G. Billy Fryman had changed all that. Under the circumstances, Jakes felt responsible to answer every query she had about the plan he had devised.

"Blackmail," he said.

"Blackmail? What . . . " Margo's question trailed off, but her questioning expression begged Jakes to continue.

"Evan and I have something in common, something very bad that he wouldn't want brought to light." Then after sucking a deep breath and releasing it slowly he began his story.

"Evan and I played football together for two years at Cal State Northridge. I was the quarterback and he was a receiver, so we spent a lot of time together and got to be pretty good friends.

"The last game of our sophomore season was an away game in Oregon. We went up there to play Portland State. We were really pumped. But I screwed up and Evan dropped a couple of passes. We lost by three points. Everybody was bummed, and Evan and I felt responsible.

"Since our flight home wasn't until the next day, we decided to drown our sorrows by club-hopping through downtown Portland all night. A girl we used to hang out with at CSUN—the team statistician—came with us. She had a rental car and didn't drink too much, so she drove us from club to club.

"In every club there were PSU students celebrating and CSUN students sulking in their beer. The PSU people didn't hassle us too much, except at a place called River Jack's. There was this rowdy crowd who called us names and really rubbed it in. The worst of it was one guy—his name was McGruder—who was especially loud and nasty. And he really ragged on our black kids, calling them 'Watts Rioters.' None of our blacks were thugs; they were all great guys.

"McGruder was being a real jerk, and the CSUN students in the club were getting rowdy. Evan and I and half our team were ready to jump the guy. But Libby didn't want to get into a race thing. She said McGruder's crap didn't bother her. So we left before anything happened."

"Libby?" Margo probed.

"The girl who was with us."

"She was black?"

"Yeah. She became quite a track star after she transferred out of CSUN. Qualified for the '84 Olympics. Libby Carroll. Ever hear of her?"

Margo shook her head.

Jakes continued. "Anyway, we hit a few more clubs, then headed back to the hotel. And who should we see stumbling along a downtown side street all alone but McGruder, the sewer mouth from River Jack's. He was seriously stoned and trying to find his way back to the campus.

"I don't remember whose idea it was, but Evan and I jumped out, grabbed him, and dragged him into the backseat of the car. He was too wasted to put up a fight. So we sat on him and roughed him up while Libby drove around Portland. We ended up in a dark corner of Washington Park where we worked him over some more and left him on a hillside. We drove back to the hotel about 3 and went to bed. There was no curfew that night, so nobody saw us come in."

Jakes paused as the fresh memory of a distant night twisted the dagger of guilt which had been embedded in his soul for over twenty years. He continued, but his voice was more sober. "We were up at 7 to catch our flight, and guess who made the early morning news on TV."

"McGruder?"

Jakes nodded. "He had been found dead in Washington Park. The reporter said he died of drug and alcohol poisoning aggravated by several blows to the head."

Margo gasped. "Geez, Nolan," she said sympathetically, reaching out a hand to touch his arm.

"But we lucked out," he continued, trying to sound positive. "A bum who had filched a wallet off McGruder's body was picked up in Hoyt Arboretum early that morning. He claimed he had nothing to do with the beating, and the public defender got him off for insufficient evidence."

Margo released a low whistle. "And you and your friends walked?"

Jakes nodded again. "After seeing the news, we were really shook. But we sucked it up and flew back to L.A. with the team, and nobody had a clue. We each swore never to tell a soul, then we split up. Libby and Evan transferred to other schools over Christmas break, and in the spring I signed with the CFL and moved to Vancouver. I haven't seen either of them since."

After a thoughtful pause, Margo said, "So now we pay a surprise visit to Dr. Evan Rider and say, 'Give us a pile of your money and drive us to Canada. If you don't and we get caught, we'll spill the real story about how McGruder died and take you down with us.' " There was a subtle, cold gleam in Margo's eyes which Jakes had never seen before. The look substantiated her verbal assertion that she was ready to run with him at all costs. She had also used the words "we" and "us," linking herself with the proposed deed and the possible negative consequences. Jakes was quietly pleased.

"Right. And when I locate Libby Carroll or whatever her name is now, I'll hit her up for a healthy contribution under the same terms."

Margo beamed a smile of admiration for Jakes' ingenuity. Then another question clouded her expression. "Since we're going to black-mail the doctor, why do we have to take him to the border with us? If he knows we will tell about McGruder, won't he let us take his car and keep quiet?"

Jakes shrugged. "I haven't seen this guy for almost twenty-two years, Margo. I don't know what he'll do. He could change his mind after we leave, decide to turn himself in, and take *us* down with *him*. I can't take that chance. So he goes with us."

Margo nodded agreement, seemingly with reluctance. Then she asked, "What do you plan to do with that?" She pointed to the .44 Magnum lying on the bedside shelf behind Jakes. "Could you shoot somebody if you had to? Could you shoot Evan Rider or a cop?"

Jakes dropped his head, churning inside at the prospect Margo had voiced. After a moment he answered without looking up, "I don't know, Margo. Shooting that guy last night was no problem; he was about to kill me. And if Fryman or one of his people came to gun me down, I could easily pull the trigger. But shooting an innocent bystand-er, like a hostage, or a cop—I just don't know. Living with one killing on my conscience all these years is bad enough. I don't think I could live with another. But who knows what I'll do if I have to shoot some-body to get free."

Sensing Jakes' discomfort with the subject, Margo let it go.

Jakes ventured a peek between the thin gold curtains. *It's past noon, Margo. You're supposed to be back by now. We've got to get out of here. Where are you?*

The most formidable task Margo had to accomplish was to secure their transportation to Ventura. Jakes had insisted that her car, a gray '94 Volvo four-door sedan, was no doubt already on the LAPD hot sheet. A simple police scan of his background would turn up the link between him and his girlfriend. They didn't dare take the Volvo.

Public transportation was also out of the question. Jakes' face was too familiar around L.A. to go unnoticed on the bus or in a taxi. And thanks to the Saturday morning TV news, which had linked him with the fatal drug bust attempt at Dodger Stadium, he was now infamous. Anyone who recognized him had only to place a 911 call and the police would be on his trail.

But Margo had amazed Jakes with a simple, workable solution to the transportation problem. She told him that her Aunt Ruby, who lived in nearby Tarzana, was currently enjoying a South Seas honeymoon with her third husband. Margo had keys to her aunt's home and car, which she often cared for while Ruby traveled. Margo suggested that she take a taxi to Tarzana and pick up Ruby's late-model Jaguar sports sedan, which they would later ditch in Ventura. Jakes praised her idea and eagerly agreed.

Margo's other tasks while she was out included buying them both a change of clothes. They obviously could not return to their apartments, which were likely staked out by both the cops and Fryman's goons. And the Unocal jacket and cap he had purchased last night could help identify him. They had to be destroyed. So Jakes had cut them up and flushed them piece by piece.

Jakes had also asked Margo to bring back some makeup to cover the abrasions on his face. And he told her to buy dark glasses, a hat, and a fake mustache or beard. For the second time in twenty-four hours, he had to disguise his appearance.

Pacing the small room, Jakes was nervous. It had occurred to him that Margo might not make it back to the motel. She was even less experienced at running from the law than he was. It wasn't that she could be easily recognized. Jakes doubted that her picture had been distributed through the LAPD computer network. After all, the police probably didn't yet consider her to be an accessory, just the girlfriend of an at-large murder suspect who could not be reached.

But what if she said something to the cab driver, making him suspicious enough to notify the police? What if she got stopped for a traffic violation in Aunt Ruby's Jaguar and the police detained her for questioning? What if a friend saw her in the store and asked what she knew about her boyfriend's crime? Jakes wasn't sure Margo could play out her role and avoid detection.

It had also occurred to Jakes that Margo might *purposely* not come back for him. *She may come to her senses about the life she is throwing away to be with me. She may return to her apartment to face the police. If she comes clean now, she probably won't be charged with a crime. I only hope she has the decency not to tell the police where to look for me.*

Jakes had already decided on a contingency plan. If Margo didn't appear by 12:30, he would assume that she wasn't coming back. He would take his chances getting to Ventura in Margo's Volvo, perhaps via the less-traveled Santa Susana pass through Simi Valley, Fillmore, and Santa Paula. If Margo turned on him, he doubted he would make it very far. But he had to try.

The sound of brisk footsteps approaching outside drove Jakes to the curtain again. It was a woman, not the raven-haired Margo who left wearing tan cotton slacks and kelly-green shirt, but a platinum blonde in bleached jeans and a plum-colored polo, hiding behind large sunglasses.

Jakes quickly opened the door and let her in. "You look terrific," he said.

Margo dropped a plastic bag of clothes on the bed, removed her sunglasses, and pulled off the blonde wig. Her face was beaming. "This is so exciting, Nolan. Everything worked exactly as we planned." Then she threw herself into his arms. "Thank you for letting me go with you.

We'll have such fun together."

She pulled his face to hers and lavished him with deep, sensual kisses. She would have taken him back to bed had he not—with great discipline—reminded her that they had already stayed at the motel too long. In fifteen minutes the platinum blonde and her artificially bearded companion in a pale-blue golf hat pulled out of the Days Inn garage in a silver-blue Jaguar. They turned south on Winnetka Avenue and headed for the Ventura Freeway.

Nineteen

Shelby Tuggle would have been lost without the calming presence and practical assistance of her friend and former personal assistant, Theresa Bordeaux. Evan and Shelby had wanted a simple garden ceremony, free of pointless pomp and circumstance, and an informal reception with a light buffet supper and wedding cake. They had planned to invite only close family and friends, and a few coworkers. It was to be more like the continuation of Shelby's fortieth birthday party than a traditional wedding.

Theresa had reminded Shelby soon after Evan proposed that even simple weddings tend to grow beyond their proposed borders. At first Shelby scoffed at her friend's prophecy, but soon she found herself the instrument for its fulfillment. "If we send an invitation to Uncle Charles and Aunt Violet from your family," she said to Evan one day, "then we have to include your cousins and their families." They agreed and addressed the envelopes. Moments later Evan said, "If we invite Bill Fawcett from King's House, we're duty-bound to include Tran Van Le and Izzy Freberg from the kitchen. And why don't we invite the entire full-time staff anyway?"

By the time the invitations were stamped and mailed (a second printing was necessary), the original game plan for the wedding had been scrapped, and a new, expanded script adopted. Borrowing a few lawn chairs from the neighbors for the backyard ceremony would have sufficed for an intimate group of twenty-five guests. Now Shelby had to order an additional fifty chairs—plus a couple of serving tables, matching plates, and silverware—from the rent-a-party store in Oxnard.

Furthermore, the plan to serve a supper of cold cuts, salads, and breads prepared by a few willing friends was also suddenly inadequate. So local caterers were engaged, a menu of salads, sliced hot meats, hot side dishes, and punch and coffee was ordered, as well as a large cake.

Evan had originally secured the photographer, a cardiologist in his office complex. Dr. Chuck Householder was the only person he knew who owned both a Nikon for slides and prints and a Sony digital handicam for action. Chuck was always popping into Evan's office to show pictures and clips of his five kids, so Evan had invited him to video the ceremony and then "slink around the reception and shoot up a couple of rolls for the album." But when the wedding plans shifted into high gear, the amateur photographer had to be replaced in the lineup by a pro, even though Chuck had insisted that he would still bring his Nikon for candid shots.

With her head spinning in details three weeks before the wedding, Shelby had issued a distress call to Theresa Bordeaux in Dallas. Would she come to California early to help Shelby lasso this bucking bronco of a wedding and tame it to the easy gait of a docile plow horse? Yes, Theresa would gladly come a week before the ceremony and take over as the event's "executive producer." Working from the "command center" of her suite at the Hilton, Theresa had spent the week methodically tacking down every last detail to assure a smooth and memorable wedding day for her dear friend.

Theresa's availability had freed up Shelby's wedding-day morning, allowing her to spend an extra couple of hours in her apartment at King's House getting ready. She had awakened as usual at 6:30. While Malika slept on, Shelby lingered over her Bible reading, sipping coffee and relishing phrases and thoughts she immediately applied to the new life she would begin today with Evan Rider. Fighting off an insistent urgency to busyness, she allowed herself several minutes of quiet prayer, although she couldn't imagine her life being better than it was on this Saturday morning.

Shelby had spent several minutes meticulously wrapping the wedding gift she had chosen for her bridegroom. As she toiled over the project, wanting her handiwork with paper and ribbon to be a work of art for her dear Evan, she imagined their first night together. They had agreed to save their gifts for each other until the party was over and they were alone. She warmed at the thought of Evan preparing a special gift for her. And her heartbeat quickened with the anticipation of being in his arms, finally allowing their passions free course of expression after so many months of painstaking discipline and restraint. *This time we will not have to pull apart and say good-night*, she thought with delight.

Shelby then treated Malika to the girl's favorite breakfast treat, sausages and homemade Swedish pancakes with lingonberry jam and a dusting of powdered sugar. They talked together about the day's events and their joy at having Evan join their small family. In reality, Shelby did most of the talking. Malika's contributions were limited to sentence fragments like "mo' 'cakes" and "goo' dadduh." Shelby's constant coaching toward complete sentences—"Malika say, 'May I have more pancakes, please?' " or "Malika, 'Our new daddy is such a good daddy' " were met with a sharp nod and a repeat of the chopped phrases.

Shelby had explained again to Malika over breakfast the schedule she had been drumming into her for two weeks. "We are driving out to Daddy's house this morning. Daddy and I will be married this afternoon in the garden, and lots of people will be there to celebrate with us. We'll have a big dinner and cake and punch. Tonight you will sleep with Grandpa and Grandma Tuggle at the hotel. Won't that be fun?

"Tomorrow morning Grandpa and Grandma are taking you to Magic Mountain for the day. Then on Monday they will bring you back to King's House before they fly back to Dallas. Wendy will stay with you here in our apartment and take care of you while Daddy and I go on our honeymoon in the RV. Do you remember our big bus with a kitchen, bathroom, and bedroom? We're going to the Grand Canyon—do you remember the pictures I showed you?—for two weeks. We're going alone this time, because it's good for Daddy and Mama to be together after the wedding. But next time we'll take you with us."

Malika had listened with her large brown eyes focused on the breakfast plate as she finished off her third jam-laden pancake. Then she answered, as if she hadn't absorbed a word of the carefully recited itinerary, "Mo' cakes, mama." Shelby reminded herself to be thankful for any kind of response. Malika often said nothing at all.

Shelby and Milaka had left for Ventura at 9:45. The warm, bright sunshine on the east side of the Conejo grade abruptly disappeared above the blotchy gray umbrella of clouds spread over Camarillo, Oxnard, and Ventura. Shelby swept down the west side of the grade, renewing her prayer that the marine layer so characteristic of Southern California beaches in early summer would evaporate in time to dry the garden before the wedding. They drove up to Evan's house at almost 11.

Shelby had come dressed in casual pants and a sweater, prepared to work. But she wasn't needed. After ninety minutes of surfing the south jetty, Evan, the detail person, had spent the morning cleaning windows and mirrors, polishing wood furniture, and sweeping the driveway and walks. The house was spotless. Theresa had marshaled the rest of the out-of-town guests staying at the Hilton to a variety of tasks such as decorating the gift table, setting up chairs, and arranging flowers. And she had the caterers hopping with meal preparations, having made them swear to cleanliness and quiet efficiency.

Insisting that everything was under control, Theresa took Malika under her wing and banished Shelby and Evan to their respective dressing rooms to primp for their soon-to-arrive guests.

Evan had decided, with Shelby's approval, to wear his newest suit for the ceremony, a medium blue-gray summer-weight wool with subtle pin stripes. The rest of the ensemble consisted of white shirt, solid blue tie, and black leather-soled oxfords. The dress shoes were new, since Evan's two pairs of black shoes were rubber-soled for comfort and a little worn. His lone piece of jewelry was an elegant Seiko watch with a bracelet-style gold band and small diamond mounted on the face. Shelby had given it to him as an engagement gift. The trim watch felt like a toy compared to the large diver's watch with digital readout Evan wore practically every day in the Ventura surf and in the office.

Shelby's wedding dress had been designed and handcrafted for her by her former seamstress in Dallas. During her years of abundance and lavish spending at Victory Life Ministries, Shelby had funneled thousands of dollars into Nita's little shop. Adrian had insisted that his wife always dress to the standards of their wealthiest parishioners. And she loved being swathed in the finest fabrics and bedecked with precious metals and jewels. Thanks to her skill with needle and thread, Nita had been the benefactor of Shelby Hornecker's "need" for a veritable storehouse of expensive clothes. The wedding dress had been Nita's gift of appreciation for years of patronage.

The dress was ivory brocade with a sweetheart neckline, fitted waist, and straight skirt. Shelby accessorized her dress with dyed-to-match medium heels and milky-white pearls — earrings, necklace, and bracelet. Her former husband had lavished her with jewelry, more to make himself look generous than to make her look beautiful, Shelby had deduced. The pearl ensemble was an heirloom passed on to Shelby by her grandmother before her death three years earlier.

When she had resigned her pastorate and sold her villa in Austin to move to Los Angeles, Shelby had liquidated the majority of her personal wardrobe and jewelry collection. She sold or gave away several closets full of dresses, gowns, suits, coats, and shoes and boxes laden with necklaces, bracelets, pins, and rings, donating the proceeds to the ministry of King's House. Surprisingly, she felt happier without the racks and racks of seldom-worn costumes than she had ever felt with them.

Shelby emerged from the guest room dressed for the ceremony at shortly past noon. Her parents and dear friends from Dallas greeted her with rave compliments for her beauty. Evan was also ready for the event, except for his suit coat. Busy rubbing a small stain out of the carpet when Shelby appeared, Evan turned at the noise and just stared, seemingly paralyzed by her radiance. When he tried to speak, his voice broke and he almost cried. Taking the cue, everyone scattered to some perfunctory task, leaving the couple alone in the living room.

Shelby sat down on an ottoman beside Evan who was still kneeling on the carpet. "Are you all right, darling?" she said, moved by his show of emotion.

"It just kind of hit me," Evan said, blinking away the tears misting his eyes. "Everything I've ever hoped for in a woman—beauty, femininity, intelligence, grace, tenderness—it's all wrapped up in you. And of all the men who would die for the chance to be your husband, I am the one you chose. I can't believe how blessed I am."

They fell into a tender embrace and playfully argued—in between kisses—about who was the more blessed.

"I hate to break up this touching scene," Theresa interrupted with a rascally grin, peeking around the corner from the dining room, "but luncheon is served. Evelyn and Eleanor have made some sandwiches and sliced some cantaloupe. Come on, you two; you're going to need your strength today."

The festivities around the lunch table were enjoyable but short-lived, since wedding guests began arriving by 12:30. Theresa and her conscripted volunteers scurried to return the dining room to order as Evan and Shelby welcomed wave after wave of friends and acquaintances, arriving in ones, twos, threes, and fours. Kisses and hugs and giggles and guffaws were abundant. Beautifully wrapped gifts were given and received, then carried to a table on the patio by Malika, with help from Wendy Ngo.

Outside, the sun had conquered half the overcast sky with the promise of a complete victory—and a 67-degree high—by midafternoon. In the garden behind the house, a medley of contemporary hymns and love songs was being played on a keyboard by a musician from a local church Evan visited frequently. Guests filtered out of the house and through the patio to inspect the beautiful grounds and take a chair on the gently sloping lawn.

Shelby heard a motorcycle winding up the hill toward Foster Road. "I'll bet that's Reagan Cole," she whispered to Evan, as another knot of guests moved passed them through the living room and toward the patio. Through the open front door she watched a tall man in an electric-blue flight suit nose his idling Kawasaki into a tiny space between cars and shut down the engine. Had he been driving a car, he would have had to settle for a parking place three blocks away.

Cole stepped out of his flight suit, folded it, and stowed it, along with his gloves, in the compartment under the seat. He brought his black helmet with him as he approached the house.

Evan and Shelby met Cole on the front porch with a firm handshake and friendly embrace respectively. "We're so glad you came, Reagan," Evan said, ushering him inside. "This day would have never happened if it hadn't been for you. You're still a hero to me for what you did for Shelby before God brought her into my life. I'd be lost without her."

Uncomfortable at another mention of his hero status, Cole shifted the attention to his own hero. "Evan, if it hadn't been for your Shelby here, I would be as lost as you were. Remember, she helped get me involved in King's House. I'd say she's been a real beacon of the faith for both of us, wouldn't you?" Evan agreed.

Evan asked how Cole was enjoying detective work. Cole complained that his surveillance work was putting him to sleep. He explained that he was leaving tomorrow for a week at his mother's place in Lake Tahoe, hoping to come back with a better attitude or an idea for a departmental transfer which would get him more action.

As he spoke, Cole occasionally glanced past the couple to the window overlooking the patio and garden as if looking for someone.

Shelby knew what was on his mind. "Beth isn't here, Reagan," she said rather apologetically. "Did she tell you she was coming?"

Blushing slightly at his hidden agenda being uncovered, Cole said, "No, I . . . I haven't talked to Beth in months. I have no idea if she's planning to be here today. I was just hoping . . . " He fell quiet and finished the sentence with a sheepish grin.

"What happened between you two, Reagan?" Shelby asked with the gentle concern of a big sister. She had asked the question dozens of times in her mind, but never felt bold enough to verbalize it to Cole. "You seemed to really hit it off, and then she disappeared."

Cole shifted from one foot to the other and wrinkled his forehead in thought. "The usual life-threatening differences, I guess. I say to*may*to, she says to*mah*to. She likes the three-point shot, I like the physical inside game. She squeezes the toothpaste tube in the middle, I squeeze from the end. . . . "

Shelby smiled at his obvious humor intended to deflect the point of her inquiry. Then she bored in again with big-sister intuition. "And you decided to turn your life to God while Beth chose to do her own thing."

Cole shifted his posture again and dropped his head. "Yeah, that's probably the biggest part of it. In fact, I *know* it is." Then, looking up, he added, "I assumed that Beth was as interested in getting close to God as I was. But those successful books of hers seemed to distract her, get her all starry-eyed about being a rich and famous writer. I guess she's just going to have to find herself and find Him on her own." He flicked a glance toward heaven to clearly identify the "Him" to whom he was referring. "And when she finds Him, I just hope I'm around to see it."

"Don't give up on her, Reagan," Evan interjected, "and don't stop praying for her."

"Oh, I won't," Cole answered with conviction. "I learned on Millennium's Eve what prayer can do. I've been in this dark tunnel praying for Beth for many months. I know God's doing something on the other side. It's just a matter of time."

Theresa Bordeaux rushed up behind Evan and Shelby. She stretched out a hand to the tall guest and said, "Hello, Reagan. It's good to see you again." Then before he could respond she said to the couple, "I hate to break up the reunion, but it's one minute to zero hour. After the ceremony you can talk to everyone for as long as you like. But right now it's time to walk the aisle." To Cole she added, "Excuse us, Reagan, but we have wedding to do. Would you like to take a seat outside?"

Again Theresa did not wait for Cole's response. She whisked the couple to the patio door where Malika waited for them, beautifully adorned in a flouncy, pale-yellow dress. The trio would walk together through the patio and down the center of the lawn to the white wicker altar after Stan Welbourn, Theresa, and the best man, Ben Heath, had taken their places.

Suddenly alone in the living room, Cole found a corner where he could stash his helmet. Then he stepped to the front door, which still stood open. He took a last look down the street, hoping for the appearance of one more guest. But he saw no one and closed the door. He made his way into the garden and took a seat alone as Evan, Shelby, and Malika started down the aisle to the familiar strains of "The Wedding March."

Twenty

From the moment he stepped out of the house onto the sun-drenched brick patio with Shelby and Malika, Evan had to battle to keep his emotions from running away with him. The scene was perfect, and he couldn't believe his good fortune to be one of the featured players.

The stairway ahead led down to the broad, sloping, manicured lawn. Dewdrops remaining in the grass from the morning mist glistened in the sunlight, transforming the garden turf into a lush green carpet sprinkled with tiny stars.

Over seventy guests, now standing respectfully to watch the procession, welcomed Evan, his bride, and fragile Malika into the outdoor sanctuary with beaming smiles of approval and happiness. At the front of the gathering stood three figures as complimentary to the garden surroundings as fine marble statuary. Rev. Stan Welbourn, tall, graying, distinguished-looking in dark suit and tie, held a small, leather-bound service book in his hands. He was flanked by Theresa Bordeaux, who wore a subtle pastel-print dress chosen to accent Shelby's wedding dress, and Evan's short, stocky friend and surfing buddy, Ben Heath, in a tan, summer-weight sports jacket and subdued plaid tie.

The garden chancel behind the minister, maid of honor, and best man consisted of an eight-foot, flower-draped white lattice arch. Evan had never seen a stained-glass window more beautiful or awe-inspiring.

The elegant miniature palms, the low shrubs of variegated green, and the shocking violet bougainvillea at the rear border of the yard formed a lovely backdrop to the scene. But the artful landscaping was no match for the stunning spectacle beyond. The blue-gray sea stretching out to distant haze shimmered in the dominating sunlight. Ponderous Santa Cruz Island hunkered offshore like a sunning gray whale, while her three tiny calves, the Anacapas, frolicked behind her. Distant Santa Rosa Island, barely in view, seemed to be the cow's mate, aloof from his family and yearning for the open sea.

Evan drank in the moment with his senses: the visual magnificence of smiling loved ones and the splendor of creation, the warm caress of the afternoon sun tempered by a fluttering ocean breeze, the fragrance of a living bouquet of flowering plants surrounding the garden, the melodious processional wafting from the electronic keyboard. And above all, Shelby Tuggle was at his side for the brief march into the garden, that would culminate in a lifetime commitment to live together as one.

A flood of joy engulfed Evan, and a lump of emotion swelled in his throat, squeezing the salivary glands and prompting tears. He swallowed with difficulty and blinked away the mist in his eyes as they stepped down the broad brick stairway to the garden floor.

For the moment, the emotional rush overwhelmed the sense of guilt and unworthiness which had menaced him for weeks on end. His happiness was like an anesthetic, temporarily dulling the discomfort while not dealing with the symptoms. Evan acknowledged that the gnawing sense of wrong from his past, like a large, benign tumor, had to be treated soon. It wasn't a life-threatening malady, but it surely had the potential to negatively affect his relationship with Shelby as well as his personal peace. Eventually it would have to be excised. For the moment, however, Evan's supreme joy at marrying Shelby numbed the pain and helped him push it from his mind.

Striding slowly down the grassy center aisle between uniform rows of chairs, Evan scanned the faces of the people who meant so much to him. His parents stood in separate rows near the front with their spouses. Evan wondered if they had ever known the happiness he knew today. Shelby's parents stood on the opposite side of the aisle. What gracious people to wholeheartedly support their daughter in her choice of a new husband and to welcome him into their family.

There was a generous sprinkling of Evan's old friends and business associates in the congregation, people from his less focused, less temperate past who didn't understand the faith which now propelled his life to greater selflessness and service to others. And there was an even larger representation of Evan's new friends in the crowd, most of them volunteers at King's House. These friends knew as little about Evan's selfish past as his worldly friends knew about his fledgling life of faith, for which he was humbly grateful.

Then there was Dr. No. Evan's eyes locked onto the diminutive Vietnamese-American, standing with his wife and children, whose heart of faith and love seemed larger than Los Angeles itself. Evan had come to King's House in run-down Echo Park nearly two years earlier searching for a clue to the meaning of life. But he found more than a clue; he found the key in a humble man who had given up his profession to serve Christ as he perceived Him in the form of L.A.'s hidden subculture of destitute throwaways—the poor, the abused, the diseased, the dying.

While volunteering his services at King's House one day a week, Evan Rider had experienced a transformation. Following Dr. No's example and heeding his gentle encouragement, Evan Rider, floundering man of medicine, had become Evan Rider, grounded man of faith.

Evan's quest had culminated one Friday in October 1999. Activity on the fifth floor of the old hospital had been unusually slow, and Dr. Rider found himself in the staff lounge drinking cold cans of diet Squirt with Dr. No. In response to Evan's probing and sometimes irreverent questions, the discussion moved from the tragedy of AIDS to the lifestyle choices behind the spread of AIDS to the question of moral absolutes to Dr. No's personal apologia which, he insisted, was merely a reflection of God's blueprint for man found in the Holy Bible.

Every objection Evan fabricated to defend himself against Dr. No's convicting message had crumbled that day under the substance of the man's convincing life. Here was someone who had walked away from the prestige and material rewards of a professional career to lose himself in an old hospital populated by the dregs of society. Dr. No obviously worked harder for less money than most people Evan knew, while Evan worked smarter and raked in a bundle in contrast to many of his peers. But the real difference between the two men lay in the intangible outcome of their endeavors. Dr. No, the servant of the helpless, was at peace; while Dr. Rider, the workaholic physician, was falling apart.

"It's a matter of simple economics, Evan," Dr. No had stated matter-of-factly, as the two men sipped soda pop in the staff lounge. "People don't invest in something that swallows up their capital and pays no dividends. For example, nobody buys stock in cellular communications anymore, now that the wireless personal phone system has been perfected. And with the dramatic advances in powerful, long-life, quick-charge batteries, an automotive investor is wise to get into electric cars and get out of anything with an internal combustion engine."

Evan nodded with comprehension at the examples. His broker had advised him similarly, and Evan had already pocketed substantial earnings from those transactions.

Dr. No continued, "In the same way, Evan, if you want a certain dividend out of life, you have to make the appropriate investment. Here, read this. Read it out loud."

Dr. No pushed a well-used Bible across the table to Evan, pointing to several lines that were highlighted in yellow. Evan's curiosity about Dr. No's point overpowered the minor embarrassment he felt at being a student reciting for the teacher. So he read aloud, "For whoever wants to save his life will lose it, but whoever loses his life for Me and for the Gospel will save it. What good is it for a man to gain the whole world, yet forfeit his soul?"

As he read, a mental picture vividly materialized in Evan's head. He saw himself alone in an elevator steadily ascending toward the top of a towering skyscraper. Yet the anxiety and futility of the climb was scraping his insides raw, overpowering the sense of exhilaration and reward his achievement had promised.

Stopping at an upper floor, the elevator doors opened and Evan gazed across the hall to another elevator standing with doors open. Inside that elevator was Dr. No, radiating the guileless smile that was as much his trademark as the oversized white lab coat he wore when visiting the floors of King's House. The red, downward-pointing arrow above Dr. No's elevator was illuminated, and the man looked more purposeful and content about descending to the bottom than Evan had ever felt about ascending to the top.

As the doors to the two elevators closed in his brief daydream, Evan had sensed a frantic desperation that his climb toward the pinnacle of his career and his ambition for wealth and happiness was a fruitless effort. He wanted the peace he saw in Dr. No's eyes, but he feared he was moving further from it, and he didn't know how to change direction.

Then Dr. No had interrupted his troubling thoughts. "Evan, the way to up is down."

Evan looked at Dr. No with furrowed brow, wondering if the man also saw elevators in *his* head. Feeling that he had missed something, he said, "I beg your pardon."

Dr. No tapped his finger on the verses Evan had just read. "The fulfillment and reward you want out of life cannot be achieved through position or prestige or possessions, Evan. It's found in becoming a follower of Jesus and a servant of people. Invest in this life and all its tempting toys and experiences, and you will lose your investment and any hope of a dividend in the life to come. But invest in eternal life by bowing your knee to Jesus, and you will realize the peace and purpose in this life you're so desperately seeking."

The truth behind Dr. No's uncomplicated yet profound solution to Evan's quest rang in his soul that day with the force and clarity of cathedral bells. Evan prayed a simple prayer in the staff lounge. In effect, his childlike supplication halted the dizzying ascent of his elevator prison and pushed the down button.

The relief Evan sensed after his conversation and prayer with Dr. No was instantaneous. His change of perspective and its impact on his behavior, greatly implemented by Dr. No and more recently by Shelby Tuggle, continued over many months, right up to this his wedding day.

As he walked past Dr. No on his way up the aisle, Evan attempted to convey to him through a prolonged glance and smile a portion of the gratitude he felt for the spiritual mentor's contribution to his life. Evan was a man of faith, due to the humble example and clear truth emanating from Dr. No's life and words. And the woman on whose hand he would soon slip a wedding band had also come to him through Dr. No's ministry, King's House. Evan could only hope that these two strong pillars would yet help him resolve the dark, insistent issue scratching at the distant borders of his immense happiness.

When the trio reached the front, pretty, dark-eyed Malika turned off to be with Grandpa and Grandma Tuggle for the ceremony. Shelby slipped her right hand into the crook of Evan's arm and pulled herself close to him. She held a small, handmade bouquet of fresh flowers from his garden in her left hand. Theresa Bordeaux and Ben Heath took their respective positions beside their friends.

When the final notes of the processional had sounded, Stan Welbourn instructed the guests to be seated. In the five seconds it took for everyone to get settled, Shelby delivered a love note to her bridegroom through a tender gaze: *I would rather be here than anywhere in the world. I would rather be with you than with any man alive. I love you, Evan.* Tear-filled eyes underscored the sincerity of Shelby's message. Evan squeezed her arm in reply and quickly brushed another tear of joy from his eye.

Shelby had heard Stan's opening remarks about the holy estate of marriage many times before. In fact, she had used them herself in some of the weddings she had performed at Victory Life Center in years past. It was a standard ceremony used by all members of the pastoral staff so that on a given day, any one of the pastors could pinch-hit as officiant if the first-stringer was unable to perform for some reason.

It was a good ceremony, which was why Shelby had encouraged Stan Welbourn to use it, instead of insisting that he come up with something new and different. The opening remarks, the Scripture recitations, the charge to the bride and groom, the vows and exchange of rings, and the presentation of the couple were always the same. But certain sections of the ceremony were purposely left open for the minister to add favorite anecdotes or to ad lib advice to the couple based on personal acquaintance with them. Over time, however, each of the staff ministers had standardized his or her ad libs in the ceremony for convenience, changing only the names of the bride and groom.

Shelby had intended to listen carefully to Stan's preamble as he delivered it so fluently and convincingly. But on such an emotionally charged occasion, the familiar words couldn't hold her interest. She gazed at Stan with a convincing expression of attentiveness, while her mind flirted with more tantalizing thoughts.

Chief among the distractions from the ceremony was the man whose arm she held so firmly. Today Shelby was stepping over the line: Evan Rider had been a warm friend, an entertaining escort, and a romantic fiancé—with no legal commitment; today she would be joined to him under God as his wife "till death do us part." She loved Evan dearly and couldn't think of living without him. But she was unable to convince herself that she was stepping over the line without a sliver or two of reservation.

What did Shelby *really* know about this virile, talented physician who applied as much skill to nurturing his hydrangeas, rebuilding the carburetor on his beach buggy, and mastering the waves on his surfboard, as he did to suturing a wound or treating an infection? After all, she had known Evan only sixteen months—barely half as long as she had known Adrian Hornecker before they were married in 1990. Had Shelby really matured in her ability to evaluate a prospective husband? Or did Evan have some chilling surprises for her too in the years ahead? She refused to believe it possible.

And what about marrying a man who was so new to the faith and still struggling with a past which haunted him and accused him? She had no doubts about the authenticity of his conversion. His diligence in Bible study and selfless service at King's House evidenced a profound devotion to Christ. But was he mature enough to assume spiritual leadership in their home? Or would he continue to defer to her as a spiritual big sister, leaving her without the priestly covering she so craved?

During the months of their courtship and engagement, Evan had shown every intention of taking the lead. He had initiated their Bible study and prayertimes as a couple. He made sure they weren't so busy with their King's House ministrations that they failed to attend worship services in the chapel regularly. Evan had provided abundant evidence of good intentions, but would another agenda emerge after five years, as it had so insidiously with Adrian? Shelby could not imagine it, nor did she want to.

"Evan Rider, do you hereby declare your love for Shelby?" Stan asked in his polished preacher's voice. It was the first point of interaction in the ceremony after the minister's opening remarks. Shelby was instantly tuned in to the exchange.

Evan turned to Shelby and held her gaze as he answered, "I do."

"Is it your desire to take her as your wife and be her husband for as long as God grants you life?"

Still locked eye to eye with his bride, Evan responded, "It is."

"Shelby Tuggle, do you hereby declare your love for Evan?" There was a touch of emotion in Stan's voice that caused Shelby to look away from Evan for a moment to appreciate the man performing the ceremony. Here was a dear friend who was also touched by her good fortune at finding a godly husband.

Regripping Evan's arm and finding his gaze again, she answered, "I do."

"And is it your desire to take him as your husband and be his wife for as long as God grants you life?"

Shelby searched Evan's eyes deeply as if burning her petition into his heart, *Yes, Evan, please be my husband for life. Wash away the scars of the past in the purity and strength of your love. And allow me to do the same for you. I love you. I need you.* Then she said with confidence, "It is."

Stan Welbourn launched into his familiar homily on marriage, beginning with an excerpt from a sonnet by Shakespeare:

Let me not to the marriage of true minds
Admit impediments. Love is not love
Which alters when it alteration finds,
Or bends with the remover to remove:
O, no! it is an ever-fixed mark,
That looks on tempests and is never shaken.

The final phrase echoed in Shelby's mind, "That looks on tempests and is never shaken." *That's what I'm praying for,* she affirmed silently, *a love that is never shaken by the tempests. God, make it so in our lives.*

As Stan continued the homily by reading Scripture verses and applying them to Evan and Shelby's life together, Shelby was captivated by thoughts of their wedding night and honeymoon. She had admitted only to herself and her mentor, Grace Ellen Holloway, the formidable anxiety she felt over her entrance into sexual intimacy with Evan. Only a small part of her hesitancy stemmed from the embarrassment and self-consciousness common to newlyweds. Shelby's greater concern loomed like a cloud in the distance, a cloud she prayed would drift beyond the horizon instead of threaten her married life with storm.

Shelby's apprehension centered on the disparity of experience between her and Evan. By his own contrite admission, Evan had been with several women—thankfully without the added complication of contracting sexually transmitted diseases—before his recent conversion and commitment to moral purity. Shelby had been with only one man, Adrian Hornecker, and she had failed to keep him interested. Would she be able to please Evan in light of his many "experiences"? Would he tell her if she didn't meet his expectations and hopes, or would his waning interest simply result in a cold distance between them? Could Evan overcome the temptation to compare Shelby to his previous "partners"? Was he mature enough in the faith to regard their sex life as part of their spiritual experience, instead of a carnal exercise?

As the days and hours had ticked away toward their first night together in Evan's bed, Shelby had been clearly aware that her sex drive was healthy and her appetite keen. She had carefully kept her emotions and urges in check throughout their courtship, waiting for the perfect, holy moment of her wedding night to release them. She was ready, willing, and able to present herself as a gift to her husband. But would she be enough for him? Only time would tell.

"As you prepare to take your vows, remember that you are standing in the very presence of God." The summary to Stan Welbourn's homily alerted Evan and Shelby that the critical moments of the ceremony were upon them. She tightened her grip on his arm, and he pressed her hand to his side with his elbow. "This is a solemn moment, a holy moment. God is listening to what you promise each other today. He will bless you abundantly if you keep your vows, and He will discipline you if you fail to keep them."

At Stan's direction, Shelby handed her bouquet to Theresa, and the couple turned to face each other and clasp their hands together. Stan had reminded them during the rehearsal, as he did every couple he married, that their vows were to be made face to face, eye to eye. "I'll feed you the phrases one by one, but don't look at me as you repeat them," he had urged with a twinkle in his eye. "You're not marrying me; you're marrying each other. So look each other in the eye and commit yourselves to one another from the heart."

Evan gazed deeply into Shelby's powder-blue eyes which, like his, were moist with tears of wonder and joy. Reciting the words with tenderness and conviction, he gratefully received Shelby Tuggle as his own. "I, Evan, take you, Shelby, to be my wedded wife, to love and to cherish from this day forward. I promise to stand with you through every circumstance of our life together—joy or sorrow, health or sickness, wealth or poverty—as long as we both shall live."

Shelby recited the same vow to Evan, twice pausing briefly to wait out a swell of emotion that blocked the words in her throat and caused her to stammer. After the ceremony the couple would laugh about the fact that Shelby, the experienced up-front person of the pair, had stumbled over her vows, while Evan had carried through like a veteran performer.

Stan Welbourn explained how the gold bands Evan and Shelby

would exchange symbolized their lives and marriage: valuable, meticulously prepared for this moment, unending in design. First Evan and then Shelby slipped a band on the other's finger, held it there, and repeated words of commitment, "With this ring, I give myself to you. All I am and all I have I gladly share with you, in the name of the Father, and of the Son, and of the Holy Spirit."

Then, Dr. No stepped forward from his seat to lay his hands on the couple and offer the dedicatory prayer. As Evan and Shelby knelt at the simple altar, he prayed an eloquent, discerning prayer over them. Theresa Bordeaux and Ben Heath also laid their hands on them in agreement.

Then the minister bid the couple to stand and he pronounced the words Evan and Shelby had longed for through the months of their engagement, "What God has now joined together, let not man tear apart. As a minister of the Gospel of Jesus Christ, I now pronounce you husband and wife, in the name of the Father, and of the Son, and of the Holy Spirit." Then with a playful wink, he added, "Evan, you may kiss your bride."

The pair had agreed beforehand not to let their ceremonial display of affection resemble a Hollywood love scene or the antics of two lovesick teenagers. Still, the lingering, tender kiss brought a wave of affected oohs and aahs from their loved ones, who thoroughly enjoyed the show.

Finally, with the beaming bride and groom facing their guests and linked arm in arm, Stan concluded the ceremony. "Ladies and gentlemen, I am pleased to introduce to you Dr. and Mrs. Evan Rider." The recessional from the keyboard was overpowered by applause and cheers from the small congregation. And the recession itself was soon abandoned as friends and family streamed forward to congratulate the happy couple.

In the midst of the festive hubbub, Evan and Shelby embraced again. Placing his lips near her ear, Evan whispered, "Whatever happens to us, my angel, nothing can take this moment away from us." His hopes and fears were bound tightly in his bold prediction.

Reflecting on her own secret anxieties, Shelby replied loudly enough for Evan's ear only, "Yes, nothing, my darling."

Twenty-one

Beth Scibelli was ready to give up her last-minute attempt to get to Ventura for the wedding. She knew she would never make it in time for the ceremony. Her flight out of Dallas to Los Angeles had been delayed, touching down at LAX at 12:40. The male clerk at the Galaxy Rent-a-Car counter was a trainee in his early twenties, slower than a tax refund and an obnoxious flirt. When she finally slipped behind the wheel of the racy, black Buick Barego sport coupe in space K-6, it was 1:30. *The ceremony is already half over,* she acknowledged with a sigh. *What's the use?*

Yet the prospect of seeing several friendly faces after such an un-friendly experience in Antigua spurred her on. *There's still the reception,* she challenged herself, gunning the Barego toward the exit gate. *I can make it for the party, and if I don't like it, I can leave.*

The next obstacle that almost derailed Beth's plan was clothes. It didn't occur to her until she was on the freeway that she had brought nothing suitable to wear to a wedding. She had left Colin Wendt's yacht with only her toilet articles and another pair of shorts, a top, and a light jacket. She expected him to ship the rest of her wardrobe to Whidbey Island when he returned to Connecticut.

Racing through the hilly pass between West Hollywood and the Val-ley, Beth realized that she might be able to find something to wear at her parents' home in Woodland Hills. She couldn't remember what she had tucked away in her old bedroom closet, but it was worth a quick stop to find out, before scurrying into a mall to buy something she really didn't want.

Beth was grateful that Jack and Dona were out of the country, barn-storming Britain with the indefatigable evangelist, Simon Holloway. Beth's relationship with her parents was better since Millennium's Eve, her dad and mom showing greater tolerance for her lifestyle, and she for theirs. But Beth was glad not to have to face them after her heartbreak in the Caribbean. They wouldn't understand, and today she *needed* somebody who understood—and cared.

Beth let herself into the sprawling ranch-style home on Adele Court with the key her father always left for her under the potted palm. Going straight to her bedroom closet, she found a smoky-gray winter dress that was a little too fancy and a gauzy peasant skirt and white embroidered tunic top that was a tad too casual. But the skirt went better with her sandals, which were the only shoes she brought from the yacht. So she convinced herself that the outfit would be adequate for a summer wedding.

She was back on the Ventura Freeway headed west by 2:10. *Party hearty and long, everybody,* she urged silently. *I'm on my way.* But in thinking about "everybody," only one face materialized in her mind. The face belonged to Reagan Cole.

Margo Sharpe drove the silver-blue Jaguar sedan westward on U.S. 101 between rolling, verdant hills which served as a backdrop to the burgeoning freewayside communities of Thousand Oaks and Newbury Park. These were among the few hills bordering the Los Angeles basin that were still green. Most had been graded, terraced, and suburbanized with prefab tract homes costing at least half a million dollars each.

Nolan Jakes sat statue still in the passenger's seat, daring not even a glance at a passing car, though his makeup, beard, wraparound dark glasses, and golf hat adequately disguised his face. The nylon bag full of bundled $100 bills and the loaded Colt Anaconda .44 Magnum lay on the floor between his feet.

Traffic on the freeway was light for a weekend afternoon, and the farther they traveled from Los Angeles, the lighter it became. Jakes frequently reminded Margo to keep her speed at or below 65 MPH, even though several cars swept past them at 75. One California Highway Patrol cruiser had eased around them at 70 near Agoura without incident. But Jakes was sweating the possibility that Margo's slightest driving lapse—an unnecessary lane change, failure to use the turn signal, tailgating—might get them pulled over, ending their escape before it had really begun.

Margo blew off his nervous harping with a laugh, assuring him that she had never been cited in fifteen years of driving. "If you don't like how I'm doing, you can always drive," she said with a playful challenge in her tone. Jakes ignored her, conceding that Margo seemed more calm about their flight than he was. He trusted her behind the wheel more than he trusted himself, but he couldn't stop kibitzing about her driving.

As they crested the Conejo grade and began the long, winding descent into Camarillo, Margo probed for the details of Jakes' plan.

"How are we going to find this Evan Rider in Ventura?"

"I got his address out of the phone book. When we get into town, I want you to ask directions to the place or buy a city map at a service station."

"Why don't you just call him and have him meet us somewhere," Margo suggested.

"He's probably seen the TV reports about me by now. He's liable to call the police as soon as I hang up."

"What about the blackmail? When you tell him about blowing the McGruder thing wide open, he won't call the police, will he?"

Jakes chanced a look out the side window to the onion fields which, like the hills, were gradually being eradicated by large swaths of tract homes stretching out from the freeway. "I don't know what he'll do, Margo. That's why I have to be there. That's why I have to confront him in person, surprise him when he's alone."

"He may have a family. Do we take them to the border with us?"

Jakes shrugged. "The last I heard about him, he was divorced. If we can get him out of Ventura alone, all the better. If he has somebody with him, we'll take them too. We can't leave any clues behind for the police or for Billy Fryman."

Margo was silent for a few minutes. Then she started down another trail of questions. "How long will it take us to get to Canada?"

Jakes calculated silently. "If everything goes right, we can leave Ventura this afternoon or tonight. We'll take Highway 126 east to Interstate 5 and head north. We should cross the border by tomorrow night."

"Driving straight through?"

Jakes nodded. "Right. We'll stop only for gas and food, which we eat on the road. The sooner we get lost in B.C., the better."

"What happens when we cross the border? Where will we go?"

Jakes tried to sound confident with his response, although the plan in his mind was sketchy at best. "I have a couple of 'acquaintances' in Vancouver who will do anything for a few thousand dollars. We can hide out with them while they get us outfitted. Then I'll get them to fly us into the wilderness to a remote cabin where nobody can find us. We'll lay low for a year or two."

Margo giggled with anticipation. "I love the wilderness. It will be so exciting to get lost with you, to be together where no one can bother us."

Jakes quietly marveled at Margo's excitement. He didn't know many women who would look forward to dropping out of society and living far from the glitter of civilization, no matter how comfortable the stolen money could make it.

"After two years, then what?" Margo asked.

Jakes' long-range plan was even more nebulous, but he kept up a positive front. "Maybe we can pull some of this money out of hiding, buy us new identities, and look for property—a place where we can settle down and sink our roots."

"And horses? Can we have some horses, Nolan? I've always wanted a ranch with horses."

Margo's girlish enthusiasm was almost too much for Jakes to stomach. To her, this was a lark, an adventure. *For being such a smart girl, she sure doesn't grasp the seriousness of what will happen to us if the cops track us down, or worse, if Billy Fryman catches up with us. She has no concept of the imminent danger. The next car outside my window may belong to one or more of Billy's many 'associates' armed for an immediate and deadly payback. A thug with an automatic weapon may riddle us with bullets in two seconds and be gone before we crash into the center divider in a ball of flames. And Margo is dreaming about a horse ranch in the serene Canadian back country.*

Jakes wanted desperately to abandon himself to Margo's naiveté, and perhaps he could—after they found Evan Rider, after they had another couple hundred thousand dollars in hand, after they crossed the border, after they crawled into a hole of anonymity and pulled the top in after them. But until then he had to watch both of their backs and keep his beautiful, devoted Pollyanna in good humor. "Sure, Margo," he answered, forcing a smile. "We can have horses, dogs, a picket fence, anything you like." Margo giggled again.

After several more minutes of silence, Margo's curiosity got the best of her again. "What if Evan Rider doesn't have any money?"

"Have you ever heard of a doctor without money?" Jakes allowed himself a small laugh at the thought.

"I mean, what if he doesn't have *enough* money?"

"A man with Evan's earning power has plenty of money at his fingertips: checking account, savings account, personal line of credit, equity line of credit, charge-card line of credit. And all he needs is the magic card and a couple of secret numbers—which he will gladly use to keep me from telling the story that could trash his career."

"But there are limits on those kind of accounts, aren't there—like $500 a day for a cash advance?"

"Not for high rollers. They have to memorize a few extra PIN numbers, but they can liquidate all their accounts and borrow tens of thousands of dollars on a plastic card in a matter of minutes. The money can be picked up at most banks with a signature."

Margo thought for a moment, then probed, "So how much money do you think Dr. Evan Rider is good for? Ten thousand? Twenty?"

"I'm hoping for closer to a *hundred* thousand, maybe more. But we'll take what we can get."

"And what about that other friend, Libby? Does she have any money?"

The image of a tall, lithe, attractive black woman in scanty running attire materialized in Jakes' mind. It occurred to him that the snapshot in his memory was over twenty years old. He had no idea if she had retained her trim physique or lost control and ballooned to the size of a football lineman.

"I don't know," he answered. "According to a *Sports Illustrated* article I read after the 1984 Olympics, she stopped competing and entered grad school at the University of Washington. That's the last I heard of her. She could be president of her own company by now or the mother of six kids or a bag lady in a slum somewhere. Or she could be dead. I'm hoping Evan Rider knows where I can reach her by phone. Maybe they kept in—"

"Oh, geez, Nolan," Margo gasped, suddenly stiff at the wheel with her eyes fastened on the rearview mirror. "There's a cop way back there, but he's coming up fast with red lights flashing."

The Jaguar was on a straight stretch of freeway from the base of the grade into Oxnard. Jakes refused to turn around to look. "Is he in your lane? Is he coming up behind you?" he pressed urgently.

Margo's eyes flitted between the mirror and the stretch of highway ahead. "No, he's in the left lane. Should I pull over?"

"No, Margo, don't do anything," Jakes almost barked. Then in a calmer tone he added, "Stay right where you are and relax. If he comes up behind you, then pull over."

Jakes wanted to look back. He wanted to look his destiny squarely in the eye if it was coming after him, but he refused to turn. Instead, he reached for the nylon bag and picked up the Colt .44, hiding it between his right leg and the door. The closer they got to Ventura and an escape plan to Canada, the more ready Jakes was to resist anyone who blocked his path, even a cop. He quietly flicked off the safety and waited.

"He's really flying," Margo reported, gripping the wheel tightly while monitoring the rearview mirror. "Now he may be slowing a little. It's hard to tell."

Jakes sat motionless, staring straight ahead, as if he hadn't heard a word. Seconds later a Ventura County Sheriff's car swished by the left side of the Jaguar at close to 90 MPH red lights flashing. The driver, a female deputy dressed in khaki, didn't even cast a second glance at the Jaguar or its occupants.

Margo and Jakes simultaneously released long, silent breaths. She reached out and grasped his hand, squeezing it and then caressing it. "We're going to make it, Nolan," she said confidently. Jakes gazed at her, looking past the gaudy blonde wig and dark glasses to the woman he loved. He felt very grateful not to be alone.

Twenty minutes later Jakes directed Margo to exit the freeway at Victoria Avenue in Ventura and turn north toward the hills. Morning clouds had scattered to reveal a brilliant sun and luminous sky.

They drove past a trendy shopping mall on the left and the expansive Ventura County government center on the right. Crossing Highway 126, they turned into an older shopping center at the corner of Telegraph Road across from Buena High School.

Jakes stayed in the car while Margo went into the Sav-on Drug Store to ask directions to the address on Foster Road copied from the phone book. She returned with a couple of cans of 7-Up, a bag of pretzels, and a fold-up map of Ventura.

"The girl said that Foster Road is up on the hill somewhere, closer to downtown," Margo said, popping the tab on a can and handing it to Jakes. "She wasn't sure. We'll have to look it up on the map."

Jakes set his soda on the dashboard without a sip and went straight to the map. He located Foster Road and plotted a rough course from the intersection of Victoria and Telegraph to a swirl of short, interlocking, hillside streets approximately three miles away. Then he said, "Let's go."

Finding the home of Evan Rider was like working through a maze. After leaving the main drag to climb into the hills, narrow streets turned and twisted and dead-ended, not always where the map said they would. Jakes navigated through the maze until they found Foster Road and followed the house numbers in the direction of the address scrawled on a scrap of paper.

Foster Road ended in a cul-de-sac which was almost too small to turn around in. For three blocks before the dead end, the narrow street was lined with parked cars. "It looks like somebody's having a big party," Margo observed, as she eased the Jaguar closer to the end of the street.

"That's the place," Jakes said, pointing, "right at the end of the street. And that's where the party is. Look at the cars jammed in the driveway." Then he muttered a curse. "So much for seeing Evan Rider alone."

Margo stopped in the middle of the street. "We're not sure that's his house. He may have moved. We'd better find out."

"How do you suggest we do that?" Jakes asked, a little offended at Margo finding a minor flaw in his plan.

"We sit and wait for someone to arrive or depart and ask them."

Jakes couldn't argue with her logic. Besides, he had no options.

"Okay," he resigned after a thoughtful moment. "Back up and park."

Margo shifted into reverse and slowly guided the Jaguar back down Foster Road to the nearest opening at the curb in front of another expensive hillside home. "And if this *is* his place," she said as she parallel parked, "we sit and wait until all his company goes home."

"That sounds like a lot of sitting and waiting," Jakes objected.

"You're the boss, Nolan," Margo said submissively, shutting off the engine. "I'm just trying to help."

Again, Jakes had no viable alternative. Without another word, he tore open the bag of pretzels and reclined his bucket seat a couple of settings to wait.

The thought of bringing a wedding gift didn't cross Beth's mind until she exited the freeway at Main Street and turned up Mills Road toward the Ventura hills. As she passed the Buenaventura Shopping Center, the sight of the Broadway Department Store jogged her mind to the fact that she was about to walk into a wedding reception empty-handed. She already felt self-conscious about showing up at all, not to mention arriving late and being dressed a little too casually. She just couldn't go without a gift, and a nice gift at that. Besides, she had already missed the wedding; what would another ten minutes matter?

But the Broadway was crowded and the selection was less than what Beth had hoped for. She finally settled on a silver fruit bowl for $135, confident that she wouldn't look like a cheapskate if Shelby and Evan decided to return it. She waited in line ten minutes to purchase it. And when she got to the gift-wrap counter, it was understaffed and clogged with customers. It took another twenty minutes to have the bowl exquisitely wrapped, giving Beth time to buy and sign an expensive card and ask directions from another waiting customer to the address in her electronic date book which, the woman said, was a home above the high school. Still, Beth left the store fuming that she was even farther behind schedule.

The directions led Beth directly up the hill to Foster Road and Evan Rider's home at the end. The sight of Reagan Cole's motorcycle parked at the curb in front of the house suddenly filled her with misgiving about coming to the reception. *Reagan could get the wrong signal from my being here*, she chided herself. *They could* all *get the wrong signal. Shelby and Dr. No and the others may think I'm repenting of my wandering ways and coming back to the fold. Reagan may think I'm still interested in him, when all I really want today is a friend. This may be a bad idea.*

After a few seconds of inner debate, she acknowledged that it was stupid of her to change her flight, rent a car and drive all this way, and buy a gift only to turn around and leave. *If it's not what you need, you can always leave*, she consoled herself. *These are good people; give them a chance to comfort you.*

Beth turned the Barego around in the crowded cul-de-sac with difficulty and retreated until she found a parking place four blocks away. She was hurrying back to the house at the end of the street with the wrapped gift in hand when she was intercepted by a female voice. "Pardon me."

Beth turned to see a petite blonde in jeans, purple polo, and sunglasses standing beside the open driver's door of a late-model Jaguar sedan. There was a passenger in the front seat also, a man with a beard and wraparound shades.

"Yes," Beth responded from the middle of the street.

"Are you going to the party down there?" The blonde pointed to the house at the end of the street.

Beth's inquisitive, journalistic mind immediately flooded with questions: *Are these guests also late? They have a better parking place than I have, so they have been here a while. But why are they sitting in the car instead of enjoying the party? Or are they even guests at all? The girl is even more inappropriately dressed than I am. On the other hand, in California people dress more casually. A pair of jeans and a jacket can pass for semiformal. If the jeans have a crease and a belt, it's a tuxedo. And why would they be sitting here if they aren't guests?*

Beth saw no harm in answering the question. "Yes. I missed the wedding completely. I hope I didn't miss too much of the reception.

Are you coming in?"

"In a minute," the blonde answered. "How do the bride and groom spell their names? We're signing a card."

"Evan, E-V-A-N, and Shelby, S-H-E-L-B-Y, Rider, R-I-D-E-R."

"Thanks," the blonde called back. "Maybe we'll see you inside." Then she returned to the driver's seat and closed the door.

Beth resumed her walk toward the house. With the anticipation of seeing old acquaintances again, especially Reagan Cole, she quickly forgot about the would-be guests in the silver-blue Jaguar.

Twenty-two

Reagan Cole engaged in small talk with many of the wedding guests about the splendid day, the gorgeous flowers in the garden, the magnificent view of the ocean, and the touching ceremony. But his heart wasn't in it, and his congeniality was superficial. The catered buffet supper of hot sliced meats, steamed fresh vegetables, pasta, potato and garden salads, and breads was delectable and plentiful. Ordinarily Cole would have gone back for thirds and fourths. But he had filled only one plate and didn't finish all of that. He wasn't very hungry, he told Evan and Shelby, when they urged him to go back for more.

All right, admit it, Cole lectured himself, as he strolled alone across the back of the garden. Guests nearer the house continued to eat and chat and congratulate Shelby and Evan. *You may have come for the wedding, but the wedding's over and you're still here. You've seen and spoken to everyone you want to see and speak to. You've complimented the groom and kissed the bride and heard about their honeymoon trip to the Grand Canyon and promised to send them a gift in a couple of weeks. You could have been out of here an hour ago, but you're still partying long after you're partied out. And there's only one reason you're here: Beth Scibelli.*

Cole nodded, as if yielding to the ironclad argument of a prosecuting attorney who had him dead to rights. *Okay, so how long do I stay around pretending to enjoy myself, while secretly waiting for her to appear?* He glanced at his watch. It was almost 3. The wedding cake was yet to be cut and served, and Shelby had invited Cole to stay until they had opened their gifts—which was the point at which he had tried to cover his faux pas of forgetfulness by promising to send a gift soon.

Four o'clock—that's it, he decided in a snap. *Beth is probably halfway around the world working on her next bestseller right now. If she*

had planned to make it to the wedding or the reception, she would have
been here by now. But I'll give her another hour. Then I'm going home
to pack for Tahoe.

Having made his decision, Cole started up the gentle hill toward the
house to refill his punch glass and try to be more sociable. Even from
fifty yards away, Cole noticed the woman in dark glasses and a peasant
skirt stepping out of the house onto the patio. He hadn't seen her at the
ceremony, and from the nicely wrapped gift in her hands, it appeared
that she was just arriving.

At first glance Cole's pulse raced, but he relaxed just as quickly. She
was tall like Beth, but this woman's dark hair was cut short and she
glowed with a Caribbean tan that would take all summer to acquire on
Whidbey Island. And her outfit was too casual. Beth would have selected something a little more—

"Beth, you're here! How wonderful!" The greeting, which Cole
heard clearly from the lower slope of the lawn, was from Shelby who
was near the patio steps. The woman responded by taking off her dark
glasses and flashing a pleasant smile. It was the same beautiful face
Cole had visited in his memory every day since he had last seen it in
person. The woman on the patio—short hair, unusually deep tan, and
all—was Beth Scibelli.

Cole's first impulse was to race up the hill, burst through the crowd,
bound up the steps to the patio, and engulf Beth in a bear hug. But he
immediately snuffed out that impulse. He was aware that such a greeting probably wouldn't be appreciated by Beth. In fact, he suspected
that she might not want to see him at all, considering that she had
quietly but firmly closed all windows of communication between them
over the last year.

But he had to at least say hello and try to talk to her. He had to find
out what was going on in her life, if she was still as disinterested in
him as her aloofness indicated. If Beth ignored him or gave him only a
superficial response, he would regard it as an answer to his prayers
about her—not the answer he wanted, of course, but an answer none-
theless, and he would learn to live with it. So he made his way toward
the house casually in order to conceal his excitement.

As Beth came down the steps into the garden, she was met and
embraced by Shelby, Theresa, Dr. No, Mai, and the Welbourns. Then
Shelby introduced Beth to Evan and the other guests. When they realized her connection to the tragic events of Millennium's Eve, they
greeted her like a celebrity.

When Cole reached the outer perimeter of the circle, introductions
were still underway, so he waited with hands in pockets. One by one
the other guests peeled away from the circle to finish their meals and
resume their conversations. Finally, he was face to face with Beth.

Seeing him, she stuck out her right hand and smiled a phony smile that drained all the natural warmth from her face. Cole noted that Beth's arm was locked at the elbow, clearly warning him to keep his distance. "Hello, Reagan," she said, with a similar warning in her tone.

Cole shook her hand, which she then quickly retracted. Beth's cool, plastic cordiality reminded him of their first date eighteen months earlier. Cole had talked Beth into meeting him at quaint Olvera Street for dinner. He had issued the invitation on the heels of his apology for endangering her life in a wild car chase in her rented car, and for saying some thoughtless, angry words to her afterward. *Somehow I was able to thaw her icy heart then,* Cole thought. *Maybe it can happen again.*

Cole determined to be friendly without appearing patronizing. "Hello, Beth. It's good to see you again. I like your hair."

"Thank you."

Cole hoped for a return compliment—"You've lost a little weight, Reagan" or "I've always liked that gray suit on you"—but there was none. The onus was apparently on him to keep the conversation going, which again reminded him of their afternoon at Olvera Street.

"How's the writing business?"

"Good, good. I've been very busy."

It was a perfect time for Beth to ask, "And how about the detective business? Caught any criminals lately?" But she didn't.

Cole pressed on. "How are book sales going?"

"Good, good. The newer books are selling well; the others are tapering off."

"And your parents? Are they well?"

"Yes, fine. They're touring the UK with Simon Holloway's road show, even as we speak."

Cole continued to probe Beth with innocuous questions, to which she responded with terse answers of basic information and no apparent interest in Cole's life.

"Have you been playing any hoops lately?" Cole remembered fondly the games of one-on-one he and Beth had played in the driveway of her parents' home the week before Millennium's Eve. Those competitive encounters, showcasing the spunk and drive in Beth which so entranced Cole, had also served to bring them together romantically.

"Nope, too busy. I haven't touched a basketball all spring. I'm really out of shape."

"How about those Lakers, missing the playoffs again."

"L.A. teams are no match for my Sonics."

Cole was getting frustrated. The conversation was all one way. He could be talking to one of the bougainvillea in the yard and feel just as fulfilled. He wanted to shake her. *Beth, it's me, Reagan Cole. We were very close at one time. We shared something very special together. We have been in each other's arms. We have confessed deep feelings for one another, feelings we thought were going to last a lifetime. Why do you act as though we've never met?*

Getting a grip, he tried to encourage his own flagging hopes. *Hang in there, man. This is a spirited, headstrong woman, not a goo-goo-eyed bimbo who doesn't have an original opinion, let alone an independent life. Keep stoking the fire and the ice will eventually melt.*

The tension was temporarily interrupted when Theresa Bordeaux called everyone to the serving table to watch Evan and Shelby cut the three-layer wedding cake. The couple carved pieces of poppy-seed cake from the bottom layer, mugged comically for snapshots, then fed each other, complete with icing purposely smeared on the nose, to the delight of their guests.

"Would you like a piece of cake?" Cole asked Beth, as the caterers began transferring generous wedges to crystal dessert plates on the table.

"Actually, I haven't had lunch yet," Beth said. "I think I'll have a plate of salad first. Have you eaten?"

Cole warmed with hope. *She actually asked me a question. It's not much, but it's a start.* "I've had a little, but I'm still hungry," he said, deciding that he could eat another plate of food if it allowed him to keep talking to Beth. "The prime rib is very good. Do you mind if I join you?"

Beth studied him as if weighing the benefits of his invitation against the liabilities. She took so long Cole reckoned that the scales could tip either way.

Finally Beth answered without emotion, "No, I don't mind. Suit yourself."

It took several minutes for Beth and Cole to move through the buffet line. Several people Beth had met before conveyed their genuine pleasure at seeing her again. The Welbourns stopped Beth to compliment her on her hair and tan. Dr. No and Mai came along for another serving of Italian rotini chicken salad and asked about her career and her parents. A few other guests she had not met before today, preparing to leave, offered a proper, "It was nice to meet you, Beth. Hope to see you again."

Beth was more amiable in her responses to the people who stopped her at the buffet table than she had been with Cole, but only slightly. She didn't appear to be having a good time. Rather, she was curt, defensive, and standoffish—a real sourpuss—while trying to mask her attitude with that bogus toothpaste-commercial smile of hers. Cole wondered why she had come at all.

Cole found them a place to sit at a table where Jimmy and Evelyn Tuggle were seated with their adopted granddaughter, Malika. Jimmy, recently retired as the chairman of the history department at Baylor

University in Waco, Texas, had read Beth's books about Unity 2000. But the opportunity to sit with Beth and Cole to probe for additional details about the event was too great for a history buff to pass up. So he asked questions, and they responded as they ate.

"You said in your book that you learned a lot about prayer during your ordeal," Jimmy said. "Do you believe in prayer as much today as you did back then?"

Beth seemed momentarily stymied. With her fork she rolled a rotini pasta spiral through a puddle of Italian dressing on her plate, then stabbed it and brought it to her mouth. Finally she said, "Well . . . I . . . I think prayer means different things to different people. Back then it meant a lot to me. Perhaps it will again some day." Then turning to Cole, she quickly added, "I'm ready for a piece of cake now, Reagan. Shall we?"

Cole suddenly understood why Beth had been acting so indifferent and withdrawn since she arrived. *You no longer feel at home in this crowd, do you, Beth?* Cole asked silently, searching her expression for confirming evidence. *Eighteen months ago, these people heard you talk about how God helped you through a traumatic experience in response to your prayers. They read in your book how you cried out to God and asked Him to spare your parents and the Unity 2000 leaders from an assassination plot. Then, you plainly wrote that you knew God intervened, that you might have died without His help.*

These people still think you're close to God, but you've drifted far away, and you're self-conscious about it. They think you're still a praying dynamo, but you probably haven't talked to God in weeks—maybe months, and Jimmy's question embarrassed you. And that's why you're keeping your distance from me, isn't it? I represent what you turned your back on over a year ago. No wonder you're so hard to reach today. You must be very uncomfortable here.

Cole felt compassion for Beth's need to get away from Jimmy Tuggle and his probing questions. "Sure, I'm ready for cake," he said to Beth. To Jimmy and Evelyn he said, "It's been nice visiting with you. Please excuse us." Then he helped Beth from her chair and they headed for the wedding cake without a word.

Cole felt like he had solved only half the mystery. He understood why Beth was uncomfortable and defensive about being at the reception with people who were more "religious" than she was. What he didn't understand was why she came in the first place—and two hours late at that! *She could have shipped her gift or sent a videogram or called with her congratulations,* he thought. *She didn't have to come, and she acts like she didn't want to come, but she came. Something must have drawn her—or pushed her. Whatever it is, she traveled quite a distance to have such a bad time.*

Theresa Bordeaux made sure that Cole didn't have time to probe

Beth for answers. Just as he picked up a plate of cake and handed it to Beth, Theresa announced that Evan and Shelby were ready to open their gifts on the patio. About half the guests had already left, mostly Evan's friends and coworkers and a group of staffers from King's House who had come together in a couple of vans. So approximately thirty family members and close friends collected their chairs and trooped up the stairs to watch.

"Are you going to stay for this?" Cole asked, nodding toward the patio.

Beth shrugged apparent indifference. "I got here so late it would be rude of me to leave so early. Besides, the gift I brought cost me $135. I want the satisfaction of hearing the obligatory oohs and aahs. What about you?"

"I forgot to bring a gift," Cole answered, with a mild look of chagrin. "But I would enjoy talking with you some more." He hoped he wasn't being too forward, but Beth was in a funk and he wanted to know why.

"I'll tell you what," Beth said. "You give me $65 and I'll let you sign your name on my card. We can ooh and aah together when they open the gift." Then she smiled—not the phony smile she had been wearing all afternoon; the real one. It wasn't a big smile, but it was promising.

In a moment it all came together for Cole again: the dark eyes and hair, the tall, shapely figure, the spunk and spirit, and that smile. *Lord, I love this woman,* he prayed silently. *If You can use me to help her, I'm willing.*

"Buy into your gift? You've got a deal," Cole said enthusiastically. Then he picked up two chairs and headed for the steps with Beth and two plates of cake in his wake. He hoped this day would never end.

Nolan Jakes and Margo Sharpe learned a lot about Dr. Evan Rider by moving the Jaguar closer to the house at the end of Foster Road. An early departing guest left a convenient parking space on the curb only a half block from the front door. Subsequent guests leaving the house thought nothing unusual about the man and woman sitting in the expensive silver sedan with the front windows down, enjoying the late afternoon sunshine. As people lingered in the street near the Jaguar discussing the wedding and the happy couple, Jakes and Margo feigned disinterest while listening intently.

"Are Evan and Shelby taking a honeymoon?"

"Yes, they're going to the Grand Canyon."

"They don't seem concerned about getting people out of the house so they can catch their flight."

"No, they're spending the night here and leaving in the morning."

"That's smart. When we got married we flew half the night getting to Maui and were almost too pooped to enjoy our first night together."

"Yeah, and I think it's kind of special that they're spending their first night in their own home."

"And by the way, they aren't flying to Arizona; they're driving."

"Driving? Why are they driving? They can afford to go first class all the way."

"They bought an RV."

"You're kidding!"

"No, they got a used one, at least a thirty-footer. Evan refurbished it, put in new floors, got it all tuned up; it's like new. They want to get into camping—well, RV camping at least. They're taking it on the honeymoon, then they plan to go camping three or four times a year with Malika, you know, a couple of long weekends, summer vacation."

"Well, I never figured Shelby to be the outdoor type, but I'm happy for them. And what a great life for little Malika."

"By the way, who's taking care of her while Evan and Shelby are gone?"

"I heard that she's spending the night with Shelby's parents at the Hilton. Then they're taking her to Magic Mountain tomorrow."

"Right. And the Tuggles leave for home Monday after they drive Malika to King's House in L.A. She will stay with one of the staff families for the two weeks Evan and Shelby are gone."

"Did you hear Shelby today? She said she couldn't leave in the morning without saying good-bye to Malika. So while Evan gets the RV ready, she's going over to the Hilton for a final kiss and a hug. If it were me, I'd say good-bye tonight and let it go at that."

"That's Shelby for you, the doting mother!"

"So where's the RV? It's not in the driveway or on the street."

"It's too big to park up here. I think Evan has it stored somewhere down the hill—an RV lot or self-storage place."

"Well, I hope they have a great time. They seem perfectly matched for each other. Shelby deserves a little happiness after all she's been through."

"Amen!"

Jakes couldn't believe his good fortune. Strangers standing in the street talking about the happy couple and their dream honeymoon had become his unsuspecting accomplices. It was going to be easier getting out of Southern California than he thought. The plan was obvious to him.

"This is what we'll do," he said to Margo, as another group of guests moved down the street to their cars. "We'll wait around until everybody leaves and Rider and his new bride are alone. Then we'll go to the door, tell them what they're going to do for us, and leave for Canada tonight. A rich doctor like Evan must have a Beamer or a Mercedes locked up in that garage of his. We can get out of town fast and in style. If we leave by 9 or 10 tonight, we should hit Oregon by midmorning, reach Washington around 3, and cross into Canada sometime tomorrow evening."

"I see a couple of problems with leaving tonight, Nolan," Margo said. Her tone was more apologetic than judgmental. But Jakes felt affronted by the comment, and he immediately second-guessed his decision to take someone with him, even someone as warm and desirable as Margo.

"What's the matter?" he said with a slightly defensive and sarcastic inflection to his voice, "Are you feeling sorry for the happy couple because they won't get to enjoy their wedding night alone?"

"Nolan, I'm just trying to help," Margo said, sounding hurt by his subtle but snide rebuff. "I thought we were in this together. Do you want me to keep quiet when I have an idea that might help us?"

Jakes didn't see anything wrong with his idea, but he also knew that Margo was a pretty good thinker. As much as he wanted to assert himself, he decided to eat crow. "Okay, I'm sorry. What's the problem?"

Margo accepted his apology and continued. "We have to take Evan's wife with us, don't we?"

"Of course. If we take Evan and leave Shelby, she'll blow the whistle on us."

"Well, if we go tonight, what happens when she doesn't show up at the Hilton to say good-bye to the little girl in the morning? Won't the parents get suspicious and report the missing couple and their car?"

Margo *had* spotted a flaw, and Jakes didn't have an answer. Resisting the urge to respond defensively, he said, "What do you suggest?"

"I think we should come back early tomorrow morning and wait until Shelby leaves to visit the little girl. Then we follow Evan to the RV and tell him what he has to do. When Shelby comes back, we take off in the RV with both of them. But instead of heading east to Arizona, we tell them to turn north."

Jakes was suddenly angry. "Take an RV to Canada? Are you crazy? Those things are too easy to spot on the highway. Besides, you can't go faster than 55 pulling a car carrier. We might as well hijack a blimp."

"Nolan, listen," Margo insisted. "We can hide in an RV. We can control Evan Rider from the inside, and nobody will see us from the outside. We stop only for gas. And when Rider is outside at the pump, we keep the gun on his wife so he won't try anything stupid. In the RV we'll be invisible until we step out on the other side of the border."

"I'd feel a lot better in a car," Jakes argued weakly, realizing that Margo had a good point. "We can make better time."

Margo touched Jakes' leg with her hand and caressed it softly, trying to assure him that she was on his side as she drove her point home. "But with every car we pass, Nolan, you'll be ducking out of sight. Tell me *that* won't look suspicious on I-5. The idea is to get to Canada without being seen, not to break a speed record on the way."

Jakes laid his hand on hers and reluctantly admitted to himself that Margo's brain was his best asset. He hated being out-strategized by a woman, especially a woman he was attracted to. But it was starkly obvious to him that he would never have made it this far without Margo's help. He still couldn't fathom her devotion to him or figure her decision to leave her life behind and run to Canada with him. But he was sobered to think that he might not make it without her. Margo was indeed his good luck charm, an angel sent to guide him safely to the promised land.

After several moments, he squeezed her hand and said, "Yeah, I guess you're right. The RV may be our best bet. Let's get out of here and find a place to spend the night. My back is killing me. I need to soak in the tub again. It feels like there's still some glass back there."

Margo smiled and nodded. Then she started the Jaguar, turned it around, and headed down the winding street toward downtown Ventura.

Twenty-three

Shelby Rider peeled silver wrapping paper off another boxed gift, a cut crystal vase, which Evan's office manager, receptionist, and medical records clerk had given jointly. "Say, look at this!" Evan exclaimed, holding up the vase until it sparkled in the late afternoon sun. "It's the piece I've been admiring at Excelsior's for months. I didn't think Maggie, Arlene, and Kim were listening to my hints." Evan's three co-workers, sitting near the sliding glass door, beamed their pleasure at putting one over on their boss. "Thank you, ladies," Evan said. Shelby echoed his appreciation.

Beth watched the festivities from her chair at the back of the small crowd, wishing she had never come to Ventura. The joy and camaraderie of the event were like salt searing her already raw emotions. Evan and Shelby's happiness taunted Beth's sudden, bitter breakup with Colin Wendt. And the sight of Dr. No and Mai caused her to recoil in embarrassment, although she felt she had adequately disguised her feelings. The kind, wise couple had befriended her so warmly and influenced her so deeply with their faith during the days before and after Millennium's Eve. They certainly had no clue how uncomfortable she felt in their presence about her very worldly pursuits of late.

Then there was Reagan Cole, who sat beside her in silence, enjoying the laughter and banter of the gift opening. Beth felt like an idiot about the way she had greeted him. Reagan had been cordial—much more so than she deserved, after having dumped him a year ago without so much as, "It's been nice, but you're getting a little too religious for my taste, so I'm out of here."

The tough, I-don't-need-you-or-anybody-else facade Beth had foisted on him when they shook hands earlier was a defense mechanism against his forgiving welcome, any freshman psychology student could have seen it. She wouldn't have blamed him for ignoring her completely or verbally blistering her for lacking the class to say a decent good-bye last year. What she *wasn't* ready for was Cole's genuinely pleasant hello that overlooked the hurt her cold shoulder must have caused him. It was a kindness Beth desperately craved. But instead of accepting it, she had come on like iceberg to the only man she had ever dated who would treat her so forgivingly. Beth could kick herself for responding in such a predictably juvenile manner.

On the bright side, Cole was still seated beside her as if she were the belle of the ball. Her clumsy, scrambling efforts at conciliation—allowing Cole to eat with her and inviting him to buy into her gift—seemed to have worked. Beth couldn't deny feeling pangs of her old attraction to him. But she wasn't ready to trust her stressed-out emotions to pursue a rebound relationship with him. *In reality,* she thought, *"St. Reagan of Los Angeles," the handsome Christian police sergeant, may no longer desire a relationship with a loose-living heathen journalist from Whidbey Island. I should thank God for small favors. He seems more interested in being my friend than in biting my head off or preaching a hellfire and damnation sermon to me. And I really need a friend right now.*

"Did you come down just for the wedding?" Cole asked Beth quietly, as they continued to watch the bride and groom open gifts.

Beth sensed her defenses stiffen to prevent Cole from knowing the truth about her recent heartbreak. She wanted to be honest, but she wasn't sure how vulnerable she could afford to be, even with a seemingly guileless friend.

"Actually, I've been on the road a couple of weeks," she answered, purposely keeping the hard edge off her voice. "I'm on my way home."

"On the road, eh? Do you have a new writing project?"

"Yes . . . well . . . I *had* a new writing project."

"Had?"

Beth nodded. "The publisher and I didn't exactly see eye to eye."

"And he fired you?"

"No," Beth corrected with a hint of triumph. "I walked out on the jerk . . . er . . . I mean, I tore up my contract, well, I *will* tear up my contract when I get home."

"Mm," Cole answered supportively. They were both silent for a couple of minutes as if more interested in the proceedings in the center of the circle.

Then, still staring straight ahead, Cole asked, "Were you very . . . close . . . to your publisher?"

Beth felt a flush of warmth color her cheeks. *Geez!* she thought. *How does he know? No wonder he's in the detective division now. He has that uncanny sixth sense.*

Beth decided to be as oblique in her answer as Reagan had been in his question. "Closer than I should have been, as it turns out," she said, refusing to look at him.

Cole hummed noncommittally again.

After several more minutes of silence, Cole turned to Beth and said, "Caribbean, right?"

She snapped her head toward him as if he had just uttered her deepest secrets for the world to hear. "What?"

"The Caribbean. That's where you've been, where you got your tan. And that's probably where you and your publisher came to a disagreement, right?"

Beth's mouth dropped open in surprise, but she caught herself and closed it quickly. She would have felt invaded if she hadn't been so curious. "How do you know I've been in the Caribbean?" she answered, instantly wishing she could take back the words which clearly confirmed his theory.

"First, the shade of your tan has been scientifically proven to come only from that part of the world." He touched the top of her arm where the tan was dark and rich.

Beth was ready to laugh in his face for pulling her leg, but his stone-serious expression caused her to wonder. For all she knew, such technology had been perfected, and a detective would know that stuff.

"Second, there is a certain scent to Caribbean breezes that remains in the pores after prolonged exposure. It's a beautiful fragrance, and you have been emanating it since you arrived." Cole leaned slightly toward Beth, closed his eyes, and sniffed. "I'd say you were in the Caribbean, somewhere around the island of Antigua, as late as yesterday."

Beth held her breath with surprise. She felt like she was back at the Magic Castle in L.A., a club where entertainment is provided by up and coming magicians in the area. She and her friends at USC loved to visit the Castle during her college days. Beth had prided herself on being able to figure out how most of the illusions were accomplished— mirrors, fake bottoms, trap doors in the floor, contortionist assistants, etc. But occasionally an illusionist would perform a stunt so mystifying that Beth could find no logical explanation for it. At those times she was tempted to believe that the illusionist was a bona fide magician exercising supernatural powers. For a fleeting moment she had the same suspicion about Reagan Cole because of his incredible revelation.

Beth studied Cole's face. It was boyishly innocent with the same large blue eyes which had caught her attention on Christmas Eve 1999. But the schoolboy qualities of his face were offset by telltale marks of maturity: a thin, sandy wave of hair, and judging by the hairline, the tide was clearly ebbing out; thick brown brows; slight creases across the forehead and at the corners of the eyes; tight lips and a distinctly masculine set of the jaw that dared anyone to call him a liar.

Finally she said, "Reagan, you've got to be jiving me. There's no way you could know that I—"

"Third," Cole interrupted, as the overture of a smile teased the corners of his mouth, "the boarding passes sticking out of your purse reveal your complete itinerary."

Beth grabbed the straw purse at her side as if a purse snatcher was reaching for it. There in the side pocket where she had stuffed and forgotten them were three computer-generated boarding passes with cities of origin, destinations, and travel dates tattling on Beth's trip from Antigua to Miami to Dallas to Los Angeles.

A "gotcha" grin consumed Cole's face, igniting an "I've been had" grin on Beth's. "Caribbean breezes in the pores. I can't believe it," she said, starting to giggle. Then she covered her mouth as the giggle escalated to a laugh. Cole laughed too. The two of them huddled behind the other guests muffling belly laughs for a full minute. Beth couldn't remember the last time she'd laughed till she cried. She thought it might have been a time when she was with Reagan Cole. He seemed to be able to touch her emotions like no other man she knew.

The gift-opening festivities continued until nearly 6 P.M. By that time the caterers had completed their cleanup and departed. The remaining guests rose, said their final good-byes, thank you's, and God bless you's, and headed for the door. Though no one verbalized it, everyone knew it was time to leave the wedding couple alone to begin their honeymoon.

Beth was humbled at the affection showered on her in the embraces and good wishes of Shelby and Evan, the Ngos, the Welbourns, and the Tuggles. They had treated her as a cherished friend instead of the unworthy wayward child she felt like in their presence. No one preached at her, and the few who said they were praying for her did so in a completely uncondemning manner, as if offering her a valuable gift.

Seeing Reagan Cole again had been more rewarding than Beth had anticipated. Embers of their romantic relationship, seemingly dead after a year of neglect on her part, had flickered briefly in the three hours they had spent together. They had been with a small crowd of people all afternoon, but for most of that time Beth felt she had been alone with the man whose disarming kindness and humor had drawn her from the parched desert of her recent despondency into a lush oasis.

The fit of laughter over Cole's uncanny "detective work" about her Caribbean visit had helped Beth recover from the defensive snit which had colored her first words with him. They had continued to talk quietly as more gifts were opened and passed around the circle of guests. In response to her questions, Cole had explained his new role in the LAPD detective bureau monitoring the activities of questionable characters for the FBI. And he had confessed that it wasn't as exciting as he had hoped, prompting him to consider seeking a transfer.

After some hesitation, Beth had queried Cole's present involvement with King's House, reasonably sure that his response wouldn't digress into a strong-arm attempt to get her "saved." He did not disappoint her. He simply reported that he spent one or two days a week—depending on his schedule—working with Bill Fawcett in the prisoner rehabilitation program, and that he participated in a very rewarding Bible study group each week led by Dr. No. In no way did Cole turn "holy joe" on Beth or make her feel like a second-class citizen because she didn't share his interest in spiritual things.

Beth and Cole said good-bye to Evan and Shelby and slipped out of the house, leaving only the Tuggles, little Malika, Theresa, and the Welbourns to finish moving all the gifts inside the house before they also departed. Beth wasn't ready for her visit with Cole to end. When he offered her a ride to the rented black Barego on his motorcycle, she eagerly accepted. He slipped into his electric-blue flight suit but insisted that she wear his helmet for the short ride. She straddled the Kawasaki behind him as modestly as possible, tucking the skirt under her legs.

Instead of stopping at Beth's car, Cole continued down Foster Road to a side street heading up the hill. Beth didn't complain. She clung to Cole tightly, relishing his strength and savoring memories of rides they had taken together when their fascination with each other was new.

The motorcycle wound through the maze of beautiful old homes until they reached a dead end. Undaunted, Cole steered around the barricade and continued up a footpath in the grass that snaked to the top of the hill. Turning the bike around toward the shore, Cole shut off the engine. Beth took off the helmet, and the two of them leaned against the bike side by side and drank in the beauty in silence for several moments.

The low-hanging sun in the northwest unfurled a gleaming golden carpet across the sea from the horizon to the Southern California shore. The Channel Islands looked like nondescript toys strewn across the carpet by a child who had toddled off around Point Conception for an afternoon nap. The breeze sweeping up the hill from the water was cool and invigorating, prompting Beth to wish Cole would wrap his arm around her. Instead he offered her the windbreaker he had pulled from the motorcycle's storage compartment under the seat. She accepted, and he draped it over her shoulders.

"I suppose you'll be heading home soon," Cole said, still appreciating the sparkling panorama before them.

"I should leave tomorrow," Beth said. "As of two days ago, I'm unemployed. I need to make some contacts and get to work on something else, or I'll soon be standing in the soup line on Whidbey Island." It wasn't really true; Beth had enough money tucked away from royalty checks to live comfortably for several months without working. But she didn't want to seem *too* eager to hang around L.A. and Reagan Cole.

"I'm leaving tomorrow too," Cole informed.

"For where?" Beth asked, successfully hiding her disappointment.

"Tahoe. I'm riding the bike up to see Mom."

"A little vacation for the bored detective?"

"Right, a week. I'll be back next Sunday."

A gust of wind rushed up the hill and swirled around the motorcycle, teasing the ankle-high grass into a rustling wave and pulling the hair back from the two faces gazing out at the sea.

After a moment of silence, Cole said, "Would you consider taking a later flight tomorrow so you could eat lunch with me at Quintero's on Olvera Street—just for old time's sake?"

It was the kind of invitation Beth had been hoping for. Still staggering at the emotional bludgeoning she had endured from Colin Wendt, she wasn't quite ready to walk away from Cole's steady warmth and uncomplicated acceptance. She didn't want to sleep with him, something they would have done shortly after Millennium's Eve, but never did because of Reagan Cole's sudden moral fortitude. Nor was she ready to resume a long-distance, Seattle-to-L.A. relationship with a man whose criteria for a female partner was now shaped by his religious convictions. But lunch at Quintero's seemed a harmless, refreshing extension of the healthy safety she felt right now just being with him.

The memory of their first meal together at Quintero's wafted pleasantly through Beth's mind like the gentle breeze caressing her face. It had been on Christmas Day 1999, following a mariachi Mass at the Old Plaza Church across from historic Olvera Street in downtown Los Angeles. The restaurant was closed for the holiday, but the family of Luis and Raphaela Quintero was there in force to warmly welcome their friend Reagan Cole and his guest. It had been one of the most enjoyable Christmases Beth could remember, especially because she had shared it with Reagan Cole.

"Won't that give you a late start for Tahoe?" Beth probed. She had already decided to accept his invitation, but couldn't resist the temptation to tantalize him.

"The saddlebags will be packed," he said. "I'll leave right after lunch and be there before midnight."

Beth lingered a little longer in feigned indecision. "I suppose I could take the 4 o'clock nonstop to SeaTac. Okay, Quintero's for lunch. Meet you there at noon?"

"Eleven-thirty," Cole said, as he mounted the bike and fired up the engine. Beth pulled on the helmet and straddled the backseat, wrapping her arms around Cole's waist. He maneuvered the Kawasaki down the footpath to the street and had Beth back to her car in four minutes.

Beth dismounted and returned Cole's helmet and jacket. "It was really good to see you again, Reagan," she said. "Thank you for being so . . . kind." It was the closest she could come to saying, *"After the way I went AWOL on you last year, you had every right to tell me to take a flying leap today. Thanks for not doing so."*

"I enjoyed it too, Beth. I'll see you tomorrow."

Cole followed Beth on the Ventura Freeway all the way to the San Fernando Valley where she exited at Winnetka Avenue for the brief drive to her parents' home. She had glanced at him in the rearview mirror often.

Twenty-four

Had it been anyone but Robert Camden Rhodes, Libby might have cancelled the dinner date. She had felt depressed and physically sick all day after her blowup with Brett. By the time Brett and Andie stormed out of the house, the morning fog had lifted from Puget Sound, unveiling a balmy, sun-soaked afternoon. But instead of enjoying the day and busying herself with a short list of errands around town, Libby had stayed indoors brooding over the volatile confrontation, wondering how she could have done better.

Her date with Robert had been on the calendar for two weeks, and she didn't want to break it. He was the only man she was currently seeing who was not involved in higher education. Dating available men in the administrative hierarchy at the University of Washington and other institutions in the Seattle area was usually unfulfilling. Conversations over a candlelight dinner inevitably digressed to shoptalk, rekindling the very stress Libby accepted dates to get away from.

Furthermore, dating administrators and professors presented other problems. Few of them were her peers in education or administration, and some of them were her direct subordinates. She had to be choosy about the men she fraternized with. After all, she was only a few years from stepping into the president's office at UW or another PAC-10 university—Arizona State, perhaps, or the University of Oregon. Getting too chummy with the wrong administrator could be almost as bad as getting involved with a person as common as Reginald Burris, the considerate but plebeian UWPD officer.

But Robert Camden Rhodes, a handsome man of forty-eight with skin the color of dark caramel and a smile as extravagant as his three classic sports cars, was different. He was neither a threat nor an embarrassment to Libby. Robert wasn't in education; he was a successful stockbroker. Furthermore, as a University of Washington alumnus with a Stanford MBA summa cum laude, Robert was Libby's intellectual equal. They rarely talked about their careers. Instead they spent evenings over dinner at their favorite waterfront restaurant discussing art, literature, politics, and interior decorating, subjects in which both shone, but neither outshone the other.

Robert was special to Libby in another way. Matrimony and/or its intimate pleasures was a subtle agenda point for her other gentlemen friends—bachelors, divorcés, or widowers in their forties and fifties yearning to enjoy conjugal bliss at the height of otherwise successful lives. Categorically disqualifying anyone in education as a potential mate, Libby had come to tolerate their quietly voiced hopes for greater intimacy as the price she had to pay to enjoy a man's company once in a while.

But Robert seemed content to offer a warm, virtually platonic friendship free of innuendos and expectations. Their dinner dates were always Dutch treat and ended with nothing more romantic than a cordial hug and a kiss on the cheek. Libby thought she might want more from Robert some day, and she suspected that he felt the same way. But for the time being, she felt safe and comfortable with Robert as a good friend.

One infrequently navigated passage remained a challenge in Libby's relationship with Robert, a topic of vulnerability and openness yet to be broached: their children. Libby's friendship with Robert began shortly after his wife died suddenly of an aneurysm in 1999, leaving him with four children, ages nineteen to twenty-six. Libby had attended a six-week financial planning seminar sponsored by his firm, and he was the instructor. They liked each other immediately.

During their first date, dinner at the Top o' the Pier after the fourth session of the seminar, the couple exchanged basic information about their families: he, widowed recently with four children; she, never-married with one son. But Robert offered little more about his kids than their names and ages. Libby would have liked to hear more, but being sensitive to his grief she decided not to pry.

Nor did Robert seem very interested in Libby's son. He never asked about Brett's progress in school, his career path, his outside interests, or Libby's relationship with him. Indeed, once Robert discovered that

Libby shared his intense interest in modern art and the literature of the South and his cynicism toward a government that created arbitrary absolutes and flaunted an imperial judiciary, he seemed disinterested in other topics. Libby figured that Robert had been as reticent to bring up the touchy topic of her illegitimate son over the two years of their friendship as she was to ask him about parenting four young adults alone.

But this would change today, Libby had decided. After her painful run-in with Brett, she was in no mood to discuss Baldwin or Faulkner or the Supreme Court's latest attempt to play God. Tonight she needed advice, counsel, and comfort—someone to tell her she wasn't unfair or unfeeling in her decision to delay Brett's desired reunion with his biological father. She had to know if Robert cared enough to be interested in her pain. If he was truly her friend, he would be at least as concerned about her trials with Brett as rough-cut Reginald Burris had shown himself to be.

Libby met Robert at the Top o' the Pier on the waterfront at 7:00 as usual. She wore a belted black print silk dress with a high collar and full skirt. Her hair was pulled back and accentuated by a black bow. Her makeup was perfect, highlighting her natural beauty, while making the slightly puffy skin around her eyes seem to disappear.

Robert, broad-shouldered and taller than Libby by two inches, always wore a suit when meeting Libby for dinner. Tonight it was a stylish wheat-colored silk with an off-white shirt and an expensive tie showing bold brush strokes of mottled browns and greens with highlights of rose. Robert's hair was naturally kinky and cut short with barely a whisper of gray at the temples to interrupt the jet-black sheen.

Elias had their table prepared for them at the window overlooking Elliott Bay. He always placed them where they would be served by their favorite waitress, Whitney, a student at Seattle Pacific University. Gulls cavorted in the breeze outside for their entertainment or posed on wooden piles thrusting up from the water. A Washington state ferry, like a huge, green and white, water-walking tortoise, inched slowly but surely out of the nearby dock, toting passengers and vehicles to Bainbridge Island and Bremerton across the Sound. Another ferry arriving from Victoria, B.C. to the north waited for an open berth.

After enjoying aperitifs, Libby ordered the Chinook salmon stuffed with crab and shrimp, while Robert opted for his favorite dish on the menu: blackened Alaskan halibut with Cajun-spiced pasta and vegetables. After Whitney had delivered Caesar salads to their table, complete with extra lemon wedges, Libby turned the conversation from the commercial art exhibit showing at a local gallery to Robert and his children. She hoped to use the conversation as a springboard for telling him about Brett and her concerns for him.

"How are your children doing, Robert?"

"My kids?" he responded, as if the question was outside the circle of his interest and expertise. "Fine, I guess. Why do you ask?"

"You haven't told me much about them. I'm just interested in knowing where they are and what they're doing." Then before Robert could respond, she added, "If it's difficult for you to talk about the children with your wife gone, I certainly don't mean to pry."

Robert shook his head with certainty as he buttered a warm kaiser roll. "No, I'm fine about Alma, and the children are too. I guess I didn't expect that my family was a topic of interest to you."

"We've become good friends, Robert, haven't we?" Libby asked.

Robert gave her a look of genuine contentment, "Yes, Libby, very good friends I'd say. You're a stimulating conversationalist. I'm quite fond of you."

Libby smiled her agreement. "As your friend, Robert, I'm interested in everything that involves you, including your children. Tell me about them."

Robert's eyebrows raised in mild incredulity as he squeezed another lemon wedge around his table knife, allowing the juice to trickle off the tip of the blade onto his salad. Libby was disappointed that he seemed so disinterested in the topic.

"Well," he began finally, "there's not much to tell. All four of them are on their own. Andrea is at Stanford finishing her MBA. Derrick still has a year of eligibility on his baseball scholarship at Pepperdine. He's a pitcher and a third baseman. Adam is taking a year off from forestry school at Oregon State to tour Europe with his girlfriend. And Damone is having too much fun playing drums in a rock band to be bothered with school." Having finished the "chore" of reporting on his kids, Robert set about to eat his salad.

Dissatisfied with the lack of depth in his report, Libby probed further. "What's your daughter going to do with her MBA?"

"She's not sure," he said, waving with his fork as if Andrea's indecision was a bother to him. "I've offered her a position in the office with a fast track into management, but she says she wants to do something more 'humanitarian,' like work on the business end of a world hunger relief organization. I told her, 'Andrea, why did I spend over a hundred grand to get you through Stanford when all you need to organize a hunger relief drive is couple of classes in marketing?' She said, 'Dad, the hungry of the world deserve as much expertise applied to the meeting of their needs as do the affluent. Your money has not been wasted. In fact, I'll probably accomplish more with my education than somebody who is in this only to make the rich richer at the expense of the poor.' "

Libby read in Robert's tone a definite but subtle discomfort talking about Andrea. The discomfort pervaded his responses to Libby's queries regarding his sons. Robert's answers were brief; he seemed clearly out of his element, like a tennis pro pressed to explain the finer points of a golf swing. He did his best to cover his uneasiness, but he was far less self-assured in his demeanor than Libby had ever seen him. Here was a man who managed a $14 million business, but was at loose ends about how to relate to his four adult children. *No wonder he hasn't said much about them before*, she thought. *He is struggling with this stage of parenting, perhaps because the backbone of the family, the late Alma Rhodes, is gone.*

"Will you see your children much this summer?" Libby continued, trying to show genuine interest and put Robert at ease.

"No," he answered without explanation.

When their entrees arrived, Robert valiantly attempted to change the subject. He had been reading about Cajun cuisine recently, he said, and the sight and aroma of his meal brought an article to mind. Libby allowed him to regale her with a formula for Cajun spices before she seized the reins of the conversation again and pressed on toward the goal of soliciting Robert's opinion about Brett.

"I had a rather upsetting experience with Brett last night and this morning. May I tell you about it?"

"Brett?" Robert said blankly, looking up from his plate.

"My son, Brett. He's twenty, attends Washington State . . . " Libby allowed her sentence to trail off hoping Robert would remember that she had told him about Brett before.

"Oh, yes, Brett," Robert acknowledged. "I hope to meet the young man some day." Then he returned to slicing the entire serving of Halibut into bite-sized chunks before tasting it, a quirk Libby had noticed since their first date.

"Brett and I had a rather heated confrontation today about a stunt he pulled last night. It opened up some old wounds between us. You've raised four children, so I thought that perhaps you might be able to give me a pointer or two on handling this situation."

Libby knew she wasn't being completely truthful about her request. She would welcome Robert's suggestions to be sure. However, from his clipped and seemingly unfeeling comments about *his* children, she had already begun to doubt whether he had anything of valid worth to offer her. What she really wanted was a sounding board, someone to hear her out without judgment or criticism. She could also use Robert's sympathy and emotional support, though she was less hopeful of realizing that bonus from someone who didn't like talking about his children.

"I'm no child psychologist," Robert said, flashing his hands in a sign of innocence and surrender. "And I can't say that I was very successful at keeping my own kids on the straight and narrow. Alma took care of things at home for me."

Libby translated his response to mean, *"I respectfully decline the opportunity to give you pointers on the grounds of ignorance and lack of interest. Now can we get back to the topics I want to discuss?"*

Undaunted, she pressed on. "May I at least tell you about what happened between us?"

Robert finally picked up on the petition for understanding flickering from his friend like a faint, distant SOS signal in a dark storm. Studying her with a what-am-I-getting-myself-into gaze, he said, "Okay, sure, Libby. What happened?"

In between small bites of salmon and sautéed vegetables and sips of dry Riesling, Libby recounted the story of Brett and Andie breaking into her office and getting caught by the University police. She purposely paused every few sentences to allow Robert an entry point for asking clarifying questions or expressing his sympathy for how she must have felt. But he simply listened and ate, saying nothing.

Libby continued by describing the scene in the kitchen when Brett bitterly threw her chastisement back in her face and smashed the platter of cookies against the wall. She was able to keep her emotions in check through the account by saving the delicate point of Brett's anger until last.

"I discovered that the bottom-line issue for Brett in this conflict is his father," she began. "I told you that Brett was born out of wedlock, didn't I?"

Robert had a faraway look in his eye, signaling to Libby that he really didn't remember. "Yes, I suppose you did," he said vaguely.

"Brett doesn't know who his father is; I have kept that information from him for his own good. But he insists that by not telling him about his father I have violated his sense of respect, so I have no right to expect him to respect me."

"Why haven't you told Brett who his father is?" Robert asked, sparking hope in Libby that the man was interested.

Libby began with all the noble, good-sounding reasons. "I have kept the man's identity a secret because, well, he was only a passing interest to me at the time. And as far as Brett is concerned, his father was nothing more than a one-time sperm donor. Besides, I never told the man that I was pregnant; he probably has no idea that he has a twenty-year-old son. I don't know where he lives; but if Brett tracked him down and barged into his life now, I'm afraid they would both be terribly shocked and disappointed—not to mention the man's family, if he has one. Brett is too immature for that now. Maybe in a few years . . ."

Robert eyed her perceptively. "And Brett making an issue over his father at this point in your career could be rather disappointing to you also, right?"

Libby nodded timidly. "That's not my sole motivation for keeping quiet, at least I hope it's not. But the complications to my life and career do add weight to my decision to leave him in the dark for a while."

"So leave him in the dark," Robert announced decisively. "You're the parent, he's the child. Tell him the way it's going to be, and get on with your career."

Libby feared that Robert was tiring of the discussion and had offered his curt, quick-fix advice in order to move on to something else. She wasn't ready to move on. "But I don't want to lose Brett over this," she argued as much with herself as with Robert. "The way he reacted this morning and stormed out of the house . . . I'm afraid he may write me off completely. That's a high price to pay for a career."

"He's a man. He'll get over it and come running home to Mama," Robert assured her a little too confidently to be convincing. "Hold your position and leave him alone. When he's ready to see things your way, he'll be back."

Libby was silent for a few moments. When Robert spoke again, she expected him to change the subject to something neutral and less threatening to both of them. But he didn't. "You said that both Brett and his father might be shocked and disappointed when they meet. I can understand the father's shock learning that he has a twenty-year-old child he never knew about. But why would Brett be so affected when he meets his father for the first time? Is his old man some kind of loser?"

Libby laid down her fork and sat back in her chair. She stared out at the bay without seeing it, imagining the father-son reunion that would surely take place in the next few years. "I doubt it," she said, still gazing across the water toward Bainbridge Island. "Knowing him as I did, I'm sure Brett's father has done very well for himself. In fact, Brett might find him to be more successful in his chosen field than I have been in mine."

"So why are you afraid Brett will be disappointed?" Robert pressed.

Libby lapsed into momentary silence again. She appreciated Robert's questions because they helped her weigh her opinions and alternatives. But she still couldn't tell if his interest was as much genuine concern as it was mere curiosity. She had told Robert more about her struggle with Brett than anyone else she knew, and he had modeled only a tentative interest, not the empathy she had hoped for. Perhaps one more key fact would pull him over the line to her side.

Finally she said, "I don't know where the man is or what he's doing. He may have doubled his weight by now and gone bald and toothless. But I do know one thing about him that Brett may have difficulty hearing, something that I know hasn't changed."

Robert leaned in with interest. Libby continued, "All these years Brett has been referring to his father as the 'black phantom,' a black man who came and went before he was born. I have never refuted him on that point, but some day I will have to, because Brett's father is white."

Twenty-five

The man was so average-looking that he was often overlooked in a crowd. He was in his mid-thirties, although a stranger might guess his age to be anywhere from twenty-five to forty. He was a solid medium: medium height, medium build, medium-brown eyes, and medium-brown hair which was regularly cut in a very ordinary style. He had a pleasant face, yet it lacked distinctly memorable features; people rarely mistook him for a long-lost friend and never for a movie star. He had long realized his uncertain appearance to be a great benefit to his work.

The man was full-blooded Hispanic—Peruvian, to be exact. But his facial features and skin color caused most whites to accept him as one of their own, especially when they heard him speaking in his accentless and comfortably colloquial brand of English. Yet when he broke into his native language, he was recognized as thoroughly Hispanic.

Though he could afford to patronize the most exclusive men's shops, the man wore clothing from J.C. Penney and Montgomery Ward—nothing too fancy, nothing too plain, mere social camouflage to aid him in being eminently forgettable wherever he went.

Despite the man's carefully choreographed commonness, he *could* make an impression one-on-one when it served his purposes to do so—specifically when he wanted to finagle a favor, coax a secret into the open, gain access to privileged information, or attract a woman. The traits which made him appear so winsome and trustworthy were a smooth, articulate tongue, a penetrating gaze, a disarming smile, and an engaging charm which—when fully activated by voice, eyes, and smile—could melt cold steel.

The man had no home, preferring to move around the country by air or rental car, and stay in comfortable, moderately priced hotels while waiting to be contacted by his clients. What little personal property he possessed, including the tools of his trade, fit compactly into one plastic carryon suit bag. Whenever he needed something more, he purchased it, used it, and discarded it before moving on to his next stop.

The man carried driver's licenses, ATM cards, and credit cards under three identities which matched his plain vanilla appearance: William Martin, Thomas Johnson, and Alberto Rodriguez. His credit cards were used only for identification and deposits, as when renting a car or checking into a hotel. Everything was eventually paid off in cash withdrawn from a variety of secure, electronically accessible accounts. His professionally doctored black-market ID packages were recycled with every move, at great personal expense. It was important to his success not to be the same person for more than a few weeks at a time.

Rennie Barbosa was not his real name but his professional name. His father, who went by the name of Oscar Ortiz, had told him as a youth that he would live longer in his business if he didn't use his real name. So he was Rennie Barbosa to his clients this year, and perhaps Charles Eggleson or Richard Bontrager the next.

Rennie Barbosa's business was killing. He had learned the basics of his trade at the knee of his father in the Peruvian jungle camps of Sendero Luminoso. But the boy surpassed his master both in skill and passion for his work early in his adolescence. He came to be regarded as the most cold-blooded and calculating of the terrorist assassins in Ortiz's camp.

Although he had become an expert in explosives and firearms, the young Barbosa preferred to stalk his victims like a shadow, confront them without weapons in an unguarded moment, and kill them in seconds with his bare hands. And he felt not the slightest compunction, often smiling in the face of his victims as he squeezed their last breath from them. Many of Barbosa's fellow terrorists, who feared him like death itself, claimed that he had been personally schooled for killing by el diablo—the devil.

One of Ortiz's best trackers and seasoned killers recounted with bitter cursing how he was startled awake one night deep in the jungle with a knee on his chest and his neck twisted to within a centimeter of snapping. Barbosa had stalked him for three days and slipped in for the mock kill purely for the joy of it. He was only fourteen at the time.

Long before the dissolution of Sendero Luminoso, Barbosa's trade had totally consumed him. To him, killing was no longer a philosophical lever employed to terrorize the Peruvian government into submitting to the demands of Sendero Luminoso. It was an extension of his identity, a compulsion born of his desire to be the best at what Oscar Ortiz had taught him.

When the cause in Peru no longer interested him and his opportunities to track and kill diminished, he found an eager welcome in the flourishing empire of his Colombian neighbor, Pablo Escobar, lord of the murderous Medellin cocaine cartel. Barbosa became the shadowy assassin of numerous Colombian judges and officials who made the mistake of opposing Escobar. Barbosa often succeeded with his bare hands, where others had failed with bombs and guns. He was rewarded with great wealth, much of which he sent by secret courier to his father and mother in Peru. Barbosa didn't need the money; his work was its own reward.

After several of the cartel's "assignments" had taken the fair-skinned Peruvian into the United States, Barbosa's life took another turn. He was fascinated by mastering the new challenge of tracking and killing in the vast concrete jungles of Miami, New York, Chicago, and Los Angeles, just as he had mastered the steamy jungles of Peru and the crowded streets of Medellin and Bogota. Enthralled by the possibilities, Barbosa moved to Miami in 1993, a few months before his former employer, Pablo Escobar, died in a rooftop shootout with Medellin police and the Colombian military.

Barbosa diligently applied himself to master English and lose his Latin accent. Meanwhile he slipped into the Florida underworld and rose through the ranks as a skilled, elusive, and fearless hit man. His fame earned him similar opportunities in larger markets. Before the end of the millennium, Barbosa had quietly established himself across the country as a nomadic hired killer who was fast, invisible, and who left no traces. He was especially feared in the underworld where territorial drug lords had no qualms about enlarging their operations through the strategic demise of a greedy rival.

Over the years of his ascendancy in the "business," Barbosa's passion for the kill gradually abated. He could go for months without a client and not feel unfulfilled. Nor did he need the money. Numbers of lucrative "contracts" had swelled his secret accounts with cash. His material needs and desires were strategically limited; too much stuff left an inconvenient trail. So he continued to divert much of his wealth to family members in Peru.

What Barbosa could *not* live without was the hunt: selecting a target—the more difficult the better, learning the target's habits by observation, slipping into the target's personal space undetected, and closing in for the kill. Two or three times a year Barbosa played the game for real, for a price: stalking a victim from the shadows until, in one swift, silent moment, a life was taken.

The rest of the time Barbosa amused himself by stalking women, not to kill them, but to entertain and pleasure himself at their expense before disappearing from their lives. And because of his wholesome appearance and lethal charm, he was as good at his avocation as he was at his vocation.

"Pardon me, ma'am, but do you know what time *The Dolphin at Sunrise* starts?"

The woman in her early thirties, standing in line at the snack bar, turned in the direction of the masculine voice behind her asking the question. Relieved to find the warm smile of a normal-looking guy instead of one of the nerdy kooks who sometimes bothered her at the movies, she answered pleasantly, "It starts at 7:35." Then she added with a slight laugh, "At least that's when they start showing the previews."

"Have you seen it yet?" Barbosa asked, easily holding her attention with his gentle gaze. The woman was not a beauty, but she was reasonably attractive—a worthy but rather easy object—and she was alone. He guessed that she lacked the social confidence to date much but would like to.

"No. Actually it's the movie I'm seeing tonight."

Barbosa raised his eyebrows in a convincing expression of mild surprise. In reality, he already knew that she had selected *The Dolphin at Sunrise* from the menu of twelve movies playing at the North Hollywood Metroplex Theater. He had been watching the ticket window unnoticed moments earlier when she approached and said, "One for *The Dolphin at Sunrise* please." It was all the invitation he needed. Moments later Barbosa bought a ticket to the same movie and found a place behind her in line at the snack bar.

After taking another step forward, the woman turned back to Barbosa and asked, "What about you? Have you seen *The Dolphin at Sunrise* yet?"

He was pleased that she wanted to continue the conversation, but he was not surprised. He had always been good at putting strangers at ease—especially women, especially *lonely* women—and gaining their confidence. "Yes, I saw it last night in San Francisco. Enzo Fabrini is so good in this one that I just had to see it again."

"San Francisco?" the woman asked with surprise. The tone of her question invited him to explain why he had come so far to see the movie again.

"I'm on a business trip," Barbosa lied convincingly. "Seattle and Portland two weeks ago; San Francisco last week; L.A. next week. I flew down today. Nights and weekends are pretty boring, though, so I see a lot of movies."

Nodding, she said, "My nights and weekends are pretty boring too, so I'm here at the Metroplex about three times a week."

You're not telling me anything new, Sarah, he thought, without changing expression. *I've seen you here twice before, even though you didn't notice me. And I followed you home one night and got your name off your condo mailbox. You're even easier to meet that I had expected.*

The woman had turned fully around to face him, glad for a few kind words from a total stranger who was a movie-lover like herself. She glanced over her shoulder occasionally in order to keep up with the slow-moving line. "So where are you from?" Sarah asked.

"Pittsburgh. I work for Alcoa Aluminum."

"You're a long way from home."

"Yeah, but it's good for my hobby."

"What hobby?"

"I collect frequent-flyer miles," he said with an impish twinkle. They shared a comfortable laugh.

"You sell aluminum pots and pans?" Sarah probed.

He smiled his devastating smile. "No, I sell industrial aluminum by the roll for commercial construction. My territory is the I-5 corridor from Bellingham to San Diego. And you?"

She shook her head with mild chagrin. "Nothing as exciting as what you're doing. I'm a court recorder at Los Angeles District Court in Van Nuys. You know, it's one of those jobs they advertise on TV as exciting and challenging. Ha! My job is so boring I need three or four movies each week to keep my blood circulating."

Sarah reached the counter and placed her order for a small popcorn with added butter flavoring and a medium diet Coke. The pimply faced, teenage clerk went through the motions of filling the order as if sleepwalking. Sarah paid for the snacks and stepped aside. Barbosa calculated that his new acquaintance would wait for him. She did not disappoint him. She loitered near the napkin and straw dispensers on the counter and continued talking as he stepped up to order.

"Have you seen many of Fabrini's movies?" Sarah asked, as he ordered popcorn and a Coke.

"All of them," he answered enthusiastically, reeling her in with his smile, "most of them at least twice. He's my favorite actor."

"And is he really good in *Dolphin?*"

"Outstanding. I don't think it's quite up to his Oscar-nominated performance as the Count of Monte Cristo, but he could get a nomination for his role in *Dolphin.*"

He paid for his popcorn and drink and stepped out of line. "It's this way, in theater number 6," Sarah said, nodding to the left. She led him down the corridor to where the title THE DOLPHIN AT SUNRISE glowed on the marquee above the double doors. Sarah walked along with him, glad for the windfall of a sane, knowledgeable companion for a change.

"Do you mind if I sit with you?" Barbosa asked, confident that Sarah was hoping for such a possibility. "I enjoy critiquing a movie with someone who knows what they like."

"Not at all," she said, sounding delighted. Then she added, "By the way, my name is Sarah Coats."

Sarah Jeanine *Coats,* Barbosa corrected silently. *You don't know it, but I've learned a lot about you in three weeks. You live in the Lankershim Colony Apartments in North Hollywood with your roommate, Ellie Kim, and two cats. You drive a six-year-old Nissan Sentra with a hole in the muffler. You step outside in your bathrobe at 6:30 every morning to pick up the morning edition of* Valley News, *which is delivered to your doorstep. You leave at 7:55 for the twenty-minute drive to Van Nuys. You arrive home at 5:30, in time to eat a quick meal with Ellie and get to the movies two nights a week. You go alone because your roommate works evenings. And you haven't missed a Saturday night movie in three weeks. I know; I've seen you here.*

"Good to meet you, Sarah," Barbosa said. "I'm Tom Johnson, your friendly Alcoa man from Pittsburgh."

Sitting in the theater eating popcorn before the previews rolled, Sarah engaged Tom in a spirited debate about which of Enzo Fabrini's seven films was his best work. From her friendliness, Barbosa sensed that the hook was firmly set. Sarah would go out for a hamburger with Tom after the movie, he was sure of it. Barbosa was already contemplating the next challenge with delight: *How many movies and hamburgers will it take before Sarah accepts my invitation to the Sheraton?*

Stalking women like Sarah Coats was a minor diversion compared to the work he loved most, but the excitement of the hunt brought him great pleasure.

About an hour into the movie, Barbosa's pocket phone sounded on a low tone. He excused himself, accompanied by a promising squeeze on Sarah's arm, and hurried to the lobby.

"Yes, this is Tom Johnson," he said, after finding a semi-private corner.

"Mr. Barbosa, this is Bishop again."

Barbosa warmed at the voice of his latest client. "Yes, what can I do for you?" he said, avoiding the use of the caller's name.

"Did you find the deposit all right? Was everything satisfactory?"

"Yes, thank you, quite satisfactory."

"Excellent. Then let me supply a few last minute instructions."

"I'm listening."

"Your target is a man by the name of Nolan Jakes. You said earlier that you have never heard of him."

"That is correct."

"Jakes will be no problem; he's a novice in the drug game and rather unskilled at dealing with someone like yourself. He has stepped way out of line, and my employer insists that he be eliminated quietly and cleanly."

"All I need to know is where to find the gentleman, and I'll take care of everything."

"I'm sure you will, Mr. Barbosa. But there are a few extenuating circumstances concerning this contract that I need to explain. I hope this won't be too much of an inconvenience to you."

Barbosa listened patiently as his client outlined a rather unusual approach to the permanent silencing of Nolan Jakes. He was slightly deflated when Bishop revealed that Jakes would not be difficult to find or track. Anything that diminished the challenge and excitement of the hunt took away from his enjoyment of it. But he had agreed to the terms, and Bishop was calling the shots. So Barbosa absorbed the details and memorized them, assuring himself that he could concoct some measure of excitement out of a routine task that promised only a couple of mildly entertaining twists.

Barbosa returned to his seat beside Sarah Coats in the theater. On the screen, muscle-bound Enzo Fabrini and his beautiful female co-star struggled to keep their damaged boat, the *Dolphin*, afloat in the midst of a raging typhoon in the China Sea. The roar of crashing waves and pulse-quickening background music poured from the speakers surrounding the audience. Sarah was transfixed by the action.

Barbosa would be leaving L.A. tomorrow to deal with Nolan Jakes, and he would not return for many months, possibly never again. On the way back to his seat, he had fabricated the story he, as Tom Johnson, would give Sarah at the conclusion of the movie.

"That was my sales manager on the phone during the movie. He wants me back in Pittsburgh tomorrow night for a big sales meeting on Monday. He says we're doing some restructuring and that I'm up for a regional position. But that means I may not be back in Los Angeles for a while. So it was good to meet you, Sarah, and I wish you the best of luck. By the way, I thought I might stop by the Hamburger Hamlet for a hamburger on the way back to the hotel. Would you like to join me—my treat?"

Sarah would accept, of course. And if Barbosa plied her sympathies and enticed her sufficiently, she might even spend the night with him. In the morning he would take Sarah's phone number, promising to call her, and give her Tom's personal number—which would be a fake. Then he would disappear from her life forever and get down to the business of Nolan Jakes.

Twenty-six

Nolan Jakes' muscular back looked like it had served as the battle ground for a cockfight. A flurry of short, dark red scabs marred the tanned skin. Jakes soaked in the tub, carefully resting his head on the edge and his elbows on the bottom to keep his sore back from touching anything but the warm water laden with Epsom salts. The bathroom of the $50-a-night motel on Thompson Avenue near downtown Ventura was dimly lit, with a cracked mirror and stains of an unknown nature streaking the dingy-green walls.

The stainless-steel Colt Anaconda .44 Magnum rested on the corner of the tub within Jakes' easy reach. The nylon sport bag containing $620,000 in stolen bills lay on the floor under the bathroom sink. Jakes was alone in the motel room while Margo scouted the neighborhood for a drugstore to buy more antiseptic lotion and some aspirin. Then she was to find a take-out restaurant and bring back something to eat—"something good, not any of that fast-food crap," he had insisted, "and get a bottle of wine too."

Margo had been cheery and accommodating since Jakes had agreed to her suggestion to hijack Evan and Shelby's RV for their escape to Canada. She was like a giddy college girl again, accentuating the ten-year difference in their ages. Where Jakes saw only trouble and danger trying to outrun the law and Billy Fryman, Margo found great adventure. She seemed to enjoy disguising their appearance and skulking through the streets of Ventura unnoticed, with a loaded .44 Magnum under the seat. Once she had checked them into the motel room under the innocuous names of Doug and Mary Jane Winters, she couldn't wait to get outside again to pick up the supplies they needed. When Jakes insisted that he keep the gun with him, Margo giggled and said, "That's okay, Nolan, I don't need a gun anyway. I'm too clever and careful out there."

Jakes had considered sending Margo after ammunition for the Anaconda. One round had been fired by Reynoso Fernandez in the fracas at Dodger Stadium, unleashing the slug that ripped into Chance, Jakes' human shield. Fernandez would have emptied the gun into Jakes as he lay on the asphalt, had the fugitive not ended the killer's life first with a burst of lucky shots from Chance's plastic Rourk.

The Anaconda, which Jakes had lifted from the fallen Fernandez, still had five rounds in the cylinder—Jakes had carefully checked it several times. But a .44 with five bullets, as deadly as it could be, didn't seem like much against the kind of firepower Billy Fryman and his posse of killers would likely bring with them. Jakes assessed that a box of shells might help reduce the odds against him a little.

But the more he thought about it, the more uncomfortable he felt about having Margo make such a purchase. He had little doubt that she could snow a clerk into believing that she had left her gun registration permit in another purse and give a convincing number "from memory." But such purchases were immediately recorded on a computer network accessible to every law enforcement agency in the country. The sale of a box of shells, noteworthy due to what would quickly prove to be a bogus gun registration number, would serve as a large and incriminating footprint in Ventura County for the police, who doubtless suspected that Jakes, the alleged cop-killer, still had Donatelli's cannon.

Jakes couldn't afford to leave any footprints. So he had dismissed the idea and never mentioned it to Margo.

Jakes leaned forward with a slight groan to turn the faucet so the hot water would dribble into his bath, which was turning tepid. Then he eased back onto his elbows as steam wafted upward from the tap. Throughout the day he had wondered about his decision to take Margo along, particularly when she challenged his plan of escape with what he ultimately admitted was a better plan. In his moments of solitude and inactivity, he thought through the lists of pros and cons again. If he was going to change his mind about Margo, it had to be soon. Once they forced their way into Evan Rider's RV and started for Canada, he would be committed. But there was still time to slip away from her tonight and find his own way out of the country—if he deemed it necessary.

Pro: Margo was a beautiful, desirable woman. Perhaps more important, she was a warm and accepting companion, who seemed no less committed to him now that he was a criminal and a fugitive than she had been when she thought he was a hard-working, law-abiding citizen. No other woman he had been with had shown him such devotion. Margo's closeness gave Jakes something to stay out of prison for and to stay alive for. He had difficulty believing that a life of exile without Margo—or someone like her, if he ever had the good fortune to find anyone like her again—would be worth pursuing.

Pro: Margo was intelligent, as evidenced by the strategic albeit humbling correction she injected into his plan. Jakes didn't regard himself as inept or helpless; after all, he *had* eluded a police dragnet and an unconscionable drug dealer by himself during the critical first hours of his escape. But he soberly admitted that he and Margo might get away from California easier and stay hidden longer than he might on his own. And who knew how else her smarts and quick wits might aid him in his flight? Margo's intelligence was not a benefit to be easily ignored.

Pro: Two runaways can cover each other's back. And, for the time being, Margo was the less sought, less recognized of the pair. Showing his face in Ventura or anywhere along the I-5 corridor to Canada to buy food or supplies would be extremely dicey. Margo was there to do it for him. And during the projected drive to the border, Margo could keep an eye on their hostages if and when he was able to sleep, and he could do the same for her. They would both need to be well rested, because their flight to a safe hiding place might continue for days after they left the RV at the border.

Con: For all her warmth and wonder, Margo increased his runaway liabilities by at least 100 percent. She was one more person to hide, to transport, to feed, and to protect. And if she was caught, there was certainly no guarantee that she would toddle off to prison in silence while he went free. There is no honor among thieves, he remembered from somewhere. What would prevent a captive Margo from spilling everything she knew about Jakes' prospective hiding places in retribution for his failure to protect her?

And if Margo stayed with him, then changed her mind in a year or five years or ten years and returned to the U.S. to face the music, Jakes would need to find an even deeper hole, one that she could not reveal to the authorities.

Con: If he ever tired of Margo, what would he do with her? He couldn't just bid her a pleasant good-bye and send her home, knowing what she knew. And he couldn't kill her, at least he couldn't imagine being able to kill her, no matter how sour their relationship became. Would he be responsible to find her a separate hiding place? Would she expect him to share the stolen money with her or support her for life with monthly payments like some kind of alimony? Would she try to extort such an arrangement under the threat of copping out on him? The staggering complications caused Jakes to appreciate the "till death do us part" commitments of marriage.

Con: Margo's Bonnie-and-Clyde sense of adventure and enjoyment in their escapade made Jakes nervous. She was confident and cool, bordering on being cocky and careless. He could imagine her now, purposely driving the Jaguar a little too fast somewhere in Ventura, just daring a city cop or county deputy to pull her over so she could experience the rush of avoiding detection. It was as if she didn't comprehend the gravity of taunting the law or the danger of playing games with G. Billy Fryman. Her theatrics could get them both captured or killed.

Jakes shut off the faucet and reclined again. The hot water on his back made him grimace, momentarily distracting him from his evaluation of Margo. He endured the discomfort, hoping that the heat would somehow purge his wounds of infection.

Thinking about the sores on his back, it occurred to Jakes that, as a fugitive, he would be unable to see a physician until he was securely ensconced in his new identity in Canada. In the meantime, any medical emergency—appendicitis, a bone fracture, a heart attack, or even an infection from the cuts on his back—would have to be ignored, possibly resulting in his death. If he chose to come out of hiding to seek treatment from a physician, he would drastically increase his chances of detection and arrest.

Then he thought about Evan Rider—*Doctor* Evan Rider, the man he would approach in the morning and blackmail into driving him to Canada. *I might as well make the most of my hostage,* he thought. *The doctor can probably lay his hands on plenty of drug samples and first-aid supplies in his office: painkillers, antibiotics, antiseptics, bandages, etc. Tomorrow, Dr. Rider will take me to his office, and I will load a suitcase full of stuff we may need in Canada. And I'll have him treat my back for infection.*

Pleased with himself for coming up with the idea, Jakes returned to thinking about Margo. The pluses and minuses of taking her to Canada clashed relentlessly. One moment he saw her as such a detriment that he wished he had never met her, never been attracted to her, never asked her out. The next moment he knew he would never meet another woman like Margo, and he could not live without her. How could he choose to leave her behind?

His thoughts were interrupted by a sharp rap on the front door, followed immediately by the sound of a key slipping into the lock. The bathroom door was closed but not locked. Jakes tensed to listen, puzzled that Margo would knock before entering.

A female Hispanic voice called out from the adjoining room, "Housekeeping, Mr. Winters." A pause, then again, "Housekeeping, Mr. Winters. There is someone here to see you."

A lightning bolt of fear shot through Jakes. *Someone to see me?! Fryman or one of his goons?! The police?!* He grabbed the gun as quietly as possible from the corner of the tub. He considered getting out of the water and wrapping a towel around his waist but discarded the idea immediately. It would make too much noise, and make him even more vulnerable. At least in the water he had the protection of one wall of the tub.

"Mr. Winters, are you here?"

Jakes lowered himself farther into the water and leveled the gun at the door. He pulled back the hammer with his thumb. His hand was shaking. He flashed back to less than twenty-four hours earlier, when Reynoso Fernandez stood over him with the .357. He had blown the man away without regret. Was he just as prepared to empty the .44's cylinder into whoever opened the bathroom door?

Jakes didn't have time to think about it. The handle on the bathroom door turned slowly, and the door opened four inches. "Mr. Winters?" the unseen Hispanic woman called in. Jakes adjusted his aim to the dark slit of the open door, head high, and nestled his finger snugly over the trigger. He could feel the adrenaline throbbing in his trigger finger.

"Mr. Winters," the voice said from behind the door, the Hispanic accent slipping away, "would you care for a drink before dinner?" Then a woman's hand came through the opening, and in the hand was a bottle of Chianti and two wine glasses. Jakes recognized Margo's laughter before she finally pushed the door fully open and stepped into the bathroom, still wearing her blonde wig.

Jakes lowered the barrel of the gun, swearing as he released a breath. "Don't ever do that again!" he snapped angrily. "I almost blew your head off! And even if I had missed you, the gunshot would have attracted every cop in the county!"

Margo seemed unfazed by the gun or Jakes' warning. "I was just testing your reactions, darling," she said, as she placed the bottle and glasses on the sink and sat down on the stool. She pulled a small corkscrew out of her shirt pocket and proceeded to assault the cork on the Chianti. "And you did very well, Nolan. You didn't panic. If I had been a cop or one of Billy Fryman's men, you were ready. I'm proud of you."

Jakes was so angry he couldn't say anything but curses under his breath. His hand was still shaking as he released the hammer on the .44 and returned it to the corner of the tub.

Margo popped the cork and filled the two glasses with deep-red wine, setting one of them on the ledge of the bathtub near Jakes' arm. She said, "As soon as you're dry, join me in the dining room for cannelloni, ravioli, and salad served in those charming take-out aluminum foil containers. It smells wonderful." Then she raised the wine bottle over the tub and, with an impish grin, poured two good swallows into the bath water. "Alcohol is good for your sore back," she giggled, as she picked up her wine glass and left the room.

This is not going to work, Jakes, he remonstrated himself, steaming with anger and trembling in the aftermath of the adrenaline surge. *This woman is going to blow your cover and get you killed. You have to get away from her tonight and find your own way to Canada. She's not worth the hassle.*

But by the time he took her to bed, after they had devoured a delicious Italian meal and polished off the bottle of Chianti, Jakes had changed his mind.

Twenty-seven

Reagan Cole spent the evening packing and repacking his saddlebags for the trip to Tahoe. It was always difficult deciding how to use the limited space to pack everything he wanted to bring. Owning a car with room for several suitcases would make things a lot easier on him when he traveled—which he did as often as his schedule allowed. But he had decided years earlier that the convenience of luggage space was no match for the thrill of riding in the open air astride 1,200 cubic centimeters of power.

Cole would have completed his packing sooner, had it not been for the mental distractions. He found himself often diverted to the kitchen for coffee and then to the lanai to sit and process the intruding thoughts as he gazed out at the lights of Santa Monica pier dancing on the black waters of the Pacific Ocean.

He thought about Rennie Barbosa, the sinister, elusive Peruvian hitman he had been assigned to track. The man's lack of activity since arriving in Los Angeles would put an insomniac to sleep, Cole concluded wryly. It upset the detective sergeant to waste the department's man-hours and equipment watching a criminal on vacation. They had a bug on his hotel phone, a homing device secreted in his rental car, and a small crew monitoring his movements twenty-four hours a day. Yet the alleged scourge of Sendero Luminoso had done nothing more incriminating since arriving in town than take extra mints from the counter of a restaurant when the cashier wasn't looking.

While watching Barbosa personally on a few occasions, Cole had caught himself praying that the man would commit a felony—an assassination, a drug deal, anything—so he could nab him and end the series of brainless stakeouts. Once Cole realized how ludicrous his request sounded—asking God to cause Barbosa to commit a crime for his benefit, he was embarrassed and had to apologize to God. Even so, Cole wished Barbosa would do what he had come to do—if he had come to do something—or just get out of town, so Cole could get on with more promising and rewarding detective work.

But most of the interrupting thoughts which drove Cole to the lanai with a cup of coffee were about Beth Scibelli. His senses were still vibrating from being with her: the striking beauty of her dark features, the melodic sound of her voice, the fragrance of her skin and hair mixed with the ocean breeze, the softness of her skin to his touch.

One moment he was thanking God profusely for allowing him to see her again. The next moment he was chastising himself for some of the desires which had been aroused by seeing Beth, desires he thought he had corralled permanently many months earlier. For minutes at a time he was giddy and excited at the prospect of being with her at Quintero's tomorrow. Then he would berate himself for placing so much importance on seeing her.

You and Beth are traveling two different paths, Cole reminded himself. *You can't let your old feelings carry you away. She must choose to come your way; you cannot choose to return to her way. Go have a nice lunch with her tomorrow; then let her go. Don't give her any false hopes, and don't let yourself get sidetracked by unrealistic expectations. She has made her choice. She has decided to serve her career and you have decided to serve God. You can be a friend to her, you can tell her how your life has changed, but you will eventually part company forever unless . . .*

The prospect of Beth's interest in spiritual values being rekindled seemed disappointingly remote to Cole. The character qualities which so attracted him to her—her saucy individualism, her competitive fire, her fearless and sometimes foolhardy daring—loomed in his mind as great obstacles to her turning to a life of simple trust in, and humble dependence on, God. *A turnaround in Beth would be an even greater miracle than getting me to head in the right direction,* he confessed with a sigh of discouragement.

By 10:45 Cole was finally packed. But the trains of thought which had consumed his attention most of the evening demanded that he place two phone calls before he turned out the lights.

The first call was to Officer Bruce Madden, one of the detectives on the Barbosa detail. "What's the latest on our man, Bruce?"

"Just another day of murder and mayhem, sarge," Officer Madden replied, tongue-in-cheek. "The Peruvian Predator stayed in his room at the Sheraton all afternoon. He talked to a couple of his girlfriends on the phone. Pretty steamy stuff. I should be able to get twenty bucks a tape from the perverts at Parker Center."

Cole didn't laugh. He felt increasingly uncomfortable with the raw humor he found to be all too common among the brothers and sisters of the blue fraternity. He recalled with remorse having perpetuated the same sordid topics in recent years.

"What about tonight?" Cole asked to move Madden along.

"He went to the movies . . . again. This time it was *The Dolphin at Sunrise* over at the North Hollywood Metroplex."

"Did he see anybody or talk to anybody?"

"He got one phone call during the movie. We couldn't pick it up, of course. Probably another member of his harem."

"Anything else?"

"He hit on a girl in the popcorn line, and they went to Hamburger Hamlet after the movie. But this time Romeo struck out and went home without her. He called her once from the Sheraton after he got in, but as far as I can tell, he's home alone tonight."

"Anything unusual at all today, Bruce?" Cole pressed. He had promised himself that at the first sign that Barbosa's work was overtaking his pleasure, he would postpone his vacation to follow it up firsthand.

"Sorry, sarge, but this guy is squeaky clean. He doesn't even litter."

Cole thanked Madden for his good work and instructed him to call Sergeant Frank Chavez at Parker Center *day* or *night* if Barbosa so much as sneezed illegally. Madden agreed.

Cole hesitated over his next call for several minutes. He wasn't sure if his motive for calling was to tell Beth of his concern for her or just to hear her voice again. Finally he pressed a two-key memory sequence on his personal phone, a sequence he hadn't used in over a year. He didn't know what he was going to say, but he needed to assure himself by talking to Beth that his motives for taking her to lunch at Quintero's were right.

"Yes," Beth said in her typical businesslike telephone voice. Cole was relieved that she didn't sound like she had been asleep.

He said in polished cop-speak, "Ma'am, this is a special security detail from the Los Angeles Police Department checking to see that you made it home safely." Then he immediately felt stupid for such a lame beginning. He feared that his late-night intrusion might wipe away all the progress he had made earlier in the day melting the icy distance between them.

There was a pause, then, "Well, thank you, sergeant. Yes, I did make it up the hill in one piece. And you?" There was a quiet welcome in her voice, more like their friendly parting on the breezy hilltop than their chilly beginning at the reception.

Pleasantly surprised at her response, Cole relaxed. "Just fine. I've spent the evening trying to pack for a week in saddlebags that only hold enough for about two days."

Beth laughed lightly, a laugh Cole had come to love during their romantic weeks after Millennium's Eve. Then she was silent, and Cole knew the ball was back in his court.

"The real reason I called, Beth . . . er, well, I'm not really sure why I called. I wanted you to know that I enjoyed seeing you again today, and I'm looking forward to meeting you at Quintero's tomorrow."

"Thank you, Reagan," Beth said, sounding genuine. "I feel the same way." Then she added with a friendly little jab, "But that can't be why you called, because we already had this talk earlier today."

Cole felt like a bumble-brained, tongue-twisted junior high kid asking a girl out for the first time. "Er . . . right." He took a deep breath and let it out slowly and quietly, giving himself precious seconds to frame his words. "Beth, I don't want you to get the wrong idea about tomorrow. I'm not trying to butt into your life or get you to change how you feel about me—or about us. I appreciate what we had and, frankly, I wonder why so much distance has come between us. But I respect your choices, even when I don't agree with them. I'm not pushing you to be something you don't want to be. I just want us to be friends."

Cole appreciated Beth's silence, hoping that she was processing his words thoughtfully. When she finally spoke, he detected neither defensiveness nor condescension in her tone, but honesty. "That's very sweet, Reagan. And since you have been up front with me, let me be up front with you. If I thought you were putting a move on me, either to get me into bed or to influence me toward your beliefs, I never would have agreed to be with you tomorrow. But your kindness today confirmed to me that being with an undemanding friend is just what I need right now."

"I'm glad you feel that way," Cole said, feeling relieved.

Beth continued. "I've just been through three days of hell, Reagan, and up until about fifteen hours ago I had no intention of coming to the wedding or seeing you. I was headed home. But while flying out of Miami this morning, I saw the notes about the wedding in my date book and realized it was today. When I reached Dallas, I changed my flight from Seattle to L.A. But it wasn't the wedding that made me come. The main reason I came to L.A. was because I needed to be with some decent people, people I trust, people who accept me for who I am rather than for what I can do for them. I was thinking of Shelby and Dr. No and Mai . . . and you."

"But you didn't seem very happy at the reception," Cole interjected. "In fact, if I may say so, you were rather cool at first. You acted like this was the *last* bunch of people you wanted to be with."

Beth sighed dejectedly. "Was it that obvious?"

"Not to everyone, I'm sure, but I picked up on it."

Beth was silent again. Cole could almost feel her embarrassment. "I didn't want to be that way," she confessed. "I felt horrible, and I just wanted a little kindness. But instead I had to put on my tough-chick exterior. It's kind of like running to the emergency room to get a cut sewn up and then snapping at the doctor for trying to help you, isn't it?"

Cole didn't want to further embarrass her by agreeing, so he said nothing.

Beth concluded, "Well, thank you again for enduring my defensive posturing today. You've always been good at seeing past that to what's really going on. If you had been any other way today, I probably would have turned down your invitation to lunch tomorrow. It just feels good to be with somebody who cares."

Cole's heart spoke before he thought about the words. "I *do* care about you, Beth; I have ever since our first lunch together at Quintero's. I want the very best for you, and if all that means is offering you my friendship for tomorrow and we never see each other again, I can handle it."

Cole's mind immediately rushed to object. *But I don't want it to end tomorrow. I think there are better things ahead for you—for us. And I'll keep praying for you—and for us—until God tells me to stop.*

"Thank you, Reagan," Beth said sincerely, "but I'm sure tomorrow won't be the end for us. Let's hope it's just the beginning."

Cole couldn't have hoped for anything better. But neither he nor Beth could anticipate the strange path their new beginning would take.

Twenty-eight

The new Mr. and Mrs. Evan Rider had been alone since 8 P.M. It had been a wonderful, unhurried evening of relaxing together and enjoying each other's company, a foretaste, they predicted, of the life that await-ed them as husband and wife.

The last car to leave the Riders' hillside home for the Oxnard Hilton contained Shelby's parents—Jimmy and Evelyn Tuggle—and Malika. The countenance of Shelby's otherwise noncommunicative adopted daughter had mirrored mixed emotions at their parting for the night. Shelby knew Malika was looking forward to spending the night in the hotel and the next day at Magic Mountain with Grandpa and Grandma Tuggle, who had been generous and caring from the first day they met her. But there had also been a flicker of fear in little Malika's eyes: the fear of abandonment rooted in a life history of neglect and abuse. Shelby assured her daughter that she would come to the hotel in the morning to tell her good-bye before leaving for the Grand Canyon.

At Evan's suggestion, he and Shelby had driven down to the beach in their wedding clothes to walk in the sand, minus their shoes and stockings. They strolled at the water's edge hand in hand as the dark blue of evening relentlessly overpowered the gold, crimson, and violet of sunset, squeezing the ever-dwindling light into the sea beyond the horizon.

The couple savored the details of the wedding ceremony and reception. They made a game of trying to name every guest present and remember what each wore and what they brought for a gift. It was great fun, and they laughed often.

For several minutes they sat on a bench by the walkway watching the joggers and skaters glide by under the lamp light. Evan sheltered his bride from the damp ocean breeze with an arm around her shoulders. They expressed their relief that the busy day was over and that they were alone. They nuzzled each other warmly and assured each other that they would not have to separate tonight or ever again.

Returning to the house by 9:30, Evan and Shelby realized that they were both famished. So they rummaged through plastic containers of sliced meats and salads from the buffet and fixed a snack. The leftovers had been packed to travel to the Grand Canyon with them in the RV's spacious refrigerator. Content that the intimate glories of their wedding night awaited them like one last, unopened wedding gift, they continued their leisurely, cheery chat at the bar in the kitchen as they ate.

"What are your greatest hopes and dreams for our life together?" Evan asked, while building a sandwich of sliced prime rib, turkey, avocado, tomato, and sprouts on sourdough bread liberally slathered with Miracle Whip.

Shelby looked at him with a curious smile as she spooned leftover pasta salad onto her plate. "My, aren't we philosophical tonight," she said with a little laugh. "Is this a portent of the effect married life will have on you—deep discussions on the meaning of life every night at bedtime?"

Evan appreciated her humor with a laugh of his own. But he wouldn't let go of his point. "I'm serious. Tell me what stirs in that warm heart of yours when you think of spending the rest of your life with me."

"Evan, nothing I can say will be new to you," she contested weakly. "We've talked about our goals and dreams. We've made plans together."

"I know, I know," Evan said, pausing to admire the gastronomic creation on his plate, then slicing it in half with a steak knife. "But it's different now. We're actually married. I want to hear the deep confessions of Mrs. Evan Rider, the married lady."

Shelby smiled broadly, loving the man sitting across the bar from her.

"Really, Evan, I—"

"Humor me, angel," he interrupted. "I just love to hear it." Then he took a mammoth bite of his sandwich.

After a thoughtful moment, Shelby complied. "All right, it's my hope that we spend as much time together as possible, both as a couple and as a family with Malika and other children who may come along. Your medical practice is important, and my involvement at King's House is important. But we have committed not to get so involved in our work that we cheat ourselves out of the time we need to grow together— several evenings at home together each week, weekends at the beach, vacations in the RV, and so forth."

"I like it," Evan commented in between bites.

"And another dream of mine for promoting family unity is to travel with you whenever you have a medical convention out of state or out of the country."

Evan raised his eyebrows in surprise. "Hey, we never talked about *that* before," he said with his mouth full.

Shelby grinned triumphantly. "I know. I just thought of it. It must be the wisdom that comes along with being married."

Evan laughed out loud. Then Shelby said, "Now it's your turn, darling. You tell me about one of *your* dreams while *I* take a couple of bites."

Evan wiped his fingers and mouth with a napkin, then sat back in the bar stool. "Okay, that's fair." Then after just a brief moment to think, he said, "One of my hopes for us is that our ministry will take increasing priority over my work. I would like to build up such a reserve of savings in the next couple of years that I can cut back from four days a week at the office to three. That way I can spend two days at King's House with you. Perhaps in a few more years I can add another day. And if I can swing an early retirement, we can spend even more time serving at King's House together."

Shelby nodded, affirming that they had had this discussion before. Then she pushed gently on the parallel topic that had remained an unresolved point of friendly contention between them. "You can always cut back sooner and retire earlier, Evan, if you allow me to contribute." She was referring to a substantial amount of money she had put aside from her previous marriage.

Evan responded with his stock answer. "Angel, I appreciate your generosity, but that money has been earmarked for our children's education and inheritance. We can't touch it." Shelby felt it was more of a pride issue with Evan. He didn't want anyone to think he had married Shelby for her money. And he needed to show that he was capable of providing for a family on his own, after so many years as a bachelor. He had steadfastly refused to consider her money as his money. Shelby had learned over the months of their courtship not to harp on the issue.

Evan picked up his sandwich and quickly changed the subject. "Your turn, angel. Tell me about another dream."

Shelby said, "I have a dream that we will be a close, caring family. I want us to provide a safe, nurturing home for Malika, replacing the horrifying memories of her early childhood with a peaceful, loving environment. And I want us to be open to adopting other children from the streets as we feel led. You're too wonderful a father to lavish on just one daughter. You need a house full of children."

"And you have marvelous mothering instincts that just won't quit," Evan interjected proudly. "I love seeing you care for Malika. But a house full of adopted children? Mm, I'm still thinking about that one."

Shelby continued with what Evan knew was next. They had talked about it many times, but he loved to watch her face glow when they did. "I want to bear a child—your child, darling—before my biological clock runs down. We'll thumb our noses at the genetic baby designers and show the medical community what a fine child we can produce on our own under God's supervision. And he will be a masterpiece."

"He?" Evan probed. "I thought we weren't going to manipulate the sex genes of our offspring."

"Of course, we're not. But we obviously need a son to keep the family name alive, so we'll surely have a boy. And I just thought of his name: James Evan Rider, named after Daddy and you. What do you think?"

Evan blinked in amazement. "You're really on a roll tonight with these hopes and dreams. James Evan Rider—*Doctor* James Evan Rider," he said, savoring the sound. "Yes, I like it!"

"But perhaps it will be *Reverend* Rider or *Ambassador* Rider or even *President* Rider," Shelby insisted.

"I still like it, even if President Rider ends up being a girl."

Evan and Shelby continued rehearsing their dreams for one another until they finished their snacks. Then, while lingering over small slices of wedding cake and tea, they exchanged the wedding gifts they had prepared for each other.

At Shelby's invitation, Evan opened his gift first. It was a beautiful Bible bound in navy-blue calfskin with his name embossed on the cover.

"It's just like Dr. No's Bible with all the study helps in the margins and the appendices," Shelby pointed out. "I hope you like it."

Evan held the Bible reverently, admiring the fine-grained leather with the soft touch of his fingers. "It's beautiful, angel; I love it," he said. "I've been looking for a Bible like Dr. No's."

"I know," Shelby beamed.

After appreciating the book several seconds longer, Evan leaned across the bar and kissed Shelby. "Thank you very much," he said sincerely.

"You're welcome, darling. I just want you to know that I regard you as an equal in the faith. I expect to learn as much from you as you have learned from me. And I respect you as the spiritual head of our home."

"I don't really feel worthy of such respect, but with God's help I'll try to live up to your expectations. Thank you."

Evan then presented Shelby's gift. She carefully removed the silver ribbon, unwrapped the silver and white paper, and lifted the lid on the box. The beauty of what she found provoked a slow gasp of surprise. It was a large personal journal bound in leather with an intricate floral pattern carved on the front. At the bottom, beautifully etched in a space for that purpose, were the words SHELBY RIDER.

Between the covers of the book were 200 white linen pages. Also in the gift box was a gold pen.

"O Evan, how beautiful! A diary to record our life together."

"Yes, and when you fill this one, you simply remove the leather cover and slip it on another book of blank pages."

"What a wonderful idea. How very thoughtful. Evan, I'm so pleased." This time it was Shelby leaning over the bar to present a thank-you kiss.

Then Shelby cocked her head and smiled. "Isn't it odd that we both selected books?"

Evan thought for a moment. "Yes, one that tells us all we need to know about living happily ever after, and the other in which to record how happily ever after we live." They smiled, then they laughed, then they embraced and thanked each other again for their gifts.

"Well," Evan said with a flutter of anxiety teasing his stomach, "I believe it's time to go upstairs."

Shelby excused herself to bathe and dress for bed in the downstairs guest room. Evan quickly put away the food and rinsed the dishes. Then he climbed the stairs to the master bedroom, showered, shaved, and donned a new pair of pajamas and a robe he had purchased for the occasion. He hurriedly lit several fragrant white candles mounted in crystal holders and placed them around the room. Then he sat down in one of two occasional chairs in the corner of the bedroom to await Shelby's appearance from downstairs.

The sight of his bride in the doorway caught Evan's breath away. Shelby had selected a modest, floor-length satin and lace peignoir in shimmering powder blue. Her blonde hair encircled her head like a halo, shining in the candlelight. Her face glowed with demure innocence and anticipation. Evan immediately stood as if in the presence of royalty.

"Good evening, Mrs. Rider," he whispered in awe.

"Good evening, Mr. Rider," she smiled back.

"You are incredibly gorgeous, my lady."

"Thank you. And you, sir, are very attractive and desirable."

Evan found himself fidgeting with the sash on his robe.

"I . . . I'm kind of nervous about this."

Shelby smiled sheepishly. "Good. So am I."

"I think there's something we need to do before we go to bed," Evan said, drinking in her beauty. "I used to make fun of religious people by saying, 'I'll bet they're so holy that they can't even have sex without dropping to their knees in prayer first.' In those days I never prayed before anything. I could have saved myself some grief if I had.

"But I'm different now, thank God, and thanks to you. This may sound corny, but I want to pray with you tonight before we turn out the lights. I want to give our marriage and our marriage bed to God. Would that be all right with you?"

"I would be honored. Thank you for being so thoughtful."

They knelt together beside the bed. Taking Shelby's hand, Evan prayed a simple, heartfelt prayer thanking God for the wonder of their relationship. He asked God to unite them in spirit and soul for their life together. He told God they would follow Him wherever their path would lead them. He asked for wisdom to be the husband God wanted him to be.

Shelby added a few lines of prayer, not the polished religious phrases she had mastered as the former leader of a vast electronic church, but as a woman eager to fill the role of wife and mother with the man God had given her.

After a quiet amen, Evan swept his lovely bride into bed.

SUNDAY
June 24, 2001

Twenty-nine

Having slept soundly for six hours, Rennie Barbosa awoke at 6 A.M. with a profound sense of anticipation. It was the same sensation that greets professional athletes on the morning of the big game, the same feeling that corporate raiders welcome on the morning of the big take-over. It was the inner tingle of anticipated competition, conflict, and conquest. Barbosa always awoke to this delightful inner buzz of expectancy on the day of the hunt.

Barbosa purposely lay in bed for several minutes, relishing the prospect and savoring his confidence. His prey was a man named Nolan Jakes. Barbosa had never met the man and didn't yet know what he looked like. But whoever he was, Jakes would be no match for the assassin's wit and skill.

The task would be a simple matter of locating his prey—elementary since Bishop had told Barbosa where to look, tracking him as invisibly as the wind, patiently waiting for the perfect moment, and moving in for the kill. Barbosa smiled at the promise of surprising Jakes in the shadows, disabling him with a couple of lightning quick chops, enclosing his neck in the vise grip of his powerful arm, and forever stilling the man's breath and silencing his voice. And it would all be finished in seconds.

Barbosa felt no more sympathy for Jakes or remorse at the thought of taking his life than a lion feels when closing in on a helpless wildebeest. Like the fierce lion, killing was what Barbosa did. It was instinctual, automatic, a matter of compulsion and expedience, not conscience. A person need feel no compunction about fulfilling his destiny on earth, and Barbosa certainly did not.

There had been a time in Barbosa's childhood when conscience had weakly protested the tutoring and experimentation in cold-blooded murder to which he was exposed. But the fanatical devotion of his father, Oscar Ortiz, to Sendero Luminoso, and Ortiz's vehement approval of assassination as a primary means to the cause's ends were infectious, hypnotizing. What little guilt young Barbosa may have felt was quickly seared in the heat of relentless brainwashing and the mandatory ritual killing of animals. By the time Barbosa took his first human life—the teenaged son of a Peruvian police captain who had arrested and tortured two of Ortiz's men—Barbosa's conscience barely flinched in protest. He had become an unfeeling killing machine.

Barbosa threw off the sheet but continued to lie quietly in the darkness of his spacious hotel room, drawing long, slow breaths as if storing strength. He knew that he might not sleep again for days. He dared not rest while on the hunt, even when his prey rested. He must alertly track until the precise moment of attack presented itself. There would be days and perhaps even weeks to rest in seclusion after the job was done. Diligence and dogged persistence were the watchwords of the hunt.

No one hunt was exactly like another, so Barbosa contemplated the unique twists of this particular contract killing. There was the matter of slipping away from the pesky police surveillance team which had dogged him since his arrival in Los Angeles. Ever since Barbosa's reputation had leaked from the underworld, the FBI—or whatever local agencies the Bureau could strong-arm into doing its legwork for them—had been continuously on his tail, at least when he permitted himself to be tailed. However, Barbosa always conveniently vanished a few days before the mysterious assassination of a drug lord who had pushed a rival too far. The Feds suspected the elusive Barbosa but could not pin him with the crime due to lack of evidence. When he surfaced in another city weeks later, they could do nothing but put a tail on him and hope they got lucky on his next hit. Barbosa took quiet delight in dragging the law around by the nose, while conducting his lucrative, fulfilling business.

On his first day in L.A., Barbosa had detected the homing beacon secreted on his rented green Corsica and the tap on his phone at the Sheraton Universal. Common, amateurish devices, he had acknowledged with the shake of his head, truly disappointed at the LAPD's lack of ingenuity. And since the LAPD hadn't come up with something more imaginative or challenging, Barbosa had in turn purposely bored them with three weeks of the vanilla existence of Tom Johnson, vacationer, entertainment-seeker, and womanizer. It would be no problem to duck out of L.A. on these simpletons. He had already planned exactly how he would do it.

Then there was the matter of Bishop's specific, curious, and almost annoying orders for tracking Jakes. Barbosa had previously been contracted to do jobs at his own pace, to strike when he deemed it most expeditious. But not this time. "Watch and wait," his present client had insisted, "and I'll tell you when to move in. Timing is everything on this job. It may take a couple of days, but you'll be well paid for your time. Stay out of sight until I give you the go. I'll be in touch."

Barbosa acknowledged to himself that such an unorthodox approach to the hunt could rob him of his advantage over Jakes and the law enforcement agencies hoping to catch the assassin in the act. But despite the annoyance and possible disadvantage, Barbosa had warmed to the challenge of proving himself again. He welcomed anything to make the hunt more enjoyable. After all, a karate master with one hand tied behind his back could still beat a rank amateur in combat. And Barbosa knew he could still take out Nolan Jakes, even with the nagging restrictions placed on him by a client named Bishop.

He had all the tools and knowledge at his disposal. He simply must be resourceful and patient.

Bishop had also mentioned the possibility that Jakes was being hidden or protected. "If Jakes is in the company of others when I instruct you to strike, they must also be eliminated," Barbosa's client had insisted. Additional funds had been promised for additional targets, but Barbosa still regarded that eventuality as a nagging loose end. He had accomplished multiple kills on several occasions before, although such contracts required him to employ weapons other than the darkness of shadows and the strength of his hands. Special preparation and tactics would be needed for dealing with Jakes' accomplices.

Barbosa rose and performed his daily ritual of mind and body exercises adapted from yoga and a variety of martial arts disciplines. Then he added thirty minutes of intense meditation which he practiced only at the outset of a hunt. Stripped to the shorts in which he had slept, the hired assassin sat cross-legged on the floor in a trancelike state, consciously slowing his respiration and circulation. He gradually and deliberately swept his arms out from his sides and arched them above his head, with fingers spread and curved like a lion's claws. Holding the pose, he called out to the predator spirits of the world, drank of their strength and cunning, and promised to honor them with a kill. Rising from his meditation, Barbosa imagined the blood of a hungry lion coursing through his veins.

After a shave and shower, Barbosa dressed in tan cotton pants, a navy polo, and top-siders, looking for all the world like Tom Johnson getting ready to tour Universal Studios. Then he packed the rest of his clothes, with the exception of a tan windbreaker, in his suit bag.

Outside, the famed Southern California sun had already driven the temperature into the high 60s on what promised to be a very warm and smoggy June day. Usually he opened the drapes to welcome the sun and announce to the morning stakeout unit that he was stirring. This morning he left the drapes closed. He didn't really think that those who were tapping his phone were also peering into his eighth-floor room from a distance with high-powered glasses, but he couldn't take that chance today.

He took his canvas shaving bag to the mahogany table and carefully spread out its contents on the surface: a cordless electric razor, a small manicure set, a half-empty tube of toothpaste, a toothbrush, a capped yellow cylinder which looked like a toothbrush container, a comb and brush set, two disposable plastic razors, a small can of shave cream, travel bottles of cologne, shampoo, conditioner, and skin lotion, and a medical kit containing aspirin, nasal spray, a few Band-Aids, and a box of suppositories.

Perhaps only one person in twenty-five, Barbosa had estimated, would view this collection of toiletries and grooming supplies and wonder, "Why do you carry an electric razor *and* blade razors?" Had Barbosa ever been asked that question—which he had not—he would have replied, "Because sometimes I need to shave in a hurry, so I use the electric, while at other times I like a more leisurely, closer shave with a blade." No one would have contested his answer, least of all another man.

In reality, Barbosa always used the blade razors for shaving. His electric razor had an entirely different purpose, which was revealed as he sat down at the table and began to work.

First, he picked up the six-inch-long yellow cylinder, which was made of a much heavier grade of plastic than was necessary to tote a toothbrush, and snapped off the cap. The inside of the cylinder had never housed anything, let alone a toothbrush. The bore was too small.

Taking the metal fingernail file from his manicure kit, Barbosa inserted the pointed end into a score in the cylinder near the closed end. After a moment of prying, a rectangle of yellow plastic, approximately an inch and a half long and three-quarters of an inch wide, popped out onto the table. He repeated the process on the other side of the cylinder. Then he poked the file through one rectangular hole and out the other, assuring himself that the opening was completely clear.

Setting the cylinder and file aside, Barbosa picked up the hair brush. It was black plastic with a thick, rubberized handle. Grasping the bristles in one hand and the brush handle in the other, he pulled with measured strength until the bristle end pulled away from the handle like a sword withdrawing from a scabbard. The bristle end of the brush now had a new, smaller handle, and the original rubberized handle was hollow.

Barbosa tossed the brush into his canvas bag, laid the handle beside the perforated yellow cylinder, and reached for the electric shaver. Using the pointed end of the fingernail file, he snapped off the metal shield protecting the blade end of the razor. But there were no tiny blades inside, and no shaving mechanism. The guts of the shaver had been removed and replaced with another mechanism made of black, high-impact polymer, as tough and serviceable as metal but undetectable by an airport X-ray scan. With thumb and forefinger, Barbosa lifted the mechanism out and set the useless shaver shell aside.

The mechanism slid easily into one slot in the yellow cylinder and out the other until a flanged end secured it in place. The hollow hairbrush handle slipped snugly over the protruding end of the mechanism at a fifty-five-degree angle to the cylinder, leaving a black trigger and safety switch exposed at the junction of the yellow plastic barrel and black rubberized grip.

Barbosa passed the assembled compact pistol from one hand to the other and back again, marveling at its simplicity. He had handled kids' water pistols that were heavier and looked far more deadly.

The gun had been serendipitous booty taken from the personal belongings of one of Barbosa's targets, a Chinese drug runner in Chicago who got a little too sloppy with company funds and too friendly with his boss' girlfriend. Barbosa had never seen anything like it: a snap-together, nine-millimeter pistol designed to pop apart and be carried unobtrusively as part of a shaving kit. He knew immediately that it wasn't a mass-produced weapon but a skillfully handmade original, probably fashioned in China by one of the dead drug runner's countrymen.

Barbosa usually took nothing from his prey; he rarely wanted anything they had, and he preferred not to encumber himself with baggage that might link him to the crime. Nor did he often carry a gun or use one in his work. Guns were noisy, left a mess, and could sometimes be traced, whereas the bare hands of a trained assassin were quiet, clean, and could be carried in plain sight without suspicion.

But there were times when a firearm—especially one which didn't look like a firearm most of the time—was fitting insurance in Barbosa's business. This was one of those times, when the timing and setting for a hit were not under his direct control. For this reason, he was glad he hadn't ignored the windfall of a snap-together pistol no longer needed by a former drug runner with a shattered neck.

Barbosa set the pistol down reverently and reached for the box of what appeared to be foil-wrapped suppositories. He emptied the box and methodically stripped the foil off each of the twelve hard-plastic, nine-millimeter bullets. Then, releasing the empty clip from the heel of the pistol grip, he carefully loaded the bullets into the clip and snapped it back in place.

Barbosa hefted the pistol again. It was a little heavier with the added weight of the twelve shells, but it still looked more like a toy than an implement of destruction. Assured that the safety was on, he slipped the pistol into a side pocket of his suit bag. Then he disposed of the scraps of foil and repacked his shaving kit.

Content at his preparation and confident about his upcoming mission, Barbosa stepped to the window of his room and pulled open the drapes. The unmarked LAPD sedan was parked in a different space, but it couldn't have been easier for Barbosa to spot if it was black and white with a "Christmas tree" of emergency lights mounted on top. Two plainclothes officers, a man and woman unconvincingly dressed like tourists in their Polynesian shirts and dark glasses, gazed up at the window. He recognized the couple on duty today. He had nicknamed them Bob and Betty, the farmers from Terre Haute. He was sure that was the image they were trying to convey.

Barbosa smiled at the sloppy attempt at secrecy. He wondered how any crimes in Los Angeles could be prevented or solved by what he considered an ill-trained, sophomoric police force. The underworld was better organized, more efficiently staffed, and more potently armed. The only thing that prevented a city like Los Angeles from becoming the crime capital of the country was the sheer numbers of officers. There were so many of them stumbling and bumbling around the city that they probably caught many criminals by accident.

But Barbosa felt completely safe. Shortly he would leave Bob and Betty and their LAPD coworkers in his dust and rid himself of this city. They would turn around and he would be gone, and they would be clueless as to where he went or how he got there. The prospect made him smile again at the couple craning their necks to look up at his window from the car.

Barbosa moved to the phone and dialed room service. "A glass of grapefruit juice—large, eggs benedict, a side order of O'Brien potatoes, and coffee, please. Send it up right away. Thank you." He was tempted to order coffee for the two spies in the parking lot, but again, as always, prudence quickly assumed control. He sat down at the table to wait for his breakfast.

Thirty

Margo Sharpe was up early to take a shower and start a pot of coffee on the wall-mounted coffeemaker. Jakes watched her from the bed in the semidarkness as if still asleep, while the aroma of hot coffee permeated the room. She hurriedly and quietly dressed and gathered their few possessions by the door in preparation for departure. Scurrying around the room, Margo looked like a little girl on the first day of vacation, excited to hit the road.

"Nolan, Nolan," she said softly, kneeling over him on the bed as he feigned waking up. "I'm going down to get a Sunday paper and a couple of donuts from the restaurant next door. It's 6:30, Nolan. Shouldn't we be up on the hill soon?"

The blonde hair of Margo's wig cascaded from her beautiful face. Her clean, feminine scent wafted near. The idea of leaving Margo behind was now a faint memory to Jakes, distanced from him by a night of love and warmth with the only person in the world he could trust. The questions about her liability to his successful escape were yet unanswered. But looking up into her face, he realized again that he wanted her more than he wanted freedom itself. They would run together and he would have her as his own until his luck ran out. He could ask for no more than that.

"Yes, we need to get going," he said, yawning. "I'll take a quick shower and get dressed."

She covered his mouth with a warm, tempting kiss. But before he could pull her to himself, she was off the bed and heading toward the door. "Oh," she said, turning back to him, "just in case . . . " She laid the loaded .44 Magnum on the pillow next to him. Then with a flirtatious wave she slipped out the door.

The sight of the gun prompted a flashback to Margo's prank of sneaking in on him while he sat in the bathtub. He had been scant seconds from blowing a hole in the bathroom door and blowing away the intruder behind it, who turned out to be Margo. He had almost killed the woman he loved and desired and needed. Last night he had been angered at her thoughtlessness. But now he was stunned by remorse at what could have happened. And he suddenly knew that if he had killed Margo Sharpe by accident, he would have reacted immediately and just as thoughtlessly. He would have turned the gun on himself. The image chilled him to a shudder.

The pulsating shower jets abruptly reminded Jakes that his back was still very tender. He reached his hand over his shoulder as far as he could and found the wounds to be warm and sensitive to the touch. He reduced the water pressure and again turned his back to the spray, grimacing and willing the heat and moisture to wash away the infection.

Jakes was half dressed when Margo returned. "Look at this," she said, waving the Sunday morning edition of the *Ventura Star–Free Press*. "You have to go clear to page 8 to find anything about you, and there's nothing about me." She sounded disappointed, as if expecting to find their pictures on the front page.

Jakes took the paper and read the one-column article on page 8 headed Ex-FOOTBALL STAR STILL AT LARGE. "Mm, this is good," Jakes said in a low voice. Then he read aloud, " ' . . . no leads as to the whereabouts of the former CSUN and B.C. Lion quarterback turned drug dealer and informant for the LAPD. . . . Fingerprint analysis at the scene and ballistics tests confirm that the slain officer was gunned down by one of the drug dealers, who in turn was shot to death with a nine-millimeter Rourk semiautomatic bearing Jakes' prints.' At least they know that *I* didn't kill the cop. 'Sergeant Donatelli's weapon, a Colt .44 Magnum, and $620,000 in unmarked LAPD drug money, apparently left the scene with Jakes, who eluded a police dragnet and is still at large.' "

"You're not going to turn yourself in, are you, Nolan?" Margo interrupted.

Jakes wasn't sure if he heard her correctly. "What?" he said, looking up from the newspaper.

"I mean, since they know you didn't kill the cop and that you probably shot Fernandez in self-defense, they're not after you for murder.

But you could still go to prison for dealing drugs and stealing the money. You're not going to give up now, are you?"

There was a disappointed lilt in Margo's voice. She sounded again like a little girl on vacation who was afraid her father was not going to let her ride the merry-go-round anymore.

Jakes' response was immediate. "No way. I'm not going to prison. No way in the world."

Margo blew a sigh of obvious relief. "Good," she said in a sober tone, "because I don't want to go to prison either."

Jakes studied her. *She does have a grasp on how serious this is,* he thought. *This may be a lark for her, but she understands what awaits us if we fail.*

He turned back to the article for a second, then snapped his eyes back to Margo. His face mirrored puzzlement. "How did you know that the man I shot was named Fernandez?"

"I beg your pardon."

"A second ago you said that I shot Fernandez in self-defense. How did you know his name? I never told you his name."

Margo cocked her head with the same baffled expression worn by Jakes, as if for a split second she was asking herself the same question. "The paper," she said at last in a tone that conveyed, *You dummy.* "His name is right there in the article."

Jakes' curious glare was suddenly swept away by a look of chagrin. He glanced back at the article before him and his eyes immediately fell on the name Reynoso Fernandez. "The newspaper, of course," he said weakly. "I knew that." He silently remonstrated himself for a moment of unfounded suspicion.

After devouring the stale donuts and washing them down with luke-warm coffee, Jakes put on his fake beard while Margo carried their few belongings and the bulky bag of money to the Jaguar, stashing everything in the trunk. When she had checked them in, Margo had insisted on a downstairs room at the far end of the motel and had backed the car practically to the door, to assure that they would be visible to as few motel guests as possible.

The city of Ventura still had its head under the covers. A blanket of low-hanging marine clouds extended from several miles offshore to a ridge of hills behind the city. The temperature was in the low 50s. Margo used a handful of Kleenex™ from the motel room to clear the outside car windows of dew while the engine was warming up.

Jakes watched her from inside. The gray sky reminded him of Canada. It rained a lot in Vancouver, a fact he had difficulty accepting during his first few years with the B.C. Lions. He was a native of sunny Southern California. He had hated playing football in the rain, especially on the artificial turf which was so necessary in a city susceptible to showers all year long. At the end of each of his first three seasons, he couldn't wait to get out of wet Western Canada to winter in California, Florida, Arizona, or Mexico.

But the beautiful city of Vancouver and the loyal Lions fans had grown on him. He had never seen anything in L.A. as lush and beautiful as Stanley Park or as unique as the Capilano Suspension Bridge. And neighboring Vancouver Island with quaint Victoria and exquisite Buchart Gardens seemed idyllic in contrast to the concrete, asphalt, and steel of Los Angeles.

Furthermore, despite the ever-present threat of rain, spring and summer in Western Canada were spectacular, free from the oppressive heat and smog that drove Southern Californians to the beaches for relief. And fishing trips on the remote streams and lakes of the Canadian Rockies and coastal mountains made Jakes feel more alive and free than anything he had ever done in L.A. The beauty of British Columbia gradually reeled him in.

Then there were the people. The Canadians seemed less complicated and less hurried than Americans, more willing to stop and smell the roses. And they seemed more sensitive and respectful than the Angelenos Jakes knew. He could take a lady to a nice Vancouver restaurant or shop downtown or work out at the club, without being hounded by a horde of discourteous autograph seekers. As one of the city's star athletes, Jakes was still recognized and stared at often, but he was rarely hassled. He liked that.

So after four years as a Lion, Jakes had made Vancouver, British Columbia his permanent home. He still wished for fewer dreary, rainy days. But the gloomy weather dwindled in significance when compared to the quality of life he had discovered in this jewel of the continent.

Most important of all, in Vancouver Jakes felt decades away from the indelible black blot staining his college career at CSUN. How he longed to be there now.

Watching Margo sponge away the droplets on the Jaguar's back window, Jakes pondered the 1,300 miles and approximately twenty-four hours standing between him and his adopted homeland. The knot of anxiety in his stomach, his constant companion for the last several weeks, cramped painfully again in anticipation of the dicey journey. So many threatening obstacles loomed ahead on Interstate 5: the Los Angeles Police, the California Highway Patrol, vengeful Billy Fryman and his trigger-happy associates, and Canadian customs. Also, there was the unsettling vulnerability of being confined to a lumbering recreational vehicle on the open highway.

His escape plan, as good as it seemed, was riddled with perplexing variables, principally the untried reliability of Margo Sharpe and the unpredictable behavior of their prospective hostages, Evan Rider and his wife, who waited unwittingly to be kidnapped. And could he even trust *himself* not to blow his cover and get caught or shot?

Jakes drained the bottom half of a styrofoam cup of cold coffee, hoping to douse the fire burning in the pit of his stomach. There was no easy way to do this, he acknowledged. Any one of a dozen or more things could go wrong, exposing him to men who had sworn to blow his head off, or to the police who were intent on locking him up for the rest of his life.

The race to the border seemed even more formidable than a fourth-quarter, last-minute drive across 110 yards of turf against a snarling defense to the end zone. How often he had faced that challenge as a quarterback in the CFL. And more often than not, he had failed to reach the goal line. An ill-conceived play against a heads-up defense, a badly thrown pass resulting in an interception, a fumbled ball or dropped pass by a teammate, a vicious sack by a rabid linebacker who would rather see his mother starve than to allow an opposing quarter-back a completed pass for the winning touchdown—the odds were always against the success of such a drive.

Today Jakes didn't see 110 yards ahead of him but 1,300 miles. By all rights, he shouldn't expect to make it. But a true competitor never succumbs to the odds. You play your heart out until the final gun sounds. That's what Jakes would do today. He would get to Canada one gut-wrenching play at a time—or die trying.

Jakes glanced at the pillow and realized that he had one advantage on his drive to the border that had been unavailable to him on the football field. He reached for the Colt .44 Magnum and cradled it in his right hand. Jakes had five potent blockers on this drive to the goal: the cold .44 slugs snuggled into the Colt's stainless steel cylinder. One or more of these allies could spell the difference between freedom in the Canadian wilderness with Margo and a lonely prison cell without her. He must pull out all the stops. He must exercise his advantages. He must be ready to kill.

Once Jakes saw that Margo was behind the wheel, he pocketed the Colt, donned his shades, pulled the brim of his golf hat low on his brow, and hurried out of the room to the passenger seat of the Jaguar. "Here's what we're going to do," he said sternly, borrowing a play-calling phrase from the huddle of a last-ditch drive to the goal. "We're going to park two blocks from the house, wait for this Shelby chick to leave, and then follow my old college buddy to his RV. As soon as we know he's alone, I'll walk in on him and tell him what's going to happen. When his wife gets back from the hotel, we'll surprise her inside the RV and leave."

"I think that's a good plan," Margo said, bolstering Jakes' confidence. "But what about the doctor's money? When will we force him to make a withdrawal?"

Jakes thought for a moment. "I want to get out of L.A. first. We can stop somewhere north of the Los Angeles County line."

"Once we leave L.A. we won't even see another decent-sized town along the Interstate until we reach Stockton. That's over 300 miles. Do you want to take U.S. 99 north through Bakersfield or Visalia or Fresno?"

"No," Jakes snapped, "I want to take the fastest route, and that's I-5. We'll find a bank somewhere." Collecting "retirement" money along the way momentarily seemed insignificant to Jakes compared to the other challenges of the escape.

Margo eased the Jaguar into gear and the car idled toward the motel driveway. "And what about your other friend, Libby? Are you still going to hit her up for some money?"

"If Evan Rider knows where she is, and we can get to her on the way to Canada, yes. But I'm not going to worry about that until we're on the road."

Margo stopped at the driveway to look for an opening in the light traffic on Thompson Avenue. She reached her hand out to touch Jakes' leg. "I'm so glad we're together, Nolan. We're going to have such a great life. I love you."

Jakes patted her hand and mumbled, "I love you" in response. But his thoughts were quickly being consumed by the face-to-face meeting he would soon have with his old friend, Evan Rider.

Thirty-one

Beth Scibelli wiped beads of sweat off her nose with her thumb as she turned into her twelfth lap around the Taft High School track. The band of the white cotton visor riding low on her forehead was soaked with perspiration, and her faded cotton tank top was damp and stuck to her chest and back. Beth was glad she hadn't waited until later in the morning to run. It wasn't yet 8 o'clock and the temperature in the West San Fernando Valley community of Woodland Hills was approaching 75 degrees. It would be a hot one in the Valley today.

Beth's internal clock was still on East Coast time, so she had been awake since 5:30 A.M. She had flopped from side to side and from back to belly between the sheets for over thirty minutes trying to convince herself that she should drop off again for a while. *It's Sunday morning and I've only had six hours of sleep. I'm still an emotional wreck from leaving Colin and then seeing Reagan Cole again. I don't have any clothes to pack for my flight, and I don't have to be at Olvera Street until 11:30. I have every right to a couple more hours of sleep.*

Still wide awake at 6:15, Beth had given up trying and decided to go run. But that decision presented additional problems. Her tights, shorts, and good Avia running shoes were with her other things aboard Colin Wendt's yacht somewhere between Antigua and Long Island Sound. She spent several minutes padding through her parents' spacious, hillside house in her underwear, trying to piece together a running outfit she dared wear out in public.

She had found an old pair of her basketball shoes buried in the closet in what Jack and Dona Scibelli still called Beth's room, even though their only child had been out of the home for more than a dozen years. The shoes were scuffed and worn but adequate—her best choice since the tennies in her parents' closet were either too large (Jack's) or too small (Dona's).

Rummaging through her father's bureau, Beth had located a pair of neon-blue nylon running shorts. They were a little baggy on her, but she could cinch them tight around her trim waist with the cord sewn into the waistband. Jack's drawer had also yielded a pair of athletic socks and a well-worn but clean white cotton visor. She recognized the visor from countless games of driveway one-on-one with her father during her teen years.

Jack and Beth were clearly the only athletes in the family. They had joked good-naturedly with Dona that she possessed the coordination and athletic skill of a beached whale.

Beth had completed her running ensemble with a pink tank top from one of Dona's drawers. It was a little small on her, but in contrast to the unflattering blue shorts, the clingy top accentuated her shapely upper body—and Beth wasn't averse to looking as feminine as possible under these conditions at the prospect of encountering a good-looking man or two on the Taft High School field. She hoped her figure and her golden Caribbean tan would more than compensate for a rather slapdash outfit.

Once attired for the track, Beth had batted around the house for several more minutes collecting a sport bottle full of water and a threadbare beach towel to throw over her shoulders during cool-down. She finally left the house at 7 for the short drive down the hill to William H. Taft High School on the southwest corner of Ventura Boulevard and Winnetka Avenue.

When Beth had stepped onto the track after several minutes of stretching, there were only two walkers, a couple in their sixties, plodding around the outside lanes. During her third lap two middle-aged women joggers joined her on the track, but their casual pace convinced Beth that they were there to socialize more than exercise. They adjourned to the bleachers for more intense conversation before Beth had completed her seventh lap. The elderly walkers maintained their slow but steady pace.

Sixteen laps, four miles. Come on, Beth, you can do it! she challenged herself around the first turn of lap twelve. Few and sporadic workouts during her months with Colin Wendt were showing on Beth. Her lungs burned for oxygen. Her quads, seemingly encased in lead, screamed at her to quit. A tender Achilles tendon nagged at her about the inadequacy of the old Nikes she was running in. But Beth was resolute in her intention to burn off a couple of the margaritas and cervezas in which she had overindulged while in Colin's company. And she wanted a good start on the project before she saw Reagan Cole at Quintero's for lunch.

The worst part about pushing herself on the track was not the physical torture. As a disciplined, successful athlete at Taft and USC, Beth was no stranger to grueling workouts. And she continued to pay the price—with occasional lapses during deadline crunches—to keep her thirty-two-year-old body toned and trim. She prided herself in being able to keep pumping iron, tromping away on the Stairmaster, or circling the indoor track when all other women in her Whidbey Island Athletic Club—and many of the men—had collapsed in a puddle of their own sweat.

The torture of the track for Beth was boredom. After the first two or three laps, the scenery became as uninteresting as the revolving video clip in the supermarket produce department describing how to cut and serve kiwi. But Beth hated working out in Valley clubs crowded with snooty Adonis wannabe's and washed-up soap opera stars. So the Taft track was the most expedient means for burning calories and achieving a good cardiovascular workout. Furthermore, monotonous though it was, running laps at the track next to well-traveled Ventura Boulevard was much safer than running alone in the quiet neighborhood—even in upscale Woodland Hills.

It occurred to Beth, as she strode and panted and perspired through the twelfth lap, that her life at the present resembled a repetitive, often wearisome series of laps going nowhere. Eighteen months ago she came to L.A. to cover the big event at the Coliseum on Millennium's Eve, Unity 2000. At that time, her relationship with her parents was strained, essentially because she couldn't stomach their religious lifestyle. Her love life was as cold as the winter breeze blowing across Whidbey Island from Puget Sound. And her career had slumped to the point that she had accepted an assignment to write a supermarket paperback about—of all things—the big religious convocation called Unity 2000.

Little did she know how potentially lethal her visit to L.A. would become. Beth almost died that week. A maniac had plotted to assassinate the religious leaders on the Coliseum platform that night. Beth had stumbled onto his scheme and helped prevent a deadly disaster.

Her narrow escape produced some unexpectedly positive results.

Things turned around for Beth as the dark horror of Millennium's Eve was swept away by the promising glow of the new millennium's dawn. A new appreciation for her parents, who might also have been the killer's potential victims, paved the way for Beth to rekindle a more positive relationship with them. And the two books she had produced from her harrowing Millennium's Eve experiences catapulted her career into an upper-atmosphere orbit.

Then there was Reagan Cole, the knight in shining armor who saved Beth from unspeakable horrors during a rude freeway encounter with the Latin Barons, and then melted the frost in her lonely heart with his rugged charm and tenderness. The new millennium had dawned for Beth with a romance that she thought might be *the* romance of her life, with a man who had captivated her like no other.

Even Beth's spiritual side, dormant since she kicked over the traces of her parents' rote Catholicism during her young teen years, showed new signs of life in the weeks following Unity 2000 in the Coliseum. In fact, all the loose ends in her life were coming together beautifully in those first weeks of the year 2000 until . . .

Beth swept out of the east turn and down the straightaway to begin her thirteenth lap. Same bleachers to her right, same complex of school buildings beyond the field, same unrelenting eight lanes of composition track stretched out before her. She had been here before, twelve times. It was boring.

And here she was in L.A. again, one of her least favorite cities on the face of the globe. Her relationship with Jack and Dona Scibelli was better than it was eighteen months ago, but she had allowed neglect and cynicism to forge a new distance between herself and her parents. Though far from needing to rely on unemployment benefits, Beth's career had suffered a costly blow when she walked out on her wealthy but despicable publisher, Colin Wendt. She felt as much at sixes and sevens about what to do next as she had that last week of 1999. There was a sudden, discomfiting sameness to what was happening in her life that was as insipid as the track she was circling.

Beth's spiritual life, which had budded briefly in the warmth of authentic, winsome, feet-on-the-ground Christians like Dr. No, Mai, Shelby Rider, and then Reagan Cole, had withered quickly. Beth had long since rationalized away the good feelings and settled contentment as emotionalism and wishful thinking. She felt as much at odds today with God—whoever or whatever He really was behind all the religious hype perpetrated in His name—as she had when she landed in L.A. eighteen months ago.

And right in the middle of this depressing déja vu she had found Reagan Cole, just as attractive and available and forgiving as he had been when they first met. The last time they had found each other in L.A., Beth's life took a turn for the better in nearly every respect. But it didn't last long, and in a few months she was back to her old independent, ambitious, lonely self. Having come full circle, the thought of being with Reagan Cole again was as appealing as before. And he seemed just as taken with *her* as before.

It's no use, Beth, she complained as she drove herself into lap fourteen. Beads of perspiration bounced from the ends of her dark hair like dewdrops from a windblown fern. *Getting involved with Reagan again will be short-lived at best. Once you satisfy your magnetic attraction to each other, you'll discover that he is still more interested in his religious experience than in you. Remember those romantic evenings early last year touring the fifth floor at King's House, visiting with emaciated AIDS victims? Is that what you really want?*

Beth spent her fifteenth lap feeling sorry for herself and trying to decide who was to blame for a life that was just running her in circles. She advanced a number of potential candidates: her parents, the Catholic church, a cookie-cutter educational system that hadn't really prepared her for life, and a few people over her thirty-two years who had abused her physically (her third grade teacher with a ruler), sexually (a high school boy during her seventh grade year), and emotionally (a junior high basketball coach and, most recently, Colin Wendt).

But as she swung around the last turn and began the final, grueling lap, Beth got real and gave herself a stern lecture. She had lashed herself with these words before, but she needed to hear them again. What's more, she needed to get beyond the inner diatribe and do something about what she knew was true.

Others may have hurt you, taken advantage of you, or influenced you unjustly, but you're a big girl now. If you stay on this treadmill of unfulfillment and disappointment, it's your own fault. You're not the victim of your past. If your career is going to get back on track after the Havercroft and Wendt debacle, you're going to have to make it happen. If you want lasting peace and a measure of enjoyment with Dad and Mom, you're capable of initiating it and maintaining it. If you hope to find the man of your dreams and convince him that you are the woman of his dreams, you can't wait for him to come to you; you have to put out. And if that man turns out to be Reagan Cole, you may need to bend a little his way instead of expecting him to dance to your tune.

Beth crossed the finish line with her head tossed back and a grimace of exhaustion creasing her sweat-stained face. Slowing to a trot she scooped up the towel from beside the track, used it to blot her face dry, then tossed it over her shoulders like a shawl for a one-lap cool-down walk. A good-looking guy in his mid-twenties jogged past and flashed a "Hi, babe" grin and wink at her. Considering what her moist, stringy hair, mismatched outfit, and faded Donald Duck beach towel looked like, Beth judged the guy to be myopic or excessively charitable. She couldn't find the strength to return his smile.

The only issue Beth had not lectured herself about during the sixteenth lap was religion. She was no stranger to poignant religious experiences. Her First Communion at age eight had been so meaningful to her that her lips trembled as she received the wafer. But the Eucharist quickly became commonplace, and she felt no more or less blessed if she received the elements with holy thoughts or made a mental game of the Sacrament. And she didn't live any differently either.

Beth had expected Confirmation at age eleven to be another launchpad into fulfilling spirituality. She took her vows quite confident that she would go on to become the first woman priest in the Catholic Church—or at least a Eucharistic Minister—by the time she was twenty. And she told God of her availability repeatedly.

But try as she might, young Beth couldn't make herself behave like a nice Catholic girl and future priest, and God didn't seem to care about helping her. She still exploded with anger and bad language, especially in the heat of competition. *God, why didn't You keep me from blowing up in the game today?* She still studied hard to keep her grades up, but took liberties when she ran out of time or discovered a dishonest means to a higher mark. *I vowed to be Your priest. Why didn't You help me find the right answers to the exam? Why did You force me to cheat?*

Beth judged that God hadn't taken her seriously, so she decided at age fourteen no longer to take Him seriously. She made up excuses to skip Mass as often as possible. And she hounded Jack and Dona mercilessly until they allowed her to transfer from the Catholic school she had attended since kindergarten to Taft of the Los Angeles Unified School District, between her freshman and sophomore years. Jack and Dona might not have been so compliant on the school issue, had they not begun privately to doubt their own faith in the Church. This fact was kept from Beth until her first year at USC, when her parents left the Catholic fold to become followers of right-wing Protestant sinfighter Rev. Simon Holloway.

Beth had no more spiritual mountaintop experiences as an adolescent and young adult. Moreover, she did everything in her power to prevent them. She stayed away from churches as if they were contaminated, going so far as to limit her attendance at weddings to those of her dearest friends. At USC, she distanced herself from students who carried Bibles or waved gospel tracts in her face. She avoided any student movement or group which used a C—for Christ or Christian—in its acronym: Campus Crusade for Christ, Trojan Christian Fellowship, even the nominal Young Women's Christian Association. She still believed that God was the Father Almighty, Maker of heaven and earth, but she no longer deemed Him sufficiently capable or concerned to play a major role in her life.

There were occasional lapses in Beth's rebellion, usually during crises of panic or pain. She did a lot of praying when she thought she had broken an ankle—which turned out to be a sprain—in the first half of a game against Stanford. Then there was the flight to Hong Kong in '93, when the 747 ran off the end of the runway and nosed into the bay on landing. Sloshing frantically through the cabin and paddling to shore with 200 other passengers, Beth renewed every vow she had ever vowed to God and promised to give Him every child she bore, if He would keep the jumbo jet from blowing up and killing them all. There wasn't so much as a puff of smoke out of the broken plane.

But Beth's devotion barely outlasted the moments of crisis that provoked them, and she quickly slipped back into her confident, self-reliant self.

Never had Beth come closer to renewing her complete trust in God than during the last forty-eight hours of 1999 and the weeks immediately following the millennium's dawn. This was not a *moment* of crisis, but *two days* of crisis. She prayed like she had never prayed in her life. And, as she discovered later, others were praying. As a result she not only escaped with her life but was instrumental in stopping the assassin.

For several days afterward, Beth had been exposed to the very down-to-earth Christian people who had prayed for her safety. These weren't the pie-in-the-sky-when-you-die-by-and-by or glitz-and-glamour kind of people who had turned Beth off to Christianity. They were the roll-up-your-sleeves-and-get-it-done kind of people who were quietly and confidently living their faith in the trenches where L.A.'s hungry and hurting were so often overlooked. The devotion and sacrifice of Dr. No and his wife and staff had made a profound impact on Beth.

She trudged back to the car, unsure of what to do with the thoughts which had occupied her mind during the run. She didn't feel that a self-inflicted lecture of spiritual devotion was appropriate. But she was strangely moved to consider praying about what was going on in her life. Beth hadn't said so much as a word to God in months.

Thirty-two

Evan had been out to the driveway twice looking for the Sunday morning paper before he remembered that he had suspended delivery service for two weeks beginning today because of his honeymoon. He could have stopped the *Star-Free Press* over a week ago for all the time he had had to read it. He had tried to get out to the South Jetty nearly every morning to surf, since he would be far from the Pacific Ocean during his two weeks away with Shelby. The remaining hours of his days were crammed with office appointments and rounds at the hospital. And every evening found him in the Flair RV until after 10 o'clock, polishing or tweaking something in preparation for the long journey to the Grand Canyon.

He hadn't watched the evening news on TV since midweek. And the daily editions of the newspaper had gone directly from the driveway to the recycle pile without being read. Now, the one morning he had a few minutes to linger over the paper while drinking his coffee, there was no paper to read.

With no newspaper, Evan had puttered around the downstairs completing a few last-minute details for leaving the house: testing and retesting the security system, programming digital timers to turn lights and music on and off as if someone was home, moving houseplants out to the patio where they could be watered by the sprinkling system. He also mixed up a batch of his famous cinnamon rolls—overflowing with raisins and nuts—to bake for breakfast.

Evan had risen early and shaved and dressed quietly in the bathroom while Shelby dozed on. Despite the misty gray morning, he had dressed for hot weather: a plum-colored T-shirt, baggy tan cotton shorts, and his comfortable Rockport walkers. He was aware that by the time they drove the RV through Orange County and turned north on I-15 toward Barstow, the outside temperature would be in the 90s. And when they reached the Mojave Desert on the hot, dry stretch of I-40 between Barstow and Kingman, Arizona, it would be in the low 100s.

The air conditioning would keep the Flair reasonably comfortable inside as they traveled, but summer apparel would be the standard uniform for the next two weeks in the stifling heat of the southwestern United States. Evan and Shelby had packed the wardrobes in the RV accordingly.

When Evan heard Shelby stirring upstairs, he put the cinnamon rolls into the oven to bake, ran a dozen oranges through the automatic juicer, and blended the ingredients of a veggie omelette for their first breakfast as husband and wife. Shelby had warned Evan during their courtship that she hated eating in bed, so he set two places on the small table in the nook with plain white china, crystal juice glasses, blue linen napkins, and a cheery arrangement of Shasta daisies freshly cut from his garden.

Shelby appeared in the kitchen just as Evan was lifting the pan of cinnamon rolls from the oven. She was dressed in knee-length shorts—blue, lavender, and green madras plaid—with a matching blue polo, white sandals, and ceramic earrings that tied the ensemble together.

When their eyes met across the kitchen, they beamed with contentment, like a couple of kids unable to suppress the giddy triumph at keeping their secret from everyone else. Their momentary locked gaze communicated volumes of wonder, gratitude, and love.

"How did you sleep, angel?" Evan asked, setting the pan on a trivet atop the counter.

Shelby crossed the room to greet him with an embrace. "Wonderfully well, my darling, the most satisfying night of sleep in my life," she cooed near her husband's ear, as he welcomed her into his arms. "I almost wish we weren't leaving for our trip today. I could really enjoy a cozy, leisurely Sunday just being here with you—alone."

"Mm, that *does* sound nice," Evan whispered, unwilling to let her go. Then, glancing at his watch over Shelby's shoulder, he said, "Unfortunately, we have a space reserved at an RV park in Needles tonight. So . . . "

"I know," Shelby said, releasing a melodramatic sigh that turned to a soft laugh. They broke their embrace but quickly linked hands and stayed close. "We have places to go and promises to keep and miles to go before we sleep, or however that poem goes. I've been a rather organized, regimented person all my life, but now I'm married to Mr. Schedule himself. Will the two of us ever be able to do anything spontaneously?"

"We can do something spontaneous every week, angel," Evan said with a grin, "as long as it's requested in triplicate along with a comprehensive cost appraisal, scheduled at least a month in advance, and thoroughly planned."

The laugh they enjoyed ended with another longing gaze which telegraphed eager anticipation for their two weeks alone and subsequent years of life and love together.

Evan occupied Shelby with a glass of orange juice, then poured the omelette mixture into a hot skillet on the range. As the eggs began to cook, he quickly transferred the warm rolls to a linen-lined basket and placed it and a carafe of coffee on the table. After folding the omelette at the perfect moment and allowing it another minute to cook, he split it with the spatula and scooped one half to Shelby's plate and the other half to his.

"Maybe during our trip I can teach you how to drive the beach buggy," Evan said as they ate.

Shelby groaned. "Why can't we trade it in for a wagon with automatic? I hate driving cars with stick shift."

"Trade in my beach buggy—my baby?" Evan responded, sounding wounded for effect. "That would be like disowning Malika and sending her back to the streets of L.A. Besides, how can you hate something you've never done? Once you get the hang of the five-speed, you may enjoy it."

"God created me with only two feet," Shelby argued weakly while lightly sprinkling pepper over her eggs, "one for the gas and one for the brake. I don't have a foot left for the clutch. And I have always been taught to keep two hands on the wheel. That leaves me nothing to change gears with. Driving a stick shift is . . . unnatural."

Evan chuckled at his bride's intentionally comic rationalization, then came back to his point. "See, if you could drive the buggy, it would even have saved us time today. You could leave your car in the garage and drop me off at the office on the way to the Hilton to get the RV fired up and ready. Then we could just load the buggy on the carrier after you kiss Malika and your parents good-bye and leave from there. As it is, I have to follow you back up the hill to drop off the Lincoln."

"Puts a real crimp in your plans, doesn't it, Mr. Schedule?" Shelby retorted with an impish twinkle. "Five minutes wasted for all eternity."

"But that's not all," Evan asserted, enjoying the humorous repartee. "What if we're out in the Arizona desert with the buggy next week, and I get captured by an Indian raiding party?"

"You've been watching too many corny westerns."

"This is hypothetical. Work with me for a minute."

"All right, so we're attacked by a savage band of those roadside Navajo jewelry sellers I've read about, for example."

"Exactly. And if I get dragged off into the Painted Desert to get scalped, how are you going to drive to the fort and get help from the calvary if you can't use a stick shift?"

"That's *cavalry. Calvary* is where the cross was."

"Whatever. How are you going to call out the cal−, er, cavalry?"

"I guess I'll have to use the car phone," Shelby said matter-of-factly, struggling to keep herself from laughing.

Evan shook his head. "Sorry, angel, but the treaty with the Indians strictly prohibits the use of car phones during a raid."

Shelby hummed plaintively. "In that case, I'm really going to miss that wavy black hair of yours. But yesterday I promised to love you forever, so I guess I'm stuck with you−baldy."

They laughed and bantered through the rest of breakfast without resolving anything about Shelby and the beach buggy. Working together, they quickly cleaned the kitchen and transferred food from the refrigerator into a cardboard box for transport to the RV. They commented often about their excitement at being together and leaving for the Grand Canyon.

They loaded the food and the last of their luggage into the back of the Datsun wagon. At 7:45, Shelby slipped a white sweater over her polo, kissed Evan good-bye, and left for the Oxnard Hilton in her Lincoln.

Evan toured the house checking windows and doors and then arming the security system from the kitchen computer. Assured that all they yet needed to do was deposit the Lincoln in the garage, he fired up the beach buggy and headed down the hill toward his office where the RV was parked. With his head swimming with the tasks he had to complete before they left, he didn't notice the silver blue Jaguar sitting at the curb two blocks from his driveway with two occupants slumped low in the front seat.

Thirty-three

Libby Carroll stood bundled in her hooded parka on the observation deck, as the giant white and green ferry, the *Yakima*, churned laboriously out of Elliott Bay into Puget Sound. The morning sun blazed brightly from a cloudless sky, but a chilly headwind kept most of the ferry's passengers inside drinking coffee or cocoa. Their vehicles, including Libby's midnight-blue Seville, stood silent and empty in the bowels of the ferry for the hour-plus westward journey across the Sound to Bremerton, Washington.

Libby welcomed the warmth of the sun on her back, the sting of the breeze on her face, and the solitude of being outside virtually alone. She stayed at the railing above the ferry's bow as other passengers, most of them out-of-towners who hadn't thought to bring a warm coat on summer vacation, ventured outside for a look only to scamper back inside after a few minutes. The monotonous drone of the ferry's engines and the vibration in the steel deck beneath her feet warmed Libby inside. It was a simple comfort she had enjoyed since she rode her first Seattle ferry as a toddler.

To her left along the eastern shore of the Sound was a crowded array of giant crane booms and rusty hulks designating the shipyards. In the middle of the Sound to the south was serene Vashon Island, home for hundreds of commuters purposely isolated from the big city by a twenty-minute ferry ride. Straight ahead was Bainbridge Island and behind it to the southwest the old navy town of Bremerton, accessible to the ferry system through Rich Passage and the Sinclair Inlet.

In the distance and slightly to the north stood a line of snowy peaks rising from the Olympic Peninsula: Mt. Angeles, Elk Mountain, Mt. Deception, Mt. Constance, Mt. Anderson, and the Brothers. Beyond them, like two proud parents nearly obscured by their large family, were Mt. Carrie and Mt. Olympus.

Far up the Sound to her right Libby could make out the southern tip of Whidbey Island. And in the near distance, at the northern rim of Elliott Bay, was Queen Anne Hill and the brown-roofed, red-brick house on West Kinnear Place where she lived. Libby prided herself in being able to spot her dream house on the hill from the ferry on a clear day, and from the air whenever a flight into Seattle employed a low, southerly approach to SeaTac over the civic center.

When she arrived in Bremerton, Libby planned to nose through a couple of her favorite galleries and out-of-the-way shops and enjoy a quiet lunch at a restaurant near the water. Then she would take a leisurely drive up the eastern finger of the peninsula to quaint Poulsbo for more window shopping, before returning to Bremerton for the late-afternoon ferry back to Seattle. There was no real reason for Libby to go to Bremerton; it was the unhurried ferry ride and mindless day away from home she craved.

She had originally considered attending church this morning, something she did occasionally when she felt steamrolled by job stress and needed a spiritual uplift. The music at University Presbyterian was inspiring, and the sermons challenged her intellectually in topic areas she didn't often think about. Furthermore, the congregation was large enough to allow her anonymity. She could slip in and out without getting buttonholed in the narthex by the Friendship Committee asking her why she wasn't in service last week or by someone from the Women's Ministry Commission begging her to sign up for a Working Women's Bible Study Group.

But Libby had discarded the idea of attending church as she sipped her first cup of coffee. Today, more than inspiration or intellectual challenge, she needed time to think about Brett's angry demand that she reveal his father's identity. Robert Rhodes, Libby's handsome stockbroker companion last night, had seemed barely interested in Libby's conflict with Brett, let alone sympathetic or helpful. "You're the parent, he's the child. Tell him the way it's going to be and get on with your career," had been the upshot of Robert's advice.

Libby wasn't sure such a hard-nosed stand with Brett would be effective. And she was increasingly ambivalent that her rigid posture of noncompliance was even fair. But after talking with Robert and wrestling with the issue through a fitful night's sleep, she was still adrift without a viable alternative. She needed a day away to mull over Brett's angry words and her options.

"Dr. Carroll, what a coincidence." The voice off Libby's left shoulder was youthful and masculine with a slight Oriental accent. She was not surprised that someone on the ferry knew her name; she had lived in Seattle most of her life. But she was immediately disappointed about her solitude being invaded.

Libby turned to find a young man approaching her wearing purple U Dub sweats and a gold stocking cap pulled over his ears. His hands were jammed into the pouch of his sweatshirt, and he squinted his eyes against the stiff breeze pouring over the bow from the west. Libby recognized him as a student who worked part-time somewhere in the administration building at the university, but she didn't remember his name.

"Brandon Yu," he said, alert to the questioning look on her face. "I work in the financial aid office at the U."

"Hello, Brandon," Libby said with a weak, forced smile. She thought she should offer to shake his hand, but quickly decided to keep her hands inside the fur-lined pockets of her parka. Instead, she offered a mildly polite, "It's a nice day for a ferry ride, don't you think?" Then she again turned her face into the wind, wishing she hadn't ended her innocuous statement with a question.

"I've been hoping to talk to you, Dr. Carroll," Brandon Yu said. "My friend, Tansey, says that you have an opening in your office for a student assistant this fall."

At the mention of Tansey Underwood, one of three student assistants in her office, Libby remembered where she had seen Brandon Yu. He had spent several afternoons a month hanging around Tansey's desk—or more correctly, hanging on Tansey and distracting her from her work. Libby surmised that Brandon wanted a job in the provost's office as an excuse to be close to his main squeeze.

Brandon continued, "May I talk to you about—"

Libby turned toward the young man again and cut him off, hoping to save his breath and to rescue her seclusion as soon as possible. "Actually, Brandon, my assistant, Sylvia Eberhard, handles those matters."

"I understand, Dr. Carroll. I've been trying to set up an appointment with Mrs. Eberhard since the end of the term, but your secretary says—"

"Yes, Mrs. Eberhard is on an extended vacation, but she will be back a week from Monday. I suggest that you call her then. There's plenty of time for an interview before fall term." Libby instantly determined to instruct Sylvia to put Brandon Yu's application at the bottom of the stack.

Brandon seemed only slightly dissuaded. "I *will* make an appointment, Dr. Carroll, but since we both have some time to kill right now, perhaps I could tell you about my qualifications."

"I'm very sorry, Brandon," Libby said, overplaying the kindness to a subtle edge that she hoped he would catch. "Maybe *you* have time to kill today but, unfortunately, *I* don't. I have some rather pressing business to attend to before we reach Bremerton. Perhaps we will have a chance to talk in the fall." *But more likely, we won't,* she added silently.

"Oh, I'm very sorry, Dr. Carroll," Brandon said, adding a slight bow to his apology. "I didn't mean to bother you. Yes, I will talk to Mrs. Eberhard next week. Thank you. I'm sorry." Then he backed away with a couple of nods and rejoined a knot of students on the port rail.

Libby wasn't sure if Brandon Yu was genuinely penitent or just kissing up to a potential employer. At the moment, it didn't really matter. She was free of an annoying distraction.

Libby used the break in her train of thought to go inside and buy a cup of cocoa from the snack bar. It was noisy in the large, enclosed observation deck. People filled every one of the booths beside the windows, eating, playing cards, or just watching the whitecaps which dotted the Sound like clumps of white wildflowers waving in the wind on a broad, blue-green meadow.

Deciding not to tempt Brandon Yu to another intrusion, Libby strolled the length of the cabin and outside to the rear deck, finding a solitary place at the rail overlooking the stern. The wind sweeping around the ferry was now at her back, flipping up the hood on the parka until it wrapped around her head and covered her ears. The sun in her face and the warmth on her cheeks felt as good as the sips of cocoa warming her stomach.

The interlude with brash Brandon Yu prompted Libby to wonder again about Brett. *Where did he spend the night? Where is he now? What stunt will he pull next to get back at me for shutting him out of his father's life?*

Libby had tried Brett's personal number twice: once last night after returning from the restaurant and once this morning before leaving home. There had been no answer. She couldn't imagine that Brett wasn't carrying his phone. He just wasn't answering it. But she had tapped off the phone both times without leaving a message. It was just as well Brett hadn't answered; she didn't know what she would have said to him anyway.

She sighed with resignation. *Maybe I should try to find Tango and break the news to him myself,* Libby thought, holding the idea of contacting Brett's father at bay while she contemplated the possible repercussions. *Brett is a clever boy. He may find some way to locate his father on his own, and the shock is liable to set them both off. Then I'll have* two *men ready to kill me.*

Kill was the wrong word to cross Libby's mind at this precise moment. A terrifying, unbidden image swept over her like a paralyzing arctic wind, seemingly turning the warm cocoa in the pit of her stomach, as well as the fiery globe blazing at her from the sky, to ice. She suddenly felt very cold and very alone.

The image was dark, just as the real event had been that horrible night in Portland's Washington Park twenty-two years earlier. With Libby sitting behind the wheel egging them on through the window of her rental car, her two friends from the football team had pummeled the obnoxious creep from Portland State senseless. Neil McGruder had repeatedly slurred Libby and other black students who had traveled north from CSUN for the game as "Watts rioters." Libby had applauded her two buddies, whom she had nicknamed Choo-Choo and Tango, for their restraint in River Jack's. Then, in Washington Park, she cheered even louder with every blow they landed to McGruder's head and body.

The three friends, somewhere on the bubble between sober and drunk, had left the park cocky and jubilant, having righted an ugly wrong by paying McGruder his due. They shared a can of beer in Libby's room at the Marriott—a toast to their accomplishment. Then the two football players left for their respective rooms.

Had Libby known that McGruder was lying dead in the park, she would never have joined the guys in the celebration. Nor would she have invited Tango into her room when he came back to pick up the letterman's jacket he had forgotten. But she did, and they shared another beer and laughed some more about McGruder waking up in the morning not knowing what had hit him.

Libby, Tango, and his constant shadow, Choo-choo, had become good friends. She had met them both at Cupid's, a popular hot dog stand a few steps from CSUN's main entrance at Nordhoff and Lindley in Northridge. Libby had worked at Cupid's while establishing California residency in preparation for enrolling at CSUN.

Her journey from her hometown of Seattle to Northridge had been a painful one. After high school graduation, Libby had rebelled against her parents' authority and followed a high school sweetheart from Seattle to L.A. The boy had been recruited to play basketball at UCLA, and Libby naively expected him to take her along for the ride and eventually marry her. To her parents' horror, Libby gave up a track scholarship at Central Washington State to become Alonzo Charles' groupie.

But even before Alonzo's first college game, he dumped Libby for an L.A. girl. Too proud to return to Seattle, Libby decided to get a job, establish residency in California, get her degree, and pursue her track career somewhere in L.A. She chose Cal State Northridge because of its respectable academics and a modest athletic scholarship. Slopping hot dogs at Cupid's wasn't Libby's first choice, but it was a job, and she got to meet a lot of students who lined up day and night for the Valley's best chili dogs.

During their first year together playing football for CSUN, Choo-choo and Tango used to come to Cupid's on Libby's shift to entertain and impress her with chili dog eating contests. She loved watching them each down "five with everything," foot-long dogs with mustard, onions, and chili, and practically gag trying to force down a sixth.

And Libby became one of her friends' greatest fans, coming out to football practices and yelling wildly for them during games. She began calling them Choo-choo, because he ran with the abandon of a runaway train on the field and Tango, for his ability to dance away from tacklers.

The following spring, Libby's two male friends reciprocated. They showed up during track workouts and warmed up with her, then attended track meets to cheer her on during the sprint and relay events.

Libby was fast enough to beat them both in the 100-meter dash. So in response to the nicknames she had given them, Choo-choo and Tango simply called her the Jet.

For the two men, the attraction to Libby was clearly more than platonic, and she couldn't deny her romantic interest in them. Throughout that first year Libby dated Choo-choo and Tango casually, aware and undisturbed that they were seeing other women. But the three of them discovered that they had much more riotous fun together as a trio than they had as dating pairs.

In the fall of '79, Libby accepted the position of statistician for the football team, sitting in the press booth during every game and keeping track of players, yardage, scoring, penalties, etc. The mundane job was simply a means to an end for Libby. Traveling with the football team allowed her and her two friends to take their fun on the road when the Matadors traveled to San Luis Obispo (Cal State), Sacramento (Sacramento State), Reno (University of Nevada), and Portland (Portland State). The party started as soon as the game was over on Saturday afternoon and often lasted until curfew—or beyond if Choo-choo, Tango, and the Jet could find a way to do it.

Libby and Tango were taken by surprise in the early morning hours at the Portland Marriott, after the three friends had roughed up the disgusting Neil McGruder. Their latent romantic attraction, temporarily magnified by alcohol and the aphrodisiac of their triumph over McGruder, subtly manipulated the conversation from their prank to themselves, their dreams, and their fears. Being alone and emotionally unguarded proved too great a temptation, and they succumbed to each other in a clumsy yet passionate rush.

Before Tango slipped back to his room at 5 A.M., the two of them confided a mutual hope that their relationship grow deeper and more intimate than the sexual encounter they had just shared. But they agreed to keep it a secret from Choo-choo until they had sorted out their feelings for each other.

However, in the morning, after the shocking revelation of McGruder's death, an even more desperate agreement to silence was forged between the three friends. Subsequently, Libby and Tango's night of passion was hidden away in a vault of secrecy which had remained locked for twenty-two years.

Libby moved to another location on the rear deck of the ferry to escape a noisy cluster of kids. She sipped the last of her lukewarm cocoa and tossed the paper cup into a nearby trash receptacle. Then she returned to the rail to appreciate the panoramic view of downtown Seattle, the city which had welcomed her home after the abrupt conclusion of her studies at Cal State Northridge.

Libby had flown home for Christmas break a week after the incident in Washington Park. That last week on campus had been a week of sheer dread. She lived in hellish fear that the next rap on her dormitory door would be the police coming to arrest her for complicity in the death of Neil McGruder. Being finals week, Libby had little time for sleep. When she did drop off for catnaps between cram sessions, her mind was tormented by visions of McGruder's ghost coming after her.

Libby had prayed frantically day and night that her friends Choo-choo and Tango would remain firm in their pledge to secrecy, although she lived in fear of accidentally breaking the pact herself during an unguarded moment of conversation.

Libby had patched up her relationship with her parents the previous summer. But when she arrived home to Kent—a bedroom community south of downtown Seattle—for Christmas break in 1979, Libby behaved like a stranger. She stayed in her room alone most mornings complaining of nausea, refusing the company and comfort of her older siblings and cheery little nieces and nephews. She had literally worried herself sick over finals, she maintained.

"Is there any possibility you are pregnant?" Libby's discerning oldest sister, Claudia, a mother of four herself, had posed the question privately on the morning of Christmas Eve. Libby had just dry-heaved at the aroma of Dad's traditional holiday flapjacks, sprinkled with red and green M&M's, frying in bacon grease downstairs.

Libby wasn't naive about human reproduction. But having survived a few incidents of experimentation with Alonzo Charles after graduation, she had naively assumed a kind of immunity to getting pregnant until she really wanted to, especially in view of the fact that she and Tango had been together only once.

However, a pregnancy test after Christmas confirmed Claudia's suspicion. Libby secretly and stoically accepted the result as God's punishment for her role in the McGruder beating. She imagined His pronouncement of judgment: *You took a life, so your life and career must be sacrificed to bring another life into the world.*

Libby's parents were informed of the pregnancy, their disappointment was expressed and received, and then their support was lovingly offered. Inquiries about the child's father were met with, "A foolish one-night stand with someone I'll never see again," and it soon became a non-issue in the family.

Dad and Mom Carroll had raised their children to abhor abortion as a heinous moral crime, "Murder of the innocent unborn, pure and simple," her father used to say. Predisposed to carry the infant to term, Libby dropped out of CSUN immediately and moved in with Mom and Dad. She had not been pregnant three months before she decided to keep the baby.

By the time Brett was born in early September 1980, Libby's fears about the incident in Washington Park coming to light had largely abated. Instead, the demands and challenges of single motherhood consumed her waking hours. Uncomfortable about living off the welfare of her parents, Libby made plans to find a place of her own after Brett's first Christmas. Unwilling to depend on the welfare system of the state, Libby began selling cosmetics door to door during the day—taking Brett with her in the stroller—and waiting tables in the evening, accepting Grandpa and Grandma's offer of free baby-sitting. And unwilling to grovel under the sentence of a purposeless existence she had assumed had been handed down by God, Libby scrimped and saved, ran and pumped iron, and was accepted to Central Washington State University in Ellensburg on a partial athletic scholarship.

In the fall of 1981, with cute little Brett in tow, Libby had bolted from the starting blocks with new resolve and sprinted headlong into her promising future. She hoped to eventually outrun the menacing clouds of the past which constantly loomed on the distant horizon of her mind.

The ferry's engine slowed, announcing the onset of its gradual approach to the dock. A voice over the loudspeaker directed passengers to return to their vehicles on the lower deck in preparation for disembarking. Libby joined a small stream of people coursing into the upper deck cabin and merging with other streams to funnel down the stairway.

And the rest, as they say, is history, she thought as she walked, momentarily cherishing the highlights of the past twenty years. Undergraduate honor student, Olympic-class sprinter, postgraduate honor student, double master of arts, doctor of philosophy, university administrator, successful single parent . . .

Successful single parent? Libby cross-examined herself critically. *I would be hard-pressed to convince an openminded jury on that count, after what happened last night.* It was stifling in the crowded stairwell, but Libby shuddered again at the chilling thought of telling Brett about his father and possibly opening the door to her carefully concealed past.

What kind of mother am I if I don't tell him about Tango? A failure. An ogre. But what kind of life will I have if I do tell him and lose my career and possibly my freedom? Libby stifled an involuntary moan at the fearful, humiliating thought of facing criminal charges for McGruder's death after all these years. The feeling was reminiscent of her terror during her last week in the dormitory at CSUN over two decades earlier. She sensed that the dilemma would tear her apart soon if she didn't resolve it.

Reaching her dark-blue Seville, Libby removed her parka and tossed it into the back seat. She wouldn't need it again until the chilly ferry ride back to Seattle.

Under the parka she was wearing designer jeans, fashionable boots, a tailored, long-sleeved plaid shirt, and colorful suspenders designed more for form than function. Her black hair was pulled back to a bow the color of her suspenders. She looked like the answer to a lonely lumberjack's prayers.

Libby slipped behind the wheel to await the docking and the single-file departure of vehicles in front of her. "Dear God, what am I supposed to do?" she whispered, gripping the wheel, surprised that she was crying again. "I have to sort this out today. I have to come up with a solution before I get back on this ferry. But I haven't a clue. I can't do this. O God, O God, O God!"

Libby dug a Kleenex out of her handbag just in time to dry her tears before following a black Toyota pickup out of the ferry's belly, up the ramp, and into the sunshine.

Thirty-four

Evan and Shelby's Fleetwood Flair was white with a teal accent stripe along the roof line on each side. A larger teal stripe and narrow gold stripe encircled the thirty-foot coach horizontally, from just below the massive bus-style windshield in front to the canvas-wrapped spare tire attached to the back wall. Below the living room windows on both sides, the two stripes broke into a group of wild, diagonal squiggles resembling artsy spikes on an EKG readout. When they first saw the Flair, Evan and Shelby had joked that the exterior must have been designed by a cardiologist.

Evan had been inside the RV only a few minutes stowing perishable foods in the refrigerator when he heard a firm knock on the side of the coach. He had left both the outward-swinging main door and the inner screen door wide open so he could toss out cardboard cartons as he emptied them.

"Come on in," Evan called out, still kneeling in front of the open fridge preparing a space for a container of cold prime-rib slices. The coach's only entrance was just behind the cab on the passenger's side at the front of the kitchen area; the refrigerator where Evan was working was at the rear of the kitchen, so he couldn't see who was knocking. The venetian blinds over the kitchen table were still drawn, further obstructing his view of the outside.

Evan assumed the visitor must be someone from the family or a small circle of close friends who had dropped by to say good-bye and happy honeymoon. Few other people knew he was here. Expecting to see a familiar face, Evan didn't bother to look up until he had stashed the Tupperware box behind a jar of sweet butter chips.

The back light from the open door cast the visitor's face in shadow, so the first detail Evan noticed was a slouchy golf hat. Next he picked out the wraparound sunglasses and a short, light-colored beard. Evan stood to face the man, closing the refrigerator door with his left hand.

The person standing beside the kitchen table six feet away was a stranger. Evan quickly assumed that the man must be a panhandler who, wandering down Loma Vista and seeing the open door on the coach, had stopped to beg for a handout—although he appeared rather well dressed for a panhandler.

Then another possibility crossed Evan's mind: the stranger might be an addict come to force the doctor to open his office in the medical building in order to steal drugs. He eyed the stranger for a moment weighing the possible threat and quietly affirming a plan he had predetermined to employ years ago in such a situation: comply with the thief's demands and save your skin, but get a good look at him so you can describe him to the police.

Finally, Evan said in a mildly hospitable tone, "What can I do for you?"

The stranger continued to stare at Evan from behind the shiny blue lenses. Then the whisper of a smile appeared on his lips. "You haven't changed a bit, Evan," he said. It was something an old friend might say, but Evan detected a note of purposeful distance in the tone.

The fact that the man had used his first name and was smiling—if only slightly—disarmed much of Evan's alarm to imminent danger. There was also something distantly familiar in the intruder's voice. Evan quickly eliminated the possibility of the man being a former patient because he hadn't used "Doc" or "Doctor" in his greeting. But when he tried to match the voice and the shadowy face with a gallery of portraits flashing onto the screen of his mind, Evan drew a blank.

"You have me at a disadvantage," Evan said at last, guardedly curious. "You know my name, but I'm afraid I don't recognize you."

The man's smile was only a few degrees warmer. "Maybe this will help," he said, removing first his hat and then his shades and setting them on the kitchen table.

Even in the dim light of the coach, the blonde buzz-cut and the shape of the deep-set eyes—added to the familiar voice—were enough to confirm the man's identity. A name leaped into Evan's consciousness, and the name and face together instantly weakened his knees and stopped his breathing.

After several seconds, Evan pushed the words out at a whisper, "Nolan Jakes." With the mention of the name, an avalanche of haunting memories thundered down on him, memories of a night years ago when the two middle-aged men facing one another were young, brash, and very foolish.

"Bingo," Jakes responded without enthusiasm. "Sorry if the beard threw you off. It's a fake, of course. I'm wearing it for obvious reasons."

"Obvious reasons?" Evan echoed, feeling dazed, as if trying to understand the meaning of a weird dream. "What do you mean? What . . . what . . . ?" He didn't know what to ask, what to say, or what to think.

"Haven't you been watching TV lately, man? Haven't you read the papers?" Jakes quizzed skeptically. "Haven't you heard about the mess your old football buddy has gotten himself into?"

Evan felt out of breath and slightly dizzy. He reached out to the refrigerator to stabilize himself. "I don't know what you're talking about, Nolan. Why are you here? What's going on?"

Jakes didn't answer him. Instead, he appraised Evan's apparent ignorance with a stare. Then, without taking his eyes off of Evan, he called over his shoulder, "Margo, c'mon in."

A petite platinum blonde wearing bleached jeans, a white sleeveless top, large dark glasses, and a serious expression stepped up into the coach. Evan barely noticed her as his reeling mind scrambled to sort through the sudden appearance of the one man in all creation he had hoped never to see again.

"Evan, this is Margo, a very good friend of mine," Jakes said. Margo peered at Evan from behind Jakes' shoulder in the narrow kitchen walkway. She removed her glasses, revealing a pretty face and alert, penetrating eyes. Evan flicked her a glance, fighting through his shock and trying to guess her role in this very bad, very real dream.

Jakes continued, "And Margo, this is the old football buddy I've been telling you about, Evan Rider—I mean, *Doctor* Evan Rider." Margo sized him up without changing expression.

"The good doctor here has been so wrapped up with his wedding that he hasn't heard our shocking news—or so he says," Jakes said, watching Evan for a telltale response.

"I find that hard to believe," Margo said. "It was in the paper this morning, so I'm sure it's been on TV."

"I haven't seen the paper and I haven't watched TV in days, so I don't know what you're talking about," Evan retorted, as anger and fear battled for supremacy within him. He struggled to get a grip on himself and press the issue, even though he was afraid he wouldn't like what he might hear. Whatever this was about, he had to get to the bottom of it in a hurry and get rid of his two visitors before Shelby arrived. "Nolan, you haven't searched me out to renew an old friendship, so let's cut to the chase. What are you doing here and what do you want?"

Jakes nodded. "You're right, doc. We don't have time for small talk. Margo and I have something very specific in mind. You might say it's kind of a proposition with definite benefits for both parties. But you might want to sit down for this."

Jakes slid into the bench seat on the door side of the dinette and motioned Evan toward the bench on the opposite side. Evan complied only to expedite the matter. Margo pulled the coach's door closed, locked it, and sat down on the corner of the sofa opposite her boyfriend.

Evan studied the face of the man sitting across from him. The false beard wasn't as convincing as it had been on first glance. And from this distance Evan could see the lines of age across Jakes' forehead and around his eyes. The eyes had lost some of the intensity from the days when the gutsy, small college quarterback relished taking on linemen twice his size.

Evan also noticed smudges of what appeared to be makeup on the man's nose, cheek, and brow, rather crude attempts at recapturing youth, he thought. The face was clearly twenty-two years older than when Evan had last seen it. But the blonde buzz-cut was exactly the same as Evan remembered it, as if Jakes' hair had grown out half an inch after birth and stopped, sentencing Jakes' head to life as a fuzzy cue ball.

"You know about my time in Canada, don't you?" Jakes began, suddenly sounding more conversational than confrontational.

"Football in B.C? Yes, I read a little about you in the papers." In reality, Evan had steadfastly tried to avoid hearing or reading anything about the more famous of his two friends from CSUN. Every encounter with Jakes' name or picture in the media activated old, painful memories.

"And you know that I moved back to L.A. in '97?"

Evan shook his head slowly. "I saw one of your car commercials down there a couple of years ago, but I didn't know you were living in L.A."

Jakes hissed derisively. "It wasn't much of a life, but I was existing. I worked for that scumbag Fryman, first in his car business and then in his 'pharmaceutical' operation, as he liked to call it."

"Drugs," Evan clarified.

Jakes nodded and looked away with an expression that Evan took to reflect a modicum of remorse.

Evan sensed a wave of mild relief, hoping that Nolan Jakes had come only to bum drugs off him. He decided that he would gladly give Jakes anything in his office just to get rid of him before Shelby returned.

Jakes continued, "Cutting to the chase, as you say, I got caught by the law. But instead of pressing charges, the cops cut me a deal: I narc on Fryman and they turn me loose. Not a bad deal for a guy facing prison until he's a senior citizen, eh?"

Evan did not respond.

"But the sting operation blew up in my face. A cop was killed. So were two of Fryman's gorillas. Are you sure you didn't hear about it?"

Evan shook his head. "When? Where?" he probed.

"Friday night in the parking lot of Dodger Stadium. It's been all over the media." Jakes stroked his fake beard absently as a child fondles the satin hem of his security blanket.

"Did *you* kill anyone?" Evan asked cautiously.

"Not the cop," Jakes clarified. "One of the gorillas—Fernandez. He was about to blow me away. Chance's gun—he was the other guy, Fernandez shot him while trying to kill me—fell into my hand. So I just closed my eyes and pulled the trigger."

Jakes' eyes darkened under an invisible cloud of pain and disbelief. But he quickly recovered. "The whole thing was over in seconds. The cops swarmed in like locusts. It was a miracle that I got away."

"Why did you run?" Evan asked.

Jakes glared at him resolutely. "I'm not going to prison, Evan—no way."

Margo added an explanation, more to hurry Jakes to the point than to contribute to Evan's enlightenment. "Since the deal to catch Fryman fell through, the Feds will send Nolan up for trafficking."

"If Billy lets me live so long," Jakes interjected. "He doesn't stand for disloyalty. He'll send somebody to get me; he probably already has. That's another reason why I can't stay around L.A." Jakes was stroking the blonde beard again.

Evan was also anxious to get to the point. He didn't want to ask the question, but he knew he must. "So what does all this have to do with me?"

"I want to cut a deal with *you*. You have a choice in the matter, but I think you will see the situation my way and go along with me."

Jakes peeked through the blinds to assure himself that the parking lot was still empty except for the red Datsun wagon and the silver blue Jaguar. When he turned back to Evan, his face was solemn. "As soon as your wife gets here—and I know where she is and what she's doing—we're leaving for the Canadian border, all four of us in this rig of yours. You're going to drive us there just like you're on your honeymoon. We're going straight through, stopping only for gas and take-out food. Once Margo and I cross the border safely, you're free to go on with your life."

"Tell him about the money, Nolan," Margo urged. She seemed impatient, as if late for an important engagement.

Jakes snapped a brief glance at her which communicated his displeasure at being hurried.

Turning back to Evan, he said, "I'm asking you to contribute to our 'retirement fund' from your surplus. Call it a substantial, long-term loan to an old friend. Once we get on the road we're going to watch for a bank, and make a withdrawal. I expect you should be good for a contribution well into five figures."

Evan sat still, unblinking, lips taut, staring at Jakes. Finally, he forced the $64 million question, even though he knew he wouldn't like the answer. "And if I refuse to help you? You said I had a choice."

"Sure you have a choice," Jakes said, indicating in his tone that it was no choice at all. "If you don't take us to Canada, or if you escape from us or tip off the Highway Patrol, and the police get us, I'm taking you down with me. Remember Neil McGruder? I'll tell the whole story, I'll name names. They can't give me much more time in the can for murder than I'm already going to get for drugs, so it's all the same to me.

"But you've got a medical career on the line. I don't imagine your patients or your colleagues or the AMA would want to be associated with you when they discover that you have a murder in your past, even if by some fluke you get acquitted of the charges. You'll be ruined. And what about your sweet little wife? I'll bet *she* doesn't know about Neil McGruder, does she, Evan? What would happen to your promising new life together if she were to find out that her doctor husband is a killer?"

In his mind's eye, Evan was already across the table at Jakes' throat, crushing his windpipe with a death-grip fueled by white-hot rage. *How dare you threaten Shelby!* he imagined himself screaming, as Jakes' face turned purple and his eyes rolled back in his head. "How dare you threaten to break your vow of silence about McGruder and ruin my life to save your own skin!" Left to himself, Evan would have hung on until Nolan Jakes was limp and lifeless on the floor. And then he would have done the same thing to his girlfriend. The fact that Evan was still on his side of the table, arms folded and staring coldly at Jakes, was to him a miracle.

"Like I said, Evan," Jakes continued, "we can all come out of this with tremendous benefits. Margo and I get to live out our natural lives in comfort where no one will ever find us, and you get to keep your career. And I won't even tell your new wife about McGruder—as long as you get us safely into Canada. Then all you have to do is report to the authorities that we kidnapped you and forced you to drive us out of the country. Doesn't that sound fair?"

Evan dropped his head into his hands, still angry but feeling helpless, trapped. *Dear God, this can't be happening,* he groaned inwardly. *Why are You punishing me? I would have told her about McGruder in a few weeks. Please don't let this happen to me. Please don't let it happen to Shelby.*

"Tell him about the money from your other friend, Nolan," Margo cut in.

Jakes' glared at her with anger. "Margo, let me handle this!" he snapped. She looked only slightly penitent.

Jakes looked back at Evan. "You remember our old friend Jet, don't you?"

The image of a beautiful, lithe black woman of twenty flashed into Evan's brain. It would have been a pleasant memory, except the image was draped in the dark colors of fear and guilt, the suffocating feelings which had dominated the last meeting of the three friends twenty-two years ago.

"Libby," Evan said at just above a whisper, looking up.

Nodding, Jakes said, "Do you know what became of her?"

Evan shrugged. He didn't want to answer. He was feeling queasy at the abrupt reunion with Nolan Jakes and the dark past which loomed over him like a bad-tempered bodyguard. But he suspected that obstinacy with his former buddy would only make things worse. "She did the Olympics in '84 as an alternate. The last I heard she was back up in the Seattle area. I don't know where she is or what she's doing."

"Well, the Jet doesn't know it yet, but she's going to help us retire too," Jakes said. "I'm going to call her sometime today and give her the same offer I gave you—at least regarding the money. If she's somewhere around Seattle, she'll have time to withdraw some money and meet us somewhere off of I-5."

"What if she doesn't have any money?" Evan advanced, feeling sick about anyone else getting caught in Jakes' net.

"Hey, you knew her almost as well as I did, Evan. Libby was one headstrong, talented woman. If she hasn't made her own mark in the world, at least she probably married into some good money."

Evan quietly agreed that Libby Carroll, or whatever her name was now, wouldn't have settled for a life of "barefoot and pregnant." He only hoped for her sake that Jakes wouldn't be able to locate her.

Jakes stood to his feet. "I assume that you have decided to cooperate with us."

Evan said, "And I assume that you have certain contingencies in case I choose to resist—for example, a weapon."

Jakes smiled a confident, overbearing smile. "No wonder you went into medicine, Evan. You always were pretty sharp. Yes, I do have a 'persuader' in my possession." He patted the bulge under the jacket on his left hip as he spoke. "I don't want to hurt you, Evan. After all, we *were* pretty good friends. That's worth something. But don't mess with me, man. I won't let an old friendship stand in the way of my freedom, if you get my meaning."

Evan measured the threat. He had been attracted to Nolan Jakes in college because he was a go-for-broke kind of guy, from his kamikaze approach to football to the cocky, in-your-face attitude that had contributed to the tragedy in Portland's Washington Park. He apparently had not changed in twenty-two years. Here he was, in trouble with both sides of the law, packing a gun, fleeing to Canada. Evan had no reason to doubt that Jakes would play every card in his hand to get what he wanted.

Evan released a heavy sigh. His stomach was in knots and his neck ached from the tension. "Okay, Nolan, I'll do whatever you want. Just let me explain it to Shelby. And don't hurt her, I beg you. Please don't hurt her."

"That's all up to you, buddy," Jakes said, reaching into Evan's pocket, removing his trim personal phone, and placing it in an inside jacket pocket. "If you do your job, nobody will get hurt."

"How soon will your wife be here?" Margo demanded.

Evan checked his watch. It was 8:35. Shelby had hoped they could be on the road by 9. "About twenty minutes," he said.

"Maybe this would be a good time to have the doctor look at your back, Nolan, before she gets here," Margo said.

Jakes weighed the suggestion. "Yeah, okay," he agreed reluctantly. Then to Evan, "Do you have a big black bag, you know, a travel kit for house calls?"

"Yes, in my office," Evan said. "What's wrong with your back?"

"Infection, I think," Jakes answered, taking off his jacket. The large gun sticking out of his waistband gave Evan a start. Jakes pulled out the gun and handed it to Margo. Then he unbuttoned his shirt, gingerly slipped it off, and turned his back toward the seated doctor.

Evan stood to inspect the muscular back which was discolored and marred with cuts. Jakes' willing vulnerability underscored his confidence in the ground rules he had established: Evan would be his ally in the escape or he would get hurt. Under this arrangement, Jakes apparently had no qualms about turning his back on his captive and submitting to his healing ministrations. Similarly, Evan realized that if he violated Jakes' trust in any way—by not treating his wounds, for example—he ran the risk of reprisal. And the .44 Magnum in Margo's hands was a sobering symbol of Jakes' overpowering advantage.

"Yes, you have a few nasty spots back here," Evan said, being careful not to touch the wounds.

"What do I need, doc?"

"I need to irrigate these lacerations with sterile saline and pick out a few glass fragments. And you need an injection of antibiotics."

"How long to do it?" Jakes pressed.

"Only a couple of minutes in my office."

"No, out here," Jakes said, pulling on his shirt again. "We'll go into your office and fill up your magic bag and do our doctoring here at the sink after your wife gets here. Then we'll take the bag along with us. It will be another contribution to our retirement."

"But in order to treat the wound properly, I need—"

"Proper is not the operative word, doc," Jakes butted in brusquely.

"Nothing I've done so far this weekend has been what you'd call proper. Fast and quiet, those are the key words. Now let's go fill that bag and get back out here."

Thirty-five

"You say there's a shuttle out of the Oxnard Airport this morning that arrives in LAX in time for the noon flight to Dallas?" Shelby was speaking on the phone in her parents' suite at the Hilton. Jimmy stood by the window watching the sun burn through the morning haze, his thoughts miles away. His wife sat on the bed dabbing her eyes with a tissue. Little Malika, dressed in a pink sweat suit with matching pink bows holding her hair in twin ponytails, was sprawled on the floor with a color book and a box of thirty-two crayons strewn on the carpet before her.

"And my parents may exchange their tickets and travel today instead of tomorrow? . . . Yes, they must return to Waco today due to a sudden death. . . . No, a close friend. . . . I understand. . . . Yes, a charge of $50 each to change the tickets. . . . That's fine. . . . Yes, will you please make the reservations?"

Shelby completed the arrangements for her parents' early departure from Southern California. Then she immediately placed another call. "Hello, Mai, this is Shelby. . . . No, but we're getting ready to leave. That's why I called. My parents received word this morning that the wife of their pastor passed away last night, a heart attack, they think. . . . Yes, very sad. . . . Thank you, I'll tell them. . . . Anyway, Daddy and Mother need to leave for home right away. They are very close to the Jessups, and Daddy is chairman of the deacon board. They want to be there to support Pastor Milt.

"I have a favor to ask, Mai. As you know, Wendy was going to watch Malika while we're gone. My parents had planned to take her to Magic Mountain today and bring her to King's House tomorrow before they left for Texas. I know this is an imposition on you, but is it possible that we could drop Malika off at King's House on our way out of town today? . . . It wouldn't be too much trouble? . . . O, Mai, you're a lifesaver. Thank you so much. That would be very helpful. . . . Yes, we're a little behind schedule, but we'll be leaving Ventura within the hour. We should be there by 11. . . . That's wonderful. Thanks again. . . . Right, we'll see you then. Bye."

To her parents, Shelby said, "Mai sends her love. They will be praying for you and Milt." Jimmy and Evelyn nodded.

"I'm sorry to spoil your plans, honey," Evelyn Tuggle said weakly from the bed. Her eyes were red with tears that came with the news of the sudden loss of her dear friend, June Jessup.

"Mother, you haven't spoiled our plans," Shelby said, sitting beside Evelyn and wrapping a consoling arm around her. "You need to be home, and Mai said they'd love to have Malika early. And Malika is very comfortable at King's House. After all, it's still her home—at least until we get back from the Grand Canyon."

"And we're disappointed not to spend the day with our beautiful Malika," Jimmy Tuggle said, bending over to pull playfully on one of the girl's ponytails on his way to the closet. The couple was packed except for two of Jimmy's shirts, which he quickly folded and laid in the suitcase. His lack of tears belied his own deep grief.

"There will be another time," Shelby consoled, though Malika seemed unfazed by the change in plans. At her direction, the girl returned her crayons to the box and stowed them with the book in her overnight bag.

"We can stay here until you two are on the airport shuttle," Shelby offered.

"Nonsense, sugar, but thank you," Jimmy said, waving off his daughter's generosity. "We can still take care of ourselves. You get on the road to the Grand Canyon and have a wonderful time. We'll be fine."

Shelby embraced her parents warmly and kissed them both. Jimmy couldn't resist tickling Malika again until she giggled. Then mother and daughter left.

"Do you know what we get to do today, Malika?" Shelby said as they walked to the Lincoln. Malika, as usual, was speechless. "We get to ride to King's House in the RV with Daddy. Won't that be fun?"

Malika walked along in silence for a moment, holding Shelby's hand. Then she said, "Vee, dadduh." Shelby broke out in a pleasant laugh. It was the first time Malika had tried to say "RV."

Holding the gun under his jacket, Jakes accompanied Evan from the RV to his office in the empty medical complex while Margo waited in the coach. Under Jakes' close scrutiny, Evan inspected the contents of the leather satchel he often carried in his car for occasional home visits and emergencies. It contained the standard items: a stethoscope, otoscope, sphignomometer, suture kit, tongue blades, gauze, skin tape, Ace wraps, telfa bandages, and alcohol swabs. In addition, Evan always carried a selection of analgesics, anesthetics, and tranquilizers: Tylenol, Xylocaine, Betadine, Demerol, and Valium.

At Jake's direction, the doctor added a variety of packaged drug samples and some supplies specifically selected for treating the back wounds: sterile saline solution, Vicodin for pain, a vial of Keflin—an injectable antiobiotic, a 5cc syringe with a 22-gauge needle, and Xerofoam gauze.

As Evan filled the satchel, he forced himself to consider ways he might be able to stop Jakes, like hitting him with something and grabbing the gun or stabbing him with a syringe of Halothane 3 to knock him out. Evan's life was being threatened, and his personal rights were being violated. What's more, Shelby was soon to be in as much danger as he was. He couldn't just let it happen without looking for a way out. Furthermore, Jakes intended to kidnap them and cross state lines, a federal offense. Evan sensed a moral responsibility to resist.

But every possible way out of the maze of Evan's predicament wound quickly to a heart-stopping dead-end. Even if he was able to disarm Jakes and subdue him—which in itself was no mean feat—what would he do with the man? If he turned his former friend in to the police, Jakes would likely make good on his threat to take Evan down with him, by blowing the unsolved death of Neil McGruder wide open.

Evan imagined three other ways of dealing with Jakes and Margo should he succeed in subduing them, each choice as ludicrous as taking the couple to the police.

One, he could bind and gag them and lock them up somewhere like animals—the basement of his house, a deserted cabin in the Angeles Forest, a rented storage shed—and keep them out of circulation. *Preposterous!* Evan thought.

Two, if indeed a vengeful drug lord had a contract out on him, all Evan had to do was expose Jakes and Margo to the hit man and be done with them. *Absurd! Such an act would make me an accessory to murder, and I already have my conscience full dealing with my part in McGruder's death. And who's to say the drug lord wouldn't kill me also to eliminate the evidence against him?*

A third option presented itself. Evan could kill Jakes and Margo himself and dispose of their bodies. *Insane! That's cold-blooded murder! Dear God, what am I thinking?*

Evan saw no way out except to do what Jakes demanded—get him safely across the Canadian border. It was the best escape plan for everyone involved. Evan could only hope that Jakes and Margo would lose themselves in the Canadian Rockies or deep in the Yukon Territory never to be seen again, the twenty-two-year-old secret disappearing with them.

The two men returned to the RV with Evan carrying the satchel and Jakes watching the street warily. Evan found himself as watchful as Jakes, hoping no one he knew saw him and stopped by to complicate his dilemma.

He also began praying to God that somehow Shelby wouldn't show up—have a flat, get stuck in traffic, even get involved in a minor accident — so he could leave in the RV without her.

Then he realized that when she arrived and found him gone, Shelby would eventually report him and the RV missing. The Flair would be easy for the police to spot on the freeway, and Evan's secret would be out. As much as he hated to admit it, Evan knew Shelby had to go with them. He could only hope and pray she would be safe.

Walking past the empty car carrier hitched to the rear of the coach, Jakes said, "Dragging the car behind us will slow us down, so we're not taking it. You might as well unhook the trailer."

Before Evan could respond, Margo stuck her head out the door. "Nolan, I've been thinking about that. Leaving the car behind is a bad idea."

Jakes showed a scowl of disapproval at being contradicted again. Evan noted that this couple might encounter serious compatibility problems living alone in the Canadian wilderness.

"Margo, we already talked about this," Jakes said. "The extra weight will hurt us, especially going over the Grapevine and through the Siski-yous into Oregon."

Margo countered firmly but respectfully. "But if the bus breaks down, we're stuck. We need the station wagon for insurance. Besides, if we leave it in the lot, somebody here might get suspicious." She waved a hand toward the office building which housed a number of medical professionals who would be back to work Monday morning.

Evan knew she was right and hoped Jakes saw it too. Jakes blew a sigh and conceded. He said to Evan, "Okay, load the car onto the carrier. And don't try anything funny."

"Don't worry, Nolan, I'll play this your way. I don't want anything to happen to Shelby." Evan couldn't have been more serious.

Jakes snorted. "Admit it, doc. No matter how wonderful your lady is, you mainly want to save your own butt."

Evan didn't respond. Instead he handed Jakes the satchel and walked to the Datsun wagon. In five minutes, as Jakes watched from a corner of the coach which shielded him from the street, Evan had run the front wheels of his beach buggy onto the carrier and strapped them down. The RV was ready to travel.

Jakes motioned Evan inside and then sent Margo to abandon the Jaguar on the street, a few blocks away. The two men sat down to await Shelby's arrival.

Thirty-six

Teach me some melodious sonnet,
  sung by flaming tongues above;
Praise the mount, I'm fixed upon it,
  mount of Thy redeeming love.

Cole stumbled over the words, singing rather self-consciously a half beat behind and an octave below the rest of the small congregation. The old Hammond organ, played by a large woman in a faded blue choir robe and silver stole, charged loudly through the chords yet another half beat ahead of the people in the pews.

Hymns like this one, which sounded to Cole like it had been written by William Shakespeare for a choir of aged sopranos, had been one of the most difficult adjustments for him since he began attending the little church four blocks from his Santa Monica condo. He loved the more contemporary songs about God and Christ and the new lifestyle he had chosen since Millennium's Eve. Those songs seemed to fit the electronic keyboard better and accommodate his limited vocal range. But every Sunday morning, just before the sermon, they always stood and sang an old hymn from the dog-eared hymnals in the pew racks. And the elderly folk in the congregation, most of them aging sopranos, warbled like contented songbirds while the younger generation pondered the meaning of terms like "flaming tongues" and "praise the mount."

Here I raise my Ebenezer,
  hither by Thy help I've come;
And I hope by Thy good pleasure
  safely to arrive at home . . .

Cole never got past the word "Ebenezer." The only Ebenezer he'd ever heard about was Ebenezer Scrooge from Dickens' *A Christmas Carol.* Cole wondered why such a character would be mentioned in a Christian hymn, even though he admitted that old Scrooge turned out all right in the end, judging by the way he took care of Bob Cratchett and Tiny Tim.

Cole was lost in thought. *But what does "raise my Ebenezer" mean? It sounds like the song is talking about Scrooge's mother and father; they certainly raised him. And before old Scrooge ran into the Christmas ghosts, he was a belligerent old goat. No wonder his parents needed divine help in raising him. But what in the world does all that have to do with being a Christian?*

The congregation was in the process of sitting down before Cole realized that the hymn was over. He sheepishly plopped into his padded pew near the rear of the sanctuary and returned the hymnal to the rack, hoping his faux pas wasn't too obvious to those around him.

A young man stepped to the podium and began to speak. Well groomed and dressed in an unpretentious blue suit, the lanky, congenial minister looked out of place among the old, blonde, wood pews, pulpit, and altar rail, the threadbare crimson carpet and drapes, and the patched stucco walls from the '50s. Cole had assumed that the upright piano in the corner of the room must have sailed with Noah on the ark. The piano had been retired from active service since twenty-six-year-old Rev. Matthew Dugan—who preferred simply to be called Matt by his parishioners—arrived at the church with his electronic keyboard and youthful, contemporary approach to worship and teaching.

Cole liked Matt. They had met at a donut shop on Pico Boulevard about the time Beth stopped coming to L.A. to see Cole and started ignoring his phone messages from her home on Whidbey Island. Losing touch with Beth had been a major blow to Cole's infant faith. He had relied heavily on his friends at King's House for understanding and support. King's House had served as something of a spiritual incubator for Cole after the dramatic events of Millennium's Eve had turned his attention toward God. But Dr. No and his staff were understandably preoccupied with human needs far more severe than a broken heart. So it was providential that Cole ran into Matt Dugan while waiting in line for a couple of apple fritters at Winchell's one morning.

In their brief initial conversation in the donut shop, which progressed rapidly from favorite pastries to the beautiful Santa Monica weather to the Lakers and basketball to "What do you do for a living?" a small bond was formed. Unaware of Cole's spiritual pilgrimage, Matt gave him a business card and invited him to visit the little church he had been pastoring for a couple of months. Cole said he would.

Cole attended Sunday morning services at Matt's church only sporadically, due to work assignments and commitments at King's House on the weekends. But on Matt's initiative, Cole and the young minister began meeting at Winchell's on Pico early one morning each week for coffee, apple fritters, and a few minutes of Bible study and prayer. They talked a lot about Beth and what might be going on in her head. Matt didn't preach at Cole about what to do, but rather coached and encouraged his new friend to evaluate his temporal trials and tribulations in the light of his new eternal values.

Those informal meetings over coffee and fritters, like a strut under a sagging beam, helped to shore up the Christian police officer's faith. Although Matt was seven years his junior, Cole thought of the young minister as a big brother in the faith.

In the months following Cole and Matt's first meeting at Winchell's, the topic of Beth Scibelli slipped to a low priority in their conversations. By then it was obvious even to Cole that she had lost interest in him, and he was dealing with it. But the two men continued to meet, deepening their friendship and providing Cole with a local spiritual resource person and confidant as he struggled through the toddler stage of his relationship with God. And whenever Cole felt like talking about Beth, Matt listened sympathetically.

It was precisely this topic — Beth and his date with her at Quintero's — which had urged Cole out of bed early enough to get to the service at Matt's church. Ordinarily, Cole would have slept later and taken his time getting ready to leave town for a week. But yesterday's serendipitous meeting with Beth had popped the lid on some old feelings, and he had determined to make himself accountable to the person who knew more about that relationship and those feelings than anyone else: his donut-shop buddy Matt Dugan.

Cole had chosen a pew in the back among the gray-hairs of the congregation, because he was self-conscious about his appearance. Instead of wearing a suit, he was dressed casually for his long ride to Reno: comfortable jeans with a wide leather belt and heavy circular brass buckle containing a big lawman's star, a long-sleeved, maroon T-shirt with narrow horizontal stripes of gold and forest green, a jean jacket — folded and sitting beside him on the pew, and low-cut Nikes, which would be exchanged for steel-toed boots once he hit the freeway for Nevada. His black helmet and visor was on the floor under the pew.

Matt's sermon — or teaching, as he liked to call it — was good, but it didn't keep Cole's mind from occasionally wandering to Beth. At the close of the service he lingered in the foyer while Matt and his wife, Cheryl, did their pastoral handshaking at the door. Finally Cheryl headed off to the nursery to collect their eight-month-old and Matt met Cole by the missionary map, on the foyer wall.

Cole summarized his reunion with Beth and their impending meeting on Olvera Street in half a dozen tight, descriptive sentences, a verbal skill the officer had learned from years of entering concise reports of accidents and crimes. "I just wanted you to know what's going on so you can pray for me," Cole concluded.

Matt acknowledged with a firm nod that he would. "How do you feel about Beth today, Reagan, having been with her again?" he asked.

Cole absently tapped several of the push pins on the map, each designating the geographic location of one of the church's missionaries. "I can't deny it, Matt. I love that woman. And it's not just emotions; I really want the best for her. And I think Beth still has some feelings for me. I don't think she would have agreed to go out with me today if she didn't."

"But what if she doesn't? What if you have lunch and then she says, 'Thank you and good-bye,' and walks out of your life again? Are you going to be all right?"

Cole slowly exhaled a lung full of air as he touched red push pins in Chile, Paraguay, and Argentina. "I don't know," he said with a disappointed lilt in his tone. "I know this sounds kind of conceited, but I really believe that I'm the best thing that could happen to Beth. I felt that way on a strictly worldly level when we first met. Now that I'm a Christian, I feel it even more strongly. Could that be God telling me that Beth and I are supposed to be together?"

Matt thought a moment. "Could be. But I think it's more likely that you can't get her off your mind because God wants you to stay concerned about her spiritual welfare and to keep praying for her. You're a great guy, Reagan, but ultimately Beth needs God far more than she needs you." Matt underscored the positive intention of his comment with a gentle, manly clip on the arm.

"Good point," Cole agreed, but only halfheartedly. "But, I think she's here for a reason, Matt. She just split up with some guy, and she was flying home to Washington when she diverted to L.A. instead. She told me that the wedding wasn't the main reason. She's really hurting, Matt, and I think she came here because she has some good memories of what happened a year and a half ago."

The scowl on Cole's face mirrored his brain's attempt to make the pieces of his relationship with Beth fit together. "But I only have a couple more hours with her. If we could be together a few more days, if we could just spend some time talking together like we did yesterday, I think I could help her, Matt. I could explain what's happened to me. I could—"

Cheryl Dugan arrived at that moment with little Ian whose insistent crying abruptly ended the conversation. "Hello, Reagan," Cheryl said, grappling with the squirming child while trying to keep the strap of a bulging diaper bag from slipping off her shoulder.

Cole nodded and smiled, unoffended at the interruption. He regarded Cheryl as a good friend too, although he only saw her at church or at their house every few weeks when she invited him to enjoy a home-cooked meal. Cole envied Matt. He looked forward to being a husband and father some day, and for the past eighteen months he could picture only one woman in the scenario of his ideal family.

"I'm sorry to interrupt, but Ian is teething, and he's very hungry." Cheryl's eyes pleaded with her husband to take them home.

"No problem, honey," Matt assured. "By the time you get Ian strapped into his car seat, I'll be there. Just give me a second to pray with Reagan."

Cheryl hurried away as Matt turned to Cole, laid a hand on his shoulder, and prayed, "Lord, thank You for what You're doing in my friend, Reagan. And right now I agree with him in prayer that You will give him wisdom and patience for dealing with Beth today. If there is something he needs to communicate to her today, I pray that You will give him the words. And if there isn't enough time today, I pray that You will somehow make a way for Reagan to open his heart to Beth in the future." Matt added a couple more sentences about Beth and her need for personal peace, then concluded his prayer.

As the two men left the building, leaving lock-up chores to a deacon, Matt said, "I can't wait to hear how your meeting goes today. Give me a call as soon as you get back from Reno. And travel carefully, man, okay?"

"Will do, Matt, and thanks." They grasped hands firmly; then Matt hurried off to his car.

Cole slipped into the jean jacket, then sheathed himself in his flightsuit and donned his helmet and gloves for the thirty-minute ride to Olvera Street. Bulging black leather saddlebags were strapped to the rear seat of the Kawasaki. Cole swung his leg over his baggage and cranked the starter. The engine rumbled to life.

Suddenly feeling lighthearted in his eagerness to see Beth, Cole found himself humming the strange tune about Ebenezer and the flaming tongues as he pulled out of the church parking lot and headed for the Santa Monica Freeway. Even more than his friend Matt, he couldn't wait to see how his meeting with Beth would pan out.

Thirty-seven

Officers Dan Gleason and Winnie Cox resorted to discussing "all-time top three" lists when they ran out of things to talk about on a boring stakeout. They had run through countless lists over the past several days while sitting in their champagne-colored Bolt 770 four-door sedan outside the Sheraton Universal Hotel.

"Okay, Winnie, tell me your all-time top three Clint Eastwood movies." Gleason's eyes surveyed the parking lot in front of them as he spoke, as did Cox's. The two plainclothes officers talked a lot while on stakeout duty, but due to the nature of their surveillance work, they seldom looked at each other.

"Mm, number three would have to be *Paint Your Wagon*." Even with her sunglasses on, Winnie squinted at the glare of the late-morning sun glancing off the hood of the Bolt. The windows of the car were wide open, but even the light cross-breeze wasn't enough to keep the occupants cool in the 80-degree weather. The two officers were grateful to be dressed in vacation gear instead of their navy blue uniforms.

"The musical? Are you kidding me? Clint Eastwood singing?" Gleason scoffed. "I'm sorry, but Clint was a real wienie in that movie. So was Lee Marvin. That was a very lame piece of film."

"Hey, Gleason, you'll get your chance. You asked me for my top three, so I'm telling you, all right?"

"Yeah, but I didn't think you would stoop to such a wienie movie."

The banter and the whining was part of the game. If an all-time top three list went uncontested, it wasn't worth talking about.

"For number two I'd have to go for *Play Misty for Me*."

"Winnie, get serious. Clint Eastwood was born to play a cop or a gun fighter, not a disc jockey."

"*Misty* was a very powerful, suspenseful film."

"I can't believe it," Gleason complained. "Two out of three choices, and you still haven't picked one of his Dirty Harry flicks or spaghetti westerns. I'm changing the category. Forget Eastwood. Give me your all-time top three—"

"Stuff it, Gleason. You know we always finish a category. Just because I pick movies that show Eastwood's broader talents doesn't mean—"

"Talent? There *was* no talent in those two movies."

"Why? Just because Clint's character didn't blow away half the supporting cast?"

"Forget it. You have one more chance to redeem yourself. Your number one pick. What will it be, Winnie: *The Dead Pool, Unforgiven, Gauntlet...?*"

"*Every Which Way But Loose*."

Officer Gleason swore. "You can't be serious. That monkey thing?"

"Orangutan."

"That was no movie; that was a cartoon."

"I liked it. It was funny. Clint Eastwood says *Pow!* and the orangutan plays dead. I've rented it five times."

Officer Cox then moaned and groaned appropriately through Gleason's list of favorite Eastwood movies, all three of them bloody, bang-bang, blow-'em-away cop pictures.

"Okay, Gleason, my turn," she said. "Give me your all-time top three musical instruments."

"Musical instruments? What kind of category is that? I'm not into instruments. Besides, all you need is an electronic keyboard and you can get any instrument you want: trumpet, harpsichord, saxophone..."

"All right, you cultural retard, I'll make it easier for you. Give me your top three instruments which can be duplicated on a keyboard."

"Easy. Bass drum, snare drum, and conga drum."

"Drum is only one instrument, retard. Pick two more and—"

"He's leaving," Gleason cut in, the game suddenly over. Both officers quickly trained their field glasses on a man exiting the main doors of the Sheraton and walking into the sunlight toward a pale green Corsica in the guest parking lot about a hundred yards from the stakeout car. The man had a black suit bag draped over his shoulder, carrying it by the hook.

"Maybe we'll finally get something worth watching," Officer Cox said, as she put her glasses aside and dialed the hotel switchboard. The automated answering system recited a series of hotel services. Cox selected guest rooms with a tap of the number two on her phone keypad, then spelled out J-O-H-N-S-O-N. From a list of four guests named Johnson recited by the computer, Winnie picked the fourth: Thomas Johnson.

As she waited for confirmation of Tom Johnson's checkout, Cox tapped the onboard computer to life and activated the tracking system. A glowing green grid of streets filled the hooded screen, and an amber, strobelike blip located the Corsica on the grid. Meanwhile, Officer Gleason continued to watch Barbosa as he lifted the trunk lid on the car and laid the suit bag neatly inside.

After listening to the recorded spiel, Officer Cox tapped off her phone. "As expected, Rennie Barbosa, alias Tom Johnson, has checked out and left no forwarding information."

"Yes!" Gleason said enthusiastically. "It looks like this may turn out to be a pretty nice day, partner."

The pale green Corsica pulled out of the Sheraton lot and disappeared from view on Lankershim Boulevard. Gleason and Cox sat patiently watching the blip on the screen. Using the electronic bird-dog system, they had the luxury of following from a distance, out of sight, as the homing device on Barbosa's car located his precise, second-by-second position on the computerized map.

"He's heading east on Cahuenga," Cox stated, as they both watched the blip. "That's plenty of lead time," Gleason said, starting the car and heading quickly for the exit. He powered up the car windows and activated the air conditioning. "We don't want to give him too long a leash."

The officers took Lankershim south from the hotel parking lot, crossing under the eastbound Hollywood Freeway, but the signal at Cahuenga stopped them. "He's turning north on Barham," Cox announced as they waited for the green light. "Man, he's really hauling. Must have something important to do after all that lolling around. You can gain on him a little by jumping on the freeway here and getting off at Barham."

"Good plan," Gleason said as the light changed. He whipped the car through the turn onto Cahuenga and then aimed left for the freeway entrance. Racing up to 70 MPH for less than a mile, Gleason took the

Barham exit, which put them back on Cahuenga for a left turn onto Barham. Again they had to wait through a long light.

"He's still on Barham, almost to Forest Lawn Drive," Cox said, as Gleason finally sped through the turn onto Barham. "Our boy hasn't been in this big of a hurry since he got here." The electronic map on the screen scrolled slowly downward, keeping the amber blip in the center of the screen. Gleason cheated the speed limit by 10 MPH pushing the Bolt up Barham Boulevard toward the city limits of Burbank.

"He's around the curve at Warner Brothers Studios heading east. Now he's slowing, slowing . . . turning north on Hollywood Way. Geez, doesn't this guy hit any red lights?"

"I'll bet he's headed for Burbank Airport," Gleason said. "I'll bet he's on a plane out of here."

"Interesting," Cox said, eyes glued to the monitor. "He came into L.A. via LAX and rented his car down there. Why would he leave via Burbank?"

Gleason said nothing, concentrating on closing the gap between them and the Corsica at a speed which was borderline unsafe for the traffic.

"He's passing Verdugo . . . now Magnolia . . . now Chandler."

"Where did he rent that Corsica? What company?" Gleason asked.

Cox opened a window on the screen and accessed Barbosa's L.A. file.

"Thrifty," she said.

"I think Thrifty's Burbank lot is just ahead of him," Gleason said.

"Right, Hollywood Way at Burbank Boulevard."

"If he drops the car off there, we'd better call it in. The Feds might want to know their man is on the road again."

Gleason swept the Bolt around the massive Warner Brothers lot at the curve on Barham. He made the left turn onto Hollywood Way on the yellow light and accelerated to near 50.

"Bingo!" Cox exulted, patting the monitor appreciatively. "He's turning off Hollywood Way just past Burbank—the Thrifty lot. Shall I get Chavez on the line?"

"Let's wait until he checks the car in and boards the airport shuttle. We should be at Thrifty in time to get a visual on him."

Four minutes later the Bolt pulled up to the curb on Hollywood Way across Burbank Boulevard from the small Thrifty rental lot. Gleason put the car in PARK but kept the engine running. Officer Cox flipped off the computer and aimed her binoculars at the customer service counter behind the large glass windows. "Yeah, he's checking in," she said. "And they're probably adding a hefty drop charge to his bill."

"Okay, I'll watch him," Gleason said, lifting his glasses. "Give Sergeant Chavez a call."

It took several minutes to track down Chavez, who had a habit of leaving his personal phone on his desk while he wandered around Parker Center. In the meantime, Barbosa boarded the Thrifty shuttle bus and left for the Burbank-Glendale-Pasadena Airport, a small but very active commercial airport bordered by the residential communities of Burbank, Sun Valley, and North Hollywood. Gleason followed at a respectable distance.

"Chavez wants us to watch him until he gets on a plane—*if* he gets on a plane," Cox said, tapping off her phone.

"Geez, good riddance," Gleason exulted. "Maybe we can do something interesting for a change."

The shuttle continued north on Hollywood Way to the airport's entrance. The bus made the left turn at the light but the Bolt didn't, stopped by the signal again. Muttering about his bad luck, Gleason waited for a break in the oncoming traffic; then he ran the red light and squealed a hard left turn into the airport and around a short S-curve to the straightaway. The shuttle had already stopped at the main entrance to the small airport a quarter mile ahead.

The Bolt pulled up to the curb just as the empty shuttle pulled away. "We can't lose him now, not after all the hours we wasted in the Sheraton parking lot," Winnie Cox said.

Jumping from their vehicle, Gleason and Cox flashed their badges at the airport security guard who was ready to bite the heads off these two yokels for even thinking about parking at the curb. Once inside the crowded terminal, the officers checked the ticket counter. Barbosa was not in sight.

"We'd better split up," Gleason said. "I'll take the south side A gates; you take the north B gates. Let's stay in touch." The two officers switched the radios in their shirt pockets to a com channel and hurried off in opposite directions.

Showing her badge again, Officer Cox hurried through the security checkpoint to the B concourse gates, which are all at runway level with open air boarding instead of covered jetways. Getting through the throng was like running a steeplechase through a maze of bodies and luggage.

"I've got him," Cox called into her nearly invisible lapel mike. "Gate B-8—I'm two gates away. He's just passing through the door. Man, he cut it close! He almost missed his flight."

"I'm on my way," Gleason answered through her radio earbud. "Keep an eye on him."

"Right."

By the time Officer Cox got to the window, the last passenger—a man with a suitbag, Cox thought—was entering the Alaska Airlines MD-80. She watched as the door swung shut, the communication lines were retracted, and the blocks were kicked away by the ground crew. She felt sorry for the next stakeout team who would be assigned to

Rennie Barbosa, but not sorry enough to echo her partner's earlier exclamation, "Good riddance."

"Is he on?" Gleason said, coming up behind her.

"Yeah, he's out of here, thank God."

The jet, which was parked parallel to the terminal, accelerated noisily out to the taxi lane.

"So where's he going?" Gleason asked.

Cox shook her head. "I never even stopped to look." Then she walked to the counter and read the electronic flight information sign as her partner watched the jet retreat toward the end of runway 16.

"Phoenix," she said. "Rennie Barbosa is off to terrorize Phoenix."

Thirty-eight

"I wonder why Daddy isn't answering," Shelby said with curiosity and concern, more to herself than to Malika. "He *always* has a phone with him. His brain must already be on vacation." She returned the Lincoln's phone to its cradle in the console without leaving a message. She had intended to warn him that Malika would be riding with them as far as King's House, due to her parents' need to hurry back to Texas. She would wait and tell him in person.

Malika, who seemed not to be listening to Shelby, responded softly, "Dadduh, phone, b'cation." Pondering Evan's atypical unavailability, Shelby didn't even notice that Malika had attempted the word "vacation" for the first time. Shelby and her daughter had just exited the freeway at Victoria Avenue and turned toward the hills on their return from the Oxnard Hilton. Shelby knew Evan would be pleasantly surprised to see Malika and welcome the opportunity to drive her to King's House in the "Bee," which was Malika's best attempt at saying "RV."

It took five minutes in moderate traffic to travel from the freeway to Telegraph Road, after which Victoria Avenue angled steeply upward into a well-established East Ventura subdivision. About halfway up the hill, Shelby turned left onto Loma Vista for a two-minute drive to Community Medical Plaza across Brent Avenue from the hospital. The morning haze had burned off, and the view of the ocean and Channel Islands from the hillside was spectacular.

As she pulled into the parking lot, Shelby was relieved to find the thirty-foot Fleetwood Flair parked where it was supposed to be. But she was puzzled to see the shiny red beach buggy already mounted on the car carrier. Evan had said that he was going to follow her home in the Datsun so she could garage the Lincoln before they left. Shelby hoped he hadn't changed his mind. She wasn't keen on the idea of leaving her white Lincoln in the medical office parking lot for two weeks. Ventura was a pleasant, law-abiding community for the most part. But leaving an immaculate, fully-loaded luxury car unattended in public for two weeks was a great temptation for vandals and thieves.

She parked the car alongside the coach, with Malika's side nearest the door. Curiously, the kitchen blinds were still drawn, keeping the inside in shadows. But as she came around the car to help Malika out, Shelby could see Evan's silhouette through the large side window in front of the door. He was sitting in the driver's seat with his high-backed chair swiveled toward the coach's entrance.

The smile of welcome Shelby expected to see on Evan's face, as Malika clambered up the steps ahead of her, was missing. Instead, the bright sunlight flooding into the coach behind her illuminated an expression of disappointment bordering on grief, an expression Shelby had rarely seen Evan display.

"What is she doing here?" Evan snapped, when his wife and daughter were fully inside the coach. There was a tremor in his voice which insinuated pain. Malika leaned back into her mother's legs at the threatening tone.

Taken aback by his uncharacteristically brusque manner, Shelby groped for the words. "My parents . . . had to get back to . . . er, June Jessup died, their pastor's wife. They're flying home early, so I told them we would drop Malika off at King's House on our—"

Obvious footsteps coming up the stairs behind Shelby interrupted her, and the slam of the coach door caused her to whirl around. She came face to face with a woman, shorter and more petite than herself, with an overabundance of platinum blonde hair. The woman's eyes were hidden behind large dark glasses, and her unsmiling expression looked anything but congenial.

Shelby had no sooner acknowledged the woman behind her with a wan smile when she was aware of another stranger in the coach: a man with a short beard sitting in the shadows in the dinette. She hadn't noticed him when she entered.

"Hello," Shelby offered tentatively to the two unexpected guests. Then she turned back to her husband for introductions. Evan had climbed out of the driver's seat and stepped down from the cab's platform to stand near her in the aisle. Shelby assumed that the serious-looking couple were associates of Evan, who had dropped by to convey their congratulations and best wishes. But from his curt manner, she judged that Evan wasn't happy about receiving visitors, especially since the newlyweds were already well behind on their departure schedule.

Facing the two strangers, Shelby felt Evan's left arm slip around her waist and draw her near. She noticed that he was collecting Malika into a similarly protective grip with his right arm.

Evan made the introductions in a cautious, measured tone, as if any animation in his voice would somehow set off an alarm. "Shelby, I'd like you to meet an old friend of mine from college, Nolan Jakes, and his friend, Margo . . ." He looked at the platinum blonde questioningly, not knowing her last name.

"Just Margo is fine," she said in a businesslike tone. Margo remained in front of the door like a sentry. She appeared to Shelby to be on guard.

Evan nodded. "Nolan and Margo are in a bit of trouble, and they have persuaded me to give them a hand."

Shelby's first thought was that the man had probably crawled out of the woodwork to put the touch on his wealthy college chum for money. Having enjoyed a measure of affluence over the years, both she and Evan were used to friends, coworkers, and acquaintances approaching them for loans. But there was something more to this. There was something peculiar about that name—Nolan Jakes, something Shelby couldn't pin down. And his face, though dimmed by shadows, seemed remotely familiar, as if she had met the man in the distant past. Jakes' friend Margo sparked no such memories.

Evan continued, "Actually, our trip to the Grand Canyon is being delayed for a day or two because Nolan and Margo need to get to Canada, and I have agreed to drive them there."

Stunned by the sudden, odd turn of events, Shelby respectfully objected with the solution she thought to be obvious. "Wouldn't it be easier to get them plane tickets or train tickets? There might even be a flight out of Oxnard today which connects with—"

"I'm sorry, angel," Evan interrupted. Though he had used Shelby's pet name, there was little warmth in his voice. "They can't use public transportation because they're in trouble with the law. They need to get to Canada without being seen. That's why we're going to take them there in the RV."

Shelby stared at Jakes. It took only a few seconds for all the tumblers to fall into place in her brain: the name, the face, the girlfriend blocking the door, and Evan's harsh, almost panicked demeanor since she walked into the coach. "You're the man the Los Angeles police are looking for," she said, a wave of fear constricting her throat and softening her voice to a near whisper. "I read about you in the paper, saw your picture on TV. Nolan Jakes, the former football player . . . caught in a drug deal. Some men were shot . . . killed . . . including a policeman. You're a fugitive."

No one in the coach moved or spoke. It was as if the scene and all the players around her were frozen in time while Shelby processed the startling revelation. She suddenly knew why Evan had been so pained at the sight of Malika climbing into the coach. She had unwittingly ushered her innocent daughter into the presence of a criminal. He probably had a gun. He might think nothing at hurting any one of them or even killing them.

"We're being kidnapped," she said at last, a chill of fear causing her to shudder. She instinctively leaned into her husband and gripped her daughter's arm. Malika stood still, sensing her parents' discomfort and secure in their nearness, but oblivious to the conversation or the real danger.

"That's one way to put it," Jakes said, as he slid off the bench and stood. The butt of the gun was visible sticking out of his belt. Shelby assumed he had left it in sight for her benefit. "But it's really just a detour for you—if you behave yourself. You and Evan just take Margo and me to Canada like we were all on one big vacation together. Except we don't stop; we drive straight through. Then you go on to the Grand Canyon and have your honeymoon. It's as simple as that."

"And if we refuse?" Shelby retorted, surprised at the sudden wave of boldness.

Jakes glared at Evan until the doctor spoke. "They have ways of hurting us, angel, if we don't cooperate. I've already told Nolan and Margo that we will do what they ask. It's not worth it to me to refuse; I don't want anything to happen to you or Malika."

Evan stared back at Jakes, willing him not to break his promise and reveal the blackmail scheme which had secured his complete cooperation.

"We're leaving now," Jakes announced. "Margo, take the woman's purse and go park the Lincoln on the street . . . behind the Jag. And if she has a phone in her purse, leave it with these in the car." He handed her the personal phone he had confiscated from Evan along with the RV communication unit he had ripped from the control panel.

Another wave of panic swept over Shelby, like a strong aftershock following a devastating earthquake. It was bad enough that she and Evan were being abducted by potential killers. The thought of little Malika being exposed to such danger petrified her. "May we leave our daughter here, please," she pleaded to Margo as the woman relieved her of the purse. Shelby hoped to arouse Margo's maternal sympathies. "We can drop her off in L.A. or let her stay with friends here in Ventura. We won't try to give you away, believe me."

Jakes shook his head and answered for his girlfriend. "We're not going through L.A. Besides, the kid will blab about what she's seen, and I don't think Evan wants that to happen, do you, Evan?" Jakes' smiling sneer showed that he was enjoying the bind he was exerting on his former teammate. Margo exited the coach to move the Lincoln.

"Malika won't say anything, Mr. Jakes," Shelby insisted politely, striving desperately to win Jakes' favor. "Actually, she *can't* say anything. Her verbal skills are severely retarded. She's been abused. Please . . . "

"Sorry, lady," Jakes cut in, not sounding sorry at all, "but we're leaving now and we're leaving together and we're not dropping anybody anywhere."

Shelby wanted to resist further but kept silent. It occurred to her that when Malika didn't show up at King's House later this morning, the Ngo's would be curious and call. After several tries without making contact, they would become worried, then suspicious. Perhaps as soon as late afternoon or evening they would call the police, and the RV would become the target of a widespread search.

Jakes took Shelby by the elbow, and she stiffened. "I want you and the girl to sit at the table, here on this bench, facing the rear," he ordered. "Don't move from that seat unless I tell you to, and don't touch the blinds."

Shelby turned to search Evan's face for answers. His knit brow, lackluster eyes, and taut lips telegraphed trepidation. She wanted to know about Nolan Jakes. Why hadn't Evan told her about him before? How close had they been as friends? Why would Jakes search out Evan to smuggle him out of the country? Their life of intimacy and bliss together was only hours old, their dream honeymoon barely begun, and it had been rudely and frighteningly interrupted. What was happening to them? What *would* happen to them? Could she really believe that Nolan Jakes wasn't going to hurt them?

Shelby craved time alone with Evan, time to talk through their crisis, to pray, and to plot a course of action together, as they had during other struggles in their courtship. They could determine a way to foil the plot, to attract the attention of the police. They could agree on a plan to break away from Jakes and Margo. But there would be no time alone, no time for questions, no time for plans, no time to pray together. Anything that passed between them would be heard and seen by two strangers with criminal intent. She would have to take her questions to Jesus silently and alone.

"It's okay, angel," Evan assured weakly. "Do as Nolan asks. Sit down with Malika and keep her occupied."

Then he squatted to speak to Malika face to face. The girl's eyes were wide with apprehension at the unfamiliar goings-on. Evan ached for her to feel secure. He determined for her sake not to let the traumatic event reverse the progress toward normal living she had enjoyed since meeting Shelby.

"We're going to take a long ride in the RV, sweet pea," he said, stroking her cheek with his fingertips. "Mr. Jakes and Ms. Margo are going with us. Won't that be nice?" Malika gave no indication that she heard him. Her eyes flitted between deep space and the butt of the Colt .44 sticking out of Jakes' pants less than two feet away.

"I want you to go sit at the table with Momma and be a good girl."
Evan encouraged. "I'll be driving the RV, and I'll talk to you later."
Then he gave both his ladies a kiss on the cheek and motioned them
toward the table. Jakes sidestepped toward the door to let them pass.
Shelby helped Malika climb onto the bench, then slid in beside her,
their backs facing the two men.

"Start the engine," Jakes commanded. Evan stepped up the platform
to the cab, sat down, swiveled his big chair forward, and turned the
ignition key. The Chevy V8 454 CID engine roared to life. Jakes
watched the fuel needle climb to just under one-quarter full. He said,
"We'll take Loma Vista back to Victoria and down to Highway 126.
Head east to I-5. We'll get fuel over there somewhere."

Evan nodded submissively.

"No hand signs to other drivers or cops, no speeding, no tickets, no
funny stuff," Jakes urged, pointing his finger for emphasis.

Evan's voice rose with irritation, "I won't screw up, Nolan. You
know how much I have riding on this trip. Just don't get overanxious
and hurt somebody."

In two minutes, Margo returned to the coach, hurried inside, and
closed the door. Jakes directed her to sit in the high-backed co-pilot's
swivel chair in front of the sweeping front windshield. "Let's do it,"
Jakes said to the driver.

Evan pulled the gearshift lever to DRIVE and eased the coach forward
to the driveway out of the parking lot. Waiting for a broad opening in
the light Sunday morning traffic, Evan accelerated gingerly onto Loma
Vista. The coach pitched and creaked slightly while exiting the parking
lot, and the trailer hitch scraped cement as the rear end dipped low
over the driveway.

Shelby held Malika close as they rocked gently through the turn. As
she felt the coach surge forward on Loma Vista, a new fear confronted
her: the danger of losing her husband, her *second* husband.

Evan Rider had been God's answer to Shelby's prayers for the husband of her dreams. She was as confident as she had been about
anything that Evan was the husband of God's design for her. Could she
be wrong? Could she be so out of tune with God's will as to marry the
wrong man?

Clutching Malika close, Shelby pushed away the dark doubts and
prayed.

Thirty-nine

California State Highway 126 ambles leisurely eastward forty-five miles from U.S. 101 at Ventura to the community of Valencia on Interstate 5, approximately forty miles north of downtown Los Angeles. The sixteen miles of four-lane freeway from the bustling seat of Ventura County on the ocean to the quaint bedroom community of Santa Paula is divided by an endless ribbon of lush pink and white oleanders. At Santa Paula, 126 becomes a two-lane highway—traversed at freeway speed by most drivers—which cuts a narrow swath through thousands of acres of farmland and citrus orchards. The lazy country town of Fillmore, nine miles from Santa Paula, slows east–west commuters only briefly on their flight between the southland's two major north–south arterials.

After leaving the medical office parking lot, the five occupants of the big Fleetwood Flair were silent until they transitioned from four lanes to two on Highway 126 outside Santa Paula. Evan had driven the RV only a few times before, and just once with the beach buggy in tow. So he forced himself to concentrate on staying in his lane and adjusting to the nuances of the cumbersome vehicle at freeway speed. He felt the additional burden of driving well within the bounds of the law to avoid any contact with the police. The RV's air conditioning was operating, but Evan still found himself perspiring under the pressure.

Malika snuggled against Shelby, seeking assurance in the tense atmosphere. Shelby kept an arm wrapped around the girl, prayed for her family's safety, and battled knotty questions about God's involvement in their situation.

Jakes alternated between pacing the center aisle, standing behind Evan and Margo in the cab while hawkishly scanning the road ahead, and sitting tentatively on the plush swivel chair directly behind Margo's elevated co-pilot's chair. Wherever he was in the coach, Jakes nervously glanced at Shelby and Malika every minute or two to make sure they were still seated at the dinette.

The sting from Jakes' back wounds had flared up again, so he was uncomfortable in any position. He would have Evan look at his back and give him something for the pain when they refueled after turning north on I-5. Jakes was wearing his blue, glare-reducing wraparound shades again, but the golf hat had been tossed to the empty bench in the dinette. The nylon bag stuffed with cash was stowed in the wardrobe to the rear of the dinette. The .44 was still snugly tucked into his belt.

Finally, Margo broke the silence. "Where was the little girl supposed to go?" she probed Evan.

"She was going to Magic Mountain with her grandparents today," Evan responded soberly.

"No, I mean *now* where is she supposed to go, since the grandparents had to leave? I'm sure your wife didn't plan to take her on the honeymoon."

Evan glanced in the mirror at his wife, who was turned away from him in the dinette. "Shelby, what plans did you make for Malika today?" he asked.

Shelby was silent, as if not hearing him. Evan realized that she didn't want to say anything and perhaps foil a possible avenue of rescue prompted by worried baby-sitters.

"Shelby," he called more forcefully, "please tell me. It's important."

Shelby delayed a few more moments until the pacing Jakes stopped at the dinette and glared at her menacingly. "I called Mai Ngo," she answered reluctantly. "We were supposed to drop her off at King's House on our way through L.A."

Jakes stepped quickly to the cab. "Call those people, Evan," he commanded. "Tell them the girl isn't coming. Tell them that you're taking her with you instead. Make it sound good, and don't try anything." Then to Margo he said, "Give him your phone."

Margo pulled a small personal phone from her purse and reached it across to Evan. He took it and tapped in the number with his thumb while keeping the coach on the road with one hand. He knew Shelby would not understand his eager compliance, but he had to do what Jakes asked—for the sake of his family and himself.

"Mai? . . . Oh, Wendy, I didn't recognize your voice," Evan began, straining to sound composed. "This is Evan Rider. . . . Fine, thanks. Say, we've decided to take Malika with us on our trip. . . . That's right, and we're on our way right now. . . . Yes, I think she'll enjoy the Grand Canyon. Will you please tell your mother not to expect us today? We'll be back in a couple of weeks."

Jakes grabbed Evan by the arm and motioned for him to end the call. Evan thanked Wendy for her help, said good-bye, and handed the phone back to Margo. Jakes let go of his arm and returned to his pacing without saying another word.

Margo spent the next few miles entertaining herself by rummaging through Shelby's purse, especially the wallet. "I see that your wife is independently wealthy," she said to Evan with a note of triumph, as if gloating over the discovery of a chest of gold. She displayed a colorful fan of bank cards bearing the name SHELBY TUGGLE issued by elite financial institutions, many of them based in Texas.

Evan glanced at the display. He groaned inwardly at the indignity of Shelby's purse being tampered with and the threat of robbery, but he said nothing and returned his attention to the highway leaving Santa Paula.

Margo swiveled her chair around and waved the cards at Jakes, who was seated behind her at the moment, "Look at these, Nolan," she said excitedly. "I think the new Mrs. Rider may be even more generous toward our retirement than her rich doctor husband."

Suddenly realizing that Margo was talking about the contents of her purse, Shelby whipped her head around and snapped angrily, "Have you been going through my personal things? I resent that. Give me my purse." Evan grimaced at Shelby's challenge and silently warned her not to push their captors too far.

"You can resent it all you like," Margo replied haughtily, unbuckling her safety belt and making her way back to the dinette in the gently swaying coach. "But like Nolan said, we're one big happy family for the next twenty-four hours. And in this family, smart-mouth lady, what's yours is mine."

"You have no right to treat us this way," Shelby argued. Malika snuggled nearer at the hostile exchange.

"Right?" Margo snapped. "As long as Nolan and I are riding this bus, we have all the rights. You have none. In fact, in case you haven't heard, you are going to use these cards to make a withdrawal for us on our way north."

"I most certainly will not," Shelby hissed. "That money is reserved for our daughter's education. I will not hand it over to aid criminals."

Evan listened anxiously as the argument escalated, while paying attention to a couple of old, plodding vegetable trucks he was passing on a stretch of open highway. He was about to intercede and try to quiet Shelby when a startling sight in the side mirror caught his attention: a white car coming up fast behind the two trucks he had just passed. Evan stared at the car in the mirror. As he had feared, a rack of red and blue lights, not flashing at the moment, adorned the roof. It was a Ventura County Sheriff's car, and he seemed eager to pass the two slow trucks the RV was leaving behind.

Evan held his breath and checked his speed: 52 MPH, well within the legal limit of 55 and far below typical speed of 60–65 on this road. Had he signaled when passing the trucks? Yes, with plenty of warning to cars behind. Had he passed in a safe area, across a dotted center line instead of a solid double? Yes, he was sure of it. Had he signaled when returning to his lane. Yes, he distinctly remembered it. He was driving as safely as he knew how, if anything *too* safely.

Evan checked the side mirror again. The white car, having waited for a break in the oncoming traffic, roared around the two farm trucks and quickly closed the gap between them and the RV. Evan glanced at the rearview mirror offering him a straight shot through the open bedroom doorway to the large rear window. He could see the roof line of the red Datsun bobbing behind the coach on the car carrier. And directly behind the Datsun was the Sheriff's car, apparently content to follow instead of pass.

I've done nothing wrong, I'm driving very cautiously and safely, he has no reason to stop me, Evan assured himself repeatedly. His eyes flicked between the speedometer, both side mirrors, and the rearview mirror. *He's just waiting for another break in traffic; then he'll pass me.* But the deputy didn't pass. Instead, Evan thought he looked like he was talking on his radio. A sharp edge of fright twisted in Evan's stomach. He feared that the officer was checking the validity of the RV's registration with dispatch in preparation for a traffic stop, standard law enforcement procedure.

Or worse yet, Evan envisioned that the fugitives he was transporting had somehow been traced to him and the RV. The cop behind him might be alerting backup units to prepare for an all-out firefight to capture Jakes and his female accomplice.

A foreboding scene glowered at Evan from his imagination. If the cops were onto them, they would eventually catch up with them—if not now, somewhere between here and the Canadian border. Jakes would be taken into custody, perhaps spilling his guts as he was dragged away in handcuffs, "Evan Rider is a killer! He's partially responsible for the death of Neil McGruder in 1979 in Portland! Look it up in the records! We were there! We did it, Evan and me!"

The evidence would be conclusive; no chance Evan would be able to lie his way out of it. If he was lucky he would get off with manslaughter and five to ten years in prison. But his medical practice would likely be ruined. And worst of all, the entire episode would deal a terrible emotional blow to Shelby. What would she think of him? The image instantly nauseated him like an unexpected, powerful fist to the stomach.

At that moment Jakes noticed the police car behind them. "How long has that cop been back there?" he demanded angrily, jumping to his feet and frightening Malika to tears. He stepped quickly to the side of the coach nearest the door to get out of the officer's line of sight through the rear window. Margo ducked, scampered to the far side of the dinette, and scooted in out of sight.

"Relax, Nolan," Evan said, struggling to control his own panic. "He's only been back there for a couple of minutes. There's no reason to—"

Before Evan could finish his explanation, the Christmas tree atop the Sheriff's car began flashing its brilliant red and blue lights, signaling Evan to pull over. Evan knew he could never outrun the cop. The best he could hope for was a minor infraction he could handle through the driver's side window. He let up on the accelerator and flashed his right turn signal, showing his intent to comply when sufficient space was available on the shoulder.

At the change in speed, Jakes bobbed his head into the aisle for a quick look back. When he saw the flashing lights, he cursed Evan loudly. Then he crouched and crawled to the driver's side. "You did this!" he growled, adding a stream of vulgar curses. "You tipped him off! You did something wrong on purpose!"

"I did nothing wrong," Evan replied just as forcefully. "I don't know why he's stopping us. But I'll handle it and get rid of him."

Malika whimpered louder at the coarse exchange. Shelby enveloped the trembling girl in her arms.

"You'd *better* handle him, or . . ." Jakes didn't finish his threat. Instead he crept low back to the dinette. "Give me the girl," he demanded to Shelby. Instinctively she swallowed the sobbing Malika in her arms. "No!" she shrieked.

Jakes whipped out the .44 and jabbed it at Shelby. His eyes flashed wildly with desperation and madness. "You give me the girl and shut up until that cop leaves. If either of you screws up, your little girl is history. Now hand her over."

He passed the gun to Margo and reached for Malika. Shelby lashed out at him like a wounded lioness with her right hand. Malika burrowed under Shelby's left arm for protection.

"Shelby, let her go!" Evan shouted from the cab. The RV had slowed to 30. A narrow turnout alongside an onion farm was just ahead. The Sheriff's car was still right behind them, lights flashing, slowing at the same rate. "Let her go, please, or he will hurt us all!"

In Shelby's moment of indecision, Jakes brushed her arm aside and jerked the girl out of her arms like a rag doll, clapping a hand over her mouth. The terror in the child's eyes wrenched a sob from the depths of Shelby's soul. Still in a crouched position, Jakes scrambled toward the back of the coach and ducked into the tiny commode, closing the door behind him.

Wailing in panic, Shelby made a move to follow him. But Margo was instantly in her face with the .44, pushing her back into her seat. "Don't you understand?" she insisted with teeth clenched. "You and your child will get hurt if you don't shut up. Do you want to see her in one piece again or not?"

"Please, Shelby," Evan begged from the cab, also shaken at the sight of Jakes' rough treatment of Malika, "for Malika's sake, get hold of yourself. This will all be over in a few hours. Let's not jeopardize her life by doing something foolish."

With great effort, Shelby complied. Margo forced her against the wall in the dinette seat and slid in beside her, poking the barrel of the gun into her ribs. "That's better," Margo said. "And if that cop comes inside, just sit still like we're having a nice little chat."

Breathless with fear for Malika, Shelby managed only a whispered response, "All right."

The coach rolled to a stop, and Evan shut off the ignition. He watched through the mirrors as the deputy wheeled his car into the turnout behind the coach and then angled the nose toward the road. *Please, don't come inside, sir,* Evan begged silently. *Please, God, don't let him come inside. Don't let my long-buried sin result in a massacre.*

The officer stepped out of his car, paused at the rear of the coach, then cautiously approached the front on the driver's side. Evan was surprised at how young the cop looked in his nicely pressed khaki uniform, short, red, flattop haircut, and freckled skin. Evan slid open the small side window at his elbow to greet him.

"Good morning, sir," the officer said pleasantly, his voice as youthful as his appearance. "May I see your holocard and registration please."

"I wasn't going too fast, was I, officer?" Evan said as he fumbled for his wallet with trembling hands. The registration certificate was clipped to the visor where he had placed it after purchase.

The young deputy said nothing until Evan had passed his holocard and certificate out the side window. Even then he didn't answer the question.

"Heading out on vacation, are you, sir?" the deputy asked as he scrutinized the documents. The scalp under his flattop appeared as red as his short, spiked hair.

"Yes, sir. Just left, in fact."

"I see that. You're from Ventura."

"Yes, sir."

"Where are you headed, Mr. Rider?"

Evan thought carefully. He could think of no reason to lie about his present destination. "Uh, north . . . Canada, eventually."

Apparently satisfied at what he saw, the deputy handed Evan's holocard and registration certificate back to him through the window.

"Well, Mr. Rider, there are a number of law enforcement districts between here and Canada, and every one of them has an ordinance against driving without trailer lights. One of them is bound to notice your car carrier lights aren't working and give you a ticket. I wouldn't wish that on any of my neighbors on vacation, so I suggest you get them hooked up before you go any farther."

A flood of relief washed through Evan. "Trailer lights? The trailer lights aren't working?"

"That's correct, sir. I noticed them back in Fillmore at the four-way stop. I checked them just now before I came up, and it looks like you forgot to plug them in."

Evan was more relieved than he could ever let on. He prided himself on remembering such details. But he wasn't surprised that the events surrounding his departure from Ventura had caused him to overlook such an important detail.

"Thank you, officer," he said, unsnapping his safety belt. "I'll get them right now."

The officer headed back toward his car. Evan stepped down from the cab and approached the side door. He touched Shelby as he passed. She was still trembling. "It's okay, angel. I'll plug in the lights and we'll be on our way. Malika will be fine." He was trying to encourage himself with the same words.

Then he looked at Margo. "Would you please allow her to test the turn signals and brakes for me when I get the trailer hooked up?" Margo nodded.

Attaching the wiring from the car carrier to the coach was as simple as plugging a lamp into the wall. Evan stood next to the kid officer and hand-signaled Shelby to test first left turn, then right turn, then stop. The lights worked perfectly. Evan thanked the deputy again and returned to the coach as the young man drove away.

Margo had already directed Shelby back to the dinette by the time Evan climbed inside. "You *left* those lights unplugged, Evan," Jakes snarled, still holding Malika tightly in the doorway to the kitchen. The girl had stopped crying, but her face mirrored bewilderment and fear. "You *wanted* us to get stopped."

"I did not, Nolan," Evan objected strongly. "I promised my cooperation, and I meant it. You know I don't want a confrontation with the police. I was so rattled back in Ventura that I simply forgot the lights."

Jakes didn't admit that he believed Evan, but neither did he contest his excuse.

"May I please have my daughter now," Shelby pleaded to Jakes with as much civility as she could muster.

"No," Jakes snapped. "She stays with us until we reach Canada. Maybe it will help improve Evan's memory while he drives. I don't want any screw-ups like that again."

Shelby choked back a fearful sob. "Please don't hurt her," she begged.

Ignoring Shelby, Jakes said, "Margo, sit over here with the kid," pointing to the side of the dinette opposite Shelby. Margo laid the gun on the range across the aisle, took the child, and slid into the seat.

"It's okay, baby," Shelby encouraged her child from across the table, forcing a smile. "Mommy and Daddy are right here."

Jakes stuffed the gun back inside his belt. Then to Shelby he said, "You sit over there, and buckle in." He pointed toward the low swivel chair he had used occasionally on the first leg of their journey.

Shelby obeyed. She grasped Evan's hand in the aisle as she passed him, and he returned an encouraging embrace. Then he said, loudly enough for their captors to hear, "Don't worry about the money. We will give them what they ask for. Your safety is more important to me than anything we have." Shelby nodded reluctantly and sat down.

Jakes motioned Evan back to the driver's seat. He started the engine, flipped on the turn signal, and pulled back onto Highway 126, leaving a swirl of dust in their wake.

Forty

Beth knew it was no coincidence that the pretty Latino hostess seated her and Reagan Cole at "their" table in crowded Quintero's on Olvera Street. Cole had brought her here several times in the months following Millennium's Eve, and he made sure they always sat in the same booth next to a window arched with adobe brick and overlooking a small atrium of lush fern and colorful bird of paradise.

Beth was wearing the only other outfit she had brought with her from Colin Wendt's yacht: a red, short-sleeve, V-neck knit top and stylish white shorts along with the white sandals she had worn for two days. Knowing she would be home tonight to a well-stocked wardrobe of clothes pleased her. Extending her short visit in L.A. to eat with Reagan Cole seemed well worth the inconvenience of her limited choice of costumes.

"You called Raphaela and reserved this table, didn't you?" Beth probed, as she slid into the booth across from Cole, trying to conceal her delight at his thoughtfulness.

Cole shrugged and grinned, and Beth thought she detected a slight blush on his cheeks. "I just know you like this table, the view of the garden and all," he said.

"Yes, I do like this table," she admitted. "Thank you."

Cole asked Beth's permission to order for them, and she consented. He selected pork fajitas for two—with extra onions, large corn tortillas, more arroz than frijoles, and a margarita for her and a cherry Coke for him. Beth was again pleased that he remembered what she liked: pork instead of chicken or beef, lots of onions, corn tortillas instead of wheat, and spanish rice instead of refried beans.

Seeing Cole across the table in such familiar, pleasant surroundings released a flood of positive memories in Beth. She recalled holding his hand across this very table a few days after Millennium's Eve. They had spent the evening piecing together the sobering events leading up to the near tragic Unity 2000 convocation in the Coliseum. And they had unashamedly confessed their anxiety for each other's safety and expressed relief that the harrowing event hadn't ended in harm to either of them.

Beth also reflected on the elation they had shared at being safe and together and in love. They saw each other as much as possible at the dawn of the new millennium. Beth spent almost as much time in Los Angeles as she did at home in Washington, and Cole took a couple of trips north to see Beth and explore her Oak Harbor hideaway. Those first weeks of 2000 were warm with affection and filled with promise for the Whidbey Island journalist and the L.A. cop whose lives had intersected strictly by chance, during an attempted car-jacking on the San Diego Freeway.

But the image of Reagan Cole across the table from her in Quintero's also carried memories which were not so happy for Beth. There were those tense moments when Beth's handsome six-foot five-inch police sergeant was late meeting her for dinner at their favorite restaurant, although he always called to let her know he was "running a little behind." And more often than not, the reason for Cole's tardiness was linked to his increased involvement at King's House. That's when Beth began to suspect that she was being edged out of first place among Cole's priorities by something more important to him. Beth soon realized that her chief rival for Cole's affections wasn't another woman or his career in law enforcement; it was, of all things, God.

The deflating nature of that realization was clear in Beth's mind. Huddled over a platter of sizzling fajita fixings, she had often chattered excitedly about the book offers she was considering and the possibilities those projects would afford her and Cole to travel and have fun. But Cole, though polite enough to hear her out and appreciate her good fortune, always seemed to turn the conversation back to his fascination for working with Dr. No and his staff, helping former offenders stabilize their capsizing lives and return to society as givers instead of takers, and learning more about God, the Bible, and prayer. And many of their evenings together ended up at King's House where Cole would proudly display a new piece of furniture or equipment in the prisoner rehab wing, or introduce her to another junkie who was getting straight at the House.

One of the last times Beth saw Reagan Cole before voluntarily losing herself in her writing was at Quintero's. As Cole bubbled about his growing faith and increasing involvement in Dr. No's home for wayward Angelenos, she finally saw the handwriting on the wall. Their paths, which Beth first thought had converged—possibly for life, were diverging. She was on the threshold of making a big splash in journalism and grabbing the renown and financial rewards that came with a byline. Cole, on the other hand, was giving more and more of himself away. He was spending much of his spare time at King's House, and he had confided to Beth that he was budgeting for the first time in his life, in order to divert a proportion of his income to meet ongoing material needs at the House.

Beth also perceived that she and Cole were wandering away from each other on the subject of God. Cole had insisted that Beth's timely escape on Millennium's Eve was the direct result of prayer. God had tunneled through a massive mountain and come to her rescue in the nick of time.

Beth had acknowledged that God may have given her a nudge or a clue here and there for her part in solving the mystery of the assassin.

But she also contended that her deliverance wouldn't have happened if she hadn't used her brain, her physical strength, and her willpower. She had said thanks to God in her own way and returned to the business of making her mark in life.

But Cole had seemingly let his gratitude to God push him over the edge. The man had changed his life in response to what happened on Millennium's Eve. He was on the verge of becoming a religious fanatic, much like her parents had become as followers of Simon Holloway. She couldn't understand why such a together individual would allow himself to become so unraveled by a religious experience.

It had become clear to Beth that Cole's priorities were God first, King's House second, career third, and Beth Scibelli fourth. But for Beth, Reagan Cole and her career were neck and neck for first place, and God wasn't even in the top five. This was a large, painful problem. She had reluctantly concluded that, despite her attraction to Reagan Cole, theirs was not a match made in heaven as she had originally thought. The expanse of distance between them in the weeks and months that followed had admittedly been her doing. It had been difficult to walk away from such a rugged, attractive man. But it would have been even more difficult to adapt to his new lifestyle.

Sitting with him now, Beth wondered if she should reevaluate her earlier conclusion. *The proof of the pudding is in the eating*, she mused, as she regarded him. *I went my way and he went his. Who's happier? Who's more successful? Who's more fulfilled? Who's better off today than a year ago?* Beth was well aware that it had been a good year for her in many ways—monetarily to be sure. But she was also painfully aware that her recent breakup with Colin Wendt had exposed a void within her that all her success and profit in the past year had not been able to fill. She wasn't sure she would fare well in a quality-of-life comparison with Reagan Cole at this point.

The waitress brought their drinks to the table along with a basket of hot tortilla chips and bowls of succulent salsa and guacamole. Beth thought she might be able to ask Cole about his life, but not right away. He seemed to have fared better than she in purposeful living—or at least he was putting on that he had. She decided to launch the conversation in the direction of less threatening topics.

"What's happening with Curtis Spooner? He didn't play many minutes for the Blazers this year."

Cole took a healthy sip of cherry Coke to wash down his first handful of chips. "Spoon has one more year on his Portland contract, and he's aware that he is in the 'twilight of his career,' as they say. Also, his knees are really falling apart on him."

"Three knee surgeries during his career?"

"Four."

"Mm, that's pretty serious. They say that every time you mess around in there, it takes a year or two off your playing life. That makes Spooner about a forty-year-old professional basketball player."

Cole nodded. "Spoon still has a shooter's touch, but he thinks next year may be his last. The Blazers have the fifth pick in the draft from a trade with the Bullets. They should be able to get a premier shooting guard—either Tyrone McKeever from Pitt or Maaseeb Dimbokro from . . . er, from . . . " Cole drummed his temple with his finger trying to remember Dimbokro's school.

"U Conn," Beth supplied.

"Right, U Conn," Cole nodded. Then he added with a big smile, "You still follow the game closely, don't you?"

"As closely as I can from *USA Today* and cable sports."

"Anyway, the Blazers are asking Curtis to stay through his option year as a player/coach to whip the rookie into shape. Then they'll probably offer him a job in the front office—community relations, player development, something like that."

"Do you really think Spooner is ready to hang up the sneakers? He'll be a free agent, and he can still hit the three-pointer. Couldn't he sign on somewhere else and play another year or two?"

Cole scooped a tortilla chip full of guacamole. "Maybe, but he doesn't want to leave Portland. He and Natty love the area. They're in a good church and active in the community. They want to raise their kids there. He doesn't think one last shot at NBA glory is worth moving the family to Milwaukee or Dallas or Orlando or Phoenix for a year."

Cole devoured the guacamole-laden chip in one bite, then loaded up another as he continued. "Besides, Spoon is still involved with T.D. Dunne—remember him?"

Beth nodded, savoring a sip of her margarita. She vividly remembered the talented black musician of the Unity 2000 gathering who had uniquely and successfully blended a pop music career and the Gospel ministry. She occasionally paused to listen to the music on his TV network while surfing the cable channels with the remote. But she always hit the clicker when the preaching or testimonies started.

"Curtis speaks at some of Dunne's concerts and appears on his show now and then," Cole said. "I think he wants to get more involved with Dunne when he retires as an active player."

Another fanatic in the making, Beth concluded silently. Then, hoping to discourage Cole from sermonizing, she moved on to another item of personal curiosity. "I didn't see that actor friend of Shelby's at the reception. Was he there for the ceremony?"

"Jeremy Cannon?"

"Yeah, that's him."

Cole's response was delayed by the arrival of a sizzling skillet of pork, peppers, onions, and spices and a stack of fresh, hot corn tortillas served in a ceramic warmer. After the waitress left, Cole asked, "Do you mind if I say a little prayer of thanks for the food?"

Beth had always regarded that question as grossly unfair. Anyone who said no to such a request would appear either uncooperative or ungrateful or un-American. "Go ahead," she said with a plastic smile. She was relieved that the prayer was short and simple and that Reagan Cole didn't make a big deal out of bowing his head and folding his hands.

Beth removed a steaming tortilla and placed it on her plate. As he had done on their previous visits to Quintero's, Cole took her plate and spooned mounds of spicy, pungent pork and vegetables into the tortilla. Then he proceeded to build his first fajita, picking up the conversation where it had been interrupted.

"No, Jeremy Cannon wasn't at the wedding. He's on location in East Africa. I think he sent them a videogram."

"What happened to him after Shelby left her church? Are they still friends? I heard they had a thing going at one time."

"Whoa," Cole laughed. "It sounds like you're writing a juicy exposé about the poor guy."

"No, I'm just curious," Beth grinned, infected by Cole's laugh. "What can I say? I'm a journalist. I possess an unquenchable thirst for knowledge."

Cole waited to speak until he had chewed and swallowed a big bite of his fajita. "According to Shelby, she and Jeremy have been and still are good friends, nothing more. When Shelby left Dallas, Jeremy—" Cole's pocket phone sounded, and he reached for it while his finished his sentence. "Jeremy stayed with the ministry at Shelby's request. He speaks at Victory Life occasionally, and he's still making movies. But I hear that he doesn't get many good roles because he refuses to do any sleazy sex-and-violence films."

Cole owned what he called a "banana phone." Folded, it was four inches long and about an inch square, convenient for a man's shirt pocket. With the mouthpiece unfolded at an angle, it was six inches long. Made of high-impact, mustard-colored plastic, the phone didn't look much like a banana, but Cole enjoyed calling it that.

To Beth he said with a smirk, "It's probably my mother calling to see if I've left yet. She still worries when I ride my motorcycle. Excuse me for a second." Then he flipped the phone open, "Hello, this is Reagan Cole."

For the next two minutes, Beth nibbled on her fajita and tried to appear politely disinterested in the call. But she couldn't help listening intently and trying to figure out the message from Cole's half of the conversation.

"Yeah, Frank . . . No, I'm eating at Quintero's as we speak. I leave for Tahoe in an hour or so . . . That's okay, no problem. What's up? . . . What? . . . You're kidding! When? . . . You're kidding! Wouldn't you know he'd pull a stunt like that the day I leave for vacation. Where'd he go? . . . Uh-huh . . . To Phoenix? Really? . . . What? . . . You're kidding! . . . You're kidding! . . . So where is he? . . . Get serious! . . . Well, who's looking for him? . . . Why not? . . . Frank, you're kidding me! . . . I can't believe it . . . What? . . . No sweat, I'll get right on it . . . That's okay, Frank, this is my pigeon. I'll find him myself. Who was tailing him today? . . . Uh-huh . . . Do you have a number for them right there? . . . Great. I've got it . . . No, don't worry about it . . . Thanks a lot, Frank."

Cole folded the phone and dropped it back into his shirt pocket with a sigh. Beth was overcome with curiosity. "Problem?"

"Not a biggie," Cole said, "but I have to leave. Something has come up at work."

There was a definite note of disappointment in his voice, which flattered Beth. But there was something else in Cole's tone, something vaguely familiar to her. She studied him closely, and his eyes flashed the same message. In an instant, she recognized it. She had seen it the night they first met. The phone call from a coworker named Frank had provoked a hint of bug-eyed, boyish excitement in Sergeant Reagan Cole, just as the attack on the San Diego Freeway had launched him into a frantic chase of an escaping gang member. Cole had been called into action, and he could barely contain himself.

He explained as he hastily filled another tortilla with scoops of pork, peppers, and onions, "A guy we have been watching for the FBI since May finally made a move this morning. But the stakeout team lost him, and I have to go look for him."

"But you're on vacation," Beth objected, trying not to sound too offended that he was about to walk out on her.

"I know, but this is my case, and I need to handle it. Besides, if I do it on my own time I can come and go as I please." As Cole spoke he wrapped another tortilla around his bulging fajita and enclosed the entire creation in a linen napkin. Beth realized that he was making a lunch to go. His skill at doing so convinced her that this wasn't the first time he had left Quintero's in a hurry.

Beth felt cheated. She wasn't ready for Cole to leave. "But your mother is expecting you," she interjected, grasping for an excuse to cause him to stay.

Cole was loading tortilla chips into another napkin as he spoke. "I'll call her. She understands these things. Dad was an L.A. cop too. With any luck I can get this settled in a day or two and still get to her place for a few days."

Then Cole stopped working on his takeout lunch and gave Beth his full attention. "I'm really sorry, Beth." Beth perceived nothing but sincerity in his apology. "I was looking forward to spending some time together before you left town. I want to hear about what's going on in your life. I was hoping our friendship could return to a better time and get moving again. Maybe we can get together when you come back to L.A."

Cole grabbed his helmet and leather saddlebags from the seat beside him, slid out of the booth, and stood, the prospect of adventure gleaming in his eye. "Relax and finish your lunch, Beth. Have another margarita if you want; it's all on me. Give the bill to Raphaela on your way out. I'll settle with her the next time I'm in."

He lifted his glass and sucked down the rest of his cherry Coke in three big gulps. Then he said with a wink, "I hate it when cops in the movies leave good food and drink on the table to go chase a bad guy."

Beth didn't hear his humorous statement. The wheels were spinning in her head. Then she made a snap decision and stood. "I want to go with you," she said firmly.

Cole blinked. "What?"

"I said I want to go with you to chase your bad guy."

"You can't do that. I'm on police business."

"You're on vacation, on your own time—you said so yourself. You can come and go as you please."

Cole looked surprised and puzzled and pleased all at once. "What about your flight?" he argued.

"I'll take another one, tomorrow or the next day. I don't have anything to get home for. Besides, I'm not finished talking with you either."

Cole picked up his napkin-wrapped snacks and started for the door. "I'm sorry, Beth. But this guy is a killer. You may not be safe."

Beth lifted her hands to her hips and glared at him. "Reagan Cole, you owe me," she called to him curtly across half the dining room. "Eighteen months ago you commandeered my rental car to chase a bad guy through West L.A. Your reckless driving banged up the car and nearly got me killed. It's payback time. Now do you take me with you, or do I cause a royal scene in your favorite restaurant?"

The scene was already in progress. Guests at several nearby tables were looking on wide-eyed as the statuesque, dark-haired young woman issued her ultimatum.

Cole stared at her, speechless. Finally, an old, mustachioed gentleman at a nearby table spoke up. He had been watching the brief exchange while downing his fourth margarita. "You'd better take her with you, big fellow," he slurred with a silly grin, "before she starts throwing the furniture around."

Cole shook his head in disbelief, but the smile overcoming his face betrayed his secret pleasure at Beth's dogged insistence. "Okay, but we have to hurry. Grab your purse and come on—and don't forget the bill," he said, heading for the door.

The man with the mustache led several other patrons in a round of applause at Beth's triumph. Beth flashed a playful victory sign to the crowd as she hurried out of the dining room, handbag slung over her shoulder.

Cole explained to Raphaela Quintero on the fly that he would pay the bill and return the linen napkins on his next visit. She laughed and shooed him on his way as she had often done before.

"Where are we going?" Beth quizzed Cole, as they stepped outside. The warmth of the noon sun felt good on Beth's bare limbs in contrast to the air-conditioned atmosphere of the restaurant.

"Burbank Airport," he said, striding swiftly through the crowd on the brick walkway which was Olvera Street. The stores and kiosks in the marketplace swarmed with souvenir-seeking tourists. "But I don't have an extra helmet, so you'll have to follow me in your car."

"Why don't you just ride with me?" Beth proposed, hustling to keep up with him in the milling throng.

"I can't leave my bike here because I don't know when I'll be back. I love L.A., but parking anything on the street for more than a couple hours is just plain foolish."

"I don't blame you."

"But you can throw my saddlebags in your back seat, if you don't mind."

Beth agreed, and they made the baggage transfer without missing a stride.

They arrived at the curb where Cole's Kawasaki was nosed in behind Beth's rented black Buick Barego coupe. He pulled on his helmet and straddled the bike.

"What are we going to do at the airport?" Beth asked, hurrying to her door and fumbling for the car keys in her purse.

"I'll explain everything when we get there." Then Cole started the Kawasaki and began backing it away from the curb.

"Which is the fastest way to the airport?" Beth called above the loud drone of the motorcycle.

"On a Kawasaki," Cole retorted with a big grin.

"You know what I mean."

"Pasadena Freeway over the hill to I-5, then west to Hollywood Way. I'll meet you in the main terminal." Without waiting for a response, Cole gunned the engine, bolted down Main Street, and disappeared around the corner onto Macy Street, heading toward the Pasadena Freeway.

In seconds, Beth had tossed Cole's leather bags into the backseat and the Barego was moving. When she squealed onto Macy, Cole and his bike were already out of sight. She tromped on the accelerator and started passing cars. "What kind of crazy ride is Reagan Cole taking me on this time?" she wondered aloud.

Forty-one

The deep-fried prawns, scallops, and french fries were tasty, but having been a fastidious monitor of fat intake most of her life, Libby had difficulty enjoying her lunch. She had ordered the greasy seafood combo to bolster her flagging spirits. But she pushed her plate away without finishing and turned her attention to the view from the porch, while she sipped her iced tea.

The Boat Shed Restaurant afforded its patrons a view of Dye's Inlet and Manette Bridge, which is why Libby chose to eat there. No matter what she was doing, Libby usually always felt better when she could see the water. But today the beautiful, sunny scene surrounding Bremerton was no more effective at breaking her dumpy mood than her fat-laden lunch had been.

Libby had spent the morning nosing through a few of her favorite Bremerton haunts: a Native American art gallery, a couple of antique shops, and an off-the-beaten-path flea market operated by a gigantic, hairy man who caused her to wonder if the myth of Sasquatch was total myth. She had also stopped at a couple of yard sales. In three hours of shopping she had bought nothing, nor had she been looking for anything in particular. The activity was pure diversion, she had admitted to herself just before turning into the Boat Shed.

But Libby's morning away from the city hadn't brought her any nearer a solution for her conflict with Brett. Sipping tea in the sunshine, she chided herself, *For all the education you have amassed, for all the success and recognition you have achieved, for all the material comforts you have acquired, you certainly don't know much about life. Your son is flirting with rebellion on a grand scale, and he's blaming you—perhaps justifiably. You are on the verge of losing him, and you don't know what to do about it. And always at your back is that dark cloud from the past, less threatening in the distance perhaps, but no less intense in its impact.*

Libby longed to confess her problems with Brett to her parents, but Hardy and Lola Carroll had passed away within six months of each other when Brett was sixteen and Libby was still trying to prove herself as the successful, single, career mother. She would have told them her long-held secret that Brett's father was white. She would have asked them how she should respond to Brett's demands that she identify the man. She would have welcomed their advice regarding the impact of such a revelation on her career. But her father and mother had gone to their graves without realizing the turmoil Libby's headstrong illegitimate son would cause her.

There was a time when Libby shared her burdens with Claudia or

Bernice. As the baby in the family, Libby had been coddled, protected, and spoiled by her five older siblings, particularly Claudia and Bernice. But Libby's rabid ambition to make something of herself after Brett was born created a rift in her family. Claudia and Bernice resented Libby for deserting their aging parents to pursue a career when, as the youngest and least encumbered, she should have moved into the family home in Kent and cared for them. Libby gladly contributed to Hardy and Lola's care, but refused to put her education and advancing career on hold to become their cook and housekeeper. Finally, a shared arrangement was agreed upon among the six adult children, but the distance between Libby and Claudia and Bernice was never recouped.

Libby's waitress refilled her iced tea glass and removed the half-finished platter of food. Libby added a lemon wedge and a tablet of herbal sweetener, stirring the mixture with her straw until the tablet, chasing a solitary lemon seed in the swirling liquid, dissolved.

She was in no hurry to leave the restaurant. Her morning of diversion and contemplation had proved fruitless. The thought of driving to Poulsbo and continuing the charade left her cold. What was the use? Who was she fooling? She was no closer to a solution on this side of the Sound than she had been in Seattle.

Libby watched the tiny seed, alone and adrift in her tea glass, as it spiraled to the bottom. She had never before linked her cherished independence with the painful isolation she felt. Staring at the seed, she was suddenly aware how isolated she was. She had doggedly battled the odds and made a name for herself in her chosen profession. She had raised a son with neither the help of a man nor the handouts of the system. But, unlike the sweetener tablet which had disappeared in her glass, she had failed to blend in with anyone.

She didn't have one person she could talk to about the part of her life where success was still hanging in the balance. Her parents were gone, and her sisters were distant. Robert Rhodes didn't seem to care about her crisis with Brett, and her other friends didn't even know what was going on, nor was she comfortable telling them. *In whom do you confide for advice when you don't have anyone close?* she pondered. *A shrink? A minister or priest? A talk-show personality? A bartender? A total stranger?*

Libby realized with twisted humor that if the advice of strangers was the solution, she was sitting in the middle of a bonanza of wisdom. The porch and dining room around her were nearly full of locals and vacationers scarfing down fish and chips, shrimp baskets, and clam strips, and she didn't know any of them. *I can go table to table, tell people my conflict with Brett, and ask them what I should do*, she mused wryly. *I'll be democratic about it: I'll go with the consensus, the majority vote.* She didn't really plan on talking to anyone in the restaurant, of course, but the thought amused her somewhat on this very unamusing day.

She gazed around the restaurant as if looking for a clue as to what to do next, a sign, something. There was a couple in their late twenties with two preschool-children. The family was clean, fresh from church, and obviously living on a budget. The Boat Shed was a big splurge for them, and they were enjoying every moment of it.

Several senior citizens — couples and singles — were spread throughout the dining room enjoying meals on their privileged diner discount cards.

Other guests in the restaurant within Libby's scope of view included a man and two teenaged boys determined to make the owners sorry they put all-you-can-eat popcorn shrimp on the menu for $5.95, a woman by the window who, like herself, had come for the view, and two uniformed police officers on lunch break.

The pair of cops looked to Libby like Laurel and Hardy. The white officer was narrow and slight with straight, dark hair that wouldn't lie down properly. The other officer was tall, thick, and black, seemingly the victim of too many all-you-can-eat episodes at the Boat Shed and elsewhere. The big man's scalp was nearly devoid of hair except for wispy, salt-and-pepper patches swept back from the temples.

Libby stared at the black officer until he happened to look at her; then she turned away, hoping he hadn't received the wrong message. She couldn't believe the idea which had popped into her head at the sight of the large black cop. He reminded her of another big man in uniform who would likely listen eagerly as she talked about Brett, sympathize with her, and try to help her. This person had already proven himself to be gentlemanly, discreet, and trustworthy. Libby realized that without Reginald Burris' timely intervention, Brett might be in even deeper trouble and she might have been disgraced among her peers at the university.

What harm could there be in just talking to him? she considered. *He already knows what happened. He's a father; he must know how I feel. Yet he's an outsider; he may be able to supply a needed objective perspective.*

This is preposterous! Libby argued with herself. *Reginald isn't a friend or a counselor; he's a police officer. I barely know him. Men like him only have one thing on their minds. If I open up to him and share my concerns about Brett and ask him for advice, I'll only encourage his hormones. Talking to Reginald Burris is a bad idea.*

Libby shook her head and twirled the straw in her tea. The lemon seed skipped in frantic circles across the bottom of the glass. Libby knew exactly how the little seed felt.

She sat for ten more minutes staring out at the inlet and glancing occasionally at the husky policeman who reminded her of Reginald

Burris. She was alone and out of options. *Which is worse*, she thought with a sigh, *a bad idea or no idea?*

After another minute she pulled a five and three singles out of her wallet, laid it across the check, and left. She guided the Seville down to the water to await the next ferry back to Seattle.

Forty-two

It occurred to Beth as she sped north on the Golden State Freeway that Cole might have given her a bum steer. He said he would meet her at the Burbank Airport. But she knew he didn't really want her to come on this chase, any more than he wanted her tagging along when he raced wildly after the escaping Latino gang member in her rented Star Cruiser the night they first met. Cole could have intentionally sent her off in the wrong direction today so he could do his macho cop thing all alone. She prepared herself to be justifiably livid if she arrived at the terminal and he wasn't there.

The Burbank-Glendale-Pasadena Airport is situated on Hollywood Way a half-mile south of Interstate 5, which is called the Golden State Freeway in the northwest quadrant of L.A. Along with Ontario Airport, Long Beach Airport, and John Wayne Airport in Orange County, suburban Burbank Airport is ballyhooed by its tenant airlines as the sane alternative to crowded Los Angeles International Airport. As Southern California continued to grow into the new millennium, Burbank Airport remained small and sleepy with a hometown feel, compared to L.A.'s mega-terminal on the Pacific Ocean southwest of the city. And being close to several major motion picture and television studios, Burbank Airport was frequently invaded by film crews using the site to represent a generic American airport.

Beth found a space on the second deck of the parking structure. She hurried toward the terminal, threatening Cole under her breath if he wasn't there. But she found him just inside the terminal's main doors, helmet in hand, pacing in front of the gift shop while he talked on his banana phone. For the second time in less than an hour, Beth eavesdropped on one side of a telephone conversation, dying to hear everything.

"So you caught up with him in the B terminal . . . Oh, you *almost* caught up with him . . . Uh-huh . . . Uh-huh . . . And you're absolutely positive it was our man? . . . Uh-huh . . . . But did you see him get on the plane? . . . Uh-huh . . . Uh-huh . . . Listen to me, Cox. I don't care that he had a ticket or that his name appeared on the passenger list.

And I don't care that you saw him go through the gate and saw the door close on the aircraft. Did you *actually see* our man go up the stairs and enter the plane?"

Cole stopped pacing and acknowledged Beth with a quick glance. When he spoke again, he sounded impatient and angry. "Yes, it *is* important, Cox, because after we called, the Feds were watching for him at Sky Harbor and he wasn't on the plane . . . That's what I want to know, Cox . . . You can't assume *anything* with a guy like Barbosa. He can lull you to sleep when he's just lying around. I think he just busted a slick move on you two, and you went for it."

Cole listened for almost a minute, occasionally plugging his free ear to block out the chatter of arriving and departing passengers echoing in the broad, noisy hallway. Beth assumed that the officer presently being called on the carpet was doing his best song and dance, trying to absolve himself or herself of the disappearance of a bad guy who had been identified only as Barbosa.

Shifting from foot to foot with impatience, Cole finally interrupted and finished the discussion. "Okay, Cox, you made your point. Just enter your report and we'll talk about it later . . . No, don't come back out here. Check in with the lieutenant for reassignment. I'll catch up with you in a day or two."

Cole snapped the phone shut, accompanied by an unintelligible grumble of displeasure. He looked up and down the hallway as if trying to determine what to do next and where to start doing it. Beth caught him by the arm before he could make a move. She was eager to hear the whole story. "You said you would fill me in, Reagan," she said respectfully. "How about now?"

Cole's body language and facial expression suggested that he wished he had ditched Beth instead of allowing her to tag along. Beth sensed the vibes and intervened before they could materialize as a command for her to leave.

"I know you think I'll be in your way, Reagan," she said. "But I'm not just along for the ride. I have an inquisitive, analytical, problem-solving mind. If you need to find this guy Barbosa, I may be able to help you. Two good heads are better than one, you know."

Cole paused, arranging his words. "I have no problem with your mind, Beth. But after what happened eighteen months ago, I am concerned about your judgment."

Beth flushed warm with embarrassment. She knew he was referring to her impulsive approach to finding the doomsday prophet of Unity 2000 which almost got her killed. "I've learned my lesson," she assured him, not really confident that she had. "I'll stay behind you. I won't keep anything from you like I did then. I'm not trying to break an exclusive story or save the world. I just want to help."

Cole gave in more quickly than Beth expected him to. "You'll do what I ask and stay out of my way when I tell you to, no questions asked?" he pressed.

Beth held up three fingers on her right hand. "Scout's honor," she said with a flirty smile. Had Cole asked her if she had ever been a Girl Scout, Beth would have had to say no, but he didn't ask. Beth felt that scout's honor from a nonscout was like a contract signed in disappearing ink or telling a lie with your fingers crossed. It gave her license to do anything she felt necessary, on the legal technicality of a secretly invalid promise.

Cole sat her down on a bench midway between the airport's main entrance and the ticket counters for the B concourse and gave her a *Reader's Digest* version of the surveillance and recent disappearance of Rennie Barbosa, the Peruvian hit man. Beth was aware that the bad guy's trail was cooling by the minute and that Cole was nearly beside himself to get after him. So she kept her questions to a minimum.

"Why isn't the FBI taking over the search?"

"When Barbosa didn't show up in Phoenix, the FBI said, 'LAPD lost him, LAPD has to find him,' " Cole said, standing. "The Feds give us a lot of junk about their office in L.A. being understaffed, underbudgeted, and overworked. That's why we were assigned to watch Barbosa in the first place. They say they only have the manpower to go after the most serious menaces to society. In his sleep mode, Barbosa hardly fits that category."

"But if he's 'waking up,' so to speak, he *may be* a serious menace," Beth verbalized the obvious.

"Exactly," Cole affirmed, edging in the direction of the ticket counters. "That's what the Feds will say after Barbosa wastes somebody. Then, suddenly, they'll have the manpower to look for him, but he'll be long gone. And LAPD will end up taking the rap for losing him."

"Then shouldn't the department be down here in force looking for Barbosa?"

"We are," Cole answered, tapping on his sternum with his index finger. "He's my responsibility. I know as much about him as anyone. So I'm the one who gets to find him."

Beth walked alongside Cole thinking out loud for both of them. "So if Barbosa didn't get off the plane in Phoenix, then he didn't get on the plane in Burbank," she advanced, pretending that she had figured it out herself instead of overhearing it in Cole's conversation with Officer Cox. "And if he didn't get on the plane to Phoenix, he must be around here somewhere."

"Not necessarily," Cole corrected. "After convincing Gleason and Cox that he was going to Phoenix, Barbosa could have hopped another flight."

"What if he didn't hop another flight? What if he slipped out into the city again?"

"It doesn't match Barbosa's method of operation. When he goes to the airport, he's usually on his way to his next assignment."

"Since when is a criminal duty-bound to comply with his M.O. like an actor following a script?" Beth pressed.

"He isn't, of course, Beth," Cole said, a little irritated at the interrogation. "We're just playing the odds. We start looking for suspects where we have found them before. If they're not there, we branch out and look elsewhere."

Beth wasn't convinced, but she decided to humor the handsome cop. "Well, it's Sunday, and there haven't been that many departures since the Phoenix flight left. It shouldn't be difficult finding out which one he took. Then all you have to do is tell the FBI where to pick up the search, and we can get on with our lunch."

"If it was only that easy," Cole interjected. "You don't know how slippery Barbosa can be. He can disappear so fast it's scary. Ask Gleason and Cox."

"But a man can't just disappear, especially in a busy airport. It's impossible. All we have to do is find one or two people who saw him. Where do we start?"

Cole turned into the public communications station near the intersection of the entry hallway and the main passageway leading to the A concourse to the left and the B concourse to the right. "We start by getting a picture of him from my office to show to ticket agents, gate agents, and ground crew."

Without another word of explanation, Cole stepped into a vacant carrel, swiped a bank card through the public computer terminal, and within seconds the monitor blinked on. As he began tapping access commands, he said to Beth, "Get me the number of an open fax-receive unit over there, will you please?" When Beth returned with a number, Cole entered it, activating the fax-send function from his office PC at Parker Center. In less than a minute from when the computer read Cole's bank card, a fax photo was spewed into the fax-receive tray.

"This is our man," Cole said, holding up the three-frame color photo, "Rennie Barbosa, alias William Martin, Thomas Johnson, or Alberto Rodriguez." Each frame showed a different angle: front, three-quarters, side. The original photos had been clandestinely shot by a surveillance team at Universal Studios Hollywood two weeks earlier. Barbosa looked like any other wide-eyed tourist enjoying the theme park.

"May I see it?" Beth lifted the fax photo from Cole's hand before he could answer. Then she stepped quickly to a color copier, fed it four quarters from her change purse, slipped in the original, and pressed COPY. The machine hummed and whispered briefly, then produced a copy identical to the original. "We can cover twice as much ground if we split up," Beth explained, passing the original back to Cole.

Cole looked a little perturbed. "All right, but you don't have an LAPD holocard, so your inquiries are strictly unofficial."

"What do you mean, officer?" Beth said, feigning dumb innocence. "I just happen to be looking for my big brother who is mentally ill and likes to hang around airports with his black suit bag. Sometimes he even buys a ticket. Have you seen this man today?"

"Geez," Cole said, almost laughing. "You're something else."

"I'll take that as a compliment," Beth returned, winking.

Cole was quickly serious again. "Like I said, my guess is that Barbosa faked boarding Alaska's 11:10 flight to Phoenix and jumped on another plane instead. I'll check the ticket counters for flights which left after the Phoenix flight. Then I'll ask around the B gates and talk to the ground crew outside B-8 where Alaska 2321 was parked."

"Good theory," Beth said. "But if this guy is as tricky as you say, he only came to the airport to make you *think* he was flying out. I'll bet he slipped away from the gate and left the airport by bus or taxi."

"I think you read too many spy novels," Cole quipped.

"Think what you like, but I'll check outside: skycaps, taxi drivers, sidewalk bums." She added with an impish twinkle, "And I'll bet you dinner that I turn over a clue before you do."

Cole scowled. "Beth, this isn't a game. We're looking for a professional hit man."

"All the more reason to be at our competitive best. Is it a bet or isn't it?" Beth knew Cole couldn't resist a challenge, especially from her. He had told her many times in their first weeks together how much he enjoyed her spirit and spunk.

Cole didn't seem eager to play along, but he agreed, obviously to placate Beth and get to the chase. "All right, memorize my number and call me if you turn up anything."

Beth pulled out her classic brass flip phone, about the size of a makeup compact. Cole recited his number and she tapped it into the phone's memory.

"Let me give you my number too, although you won't need it since I'll probably find him before you anyway," Beth said with a confident swagger in her tone.

"Not necessary," Cole said, grinning self-consciously. "I still have it." He patted the banana phone in his pocket. "I never erase important numbers out of memory."

Beth smiled. "I'm touched."

Cole took her hand. He was serious again. "I'm probably nuts for letting you do this with me. Please don't make me sorry too. Be careful." He tapped his picture of Rennie Barbosa. "This guy looks as harmless and innocent as a nun, but he's a professional killer. He has no qualms about snuffing out anyone who may be his way. If you see or hear anything that may lead us to Barbosa, please call me right away."

"Don't worry, Reagan. I can take care of myself."

Cole looked at her disbelievingly. "You said that once before and I trusted you. Then you almost got yourself killed."

Beth shook off the chilling memory. "Believe me, Reagan, I've learned my lesson. I'll be careful."

Beth stepped out of the main doors into the warm sunshine armed only with a photograph and a growing resolve to prove to Reagan Cole that she *could* be trusted and *could* take care of herself. His kindness and attention to her were as relentless and captivating as ever. And if he had indeed turned into a religious fanatic over the last eighteen months, he sure didn't act like one. On the contrary, in the few hours Beth had spent with him since yesterday, Reagan Cole seemed more centered, more substantial in character, and more at peace with himself than any man she knew. She was increasingly convinced that he deserved a serious second look.

Beth slipped on her sunglasses to fight the glare of the bright, midday sun. Then she surveyed the scene before her, plotting a strategy for interviewing the most people in the least amount of time.

The Burbank Airport building is a giant L with the one-way access road running along the inside of the right angle. The building's main entrance stands near the sweeping left turn in the angle. From her vantage point at the top of the stairs, Beth could look left along the tall, vertical stroke of the L which housed the B gates. To the right, the shorter foot of the L housed the A gates and had its own entrance and ticket counter.

Traffic swept into the airport complex from Hollywood Way on the left, dropping off or picking up passengers curbside on either side of the bend in the L, then exited onto Vanowen Street. Across the access road from the A gates was an island dedicated to taxis, buses, and shuttle vans for a few off-campus car rental lots and even fewer local hotels. Beyond the island stood a multilevel parking structure flanked by single-level parking lots.

Beth decided to start on her left and sweep the broad sidewalk around to the right, talking to skycaps, airport security officers, and any loiterers who admitted to being at the airport more than an hour. She would keep to the fictional story she had told Cole: her mentally ill brother, who loved to hang around airports, had disappeared and was thought to have come to the airport. She knew she could work up enough of a sense of mild panic to appear believable.

Beautifully tan and attractive in her white summer shorts and red top, Beth had no trouble getting the attention of the service personnel who had worked the sidewalk all morning, especially since most of them were men. Furthermore, most of the men she talked to wanted badly to ingratiate themselves with the grieving statuesque beauty by stating that they had seen the man in the picture. But when pressed to make a positive ID, including his black leather suit bag, they all shook their heads and lamented their inability to help her. By the time she reached the end of the sidewalk on the B side of the terminal, she had no leads.

She crossed the road to the island of shuttle vehicles and launched into phase two of her plan. She worked her way down a short queue of taxis showing the picture and telling her story to the drivers, all of them clearly immigrants from the Near or Middle East. They seemed less interested to help her than the men on the sidewalk. But each one heard her out, studied the picture, then shook their heads.

Whenever an RTD bus, shuttle van, or limo lumbered up to the curb, Beth broke from the taxi line and ran to the door to interrogate the driver. Her hopes spiked upward when the driver of the Thrifty Car Rental van, a young Iranian, recognized the picture. But he haltingly explained that he had transported the man *to* the airport almost two hours ago, not *from* it. Seeing Beth's disappointment, he apologized profusely and wished her good fortune in finding her sick brother.

Other vans servicing rental car companies, hotels, and motels came and went. Beth talked to every driver, but with no success. And with every new taxi driver adding his rig to the end of the chain, she repeated her brief interview to no avail.

After half an hour on the sidewalk in the hot sun, both Beth's energy and confidence that Barbosa had left the premises on wheels were beginning to wilt. She wanted something cold to drink. She wanted to get into the shade for a while. But since Cole hadn't called her, she was spurred on by the realization that he must not be faring any better inside than she was outside. There was still a chance she might get lucky, so she kept going.

The Burbank Airport Hilton van arriving at the curb was one of those new Swedish twenty-passenger electric jobs. It was designed to look sleek, aerodynamic, as if hurtling into the twenty-first century at Mach Six. But Beth thought that a 50-MPH bus trying to look like a stealth bomber was very hokey. The vehicle looked more like a bulbous cartoon space ship on wheels.

It was the first time the Hilton van had stopped at the shuttle island since Beth had been interviewing drivers, so she quickly slipped into line at the side door behind five boarding passengers with luggage. The driver, a chubby Filipino woman in her forties, was barely tall enough to reach the pedals.

Once inside the bus, Beth worked her way to the front as other passengers stowed their luggage and looked for a seat. Screwing her face into a look of concern, Beth said to the fireplug of a woman in the driver's bucket seat, "Excuse me, ma'am, but my mentally ill brother has disappeared, and he sometimes comes down to the airport." She thrust the fax photo of Rennie Barbosa in the woman's face. "Have you seen him around the airport in your travels?" She was about to add that the man might be carrying a black suit bag, but the woman spoke first in a thick Filipino accent.

"Yes, I see that man. He ride my bus."

Beth was so stunned at hearing a positive response that she didn't know what to say. "Th-this man . . . rode y-your bus?" she stammered excitedly. "Are you sure it was th-this man?" She moved the picture closer to the woman's face.

"Yes, that man ride my bus. I know. I look who ride my bus every-day. I look very good in case a robber ride my bus."

"When did he ride your bus? Was it today?"

"Yes, today. I watch him come on with black bag. He go to hotel this morning. He your brother?"

"Er, yeah, he's my brother. He's, er, mentally ill."

"Well, your brother at Hilton Hotel right now. You want to go?"

An urgent, icy chill traced Beth's spine. *I have to call Cole. I promised . . . or sort of promised . . . that I would. But what if this lady is nuts? What if the man she saw wasn't Barbosa? I'd look foolish calling Reagan out here on a wild-goose chase. I have to make sure.*

"I go to hotel now, lady. You go or stay?" The driver's short, fat finger was poised above the door switch.

Beth held her breath, her mind churning in indecision. "Okay, I'll go," she blurted before really thinking about it. The driver closed the door and pulled away from the curb, with Beth still standing in the aisle.

Reagan Cole acknowledged that if he had been wearing his pressed navy blue LAPD uniform bearing his gleaming badge, he would have moved more quickly through his interviews. As it was, airline ticket agents, gate agents, and ground crew members busily expediting passengers and baggage to and from their flights tended to ignore the tall man in jeans and the striped, long-sleeve shirt. Only when he thrust into their faces the laminated LAPD ID card bearing his holograph and insisted in solemn cop-speak, "Police officer," did he gain their attention long enough to show his picture of Barbosa.

The first few encounters at Gate B-8, where Barbosa had led Gleason and Cox to believe he was boarding an Alaska Airlines flight to Phoenix, were hopeful. One gate agent thought she remembered the man turning in his ticket and heading for the plane. A check of canceled tickets for that flight turned up one issued to a Thomas Johnson.

Furthermore, a baggage handler for Alaska to whom Cole spoke on the sunny tarmac clearly recalled a man fitting Barbosa's description and carrying a black leather suit bag. The ground crew member, wearing khaki shirt and shorts, a black L.A. Raiders cap, and scuffed knee pads, reported that the man in the photos fell out of line just before mounting the portable stairway to the aircraft.

"He said something about being sick, ready to barf," the baggage handler told Cole. "He hustled back into the building like he needed a bathroom in a hurry." Then the man added, "What's the problem? Was this guy a skyjacker or something?"

Cole ignored the question. "Did he reenter the building there?" he asked, pointing to the door clearly marked B-8, the same door Barbosa would have passed through on his way to the plane.

The baggage man shook his head. "He went that way," he said, nodding toward B-4. "Our flight from Vegas had just arrived. He went inside with the deplaning passengers." Cole pictured Gleason and Cox searching so intently for Barbosa around B-8 that they failed to see him slip back into the building behind them at B-4.

After his inquiries had begun so hopefully at B-8, Cole abruptly reached a dead end inside B-4. None of the gate agents on duty at the time of the Las Vegas arriving flight remembered seeing Barbosa. The next plane to leave from the B concourse after Alaska's Phoenix flight was a Southwest Airlines flight to Oakland. Cole interrogated the Southwest personnel who had worked the Oakland departure at B-14. But the photo of Barbosa prompted only blank looks, and a review of the passenger list turned up no one using Barbosa's aliases.

Cole had the same results at B-16 for Alaska's noon flight to San Jose. No one remembered seeing the man in the photo or his black suit bag, and no suspicious names appeared on the passenger list for the flight.

There were only two more flights on the B concourse to check out: an American flight to Portland and a United Express puddle jumper to Santa Barbara. As he worked his way to their respective gates, two conscious pursuits vied for attention in his mind. First, Cole tried to pray for success in picking up Barbosa's trail. Praying about job-related problems was not something he did automatically, nor did he feel very confident that he did it well. But his friend Matt Dugan had coaxed him lovingly to take God with him on the job and call on Him for daily protection and help. So Cole forced himself to say silently as he walked and scanned the crowd, *Lord, Rennie Barbosa can't hide from You. Somehow let me know where he is, and I'll take care of him.*

Cole's thoughts about God and Barbosa were continually challenged by his concern for Beth. More than once he reached for his phone to call her off the search. "I just don't feel good about you being out there alone," he had decided to say. "If you ran into Barbosa and he hurt you, I would never forgive myself." But Cole never called. The image of Beth's brimming confidence and solemn promise to be careful made his concerns seem like meddling overprotection. So he prayed for Beth instead.

Neither of the departed Portland or Santa Barbara flights yielded a clue as to Barbosa's disappearance. In the process of checking specific flights, Cole had talked to every other gate agent and ground crew member he saw on the B concourse without success. It was as if Rennie Barbosa had dematerialized as he passed through the doorway at B-4 with the Las Vegas passengers.

Cole was on his way to the smaller, less active A concourse when his banana phone sounded. He was sure it was Beth calling to say she had struck out in her search for Barbosa outside the terminal.

"Yes," Cole answered, as he approached the security checkpoint leading to the A gates.

"Reagan?" Beth said in a strained and quiet voice.

Cole recognized her. "Beth, where are you?"

"The Airport Hilton, you know, just across Hollywood Way from the airport entrance." She was forcing herself to whisper.

Cole was puzzled. "What are you doing at the—"

Beth whispered right over the top of his question, cutting him off. "I'm calling to check in as you asked," she said. Despite the softness in her voice, Beth conveyed a sense of controlled urgency. "I need your advice."

"What—"

"I'm drinking iced tea in the Hilton coffee shop as we speak, and there's a man across the room eating lunch by the window. I'm positive it's Rennie Barbosa. What should I do?"

Forty-three

It was a little past 1 P.M. by the time Evan and Shelby Rider's RV reached Gorman on Interstate 5 near 4,200-foot Tejon Pass on the border of the Los Padres National Forest. The gradual, sweeping, thirty-mile climb from the intersection of 126 and I-5 had kept the big RV in the slow lane at an average speed of under 50 MPH. They had made it to the service station with the fuel gauge needle resting on E.

The windblown town of Gorman served as a refueling and brake inspection station for northbound eighteen-wheelers preparing to crawl down the dangerously steep Grapevine for the flat, dry, boring drive through central California. Evan stood in the blazing sun at the rear of the RV for several minutes, resting one foot on the car carrier while pumping seventy gallons of premium unleaded fuel into the Flair's tank. He regarded summer's hot, dry breath as a blessing compared to the bitter, biting winds that swept over the pass in the dead of winter.

He subconsciously moistened his lips against the dry breeze as he gripped the nozzle handle and watched the digital fuel gauge race past the forty-gallon mark. Beads of sweat crawled down his back underneath his shirt.

Evan knew that Shelby and Malika were probably sweltering inside the RV along with their captors, Nolan Jakes and Margo Sharpe. Evan had used the air conditioning sparingly during their long climb toward the brink of the Grapevine to avoid overheating the engine. And with the engine and air off now, the temperature inside was probably approaching 90 degrees. It was almost 100 where Evan stood, but at least the air was moving here. Jakes had allowed no one outside at Gorman except Evan to refuel the RV and Margo to watch him, especially when he was inside the mini-market paying the bill.

Jakes had reminded Evan that he would hold little Malika at gunpoint during the fuel stop. Evan had promised to fill the tank and pay for the fuel without a problem, without trying anything sneaky. And he meant it. He would do anything Jakes asked and give him anything he wanted. He was not about to jeopardize the safety of his bride or daughter—or his career as a medical doctor—by doing something foolishly heroic. All he wanted to do was drive them all quickly, quietly, and safely to Canada and watch Jakes and his girlfriend disappear forever.

Evan's greatest fear, aside from physical harm to his family, was that his complicity in the death of Neil McGruder would be leaked to Shelby by someone other than himself, namely Nolan Jakes, his companion, Margo, or—if Jakes was able to find her—Libby Carroll. Evan had intended to tell Shelby, and now he bitterly rued the fact that he hadn't confessed much sooner in their relationship. In the almost five hours since Jakes and Margo had barged into his life, Evan had begged God for their lives to be spared; and he promised Him dozens of times that he would confess his buried misdeed to Shelby. *Only please don't let Shelby be hurt by this terrible revelation*, he pleaded silently in prayer.

It had occurred to Evan that Shelby might react severely to news of his part in a murder, no matter where she heard it. He acknowledged that his new bride might even leave him for such a heinous act and for keeping it from her. In one dark moment he had contemplated the taunting scenario of Shelby walking out of his life and Jakes turning him in to the authorities, destroying his career and ending his life as a free man. In that frightening moment, suicide entered Evan's mind for the first time since before he discovered Shelby and God and faith. He did not want to think about life without his Shelby, his career, or his freedom.

But every thought of fearsome consequences urged Evan to strengthen his resolve. He would play out Jakes' script and act his part well. No court in the land could find him guilty of complicity for anything he did as a hostage to save his own life and the lives of his wife and daughter. And as soon as he could, as soon as God gave him the opportunity, he would explain to Shelby exactly why Nolan Jakes had selected him for this role in his frightful drama. Until then he would pray that she would hear him out at that time with compassion and understanding.

Evan topped off the tank, screwed on the gas cap, and returned the nozzle to the pump. Margo was waiting for him inside the mini-market where his bank card had already been scanned. Jakes had instructed her to get some food and drink for their journey, items they could heat and eat without pulling the RV into a rest stop. The groceries would be added to the fuel bill.

"Great day to be leavin' L.A., ain't it?" quipped the clerk, as Evan entered the market and met Margo at the counter. "It's hotter than the furnace room in hell out there." He was a young kid barely out of high school, although his grammar contested any claim that he had graduated. He was missing several teeth—including three in the front, and his weathered skin suggested that he had lived most of his eighteen or nineteen years outdoors on the dry, brush-strewn slopes around Gorman. He wore the faded black T-shirt of a cultic rock band. A name tag pinned hastily to the shirt read Bron.

Evan didn't feel like bantering with the clerk, but neither did he want to annoy him in any way or provoke suspicion. "How hot will it get here in the dead of summer?" he asked pleasantly, as Margo unloaded a plastic basket of groceries on the counter: frozen mini-pizzas, bread, luncheon meats, cupcakes, beer, soda pop. Evan had assured Jakes and Margo that there was already plenty of food in the RV's pantry and refrigerator for the trip. But Jakes had insisted that Margo buy their own stuff. Evan wondered if Jakes suspected that he had somehow poisoned the food in the RV.

Bron swished the groceries across the beeping scanner as he spoke. "Last year we got up to 109 in July, hot enough to boil your eyeballs right in your head. It don't get that hot most days, though. But it'll be 100 or more half the summer. Where are you folks from?"

Evan's head was so crowded with thoughts that he almost didn't notice Bron's question. "Er, Ventura," he said.

"I ain't never been to Ventura. Hear it's nice, though, nicer than Gorman. 'Course, just about every place is nicer than Gorman." Bron laughed at his own joke. Evan smiled to accommodate him. Margo kept pushing groceries toward the scanner. She was clearly in a hurry to get back on the road.

Evan realized that he and Shelby had not packed any special food for Malika, since they hadn't expected her to be traveling with them. He asked Bron, "Do you have any bottled fruit juices, like cranapple or cranraspberry?"

"Sure do," Bron said without looking up from his task. "The other side of those boxes of cereal sticking up."

Evan turned to go collect a few things for Malika. "Hurry up," Margo ordered, showing her impatience.

Evan found the juices and selected a few bottles. Then he walked by the dairy cooler and picked out a quart of low-fat milk. On the way back to the counter he grabbed a box of Lucky Charms breakfast cereal. He and Shelby had agreed that they would purchase sugary kids' cereals for Malika only occasionally, as a special treat. Evan felt that poor little Malika could use a lift, after the distressing start to her day.

As the two of them carried the bagged groceries to the waiting RV, Evan assessed Margo with a long glance. He had barely noticed her in the rush to get out of Ventura. Nolan Jakes had commanded all his attention, and Evan had regarded Margo as little more than an android programmed to help Jakes complete his plan. But now Evan noticed her: a petite young woman with a pretty but hard face and platinum blonde hair that didn't look real. She didn't look like a criminal or a criminal's mistress. Evan wondered how she had become tangled up with Nolan Jakes, how she found out about his dark past, and why she was throwing away her life for a fugitive. Evan was surprised by a twinge of compassion for Margo, a feeling he had yet to experience for Nolan Jakes.

"How long have you known Nolan?" Evan asked her, a few steps from the door of the RV, curiosity getting the better of him.

Margo turned to Evan with a suspicious gaze. He translated the distance in her eyes to read, "Butt out. It's none of your business. Just get us to Canada, then get lost." But after a silent moment she answered simply, "Long enough."

The ambiguous inflection in Margo's words left Evan wondering what she meant: long enough *to know what I'm doing,* or long enough *to doubt that I'm doing the right thing.* But there was no time to ask, and Evan was sure Margo wouldn't have explained her cryptic response to him anyway.

At Jakes' direction, Evan moved the RV from the fuel pumps to a temporary parking space away from other vehicles at the perimeter of the service station's lot. He left the engine running to allow the air conditioning to draw the stifling air out of the coach and inject some welcome refrigerated air. The reason for delaying their return to the freeway was Jakes' back. He wanted Evan to look at it, treat it, and give him something for the pain.

Jakes permitted Shelby to make cold prime rib sandwiches for Evan, Malika, and herself. Once Shelby delivered the sandwiches, glasses of cranapple juice, and a napkin full of Lucky Charms to the dinette, Jakes motioned for her to sit down with Malika. The sober-faced little girl glued herself to her mother's side for several minutes of assurance before she was ready to eat.

Margo stationed herself in the bucket seat nearest the door of the coach, and Evan asked Jakes to stand by the kitchen sink for treatment. Jakes laid the .44 on the sink, keeping himself between the gun and the doctor. "Let's make this fast, Evan," he said, unbuttoning his shirt. "I want to get out of here."

"I need better light," Evan said, lifting his satchel to the sink. "May we raise the blinds on the kitchen and dinette windows?"

"Kitchen only," Jakes replied. "I'll turn my back toward the light."

Evan pulled up the blinds covering the small kitchen window, and the area around the sink glowed with light. He opened his leather satchel, tore open a package of sterile, disposable latex gloves, and pulled them on. He stood behind Jakes and inspected the wounds on his back thoroughly. "You have a couple of wounds that are still draining," he said, "here and here." The doctor lightly touched the two reddened areas, one near the point of the left wing bone and the other on the fleshy right lower portion of his back. Jakes stiffened at each touch.

"I will have to wash these out with saline," Evan informed. "You may want to sit down for this."

"Just do it, doc, I'm ready," Jakes ordered. "We don't have time for bedside manner."

Evan lifted a stack of gauze pads and a syringe from his bag. He filled the instrument with saline solution.

As Evan prepared to irrigate the wounds with a steady stream from the syringe, he was fully aware of his potential for hurting Jakes. The syringe in his hand was not equipped with a needle at the moment, but it had a pointed end or nozzle. With two or three sudden strokes, he could slash open Jakes' back or possibly reach his face or neck and puncture the jugular. In the instant of Jakes' excruciating pain, Evan might be able to grab the gun from the sink and take control of the situation.

But Evan's momentary temptation quickly stalled. *Then what?* he asked himself. *I would be back to the same crossroads. I would either have to turn him in and run the risk of my secret being exposed, or I would have to kill him, thus doubling my chances of going to prison as a murderer.*

As if sensing Evan's contemplation during the brief hesitation, Jakes, who was now facing the front of the RV with his back to the light streaming in over the sink, picked up the .44. He held the gun at his right side, mere inches from Shelby and only two feet from Malika. "If you try to hurt me, man," Jakes said softly, "I swear I will hurt you in a way you will never forget."

Evan had already banished the tempting thought of retaliation from his mind. "No problem, Nolan," he said with as much assurance as he could muster. "I'm not going to hurt you. I promise that I'll do everything in my power to take care of your back and get you to Canada."

It took Evan only a few minutes to irrigate the two most serious wounds and apply a small dressing to each. Jakes grimaced and hissed at the pricks of pain but remained standing. Meanwhile, Shelby kept Malika distracted by urging her to eat half a sandwich and rewarding her for each bite with a colored marshmallow piece from the napkin full of cereal.

Evan mixed 1 gram of Keflin in powder form with 5cc's of sterile saline and injected it into Jakes' hip with the 23-gauge needle. Then he supplied him with Tylenol. Jakes took four.

Evan cleaned up his instruments and repacked his medical bag, while Jakes slipped into his shirt and returned the gun to his belt.

"How large is the fuel tank?" Jakes asked Evan, motioning the doctor toward the driver's seat.

"Seventy-five gallons," he answered.

Evan touched Shelby and Malika affectionately as he passed them in the dinette. Then he picked up his sandwich and glass of juice to take to the cab.

Shelby said to Jakes, "Malika needs to lie down for a nap. May I please stay here with her?"

After a moment of thought, Jakes gave his permission with a nod. At Shelby's invitation, the little girl curled up on the dinette bench with her head on Shelby's lap.

"And what kind of mileage does this rig get?" Jakes asked, following Evan to the front of the coach.

"On the level highway dragging the car carrier, about ten miles per gallon. When we're climbing or running the air conditioning it drops to eight or seven," he said while buckling in.

Jakes calculated for a second. "So we shouldn't have to stop for gas again until Sacramento or maybe Redding."

"Redding might be pushing it," Evan offered. "That's about 500 miles."

"We'll see," Jakes challenged. Then, motioning toward the frontage road leading back to the Interstate, Jakes added, "Let's roll."

Evan donned his sunglasses and pulled the gearshift lever to DRIVE. As the RV approached the on-ramp, he saw Jakes whisper something to Margo out of the corner of his eye, kiss her, and hand her the gun. Then, without a word, Jakes made his way to the bedroom at the back of the coach and lay down on his stomach atop the comforter, leaving the door open. Evan realized that Jakes' wounds combined with the strain of the ordeal were wearing on the man. He was actually thankful to see Jakes go lie down. The rest would probably keep him from getting more hostile and punitive as the day wore on.

Sleep well, Nolan, and have no fear, Evan encouraged silently. *You couldn't be in safer hands than mine.* The RV entered the freeway and slowly gained speed up the last mile of incline toward the precipice overlooking the Grapevine.

Forty-four

The Burbank Airport Hilton, a moderate-sized hotel serving a small airport, sits directly across Hollywood Way from the airport's entrance. It took Reagan Cole three minutes after Beth's alarming call to jog to his Kawasaki in the parking lot, pay his fee, and drive a quarter mile on the airport exit road and across Hollywood Way to the hotel. He parked in the underground garage and climbed the stairs three at a time to the hotel lobby instead of taking the elevator. Then he stepped through the door cautiously, assuring that if Barbosa walked by, they wouldn't meet by accident.

Beth had explained in her call from the Hilton that she had taken the shuttle van to the hotel to check out the lead given her by the van driver. When she arrived at the hotel she went straight to the coffee shop, partially to begin her inquiries about Barbosa or his look-alike and partially to quench her thirst with a glass of iced tea. Sitting down in her booth, it was all Beth could do to contain her excitement when she spotted the man in her fax photo sitting across the room from her.

Beth met Cole by the stairway door as he had requested. He was slightly annoyed at her for going to the hotel without notifying him. But his excitement at the possibility of picking up Barbosa's trail overcame his irritation. "Is he still in the coffee shop?" Cole asked, just above a whisper.

Beth nodded. "The waitress brought his entrée just as I walked out."

"Are you *sure* it's Rennie Barbosa in there?"

Beth nodded again. "Especially after I stopped at the front desk just now and found out that he's registered under the name of Alberto Rodriguez."

Cole looked stunned. "How did you get that information?"

Beth cocked her head self-assuredly. "By doing what any good detective or investigative journalist would do: I lied. I told the desk clerk that I was meeting three coworkers here for a conference—Bill Martin, Tom Johnson, and Al Rodriguez—and wondered if any of them had arrived yet. The guy said he had no reservations for Johnson or Martin, but Alberto Rodriguez had checked in about an hour ago."

"You remembered the three aliases?" Cole was incredulous.

"Of course," Beth replied, inferring in her tone that he was some kind of jerk for thinking otherwise. "I told you I was coming along to help."

A smile slowly overtook Cole's stunned expression. "Nice work," he said, then adding, "just like I expected."

Then Cole looked serious again. "I hope you don't mind, but I really need to positive-ID Barbosa for myself."

"Don't you trust me?" Beth pouted playfully. She had expected Cole to insist on a firsthand look at Rennie Barbosa. Had she been in his shoes, she would have done the same.

Cole couldn't keep from smiling again. "You know what I mean," he said. "Now will you show me where he is, Ms. Star Detective?"

Beth led him to a window off the main hall where they could peek in on the coffee shop without being noticed. There was Rennie Barbosa, alone in a booth facing the entrance with his back to the wall, a position characteristic of both cops and criminals who fear being surprised from behind.

"Mm, he's packing away quite a meal," Cole said, watching Barbosa closely. "Looks like he ordered from the dinner menu."

"Which means. . . ?" Beth quizzed.

"One, he's a hungry man," Cole answered, thinking aloud, "which is surprising since Cox told me that he ordered a big room-service breakfast before leaving the Sheraton. Or two, he likes his big meal in the middle of the day instead of at dinner time. But that's not really his pattern. He always goes for a big dinner, especially when he has a sweet young thing on his arm."

"So much for one and two; how about three?" Beth probed eagerly.

"Three, he's not planning on being near the table at dinner time. He has an appointment, or he plans to be on the road."

Beth hummed with insight. "That may explain the desk clerk's question about a car."

"What car?" Cole asked, looking from Barbosa to Beth.

"When the clerk told me about Rodriguez checking in, he asked if I would *also* need a car this afternoon. I just looked at him as if I didn't understand. Then he said, 'If you need a car during your stay, we can order it for you through Budget, and they'll deliver it to the front door.' I'll bet Barbosa has already ordered a car, and the clerk was checking to see if I needed one too."

Cole shook his head in wonder, saying nothing. Beth prompted him, "You're supposed to say 'Nice work' again."

Studying her for a few seconds, he said, "*Very* nice work, Beth."

Cole looked back at Barbosa, who was eating as if he would never see food again. "So you turn in your car and fake a flight to Phoenix to shake us, then you sneak over here to get a room and another car and start all over again. Very clever."

The pair stood in silence and watched the man eating for another minute. Then Cole led Beth back to their quiet corner by the stairway. As they walked, Cole's brain was busy processing information and plotting contingencies.

He dismissed the idea of calling Gleason and Cox out to resume their stakeout. *Barbosa is up to something or he wouldn't have attempted the slick evasive maneuver in the Burbank Airport,* he deduced. *And if he has ordered a car, he may not be planning to stay here long. I have to stick with him until he tips his hand.*

It was clear to Cole what he needed to do next, so he informed Beth, "I'm going to call Gleason and have him bring me one of our portable Hawkeye units." He pulled out the banana phone, flipped it open, and prepared to dial. "I need to keep tabs on Barbosa until he shows his plan. Only this time I hope he thinks he's not being followed."

"Hawkeye—that's a portable satellite locater device, isn't it?" Beth queried with interest.

"Right. When Barbosa's car is delivered, hopefully I'll be able to stick the homing beacon under the bumper and find out what he has up his sleeve."

Then Beth announced what she needed to do next. "While you're waiting for the Hawkeye, I'll ride the hotel van back to the airport and get my car so we have something to follow Barbosa *in.* See you in a few." She slipped on her sunglasses and took a step toward the front door where the van stood waiting.

"Wait a minute," Cole said, grabbing her arm. "I can't let you do that. I am *not* commandeering your car again to chase a criminal. You remember what happened the last time." He didn't feel the need to go into detail about banging up her candy-apple Star Cruiser and endangering her life on Christmas Eve 1999 in the pursuit of an L.A. gang van.

Beth lifted her shades to look him squarely in the eye. "Yes, as a matter of fact, I do remember that some rather wonderful things happened as a result of that wild chase." Cole blushed at the clear reference to the romance that had budded in the days after their first meeting. "So you don't have to commandeer my car this time, Reagan; I'm volunteering it for service."

"But you could be in danger. Barbosa knows who you are now. He saw you in the coffee shop."

"He may have *seen* me, but I'm sure he didn't *notice* me. I was just another customer in a crowded dining room."

"But didn't he see you talking to me on the phone?"

Beth gave him an are-you-serious? kind of look. "Reagan, it's the twenty-first century. Half the people in that room were talking on their personal phones, so I doubt that I looked suspicious."

Cole made one more weak attempt at dissuading Beth from her

obviously clear resolve. "Remember, I'm on my own in this operation. I'm not officially on the LAPD's clock. I can't guarantee your safety or promise that the city will cover any damages or personal losses."

Beth smiled her disarming, mischievous smile. "That's okay, because if I get another best-seller out of this, maybe I'll just buy the city of L.A. and cover my own expenses."

"But Beth, I—"

"Are you trying to get rid of me?" Beth's smile was gone. "Are you saying that I do nice work but you really don't want me around?"

Cole remembered Matt Dugan's prayer only a few hours earlier when he asked God to give his friend the time he needed with Beth to sort out their relationship. "No," he said firmly, "the last thing I want is to get rid of you."

In a second, Beth's smile returned. "That settles it, then. I'll be back in a flash." Then she snapped down her glasses and strode confidently out the door.

Cole watched after Beth longingly. He felt himself falling in love with her all over again.

By the time Beth returned, Cole had contacted Officer Dan Gleason and ordered a portable Hawkeye and a pair of high-powered binoculars brought to him on the street a distance from the Hilton. "Don't bring the car you've been tailing him in," Cole insisted. "He's probably seen it. Drive out in your own car, or borrow something that doesn't look so obvious." Gleason, still humiliated from his part in losing Barbosa, quickly agreed, promising to be there in an hour. "Make that forty minutes tops," Cole ordered, then he hung up.

Cole had also called Budget and, posing as a hotel employee, obtained a description of the car Barbosa had rented and when it would be delivered. He also found out that Barbosa had specified a week's rental.

"We're waiting for a burgundy Lincoln Town Car," he informed Beth. "It's supposed to be delivered to the main entrance sometime before 3 o'clock."

They were sitting in Beth's rented Buick Barego, with Beth in the driver's seat, over three blocks from the Hilton's front door. Cole's motorcycle was still in the hotel's garage, but his helmet and saddlebags were in the back seat of the Barego.

Cole was watching the driveway leading to the hotel entrance. His bucket seat was pushed back as far as it would go, but he still had to recline the seat a couple of notches to keep his head from grazing the headliner. The coupe was certainly not built for six-foot-five-inch frames. The black coupe was parked in the shade, but the temperature had reached the high 80s, so Beth kept the front windows down.

"Mm, Town Car. Our man likes to travel in style," Beth said.

"Curiously, that's not his M.O.," Cole answered, still watching the hotel. "He usually selects rental cars that are as vanilla as his Tom Johnson or Bill Martin personas: Chevy Corsicas, Ford Tempos, Bolt 600s, your basic econo-boxes. He must have a dozen upgrades by now, but he never uses them."

"Maybe his Alberto Rodriguez alter ego is a little more dashing," Beth advanced, dabbing perspiration away from her face and neck with a Kleenex. "You know those hot-blooded Latins."

"Or he needs a larger car for some specific reason." Cole was also perspiring. His thin, sandy hair was matted to his scalp in several places. He allowed the beads of sweat to course down his neck.

Beth made a guttural, gagging sound. Translated into intelligible English, it might have been pronounced, "Yuk! You mean large enough to stash a body or two in the trunk?"

Cole glanced at her with one brow arched. "Bodies in the trunk? You're really getting into this crime-scene detective stuff, aren't you?" Then he quickly resumed his surveillance of the Hilton's entrance.

Beth wasn't intimidated by Cole's questions. "Well, why else would he have a big four-door luxury sedan, if not for transporting bodies or drugs or other contraband or gang members?"

"Comfort."

"Comfort? You're kidding me. Why would Barbosa be concerned about comfort at a time like this, especially if he's springing into action?"

"Because he may be hitting the road," Cole theorized, looking at her. "If you had to travel a distance and couldn't fly, wouldn't you choose something comfortable like a Caddie or a Town Car instead of a hard-riding econo-box or a sporty coupe with no head room or leg room?" Cole was back to watching the hotel before he had finished his question.

Beth considered the idea. "Do you really think he's getting ready for a long drive, I mean, out of state or somewhere?"

Cole released a sigh summarizing his frustration with the enigmatic and, until this morning, sedentary Rennie Barbosa. "I don't know, Beth. I don't know what Barbosa's going to do. That's probably why he's survived so long in his profession. Just when you think he's retired, he slips under the carpet like a roach and crawls away to another dark corner to do his dirty work."

They remained silent for several minutes, Cole surveying the Hilton and Beth thinking about Barbosa. Then Cole spoke again. "Are you still in?"

Beth studied him questioningly. "I thought we already settled that."

Cole looked at her again. "What I mean is, do you still want to go along for the ride if Rennie Barbosa is headed out of state? For all I know he may drive that Town Car to Phoenix or Salt Lake City or

Dallas or Detroit. If you're going to change your mind somewhere out on the highway, I'd better arrange my own transportation now."

This time Cole did not return to his surveillance. He stared at Beth, waiting for an answer.

Beth deflected his question with one of her own. "How long will *you* stay with him? I mean, if he's planning a cross-country tour, will you follow him to the east coast or wherever?"

"Yes," he answered without hesitation.

"Officially? As a police officer?"

"Officially, I will follow him to the city limits. Beyond that, I'm on vacation. I just happen to be going wherever Rennie Barbosa's going."

"But you're supposed to be on your way to Lake Tahoe for vacation—your mother's place."

"I'll get there eventually, but not until I find out what Barbosa is up to. If I don't get closure on him, these past five weeks spent watching him are wasted, as far as I'm concerned." Without letting Beth inject another question, Cole pushed the issue back to her. "I still can't believe I agreed to your coming along, but I did. So what's it going to be? Are you in or out?"

Beth was enjoying Cole's intensity, so she kept stalling on purpose. "He may only be driving to Pacoima or Van Nuys or San Fernando or Granada Hills."

"In a Town Car? I doubt it."

"East L.A., Orange County, Diamond Bar, Yorba Linda."

"But if he's traveling farther, I need to know what you're going to do now. Oh, by the way, Barbosa rented the Town Car for a week."

Beth blinked with surprise. "A week? Maybe that's because he's a cheapskate. A Town Car is cheaper on the weekly rate."

"Not if he only needs it for two days. Having the car for seven days, he can burn up a lot of miles. He can get to Boston and back in a week. So, do you want to go to Boston?"

Beth had made up her mind in Quintero's. Nothing Cole had said since then had seriously dampened her resolve. If anything, the thought of a cross-country pursuit intrigued her. She would get to spend several days with Reagan Cole trying to figure out why she was still attracted to him, despite the lifestyle changes that formerly annoyed her. The alternative, Cole leaving for Lake Tahoe while she flew home to Seattle alone, seemed cold and unappealing.

Tracking Barbosa and figuring him out sounded exciting—and potentially rewarding, should a book come from the experience. But tracking Reagan Cole and figuring him out was what drove Beth to her conclusion.

"Like I said, I'm in—for the duration," she stated confidently.

"The chase may go on for a week or more," Cole warned again. "I don't know what to expect."

"I'm on vacation too. No problem. I'm in. We can share expenses."

"Or it may be over today."

"All the better," Beth lied convincingly. "We can both get on with our lives."

"You'll follow my lead? You won't go freelancing on me and get yourself hurt again?"

Beth dropped her head slightly and put on a sad-eyed, scolded puppy look. She hoped Cole would accept it as a token of submission so she wouldn't have to lie outright. Beth admired and trusted Reagan Cole, and at this moment she suspected that she was still in love with him, in spite of herself. But she wasn't about to commit herself unreservedly to someone else's lead, even Reagan Cole's. When push came to shove, Beth Scibelli was her own person. Bottom line: Right or wrong, she could trust only herself.

Cole accepted her silent comment and turned back to the hotel without saying a word.

Forty-five

Officer Dan Gleason, still in the hokey outfit of a vacationing Indiana farmer, didn't stay more than thirty seconds. He pulled alongside the black Barego coupe in a rust-colored Bronco IV with a caved-in door—his own car—passed a small briefcase and a pair of high-powered binoculars through the open window to Beth, and sped away. Gleason was still embarrassed in the presence of his sergeant over losing Barbosa, so he was happy to drop off the Hawkeye and run. Furthermore, Sergeant Reagan Cole wanted Gleason gone as quickly as possible, in case Barbosa happened to see him on the street and recognize him.

Keeping one eye on the Hilton in anticipation of the arrival of Barbosa's rented car, Cole opened the case on his lap and enthusiastically explained the Hawkeye to Beth. "This is the monitor and this is the receiver and brain," he said, tapping first the dark screen in the lid then the metal case and compact keyboard filling three-fourths of the case. "It runs on state-of-the-art extended-life batteries, but it also has an adaptor which plugs into the car's cigarette lighter." Cole opened a compartment in the case containing the adaptor and cord to verify his claim.

It was just another high-tech gadget to Beth, and gadgets didn't exactly thrill her. But she was captivated by Cole and his excitement with the crime-fighting toy sitting on his lap. It was another opportunity to observe his boyish awe and wonder, qualities which had attracted her to him within minutes of their first meeting a year and a half ago. So to humor him and encourage him, Beth looked and touched and hummed and ooed and aahed appreciatively as he demonstrated the Hawkeye's features.

"First, you boot it up and bring up your present location." At Cole's touch, the monitor flashed on and blinked through several colorful pages of introduction and instructions which he didn't pause to read. "The default system for all of our Hawkeyes, of course, is Southern California. But you have to tell the hawk the general area in which to start looking for the rabbit."

"Rabbit?" Beth queried. She knew what Cole was referring to, but she played dumb to further enjoy his schoolboy excitement.

"The homing beacon," Cole explained, quickly opening another compartment in the case and pulling out a burnished metal hemisphere about the size of half a baseball. "This little jewel sends out a continuous signal to the satellite, which in turn relays it to the 'hawk in the box.'" Cole patted the computerlike unit in the case respectfully. "The Hawkeye program integrates the signal with its internal map by longitude and latitude, and the rabbit's location appears on the screen as a blip. It's accurate to within ten feet."

"So your box there is kind of like an electronic Thomas Guide," Beth interjected, showing her interest.

"Better than a Thomas Guide," Cole boasted, "because the hawk tracks the rabbit for you wherever it goes. You don't have to keep turning pages or referencing the index. Watch this."

Cole tapped the keys until the broad aerial view of Southern California zoomed down to Los Angeles County, then to the city limits, then to the incorporated city of Burbank which nestles into northwest L.A. A grid of major arteries appeared as brilliantly colored lines on the dark background. The map also pinpointed major landmarks such as the Burbank Airport, identified by its two intersecting runways.

"All right, the hawk is airborne," Cole announced. "Now let's turn the rabbit loose."

Cole snapped open a small door on the flat side of the metal hemisphere and activated the beacon with a couple of taps of his finger. "Now look," he said, directing Beth's attention to the screen, which he had rotated toward her.

Beth leaned in. "Yes, I see it," she said, trying to sound impressed. "There's the rabbit, just east of the airport off Hollywood Way." She touched her finger to the center of the screen below a steady blip of light.

Cole held up the hemisphere. "In a fraction of a second, the signal leaves this little transmitter, bounces off a satellite, and shows up on the map as a blip."

"The hawk can follow the rabbit all over L.A.?" Beth quizzed.

"All over L.A., all over the state, all over North America."

"Do you mean to tell me—"

"Yep, this little box contains an electronic road map for the entire continent. Anywhere our little rabbit Barbosa may go in the contiguous forty-eight, Canada, or Mexico, the hawk will keep him in the center of the map which tells us exactly where he is."

Beth stared at the blip on the screen a few seconds longer. "Truly, *truly* amazing," she breathed, anticipating Cole's desired response.

Cole basked in her apparent awe a few more seconds, but he soon returned to the task at hand. "But the whole package does us no good if we don't get the rabbit into Barbosa's car," he said.

"So far he doesn't even have a car," Beth reminded them both.

"Right," Cole sighed. He switched off the tracking device, lowered the lid on the case, and returned to the mundane chore of watching the Hilton for the arrival of a burgundy Town Car, now with the benefit of binoculars. He lifted the glasses to his eyes and focused them on the hotel's entrance.

The two occupants sweltering in the black Barego didn't have long to wait. "Here we go, here we go," Cole mumbled as he trained the binoculars on the big car turning into the driveway leading to the Hilton's entrance. Beth craned her neck to get a better view of the gleaming burgundy Town Car easing to a stop near the hotel's front door. It was almost 3 o'clock.

The Town Car was followed up the driveway by a tinny-looking, white Zap Runabout with the orange Budget logo on the door. The driver of the Runabout stayed behind the wheel while his associate, a chubby black kid in slacks, shirt, and tie who had already stepped out of the Town Car and entered the hotel lobby, completed the paperwork on the rental.

Cole's binoculars were locked on the Town Car. "If Barbosa leaves now, it might be tricky planting the transmitter on the car. We may have to track him visually until he leaves the car unattended somewhere. But if he's going to park it for a while, it will only take a minute to put the rabbit in place."

"Where does the transmitter go?" Beth asked, curious now instead of merely humoring Cole.

"Anyplace where it's in contact with metal. The flat side is strongly magnetized, so it will stick to the frame or under a fender or—" Cole abruptly ended his explanation and began describing the action in his view. "There's the Budget guy coming out. He has the papers in hand, and he's getting into the little car. So who will come out for the Town Car? Will it be Rennie Barbosa himself or . . . or . . . The door is opening and . . . "

"Who is it? Tell me," Beth demanded impatiently.

"It's a bellboy," Cole announced, sounding disappointed. "A bellboy is coming out to move the car."

"But that's good, isn't it?" Beth probed, hoping to encourage. "It means we may have a window of time to hide the rabbit."

"You're right," Cole agreed, watching the bellboy slide behind the wheel of the four-door boat of gleaming burgundy and chrome. "But if he's not leaving now, when will he leave? We may end up sitting here all night waiting for Barbosa to move out. I'm ready to get on with the chase."

Cole's boyish eagerness was showing again, and Beth loved it. She understood his anxiety and shared it to a degree. But she didn't mind the prospect of spending more time with him. Being with Reagan Cole pushed images of Colin Wendt and Antigua—and the dreary, painful feelings that accompanied those memories—far into the past. Beth was feeling more like her old self with every minute by Cole's side.

The big Town Car eased out of the shaded driveway and into the sunbathed street, heading toward the parked Barego. But in only half a block, the bellboy cut sharply into another driveway, and the Town Car disappeared into the Hilton's underground parking garage.

"Reagan, I want to hide the rabbit on Barbosa's car," Beth announced eagerly.

Predictably, Cole dropped the glasses and launched into a stern protest. "Beth, you—"

But she cut him off immediately by advancing a strong case in her favor, which she made up as she went along. "Listen, Reagan, it's a proven fact that a woman is less suspicious-looking than a man. If the hotel people see you hanging around that car, they'll think you're up to no good—especially somebody as big as you. But they won't bother me because I'm dressed like a woman on vacation. And if Barbosa comes out while you're in the garage, he may recognize you. He's already seen me in the coffee shop, so he'll think I'm a hotel guest. Besides, what's so hard about reaching under the car to attach a magnet?"

"The hard part isn't sticking the transmitter to the car," Cole returned. "The hard part is not letting anybody see you do it. How are you going to do *that?*"

Beth was quietly elated that Cole hadn't flatly refused her request. He was dialoguing with her, and she knew she had a chance. She looked him straight in the eye and confidently outlined her plan, which came right off the top of her head.

Five minutes later she stepped out of the Buick Barego, sunglasses in place, into the brightness and began her three-block walk to the Hilton. Her overnight bag, containing the few clothes she had brought from Colin's yacht plus some of Cole's clothes transferred from his saddlebags to fill it up, was slung over her shoulder by its two straps. In the middle of the bag, wrapped in one of Cole's T-shirts, was the hemispherical transmitter—already switched on.

Beth couldn't believe that Cole was actually letting her do it. "I don't know how much Barbosa knows about me," he had said in response to her pitch. "He may recognize me on sight, and if he saw me in the garage, he surely would be suspicious. We don't have time to call in another undercover cop, so I guess I have to go with you on this."

Cole had made Beth promise—and she did, "Scout's honor"—that she would not go near the Town Car if Barbosa happened to be in the garage. Walking up the sidewalk toward the hotel with Cole watching her from behind, Beth affirmed that this was one promise she would keep. She remembered the last time curiosity and a sense of adventure pushed her beyond the limits of common sense. It was a miracle that she had escaped alive. She was not about to take a foolish risk like that again.

Following the plan she and Cole had agreed upon, Beth entered the hotel through the main doors like a hotel guest returning from a day trip to the beach. She pushed her glasses to the top of her head and strolled casually through the lobby. Thankfully, there was no sign of Barbosa, so she walked to the elevators to ride down to the parking garage. An elderly couple stood patiently waiting for an upward-bound car.

The elevator door behind her opened. Beth turned to enter, then stopped abruptly, finding herself face to face with a man of medium build and pleasant features. She had no doubt about who he was; his photograph was burned into her memory. Rennie Barbosa was standing just inside the elevator next to the control panel. His dark eyes were magnetic, and he looked straight at her.

Beth felt her heart rocket into her throat and her skin turn to ice. She suddenly forgot how to breathe. "Going down?" she said with a slight squeak in her voice. She hoped she didn't look as panic-stricken as she felt.

Barbosa cast out a warm smile clearly designed to lure a lovely lady. "Sorry," he said, gesturing to the illuminated arrow above the car aimed upward. "But if you would like to change your mind, there's plenty of room." The elderly couple entered the elevator.

For a heady split second, Beth's investigative nature tempted her to go for the jugular: "What are you up to, Barbosa? Where are you going, and who are you planning to kill this time?" The questions were already formed in her mind, ready to burst out. *What would he say if I blew his cover? What would he do?* Beth wondered breathlessly. She could feel her fingers trembling as they gripped the strap on her bag.

Beth quickly backed away from the preposterous temptation and forced a nonchalant reply, "No thanks, I'm going down."

The doors began to close. "Too bad," Barbosa said, his voice dripping with syrup. And then he was gone.

Beth braced herself against the wall, suddenly lightheaded. She wanted a drink, a stiff drink. But she had little time to pull herself together, let alone make a stop in the lounge. The bell behind her signaled the arrival of the elevator headed for the parking garage. She knew she had to move fast.

He may be in the process of loading his car, getting ready to leave, Beth thought, as she stepped shakily into the elevator and pushed P for parking. *He may return to the garage in a few minutes with that black suit bag of his. I've got to find the Town Car, plant the transmitter, and get out of here now!*

Beth had concocted a simple scheme for attaching the hemisphere without looking suspicious to anyone who might be in the garage or to the security cameras sweeping the area. Perhaps her urgent need for haste would make the ploy even more believable.

She exited the elevator and looked for a burgundy roof among the sea of cars stretched out before her. She had to appear purposeful for anyone watching, not like she was looking for a car to steal. But she couldn't look purposeful if she couldn't find the car. *Hurry, Beth!* she urged herself. *He may step off the next elevator.*

As Beth visually swept the garage, she saw no one except the female parking attendant in the tiny booth near the exit. Finally she spotted Barbosa's rented Town Car. It was nearer than she expected: four cars to her left from the elevator. She immediately sprang into action.

Beth moved the straps of her bag from her shoulder to her wrist. Then, jingling her own keys from her fingers, she hurried down the row of cars where the Town Car was parked as if heading for her own car. Reaching the big burgundy sedan, she brushed the rear fender with her bag and "accidently" dropped it along with her keys. The bag was purposely unzipped, allowing its contents to spill out on the garage floor behind the Town Car.

Beth cursed her clumsiness loudly enough for the attendant to hear. The woman, a middle-aged Latino reading a tabloid, didn't even turn toward the minor disturbance. Beth quickly dropped to her knees to scoop up the contents of the bag. In the process, she slipped the transmitter from its protective cushion and thrust it under the car until it adhered to the fuel tank with a soft *clunk*. Then she shoveled the rest of the clothes into the bag, scooped up her keys, and hurried on.

Instead of returning to the elevator, Beth kept walking through the garage to the exit. Nodding cheerily to the attendant—who peeked up from her tabloid for two seconds to acknowledge her—Beth scampered up the ramp and into the sunlight.

"I think we'd better get away from here," Beth said, after throwing the bag and herself into the Buick. Her obvious haste communicated urgency, and there was a taut fear in her voice.

"What's the matter? Did he see you?" Cole pressed.

"Yes and no," Beth replied. She didn't explain until she had started the Barego, squealed through a tight U-turn, and accelerated east on Thornton, leaving the Airport Hilton in her dust.

" 'Yes and no' what?" Cole demanded. "What happened back there? Where's the transmitter?"

Beth cleared her lungs with a deep breath. "The transmitter is on the Town Car, under the trunk somewhere. It worked just like I said it would."

"So what's the problem? What about Barbosa?"

Stumbling often over her words, Beth hastily explained her shocking meeting with Barbosa at the elevator. But she assured Cole that, despite her panic, she played the role of the naive vacationer well. "He even tried to hit on me," she said, allowing herself a strained laugh.

Then she expressed her concern that Barbosa might have been going to his room to collect his things and leave in the rented Town Car. She concluded, "So I think we need to put a half-mile or more between us and the hotel and let the hawk take over the on-site surveillance."

Cole glanced at the monitor staring up at him from the floor between his feet. The rabbit's blip was strong and steady. "So you think he could leave at any minute?" he asked.

"I couldn't tell, Reagan," Beth said as she turned right on Buena Vista. "He could be checking out right now or lying down for a nap. I just don't want to bump into him like that again. I don't know if my system can take it."

"Well, thanks to the Hawkeye here, you won't have to get close to him again," Cole consoled. Beth felt his large hand light on her shoulder and stay there. "Nice work—again," he said. There was genuine appreciation in his compliment, and the warmth of his touch instantly calmed her jangled nerves.

Forty-six

Libby took the University Bridge over Portage Bay to the southwest border of the 700-acre University of Washington. She turned right on Pacific Street and right again on Boat Street to the Bryant Building on the bay. She eased the Seville into a visitor's space in the parking lot near the sign which read UNIVERSITY OF WASHINGTON POLICE DEPARTMENT. The late afternoon sun flooded through the windshield, raising the temperature in the car almost as soon as the air conditioning was turned off.

Libby sat in silence for several minutes wondering if this was really a good idea. She had contacted Officer Reginald Burris on her personal phone from the Bremerton-to-Seattle ferry. She just missed the 1:05 departure, requiring her to park the Seville in line over an hour and a half waiting for the 2:45 ferry. She made the most of the delay by exploring the ferry dock and the surrounding shoreline in the breezy sunshine.

Libby had told Officer Burris that she wanted to stop by UWPD to get the key card to her office recoded this afternoon, instead of waiting until morning. Would he be able to help her with this task personally? she had asked. She was not surprised when Reginald said he would be delighted to help her. He reminded her that he was working the P.M. shift—2–10—and that he would plan to be in the com center on Boat Street between 4 and 5 to perform the recoding for her.

What she *hadn't* mentioned on the phone was her real reason for visiting Reginald in person: to see if he could offer any advice for untangling her relationship with Brett. If the congenial officer proved to be as sincere and helpful as he seemed on that issue, she thought she might even ask his opinion of telling Brett about his father.

Why are you coming to Reginald Burris with these questions? she asked herself for the umpteenth time since boarding the Bremerton ferry. *He's not a friend or a family member or even a coworker. He's only a U Dub cop; you barely know him. And he acts like he wants to ask you out.*

And for the umpteenth time, Libby recited the reassuring answers that had kept her heading toward the university instead of toward home as soon as the ferry docked.

First, Reginald Burris is one of the few people who knows about the trouble I'm having with Brett, having walked in on him after he broke into my office and tampered with the university's student data base system.

Second, Reginald was kind enough not to arrest Brett for the break-in, calling me at home instead and allowing me to deal with Brett personally. An arrest could have been a disaster to my career.

Third, the man is a mature father of young adults himself—and a black father at that. He's been through the wars. He has already expressed empathy for my situation and asked if there was anything he could do to help. He will probably ask again today. He may have some wisdom to share from his experiences and from a man's perspective.

Fourth, he's a gentleman. He may be interested in me beyond my conflict with Brett, but he's not beating his chest like Tarzan trying to impress me, like so many other men at my heels. Reginald seems genuinely sympathetic to my plight. I think he really wants to be a friend.

Libby the skeptical interrogator pressed in a little harder. *But what if Reginald Burris interprets my vulnerability as a romantic interest? What if he begins hounding me with invitations to join him for a chili size at a greasy diner or for a Seahawks' game in the nosebleed section at the Kingdome? He could become a real pest if he thinks I'm available and interested.*

Libby wasn't perturbed at all by the question. *If he turns out to be a creep or a pervert, which I seriously doubt, I'll turn him in to his superior officers. On the other hand, if he's the gentleman he purports to be, he understands what it means when a lady says no. And besides, I've been subjected to a lot worse than chili sizes and football games with men of higher breeding and station. Who knows? An evening out with Reginald Burris might be a welcome change from many of the ordeals to which I've been subjected in the name of social activity.*

Libby stepped out of the Seville, locked it electronically with a tap on her key, and entered the police station. At her request, the desk officer summoned Burris from the com center. The mammoth policeman joined her in the lobby and greeted her with a pleasant smile. "Hello, Dr. Carroll."

"Good afternoon, Reginald." Libby extended her long, slender hand. Once again it disappeared in the officer's massive, gentle mitt. "Thank you for taking time for this little job."

"No problem at all," Reginald assured. "Give me your key card and I'll run it through the coder and get you a new PIN number. It won't take but a minute."

Libby fished the card out of her purse and handed it to him.

"Would you like to watch how we do this?" Reginald asked. He had already taken two steps down the hall when he turned and posed the question.

Libby warmed at his consideration. "Why not?" she said cheerily.

Reginald led her from the lobby to the west end of the Bryant Building which headquartered the university's custodial services. In a small office accessible both to the UWPD and custodial department heads was the hardware for the university's new electronic entry system.

With Libby watching over his shoulder, Reginald booted the system and slipped her key card into a slot like a diskette. His huge sausage fingers moved over the keyboard deftly, burning a new security code into the card as it erased the old one. Then the computer spit out a new PIN number on a sticker the size of a large postage stamp. The process took less than two minutes.

"Now, memorize this number, and don't stick it on the key card, okay?" Reginald said, mimicking the lecture he often gave to freshmen receiving a key card for the first time. "We don't want to give the local burglars and pickpockets an advantage."

"Yes, sir, I'll remember that," Libby responded in the same tongue-in-cheek mode.

Reginald escorted Libby back toward the com center. He didn't seem anxious to prolong the visit. Libby wondered if her aloofness during their recent conversations had cooled his interest. Libby feared that the brief visit might end without Reginald asking the question she had hoped to hear once more.

"So you spent the day in Bremerton," Reginald said, keeping the small talk barely alive. "I'll bet it was nice out on the water today."

"Yes, lovely," Libby responded. "Getting away from home, riding the ferry, feeling the wind and the sunshine—it's therapeutic for me. Takes my mind off the daily pressures. Helps me clear my head."

"And with a pressure job like yours, Dr. Carroll, I'm sure you need a little break now and again. I can't imagine taking on the responsibility of a university administrator." Reginald shook his head in amazement. "It's not the job for me. I admire your commitment."

"Talk about commitment, look at you," Libby responded. "I've always admired people in law enforcement. I spend my day dealing primarily with significant contributors to society—scholars, graduate students, university officers—while you deal with the dark side, the takers, people who are a threat to society. My hat's off to you and your colleagues, Officer Burris. I wouldn't trade jobs with you for all the gold in Ft. Knox."

I have pressures at home too, Reginald. You know about them. You asked about Brett yesterday, and I pretended everything was okay. Everything is not okay. Please ask again. I would welcome your counsel.

They arrived at the front doors. Being a Sunday, it was quiet in the lobby. A police science major from the U, a nerdy-looking kid who had chosen a career in law enforcement from watching TV cop shows, stood at the counter bending the ear of the desk officer. Otherwise, no one else was in sight.

"How's that young man of yours doing today?" Reginald asked, ready to open the door for his guest at the slightest indication she was ready to leave.

At his words, Libby's flickering hopes and taunting fears concerning this moment of vulnerability collided again within her. The conflict produced such a sudden inner furor that she wondered if Reginald Burris could hear the roar.

"I don't know, Reginald," she said, drawing a long breath. "In fact, I must confess that I misled you yesterday when I said Brett and I were doing well. Actually, we had a horrible fight just before you called, and he walked out—took his things and left with his girlfriend. I don't know where he's gone. He's not answering his phone."

Libby felt a knot of emotion growing in her throat and she steeled herself against it. She would *not* break down in the lobby of the police department in front of Officer Reginald Burris. She simply would not.

Reginald studied her with compassion and understanding in his gaze. "Please forgive me if I'm being too personal, but is there more to your conflict with Brett than the episode in your office the other night?" he probed.

Libby marveled at his perception. It was the opening she had been hoping for, but she balked at the threshold. The battle in her head between trusting Reginald as a friend and pushing him away as a threat or a detriment to her career seemed deafening.

Had Libby gone with her defensive instincts, she would have answered, "Yes, you *are* being too personal, Reginald. I appreciate your concern, but I must be on my way." But she couldn't do it. She needed answers. She had no one else to talk to, at least no one she wanted to talk to, no one she felt would truly listen to her. Despite his rough edges and inferior status, Reginald seemed to be a godsend. In one anxious step, she opted for vulnerability.

"It's funny that you would ask, Reginald, because there *is* more between Brett and me than the break-in." Libby was aware that her nervous mannerisms were working overtime: avoiding eye contact with the big policeman, fidgeting with her handbag, tapping the toe of her shoe rapidly on the terrazzo floor. But there was no turning back now. "I was hoping to talk to you about Brett, to get a man's opinion, if you don't mind."

Reginald's face registered mild surprise, as if he had just scratched off a lottery ticket and realized he was a $20 winner. "I don't mind at all," he said, obviously pleased. "When would you like to talk?"

Now, Reginald, now, before I chicken out and pull back into my shell! she insisted silently. But she couldn't bear to be so forward, so she shrugged and looked to him for a suggestion. He quickly picked up the slack.

"I'm off tomorrow and Tuesday. I could meet you for lunch."

Libby was disappointed. Tomorrow sounded like the distant future. She wanted to talk to Reginald tonight, but she didn't know how to tell him. So she said nothing.

Reginald seemed to hear her silent plea. "Or if you want to talk a little today, I could clock out for a dinner break at about 5 o'clock," he said, checking his watch. "It's a slow day, and the Department owes me some time. We could get something to eat in the district while we talk. How about Zelda's?"

"I don't want to rob you of your dinner break," Libby objected, lying through her teeth.

"It's no problem for me, Dr. Carroll. Whatever works best for you. I'm open for dinner or sometime tomorrow. It's your call."

Libby looked at her watch as if searching for the courage to tell him she very much wanted to talk with him now. "Well, if it's no problem, getting together over a light meal right now would be great."

"I'd like that," Reginald said. "Why don't you take the new key card up to your office and make sure it works. I have to check out a couple of vandalized trucks up at the Motor Pool. Then I'll meet you at Zelda's in half an hour. Okay?"

"You're sure about giving up your dinner break?" Libby persisted, feeling almost as guilty as she did grateful. "We could always put it off."

"There's no time like the present," Reginald said, opening the glass door for her. "Get us a table at Zelda's. I'll be there about 5."

Libby took her time driving through the quiet campus to the Central Plaza Garage. She walked to the Administration Building and tried her key card and PIN codes on the outside doors. They allowed her entry without incident, and the computer greeted her as usual. She had no reason to climb to her third-floor office other than to try out the key card there too. But with a little time to kill, she did so anyway. Again, she was admitted on the first try.

The building was empty, eerily quiet in contrast to the normal weekday hum of activity in this the nerve center of the university. Many administrators and staffers came in on the weekends to pick up loose ends from the previous week. But rarely was anyone so committed as to stay into Sunday evening, especially on a beautiful afternoon like today. Libby didn't like being in the building alone, so she checked her voicemail, made herself a couple of notes, and left.

Zelda's is a quiet soup, salad, and mineral water restaurant at Forty-Third and "the Ave"—University Way. Zelda's is more popular with university staff than with students who prefer the conviviality of the pizza and microbrew places in the District. Libby arrived a few minutes before 5 and took a booth away from the window. She was reasonably comfortable about being seen with Reginald Burris, especially with him in uniform. But she saw no reason to put their meeting on display for students or coworkers looking in from the Ave.

She had sipped down nearly a full glass of Liebfraumilch by the time Reginald arrived at 5:10. He apologized for being late, explaining that the weekend guy in the Motor Pool wanted to chew his ear off about the damage done to two of the university's new pickups. When Reginald sat down, he had to move the table six inches Libby's way to accommodate his huge frame.

The restaurant was about half full. A U Dub student straddling a stool struggled through a rendition of *Classical Gas* on his guitar in the corner. His guitar case lay open, primed with several bills and coins from his own pocket.

Libby ordered a small Caesar salad. Reginald went for a large bowl of beef barley soup, three dinner rolls, and a cup of coffee. Their meals were delivered in minutes.

Reginald made it easy for Libby to talk by asking nonthreatening questions about her background: schooling, running, career. Libby gave him a sketchy history. She said nothing about the incident in 1979 which had left such a deep scar in her memory. Her story had been repeated so often over the years with that part edited out that she sometimes wondered if it had really happened. She hoped that some day she might forget about it completely.

The conversation quickly and easily turned to Brett. Aware of Reginald's time constraint, Libby concisely explained that Brett was illegitimate, that she had kept his father's identity a secret, and that Brett had demanded to know where he could find the man. Libby admitted that she had never told Brett's father about her pregnancy. But she purposely omitted the fact that Brett's father was white and that her career goals had prohibited her from disclosing the information Brett wanted. Instead, she tried to sell Reginald the flimsy rationale that Brett and his father really wouldn't want to know each other, given the conditions of the boy's conception.

Reginald ate his soup and bread rapidly while Libby talked. He always hurried through his meals while on duty, never knowing when an emergency call from dispatch might summon him away from the table, even on a slow day.

"So when I confronted Brett yesterday about his behavior Friday night," she concluded, having barely touched her salad, "he threw the issue in my face. He said that my silence on the subject was a painful slap of disrespect. He said that he couldn't respect me if I didn't have the decency to tell him what he needed to know."

"Did your son threaten other acts of retribution?" Reginald sliced and buttered the third of his dinner rolls as he spoke.

Libby shook her head. "He didn't threaten anything. He just blasted me and left. I haven't talked to him since."

Reginald chewed on his thoughts along with a large bite of his roll. Finally he said, "Just to clarify, the reason you don't want to tell your son about his father is . . . " He left the sentence dangling for her to complete.

Libby suspected that Reginald was interrogating her, though clearly more as an ally than as a police officer. He seemed to be pressing her back to the central issue to make sure her story held up. Lies eventually eroded under such pressure. She was glad this was a friendly visit. Had he not been so kind and conversational, his tactic might have seemed like the third degree.

"I don't think Brett is mature enough to handle a relationship with a father who as yet doesn't know he exists."

"How old is Brett?"

Reginald had asked the question already, Libby remembered. It apparently was either his nature or training to chip all the fiction away from the facts through repeated questions.

"Twenty."

Reginald just looked at her, as if inviting more information.

"Actually, he'll be twenty-one in August," Libby supplied finally.

"When do you think your son *will* be mature enough to interact with his father?"

"I don't know. He just doesn't seem mature enough yet. I think he proved that yesterday when he threw the platter of cookies against the wall and chewed me out."

"So you think that in five years he'll be able to handle it? Or maybe seven years? Or ten?"

Libby pushed around bits of shredded Parmesan on the romaine lettuce with her fork as she considered his question. She wanted to come up with something more intelligent than "I don't know," but she had already spent twenty-four hours trying to answer that question without success. "I don't know, Reginald. I guess that's what I want to hear from you. What do you think?"

Reginald started to dip his last hunk of bread into the bowl to mop up the final drops of beef broth in the bottom of the bowl. Then he remembered who he was with and popped the dry bread into his mouth instead. After chewing it a while, he said, "Suppose Brett called you tomorrow and said, 'Mom, my girlfriend is pregnant, and we're going to get married.' Is he mature enough to be a husband and father?"

"Not at all," Libby answered quickly.

"But suppose he got married and had the kid anyway. Is it possible that he might knuckle down and do an okay job of being a father?"

"It's hard for me to imagine that Brett—"

"Libby, how old were you when Brett was born?" Reginald broke in, forcing the point.

It registered in the back of Libby's brain that Reginald had called her by her first name for the first time, instead of Dr. Carroll. It sounded perfectly appropriate for the brother-sister conversation they were having. She certainly would have asked him to use her first name eventually, had he not done so on his own.

In the front of her brain, Libby found herself yielding to Reginald's line of reasoning. Her answer would put her rationale in jeopardy, and she knew Reginald knew it. "I was twenty-one," she admitted softly, quickly adding, "and a half."

"You had better resistance than I did," Reginald said with a small laugh. "My wife got pregnant with our first daughter at nineteen— except she wasn't my wife yet. I was barely twenty."

Libby tried to imagine what the big, bald officer looked like as a twenty-year-old. She guessed that he had been a real bad dude, a lady-killer.

"Were you mature enough to become a parent at twenty-one?" Reginald asked.

Libby lifted her brows in submission. "No, but I didn't have a choice, at least not after I became pregnant."

"But you sucked it up and did all right for yourself and your son, didn't you?" Reginald's tone was affirming instead of condemning.

Libby nodded thoughtfully. "I could have done a better job in some ways, but, yes, I managed."

"Same with me. My marriage didn't last, but that wasn't all my fault. And my girls turned out all right. You and I managed with our responsibilities because we had to, not because we were really ready to, wouldn't you say?"

"Yes, I suppose so."

"For the record, Libby, I think you did much better than just manage. Look at you. You're a beautiful, highly educated, sophisticated woman occupying a very responsible position at the university. You're going to be a university president some day. You have a good-looking, obviously intelligent son who has the world by the tail. He's going to do better than just manage too."

Libby wilted slightly under the adulation, dropping her gaze. She had received kudos like these before, but usually from subordinates bucking for promotion in her branch of the organization chart or from male peers hot for a date. Reginald was neither her subordinate nor her peer. His compliment sounded genuine. "Thank you," she said just above a whisper.

Reginald kept on. "Here's another scenario. Suppose, God forbid, you died tomorrow—heart attack, bang, you're suddenly gone. Could Brett get along without you?"

Libby laughed off his question as purely rhetorical. "Of course he could, Reginald. Brett has been on his own since he started at Washington State— even before that, actually. I raised him to think and do for himself. Despite his rebellious streak, he is a very capable young man."

"Exactly," Reginald said, leaning across the table for the kill. "He may not be as mature as he will be in a few years. But just like you and me, the boy is smart enough and strong enough to handle whatever comes at him, including dealing with a father he has never met, even a father who doesn't know he has a son named Brett."

Libby sat back, reeling from Reginald's directness. "You don't pull any punches, do you?" she said with a weak smile.

"You asked my opinion, so that's my opinion," Reginald said with his arms folded, resting his elbows on the table. "I hope I didn't come on too strong for you, but I assumed you were looking for honesty."

Libby appraised him from across the table for a moment. "Yes," she agreed finally. "I appreciate very much your honesty, even though it wasn't exactly what I wanted to hear."

"I admire you for that," Reginald said. "But let me push my luck a little further. I really don't believe your son's level of maturity or his father's response are the core issues with you. I suspect there's another reason why you're holding back on Brett, something much deeper. I have some ideas on what that reason may be. Do you want to tell me about it?"

Libby suddenly felt violated, as if the kind officer across the table had just asked her to submit to a strip search for hidden weapons or illegal drugs. She had sought his opinion, and now he was turning the opportunity into a quest for truth. She wondered again if her willingness to involve Reginald Burris in her problem was really a good idea.

She quickly decided on a compromise, a concession. She would tell Reginald something he might already have guessed, then she would thank him for his advice—which she would agree to follow without saying when—and bring the interrogation to a close. She didn't need this kind of pressure, at least not any more today.

Libby pushed her unfinished salad aside, signaling her intention to wrap up the conversation. "All right, the primary reason why I don't think Brett is ready for this news relates to his father." She noticed that her tone was cooler, and she hoped Reginald noticed it too. "Brett has always assumed that his father is black. The truth is that Tango is Caucasian."

"Tango?"

"A nickname for the man, and Brett doesn't even know *that* much about him."

"So you think that Brett might be able to relate maturely if his old man were black; but since he's white, you expect Brett to go off when he finds out?"

"Well, what would you do if you suddenly found out that your father was as pale as this tabletop?" she demanded, tapping her finger on the off-white Formica.

Reginald grinned, then smiled broadly. "I'd start believing in miracles," he said with a laugh, stroking his near-ebony cheek with his huge hand.

"Reginald, I'm serious," Libby scolded, ignoring the joke. "I don't know what Brett will do, but I expect the worst. That's why I have resisted telling him."

"Don't you think that somewhere in that clever brain of his Brett has considered the possibility that his father is white, Libby?" Reginald posed, abandoning his attempt at humor. "He's light-complexioned, even lighter than you."

Libby shook her head. "I doubt it. We have Latin blood in our background. Brett has older cousins with skin tone very similar to his. Furthermore, he grew up talking about a black father and I never corrected him. I'm sure it will be quite a shock to him."

The conversation lapsed as the waitress came by to clear the table.

The girl offered Reginald more coffee, but he refused. He appeared eager to return to patrol.

"Do you want to know what I think?" he said after nearly a minute of silence. Reginald's tone and expression were pleasant. He still seemed intent on being Libby's friend, even though his words were hard for her to hear.

Libby suspected that he was going to tell her what he thought whether or not she wanted to know. "What?"

"Your concern about Brett's reaction to his father's race bolsters my theory."

"And your theory is. . . ?"

"That your biggest problem with Brett's demand is how the truth might reflect on you. You were very edgy the other night about the administration finding out about the break-in. I think you're edgy about Brett for the same reason. I'm guessing that you want to keep his father in the closet as long as possible, because you think stirring up that part of your life may hurt your career. The fact that Tango, as you call him, is a white man simply adds an extra spin to the main issue. You want to keep Brett in the dark so he won't rock your boat."

Libby couldn't imagine Reginald delivering his conclusion more positively and considerately than he did. This was not a cop shoving the evidence in the face of a suspect caught dead to rights. This was a friend confronting a friend with the painful truth for the healing of all parties. It was the kind of treatment she would expect from someone like Robert Rhodes or another good friend, except that all her friends, Libby realized, were too busy covering their own backs to care about the betterment of others.

Nevertheless, Libby didn't like what Reginald had to say. His indictment stung her with the reality of her selfishness. Yet he clearly hadn't assumed the role of judge. He wasn't declaring, "Libby, you're a proud, self-centered, ladder-climbing tyrant, and your son is suffering because of it." He had merely conveyed that verdict at Libby's invitation, based on the preponderance of evidence she had supplied herself.

She *was* a proud, self-centered, ladder-climbing tyrant. Perhaps everyone around Libby had acknowledged it except her. It took immense fortitude for Reginald to say what others closer to her would not.

Stunned and struggling to maintain her composure, Libby could muster a few words, "I don't know what to say."

"You don't have to say anything, Libby," Reginald consoled. It would have been entirely appropriate for him to underscore his assurance by enveloping Libby's hands in his. But he didn't touch her, and Libby appreciated him for honoring her pain and vulnerability with respectful distance. "Just promise me that you will give some thought to what I've said. Brett is no longer a boy. He's a man who needs to come to grips with his roots, warts and all, ready or not. Keeping him from his past is the same as trying to abort him as an adult. Let the boy live, Libby. You'll survive the consequences. A person of your stature always does."

They left Zelda's without another word. As they reached her Seville, Libby wanted to at least say thank you. But she dared not open her mouth, afraid that the dam holding back her emotions would burst and she would bawl, something a proud, self-centered, ladder-climbing tyrant never does in public.

Instead, Libby offered Reginald a safe businesslike handshake. But once the policeman's large, tender hand surrounded hers, she didn't ever want him to let go.

Forty-seven

Bishop's greeting was thick with sarcasm. "I hope I didn't interrupt your dinner, Billy. What are we having tonight? Stuffed gulf shrimp? Grilled swordfish you caught yourself? Or are you celebrating your retirement to the Yucatan with a liquid diet: margaritas, tequila sunrises, Tecate, Dos Equus?"

G. Billy Fryman bristled at the voice coming over the phone. "Where are you, Bishop? What's happening with Jakes? Where's my money?" Fryman was stretched out on an oversized chaise longue in the dark. A pleasant Gulf breeze swept across the veranda, cooling the fat man's exposed legs and arms, which were the color of a rare steak from too much time in the sun. Half a dozen iced bottles of Mexican beer rested in a cooler at Fryman's right elbow. Another half dozen empty brown bottles littered the floor around the cooler.

"Everything is going just fine, Billy," Bishop assured with syrupy sweetness. "I just called because I enjoy our daily chats so much."

"What about Jakes? Did you finish him yet? Did you get my money?"

"Billy, quality work takes time. Everything will be done in good order. After all, I learned from the best in the business—you."

Fryman knew that Bishop was taunting him, and he didn't know what to do about it. In his haste to leave Southern California after the sudden meltdown of his drug operation, Fryman had neglected to effectively contain his elusive and sometimes uncooperative junior partner. The former drug lord had left Bishop in L.A. on an assignment, with no effective way of keeping his close associate on task.

Now Fryman was secluded deep in Mexico, and Bishop was in L.A., ostensibly tidying up the loose end of Nolan Jakes and the drug money he snatched during the busted buy. But Fryman was uncomfortably aware that he no longer had control over his lieutenant, except through angry threats and exaggerated promises. Fryman was determined to employ his only two remaining weapons, with no guarantee that Bishop would comply.

"Listen to me, Bishop," Fryman said in his most authoritative tone. "I want Jakes finished off now, by the most expedient means. No more stalling. Do you know where he is?"

"Billy, I was the smartest soldier in your army, even smarter than you. You know Jakes can't hide from me. Of course, I know where he is."

"Is he on to you? Does he know you're tailing him?"

"I wasn't only the smartest soldier in your army, I was the sneakiest. I'm quiet as a shadow. I'm invisible as the wind. Jakes thinks he's as safe as a baby in a crib. He just doesn't know that there's a black widow creeping up the blanket toward his face."

"Then quit screwing around and get him," Fryman demanded angrily.

"All in good time, Billy. My subcontractor is an artist. You can't hurry a masterpiece."

"Forget about the best time. Tell your trigger to take him out tonight; then bring that money down here by tomorrow night. That's an order."

Bishop responded in a melodramatic quaver, "And if I can't pay the rent on time, Mr. Legree, are you going to beat me again? Oh, please don't beat me, master. Please, oh please, oh please . . ."

Fryman quivered with rage. "Listen, you slimy little leech. You were nothing, and I made you something. I dumped tens of thousands of dollars into you, afforded you every comfort, lavished on you every opportunity for a life of ease. Everything you have you got from me."

"What about my HIV infection, Billy?" Bishop interjected, suddenly serious. "Did I also get *that* from you during our moments of forbidden love?"

Fryman was silent, paralyzed by the words. "You—you're infected?" he breathed at last.

"I can't hear you, Billy," Bishop said soberly. "What did you say?"

Fryman spoke louder but with difficulty due to a severely constricted throat. "When did you find out? How long have you known? When did you—?"

"When did I contract the disease? The doctor says it's been in my system for months, Billy, perhaps a year or more, long before that last time at your house with you and those other weird guys from your office."

Fryman moaned, "But it can't be me. I haven't felt any symptoms. I don't—"

The burst of laughter over the phone actually hurt Fryman's ear.

"Just kidding, Billy, just kidding," Bishop said after gaining control. "HIV—what a great line, eh, Billy? Had you going though, didn't I? You always were a sucker for a good prank."

G. Billy Fryman sprang from the chaise longue, suddenly oblivious to his sunburn pain, and erupted with a stream of foul curses. He curtly issued an ultimatum, "Finish Jakes immediately and bring the money to Mexico or I will contact someone else in L.A. to do the job." Then he snapped off the phone before Bishop could respond.

Fryman stormed back and forth across the dark veranda in bare feet, shaking and cursing uncontrollably. He had hoped to lure Bishop to Mexico with sugar: the promise of seclusion and shared riches, the titillation of renewed intimacy between him and his closest aide. The sugar would have been laced with arsenic trioxide, of course, in the form of a bullet to Bishop's head in an unguarded moment.

But Fryman now clearly understood that his former associate was merely toying with him. He had sweat blood too many years to allow a trusted, intimate subordinate to make a fool of him in the end. He lowered his overweight, perspiring body to the chaise longue, popped the cap on another beer, and began making phone calls.

Bishop held the phone and savored the humorous HIV gag a little longer, then tapped another number on the keypad.

"Yes," came the terse answer through the speaker.

"Mr. Barbosa, this is Bishop."

"Yes," Barbosa said flatly.

"Where are you?"

"The Airport Hilton in Burbank."

"Very good. Do you still have company?" Bishop was referring to the police stakeout team glued to Barbosa's coattails over the past several weeks.

"I told you I would lose them, and I did," Barbosa said, sounding a little testy.

"Excellent, Mr. Barbosa. And do you still have a car?"

"The first car was bugged. I have a different car now. It's out of sight in the hotel garage."

"And are you ready to travel?"

"Yes, I'm ready. Let's get on with it."

"Very good," Bishop said, exuding warmth. "Our strategy to eliminate Nolan Jakes is proceeding nicely, but we still need to be patient. Timing is very important to me. Here's what I want you to do next."

Bishop detailed the next phase of the plan, specifying again that communication between the two of them would be limited and initiated only by Bishop. Barbosa listened, then rehearsed the plan almost word for word at Bishop's insistence. Bishop thanked him and said good-bye.

Once off the phone, Bishop returned to the image of Billy Fryman's panicked response to the HIV bit and laughed again. Then Bishop counseled the fat man silently, *If you don't smell a double cross by now, Billy, I'm disappointed in you. But when it finally dawns on you that neither I nor your money will be joining you in Mexico, you might as well give up. You can call out every goon you know and send them after me, but they won't find me. And by the time you figure out how I got away from you, I'll be so far out of reach that I might as well be on Mars.*

So long, Billy Fryman. Thanks for the memories, and thanks for your contribution to my retirement.

Though it was just off the line of flight for aircraft departing the Burbank Airport, the little neighborhood park seemed as peaceful and soothing as a private garden. The air was warm and dry enough to allow the couple to stretch out on the grass under a canopy of blue, without the discomfort of dampness from the earth. Yet the subtle breeze and the shade of oak and poplar trees prevented the stifling summer heat from asserting itself. A lazy afternoon in the park seemed to be what Sundays were made for.

Reagan Cole had enjoyed the last two hours with Beth so much that he was tempted to forget why he had come in the first place. He could *not* forget, of course, that a known Peruvian assassin—who had yet to be charged in the United States, for lack of evidence—was sequestered in a hotel room only half a mile away. Yet the blip on the Hawkeye monitor propped open near Cole's elbow hadn't moved since the transmitter—the rabbit—had been attached to the underside of Barbosa's rented Lincoln Town Car earlier in the afternoon.

Cole and Beth had parked beside quaint Vickroy Park off Buena Vista Street expecting Barbosa's imminent departure from the Hilton. They sat in the car watching the steady blip on the screen with the concentration of cats stalking an unwary field mouse. But after thirty minutes, they moved the battery-powered Hawkeye out to a shady patch on the grass and kept an eager eye on the flashing light, while they finished off the cold fajita and chips Cole had brought wrapped in linen napkins from Quintero's.

After an hour they had begun to theorize on Barbosa's lack of movement. Beth advanced that the Town Car might have been a decoy and that Barbosa had slipped away from the hotel by another means. Cole dismissed the idea, claiming that most criminals, even professionals like Barbosa, aren't that clever. He suggested instead that in her haste, Beth might have stuck the rabbit on the wrong car, a comment he spent the next twenty minutes wishing he could retract in the heat of Beth's rebuttal. She settled the question of Barbosa's location quickly by dialing the Hilton, asking for Alberto Rodriguez, and fumbling convincingly through, "Sorry, wrong room," when Barbosa actually answered.

As the afternoon wore on, Cole and Beth had gradually relaxed their rigid sentry postures over the high-tech briefcase and stretched out on the grass. A couple of neighborhood boys, calling themselves Malcolm and Cheyenne, came through the park selling cold drinks out of a plastic cooler they could barely carry between them. Cole bought four bottles of flavored iced tea and tipped the boys generously, instantly transforming them from stern-faced peddlers to giddy chatterboxes.

Malcolm and Cheyenne said that between them they owned almost every video game in the world, but they had never seen the one in the briefcase. Cole played along, letting them think that it was very new and very expensive and that some day it might be available at the local video arcade. The boys said they might not be interested, since the game looked more like a geography lesson than a blood-and-guts battle with space aliens. Then they resumed their tour of the park arguing how to spend the $5 Cole had given them.

As they sipped iced tea, Beth and Cole digressed from second-guessing Barbosa's plans to discussing more personal topics—always with one eye on the pinpoint of light flashing from the Hawkeye's monitor. Cole asked about Beth's parents, and she filled him in on their latest exploits tagging after televangelist Simon Holloway. Beth in turn asked how Cole's mother, sisters, nieces, and nephews were doing. She had met his family once on a ski trip with Cole to Lake Tahoe in February over a year ago.

The ensuing conversation was pleasant and purposely general, including such topics as the whereabouts of mutual friends, reorganization problems within the Los Angeles Police Department, fluctuating property values in Southern California and Western Washington, and highlights of their respective alma maters, UCLA and USC, in the recent PAC-10 basketball season.

Cole yearned to get beyond the small talk and pry into Beth's thoughts about the silent months since she slipped away from him. He wanted to know what he could have done differently—what he could do differently this time—to demonstrate his devotion to her. He wanted to explain where he was coming from, to somehow communicate the treasure of spiritual peace he had found through his involvement with Dr. No and his friend in Santa Monica, Matt Dugan.

But he felt checked about crowding Beth's threshold for intimacy right now. The "check," a term he had picked up from Matt Dugan, was the warning of an internal guidance system, like a traffic light deep inside him. Thanks to Matt's teaching and counsel, Cole understood that his internal guidance system was complementary to—and definitely subservient to—the Bible. "The more you internalize God's truth," Matt had often said during their donut shop Bible studies, "the more reliable will be your inner traffic light. Pay attention to the twinges of your conscience and let them drive you back to the Word to make sure they're authentic." Cole had taken his advice to heart.

Most of the time Cole perceived a bright green light in his conscience, as if God were saying, "It's okay. Go for it. Full speed ahead." But there were times when he sensed a flashing amber light warning him to slow his progress, alerting him to possible dangers. He had learned not to floorboard it through an amber warning, but to wait and watch for clearer direction.

And there were occasional bright red lights, which Matt said usually corresponded to strict prohibitions in the Bible. "At those times," Matt had told him, "don't move ahead, even if things appear to be okay. Wait, watch, and pray. God may be saving you from something you can't yet see."

Matt Dugan had told Cole that many new Christians interpret Christianity as a series of red lights—lists of don'ts and no-no's—with an occasional green light thrown in. The young pastor didn't buy that view. "That's not the freedom the New Testament proclaims; that's bondage to law. Paul said everything was lawful for him, but not everything was expedient. St. Augustine said, 'Love God and sin boldly.' The Christian life is a series of green lights when we walk in harmony with God's Word, with occasional amber and red lights to direct us away from pitfalls of disobedience.

"It's the difference between tiptoeing through life fearful that you're going to step on a spiritual land mine, and striding confidently within the parameters of God's revealed will, knowing that a slip or a fall isn't terminal. When you miss one of God's stop signs, you confess your sin, make it right, and move on confidently, better prepared to negotiate that intersection in the future."

Cole was confident that the amber light he sensed on the issue of plying Beth with personal questions didn't signify a major moral problem ahead. He took it as a whisper of advice from God that she wasn't ready yet. And, having earnestly talked to God about Beth and her needs for nearly a year and a half, Cole took the advice and allowed the conversation to remain comfortable and harmless.

By 4:30 Cole seriously doubted that Rennie Barbosa was going anywhere tonight and verbalized his thought to Beth. "After all, why would he take a room at the Hilton unless he planned to stay there at least one night?" he wondered aloud as he stood up to stretch.

"Because he needed a place to hide out after his disappearing act at the airport," Beth answered, as if Cole should have known it. She stood also, brushing grass clippings from her shorts. "I still think he's going somewhere tonight. Why would he have a car delivered today if he didn't plan to use it?"

"Yeah, he's probably going out to dinner or to a movie with some sweet young thing he met in the hotel lobby. That's been his pattern for over a month." Then Cole laughed. "Just think, you could have been his date tonight. He probably spent the afternoon walking the halls trying to find you again."

"Not very funny, Reagan," Beth retorted, more than half serious. "He's a killer; I could see it in his eyes. I spent all the time with him I care to, by the elevator."

"Right," Cole agreed soberly. "I'm sorry you even got *that* close to him."

"Besides, he's leaving the Valley tonight. I'd be willing to bet on it." Beth poked Cole playfully in the ribs as she spoke.

"You believe that he's leaving because he rented a car today?" Cole clarified.

"Just as firmly as you believe he's spending the night because he rented a room for the night."

"I wouldn't say I believe it *firmly*," Cole backed down.

"Neither would I, but I'm willing to bet on it. And it looks like we're going to need some competition to get us through the next few hours. What shall we bet?" Beth held out her hand, ready to shake on it.

"Well, either way, I'm not spending the night in the park waiting for our man to make his next move," Cole said, leaving Beth's hand outstretched. "I'm calling out the detectives to stare at the Hawkeye all night."

"All right, here's the deal," Beth said firmly, hand still extended. "If Rennie leaves by 9 tonight, you buy me dinner—and I mean a *great* dinner tomorrow night. If he leaves anytime after 9, I buy you dinner."

"A *great* dinner?" Cole queried with a smile, grabbing her hand.

"The greatest," Beth assured, unwilling to release his hand.

"But if he just goes out for a spin and comes back for the night tonight, I win."

"Of course. He has to leave L.A. for me to win."

"But I can't go out tomorrow night; I'm supposed to be at my mother's place in Tahoe," Cole thought aloud. "In fact, I'm supposed to be on my way to Tahoe right now. And you have a plane to catch to Seattle."

Beth gripped his hand more tightly. "A bet's a bet, sergeant," she said, grinning. "We're shaking on it. You're committed."

Cole studied the beautiful, tan, inviting face looking up at him. All he had to do was tug on her soft hand and she would be in his arms; he was sure of it. It had happened almost that way eighteen months ago in the driveway of her parents' home at midnight after a game of one-on-one. The sudden thought, combined with the warmth of her hand in his, released an avalanche of desires within him, and he impulsively tightened his grip to draw her near.

Then he felt another check, a subtle amber light flashing unseen within him as insistently as the blip flashing on the Hawkeye monitor at their feet. *Slow down, be careful, back off, wait,* came the impulse. Reagan Cole had never wanted to run a yellow light more than he did right now.

But he couldn't do it. He was not about to sacrifice his prayer investment over the past many months, nor would he tempt Beth to compromise herself for him in a tender, unguarded moment. How could he do it and face Matt Dugan? So he gave Beth's hand one last shake and pulled away. "Okay, you're on," he said. "But I have to eat before 9, so what do you say we take the Hawkeye for a sandwich?"

Wide open eyes and arched brows loomed above a curious smile possessing Beth's lips. Cole couldn't detect whether she was surprised, shocked, disappointed, or pleased at his abrupt withdrawal from the imminent embrace. Nor did she explain her expression. "A sandwich would be great." Pointing to a small building near the center of the park, she added. "But I need to visit the restroom first."

"Me too," Cole said. Then remembering the Hawkeye on the grass, he said, "After you."

While Beth was away, Cole watched the blip on the screen which had been flashing at the corner of Hollywood Way and Thornton since Beth attached the rabbit nearly three hours earlier. "Let's go, Rennie," he said to the little blinking light. "Make your move. And if you have evil intentions, I'm going to make sure you can't fulfill them."

Beth returned from the restroom to baby-sit the Hawkeye while Cole took his turn. He was washing his hands at the basin when he heard Beth calling excitedly, "Reagan! Reagan!" He ran outside with his hands dripping with soap and water. Beth was standing over the Hawkeye. When she saw Cole, she waved him over excitedly. "He's leaving!" she called. "He's on Hollywood Way heading toward the freeway!"

Cole patted his hands dry on his jeans as he ran. When he reached her side the blip on the screen was approaching a heavy glowing line on the map identified as Interstate 5. In seconds the flashing light turned north on the freeway.

"If he's just taking someone out to dinner, he's certainly going out of his way," Beth said, scooping up their empty bottles and heading toward one of the park's recycle barrels. "There are plenty of restaurants right here in Burbank. This is it, Reagan. He's on his way."

"Don't order your free dinner yet," Reagan followed her with his voice. He was gathering up the Hawkeye as he spoke. "Magic Mountain is out I-5 just past Valencia. He's probably found a woman friend to ride the roller coaster with him."

"I guess we'll know soon enough," Beth called back, dropping the bottles in the barrel and angling toward the Barego on the curb.

Cole met her at the car. "Here, take the Hawkeye," he said. "I'll drive."

Beth opened the passenger door and glared at him. "No chance," she stated firmly. "You drove on the last chase, and I nearly got killed. It's *my* turn to scare a few years off *your* life." Then she pointed to his seat. "Get in."

Cole hesitated. "Beth, this could get dangerous. I'm a professional, so I think I should drive."

"That's fine with me," Beth said curtly, slamming the passenger door and heading around to the driver's side. "But you won't get very far without a car." She jumped behind the wheel and started the engine.

"Okay, okay," Cole called into the window, admitting defeat. "Just let me get in." He hurriedly climbed in the passenger side and balanced the Hawkeye on his knees. Beth moved the gearshift to DRIVE but kept her foot on the brake.

"Just for good measure, why don't you call the Hilton and see if Rodriguez has checked out," Beth suggested.

Cole looked at her, shaking his head in amazement. "Did you ever consider a career in law enforcement?" he asked with a sheepish grin. Then he called the Hilton. Alberto Rodriguez had checked out, leaving no forwarding information.

Cole inserted the Hawkeye's adaptor into the cigarette lighter. "Let's follow him, but at good distance," Cole said.

"That shouldn't be a problem," Beth said, pointing to the blip on the screen. "He's really moving." The monitor's margin display showed the "rabbit" moving at a speed of 68 MPH.

Beth circled the park, bringing them back to Buena Vista. She turned right toward the freeway.

Cole pulled out his phone again and tapped one of his memory codes. "Hello, mom . . . Yes, it's me . . . Say, mom, it looks like I might be a little late."

Forty-eight

Interstate 5 is a 1,500-mile ribbon of asphalt which connects three countries, Mexico, the United States, and Canada, and passes through three state capitals, Sacramento, Salem, and Olympia. With no stop signs or signal lights its entire length, I-5 affords uninterrupted border to border travel—with the exception of stringent California, where motorists entering must pass through an agricultural inspection station and discard quarantined fruit.

Northbound I-5 begins just above the Mexican border at Tijuana and follows the California coastline for about eighty miles through San Diego and Oceanside to southern Orange County. There the highway turns inland, parting company with the Pacific Ocean for approximately 1,200 miles, and slices through the center of greater Los Angeles.

After cresting the Grapevine sixty miles north of downtown L.A., I-5 drops into the expansive San Joaquin Valley for a 300-mile straight-away through central California.

After a 60-mile respite through urban and suburban Stockton and Sacramento, I-5 streaks due north 160 miles through the sparsely pop-ulated Sacramento Valley to Redding at the southern border of the Whiskeytown-Shasta-Trinity National Recreation Area. North of Redd-ing, I-5 is transformed from a functional straight line between points to a scenic mountain highway winding through the Cascade Range into Southern Oregon. Sprawling, meandering Lake Shasta, stark, snowcapped Mt. Shasta, and the Siskiyou summit near the state border transition the I-5 traveler from the flat, dusty farmland of Central California to the green hills and mountains of Western Oregon and Washington.

Angling to the west from Ashland and Medford to Grants Pass, I-5 resumes its northward trajectory between the Cascade Range on the east and the Coast Range on the west. Flanked on either side by a panorama of evergreens, lush rolling hills, and mountain peaks, I-5 traverses the 300 miles of Oregon to Portland, at the confluence of the Columbia and Willamette Rivers. Crossing the Columbia into Washing-ton, the greenery continues past Mt. St. Helens.

One hundred miles north of the Oregon–Washington border at Olympia, the Interstate yields to the southern tip of Puget Sound and angles eastward through the port cities of Tacoma and Seattle. The last 100 miles of the freeway flirts with the Sound through Bellingham to Blaine on the Canadian border.

Consulting a road atlas during the first few miles of straight highway after descending the curvy Grapevine, Evan had attempted to plot distances between major cities and estimate the RV's times of arrival. Jakes had instructed him to set the cruise control for 60 MPH and leave it there on the open highway. Covering approximately a mile a minute made hourly increments of travel easy to figure.

Evan had guessed they would traverse the long stretch up the San Joaquin Valley to Stockton in about four and a half hours. It was now just past 6 P.M. and the RV was twenty miles south of Stockton, right on schedule. At this present rate, Evan predicted they would reach Sacramento by 7:30, where he hoped he could convince Jakes to stop for gas. They should hit Redding by 10:30 and cross into Oregon about 1:30 A.M. Ideally, they would refuel in Portland and enter Washington around 7:30. Keeping up the pace, they could be in Seattle by 11. From there it would be a mere 100 miles to the Canadian border. The ordeal could be over by shortly after noon tomorrow.

Evan knew, however, that there were several unknowns and variables locked in the mind of his captor, Nolan Jakes. What would he do about trying to contact their old friend Libby? How much of their precious escape time would he sacrifice to find her and convince her to part with some of her money? What other tricks did Jakes have up his sleeve during the long drive north? Evan came to terms with the fact that he might not be rid of Nolan Jakes and his girlfriend until late Monday.

Evan had been in the driver's seat since they left Gorman over four hours earlier, and his legs and back ached for a change of position. Traffic on Interstate 5 was moderate throughout the afternoon. Evan kept the RV in the slower of the two northbound lanes. Traveling at a controlled pace of 60 MPH on flat, straight highway, the coach was constantly being passed by cars, vans, small trucks, and eighteen-wheelers traveling at speeds up to 80. Occasionally Evan would come up behind a slower moving vehicle. After passing with caution, he would quickly return to the slow lane just before another fleet of freeway fliers raced by.

Jakes had slept until 4 o'clock while Margo, with the .44 at her side, kept a close watch on Evan and Shelby, sitting between them in the swivel chair near the door. After Jakes emerged from the bedroom, he checked their progress on the map and assured himself that his money was still tucked safely in the wardrobe. Then Margo passed the gun to him and went in to lie down, while Jakes settled into the chair by the door. Jakes had left the bedroom door open during his nap, but Margo closed the door for the two hours she occupied the room at the rear of the coach.

Malika had napped on Shelby's lap in the dinette for a couple of hours during the afternoon. Then Shelby had quietly occupied her at the table with books and crayons and occasional handfuls of Lucky Charms when the little girl's concentration waned. The road noise in the coach prohibited normal conversation, so Evan and Shelby had not spoken since leaving Gorman. And Margo and Jakes were each silent and pensive during their respective shifts of guard duty.

So for four long hours Evan had nothing to do but to drive and pray, and he prayed almost constantly on the long trek through the Central California farmland. Chief among his requests was a prayer for survival. In every way he knew how, he asked God to keep his wife, his daughter, and himself safe from harm. And he begged God to allow them clear passage to the Canadian border, undetected by the police or by any thugs who might be searching for his college friend, Nolan Jakes.

What Evan could *not* bring himself to pray was that justice would be meted out to Nolan Jakes. He realized that such a prayer, if answered, would result in justice being meted out to him as well. Jakes had made Evan a promise: If he was captured and given his due for kidnapping and other crimes, he would dredge up the Neil McGruder affair and nail his old buddy as a co-conspirator. Justice for Evan could translate into a murder conviction, imprisonment, and, most assuredly, the end of his medical career.

Furthermore, he could only wonder if an exposé of his past would also cause Shelby to renege on her hours-old promise to stand with him "through every circumstance of our life together—joy or sorrow, health or sickness, wealth or poverty—as long as we both shall live." Fearing that she might consider him damaged goods and return him to the manufacturer for a refund, Evan also prayed for her understanding when he had the opportunity to tell her his sad story.

A few minutes after 6, Margo appeared from the bedroom and greeted Jakes in the swivel chair. He playfully pulled her into his lap and smothered her cheeks and neck with kisses while she giggled and squirmed. Malika, who was still with Shelby in the dinette, scrambled to her knees and watched the spectacle wide-eyed.

Evan perceived that the tension gripping Nolan Jakes in Los Angeles was easing as the miles between him and freedom in Canada passed beneath the RV's wheels. Jakes apparently felt that he had outwitted the police and his former drug boss and made good his escape. After the scare on Highway 126, the journey north had been uneventful. Evan had seen only one California Highway Patrol cruiser in four hours, and it had been going the opposite direction. He felt almost as relieved and as hopeful as Jakes that they would make it to the border without incident.

The radiant orange sun was still perched above the western horizon, but Evan switched on the RV's halogen headlights in anticipation of sunset. He hoped the car-carrier lights were still securely plugged in. He would check them again when they stopped, which he hoped would be soon.

"My legs are getting numb, Nolan," Evan called over his shoulder to the cooing lovebirds. "I need a break."

Jakes reluctantly broke his romantic grip on Margo and motioned for her to stand up. "Where are we?" he asked, moving in behind the driver.

"Almost to Stockton," Evan reported. "We'll be in the suburbs now until we leave Sacramento. We could stop for gas and—"

"No," Jakes cut in, pointing at the fuel gauge, "we don't need gas yet. You still have almost a half a tank. How far to Redding?"

"Over 200 miles from here," Evan said.

"We'll get gas in Redding," Jakes announced. "Then we only need to refuel once more."

"But I still have to stop," Evan persisted. "Maybe you or Margo can drive for a while."

"And we need something decent to eat," Shelby interjected from the dinette. "May we please look for a rest stop so I can prepare dinner for my family?"

Evan warmed at Shelby's reference to him and Malika as her family. *Yes, thank God, we are still a family, no matter where we go or what Nolan Jakes does to us,* he thought. *This traumatic ordeal will end, but we will endure. And hopefully Shelby will forgive me for not telling her about my stained past. But I still must tell her soon.*

"No stops," Jakes said forcefully, raising his voice above the constant hum of six RV tires on pavement. "We'll get off the freeway long enough to change drivers and then keep on going. Whatever we eat, we eat on the road." Leaning over Evan's shoulder to scope out the freeway ahead, he added, "Take the next exit you come to and look for a place to pull over."

At Shelby's request, Jakes allowed her to take Malika to the bathroom with a warning not to try anything.

"What about the money," Margo interjected. "Where are we going to stop and withdraw more money?"

"We'll stop at a bank in Seattle tomorrow and have these two withdraw their cash in person," Jake said with authority. "One stop and it's all over."

"But won't that be chancy, letting these people out in public?" Margo objected, obviously displeased with the decision.

"Not everyone will be out in public, Margo," Jakes answered. "I'll be here in the RV with the little girl while you escort the happy couple to the window. I'm sure that will keep everyone in line, won't it, dad?"

Evan's silence was a tacit expression of submission.

"And what about your other friend, Nolan?" Margo continued. "When are we going to contact her about the money?"

Evan noted that Margo was even more preoccupied with the money aspect of their escape than was her boyfriend.

Margo's question seemed to catch Jakes off guard, as if he had forgotten about that facet of the plan. His answer appeared to be from the hip. "As soon as we're back on the freeway, I want you to get on the phone and try to find her number for me. If she's somewhere in Washington, I'll tell her to meet us in Seattle tomorrow with her bank cards."

"All three of them in the bank at the same time? Nolan, I don't think—"

"I'll handle it, Margo," Jakes insisted. "Now just back off about the money, okay?"

Margo backed off immediately, turning to inspect the grocery sack of food she had purchased for something to eat. Shelby and Malika emerged from the bathroom and returned to their seat in the dinette.

The next exit from I-5 was a quiet country road with no freeway services available. Evan flipped on the right-turn blinker and aimed the Flair up the off-ramp, slowing gradually. After stopping at the stop sign, he turned right and found a turnout within a quarter of a mile in front of a fresh fruit and vegetable stand that was closed for the evening. He eased the Flair into the dirt parking lot and stopped.

"Leave the engine running," Jakes directed. Evan lifted the gearshift to PARK.

Then to Shelby, Jakes said, "Have you ever driven this rig?"

Shelby blinked in surprise, glanced at Evan, then answered confidently, "Yes, I can drive it."

Evan stiffened with fear. Yes, Shelby had been behind the wheel of the RV a couple of times and was a confident, capable driver. But she was also the only driver in the coach who might look for opportunities to attract the attention of the Highway Patrol. She may be more committed to seeing Jakes and Margo apprehended than Evan was, perhaps thinking that she could tip off the authorities before her captors could harm Malika.

"All I need is an hour of rest and I'll be ready to drive again," Evan advanced, swiveling his chair to stand up.

"We'll see about that," Jakes said, clearly asserting his intention to decide who did what. "For right now, your wife drives. Let's move it."

Jakes and Margo stepped aside while Evan and Shelby changed places. As his bride stepped past him, Evan said loud enough for Jakes' ears, "Please be careful, angel. Don't let us get pulled over by the police. I don't want anything to happen to any of us."

As Shelby looked at him, the shadow of a question clouded her face, a question she could not verbalize. But Evan translated the expression, "Why are you being so completely agreeable for this man? What's wrong with trying to alert the police? Why are you so hesitant to stop him?"

It was a question Evan could no more answer than she could ask. So he gripped her by the shoulders and gave her a peck on the cheek before she stepped up into the cab to assume the controls.

"I need to check the trailer lights once more," Evan announced, taking a step toward the door.

"Stay put," Jake's ordered. "I'll check them."

"But someone might see you," Margo said.

"Nobody is going to see me out here in the sticks," Jakes countered. "Besides, I need to get outside for a minute." Then he donned his golf hat and shades, patted his fake beard firmly in place, passed the .44 to Margo, and stepped out of the coach.

Evan slid into the dinette next to Malika. The warm breeze flowing in through the open door felt good after nearly five hours of manufactured air from the roof-mounted air conditioner.

Surprisingly, Jakes took a brief walk around the small shanty serving as a produce stand. Evan hoped he wasn't becoming claustrophobic, because they had many more hours to spend together inside the coach. Jakes was unpredictable enough without the added anxiety of feeling closed in.

Once he reached the rear of the car carrier, Jakes signaled Shelby to test the brakes and blinkers. As she complied, watching him through the mirrors, Shelby posed a blunt question to Margo, who was standing at her shoulder, "Do you really want to go through with this? Are you serious about running for the rest of your life?"

Margo was silent for a moment. Evan didn't expect her to answer. "I'm *dead* serious about it," she said stoically. With the loaded Colt .44 in her hand, Margo's answer seemed to be issued as a threat.

Shelby was unfazed. "If you turn yourselves in now, the police will go easier on you," she said, still watching Jakes in the side mirrors. "And if you do give up, we will help you through the process. We're Christian people, Margo, and we care about you. Will you let us help you?"

Evan couldn't believe what he was hearing. Shelby had obviously taken a different approach to her prayers during the four silent hours since leaving Gorman. Though her trauma at being abducted couldn't possibly be as great as Evan's unspoken dread, Shelby was clearly disturbed and fearful. But while Evan was begging God to save his skin and make Jakes and Margo disappear, his wife had been praying for the salvation of their souls!

Evan almost spoke up to stop Shelby, until he realized how pure her motives were and how shallow his were. Shelby's desire to reach out to the unlovable was the most noble and benevolent response to her predicament. Serving others had been her passion since college days, motivating her through more than ten years of pastoral ministry in Texas and a year and a half of selfless caring for the disadvantaged at King's House. Despite her fear, how else could she feel toward the very people she had committed herself to love?

But at this moment Evan did not share his wife's concern. Were Margo and Jakes to turn themselves in at Shelby's insistence, or were they to bolt foolishly in response to Shelby's offer and get themselves captured, Evan's secret would be in jeopardy. *It can't happen that way, Shelby*, Evan insisted silently. *God will have to reach them some other way, perhaps by using someone in Canada after they have disappeared— and after I've had a chance to unburden my soul to you about my history with Nolan Jakes.*

Following another moment of silence, Margo replied, "I'll think about it." Again, the lack of conviction in her voice obscured her true meaning to Evan. Was she serious or just stringing Shelby along? He couldn't tell.

Jakes stepped into the coach before Shelby could speak again. He closed the door and locked it behind him. "The lights work fine," he announced, taking the gun from Margo's hand. "Let's go."

Reflective of his inflated sense of confidence in the mission's success, Jakes took the "shotgun" seat, the high-backed bucket opposite the driver's seat in the front window. Before swiveling it forward, he said, "Go ahead and fix dinner for your family, Evan, something the lady can eat while she drives. But no lights back there except the small light above the stove."

He waved Shelby to head the RV back toward the freeway. She buckled in and pulled the gearshift down to DRIVE, beginning a slow, wide U-turn from the turnout onto the westbound two-lane road leading back to I-5.

After a short conference with Malika, Evan stood in the kitchen and opened a can of minestrone and sliced cheddar cheese for melted cheese sandwiches, one of her favorite meals. He thought he should begin praying again, but since Shelby's attempt to "rescue" Margo, he was confused about what to pray.

As they gathered speed down the on-ramp, Jakes said to Margo, who had taken her place in the smaller chair behind his, "Call information in Washington and see if you can find a number for someone named Libby Carroll. First try the area codes in the west, then the east. By the time you finish, Evan should be done in the kitchen and you can make us a sandwich or something." Then he turned forward and tugged his hat low on his forehead.

Margo opened up her phone and began dialing.

Forty-nine

Beth had clearly won the bet, and she felt properly smug about it. According to the Hawkeye, Rennie Barbosa's Lincoln Town Car had departed Los Angeles County via I-5 North, at shortly after 5 P.M. Beth had whooped up her victory at the time and tossed out the names of a couple of spendy West Hollywood restaurants she was considering for collecting her prize from Cole.

But her celebration was short-lived in light of the story unfolding before their eyes on the Hawkeye monitor. The Town Car had not only left greater L.A. but had streaked past Gorman and over the Grapevine. Rennie Barbosa was going somewhere all right, and he was in a hurry. The Hawkeye had clocked him at speeds up to 80 MPH on the open highway between Castaic and Gorman and even higher sweeping down the grade.

In contrast, Beth had nudged the Barego up close to 75 after passing Magic Mountain at Valencia but was still losing ground. According to the statistics displayed by the Hawkeye, the Barego had dropped a full twenty minutes behind the Town Car, and the gap was increasing. Beth and Cole had fallen silent as they raced along after the blip on the computer's scrolling electronic map.

The sun descending behind the western hills had already cast much of the northbound lanes of the freeway in shadows. With the light seeping from the sky and the town of Gorman in view ahead, Beth sensed she was nearing the point of no return. The little valley drawing her toward the precipice of the Grapevine's descent was now the valley of decision.

This was not the time of day for Beth to be leaving L.A. if she intended to be back to her parents' home by bedtime. But it appeared now that Rennie Barbosa was bound for the Bay Area or perhaps farther. He had tried to shake his police tail, apparently believing he had succeeded. What did he have in mind now? Was it something she could write about and sell? Was it worth pursuing?

She and Cole had joked about following the Peruvian hit man to the East Coast and back. But was Sergeant Reagan Cole serious about staying with him to his destination? If so, was she interested enough in the story—and in the company of the man sitting next to her—to stay with him for the chase?

Beth knew she had to make up her mind before they reached Gorman. If she decided to go on, they needed to fill her tank for the long journey from the Grapevine to San Francisco or Sacramento or who-knows-where. If she decided to call it quits, they needed to find a car for Cole to rent in Gorman before she turned around and headed back to Woodland Hills.

Apparently Cole was considering the same options. Still two miles from the Gorman exit, he said, "We may be in for a long haul, so we better stop here to top off the tank and get something to eat." Then he added, "Are you sure you want to do this?"

"You mean, am I sure I want to follow this guy to San Francisco or wherever, because it looks like he's going to be traveling awhile?"

"Yes, that's what I mean."

Buying time, Beth tossed Cole's question right back to him, 95 percent sure of his answer. "Are you sure *you* want to do this?"

"Positive," he said without hesitation. "I'm going to stay with him all week if I have to—unofficially, of course. But you don't have to. You can take me back to Valencia or the Valley and I'll get a car."

"What about Gorman? Couldn't you get something here?"

Cole snorted a laugh. "I may be able to talk one of the locals into loaning me his pickup. But no, I don't think Hertz or Avis have satellite offices in beautiful downtown Gorman."

"But it's an hour back to the Valley. That would put you over two hours behind Barbosa."

Cole shrugged. "I know. I thought about that when we passed Castaic. I guess I just didn't expect him to keep going. If you want to turn back now, I'll keep him on the screen and hope I can close some ground before he does anything." Then after blowing a heavy sigh over his upper lip, Cole added, "Or maybe I should just call in the FBI and let them put a tail on him."

"Is that what you really want to do?"

"Of course not. I started this surveillance, and I want to finish it. But if you want out, it's one of my options. What do you want to do?"

Beth thought for a moment. The Gorman exit drew nearer. "What do *you* want me to do?" she asked. She wasn't as sure of his answer to this question as she had been about his intention to stay on Barbosa's trail. He had always cautioned her to safety, and he might want her to stay behind because of the possible danger ahead. On the other hand, their delightful afternoon in the park—especially that electric moment when she expected him to fold her in his arms, an embrace she would not have resisted—proved to her that Cole was still interested in her. Beth wasn't sure if he would opt for her safety or her continuing company. But his answer was important to her decision.

"I can't make that decision for you, Beth," Cole said after a moment's thought.

"That's right, you can't," Beth said with a purposeful edge of independence in her voice. "I'm asking your preference in the matter."

Again Cole paused to think as they raced past a sign announcing GORMAN — EXIT ½ MILE. "There could be a great story at the end of this chase," he said.

Beth smiled, perceiving Cole's preference through his poorly veiled comment. "So it would be okay with you if I came along to follow up this potential blockbuster story?" she asked, as she moved the Barego into the right lane and prepared to exit the freeway.

"Actually, I would enjoy your company and your help very much—*if* I can count on you to follow my lead," Cole said. "Technically, I may be on vacation, but I still want to do this operation by the book. The last thing I want is for your life to be endangered again."

Beth decelerated down the off-ramp. "That's the last thing I want too," she said, flashing back to her close call with death on Millennium's Eve. "I'll try to be a good partner." Then to make her decision completely clear, she added, "I want to go with you."

"Good," Cole said. "I'm glad."

The couple decided that their stop in Gorman should imitate a pit stop at the Indy 500 as nearly as possible to save time. After a coin flip to decide on tasks, Beth filled the tank at the Shell station while Cole ran next door to a burger stand for a fast-food, takeout dinner for two. By agreement, Beth paid for the gas and Cole paid for meal, with Beth insisting that this dinner did not count toward her reward for winning their little bet. They were back on the road in twelve minutes. Beth took the wheel again but agreed to switch off with Cole every couple of hours.

Speeding down the long, sweeping curves of the Grapevine toward the valley floor, Cole wolfed down a double cheeseburger, a chicken sandwich, a bag of fries, and a 32-ounce Pepsi, while helping Beth deal with her dinner one-handedly. She laughed about the two drops of mayonnaise decorating her top and the french fries she had dropped between the bucket seats and the center console. And she snickered at Cole's compulsion for a clean car, watching him pick up every loose sesame seed on his lap and place it in the trash bag. Meanwhile, Rennie Barbosa continued his trek north, as evidenced by the steady progress of the blip on the Hawkeye monitor.

With the sandwich wrappers and napkins efficiently bagged and stuffed behind the seat, Cole opened a window on the briefcase computer and did some figuring. "Barbosa must have his speed set at about 78 MPH," he said, studying the figures on the screen. "In order to close the gap between us and Barbosa to less than ten minutes before we reach Stockton, we have to maintain a speed of about 83."

"Eighty-three?" Beth questioned skeptically. "We're going to attract the 'chippies' like flies to garbage."

"Not likely," Cole said. "The CHP has practically conceded this stretch of I-5 to the freeway fliers, especially at night. We are now traveling California's version of the Autobahn. Our motto is, go as fast as you can for as far as you can, and if you wipe out, the Highway Patrol will send out a meat wagon to clear the track for the next race."

"You Californians keep thinking up new ways to kill each other off, don't you?" Beth said tongue in cheek as she adjusted the Buick's cruise monitor to almost 85 MPH.

"We don't need any help in that category," Cole responded with a hollow laugh. "The earthquakes, fires, floods, and riots are already doing a great job of population control."

After a few silent minutes, Beth offered what she regarded to be a hopeful insight. "We should make up some additional time on Barbosa when he stops for gas."

Cole shook his head. "If he's heading for Frisco, I don't think he'll need to stop." He busied himself for several seconds with computations as he spoke. "That big boat of his has at least an eighteen-gallon fuel capacity and gets around twenty-five miles to the gallon, a 450-mile range. Assuming that Budget started him with a full tank, that puts him in downtown San Francisco with fuel to spare."

"What about us? Will we need to refuel before the Bay Area?"

Cole tapped the keys as he thought aloud. "Let's see, these aerodynamic little GM coupes are great on fuel efficiency. We carry about thirteen gallons, but we won't get the best gas mileage at 80-plus miles per hour. Figuring thirty miles a gallon, that gets us into Frisco . . . hm, just barely, on fumes."

Beth then voiced a question which had been on both of their minds. "What if Rennie isn't going to San Francisco? What if he's going farther, like Portland or Seattle?"

"Or even Canada," Cole added.

"Right. Or maybe he will head east toward Reno. An unemployed hit man could probably find plenty of work in Reno."

Cole didn't laugh at Beth's little joke. "My gut tells me that if Barbosa is going beyond the Bay Area, he would fly instead of drive."

"Yeah, but your gut hasn't been too accurate today," Beth quipped, thoroughly entertained by her own wit. "Do you want to go double or nothing on our dinner bet? I say he's going farther than the Bay Area. Bet?" She reached out her right hand, offering to shake on it.

"Of course not," Cole insisted, backing off quickly to add, "at least not yet, not until I can think of a reason why he would waste so much time driving when he could fly."

"Because you detective types *expected* him to fly, and Rennie is pretty good at not doing what you expect," Beth said, shaking her finger at Cole to emphasize what was so obvious to her. "He's convinced that he left the LAPD standing at the airport trying to figure out which flight he took. So he's content to take the scenic route and show up for his next appointment with the element of surprise on his side."

"Maybe," Cole conceded. Then he closed the calculations window, allowing the electronic map to fill the Hawkeye screen again. He lowered the briefcase to the floor between his long legs, reclined his seat back a couple more notches, and lapsed into silence.

The black Buick Barego raced along the fast lane passing a well-spaced convoy of eighteen-wheelers in the deepening twilight. Signs ahead announced the junction of Interstate 5 and California 99. At that point I-5 angles slightly to the northwest for a faster, more direct trajectory to Northern California, while 99 takes a wider, slower turn through the more populous areas of Bakersfield, Visalia, Fresno, and Modesto. The two major highways meet again in Sacramento.

Beth guided the Barego into the lanes designated for I-5 and swept over the overpass as 99 gradually peeled away to the east. The Hawkeye had reported that Rennie Barbosa had made the same turn twenty-six minutes earlier. They were already beginning to gain on him.

In the absence of conversation, Beth tried to find something decent to listen to on the radio: classical, smooth jazz, even a public radio station with a stimulating interview. All she could pick up from the Bakersfield area were four country/western stations, two broadcasts in

Spanish, a Top Forty station blaring "C'mon baby, c'mon baby" repeatedly, and a farm station discussing the virtues of a popular pesticide. After five minutes of station-hopping, Beth switched off the radio.

Picking up the thread from their last conversation, Cole said, "Speaking of the element of surprise . . . " Then, from the corner of her eye, Beth saw him reach into the back seat, fumble in his saddlebags, and bring an object forward in his left hand. "Here's something you need to be aware of," Cole finished his sentence.

Beth glanced over in the diminishing light. Cole was holding a black, squared-off, plastic pistol fashioned on the order of the old .45 military automatic, only smaller. It could easily pass for a child's squirt gun or a spring-loaded pistol for launching rubber-tipped darts.

"Just in case something goes wrong, I want you to be ready to use this," Cole said solemnly.

Beth looked again and recognized the weapon from her first meeting with Cole on Christmas Eve of 1999. "Your DAB gun, right?" she said, mirroring Cole's serious approach to the subject.

"Right."

"What does D-A-B stand for again?"

"Drop and burn. It's not a lethal weapon—at least not usually. It fires a gel capsule at such high velocity that it drops the target, knocks him right off his pins. The capsule bursts on contact and the gel—an acidic substance—burns through the clothes and a few layers of skin, distracting the target until he can be handcuffed. It's very effective."

"I remember," Beth said. She pictured the Latino gang member who attempted to drag her from the rental car on the San Diego Freeway at midnight. Cole had happened along in time to disable him and one of his partners with the very pistol he was showing her now.

Cole continued with a brief lesson while Beth glanced between the weapon and the freeway ahead. "This is the safety, which is on. If you need to fire the gun, you must first flip the safety off. It's semiautomatic, meaning that every time you fire, another bullet is automatically loaded into the chamber. The 'semi' part means that you have to pull the trigger for every shot, instead of holding it back to fire a burst of shells.

"This baby has a pretty good kick, so grip it with both hands if you can. Aim at the target's midsection—the chest or belly—for the best chance of hitting him."

"You keep talking about the target being a 'him,'" Beth interrupted. "Have you ever shot a woman with this gun?"

Cole was silent a few seconds. "No," he said finally. "I had a chance to just before I met you: a girl about fourteen years old, a hooker high on drugs. She was waving her pimp's loaded .38 at us on the street. I hesitated, but my partners didn't. She took about five rounds in the chest and face before hitting the ground. She was hurt pretty badly. It made me sick. She was just a kid."

"But she could have killed someone," Beth said, appreciating Cole's tenderness but stung by the obvious danger the situation presented. "Somebody had to stop her."

"You're right, and I learned something that night: Never underestimate anyone's capacity for violent crime. I just hope I never have to shoot a girl, but I know I can if I have to."

Cole quickly abandoned the uncomfortable topic and returned to briefing Beth on the use of the DAB pistol. "The clip holds twelve rounds, but I've never seen anyone—no matter how tough or wigged out on drugs he was—take more than five rounds without hitting the deck screaming."

Beth noted the location of the safety button and the placement of Cole's hands as he demonstrated the firing position. Then Cole flipped open the compartment in the console designed for holding CDs, placed the pistol carefully inside, and snapped the lid closed. "It's there if you need it," he said.

"What about you?" Beth wondered aloud. "What if *you* need it?"

"Well, it's there for me too. But if for some reason I'm out of the picture . . . " Cole's meaning was clear, and Beth nodded her grasp of it.

"What about spare bullets?" she asked.

Cole shook his head. "I only have this one clip," he said. Then, hoping to lighten the suddenly serious topic with a little humor, he added, "So if you take on a big gang, shoot the fastest ones first, because you'll have to outrun the rest of them."

Beth laughed at the mental picture and smiled inside at her good fortune of having Reagan Cole to herself for the night.

Fifty

Evan hadn't intended that his bride drive for so long. After serving Shelby and Malika mugs of minestrone soup and grilled cheese sandwiches as the RV rolled past Stockton, he had unfolded the sofa bed directly behind the driver's seat. He planned to lie down with Malika for thirty minutes and read books to her by flashlight, the only light Jakes would permit in the dark coach. Then he would be ready to take the helm again so Shelby could prepare their daughter for bed and stay with her as she fell asleep.

Malika had snuggled closely to Evan as he read through a few of her favorite books—classics Shelby had been saving for her first child for more than ten years: *The Berenstain Bears and The Missing Dinosaur Bone, The Berenstain Bears Go to School,* and *Curious George Learns the Alphabet.* Malika's large black eyes flitted occasionally to the two silhouetted figures on the right side of the coach—Jakes in the tall bucket seat across from Shelby and Margo who, when she wasn't pacing the short aisle from the kitchen to the bedroom, sat in the smaller seat behind Jakes. With each fearful glance, Malika tightened her grip on the arm her daddy had draped around her. And whenever Evan made like he was finished visiting with her, Malika thrust another book in his hands and silently begged him not to leave.

Evan had listened out of the corner of his ear as Margo dialed directory assistance in Washington state hoping to locate either the office or personal phone number of Evan and Nolan's college friend, Libby Carroll. Evan prayed that Libby had married and changed her name, or that she had moved away from Washington. Not only did he wish to spare Libby the trauma he and Shelby were presently experiencing; he also wished to spare himself the awkwardness of introducing Shelby to a beautiful old college chum, worried that his wife might jump to jealous conclusions.

To Evan's disappointment, finding a number for Libby Carroll couldn't have been easier. Directory assistance had only one Libby Carroll in the state, spelled the way Jakes remembered it. Margo obtained both a personal and professional number for a *Dr.* Libby Carroll, associated with the University of Washington. Jakes told Margo that he would wait until later in the evening to contact Libby. Evan began praying that Libby would be out of communication range for some reason.

By 7:30, the steady, vibrating hum of the tires in the near darkness had lulled Malika and road-weary Evan to sleep. At Shelby's request, Margo collected an afghan from the bedroom during one of her pacing fits and draped it across the sleeping pair.

Now, about an hour and a half later, Evan was awake again. He experienced a brief moment of disorientation as the reality and gravity of his situation rushed quickly back to him. Malika was pressed against his left side, reposed in the cradle of his arm, breathing heavily. But instead of stirring, Evan continued to lie still with his eyes closed listening, praying, wondering, and worrying in the dark privacy of feigned sleep.

For perhaps thirty minutes after he awoke, there was no sound in the coach aside from the drone of the tires and the occasional roar of a truck or car in the left lane overtaking the relatively slow-moving RV. Evan felt Margo squeeze past the sofa bed several times as she walked the aisle in her stocking feet. And whenever he ventured a peek, Evan saw wisps of Shelby's blonde hair above the headrest of her tall seat and the dark outline of Jakes' muscular left side, bearded chin, and frumpy golf hat in the seat opposite her.

Then Evan heard Shelby speak, apparently to Jakes, who was nearest her. There were a couple of sentences, but the road noise muffled most of what she said, and Evan couldn't understand it. Jakes either ignored her or didn't hear her, because he didn't answer. Margo was retrieving a can of beer from the refrigerator at the moment and heard even less than Evan did.

After a minute, Shelby spoke again, half a dozen sentences this time. Her tone seemed conversational instead of adversarial, as if she was asking her fellow traveler's opinion on the road conditions or commenting on the number of RV's on the road heading for vacation spots in the Northwest. But this time Jakes responded. His terse comment, which Evan heard clearly since Jakes' head was turned toward Shelby, told him what she had been talking about. "You can save your breath, lady," Jakes said, "because I'm not interested."

Shelby is trying to convince him to give up and turn himself in, Evan realized, his stomach knotting with fear, *just like she did with Margo. She is counseling him, offering our prayers and help, urging him to abort his escape plan.*

Ignoring Jakes' comment, Shelby spoke again. Evan listened closer but was still unable to hear. This time Jakes interrupted her, raising his voice slightly. "I said I'm not interested. Now just shut up about it."

Hearing the commotion from the kitchen, Margo made her way forward. "What's going on?" she asked, leaning over Jakes' shoulder. He explained in two short phrases Shelby's attempt to persuade him to surrender to the police in Redding, only a short distance ahead.

Evan cringed at the exchange, still pretending to be asleep. It was the perfect opportunity for Margo to divulge that Shelby had tried the same tactic with her outside Stockton while Jakes was checking trailer lights. *Margo had said she would think about what Shelby said,* Evan recalled. *Could she possibly have been serious? If so, she will likely keep quiet now, allowing Jakes to remain in the dark about the treasonous thoughts Shelby has sown. If not, she will certainly expose Shelby's attempt, possibly inciting Jakes to greater anger and even retaliation.* Evan held his breath, expecting Margo to tell everything.

But she didn't. She simply muttered a curse, apparently directed at Shelby for her audacity, and dropped into the chair behind Jakes to sip from her can of beer.

Evan's stomach tightened with anxiety. If Margo was already tiring of the fugitive's life, if Shelby had indeed piqued her conscience to consider insurrection against Nolan Jakes, and if the seed of the idea had rooted in Margo's consciousness over the past three hours, Evan knew he was in trouble. If Margo weakened and allowed herself and Jakes to be captured, his secret would be exposed. *How will Shelby feel when she realizes that her attempt to help Margo forsake a life of crime may result in my arrest and imprisonment? For all her benevolence and helpfulness, Shelby is working against me, our marriage, and our future without knowing it!*

As Evan pondered the situation, Shelby spoke to Jakes again, offering another reason why his flight was futile and his capture inevitable. And Jakes again interrupted her, this time clearly angry but without raising his voice higher, in apparent deference to the sleeping child. "Lady, we're going to Canada, and that's the way it's going to be. If you have any doubts that we will make it, you'd better ask your husband, because he wants us to get there as badly as we do. Now shut up or I will make this more painful for you and your little girl than it already is."

Shelby said no more, and the coach was again occupied with the sounds of the road. Yet Evan could almost hear his wife's mind processing Jakes' words. *How will she interpret the man's insinuation that I am working for the fugitives instead of against them? Will she merge his words with that questioning expression I read on her face earlier, that look that asked, "Why are you being so agreeable with Nolan Jakes? Why aren't you doing something to thwart his escape?" Will she begin to suspect that Jakes has a more poignant reason for selecting me to get him out of the country?* Again Evan prayed for an opportunity to tell his bride the truth before Jakes blurted it out in response to one of Shelby's attempts to solicit their surrender.

At 9:50 P.M., the RV pulled off the I-5 freeway at Red Bluff, California, about thirty miles south of Redding, the gateway to the mountains spread over the California–Oregon border. At Nolan Jakes' direction, Shelby maneuvered the big Flair into a roadside service station and lined up behind two cars at the outer pump island. Then Jakes retreated to the coach's kitchen to avoid being seen under the brilliant yellow lights shining into the cab.

Evan "woke up" as they exited the freeway, and Malika stirred slightly as he slipped out of her grasp to a sitting position on the sofa. But as he arranged the afghan over her and patted her gently, she was still again.

Jakes ordered Shelby to stay at the wheel and pull the RV forward when the pump was available. "Then you fill this thing to the top and get us back on the road again," he said, pointing to Evan. "You're driving the next shift."

Margo excused herself to use the restroom in the station, complaining that she didn't like the tiny bathroom in the RV. Jakes urged her to be back in time to go to the window with Evan and stay with him until he had filled the tank and paid the bill. She agreed and left.

Evan stood up behind the driver's seat and reached out to touch Shelby's shoulder. Jakes didn't intervene. "How are you holding up?" Evan asked.

Shelby turned, and Evan read the strain in her face. He was suddenly and deeply pained at the trouble he had unwittingly brought into her life. They had been married little more than twenty-four hours and were supposed to be on the honeymoon of their dreams. They had planned to be halfway to the Grand Canyon by this time, settling in for a romantic dinner and a night of tender love and intimacy in the RV near the Colorado River on the border of California and Arizona. Instead, two fugitives from the law were leading them on a forced march to the Canadian border, and Shelby didn't even understand why she and Evan had been selected for the duty. Evan hoped to explain it to her soon, and he prayed that his life would be intact when it was all over, in order to give her the honeymoon she had hoped for.

"I feel like I'm trapped in someone else's bad dream," Shelby answered, reaching a hand up to touch Evan's. Garish yellow light flooding the cab cast a sickly pall on her fatigue-lined face.

"I'm so sorry this happened, angel," Evan consoled. Aware that Jakes was listening in, he continued, "But if we just cooperate with Nolan and Margo, by this time tomorrow it will be all over, and we'll be on our way."

The cars ahead pulled away from the pump and Shelby gunned the Flair into position for refueling and shut off the engine. Evan turned to leave the coach, but Shelby kept hold of his hand, pulling him toward her as she swiveled her seat around. "Is there something you're not telling me about all this, something I need to know?" she asked.

Shelby's tone was free of blame and her intention clearly guileless, but the directness of her question stunned Evan. He surmised that it was the result of Jakes' hasty comment in response to her pestering.

He wished he could tell her the whole story right now, about his past with Nolan Jakes and Libby Carroll, about that night in Portland, about poor Neil McGruder. More than unburdening his soul, Evan wanted to hear from the spiritually mature woman he had married about what his past meant to his faith and his future. Most important to him right now, Evan wanted to know how the truth would impact his relationship with the wonderful woman he had taken as his own.

But all Evan could say in response to Shelby's piercing question was, "I need to talk to you." Then he squeezed her hand and hurried out of the coach to fill the tank.

Two and a half hours south of Red Bluff, Rennie Barbosa flipped open his phone to receive the call as his rented, burgundy Town Car raced smoothly and quietly northward on Interstate 5. Soft Latin music drifted from speakers all around him.

"What is your present location?" Bishop asked without greeting him.

"Just past Sacramento," Barbosa said. Then with obvious impatience in his voice, he asked, "How soon until I reach my target?"

"Patience, please, Mr. Barbosa. I reiterate, the timing of this arrangement is very important to me. And I remind you that I am compensating you for this inconvenience." Then, recalling that Barbosa's prime motivation came from the adventure of the hunt, Bishop said, "Also, please keep in mind the unique nature of this assignment. Consider Mr. Jakes a moving target, a greater test of your cunning."

Barbosa was silent. Bishop continued, "And think of the challenge of multiple targets requiring stealth to surprise them and cat-quickness to eliminate them before one can escape."

Silence again for several seconds. Then Barbosa said without enthusiasm, "I will follow through on our arrangement. Just keep me informed."

"Very good, Mr. Barbosa, very good," Bishop said, trying to sound encouraging. The caller provided an update on target information to keep the Peruvian trigger man content, and then hung up.

Barbosa turned up the volume, encouraging the heavy beat of the music to overpower the sleepy monotony of I-5.

The white Flair RV pulling a shiny red Datsun wagon on a car carrier returned to the freeway with a full tank after the fuel stop at Red Bluff. Evan Rider was again at the wheel with Nolan Jakes sitting in the other front seat. Margo Sharpe took her seat behind Jakes, and Shelby slipped under the afghan beside Malika who was deeply asleep on the sofa bed behind Evan's seat.

In about thirty minutes they would pass Redding and begin the winding, climbing, 165-mile departure from I-5's normal, straight-as-a-string pattern. The next leg of the journey would lead the travelers into the craggy domain of sprawling, many-fingered Lake Shasta and 14,000-foot Mt. Shasta, both of which would be invisible during night passage. Shortly after crossing into Oregon, they would crest Siskiyou Summit at 4,300 feet near Mt. Ashland and descend into the Rogue Valley past Ashland, Medford, and Grants Pass.

While I-5 through the mountains features good roads and maintains freeway conditions, the many winding grades drop the average speed of large vehicles to 45 MPH. Passenger cars, however, are able to complete the mountainous transition from California into Oregon sacrificing little speed.

Shelby was grateful not to be piloting the RV over the winding mountain road. Driving from Stockton to Red Bluff on cruise control with virtually nothing to do but keep the rig between the dotted lines was no problem, even though she had never driven I-5 before, nor had she logged many hours behind the wheel of their thirty-foot-long, eight-foot-wide motorhome. Even dragging a car carrier behind the RV on the straightaway didn't bother her.

But the thought of navigating the RV through the mountains at night with a trailer in tow, while evading slow-moving semis and speeding cars, made the lanes hugging the mountainside seem very narrow to Shelby. And when she heard about the possibility of deer darting onto the highway, she quickly decided that Redding would be as far as she would drive. She was relieved when Nolan Jakes made the decision for her by ordering Evan back into the driver's seat after their fuel stop.

Shelby didn't expect that she would be able to sleep, however, as Evan took them through the mountains. Not that she doubted his competence at the wheel; to the contrary, she regarded him as a wise and cautious driver. Rather, the whole ordeal was weighing heavily on her. It was bad enough that her honeymoon with Evan had been so rudely and frighteningly interrupted by the abduction. But the threat of physical harm to them and their daughter, at the hands of someone who was running in terror from both the police and a mob of gangsters, was a constant worry to her.

Shelby also pondered and prayed constantly about her moral and spiritual responsibility to their captors. Her natural reaction was to hate them for what they were doing and fear them for what they might do. And she had experienced the full range of these emotions in the first several hours of their flight from Ventura. There were moments when, had she found opportunity, Shelby would have tried to kill Nolan Jakes and Margo Sharpe out of holy rage.

But Shelby had had plenty of time to penetrate her turbulent feelings with thoughtful questions aimed at evaluating how she *should* respond to Jakes and Margo in the face of how she *wanted* respond to them. She had an occasion—indeed, a responsibility, she realized—to be God's instrument of love and justice in the situation. She was doing her captors no service contributing to their escape, without confronting them about their behavior and offering to help them atone for their crimes and eventually reenter society. And even this charity would be incomplete without assuring Jakes and Margo that God loved them and would forgive them if they turned to Him.

Had there been opportunities to discuss her intentions with her husband, Shelby would have done so eagerly. But there were none. Yet Shelby was so deeply convicted of her responsibility and convinced that her husband would agree that she decided to act on her own whenever the window to speak her mind opened to her.

Shelby was disappointed though not surprised when Jakes rebuffed her so quickly and harshly. But Margo's response caused hope to rise within her. Instead of slamming the window in her face as Jakes had, Margo left it open with her response to Shelby's offer of help, "I'll think about it." Shelby prayed she would have another opportunity to talk to Margo alone during the night. She dare not sleep and miss such a prospect.

There was another element keeping Shelby from dropping off to sleep, an unsettling and puzzling question: *What is troubling Evan?* "I need to talk to you," he had said in their brief interchange at the service station. There was a flicker of desperation in his eyes as he delivered his message. She could appreciate such a look in light of their ongoing crisis as kidnap victims of an at-large criminal with a loaded gun. But Shelby had sensed a deeper fear in Evan's brief gaze, a fear she had never known in him before. And the distraction served to amplify two subtle, nagging questions which otherwise might have evaporated as inconsequential.

The first question, really a batch of questions on the same thought, had buzzed at the back door of her mind most of the day: *Why is Evan being so cooperative with the attempted escape? Have I unfairly projected onto him my desire that Jakes and Margo be brought to justice and directed toward God? Does Evan have another agenda? Is he so terrified at the threat of violence to him and his family that he has decided to play the role of an accomplice? Or is there another motivation behind his apparent complicity?*

The second question formed in Shelby's mind after Nolan Jakes had told her to shut up, adding that Evan was just as anxious for the escape to succeed as he and Margo were. *What did Jakes mean by that comment? Why did he say that I should ask Evan why the race to the border would succeed?* It was this puzzling thought that prompted Shelby to ask Evan if there was something she needed to know. And it was his reaction to her query that sparked a suspicion she did not want to pursue.

The thought that Evan might be hiding something from her—something important, even sinister—was almost too frightening for Shelby to contemplate. The suspicion that Evan was withholding something from her was like a finger pressing on deep inner scars from her first marriage that, while healed, were still tender to the touch. There was no way she would be able to sleep with such a gnawing discomfort.

The familiar line from Shakespeare, recited by Stan Welbourn at her wedding mere hours ago taunted Shelby: "Love . . . looks on tempests and is never shaken." Before today, she could not imagine a tempest great enough to threaten her seemingly rock-solid love for Evan. The fact that she was shaken now, so soon after her commitment of love, caused her to wonder if what she felt for Evan was the real thing.

Forty minutes after leaving Red Bluff, the RV announced to Shelby that the major mountain climbing portion of the I-5 trip had commenced. Lying on the sofa bed with her eyes closed, she listened as the RPMS from the big Chevy 454 CID engine gradually declined from a hum to a whine to a growl before the transmission kicked into a lower gear. The coach began to sway as the straightaway yielded to the gentle, persistent curves in the mountain road.

Jakes turned back to Margo. "Give me your phone," he said. "I think it's time to make contact with Libby Carroll and let her know she's going to have company."

As Margo passed the phone forward, Shelby was captured by a curious thought. *How does Nolan Jakes intend to convince Libby Carroll to do what he wants? He's not holding a loaded gun to her head. He hasn't kidnapped her, her husband, or one of her children and imprisoned them in an RV. What would prevent her from laughing at his demands over the phone or simply calling the authorities to await his arrival? What power does he hold over her?*

Shelby kept her eyes closed but listened closely as Jakes snapped open Margo's phone and dialed the number she had scribbled on a napkin for him.

Fifty-one

"Dr. Libby Carroll?"

Libby tensed at the use of her title over the phone at such a late hour, especially since the man's voice was unrecognizable. Her first thought was of Brett, that he had pulled another foolish stunt and was in trouble with the law, or worse, that he had been hurt and the hospital was calling to inform her. "Yes?" she answered cautiously, laying aside her book and sitting up on the sofa.

"Libby Carroll the sprinter, the alternate for the Olympics in '84?"

It had been a long time since Libby was interviewed by the media as the former athlete who went on to prominence in the world of higher education. She had pages of articles in her scrapbook and many clips in her video library to remind her of the gratifying occasions when she was recognized for achievements *after* her sports career. Usually Libby welcomed the opportunity to tell her story to a reporter or feature writer. But the lateness of the hour prompted her to respond coolly, "Yes, what can I do for you?"

The caller paused, then asked, "Is this the same Libby Carroll who once attended Cal State Northridge and worked at Cupid's?" The words came as a friendly tease from an old friend, but the tone of voice twisted the tease into a poorly veiled taunt.

Libby stopped breathing. She had avoided talking to anyone about her two and a half years in Southern California prior to enrolling at Central Washington State. It was a part of her life she had tried to forget, and she had hoped that those who knew her during that period had forgotten also. But someone hadn't. She was tempted to snap off her phone and never answer it again. But instead she sat frozen and mute.

After several seconds of silence, the caller pressed smugly, "Am I talking to the same Libby Carroll who was known to her two best friends as the Jet?"

Libby instantly knew the caller's identity. There were only two people in the world who had used that nickname, and she now recognized the voice on the phone as belonging to one of them. The past, which Libby had hoped was dead and buried, had just invaded her beautiful world.

Libby didn't want to talk to him, didn't want to listen to him. She would have hung up, but she was afraid that, having tracked her down after twenty-two years, he probably wouldn't go away. He would likely call her again and again until he said what he had to say, something Libby was sure she wouldn't want to hear.

She succeeded in sounding composed and confident when she spoke his name, though she felt quite the opposite. "Nolan . . . Nolan Jakes."

"You remember. I'm impressed."

"Yes, I remember."

"I remember you too, Jet," Jakes said. "We had some good times together back at CSUN, didn't we?"

Libby didn't answer. There *had* been good times, Libby acknowledged silently, but they were permanently stained in her memory by confusion and terror from the last time she had seen Nolan Jakes.

"And you're still Libby Carroll," Jakes continued, "not Libby Jones or Libby Smith."

"I'm not married, if that's what you mean."

"Yeah, that's what I mean. Too bad, though. I might not have found you if you had changed your name."

Too bad. Libby cringed at the words. By them Nolan Jakes revealed what she had feared the moment she recognized his voice: She was not going to like the reason for this surprise reunion.

"So you're not married. That means you don't have any kids."

Libby was unsure how much to tell Jakes about Brett. She opted for information he could easily obtain. "I have a son. He's twenty."

"Good for you, Libby," Jakes said without feeling. "I'm single too, but I don't have any children—at least none that I know about." He permitted himself a wicked little laugh.

"And I see that you are *Doctor* Carroll now," Jakes continued, filling the silence Libby allowed.

"Yes."

"What are you doctor *of?*"

"I have a Ph.D. in public administration." Normally Libby would make the statement with a glow of pride in her voice. To Nolan Jakes it was delivered in a monotone. She was waiting for him to reveal his agenda.

"So you're doctor of public administration at the University of Washington?"

It wasn't her actual title, but Libby didn't bother to correct him. "Yes." She wondered what else Jakes knew about her private life.

"Our old friend Evan Rider is a doctor too," Jakes informed in a calculating tone that seemed to be leading to a point, "only he's a medical doctor, an internist."

The knot of anxiety in Libby's stomach wrenched tighter at the mention of the third member of the old Cal State Northridge triumvirate. But she said nothing.

"Did you know that our old friend Evan is married now, and that he has an adopted daughter?"

"No, I haven't been in touch with Evan."

"In fact, Evan is here with me now," Jakes continued. "He's actually on his honeymoon. We're in Northern California right now on our way to Seattle. We're coming to see you, Libby."

"What?" Libby snapped, hoping she had heard incorrectly.

"I said Evan Rider and I are coming to Seattle to see you. Here, I'll let him say hello."

There was a rustling sound as the phone was passed from one hand to another. Then Libby heard the unmistakable voice of Evan Rider through the receiver. "Libby, this is Evan," he said solemnly. "I'm sorry about this, but I had no choice about—"

Evan's voice was overpowered by Jakes saying, "That's enough," and Libby heard the phone being passed again.

"I just wanted you to hear his voice, Libby, so you know I'm not jerking you around," Jakes said. "We're coming to see you all right. Won't it be great: Tango, Choo-Choo, and the Jet together again after all these years?" His voice was thick with sarcasm.

Libby rolled her head back, squeezing her eyes closed and clenching her teeth in silent protest. Then she pushed out the question that had been boring into her since she first recognized Jakes' voice, "Why are you doing this, Nolan? We agreed never to talk to each other again. What do you want with me?"

Jakes released a little laugh which was devoid of humor. "Yes, I guess you need to know what this little reunion is all about. So here's the deal."

Jakes recited in succinct sentences the bare facts of his trouble with the law, his escape from Los Angeles with Evan's "help," and his intention to disappear into Canada with his girlfriend. He told her that Evan had agreed to drive him to the border. He explained without apology that he expected Libby and Evan to provide generous contributions to his retirement fund from their abundance, adding, "It's the least you two successful doctors can do for your old friend after all we've been through together."

Libby didn't need to hear the punch line; she had already figured it out. But Jakes gave it anyway. "I make the same promise to you that I made to Evan, Libby: If you don't help me and I get caught, I will tell our story to the police—the whole story, names, places, everything. It's as simple as that. Do I make myself clear?"

A wave of anger and despair rolled up Libby's throat from deep in her soul. "I can't believe you would do that," she said, forcing the words through the bitter taste of her inner turmoil.

"Oh, I'll do it all right, Jet," Jakes answered. "I'm a desperate man. I'll do anything to stay alive and out of prison. If you two don't give me what I want, so help me I *will* take you down with me. We're going to be just like the Three Musketeers on this deal, Libby—all for one and one for all. Either we all get out of this or we all go to prison."

Libby said nothing as she rapidly searched for a loophole in Jakes' logic. In his college days, Jakes wasn't known for his wit or intellect. *Perhaps he has left something undone,* Libby thought frantically. *There must be a way out.* But she came up empty.

Jakes said, "Think about what I've said, Libby. I'll call you in a few hours to tell you what I want you to do. You would be a fool to call the police—unless you want to throw your life away as well as your son's."

There was a brief, muffled conversation in the background, then Evan was on the phone. "Libby, Nolan has allowed me to tell you that he has a gun. He's holding my wife, my daughter, and me hostage. I beg you to cooperate for their sake."

Then Jakes took the phone again. "I'll call you when we get closer to Seattle. Don't do anything or talk to anybody, do you understand?"

Libby forced her response. "Yes, I understand." Then the phone went dead.

Libby put down the phone and covered her mouth with her hands. She had every right to fall apart and burst into tears, but she didn't. Instead she sat on the sofa and trembled, taking breaths in short, noisy gulps. As she searched for reason in the attack and scrambled for a way out, she was overcome by an old, familiar scene.

She saw herself again precariously balanced atop a high wire, inching cautiously toward her career goals. Brett's break-in Friday night and his vehement personal attack Saturday had seriously disrupted her balance. Libby was afraid Brett would continue to hurt himself and her if she didn't yield to his demands to know the identity of his father. Little did Brett realize that such a revelation—that he was the product of her union with a white man—might be one too many obstacles between her and the coveted prize of university president.

But remarkably, Libby had recovered from Brett's emotional blow. Thanks to the wise, timely words of Reginald Burris, she had gained a new perspective on the issue of Brett and his father. Brett needed to know about the man, and Tango needed to come to terms with the consequences of the passionate act which resulted in Brett's conception twenty-two years ago.

Furthermore, Libby had determined in the few hours since being with Reginald that she would likely be less hurt by telling Brett the truth than by withholding it as he continued to sabotage her career. It all seemed so logical and appropriate after talking to Reginald. Libby had decided to tell Brett about Tango as soon as she could contact him and arrange a meeting. She had tried to call him again, but as before there was no answer and his voice mail was still apparently shut off.

Now, in her first moment of peace about Brett in months, here was an even more serious threat to her tenuous perch. Nolan Jakes stood on the platform threatening to cut the wire and send her plunging out of control to the floor below. She had been only an accomplice in the unfortunate killing of Neil McGruder, and perhaps she would get off with a reduced or suspended sentence if she went to trial. But the impact on her career couldn't be worse if she was convicted of first degree murder and sentenced to life imprisonment. Her reputation would be shattered. She feared that she would be fired by the university and blackballed from higher education. Everything she had worked for would be lost forever. Life for her would be over.

And what would happen to Brett? What personal pain and emotional damage would he suffer upon discovering that his mother, and his father whom he had yet to meet, had contributed to someone's death on the night he was conceived? How would he deal with the shame of his parents going to prison for murder? What impact would such baggage have on his pursuit of a career and a peaceful, happy life? It seemed unfair that a young man who had suffered so much from not having a dad should be subject to further humiliation.

And then there was the issue of Evan Rider and his family, whose lives might be jeopardized by Libby's failure to comply with Jakes' wishes. The thought of a gun being involved sent a chill down her spine. Was Nolan Jakes desperate enough to resort to physical harm if he didn't get his way? Libby must think not only of herself and her son, but also of the other family being threatened in Jakes' plot. The stakes in the cruel game were not limited to a career and a mother-son relationship. There was the potential of someone getting shot. Did Libby really want to be an accomplice to another killing?

At the end of all her frantic reasoning, Libby was still face to face with a man she hadn't seen in twenty-two years standing at the end of her wire with a cable cutter ready to send her tumbling. If Libby didn't do what he wanted, she feared that all hell would break loose—on herself, on Brett, and on Evan Rider and his loved ones.

Libby stood and tugged her robe tightly around her. She drew a long breath and released it. Her trembling subsided. There was really only one choice: Do whatever Jakes asked. It would cost her some money—perhaps a lot of money. But all the money and treasures she had accumulated couldn't buy back what she would lose if Jakes cut her life out from under her. She would cooperate with the plan to get Jakes out of the country.

As to the morality of such a choice, Libby assessed that she was no more immoral or criminal by helping Jakes escape than by living a lie over the past twenty-two years. She was not numb to her part in Neil McGruder's death, but she had succeeded in compromising with her conscience to delay confession to a more convenient time in the distant future. Complicity in Jakes' escape would simply be added to the list of crimes and sins she would have to atone for some day.

Having reached the decision to cooperate, Libby headed for the kitchen to get something for the massive headache which had overtaken her in the last ten minutes. But another staggering realization stopped her dead in her tracks: Brett's father would be in Seattle in a matter of hours, perhaps never to pass this way again. Was this the time to try to get them together, despite the unusual circumstances of their meeting? If so, she would have to reveal to Brett the reason for his father's coming. Was she ready to tell Brett everything? Was she ready to arm him with the same information to destroy her that Nolan Jakes now possessed, in order to get father and son together?

Libby continued toward the kitchen with the questions swirling through her mind like leaves at the mercy of a whirlwind. She decided that she had plenty of time to consider every one of them, because she knew she wouldn't sleep a minute until she heard from Jakes again.

The words she had overheard continued to assault Shelby as she lay on the sofa bed in the dark, while the coach swayed through the turns in the mountain road.

"Won't it be great—Tango, Choo-Choo, and the Jet together again after all these years?"

Where did those names come from, Evan? Shelby demanded silently. *You were apparently very close to Nolan Jakes and Libby Carroll at one time. Why haven't you told me about them before? Who are they? What power does Nolan Jakes hold over you?*

"I make the same promise to you that I made to Evan, Libby: If you don't help me and I get caught, I will tell our story to the police—the whole story, names, places, everything. It's as simple as that."

What story, Evan? And why didn't I hear about Nolan Jakes' threat to tell "the whole story"? What are you keeping from me about taking Nolan and Margo to Canada?

"If you two don't give me what I want, so help me I will take you down with me. . . . Either we all get out of this or we all go to prison."

Why would Jakes threaten to "take you down" with him? How could he promise that all three of you might go to prison? What have you done, Evan, that could send you to prison?

With each distressing question, Shelby pushed away the idea that her new husband had a past that could be used against him. Evan had argued with her during their courtship that he wasn't a saint, that he struggled with feelings of guilt about his past. But Shelby always assumed that he was referring to sins common to many unbelievers—hatred and jealousy between coworkers, shades of dishonesty on an income tax return, an occasional moral indiscretion—never anything worthy of a prison sentence. *It can't be so of Evan*, she argued with herself. *He's not a criminal*. But the conversation between Nolan Jakes and Libby Carroll left her with sizable doubts.

Evan had attempted to catch Shelby's eye in the mirror several times since Jakes ended the conversation with Libby Carroll. She guessed that he wanted to assure her of his concern for her or be assured himself that she was not disturbed by what she heard. But Shelby had blocked his view craftily with a corner of the afghan, as if avoiding the intruding gaze of a stranger.

Fifty-two

At precisely 8:37 P.M. the complexion of the surveillance of Rennie Barbosa changed dramatically. At that moment, according to the display on the Hawkeye, Barbosa reached the junction of Interstate 580, which veers westward to the Bay Area. If the Peruvian had business in San Francisco or Oakland, the blip on the Hawkeye monitor would follow the line identified as I-580. If the blip continued north on I-5, it meant he was headed for Stockton, Sacramento, Reno, Redding, Oregon, Washington, or perhaps even Canada.

Cole watched the monitor eagerly from the passenger's seat of Beth's rented Barego, which had closed the gap between it and the Town Car to sixteen minutes. Cole had predicted unequivocally that Barbosa would take the cutoff to the west, but he stopped short of wagering Beth on the issue despite the razzing he took from her.

"He's headed north," Cole said with a sigh, as he watched the blip sail past I-580 without hesitation. Beth gave another victory whoop, even though she hadn't won anything. Cole secretly wished he *had* wagered Beth, assuring him of another date with her.

When the Hawkeye tracked the Town Car to the junction of I-5 and I-80 at Sacramento an hour later, Cole let Beth twist his arm into betting her another dinner. Beth maintained that Rennie Barbosa would keep going on I-5. She was convinced that the man was headed for Portland or Seattle. For the sake of competition, Cole wagered that Barbosa would take the I-80 cutoff east toward Reno, even though he secretly agreed that their runaway must be headed north.

As he expected, Cole lost the bet. The Town Car, which the Hawkeye reported had dropped its speed to 70 through the more densely populated area of California's state capital, continued north on I-5. Beth had also reduced her speed through the area.

As soon as the blip left Sacramento, resuming a speed of almost 80, Beth started talking about restaurants again, this time mentioning some of her favorite spots in Seattle, "Which is where we will be for dinner tomorrow night," she predicted, adding, "Want to bet?"

Cole diverted her attention to the Barego's fuel gauge, which had been touching the empty line for several miles. "We have to stop in Sacramento," he said, watching the distance grow between the blip on the screen and the city it had just left. "Barbosa will have to stop somewhere between here and Redding. He's got to be under a quarter of a tank."

Twelve minutes later they took the Florin Road exit south of the Sacramento city center for another Indy 500-style pit stop. This time Cole filled the tank while Beth raced into the AM/PM for a couple of jumbo javas and a bag of pretzels.

It was still in the mid-60s at 10 P.M. in Sacramento, a pleasant night after a day in the 90s. Unable to hurry the pump, Cole stood at the rear of the Buick stretching the kinks out of his back and legs as the gasoline flowed into the tank. Beth had driven the entire trip so far, despite his offers to spell her.

With the junction of Interstate 80 just a few miles ahead, Cole sensed he was at a crossroads again regarding the pursuit of Rennie Barbosa. When he really thought about what he was doing—something he had tried to avoid thinking about since he left L.A.—he was a little embarrassed with himself. Here was a Los Angeles police detective nearly 400 miles from the city using a civilian vehicle—and its civilian driver—for an unauthorized surveillance pursuit of an FBI suspect. Even the LAPD Hawkeye locater unit had left Southern California without the approval or knowledge of his supervisors.

You have overstepped your jurisdiction on this one, buddy, he addressed himself squarely. *You should have alerted the FBI hours ago, whether they did anything about Barbosa or not—and they wouldn't have, not until he struck again. Face it: You're hooked on a game of Chase the Bad Guy and you can't let go of the joystick.*

Cole switched hands on the nozzle to stretch out his other arm. As he did, he mounted a defense. *On the other hand, I'm on vacation. I can do what I want, go where I want, and follow whomever I want. I will return the Hawkeye in one piece when I'm finished playing with it. And if in the process of watching Rennie Barbosa I prevent another murder somewhere, I'll probably receive a commendation from Chief Robinson.*

But this time chagrin over his boyish actions got the best of him.

Staying with Barbosa seemed like a dumb thing to do. At I-80 he could turn to the northeast and be at his mother's Lake Tahoe home, just across the California–Nevada border, before 1 A.M. He could probably talk Beth Scibelli into spending the week with him, especially if he spaced out the two dinners he owed her. He could show her a wonderful time around the lake. And they would have time to talk—plenty of time for him to explain how the events of the last two years had brought him to a place of faith and peace, time for him to encourage Beth in the same direction—if he could.

His mother would love having Beth around for a few days, Cole knew. In point of fact, Jacqueline Cole would welcome the company of any young woman who looked interested in rescuing her son from the ranks of the unattached. Cole would have to warn Beth to ignore Jacqueline when she pried about bedroom colors, china and silver patterns, and how many children she planned to have "if and when you marry."

Yes, as much as he wanted to stay with Barbosa, the idea to call off the hunt, notify the FBI, and head east to Tahoe with Beth seemed like a good one. He needed some time off. He wanted some time with Beth. And he didn't have a valid reason for playing super sleuth all the way to Canada or Alaska.

Cole didn't tell Beth about his decision to head east. They reentered northbound I-5 with Cole behind the wheel at Beth's request. Beth was in the passenger's seat with the Hawkeye monitor glowing from the floor. Cole pushed the Barego up to 70 MPH to merge with the flow of light traffic in the fast lane. They didn't talk for several minutes as they nibbled on pretzels and sipped coffee, which was strong and hot.

They breezed through the city, past Old Sacramento and the capitol building and across the American River. The junction of Interstate 80 was three miles ahead. Cole planned to surprise Beth by taking the I-80 transition road. When she tried to correct him, he would tell her he was giving up on Barbosa and going home to mother. She would be pleased.

When he moved into the right lane to position himself for the I-80 exit, Cole felt another check inside. It was a quiet flashing amber light calling him to evaluate his decision. He had little more than a mile to respond, barely a minute.

Is there something wrong with going to Tahoe? he questioned himself. *No, I planned to go there long before Barbosa headed north and changed my plans.*

Is there something wrong with taking Beth to Tahoe? No, my motives are right. I'm not taking her there for immoral purposes. I wouldn't take advantage of her.

Then am I being cautioned about giving up the chase? he thought incredulously. *Am I supposed to keep going north for some reason?* The sign for I-80 East was coming up fast. If he was going to change the plan, he had to do so in the next fifteen seconds. Beth was oblivious to his inner turmoil, playing with the tuner on the radio in search of some decent music before Sacramento was out of range.

It wasn't a feeling and it wasn't a voice. But Cole was clearly aware of an intelligible inner impression which communicated a simple idea: *You followed Barbosa this far for your reasons. I want you to keep following him for My reasons.* Cole didn't have time to ponder the concept, and he certainly didn't have time to discuss it with Beth, who would surely think he was nuts if he did. He didn't understand it himself, but for some reason—God's reason, he assumed, although he couldn't understand why God would be interested in Rennie Barbosa—he was supposed to keep following the blip on the Hawkeye monitor. With little to go on but an inner directional arrow, Cole moved back into the fast lane and sped past the I-80 exit.

Cole was suddenly back in the Chase the Bad Guy game, except it was no longer a game. There was something more to the pursuit than trying to outsmart a criminal. There was a deeper purpose. Cole didn't know what that purpose was, but he felt exhilarated at the prospect of finding out. He breathed a few phrases to God about what he was thinking and feeling. He asked for patience and insight. He committed himself to stay with the pursuit until he felt an inner release from the assignment. And he wondered if he would ever be able to tell Beth about what had transpired in his mind as they approached and then passed I-80.

"How much time did we lose during our pit stop?" he asked Beth, over the strains of Haydn's "Symphony 44 in E Minor" pouring from the Barego's speakers.

Beth leaned toward the monitor on the floor for a better look. "Barbosa is sixteen minutes ahead of us," she reported. "He's cruising at 78 again."

"I want to reduce the gap. I want to get closer."

"We'll gain on him when he stops for gas," Beth reminded.

"Yes, but I don't count on him stopping for long." Cole accelerated to 83 and engaged automatic cruise as the city lights faded distantly behind them. "And after he refuels, I want to stay within five minutes until he gets where he's going."

"You must be catching your second wind," Beth said, laughing lightly. "What did it for you? The industrial strength coffee? Getting behind the wheel?"

Cole thought of the inner challenge to go north instead of east. He also thought of the beautiful woman with him and the curious circumstance that had brought them all this way together. "Inspiration," he answered without explanation.

For several minutes they were silent, enjoying music from a classical station that was rapidly losing strength. Beth reclined her seat several notches and propped her bare feet up on the dashboard, relieved to be out of the driver's seat. Miles of farmland in every direction was shrouded in darkness with only an occasional twinkle visible from a farmhouse. The inside of the car was also dark except for the faint glow of the display panel and the Hawkeye monitor, and the periodic, momentary invasion of an overhead light from the freeway.

With every mile that passed under the Barego's wheels, Cole felt better about his decision to keep after Barbosa. The flashing amber light inside had faded to black soon after he passed I-80. It had been replaced by a sense of anticipation and confidence—bordering on boldness—which seemed to energize him even though he couldn't identify its source or purpose.

It was this surge of confidence that prodded Cole to turn off the crackling radio and introduce a subject which had been in the forefront of his mind since he first said hello to Beth at the Riders' reception little more than thirty hours ago. In reality, Cole had been thinking these thoughts and mulling over the questions since he last heard from Beth over a year ago.

"What happened to your faith after Millennium's Eve, Beth?" he asked, trying not to sound threatening. He was glad that he had to keep his eyes on the highway. His question was invasive enough without him prying further through eye contact. The darkness around them also seemed to work in favor of Beth's privacy.

The hum of the tires and gentle whish of the air conditioning reigned for several moments before Beth responded. "You're assuming that I *possessed* faith after Millennium's Eve."

Cole was relieved that Beth didn't sound defensive or evasive. "Well, didn't you?"

Beth allowed another gap of thoughtful silence. "I don't know, Reagan," she said with a sigh. "I'm not sure if what I had was a religious encounter, an emotional high, or just a sense of relief after a near-death experience."

"But you prayed when you were in trouble."

"Oh, yes," Beth agreed emphatically. "I prayed like I've never prayed in my life."

"So did I and a lot of other people. And you thanked us and told us that God pulled you out of a terrible mess and spared your life."

"Yes, although I like to think that God and I worked together during that crisis. I did what I could. He did what I couldn't."

"Okay," Cole said, smiling at her independence. Then he needled her good-naturedly, "But if God hadn't stepped in, what you could do wouldn't have been enough, right?"

Beth laughed. "All right, you've got me there. I confess, God pulled me out of a terrible mess and spared my life."

"And you thanked Him for it, right?"

Beth responded thoughtfully, as if processing her answer for the first time. "Yes, I thanked Him every day. I thanked Him for everything: for my life, for the two books I was able to write about my experience. I even thanked Him for you."

Cole beamed inside. He was pleased that Beth was dealing with the subject so candidly. The last thing he wanted to do was drive her further away from himself or from God with his bold probing. But neither did he want to squander an opportunity to peek into her soul and try to help her if he could. His early success prompted him to move ahead. "So what happened then?"

Beth crossed her feet on the dashboard and crossed her arms at her chest. Cole interpreted her body language to mean that she might be threatened by the question. He waited.

"I don't know what happened, Reagan," she said softly. "Those first two months after Millennium's Eve were really wonderful. I felt very close to God—I really did. Spending time with Dr. No and his wife at King's House, getting reacquainted with my parents and learning to understand their faith, hearing Shelby Hornecker—what's her name now, Rider?—tell about how God sustained her through her ordeals, all made a positive impression on me. And being with you and watching you interact with Dr. No and sort through your own relationship with God was a big plus too."

Cole kept his eyes trained on the road ahead illumined by the Buick's headlights. He did this to communicate his respect for Beth's privacy while welcoming and affirming what she wanted to tell him. He sensed her discomfort for the transparency he was requesting of her, and he loved her for continuing.

After several moments of silence, Beth said, "I suppose if I had stayed in Los Angeles and gotten involved at King's House, things would have turned out differently."

"Things?" Cole probed gently.

"My life," Beth clarified. Then she sighed heavily. "Despite the success and the money, it's been pretty crummy since I saw you last."

"But you couldn't stay in L.A.," Cole said, leaping to her defense to show his support. "You had books to write. You had a career path to follow. You had a home in Washington to maintain."

"I could have stayed. I didn't need to be home or anywhere else. I can write wherever there's electricity for recharging the computer and a good restaurant for celebrating a completed manuscript. As you know, I'm not very fond of L.A. But there were very good reasons for me to stay last year. I just didn't see them—or maybe I didn't want to."

Cole waited silently, allowing Beth to continue at her own pace. She shifted her feet on the dashboard again and cupped her hands between the back of her head and the headrest.

"What I *did* see was the glory of being a bestselling author. So I went after it and forgot what happened to me on Millennium's Eve. I guess that's the answer to your original question. My faith didn't leave me; I left it behind in pursuit of greener pastures."

Cole was amazed at how emotionally detached Beth seemed from what she was telling him. She was able to process her thoughts and report the conclusions—including concessions of weakness—with the same honesty and confidence that she would evaluate a position-by-position match-up between the Seattle Supersonics and the Los Angeles Lakers.

"And how do you feel about that choice now?" Cole pressed.

Beth released a low hum as she framed her response. "Up until a few days ago, I might have defended it—perhaps naively."

"A few days ago? You mean the 'disagreement' with your publisher in the Caribbean?" Cole asked.

"Right. The experience kind of burst my bubble, blew me out of the water, whatever metaphor you want to use. Before last week I guess I had convinced myself that I could get along very well without L.A., without King's House, without . . . certain people I once regarded important to me—"

"And without faith?"

"Yes, I was making my way in the world very nicely without faith, without God—or so I thought. I had a couple of books out and others on the way. I had my choice of assignments and companions. Then last week—*bam!* Somebody pulled the plug on my virtual reality unit. The fantasy was suddenly over, and I was back to where I started last year."

"Is that why you came to L.A. from the Caribbean instead of going home?"

Beth squirmed under the question. Then she nodded, perhaps hoping Cole wouldn't see her in the dark. He did. She added, "They say that when children from dysfunctional homes are under stress, they regress to their last secure activity or environment—thumb-sucking in a dark corner in the closet, assuming the fetal position. It's like they never got past that part, so they snap back to that behavior when something goes wrong.

"Flying out of Miami yesterday, when I saw Shelby's wedding note in my calendar, I just knew I had to get to L.A. Maybe it's because I felt good about being here last year before I screwed up, and I had to come back and get it right."

Cole was silent, mostly because there was a lump forming in his throat that would have choked off anything he wanted to say. He was deeply moved by Beth's uncharacteristic honesty and transparency. He was moved at the hurt and disappointment she had suffered since he had last seen her. He was moved by the sudden realization that his simple daily prayers for her were being answered. Her efforts at finding peace had failed. She had returned to the place where she last experienced it.

Cole reminded himself that his relationship with Beth and her relationship with God were mutually exclusive. As much as he loved Beth and wanted her for himself, he knew that it was possible for her to rekindle her faith without rekindling her love for him. Yet as soon as he had regripped his emotions, he couldn't help but ask the other question which had plagued him for well over a year. "What happened to *us* after Millennium's Eve?"

Beth released a light, one-syllable laugh, assuring Cole that she wasn't agonizing under his relentless interrogation. "I figured you'd get around to that eventually."

"You don't have to answer, Beth. I'd just like to know if . . . " Cole let his words trail off. He wasn't quite sure what he wanted to know and if he really wanted to know it. But he had to ask.

For the first time in their conversation, Beth brought her seat forward and turned to face the driver's side of the car. Cole looked her way just long enough to make brief contact with her eyes, which glistened in the darkness. Then he turned back to the road, expectant of her response.

"I've been asking myself the same question since I saw you yesterday," she said. "All these months I believed that *you* were the reason we didn't stay together."

"Me?" Cole pondered aloud.

"You changed in those first months after Millennium's Eve, Reagan. You weren't the same man I fell in love with the week between Christmas and New Year's. Instead of talking about basketball and food and motorcycles and running away to Mexico, all you wanted to talk about was King's House and God and prayer. As far as I was concerned, the more interested you became in those things, the less interested you became in me."

Cole jumped in. "But I wasn't less interested—"

"Let me finish," Beth interrupted, touching him on the arm. Cole nodded.

"I'm not saying I was *right*; I'm saying that's what I *believed*. I thought your involvement with God took something away from you as a person and took something away from us. I was afraid that if I stayed involved with you, our relationship would take something away from me, and I wasn't about to give up anything, especially on the threshold of a career breakthrough. So I thought it best to ride quietly into the sunset."

It was Beth's turn to wait quietly as Cole processed her confession.

"You suggested that you have been reevaluating that decision since we met again yesterday," Cole said. "What did you mean by that?"

Beth looked up the freeway for a moment, then turned back to Cole. "I mean I'm questioning my decision to walk away from you."

Cole could feel his heartbeat accelerating with anticipation. "What makes you question that decision?"

Beth answered quietly, "First, the way you treated me yesterday." Then she dropped her head as she continued. "Last year, I walked away from you without so much as an explanation or a good-bye. If you had dumped me that way, your name would have been dirt in my mouth. So when I arrived at the reception yesterday, I wouldn't have blamed you for blowing me off completely, not having anything to do with me.

"But you were as kind and approachable as ever. I couldn't believe it. You're either very naive and gullible or very forgiving. I think it's the latter, but that's a hard pill for my pride to swallow. Anyway, I was touched by the way you welcomed me as if I had never hurt you. Thank you."

A thousand macho, romantic quips crowded into Cole's brain, begging for expression. He also wanted to reach out to embrace Beth for her honesty. But it wasn't the right time for him to respond, so he said nothing and kept his hands on the wheel.

Bolstering her courage, Beth looked at Cole again and continued. "Second, I was wrong about how your new interest in God would affect you. I thought your involvement at King's House would take something away from you, diminish your value to me. I was wrong. It's *added* something to you, Reagan. I can't put my finger on it exactly, but there's a quality of strength and self-assurance about you that I didn't notice last year. And it's a very attractive quality."

Beth's compliment astounded Cole, both in its content and in her forthrightness to give it. In his self-consciousness, he was tempted to defend his unworthiness of such a comment. But he restrained himself and simply said, "Thank you."

"This is very hard for me to say, Reagan," Beth said, dropping her head again, "but I'm at fault for the disintegration of our relationship. I'm sorry for walking out on you last year without saying something. It was very thoughtless and selfish of me. I hope you can forgive me. I'd like to forget about last year and see if we can at least be friends again."

Having painfully delivered her soul, Beth turned forward in her seat again, straddling the Hawkeye on the floor. That's when she noticed that the blip on the screen was stationary. Before Cole could respond to her apology, she blurted out, "He stopped!"

Cole craned his neck for a view of the monitor. The steady flashing light on the map was camped in Williams about eleven miles ahead of them, one of a number of small towns clinging to the Interstate between Sacramento and Redding. The time according to the monitor was 10:41 P.M. The distance between the two cars had dwindled to nine minutes, and it continued to shrink with every second the Town Car sat at the pump.

"Great!" Cole exulted. "We've almost caught him. We may even have his taillights in sight when he leaves Williams."

Then the car was silent again and Cole returned to contemplating Beth's apology. Finally he said, "If you're looking for assurance of forgiveness, Beth, you've got it—both from God and from me. As for starting over, I'd like that very much."

Their hands found each other in the dark across the console as if they had never let go.

MONDAY
June 25, 2001

Fifty-three

Evan worked the brake cautiously as the RV descended the winding freeway from 4,300-foot Siskiyou Summit toward Southern Oregon's Rogue Valley. He felt uneasy about constantly reining in the nearly nine tons of motorhome, cargo, and trailer which gravity beckoned to the valley floor at runaway speeds. Signs announcing TRUCK ESCAPE, designating a sand-filled ramp up the side of the mountain—a safety net for runaway rigs, soberly reminded Evan of the frightening consequences of brake failure during the long descent.

At one point he was startled by a cruel, unbidden thought: *A fiery, fatal crash at the bottom of the mountain would certainly solve everything. Nolan Jakes and Margo Sharpe would be judged for their criminal acts, and I would be spared the embarrassment of revealing my secret past to Shelby or anyone.* But he quickly rebuked the ugly thought. He dared not wish such a catastrophe on his wife and daughter to effect such a selfish solution to his problems.

It was a little past 2 A.M. Jakes had been at his post in the other front seat since they left Red Bluff, remaining awake but rarely speaking. Margo had stayed up until the swaying coach got to her stomach. She had been lying down in the bedroom since before midnight. From what Evan could see, Shelby had been asleep on the sofa bed with Malika for the past three hours.

Behind them lay 150 gas-guzzling miles of mountain highway which skirted Lake Shasta and Mt. Shasta and such communities as Dunsmuir, Weed, and Yreka, California. They had passed the WELCOME TO OREGON sign at 1:35. The up-and-down mountain trek had slowed the RV to an average speed of under 50 MPH. And the concentration demanded to negotiate the ups, downs, curves, and slow trucks in a large and unfamiliar vehicle had sapped Evan of strength.

Emerging from each new curve down the hill Evan searched the darkness for the lights of Ashland, which he knew was only a few miles ahead. But he saw nothing, as if the foothill community had suffered a massive power failure. Passing the twelve-mile post near the base of the mountain, Evan and Jakes both discovered the reason for the darkness.

"Fog," Jakes muttered, adding a curse.

Evan again went to the brake as the big RV descended into the wispy fringes of a fog bank like an airliner descending into a cloud. Within a minute they were engulfed in the soup. Visibility immediately dropped to mere feet beyond the massive curved windshield, forcing Evan to slow to 20 MPH. The coach's powerful halogen headlights could do no more than illuminate the thick gray curtain before them, not penetrate it.

"I don't want to go this slow," Jakes said. "Push it a little."

"Are you crazy?" Evan snapped, raw with fatigue and tension. "We're already going too fast. If we come up on a stalled car or an accident, we'll plow into them for sure. I'm not taking that chance." Then he let up on the accelerator a fraction more.

"It's the middle of the night; there aren't that many cars on the road," Jakes insisted, cursing. "Keep it moving, Evan. Get back up to 25."

Evan realized that the pressure of the escape and the strain of the winding mountain road was taking a toll on his former friend. But he wasn't about to jeopardize his family to humor him. "I'm not going to do it, Nolan," he said, raising his voice. "The fog will only last a few miles, and we'll be back up to 60 again—or 70 if you like, to make up the time."

The reduced speed allowed for reduced road noise. Margo came forward from the bedroom at the sound of conflict in the cab. Shelby also lifted a sleepy head from the sofa bed to investigate. Malika slept on undisturbed.

"I want to go faster," Jakes said, clearly on the ragged edge of control. Then he jumped out of the cab and brushed Margo aside. He grabbed Shelby by the back of the neck, jerking her up to a sitting position while brandishing the pistol in his free hand. Shelby squealed in pain and fear. Malika stirred but did not waken.

"Listen, Rider, I'm tired of this trip, and I want to get where I'm going," Jakes growled. "You don't have any bargaining chips, but I do." He gave Shelby a gruff shake until she hissed at the pain. "Now get that speedometer up to 35 or your bride is going to be very uncomfortable for the rest of the trip."

Evan gripped the wheel in anger at Jakes' treatment of Shelby. He wanted to slam on the brakes right now and send the man flying through the windshield or at least into the dashboard where Evan could pound his face. But he couldn't do it with the loaded pistol in Jakes' grip and with Shelby and Malika likely to get injured in a sudden stop. Furthermore, hurting Jakes without killing him wouldn't solve the ultimate problem of his blackmail threat.

Margo, who had been standing behind Jakes, took his gun hand gently and pulled it away from a threatening position. "Honey, the fog frightens me," she said in a syrupy, pouty tone. It was the first time Evan had heard her call Jakes "Honey." "If we crash in the fog, the trailer will roll over or come through the back end, and we won't have a car or a bus to get us to Canada. Let's go slow, honey, please, at least until the fog lifts."

Evan watched in the mirror to see if Margo's clearly manipulative sweet talk would do any good. Amazingly, Jakes gave in, though not without a brief squall of profanity directed at no one in particular. He released Shelby, gave the gun to Margo, and stormed back to the bedroom to lie down, grabbing a can of beer from the refrigerator on the way.

"Thank you," Shelby said to Margo when Jakes was out of earshot. She rubbed her sore neck and sat up on the edge of the sofa bed, tucking the afghan around Malika.

Margo ignored Shelby's thanks. Turning to Evan, she said, "I wouldn't try that again if I were you. It could be bad for everybody."

"He wants us to play Russian Roulette with the fog," Evan responded, still upset. "And that could be *deadly* for everybody."

Margo dropped the conversation and retreated to the kitchen to make coffee. The RV pushed steadily through the fog at 18 MPH as if wrapped in a giant, dirty cotton ball. Evan could barely see the center line six feet in front of the coach.

Taking advantage of Jakes' departure and Margo's preoccupation in the kitchen, Shelby moved into the front passenger's seat, still rubbing the back of her neck. She kept the seat swiveled toward the driver as she buckled in. Margo saw her but seemed not to mind.

Evan spared her a quick glance. "Are you all right?"

"My *neck* is all right," she answered.

Shelby's inference was clear to Evan. She was not *completely* all right. He feared that his bride had heard too much of Jakes' earlier phone conversation with Libby Carroll. Evan had winced then as Jakes used phrases like "tell our story to the police," "take you down with me," "we all get out of this or we all go to prison." He feared that Shelby would be confused, suspicious, and alarmed that Jakes had implicated him in such mysterious activities and drastic consequences.

"Did you sleep?" Evan asked, further assessing Shelby's emotional state. He could feel her eyes studying him.

"Not much," she said.

Evan recognized that the opportunity he had prayed for was upon him. He and Shelby were alone in the cab. The limited road noise allowed for a nearly normal level of conversation. But he hesitated at taking advantage of it. Margo would doubtless hear everything—if she didn't break up the visit before it began. And Evan wasn't sure he wanted to bare his soul in front of a stranger.

Shelby abruptly ended his hesitation. "A few hours ago you said that we needed to talk," she said. "I overheard what Nolan told your mutual friend, Libby Carroll. I think we need to talk now." There was an urgency in Shelby's voice Evan could not dismiss.

For the next half hour, as the RV edged northward on I-5 past Ashland and Medford in the dense valley fog, Evan haltingly described the fateful night in Portland twenty-two years earlier. He decided early in his story not to compromise the details of the event which had left such a blot on his soul. He told Shelby everything: his blind hatred for

Neil McGruder, the beating he and Jakes administered while Libby drove and watched, the horrifying discovery of McGruder's death, the frantic cover-up, the years of haunting guilt and rationalization.

The more Evan talked, the more he wanted to tell. Like a pent-up flood at the opening of a giant valve, the past gushed from him. It was cathartic, healing, freeing. It didn't matter to him that Margo listened from the dinette after surprising Evan and Shelby by bringing them mugs of hot coffee. Margo likely knew most of the story anyway, Evan surmised, so there was no need to hold back.

Shelby was clearly stunned by Evan's revelation, weeping softly from the moment she realized that he had helped kill a man. But she stilled his fears of rejection and encouraged his confession with affirming nods and appropriately placed comments like "Yes," "I understand," "O Evan, I'm so sorry," "It's all right."

Apology and supplication for forgiveness rolled out with Evan's contrition, and Shelby generously complied. Evan could have cried through his story, but he denied himself the luxury. He had to get it out, all of it, without pausing for an emotional breakdown. And he had to keep the RV safely on the road in the perilous fog. He would cry someday when this was all over, and cling to angelic, forgiving Shelby as he did so.

"So Nolan blackmailed you into this trip by threatening to confess to the Portland affair, naming you and Libby Carroll as accomplices," Shelby summarized, dabbing her eyes with a handkerchief from her purse.

"Yes," Evan said, "that's why I have to cooperate."

"But darling, you can't hide your crime forever," Shelby said, sounding surprised that he hadn't grasped that point already. "Whether Nolan brings it up or not, you're going to have to face the music for what you've done."

"What do you mean? I've confessed it to God—repeatedly over the last two years, and now I've confessed it to you. You don't expect me to confess to the police, do you?"

When he glanced at Shelby for a response, Evan saw a strained expression on her face, as if she had been suddenly saddled with an enormous weight. "Evan, it may have happened a long time ago, and it may not have been entirely your fault. But a man died because of your actions. The statute of limitations doesn't expire on murder. It's still an open case." Shelby bit her lip at the seriousness of the subject matter. "You have to make it right. You have to turn yourself in."

Evan suddenly felt betrayed by the only person he felt he could trust. "But that was a long time ago, Shelby. I've changed. I'm a new person. My life belongs to Christ now. You said yourself that the past is forgiven and forgotten. We've talked about all that, remember?"

Shelby gripped the handkerchief to her mouth as she weighed Evan's words and considered her response. "You really don't understand, do you?" she said at last. Her question was free of condemnation.

"Understand what?" Evan pressed, anxious to clarify the issue.

Shelby framed her words carefully. "Darling, being forgiven for our sins is one thing. Making retribution for the consequences of our sins is quite another. God has forgiven you for what you did back in Portland, and I forgive you. But, as much as I hate to think about it, you have to make it right. You have to face the legal consequences. You have to face . . . " Shelby broke down and buried her face in the handkerchief. But she recovered quickly to finish. "You have to face the young man's family."

"That's ridiculous, Shelby," Evan retorted. He was irritated that his newfound liberty from the shackles of his past was so quickly threatened. "What I did back then is either forgiven or it's not. If it's forgiven, why do I still have to pay for it?"

Shelby seemed to be struggling as much with the pain of the concept as Evan. "It's just a biblical principle. If I steal something from someone, I ask God's forgiveness and pay back what I stole. If I commit a crime, I ask God's forgiveness and submit to the punishment. Because of Christ, my sin is forgiven. But the consequences of my sin must be made right. It's part of living righteously. I thought you knew."

Evan's head swam with turbulent, conflicting thoughts. "But I'll lose my career," he said feebly. "I could go to prison. McGruder's family may file a civil suit and clean us out. I can't let that happen, Shelby. I have a responsibility to you and Malika. Isn't that more important than something buried in the past?"

"All the success and money in the world won't matter if you don't do the right thing," Shelby said. "You won't be happy. *We* won't be happy. We'll be running from what you did all our lives, as if trying to hide Neil McGruder's body in our closet. And if the truth is ever discovered, you'll be in even greater trouble for withholding it. By turning yourself in, you may get a more lenient sentence."

Evan felt angry, trapped. He responded cynically, "So what am I supposed to do—drive into the next town and turn everybody in?"

Shelby didn't have a chance to answer. Nolan Jakes, who had been listening from the dark kitchen, rushed forward, startling even Margo as he scooped up the gun from the table. He angrily threw the afghan aside and grabbed sleeping Malika by the arm. Jakes jerked her up from the bed and dangled her in front of him like a plush toy. She screamed with pain and fright in her half-asleep state. Jakes' eyes flashed madness even in the dark coach.

"If you want to talk about consequences, Mrs. Righteous-and-Holy," Jakes snarled toward Shelby, "talk about this. If you make one move to turning us in, I'll kill this little brat." He gave another jerk on Malika's arm, and she shrieked at the pain.

Shelby reacted instinctively. She unsnapped her safety belt and sprang from her seat in the cab. Evan went for the brake and aimed the RV toward the freeway's shoulder in the fog. Margo remained at the table watching.

"You sit down!" Jakes yelled to Shelby, waving the gun at her.

Shelby did not obey. She lunged at Jakes in a blind panic to save her child. Jakes swiped at her with the weapon, cuffing her on the side of the head. The blow buckled Shelby's knees and the momentum sent her sprawling across the sofa bed. Jakes dropped the struggling, howling child on top of the stunned mother.

Evan cursed loudly at Jakes as he attempted to stop the coach. He was two seconds from pulling the emergency brake and charging the gunman himself.

"Stop this van and I'll hit the girl, Rider," Jakes roared. "I'll hit them both. I'll keep hitting them until we're moving again. And if you come after me, I'll shoot you—I swear I will." He raised the gun over Shelby, who had collected the terrified, whimpering Malika in one arm while holding the side of her head with the other hand.

"Don't you dare touch them, Nolan," Evan commanded, adding curses he hadn't uttered in two years. He watched Jakes through the mirror. The RV was barely rolling along the shoulder of the freeway.

Evan's rage demanded that he leave his seat and throw himself at the evil man who was menacing his wife and daughter. But he quickly considered the stakes and calculated the odds. With great restraint he returned his right foot to the accelerator and slowly increased speed in the fog. Checking the side mirror, he eased the coach back into the right lane at 20 MPH. His arms and legs trembled from the massive adrenaline surge.

Jakes relaxed his threatening pose over Shelby and Malika. "You're a smart man, Rider," he sneered.

"Shelby, are you all right?" Evan called out, unable to see her clearly in the mirror.

"I'm . . . I'm okay, Evan," Shelby called back in a quavering voice. She lay on her stomach with Malika halfway under her. The girl's sobs and sniffs were muffled by the afghan. "Keep going, darling," Shelby encouraged. "We'll be all right."

Jakes called to Evan, "I don't care what your wife or your conscience tell you to do about our little incident in Portland, Rider. But if you try to turn yourself in before Margo and I are safely across the border, you won't have to worry about the consequences, and neither will your wife or daughter. Do you understand me?"

Evan didn't want to dignify Jakes' threat with a response. But for the sake of his family, he responded almost civilly, "I understand, Nolan."

Jakes turned to Margo. "Take these two to the back and make sure they stay there," he said. Evan watched in the mirror as Jakes pulled Shelby, with Malika hanging around her neck fearfully, up from the bed onto wobbly legs. She had the handkerchief pressed to the side of her face. Evan thought he detected a dark blotch on the hanky.

Margo ushered them back to the bedroom and directed them to lie down on the bed. Making sure the blinds were securely drawn, she turned on one of the reading lights on the headboard. As Evan watched, Margo closed the door from the inside.

Without another word to Evan, Jakes took a beer from the refrigerator and sat down at the dinette to drink it in the darkness.

Evan gripped the wheel to calm his nerves. I-5 was climbing out of the valley and the low-lying fog was breaking up, easing at least one point of tension on the trip. Evan figured they would be in and out of the fog all the way to Roseburg, with the freeway winding through the hilly terrain of Southern Oregon.

Disillusionment clouded Evan's brain like the gray soup swirling around the coach. He was in a no-win contest. Shelby and Malika were still in mortal danger, and he had come within seconds of being shot himself. Even if he succeeded in getting Jakes and Margo across the Canadian border, Evan now faced a new crisis. Shelby had in effect issued an ultimatum: Plan on confessing your part in the Neil McGruder murder or forget about calling yourself a decent Christian. Any way he turned, it seemed that a ruined career and prison awaited him. The darkness surrounding him was stifling.

As the RV increased speed over a fairly clear hilltop, Evan took a halfhearted attempt to plow through the foggy, dark thoughts pressing in on him. It was one of the most difficult but logical responses he could imagine. He started praying again.

Fifty-four

Cole crawled right by the first Medford exit without seeing it in the fog, and he nearly missed the second. Then he almost hit a pickup truck which emerged from the fog just as Cole made a left turn across the highway into the service station.

The herky-jerky motion of the car awakened Beth, who had been dozing in the passenger's seat for about an hour. "Where are we? What time is it?" she asked, unwilling to open her eyes under the brilliant lights of the service station.

"It's 3:15," Cole said as he stopped at the pump, "and we're in Medford to get gas."

Beth opened one eye to a slit to check out the Hawkeye monitor at her feet. It located Barbosa's Town Car a few miles north of Medford traveling at 27 MPH. "The guy is barely moving," she said, quickly shutting her eye against the brightness. "What's the problem?"

"Take a look for yourself," Cole said as he got out of the car and closed the door. The cool, moist air which had rushed inside touched Beth's bare legs, prompting her to sit up and force her eyes open.

"Fog," Beth said to herself. Then, stepping out of the car and embracing herself in the chill, she asked, "When did this start?"

"Coming out of the mountains, about twenty miles back," Cole said as he removed the gas cap. "Barbosa was a couple miles ahead of us when his taillights suddenly disappeared and his speed dropped to 25. I didn't see this stuff until I drove into it. We've been creeping for half an hour."

Beth excused herself to race to the warmth of the rest room. Cole reached for the nozzle of unleaded fuel, but an attendant serving a minivan at the next island, a chunky girl wearing grease-stained jeans, a flannel shirt, and a stocking cap, called out, "I'll be right with you, sir."

"That's okay, I'll do it myself," Cole assured.

"Not in Oregon, sir," the girl reprimanded, clearly pleased at the chance to one-up a Californian. "State law. I have to pump it for you."

Cole remembered. Oregon and New Jersey remained the only two states in the country to deny motorists the convenience—or save them the chore, depending on the driver's outlook—of a self-serve pump. The issue appeared on the state ballot every couple of years, but independent Oregonians steadfastly refused to change.

Cole acquiesced with a shrug. "Okay, but I'm kind of in a hurry. Fill it with unleaded." Then he hurried inside for a personal pit stop.

Beth took the wheel as they returned to the freeway at a snail's pace. She was invigorated after standing for several minutes in the misty night air. The two travelers sipped from twenty-ounce cups of coffee. Beth hoped the potent brew would help keep her awake during her turn at the wheel. Cole welcomed the warm liquid to relax him and perhaps allow him an hour of sleep.

They had lost several minutes while the slow-moving attendant filled the tank. Then the cashier, who proudly boasted to Cole and Beth about being the pump jockey's mother as she processed the bankcard, had droned on and on about the fog. "It can hit us any time of the year," she had said, "and sock us in to a standstill." The woman, who was twice the size of her daughter and equally interested in enlightening travelers, was still talking as the couple walked out the door with the receipt. "The fog isn't so common during the summer months, but when it rolls into the valley it can be deadly. I remember a wreck out on the road to Eagle Point—"

Watching the blip on the screen, Cole could tell that the fog was dissipating ahead. Barbosa's speed fluctuated between 25 and 50 over the winding, hilly freeway between Medford and Grant's Pass. Cole cautioned Beth not to drive faster than her limited visibility, reminding her that they would catch Barbosa again after they cleared the fog. And Beth reminded *him* that she lived in the Northwest and knew how to drive in the fog and that he didn't have to worry about her, thank you very much. Cole smiled with deep pleasure, saluted her with his coffee cup, and reclined his seat to relax.

"I don't want to sleep with you, Reagan." The comment came after ten minutes of silence. Cole was so surprised at what he heard that he thought he must have dreamed it.

"I beg your pardon," he answered.

Beth laughed an almost giddy laugh. "I mean, I *want* to sleep with you, but not now—not until we're married, except it's a little early to know if we will get married."

Completely nonplussed, Cole shook his head to clear the cobwebs. "Did I miss something? Did I drop off for a while? Did I propose to you—or proposition you—in my sleep?"

Beth laughed again. There was a little-girl quality in her voice, a relaxed naiveté Cole had never heard in the year and a half he had known her. He loved it; it suited her. He hoped it reflected the personal peace she was beginning to taste, in response to the many months he had prayed for her.

"No, I've just been thinking about us," she said.

"Thinking about sleeping together or not sleeping together? Thinking about getting married or not getting married?"

"Not exactly. I've been thinking about what we discussed earlier, about our relationship getting back to where it was over a year ago. We almost slept together after Millennium's Eve—at least I expected us to sleep together. But I don't think it would be right now. I just want you to know how I feel about it."

Cole still couldn't believe what he was hearing, but he decided to accept it at face value. "I'm glad you feel that way," he said. "Thanks for telling me."

"What I mean is," Beth pressed on energetically, "since we're starting over, I think we need to focus on our friendship instead of our physical attraction."

"Yes, that's a good idea."

"But you are still attracted to me, aren't you?" Beth said.

Cole couldn't remember being asked by a woman if he was physically attracted to her. It was refreshing. "Well, er, yes," he answered. "I'm very much attracted to you."

"Physically? Sexually? Personality?"

"All of the above. Most definitely."

"Good. So am I. But we can't think about the physical and sexual part now. We need to build on our other strengths, identify our common interests."

"Like Mexican food and Kawasakis?" Cole suggested, enjoying the repartee.

"Yes, and pizza with artichoke hearts and sun-dried tomatoes."

"The West Coast."

"Fast breaks and slam dunks."

"Telemann trumpet concertos."

"Tulips and tall doorways."

"Books by Beth Scibelli."

"Amen!" Beth laughed. "We're on a roll now."

"Marimba music and kung pao chicken."

"Laurel and Hardy movies."

"With popcorn."

"Buckets of popcorn."

"Buckets of *hot, buttered* popcorn."

"While we're at it," Beth said, "we might as well identify our common *dis*interests."

"The East Coast, like east of Colorado."

"Ticky-tack fouls."

"Athlete's foot and biased news reporting."

"Polka music and professional wrestling."

"Apartheid and secondhand smoke."

"Anything made out of styrofoam."

"Anchovies and junk mail."

"Shopping carts that don't roll straight and garden hoses that kink up."

"Hold it," Cole interrupted. "We also have to talk about interests we *don't* agree on."

"Absolutely," Beth agreed. "Like they say, opposites attract."

"Like they also say, if two people are the same, one of them isn't necessary."

"Absolutely," Beth reiterated. "That's why I like living on Whidbey Island and you like living in L.A."

"I would enjoy living on Whidbey Island," Cole objected playfully. "We could agree on that."

"Yes, but I could never like living in L.A.," Beth countered.

"That means we disagree on something. That's good. That's healthy."

"I'm a Democrat, and you're a Republican."

"But we both vote for the man, not for the party."

"You may vote for the *man.* I vote for the *candidate."*

"Same thing."

"I disagree."

"That's healthy," they chimed in unison.

The lists went on for several minutes. The laughter rolled and rolled.

"Here's a big one, Reagan," Beth said. "If we end up getting married, I'm keeping my maiden name. I want to be known as Beth

Scibelli-Cole, except for my by-line which will remain Beth Scibelli. Is that something we agree on or disagree on?"

The recurrence of the "M" word in the conversation sobered Cole a little. He had thought about marriage often over the past eighteen months. And when he did, Beth's face was always the one he saw when he lifted the veil. But he had practically given up hope that he would actually be talking with her about it.

Encouraged by Beth's directness, Cole was inspired to respond in kind. "Before we talk about that, I need to understand something else about us, Beth. It's about God and faith and following Christ. Is it one of the common interests we're going to build on, or will it always be one of our points of disagreement?"

He thought about adding, "Because if you're not interested in a life of faith, all the common interests we have won't be enough to hold us together, so we might as well part company now." But he decided not to apply unnecessary pressure. He wanted to hear Beth's opinion without hanging an ultimatum over her head.

Beth was silent for a moment. Large holes were opening in the heavy blanket of fog, allowing her to increase speed as the highway rose from the valley floor. It appeared as if the worst was behind them.

When Beth finally spoke, she was serious. "Well, without a common interest in following Christ and living by the Bible, all our other interests don't amount to much, do they? What's the use of staying together if we don't agree on the essentials?"

Cole shook his head in wonder. *Among her many other talents,* he exclaimed to himself, *this beautiful woman is also a mind reader!*

Dawn was a welcome sight after half a night of oppressive, irritating, progress-hindering fog. Barbosa rubbed his grainy eyes and dismissed the temptation to close them for longer than a blink. It was 5 A.M. He had been awake almost twenty-four hours now, and he would likely be awake another twenty-four before he had finished his work and found the safe haven which had been offered to him during the night. To go long stretches without sleep was difficult and at times unpleasant, but it was part of the hunt.

He passed the fish hatchery on the South Umpqua River almost to Roseburg. The sun was up beyond the Cascades to the east, but most of the landscape was still shrouded in mountain shadows. The sky was clear over the entire state. The temperature would hover around the mid-70s in Western Oregon today with negligible humidity and an inviting breeze. It would be one of those pleasant summer days that tempts the residents of the parched Southwest and the steaming Northeast and Southeast to consider moving to the temperate Northwest. And it would be one of those days that makes residents fear that others *will* invade the Northwest.

Barbosa's personal phone was on the burgundy leather passenger's seat. He answered it after the first tone. "Go ahead."

"Did you negotiate the fog all right, Mr. Barbosa?" Bishop said;

"Yes," he answered with no interest in chitchat.

"And where are you now?"

"Roseburg."

"You're making excellent time! You should have the motorhome in view in less than an hour. Remember: It's a big white rig pulling a small red station wagon on a car carrier."

"Yes, I remember. How soon can I move in?"

"Probably somewhere north of Seattle," Bishop informed.

"Seattle?" Barbosa snapped. "That's at least another five hours. Why not sooner? Why not now?"

"I remind you, Mr. Barbosa, that timing on this transaction is critical. Taking out Mr. Jakes and his party too soon is counterproductive to my purposes. I must have your assurance that you will not move in until I give the word."

It took a few seconds for Barbosa to quiet his negativism. But he had to sound cooperative for his client.

"Yes," he said. "You have my word."

"And is it clear that Jakes and all his companions must be eliminated at the same time?"

"Yes, it's clear."

"Do you have any problem taking out women and children?"

"No."

"Excellent. I know I can depend on you. Just keep the motorhome in sight, and I'll talk to you again closer to Seattle. In the meantime, enjoy the beautiful scenery."

Barbosa hung up without responding.

Fifty-five

Shelby awoke with the left side of her face throbbing. Before opening her eyes, she took a sensory inventory of her surroundings. Light permeated her eyelids. She was lying on the bed in the RV which, judging by the loud hum and steady vibration, seemed to be moving again at freeway speed. Malika was still pressed against her and asleep. Her left cheekbone was bruised or broken from the blow she had received from Nolan Jakes during the night.

Hazarding a look, she noticed that the reading lamp above her was on. Light was also visible seeping through the drawn blinds on the right side of the coach, telling her that dawn had broken. She saw that she and Malika were alone in the bedroom; Margo had apparently left while she was asleep. The bedroom door was now open, allowing Shelby to gaze the length of the coach to where her husband sat at the controls. Sunlight streamed into the cab through the giant windshield.

Shelby also saw Nolan Jakes hunched at the dinette with his back toward her. Margo was not visible in either of the passengers' seats up front, nor did she appear to be lying in the sofa bed behind Evan. Shelby guessed that Jakes' girlfriend was in the bathroom, where she seemed to spend an inordinate amount of time.

Shelby moved her hand slowly up to her face. The left side was swollen and tender to the touch. Her left eye also seemed a little puffy. She ran her finger lightly across a thin scab about an inch long that followed the ridge of her cheekbone. She tried to be grateful that Jakes' pistol had hit her there instead of cracking her skull, breaking her jaw, or knocking out a few teeth. She was *truly* grateful that Jakes had hit her instead of striking Malika.

Shelby lay still, trying to remain unnoticed by her fellow travelers as she gathered her wits. She was aware of an ache even more painful and pervasive than the laceration and contusion on her face. *Evan killed a man twenty-two years ago. He has concealed the truth from me ever since I've known him. He's planning to take Nolan and Margo to Canada and keep his crime a secret. If he's caught, he'll likely spend years in prison. As long as he succeeds in his subterfuge, I have to live a lie to protect a criminal. What kind of future is that for me and Malika? Dear God, are You still punishing me for my failures? Will You ever allow me to love a man of purity and integrity?*

She had been sympathetic and affirming as the secrets of Evan's dark past tumbled into the light a few hours earlier while the RV crept through the fog. *That's what a good wife is supposed to do,* she reminded herself. *I vowed before God to love Evan in good times and in bad, for better or for worse.* But now, as dark thoughts rolled through her mind like the waves of a tropical storm, Shelby felt deceived, betrayed, abandoned. She wasn't sure what her responsibility was to her Christian husband if he persisted in his deceit. She wasn't sure God expected her to stay married to a murderer who refused to confess his crime and endure the consequences.

Mercifully, Shelby was rescued from the inner storm by the stirring of the little body lying next to her. Malika rolled to her side and whined. Opening her eyes in Shelby's face, she winced and said simply, "Mama, ow. Mama, ow." The sounds were muffled by the loud hum of tires on pavement. Malika reached her little brown right hand to touch her opposite shoulder. Shelby recalled with anger the gruff treatment she had suffered at the hands of the maniacal Nolan Jakes.

Shelby reached out to enfold the frail little girl, who was still wearing a pink sweat suit. She stroked Malika's shoulder and arm gently and whispered comforting words of love. Shelby only hoped the inner bruises from Malika's terrifying experience would go away as easily as the soreness to her young muscles would.

Jakes drained his third cup of coffee and checked his watch. It was 5:30. The four Tylenol he had tossed down with his first cup were taking effect, numbing the wounds on his back.

Bundles of $100 bills were lined up and stacked on the table. Jakes had hoped that recounting the staggering amount of cash would quiet his nerves as the pain reliever had soothed his back. But it hadn't. Even half a million dollars couldn't wipe away the nerve-racking awareness of the obstacles yet standing between him and sanctuary across the border with his reward and his woman. The foolish stunt Evan's wife pulled in the middle of the night was a solemn reminder of everything that could go wrong. The money in front of him only made Jakes more anxious to get where he wanted to go.

Margo stepped out of the bathroom between the kitchen and the bedroom and slipped up behind Jakes. She wrapped her arms around his shoulders, careful not to touch his sensitive back, and kissed him warmly behind the ear and down his neck. Her dark hair was cool and damp, and she smelled of soap, moisturizing lotion, and fresh nail polish.

"You've been in there an hour," Jakes said, soothed by Margo's fragrance and sudden affection, but trying not to show it.

"Forty minutes tops, Nolan," Margo cooed, nuzzling him softly from behind. "Besides, today is our big day. I wanted to look and smell my best for the beginning of our new life."

"Did you take a shower?"

"No, I just washed my hair and took a Marine bath."

"You still have to wear that wig."

"I know, I know," Margo giggled. "But at least I'll be squeaky clean underneath it." Then she moved into the center aisle where Jakes could see her. "And how do you like my new outfit?" She struck a model's pose in tan cotton shorts and a lightweight, V-neck, forest green pullover sweater pushed up at the sleeves.

"Where did you get that?" Jakes asked, surprised by how desirable she looked.

"Mrs. Rider's wardrobe," Margo announced proudly. "I even found a few things to take along, including a couple of very sexy nightgowns for a brand new bride."

Jakes nodded and allowed himself a brief smile. "Sounds great," he said. Then he was again crowded by the details of getting out of the country in order to enjoy the vision before him. He began returning the bundles of bills to the nylon sport bag which had traveled with him from Dodger Stadium. "I want to call Libby Carroll now and tell her where to meet us," Jakes continued, more businesslike.

Margo retrieved her purse from the bathroom and sat down in the dinette opposite Jakes. "I made a few calls to directory service while my nails were drying," she said. "I found an InterCorp Bank in Seattle near the university and not too far off the freeway. It takes all the major cards. Your friend in Seattle should know right where it is."

Digging for the phone and her notes while trying not to scratch her nails, Margo knocked her purse over. Several items tumbled out on the table, including the phone, a makeup bag, and Margo's billfold, which flopped open to her California driver's license.

Jakes stopped packing the money to look at it. "Why does it say Margo Rene *Bishop?* Your name is Sharpe."

Margo collected her billfold and returned it to the purse. "Sharpe is my maiden name," she said. "My husband's name was Bishop. When I divorced him, I took my name back. I was going to change it when I renewed my license."

"You've never told me anything about your husband," Jakes said. "What was he like?"

"Gary Bishop was a first-class low-life," Margo spat, "the scum of the earth."

Jakes stared at her, silently inviting more information. Margo complied.

"He was a bush league club singer in Hollywood. Our talent agency represented him. I saw him in the office once or twice a week. He fed me a lot of bull about getting recording contracts and scoring a few bit parts in cable movies. He showed me a good time and flashed around some big money. I fell for him, and we were married about two months after we met.

"Come to find out the contracts and movie deals were lies, and the big money was from drug deals. He was in pretty deep. For all I know he could have been working for your old boss. Do you recognize the name?"

Jakes shook his head. He had never heard of Gary Bishop before.

"Anyway, I caught on to his secret life and dumped him fast."

"Where is he now, this Bishop?" Jakes probed, as he finished packing the money in the bag.

"I don't know. The company tore up his contract about two years ago, and I haven't seen him since. He's probably dealing drugs somewhere in the sewers of L.A."

Jakes studied the pretty face across from him. "Well, in a couple of days Margo Bishop, Margo Sharpe, and Nolan Jakes will also disappear forever. We will both need to find new names."

"I've been looking forward to it," Margo said with enthusiasm. "We can be a married couple, of course. Less suspicious that way. I kind of like Dressler for a last name—not too common, not too uncommon.

Rather believable, don't you think?"

Jakes zipped the sport bag closed and pushed it to the window on the table. The blinds had never been opened during the trip. "We'll have plenty of time for names, Margo. Right now I need to call Libby Carroll. Where is the bank you found?"

"Here it is," she said, shoving a small notebook across the table. "InterCorp Bank, University Branch. Thirteen hundred Northeast Forty-Fifth at the corner of Brooklyn Avenue. It's in the University District. She'll know right where it is."

"And they take all the cards for savings, line of credit?"

"Yes. They run your card, you tell them how much you want and sign the form, and they bag it up for you. No limit. It'll be easy."

Jakes sighed heavily at the thought of such a chancy maneuver. There were so many variables. Any one of the hostages could get cold feet or suddenly feel heroic. Last night Shelby almost had her husband talked into driving the bus up to a police station and turning everyone in. So many things could go wrong. Yet a mass bank withdrawal seemed substantially more efficient and profitable than any other method he could think of for tapping into his former friends' wealth. And Jakes wasn't about to leave the country without as much money as possible.

"Easy? Let's hope so," Jakes said. "Give me the phone."

Evan lowered the shade on the windshield to block some of the glare pouring into the RV from the sun cresting the eastern mountains. Still he squinted his tired eyes against shafts of light coming through the side passenger window. When they made their final fuel stop, which Evan guessed would be in Salem or Portland, he would adjust the shades better. He doubted that his two captors would show themselves in the cab in daylight, even to pull a shade for him. And he was sure they wouldn't let Shelby ride up front with him. He would have to handle everything in the cab himself.

A sign along the freeway announced that they were nine miles from Eugene, Oregon, home of the University of Oregon, graced by the Willamette and McKenzie Rivers. Freeway traffic at this time—still an hour away from Monday morning rush hour—consisted mainly of eighteen-wheelers and vacationers in minivans and motorhomes. The most notable exception was the dark red Lincoln Town Car Evan had noticed in the sideview mirror. The luxury sedan had been traveling about 200 yards behind the RV for the past several miles. It was the only vehicle on the freeway which didn't pass him. Why a big, smooth-riding boat like that would be content to poke along at 63 MPH. was a puzzle.

Evan had spent the last 150 miles, while the fog and dark gave way to summer's early light, thinking and praying about his confession to Shelby. He had been both encouraged and troubled at her response.

Her tearful sympathy and concern had touched him and spurred him on to "full disclosure." But he was taken aback by her dogged insistence that he tell the world about his part in Neil McGruder's death. And the idea that her argument might be theologically correct was a painful blow, prompting a prolonged, predawn conversation with God.

Why would You want me to turn myself in? You forgave me for my sins. You made me a new person. You said old things are passed away. You said my sins are buried in the sea, as far as east is from west. I have made things right with You and with Shelby. Atoning for my mistakes is a mockery of faith and forgiveness.

God didn't seem to answer him. At least, Evan didn't want to believe God had answered him. The only thing that came to his mind was a story he had heard Shelby read to Malika once from a Bible storybook. It was about a weasel of a tax collector with one of those strange Z names: Zedekiah, Zacharias, something like that. The Z-man was a real crook, squeezing extra tax money out of people to line his own pockets. Everybody hated him.

Then the Z-man met up with Jesus and became a man of faith. The astounding thing was that he paid back his victims *four times the amount he had extorted from them.* Evan thought he remembered that the Z-man did this of his own free will. Jesus hadn't required it of him.

Still unsettled about the idea, Evan tried another tack with God. *Going to the police with my story isn't very considerate of Shelby and Malika. I just committed myself to love them and take care of them "till we are parted by death." I will not be able to fulfill that vow from a prison cell. I will not be able to provide for them if I lose my practice. You certainly don't expect me to forfeit my commitment to meet a stiff biblical requirement. I know You prefer love over law.*

After several minutes Evan had exhausted that approach without sensing any peace. He was left with only one plea. *God, I've worked so hard for my practice, my home. And now You have brought the most wonderful woman into my life. If I come forward with the story of Neil McGruder, I'll lose everything. I'll be humiliated in front of my peers. I'll bring shame on Shelby and her family and her former church. And I'll be unable to continue the work You gave me to do at King's House, and perhaps Shelby's ministry will be curtailed. Please don't allow such a horrible blot on our lives. We have so much we want to do for You.*

As he rolled into the Eugene city limits, Evan's back and legs were sore from inactivity. His eyes burned from hours of constant alertness. He was distressed about the pain and anxiety he had caused his wife and daughter. The only hope appeared to be on the northern horizon: the Canadian border. Delivering Jakes and Margo seemed the most logical and expedient means to getting his life back on an even keel.

Evan sensed that he hadn't heard from God, and he wasn't even sure that God had heard him. God seemed no more interested in Evan's plight than did the driver of that burgundy Town Car lazing behind the RV. Evan wasn't happy about the distance he perceived between himself and God, but he decided it would not keep him from contending with God until he received some kind of answer.

In the rearview mirror he saw Shelby and Malika stirring in the bedroom. How he wanted this to be over for them, and how he prayed that God would spare them any more pain.

In the dinette, Jakes was making a phone call, most likely to Libby Carroll. Evan prayed for her too, that somehow she would survive such a cruel invasion of her life.

And in the side mirror he noticed that the big Town Car was exiting the freeway. Eugene must be the driver's destination. Evan rather hated to see his fellow freeway traveler leave. He only hoped God wasn't ready to abandon him too.

Fifty-six

Libby's phone sounded just before 6 A.M. She had been expecting the call for seven hours, ever since Nolan Jakes shocked her with his first call and assured her that he would call back. She had paced and worried and prayed most of the night, hoping the threat had been a hoax, a cruel stunt by Tango and Choo-choo. The beeping phone dashed those hopes.

But the call she had been expecting turned out to be the call she had all but given up hope of receiving.

"Yes," Libby answered.

"Mom." Brett's tone was cool but not hostile.

Libby tried to contain her relief at finally hearing her son's voice. "Brett, I've been trying to reach you."

"I—I shut off the phone, mom. I didn't want to talk to you."

"I understand. I'm sorry about the other day. I'm glad you called. I need to talk to you."

Brett pressed on with his agenda. "Sorry about calling so early, but I wanted to catch you before you got to work."

"It's all right, I've been up for a while. Where are you?"

Brett hesitated. "That's why I called. Andie and her parents convinced me that I should at least let you know where I am. I'm in Spokane—at Andie's mom and dad's. We came on the bus last night. I'm going to spend the rest of the summer here. You can forward any personal mail—no ads or stuff—to their address. It's in the file on the kitchen computer."

"Brett, I have something to tell you," Libby interjected hastily, fearful that, having delivered his message, Brett would hang up on her. "Something very important."

Brett was silent a moment. Libby heard a sigh of reluctance coming through the phone. "What is it, mom?" Brett said, sounding unconvinced that what she had to say would be important to him.

Libby began slowly and deliberately with the monologue she had formulated and rehearsed through the night. She hoped she could do it without breaking down. "I've been thinking very seriously about what you said Saturday. I've come to realize that I have been selfish. You deserve to know about your father." The tears Libby feared filled her eyes, but she kept moving ahead. "I'm prepared to tell you everything you want to know."

"Are you serious?" Brett's response was rife with skepticism.

Libby swallowed hard to continue. "Yes, I'm serious. You want to know, so I have decided to tell you."

"So what's his name? Where does he live?"

"I can't tell you over the phone, Brett. I want you to—"

"I thought you were serious," Brett snarled.

"I'm completely serious, honey. Please hear me out. Late last night I learned that your father will be in Seattle today."

The momentary silence communicated Brett's shock. "You talked to my father?" Brett's tone had changed to reflect acute interest. "I thought you two didn't communicate."

"We haven't talked for almost twenty-two years. Then last night I got this phone call. It came out of the blue. I had no idea where he was or that he was on his way to Seattle."

"Did you tell him about me?"

"Not yet, but I plan to."

"Are you going to see him?"

It was difficult for Libby to continue. She was afraid that Brett would be disappointed in what she would tell him about Tango. And she was afraid that what she told Brett might ultimately come back to hurt her. But she had made the decision in the middle of the night to tell Brett everything. She could not back down now.

"Yes, I've been waiting for another call to tell me where and when. If you can get back here this morning, I'll take you with me. I'll introduce you to him today."

Brett whispered an expletive which Libby barely heard. "Really, mom?" The skepticism in Brett's voice was melting to boyish expectancy.

Libby wiped tears from her eyes. "Yes," she answered in a shaky voice, "but I must warn you—you aren't going to like everything you learn today about your father and me. But I won't keep it from you any longer."

"Mom, are you all right?" Brett asked with genuine concern.

Libby started to cry. "No, I'm not all right, honey. But I'll be much better when you get here. Will you come?"

There was a break in the conversation. Libby could hear voices in the background. Then Brett was back on.

"Mom, Andie's dad is going to loan us a car. We'll be back as soon as we can. It'll take us about four hours. I should be home before 11."

"Please leave your phone switched on, Brett." Libby wiped her eyes and nose with a tissue as she spoke. "I may need to call you again."

"I will. We'll leave right away. Don't worry." Then Brett added, "I'm sorry about Saturday, mom. Things built up. I really thought you were against me."

"We'll talk about it, honey. Drive carefully."

Libby barely had time to compose herself before Jakes called.

"I've been trying to get you for several minutes," he said threateningly. "You haven't been talking to the police, have you?"

"No, not the police." She almost told him who she had been talking to, but changed her mind. "I promise I'll do whatever you ask."

"Do you know where the InterCorp Bank is in the University District?" Jakes was serious, all business.

"Yes. Forty-Fifth and Brooklyn."

"Is there a parking lot near there?"

"There's a big lot right behind the bank on Brooklyn."

"Be there at 10:30 this morning. What are you driving?"

"A blue Seville, dark blue."

"Wait in your car until I arrive. And bring all your bank cards."

"I will."

"And remember, Libby, if you mess with me, somebody will get hurt. I'm sure you wouldn't want a child's injury or death on your conscience. Besides, if I go down in this deal, you and Evan are coming down with me. Are we completely clear on that?"

"Completely, Nolan. I will cooperate."

"Good choice. Ten-thirty, then, behind InterCorp."

"I'll be there."

Jakes snapped the phone closed, stood, and worked his way forward to the cab. "The Jet is ready to cooperate with me, Rider," he said spitefully. "She has no problem with conscience, and she has no holy joe boyfriend who thinks she should blow the whistle on us. I think she's going to be a big help to my retirement. I hope you're planning to follow her example."

Evan did not respond to Jakes' comments. Instead he said, "We're getting low on fuel, and I need to take a break. Where do you want to stop?"

"What's coming up?"

"Albany in about forty miles, Salem in another twenty."

Jakes inspected the fuel gauge. "Rider, we have another 100 miles before we start running on fumes," he said condescendingly. "And you're tough; I know you can hold out for an hour or so. We'll stop at Salem, no sooner." Turning toward the dinette, he said, "Margo, fix the man another cup of coffee."

"Ms. Scibelli, I'd like to introduce you to Mr. Rennie Barbosa," Cole said, tongue in cheek. "Mr. Barbosa, this is Beth Scibelli."

Cole and Beth stood outside the black Barego coupe in a service station near the freeway in Eugene as the attendant topped off the tank. The couple watched the service station across the street where a burgundy Town Car was loading up on fuel. Cole and Beth had discreetly shielded themselves from the view of Rennie Barbosa, who neither saw nor heard them as he paced around his big car impatiently.

"It's a pleasure to be formally introduced, Mr. Barbosa," Beth said for Cole's amusement, "but I believe we have already met. Remember the elevator back at the Airport Hilton in Burbank?"

"Of course, Señorita Beth," Cole said in a weak Latino accent. "If you had been just a little friendlier in Burbank, you could be riding in my luxurious Town Car now instead of that cramped little Buick."

"Thanks, but no thanks, Rennie old friend," Beth kept up the patter. "I have always believed that being crowded into a coupe with a good friend is ultimately safer than riding in a big limo with a killer."

Despite the brightness of the morning sun, it was chilly in the shade of the service station's awning. Beth kept seeking patches of warm sunlight to stand in as they observed Barbosa. Cole kept a low profile as he scrubbed petrified bug guts off the windshield with the sponge side of a squeegee. While motorists were not allowed to pump their own gas in Oregon, the law didn't apply to cleaning windows. Do-it-yourself squeegees were abundant, but windshield service was not.

"I have a question for you, Mr. Barbosa," Cole mused aloud. "Why are you in such a hurry over there to get back on the freeway when you have kept your speed at just above 60 for the last several miles?" He and Beth had theorized about Barbosa's significant drop in speed coming into Eugene, which had also forced them to slow down in order to stay a safe distance behind. The idea that Barbosa had reduced his speed to improve gas mileage was thrown out early by the pair. Other ideas were similarly discarded. Had the slowdown been the result of car trouble, Barbosa would have stopped miles back at Cottage Grove or Creswell. If he was leery of getting a speeding ticket from the Oregon State Police, he had overdone his reaction. He was almost as conspicuous to the police at 60 as he would have been at 80.

For lack of a better idea, Cole and Beth agreed that the Peruvian must be ahead of schedule for his next appointment, so he pulled in the reins on the Town Car to make up for it.

Cole's interest in Barbosa had waned through the night. The urgency he sensed outside Sacramento to keep on the hit man's trail had obviously been for Beth's sake. The deep, meaningful conversations the two travelers enjoyed during the long night on the road might not have happened if Cole had turned east to Lake Tahoe. Beth had not only flung open the door to reestablishing their relationship, but had also expressed a genuine interest in reestablishing her faith in God. Cole had quietly thanked God several times for keeping them on I-5 and using him to encourage Beth. It was the most productive sleepless night he had ever spent.

As for Barbosa, Cole wasn't as constrained to follow him as he was curious about the man's final destination. They had followed the Town Car almost 1,000 miles from Los Angeles and knew no more about his objective than when they started. But they would know within the next few hours. If the man had a job to do in Portland, they were little more than 100 miles away from finding out what it was. If his destination was Seattle, another 180 miles would tell the tale.

If Barbosa was headed out of the country via Canada, Cole would need to drive only 100 miles beyond Seattle to know it, at which point he would notify the FBI to call the RCMP. Then he and Beth would head for her place on Whidbey Island—Beth had already invited him for a visit. In a day or two he would drop Beth's Barego at the SeaTac Galaxy Rent-a-Car lot and fly down to Lake Tahoe before returning to L.A. Cole felt that he was too close to the end of the book not to read the last couple of chapters, even though he doubted that the conclusion would be any more exciting than the dull story so far.

Cole and Beth watched Barbosa pay for his gas and leave for I-5, oblivious to their casual observation. "Looks like he's ready to blow out the carbon again," Cole said as the blip on the Hawkeye monitor raced up to 75 MPH. They paid for their gas, raced through the drive-up window of a McDonald's for breakfast sandwiches and coffee, and hurried after the Town Car. Barreling up the onramp, Cole saluted the experience by ad-libbing through a couple of lines from an old Willie Nelson tune, sung with appropriate nasal twang:

On the road again, we're back on the road again.
What I like is traveling I-5 with my friend;
Yes, we're back on the road again.

Fifty-seven

Jakes insisted that Evan drive through Salem, even though the fuel gauge warned that the RV was dangerously low on fuel. The freeway and surface streets in the state capital bustled with rush hour traffic at 7 A.M. Jakes did not want to deal with the crowd. So the RV joined a mass of commuters leaving Salem for Portland, less than an hour north via I-5.

For twenty-five minutes the RV traversed the lush green farmland of the upper Willamette Valley with a river of traffic flowing northward. Snowcapped Mt. Hood, a majestic 11,000 feet tall, was clearly visible ahead. It stood guard over the greater Portland area from sixty miles to the east like a white-haired giant.

Jakes directed Evan to exit the freeway at the little town of Woodburn, about halfway to Portland. They pulled into the first service station they came to, which was far less crowded than the stations they had avoided in Salem.

After the refueling, which was superintended by Margo wearing Shelby's clothes and the platinum blonde wig and shades, Evan pulled the rig to the back of the lot to park. Jakes had insisted that Evan shave his dark twenty-four hours of stubble in preparation for their visit to the bank. Evan convinced Jakes to allow him a fifteen-minute break to clean up and look at Shelby's cut. Then he promised to drive the rest of the way to the border so Shelby could take care of Malika.

Evan determined that Shelby's cheekbone was not broken, just severely bruised. The cut could have used a few small stitches, had Evan gotten to it soon after it had opened. But the wound was already scabbed over. He told his wife that it would heal nicely, leaving only a slight scar. And he assured her that the blow would not result in a black eye.

As Evan checked Shelby's face, they searched each other's eyes for answers, hope, and encouragement. Evan's turmoil over Shelby's response to his confession had diminished very little over the past five hours. Thankfully, love and acceptance was present in her gaze and her touch, though Evan wondered how Shelby would deal with his continuing reluctance to turn himself in. He tried to communicate through his eyes that their ordeal with Jakes and Margo would be over in just a few hours. Then he, Shelby, and Malika would have a good cry and sort out what to do next.

Evan washed and shaved, then changed into summer cotton slacks and a short-sleeve print shirt with a collar, more acceptable attire for visiting a bank to withdraw tens of thousands of dollars in cash. As Evan hastily dressed, Shelby brewed fresh coffee for everyone and prepared a meal of hot cereal and fruit for her family. Jakes allowed Evan only a few bites of breakfast before herding him back to the driver's seat. They were back on the freeway before 8.

Margo moved into the kitchen next to fix scrambled eggs and toast for herself and Nolan Jakes, a "first day of the rest of our lives celebration breakfast" she called it. Jakes celebrated very little, keeping a wary eye on Evan at the wheel and Shelby in the bedroom as she helped Malika with a sponge bath and a change of clothes. When Shelby asked permission to close the bedroom door so she could change clothes, Jakes ordered Margo to go in with her. Little Malika, wearing a Minnie Mouse T-shirt under a pair of floral print overalls, sat on the bed brushing the hair of a small doll.

As Shelby slipped out of her shorts and polo beside the bed, she said to Margo, "Last night, when I talked to you about turning yourself in, you seemed interested. Have you thought about it?"

Margo walked to the rear window on the other side of the bed and peeked out of the drawn blinds, seemingly deep in thought. After spending a minute watching the freeway behind the RV, she turned and said, "You really have a lot of nerve, lady." The statement came out as much as a compliment as an indictment. "All I have to do is open the door and tell Nolan what you said and he would probably hit you again."

"I know he would," Shelby said soberly. "But I don't think you will tell him. I don't believe you're convinced that running away is the right thing to do."

"You know that if I turn myself in and Nolan gets captured, your husband will be in deep trouble with the law. He'll have to answer to a murder charge. And yet you're still campaigning for me to bail out on this deal. Do you *want* your husband to go to prison?"

Shelby pulled a sleeveless white blouse from the wardrobe by the head of the bed, slipped into it, and buttoned it up. "No, I don't want Evan to go to prison," she said with obvious inner pain. "But I want even less for him to spend his life running from the past. I'd rather have him suffer the consequences of his acts now and be cleared, than to live in torment. If he doesn't face up to what happened in Portland, he will always be looking over his shoulder, always waiting for another skeleton to jump out of the closet. That's no way for him—or us—to live."

"You call getting him blackballed from his profession and saddled with the label of a murderer any way to live?" Margo seemed to taunt Shelby with the words.

Shelby stepped into a pale-blue cotton skirt and buttoned it around her waist with the blouse tucked in. "What you don't understand, Margo, is that living with the consequences of doing right, even if they are difficult, is infinitely better than persisting in doing wrong. It's called integrity—doing what's right *every* time, not just when it's convenient, comfortable, or profitable."

Margo released a mocking little laugh. "From what I heard earlier this morning, you and your man seriously disagree on what's right in this situation."

Shelby stared at Margo, unsure of what her interest in the topic really was. Finally she said, "Evan is a wonderful man, a godly man. This is a difficult challenge for him, but I know he will eventually do what is right, even if it causes him pain. Consequently, he will come out of this okay—*we* will come out of this okay."

"Life doesn't always turn out the way we expect," Margo said, as if issuing a warning to Shelby.

"You have a choice in how your life turns out, Margo," Shelby said. "And the sooner you turn around, the better things will be."

Margo glared at Shelby coldly. Any softening Shelby may have perceived in her, real or imagined, had vanished. "You pathetic fool with your pathetic husband," Margo murmured. "You haven't a clue about what's going down here." Then she snapped open the door and left the room, leaving Shelby with her brow furrowed in disappointment.

Evan was relieved that Jakes had agreed with the suggestion to take the I-205 bypass east of Portland, to avoid traveling I-5 through the heart of the city on a business morning. For all its charm and personality, the city perched on the banks of the lazy Willamette River held no allure for Evan. Since his last visit in early December 1979, Evan had avoided Portland as if it had been overrun by a deadly, infectious disease.

The farther away he was from the city, the easier it was to ignore the voices in his head, imagined voices that seemed so real they had often brought chills of grief and fear. They were the voices of Neil McGruder's family and friends mourning his senseless death and crying for the arrest of his unknown assailant.

Even now, traveling I-205 ten miles east of the city center, Evan wondered about Neil's survivors twenty-two years after his death. The brash young man would have been in his forties by now, perhaps an accountant in Lake Oswego, an Intel engineer in Beaverton, or a utilities executive or timber broker downtown. He might have kept a small boat in a slip at the Riverplace Marina or maintained membership at the Columbia Edgewater Golf Club. He could have been married with children, perhaps a daughter who would have been selected as a junior princess at the city's annual Rose Festival.

Evan glanced left beyond the town of Clackamas toward the downtown Portland area. McGruder's parents might still be alive somewhere in the city or the state, he knew, perhaps saddened at every memory of a son who had been cruelly prevented from fulfilling their hopes and dreams by a nameless, faceless assassin. How often Evan had silently explained to the McGruders that he never intended to kill Neil. And how often Evan had begged them to forgive him for his act.

Driving now, battling fatigue, Evan tried to console himself as he had for more than two decades: *Coming forward to admit my guilt will do nothing to bring Neil McGruder back. On the contrary, a confession at this time will only serve to reopen old wounds and inflict new pain for those who knew and loved him. There will be charges, a plea, a trial, a conviction, a sentence. The family's peace will be disturbed, the judicial system in Portland will be taxed, my life will be ruined, and for all our trouble Neil McGruder will still be in his grave. His parents' hopes and dreams for him will be no closer to fulfillment. Leaving well enough alone seems the most charitable response.*

But now as before, Evan was not consoled. If anything, he was more agitated over the issue, especially with Shelby's words ringing in his ears: *"You have to make it right. You have to face the legal consequences. You have to face the young man's family."* Her response flew in the face of his admittedly contrived conviction that it was okay to let this sleeping dog lie. Evan wanted to sneak by the issue again this time, just as he was trying to slip quietly around Portland. But he couldn't quiet his suspicion that the vicious guard dog he had feared all these years was awake.

Soon Evan passed the exit for Portland International Airport, situated to the west of I-205 along the broad Columbia River separating Oregon from Washington. Then the RV was atop the Glen Jackson Bridge spanning the river to Government Island and beyond to Vancouver, Washington, leaving Portland and Oregon behind.

In a few miles, I-205 reunited with I-5 north of Vancouver for the nearly three-hour drive through the Evergreen State to the Emerald City of Seattle. As he negotiated the merger of the freeways, Evan thought about Libby Carroll. At one time he had nurtured a romantic interest in her that might have grown to a lasting relationship. He knew that Nolan Jakes had felt the same way. Who knows—one of them might have married her.

But one night in Portland ended everything between the three friends. Now Libby was just another reminder of Neil McGruder. What's more, meeting up with her at the InterCorp Bank in Seattle was just another unpredictable and potentially dangerous step in the race to reach the border undetected. Evan was not looking forward to seeing Libby, especially under these conditions.

Apparently Libby had assured Nolan Jakes that she was just as eager to help him on his way as Evan was. And from what Evan could make of the telephone conversations, Libby had as much or more to lose as he did if the true story of Neil McGruder came to light. But what if she had a change of heart? Libby could be meeting with the police right now to confess her role in the crime—clearly the least punishable role, since she hadn't laid a hand on McGruder—and agreeing to testify against her two former friends in exchange for a lighter sentence.

Evan didn't want to think about such a double cross or the explosion it might ignite in Nolan Jakes. Instead he set the cruise function at 63 MPH and steeled himself for the inevitable rendezvous awaiting them 160 miles up the freeway.

Fifty-eight

Cole and Beth were still trying to make sense of Barbosa's puzzling antics in Woodburn long after the burgundy Town Car and the black Barego coupe had cruised around Portland on I-205 and crossed the Glen Jackson Bridge into Washington. The Town Car was back to traveling at a baffling 63 MPH, and the Barego rolled along at the same speed three minutes behind.

"He pulls off I-5 for no apparent reason," Cole summarized to himself as Beth drove. "He drives down the street a half mile from the freeway. He turns around, comes back, drives a half mile on the other side of the freeway, comes back again, and parks under the bridge for fifteen minutes."

"Mt. St. Helens is just beyond these mountains on the right," Beth informed, proud of the features of her adopted home state and tired of rehashing Barbosa's unspectacular stop in Woodburn. "It blew in 1980. They say the ash cloud traveled around the world. You can drive right up to the crater now. We ought to do that some time."

Cole continued his review without hearing her. "He doesn't need to stop for gas. He didn't stop to eat or visit the john. He sees no one, talks to no one, doesn't even get out of the car."

"That's the Toutle River," Beth said, pointing out the window. "After the eruption, it was clogged with ash and debris all the way to the Columbia."

"Then he jumps back on the freeway and resumes his snail's pace in the slow lane," Cole continued, analyzing Barbosa as if he was alone in the car.

"See those big berms running along the freeway?"

"Maybe he was waiting for a contact person who never showed up," Cole thought aloud.

"Maybe he just needed a catnap," Beth said, hoping to derail Cole's one-track mind. "After all, the guy has been driving for over fourteen hours." Then she jabbed him in the arm to make sure he was paying attention. "Now look at the grassy berms before we pass them."

"Yeah, neat little hills by the freeway," Cole said, trying to sound interested. "I see them."

"They're made of ash dredged out of the Toutle. They piled it out here like so many giant anthills, and before long the grass sprouted and covered the gray mounds with beautiful green. It's just like the mountain up there that blew its top. After all that devastation, it has been completely reforested over these two decades."

Cole stared at the grassy ash berms and hummed his appreciation for them. Then he said excitedly, "I know. He's waiting for someone. He's lazing along in the slow lane waiting for his unsuspecting victim to fly by him. Then he slips in behind the guy and follows him to a place where he can do him in."

"Waiting for someone?" Beth wondered aloud, suddenly intrigued with a new twist on a boring puzzle. "But that still doesn't tell us why he stopped in Woodburn."

"Simple. Somebody alerted him by phone that his target was coming up behind him. Instead of slowing to 45 on the freeway, he pulled off just to let the car catch up a little."

"So why didn't Barbosa wait until whoever-it-is caught up with him so he could just follow him?" Beth asked.

"Like we're following Barbosa?"

"Right."

"He can't just sit on the target's tail. He's likely to be seen. But if he lets the target pass him—"

"Barbosa won't look so obvious," Beth butted in to finish Cole's sentence.

"Seems reasonable to me," Cole said.

Thoroughly involved in the challenge again instead of the scenery, Beth advanced another idea. "Maybe he's been trailing somebody all along—you know, playing leapfrog. He goes ahead for a while, stops and waits, follows for a while . . . "

"If he is, he must have a locater in the car like we do. You could easily lose somebody playing leapfrog."

"Or, like you said, he's working with someone who knows where the target is."

"That guy could have a locater," Cole repeated.

"Right. Barbosa's accomplice calls him from time to time and says, 'Slow down' or 'Speed up' or 'Pull off the freeway for fifteen minutes.' "

Cole shook his head and smiled. "I'm telling you, Beth, you should have been a detective."

"I *am* a detective," she insisted. "What do you think investigative journalism is? I'm always digging up something on somebody, except my subjects are not all criminals—at least *they* don't think they're criminals."

The pair was silent for a minute as they contemplated the new theory. Then Beth spoke again. "Do you think Barbosa has been trailing someone all the way from L.A.?"

Cole pondered the question for a moment. "It seems unlikely from the way he blasted out of the city. At 80-plus MPH, he wasn't following *anyone;* he was passing *everyone.*"

"Maybe he got a late start."

"You mean he blew out of L.A. like a bat because his target was already half way to Fresno?"

"Sounds a little far out, doesn't it?" Beth said, a little embarrassed at the idea. "A professional hit man isn't likely to get lazy and miss an appointment."

Cole's mind was churning on the new idea. "True, especially someone as polished as Barbosa. But getting a late start—perhaps on purpose—would explain his sudden drop in speed just past Eugene."

"In other words, he finally caught up with whomever he was chasing all night," Beth advanced.

"Could be."

"And now he's playing leapfrog or cat and mouse until. . . ?" Beth deferred to the professional detective for a theory.

But Cole just shook his head and released a yawn. "I haven't a clue. In fact, we would probably get laughed out of an FBI ready room with such a theory."

"So you think Barbosa is just on his way to Seattle for vacation, and we burned three tanks of gas and lost a night's sleep for nothing?" Beth's tone of voice issued a subtle challenge.

Cole recognized the open door and walked right in. "Not 'for nothing,' " he said, reaching across the console for her right hand, which rested conveniently on her leg. "That was one of the best night's sleep I never had."

She welcomed his grip and their fingers intertwined. "Nice shot," she said, grinning.

They rode along in cozy silence for a couple of minutes. Then Cole was struck with an idea he knew Beth would eagerly welcome. "Let's pass him."

"Are you kidding?" Beth queried, clearly hoping he was not.

"No, I'm not kidding. Move into the fast lane and go with the flow of traffic. Let's ease on by him and see if he's following anything interesting." Beth began changing lanes before he was finished speaking.

They cruised along at 75, passing a steady stream of trucks, motorhomes, pickups with vacation trailers, and a few old clunkers whose drivers feared the wheels would fly off at speeds greater than 65. They followed by several car lengths one of the newer electric sports cars with a driver trying to prove that the little sewing machine on wheels belonged in the fast lane. Behind them was a streamlined red, white, and blue Greyhound maxibus with VANCOUVER, B.C. displayed above the massive, sweeping windshield.

Cole lifted the Hawkeye to his lap and tapped in a command. A second blip, colored electric blue to distinguish it from the blip representing Barbosa's car, appeared on the map of I-5 filling the monitor. The readout in the margin silently announced that a distance of one minute and thirty-eight seconds separated the two blips, but the digits on the right were dropping steadily.

When they passed the second Centralia, Washington exit there was less than a minute between the rabbit and the hawk. "I think I see him up there," Beth said, "tucked in between a tractor-trailer and a tan Winnebago."

"At this rate, the Hawkeye says we will be alongside him in two minutes and ten seconds," Cole said.

Beth emitted a small gasp. "What if he recognizes me?" she said. "He had a pretty good look at me yesterday by the elevator."

"Good point," Cole responded, "although I doubt that he's focusing very well after driving all night." Then he reached into the backseat, rummaged through his saddle bags, and brought two items forward: a sweatshirt and a cap. "Here, put these on."

Cole took the navy blue sweatshirt and turned it inside out so the words LAPD BASKETBALL—PARKER CENTER were not visible. He helped Beth slip the sweatshirt over her head. Then he held the wheel while she stuck her arms in one at a time and pulled the shirt down to cover her top.

Then Cole handed her a worn and soiled, medium blue baseball cap with the word BRUINS stitched in gold script above the bill. "A UCLA cap? USC alumni usually don't stoop to such depths," Beth complained. "Can't you do better than this?"

"It will look more believable than a motorcycle helmet," Cole said without sympathy. "C'mon, we don't have much time. Put it on and stuff your hair inside."

Beth grumbled unintelligibly as she donned the cap. Cole again held the wheel as she hastily pushed handfuls of her dark hair up into the cap.

"The finishing touch," Cole said, handing her his wraparound shades. As Beth put them on, he slipped on her gold-rimmed dark glasses. Then he reclined his seat several more notches until he was invisible to the outside from his nose down.

Cole and Beth watched in silence as the Barego crept up on the boxy, tan Winnebago which lumbered behind Barbosa's sleek Town Car like a Saint Bernard galloping after a German shepherd. Slowly passing the big motorhome, the couple stared ahead to the figure at the wheel of the burgundy sedan. In his casual clothes, Barbosa looked like an executive on his way to Seattle for a business conference which promised plenty of free time for golf.

Cole and Beth kept looking at him until they were almost alongside the car. Then they snapped their eyes forward and played the role of the vacationing couple from California exploring the Northwest.

"This is eerie, driving by a known assassin," Beth said. Then she quickly added, "What a rush!"

"*Known* perhaps," Cole retorted, not sharing her emotional buzz, "but still to be caught in the act, tried, and convicted. Sooner or later he will slip up and we'll get him."

The Barego kept rolling past four long-range freight haulers—a triple trailer and three doubles—in line nose to tail like circus elephants on parade. In front of the truck convoy was a classic '72 Buick Riviera. The body had been nicely kept, but the Rivvie showed its age with a light but steady spiral of blue-white smoke flowing from the exhaust pipe.

Next came a white motorhome—Flair, it said above the rear window—dragging a car carrier with a cherry-looking red Datsun station wagon strapped on by the front wheels. Both vehicles had California plates. "Nice looking wagon," Cole said. With Barbosa well behind them, he pulled his seat up again to admire the vehicle as they passed it.

"Those crazy Californians must be allergic to sunlight," Beth said, inspecting the RV in quick glances. "A beautiful day like this, and they keep the blinds down. What a waste of scenic Washington."

Cole hummed his agreement.

As they passed the front of the RV, Cole glanced up at the driver's window. He saw the silhouette of a man at the wheel but did not see him clearly. The glare on the Barego's window also kept the Flair's driver from recognizing Cole. Beth kept her eyes on the road as they continued to move past slower traffic in the right lane.

After several more tractor-trailer rigs and motorhomes, they were two miles ahead of Barbosa. The Hawkeye showed the Town Car to be plodding along at 63. Beth pulled into the right lane and dropped her speed to match the trucks and RVs. She said, "I didn't see anything in that stretch of vehicles that would attract an international hit man, did you?"

Cole yawned and flopped his head back on the headrest. "Not even close," he said, "unless that furniture truck back there happened to be carrying a drug shipment for the Godfather."

"Are you ready to bag this nonsense and head for Whidbey Island?"

Cole shrugged. "I suppose. Mr. Barbosa has been a real disappointment. But we have to stay on I-5 for a while to get to your place, don't we?"

"Yes, past Seattle to the Mukiteo Ferry, or on up to Mount Vernon if you'd like to take the bridge at Deception Pass."

"Then it wouldn't hurt us to keep Barbosa in sight, at least to see if he makes it through Seattle."

"True," Beth answered, adding a sigh. "But I'm sure getting tired of 63 MPH."

"I hear you," Cole said, squirming in his seat. "Let's pull off for coffee; then we can play catch-up in the fast lane."

"I'm ready," Beth exulted. "Besides, it's your turn to buy."

Four miles later they took the exit for Tenino, Washington in hopes of finding a coffee shop. By the time they did and parked, the white Flair with the red Datsun caboose had rolled by on the freeway followed by a '72 Riviera, a small convoy of trucks, and a burgundy Town Car.

Fifty-nine

As Libby stood in front of her closet, she was surprised by the question that popped into her mind: *What do you wear to be robbed of thousands of dollars and to introduce your son to the father who doesn't even know he exists?* She had been in baggy slacks, a blouse, and a warm robe since Nolan Jakes first called late last night. There was no use in changing into pajamas when she knew she wouldn't sleep.

Now, at 9:25 A.M., Libby must prepare to leave the cocoon of her beautiful brick Tudor home and deal with the nightmare which had tormented her imagination for hours. Two nightmares actually, blended into one: The sudden reincarnation of Neil McGruder in the form of Nolan Jakes' demand for her assistance, and the bizarre, coincidental reappearance of Brett's father after twenty-two years. But even for a nightmare, Libby was determined to be properly attired.

Libby had called her secretary at 7:45 to announce that she would not be in today. She gave no reason, nor did she need to. It was one of the privileges of her rank. "I won't be in. Reschedule my appointments. Good-bye." It was that easy for the provost. Depending on how the day went, Libby thought she might take the whole week off. Call it a mental-health leave. She assessed that a trauma of this magnitude deserved a little time for R and R.

Libby selected a summer skirt, blouse, and frilly vest in pastels and white—an ensemble she hoped would serve as a pick-me-up for her less than bouncy mood. She showered, dressed, applied her makeup, and tied her hair back with a bow. She needed to look thoroughly together and in control in order to help herself believe she really was.

As she thought about it, Libby was amazed at how unconcerned she was about withdrawing a large sum of money to send Nolan Jakes on his way in silence. She looked at it as a maintenance investment, money well spent to keep the machinery of life running smoothly. Libby had long believed that when a needed or greatly appreciated possession had to be fixed or replaced, you ante up no matter what the cost. When the Puget Sound storm of '97 blew down her patio and ripped away half the shingles on her roof, Libby spent $12,000 for repairs without a qualm. When she was appointed provost, the four-year-old Buick Park Avenue had to go. A new Cadillac Seville at $50,000 and change was practically a necessity. Libby wrote the check with pleasure.

Jakes' proposition was a straightforward damage-control issue. If she paid what he asked, she remained on track for the president's chair. If she ignored his request, everything her brick Tudor home and midnight blue Seville and plush office represented went up in smoke. She was no more emotionally involved in paying off Jakes than she would be in ordering a new heating system for her home. It had to be done. Some might call Jakes' threat blackmail or extortion, and perhaps in a strictly legal sense it was. To Libby it was a job-security insurance premium, and the sooner Jakes was paid and sent on his way, the sooner the stirred waters of her life would calm.

Her deepest feelings in the matter revolved around Brett. Introducing him to his father—and his father to him—under these conditions would be awkward. But she had deprived her son of this knowledge all his life, and now she was making it right. Whenever she thought about it she teared up.

Jakes had set the agenda, but hopefully the 10:30 meeting at the bank would be civil enough to permit Libby's surprise introduction without provoking him to do something careless and hurtful. After all, they would be in a public place. How father and son worked out their future relationship—if indeed they chose to after meeting each other today—was their own business. At least she would have done her job.

Thinking of Brett again, Libby checked her watch. It was almost 10. She had planned to leave early to get to the bank, normally about a fifteen-minute drive. Brett was due to arrive home at any time, but Libby couldn't wait for him any longer. She decided to have him meet her at the bank, so she dialed his personal phone.

"Where are you?" Libby asked without responding to Brett's greeting.

"Just past Issaquah. We'll be home in about twenty-five minutes."

"I want you to meet me at the InterCorp Bank in the District," she said. "Do you remember where it is?"

"Yeah, Forty-Fifth and Brooklyn. But why there?"

"That's where I'm meeting your father."

Brett was silent for a moment, as if savoring the sound of the word *father*. "When?"

"At 10:30. I'm leaving right now. You can be at the bank in about fifteen minutes, can't you?"

"Right, depending on traffic."

"Good, because we need to talk first. Meet me in the parking lot. I'll be waiting in my car."

"Okay."

Libby collected her purse and headed for the garage as she concluded. "And Brett, please don't take this the wrong way, but we need to talk in private. Would you please have Andie wait in her father's car or drop you off and go shopping for half an hour?"

Brett hesitated, hinting displeasure at his girlfriend being specifically excluded. "All right, mom, if it's that important to you."

"Thank you, honey. Yes, it *is* that important—to both of us. You'll see."

As Libby backed out of the driveway onto West Kinnear Place, she wished she didn't have to do what she was about to do alone. *This is where a devoted husband would step in,* she told herself. *Right or wrong, I could depend on the support of a man who loved me. No matter how strong an individual may feel, when it comes to facing a crisis, two are better than one. You can endure practically anything if you know that someone is standing beside you.*

But Libby didn't have a devoted husband—or a husband of any description. Even the father of her only child was one of the complications in her enormously problematic morning. Nor did she have a friend—male or female—who understood the complex burden she was carrying. And at this late date, you don't just call someone up and say, "By the way, I just wanted you to know that many years ago I was an accomplice to a murder, and that today I'm being blackmailed out of thousands of dollars and introducing my twenty-year-old son to his father, who doesn't even know he has a child. If you can't go with me to hold me up, please keep me in your thoughts."

If Libby *could* select such a person—a combination of confidant, counselor, and bodyguard—she knew it would be Officer Reginald Burris. She was surprised at how readily she acknowledged that fact. Here was a man to whom she had revealed more of herself over a weekend than many of her friends had discovered about her over years of relationship.

But why Reginald? Libby didn't have an answer. Perhaps it was because the plebeian campus policeman didn't deserve access to her private world—and apparently didn't crave such privilege—that he was an unwitting candidate. Reginald seemed content to be a friend indeed. Libby had told him no more about the dark blot in her past than she had told anyone else. But she sensed that she *could* tell Reginald and that he would be as forthright in his counsel and as gentle in his support as he had been with her admissions about Brett.

Is this how real love begins? The question took Libby by surprise, and she felt suddenly flushed even considering it. *Is this the stuff of lasting, devoted relationships — friendship, trust, acceptance, openness? Does devotion of this nature transcend differences in intelligence, education, and life station? And if it does, what would I give to know such devotion?*

As she turned off Queen Anne Avenue onto Florentia to approach the Fremont Bridge across the ship canal, Libby forced herself to abandon such thoughts in the face of more pressing immediate concerns. She would have only a few minutes to explain to Brett both how he came to be and why she was meeting with Nolan Jakes and Evan Rider under these circumstances. On both counts, Libby's dilemma was how much of the truth to reveal to her son.

On the topic of Brett's conception, she would have no problem explaining the one-night stand. But regarding her flight to Seattle and total separation from Tango, she could not bring herself to reveal the real reason: the death of Neil McGruder and the three-way vow of silence. Brett had already accepted that his mother's naiveté and embarrassment pushed her to end the relationship with the father of her child. She would let him continue to believe it — for now, at least.

On the topic of the rendezvous at InterCorp Bank, Libby had experimented with a number of plausible explanations, each of which contained a shred of truth: "Nolan Jakes is in financial trouble and has asked me for a sizable, long-term loan." "Nolan, Evan, and I are partners in a business deal that went sour. We're putting our money together to pay off our debts and get out." "Nolan has found a very hot investment opportunity in Canada, and Evan and I are buying in."

There would come a time when Libby could tell Brett the whole truth, but for now he would have to live with a partial truth. She expected that Brett would be so focused on meeting his father that the bank transaction would not even need an explanation. If she was wrong, she decided that the failed business deal story was as believable as any.

She crossed the Fremont Bridge and turned east on Thirty-Fourth, which runs along the northern shore of Lake Union. Elevated Interstate 5 was visible in the distance ahead, and on the other side of the freeway was the University District.

A startling dark thought darted through her mind, producing a chill of fear. She had not considered before that Nolan Jakes' desperation might push him beyond extortion to physical harm. *Does he have more planned for Evan and me than taking our money?* she wondered. *Evan said he had a gun, that his wife and daughter were being held hostage. Is Nolan planning to take our money and then kill us all? Is he intending to bury the past completely by silencing the only other living witnesses? Is Nolan Jakes prepared to elevate the cover-up to murder?*

Again the face of Reginald Burris materialized in her brain, Reginald the strong, imposing policeman, Reginald the closest thing to a bodyguard she had ever met. She had the sudden urge to call him and ask him to meet her at InterCorp Bank. He had volunteered to help Libby in any way she might need him. Could she trust him to stand by her during the father-son introductions and the money withdrawal without telling him what she was really doing? Would he even be able to get there in time? Would he even want to come on his day off?

She decided to find out. As she picked up her phone she realized that she didn't know his number, didn't even know where he lived. She tried directory assistance and, as she expected, Reginald's number was unlisted—understandable for policemen who didn't need disgruntled suspects bringing trouble to their front door.

Libby dialed UWPD and introduced herself to the desk officer. "May I please have the personal number for Officer Burris?"

"I'm sorry, Dr. Carroll," the officer explained cordially but firmly, "but we're not allowed to give out that information to anyone."

"But I'm the university's provost," Libby argued. "Officer Burris and I are friends."

"I'm sorry, ma'am. No exceptions. However, I will be happy to try to contact him for you and ask him to call *you*. May I do that?"

"Yes, officer, thank you," Libby agreed with relief. "Please call him for me right away, and tell him that it's rather urgent." Then she recited her personal number and hung up.

Libby turned left onto North Pacific to follow the arc of the Lake Washington Ship Canal underneath I-5 to the University District. She was five minutes from InterCorp Bank. It would be a miracle if Reginald Burris would even call her, let alone drop whatever he was doing to be with her. But she reasoned that their budding friendship was already something of a miracle, so she wished for one more.

Nolan Jakes had been hovering over Evan's shoulder since the RV entered Tacoma, thirty miles south of Seattle on I-5. Jakes seemed more tense with every mile closer to downtown Seattle, shifting from foot to foot, running his hands over the stubble of his blond buzz-cut hair, touching frequently the butt of the Colt .44 tucked into his waistband.

Freeway traffic in the city was heavy, so Jakes took it upon himself to backseat drive. He chipped at Evan about his speed and told him when and how to change lanes. When a Pierce County sheriff's car passed them, Jakes dropped to a squat behind the driver's seat and threatened Evan with vile curses if he did anything to get them pulled over.

Evan tried to let Jakes' nervous paranoia roll off his back. He couldn't seem to assure his captor that he was intent on cooperating fully. Yet he kept trying in hopes of preventing Jakes from another angry outburst against his wife and daughter, who were still confined to the back bedroom with Margo Sharpe standing guard like a jailer. Getting through the bank transactions unharmed and reaching the Canadian border as quickly as possible were his primary goals. Dealing with the mounting inner conflict over the morality of his cooperation with Jakes would have to come later.

As he glanced at Boeing Field to the left, Evan thought about the imminent reunion with Libby Carroll. Under more favorable circumstances he would welcome the chance to see her again and catch up on each other's life. Judging from what Evan could hear of Jakes' brief conversation with her, Libby had also made a name for herself beyond the transitory world of athletic achievement which had brought the three friends together at Cal State Northridge. A doctorate. The upper echelon at the University of Washington. And doubtless the appropriate monetary and material rewards that come to those who measure their career educational investment in decades instead of years. As professionals, Evan and Libby would likely have much more in common with each other than with Jakes.

On the topic of money and brains, however, Evan realized that Jakes, hardly MENSA material, had earned and spent millions more than his two published and educationally polished friends combined since they parted company. And Jakes was clearly in the power position now, preparing to bleed his smarter friends of thousands of their hard-earned dollars to rescue himself from the consequences of his stupidity. *So much for the advantages of intellectual superiority*, Evan mused.

No, this would not be a joyous or lingering reunion for any of them. Regardless, Evan couldn't deny a pang of curiosity about the girl both he and Jakes had dated and fantasized about. He wanted Libby to know how sorry he was that his brash ego and immaturity twenty-two years ago made this forced reunion an unpleasant one. He wanted her to understand that his foolish actions as a young man did not mean he was without respect for her now as a person and a fellow professional.

Evan also wanted Libby to meet Shelby. And he wanted his former, fleeting flame to know that something eternally significant had buoyed his sinking life a couple of years ago. He hoped Libby had somehow found faith as he had. If she had, Evan wondered if she was also struggling with her conscience over the soul-grating dissonance between past actions and present consequences. Evan hoped that, after the storm of today had passed, he and Shelby might spend some time with Libby. Perhaps they could all help each other put the pieces of their disrupted lives back together again.

Evan noticed the Kingdome on his left and the adjacent King County train station with its 150-foot tall brick clock tower. They were crossing the southern perimeter of the downtown district now. From the directions he received from Margo, who had been on the phone to the bank operator, InterCorp was just a few miles ahead and off to the right, on the other side of Portage Bay.

The long night and torturous drive on endless I-5 now seemed like an eye blink, a momentary hallucination. The trip was down to two critical stops: InterCorp Bank, which was dead ahead, and the Canadian border less than two hours farther north. Evan began praying for calm for himself, Shelby, and Libby, and for restraint for the man crouched behind him with a loaded .44.

Sixty

Libby had been parked in the InterCorp lot only two minutes before a little red GM Star Chaser pulled up to the curb across Brooklyn Avenue. She watched Brett jump out stern-faced and wave good-bye as Andie drove off. Libby was relieved that Brett's girlfriend wouldn't be hanging around the bank during the unusual and potentially dangerous goings-on.

It had been nearly ten minutes since Libby had asked the UWPD officer to contact Reginald Burris for her, but Reginald had not called back. Perhaps he was out of the city for his day off. Perhaps he was sleeping late, not answering his phone. Even if Reginald could not meet her at the bank, Libby knew she would feel better just talking to him.

Neither had there been any contact from Nolan Jakes. Libby hadn't seen anyone resembling him in the parking lot, nor had her car been approached. She was fourteen minutes early for her 10:30 appointment and grateful to spend that time with her son in what she expected would be one of the most emotional conversations of their lives. She had to make the most of every undisturbed moment.

Brett climbed in the passenger side. He wore a snug-gray WSU T-shirt which revealed his modestly developed upper body, threadbare denim shorts, and huaraches without socks. Two days worth of heavy stubble darkened his creamy-mocha face.

Mother and son embraced briefly across the console, reassuring Libby that she had made the right choice in response to Brett's demands. They were, and perhaps always would be, the only members of their two-person family. Libby now was determined to keep them together, despite the potential cost to herself and her career.

"Your father and his friends will be here any minute, so I want to cover as much ground as I can before they arrive." Libby reached out to grasp Brett's hands, a gesture she feared he would judge corny or maudlin. But she exerted her maternal privilege and did it anyway. Looking at her handsome son, she could already feel the emotion beginning to constrict her throat. She had to hurry on with her words before a storm of tears rolled in.

"First, I want to say again how sorry I am for keeping this information from you," Libby began. "I know now how important this is to you—maybe I've always known and just ignored it. But, honey, I apologize and ask you to forgive me."

Brett's dark eyes glistened with a mist of tears and he swallowed hard. "I forgive you, mom," he said, gripping her hands tightly. "And I want you to forgive me for being such an adolescent about this whole deal. I feel terrible about how I acted Friday night and Saturday." He could speak no more.

Libby nodded. "You had a right to be angry, but it's all over now." They gripped each other's hands until they hurt and loved each other through tear-filled eyes. After several moments they broke their connection and Brett retrieved a travel box of tissues from the glove box. They even laughed a little about how emotional they were becoming in their old age.

"Now to the important part," Libby pressed on. She reached into a side pocket of her purse and pulled out a square of paper with a photograph on it. The paper, yellowed and frayed at the edges, had been snipped from the intercollegiate athletics section of a Cal State Northridge yearbook over twenty years earlier. It contained a black-and-white photograph of a football player. The player was in a clean uniform—no helmet—with a large block number six on his jersey. He was posed and smiling with a football in his hands. A faint autograph was scrawled across the picture. The player's name was printed at the bottom.

Libby took a deep, calming breath and locked onto her son's gaze. "Brett, I wish I had more time to prepare you for this," she said, "but here is what your father looked like almost twenty-two years ago when you were conceived." Libby handed him the photograph.

Brett received the limp square of paper like it was a check for a million dollars. Then he looked upon his father's face for the first time. Libby allowed him to stare at the photograph undisturbed, ready to respond to his questions.

"He's white," Brett said without looking up. "My dad is a white man." His tone was marked by surprise, but it was free of disappointment.

"Yes, he's Caucasian. How do you feel about that?"

Brett couldn't take his eyes off the photograph. "It's okay," he said at last. "I've thought about the possibility before. I'm still surprised, but it's really okay."

Libby remained quiet, giving Brett his space. Then he said, "What does this writing across the picture say?"

" 'To the Jet, from your friend, Tango.' Those were funny little nicknames we had for each other. The other man you will meet today was also a friend of ours. We called him Choo-choo."

"Where was this taken? Where did he play football?"

"Cal State Northridge, near L.A."

"Did you go there?"

"Yes, for a couple of years. I transferred to Central Washington after taking a year and a half off to have you."

Brett touched his finger to the name printed at the bottom. His next comment was for Libby's benefit. "It doesn't matter what his name is, mom. I've already decided that I'm not changing my name. I've always been Brett Carroll, and I always will be. I'm not going to be—" he paused to read the name on the photograph again "—Evan Rider, Jr."

Libby smiled proudly. "Thank you, honey. I'm pleased that you want to keep our name."

Libby quickly capsulized the story of her friendship and one-night romance with Evan Rider at Cal State Northridge. She explained how she returned home to Brett's "Nanny and Papa" in Seattle without telling Evan that he had fathered the child she carried. She carefully avoided intimating to Brett that an even darker secret prompted Libby and Evan's sudden and permanent separation.

The telephone call Libby had been waiting for interrupted the conversation. Libby explained to Brett that the call would take just a minute. He offered to step out of the car, a courtesy Libby had taught him when he was very young, but she shook her head and motioned him to remain seated.

"I'm sorry to bother you on your day off, Reginald," she began.

"It's no bother," he replied convincingly. "I've been doing my housework, and I'm ready for a coffee break."

"Reginald, I have a favor to ask, but I'll understand if you have other plans."

"I'll be glad to help if I can, Libby. Shoot."

"In a few minutes I'm meeting an old . . . business partner . . . at the InterCorp Bank in the District. Do you know the place?"

"Sure," Reginald said. "I bank there myself since it's so close to the U."

Libby glanced at Brett, who was still staring at the old photograph while hearing every word. "Well, I owe this man a substantial amount of money to pay off some old business debts. We didn't exactly part as friends, so I'm not sure what kind of mood he'll be in. I would just feel a little better if I had someone—"

Reginald interrupted her. "When will you be at the bank?"

"I'm here now, waiting for him in the parking lot."

"I'll be right there. I'm only about fifteen minutes away."

"I don't want to put you out, Reginald."

"Nonsense, Libby. I'm glad you called. Sit tight, I'm on my way."
Then he hung up.

Libby snapped her phone closed. Brett looked up with his brow
furrowed in bewilderment. "Who is this business partner?" he asked.
"Do I know about this?"

Libby squirmed inside, wishing she didn't have to perpetuate the
cover-up any longer. But she knew she had to. "He's the college friend
I mentioned a minute ago. The three of us got involved in a foolish
venture back then. It's been losing money ever since. He's insisting
that your father and I pay our share. I have agreed, and apparently
Evan has also."

"Has he threatened both of you?" Brett asked, hardly believing his
mother could be involved in such a relationship.

"I'll just say he's very insistent that we give him what we owe him
today."

"And who was that you called to come over, some kind of bouncer?"

"Just a friend, a new friend," Libby answered. "You and Andie were
introduced to him Friday night in my office."

"That big campus cop?" Brett exclaimed. "Geez, Mom, you had to
call a cop in on this deal?"

"I didn't call him because he's a policeman, Brett. I called him
because he has been a very supportive friend since the other night. I
just feel better having someone like him—"

Libby was interrupted by the awareness of a petite platinum blonde
in summer wear and sunglasses approaching her car. "I think our
company has arrived," Libby said to Brett. "Please follow my lead in
this, all right?"

"Whatever you say, mom," Brett answered, sensing her anxiety.

The blonde came up to the driver's window. Libby touched the power button and zipped it down.

"Libby Carroll?" the blonde inquired impassively, bending down to
inspect the car's occupants through her dark lenses.

"Yes."

"And who's that?" the visitor probed, nodding toward Brett.

"He's my son."

The blonde surveyed the young man for several moments. Brett returned her stare. Then she turned back to Libby. "I'm with Nolan," she
said, all business. "He's parked in the lot across the street. He wants to
talk to you. Bring your son."

"Is Evan Rider with you?" Libby asked.

"Yes," the blonde said. "Come on. We're in a hurry."

Libby turned to Brett, who was puzzled by the cryptic exchange.

"Let's go meet your father," she said, trying to sound positive. "And don't worry about anything."

Libby and Brett got out of the car and followed the blonde—jaywalking across Brooklyn Avenue—into the large parking lot behind the Meany Tower Hotel. Near the back of the lot, closer to Twelfth Avenue than to Brooklyn, stood a white motorhome with its nose pointed toward the InterCorp lot. The coach had a car carrier hitched to the rear and a red import station wagon mounted on the carrier. The blonde was leading them directly toward the side door of the big white rig.

Libby's blood suddenly ran to ice. She hadn't expected Nolan and Evan to be traveling in a motorhome, a virtual fortress on wheels where not only she but Brett could be imprisoned. She pictured Nolan inside holding a gun to the heads of Evan, his wife, and his daughter. Libby realized with horror that she had unwittingly brought Nolan another hostage in the person of her own son. She could not let him go inside with her.

She called to the blonde, "I'd like my son to wait in the—"

Turning around, the blonde cut her off. "No, we're all going in," she insisted coldly. Then she continued toward the RV.

"What's going on, mom?" Brett whispered, obviously perplexed.

"It will all make sense in just a minute, honey," his mother assured. Libby winced at the knowledge that she was leading her son into a trap. But if she didn't do what Nolan wanted, terrible things might happen to all of them. Nolan sounded like a man on the edge. Libby could only hope that her full cooperation would result in their swift release. And she prayed that Brett would also cooperate—and that he would forgive her again for purposefully misleading him.

When Evan parked the RV in the big lot behind the hotel and turned off the engine, a very nervous Nolan Jakes took the keys and told him to stay in the driver's seat. Then Jakes ordered Margo to bring Shelby and Malika forward to the dinette. Gripping the gun in his right hand but keeping it at his side, Jakes again warned Shelby and Evan to cooperate. Evan assured him that they would, imploring Jakes not to hurt his wife and daughter. Shelby said nothing, and perpetually silent little Malika clung to her mother while glaring frightfully at the man who had been so rough with her during the trip.

After his brief threatening lecture, Jakes sent Margo across the street to find Libby Carroll in the InterCorp lot and bring her back. Jakes hung over Evan's shoulder to watch anxiously as Margo snaked between several parked cars in the lot, crossed the street, and approached a dark blue Cadillac Seville.

When Libby stepped out into the sunlight moments later, even from a distance Evan quickly recognized her as the fortysomething version of the willow-limbed beauty he had partied with and dated and once taken to bed in the late '70s. He was pleasantly surprised that the sight of her triggered no fleshly desire for her. That part of their relationship had been fleeting and was now long buried. Instead, he felt another pang of pity that such a beautiful and obviously successful woman had also been trapped in Nolan Jakes' web.

"Who's the kid?" Jakes snapped to no one in particular. Both men were looking at the lanky, handsome, caramel-colored young man climbing out of the Seville on the other side. Jakes seemed to welcome another reason to vent his anger. "I didn't tell her she could bring someone," he snarled.

"It'll be all right, Nolan," Evan said in a calming tone. "He's just a college kid, maybe one of her students. He won't be any trouble."

"He already *is* trouble," Jakes muttered sourly. "I don't need another complication like this."

As Margo escorted Libby and the young man across the street, Jakes scrambled back to the kitchen where he could have everyone in front of him. He patted his fake beard to make sure it was in place and put on his wraparound shades and floppy golf hat. Evan swiveled the driver's seat around, but after a threatening wave of Jakes' gun, he remained seated.

When the door opened, Jakes hid the gun behind his right thigh. Libby was the first one up the stairs. Evan caught her eye and they exchanged pallid smiles. The young man was next. He gave Evan a measured glance, then quickly looked away. Margo closed the door and followed him up the stairs where the three of them stood in the suddenly cramped area between the cab and the dinette.

"What's with the kid, Libby?" Jakes demanded from the shadows at the back of the kitchen.

Libby put her arm around Brett's waist. "This is my son, Nolan," she said. "His name is Brett. I asked him to come along today for a special reason." Then, turning to Brett, she said, "And this is an old friend of mine from Cal State Northridge, Nolan Jakes."

Evan saw the young man stiffen at the name. "Nolan Jakes, the football player from Canada?" Brett said in disbelief, staring at the man standing nine feet away. "Mom, this guy is in trouble. I saw the story on CNN. He's wanted by the police in L.A. for dealing drugs. There was a shooting Friday night. A cop was killed."

Evan anticipated Brett's move just in time to act. He sprang from the driver's seat and bear-hugged Brett around the arms and chest. The kid had cocked an elbow to knock Margo aside, clearing an escape route to the door for himself and his mother.

Brett instinctively fought to resist the arms encircling him, but Evan tightened his grip and bounced him off the floor. "This won't help your mother," he hissed into the young man's ear. "It won't help any of us. Now just relax."

Jakes had also reacted to Brett's sudden move by swinging the gun into view and leveling it at the suddenly wild-eyed kid. Evan quickly spoke again, this time to the man holding the gun. "It's okay, Nolan, I've got him. He'll be all right. Don't do anything rash."

For a few tense seconds the seven persons in the coach seemed suspended in time. The enraged gunman in the kitchen dared the kid to move. Evan maintained his powerful bear hug and willed him to be still. And the four females were frozen in place, powerless to alter the outcome of the confrontation.

After what seemed to be a millennium, Brett relaxed submissively. Evan lowered him to the floor and loosened his grip without completely releasing Brett. Libby was immediately at Brett's ear with a tearful apology. "I'm sorry I couldn't tell you about this, but I—"

"That's enough," Jakes shouted, waving the gun. "We have work to do. Evan, bring the kid back here. Everybody else stay where you are."

As Evan escorted the young man through the kitchen, Jakes fumbled in the doctor's satchel on the sink and pulled out a large roll of adhesive tape. Keeping the gun barrel between himself and the two men, he said to Evan, "Tape his mouth shut."

Evan felt for the kid, whose expression mirrored an odd mixture of confusion, defiance, and fear. But he knew he must follow Jakes' order without questioning. He ripped off several short lengths of tape and firmly sealed Brett's lips.

"Now use the tape to hogtie him face down on the floor next to the bed," Jakes directed. Evan knew exactly what he meant. During their time at CSUN, Tango and Choo-choo had hogtied their share of freshman athletes in the shower room using trainer's tape.

As Jakes watched, Evan put Brett face down on the bed. While he fused the young man's wrists together with several lengths of adhesive tape, Evan tried to make a point. "My family and I are in this against our will, just like your mother is—and now you. If you play along without making trouble, we'll all get out of this all right. But if you make Nolan mad, it could get bad for all of us. Do you understand?"

Brett grunted yes.

Evan assisted the kid to a prone position on the floor, adjusting a pillow under his head. Then he taped Brett's ankles together, bent his knees, and linked the wrists and ankles with several loops of tape. The prisoner was effectively immobilized.

"You don't want your mother or that little girl out there to get hurt, do you?" Evan continued.

Brett grunted no.

"Good. Then you lie here and forget about trying to be a hero," Evan said. "We'll make some sense out of all this for you when it's over." Then Evan leaned down and gave him a reassuring pat on the shoulder.

Seeing that Evan had finished, Jakes waved him into the dinette.

"Let's get this over with and get back on the road," he said nervously.

Libby was already seated at the table opposite Shelby and Malika. Evan slid into the bench next to his wife and daughter. Malika transferred her panic grip from Shelby to him. Evan wrapped strong arms of security around her.

When Evan's eyes met Libby's, which were misty with tears, the woman seemed desperate to communicate something to him—a warning, a vital shred of information. She wasn't about to speak with Nolan Jakes hovering over them. Evan searched her face for a clue, but he could read only the anguish of her forced silence.

The unspoken exchange lasted only a moment, interrupted by Jakes' words, "It's time to go to the bank. Here's how we're going to do it."

Sixty-one

"I just *knew* Rennie was heading for Seattle," Beth said, feeling smug about her guesswork. "It's just my luck to have an international trigger man prowling the streets across the Sound from my island."

"We *both* figured out that he was headed for Seattle," Cole corrected, as he eased the Barego toward the right lane of I-5 in the middle of the city. "The question is, is he stopping to do business here or is he just getting a sandwich before moving on to Canada?"

Cole and Beth had stayed two to three minutes behind the Town Car since their brief stop to get coffee and change drivers near Centralia, Washington. As their man passed first the state capital of Olympia and then Tacoma, the pair agreed that the port city of Seattle was the next most likely destination for a man connected to the international drug business.

Of course, they had already been wrong about San Francisco and Portland, two other west coast hotbeds for the mayhem and murder connected with the drug industry. But they were down to their last strike. Barbosa was headed for either Seattle or Vancouver, B.C. Neither of them were surprised when the blip on the Hawkeye's map of Seattle peeled off the freeway just north of downtown and entered the University District.

"But why the District?" Beth wondered aloud. "I would expect a guy like Barbosa to head for a downtown hotel or some dive on the waterfront, not the District."

"The man has made a living out of concealing his motives and actions," Cole reminded. "That's why we'd better take a closer look."

By the time the black Barego had crossed the University Bridge, the

Hawkeye revealed that Barbosa's Town Car was stopped on Twelfth Avenue between Forty-Seventh and Fiftieth Streets. Having spent time at the University of Washington logging credits toward a master's degree, Beth knew the District well. When they left the freeway, she assumed the navigator's role.

"Angle left on Eleventh Avenue," she said, glancing between the electronic map on her lap and the landmarks around them. "Stay on it to Fiftieth Street."

"What's this area like?" Cole asked as he followed the one-way traffic onto Eleventh.

"It's a neat little shopping district—restaurants, stores, galleries, banks. Being adjacent to the U Dub campus, many of the places cater to the college crowd."

"Husky T-shirts and beer steins for sale everywhere," Cole quipped.

Beth ignored his attempt at humor. "Turn right on Fiftieth, then another right on Twelfth. According to the map, he's parked at the curb on the right side of the street."

"I don't want to park right behind him," Cole said. "He may remember us from passing him on the freeway."

"You're kidding. He's seen hundreds of cars on the freeway. How is he going to remember this one?"

"I'm telling you, Beth, these guys have their radar tuned to this kind of stuff. The ones that don't are dead meat."

"Okay, okay," Beth surrendered. "You can park on Fiftieth, around the corner from him. But how are we going to see if he's out of the car—and if he *is* out, what he's up to?"

"I'll have to take an undercover reconnaissance stroll around the corner," Cole said, slowing the car as he approached Fiftieth Street. "Barbosa has seen more of you than he has of me. And I'm *sure* he would remember someone like you."

"I'm flattered, but I'm not very happy about getting shut out of the action," Beth pouted.

Cole made the right turn and parallel parked near the far end of the block across from the YMCA. "I'm only going to be around the corner," he explained. "I'll give you a full report as soon as I get back."

"Better yet," she said, pulling out her phone, "dial my number and give me a running commentary."

Cole paused, and Beth guessed he was thinking up reasons for not taking his phone with him around the corner. But he surprised her when he said, "Fair enough."

He took back his wraparound shades and pulled a windbreaker out of his saddlebags. It was a pleasant, breezy 68 degrees outside, but Cole maintained that the jacket would help him keep the phone out of sight. Beth offered him the UCLA cap, which she had stowed between her seat and the console right after they passed Barbosa on the freeway over an hour ago, but he declined.

Cole stepped out onto the sidewalk and donned the jacket. Foot traffic in the District was heavy on such a nice day, giving him a crowd to blend into. With the car door still open, he tapped Beth's number into his personal phone, and she answered after the first tone. "Sit tight, I'll be back in a few," he said into the phone.

"Just don't hang up," she insisted into her instrument.

"Roger, but I'm turning off my receiver while I'm out there," Cole said. "I don't want a woman's voice coming out of my pocket when I'm trying to stay incognito."

"Roger yourself," Beth responded. Then Cole stuck his hand and phone into the jacket pocket with the line still open and headed off, disappearing around the corner after a dozen steps.

Beth propped her phone up on the console next to her. She was tired. She knew that if she relaxed just a little and leaned her head back, it was all over for an hour or so. And even though much of the novelty of the I-5 chase had evaporated, she couldn't doze off on Cole now. She had to stay interested as long as he did.

She pulled down her window with a tap on the power switch. The noise of shoppers and cars outside was a pleasing reminder of the many days she had spent hanging out in the District between classes at U Dub. And the touch of the breeze—lightly scented by Puget Sound a few miles to the west—made her glad to be home in the Northwest.

More than being home, she was home with Reagan Cole. *This is amazing, really bizarre,* she mused with wonder. *A week ago I was gliding through the Caribbean in the embrace of a rich, powerful man. I had a book contract well into six figures with Havercroft and Wendt and others on the horizon. I was better off than I've ever been, and it only promised to get better. Then—shazzam!—in a few hours it was all over. The trap door underneath me snapped open, I dropped into the pits, and my storybook life disappeared in a puff of smoke.*

Now look at me. I've been up all night. I've worn the same clothes for twenty-four hours—makeup long gone, hair a mess. I have no job. I'm sitting in Seattle's University District listening for a Los Angeles policeman to tell me that the Peruvian hit man we've been following all night—I can't believe this!—is stalking a victim or sitting in Hot Beans sipping an espresso before resuming his trip to Canada.

Beth laughed to herself at the astonishing contrast. Then she was struck by an even more startling realization. She was happier than she was a week ago—poorer, more fatigued, less in control of her life, less sure about her future to be sure, but happier. And it was all because of Reagan Cole. Like serene Whidbey Island anchored in the Sound for millennia, Cole had waited silently and patiently for her to return from more than a year of selfish wandering. And in the meantime, he had become more of a rock than he had been when she slipped quietly away from him.

Substance, that's what it is, Beth reaffirmed. *I don't know what else to call it. The man has substance to his life. He's solid, well-grounded. I spent the last year building my life over a trap door; Reagan has positioned himself on a rock. Thank God my abrupt tumble through the floor landed me next to him.*

Beth suddenly felt the warmth of a hand resting on her right shoulder. It was as if someone sitting in the backseat had reached up to touch her, but Beth knew there was no one in the backseat. The hand seemed so real that she snapped her head left to see if Cole—or worse yet, a stranger—had reached through the window from the street. There was no one, but the sensation of warmth on her shoulder remained.

You're welcome. It came from behind her. It wasn't a voice, but neither was it a projection of Beth's mind. Her heartbeat, already accelerating from the touch, jumped another level at the strange impression. Icy droplets of fear which had trickled down her spine raced back up to her neck.

Ordinarily, Beth's response to such a fright would be autonomic, launching her from the car as if a snake was coiled around the headrest. But she didn't move, didn't even breathe for several seconds. The unseen hand steadied her without restraining her. The calming warmth on her shoulder disarmed the chilling fear.

Beth pondered the vivid impression, grasping for an explanation. *My last thought was, "Thank God my abrupt tumble—"*

The invisible hand squeezed her shoulder. The silent voice said again, *You're welcome.*

Beth instantly knew. A wave of wonder crashed over her, driving the breath from her lungs. It was the God who had spared her life on Millennium's Eve. It was the God who had briefly attracted her attention through the selfless, serving acts of Dr. No at King's House in Los Angeles. It was the God who had been waiting beneath the fragile scaffolding of her self-centered life, ready to catch her and set her again beside a man of irrefutable substance. It was the God she had almost flippantly told Cole she would obey.

During the night, as Cole had talked about his faith and asked Beth about hers, it all seemed so logical. There is indeed a God and He is vitally interested in His human creation. Beth had never denied that. People have a choice in the matter, either to do God's thing or blow Him off. In the nearly forty-eight hours since she first faced Cole at the reception in Ventura, Beth had acknowledged to herself that she might need to rethink her decision to walk away from God, as she had walked away from Cole early last spring.

Cole's well-timed, poignant words, as they crawled through the Southern Oregon fog in the wee hours of the morning, had brought her to a logical conclusion: She would choose to do God's thing. It had done wonders for Cole, and it had to be better than falling through the floor.

But unlike the inner warmth of being drawn back to Reagan Cole, Beth's choice to reignite her barely flickering faith had been just that — a choice. She had been stirred very little emotionally, either as she pondered the options or as she voiced to Cole her decision. For all she felt, her decision was no more earthshaking than deciding to start flossing again after having ignored the practice for over a year.

Now Beth knew, as deeply as she knew almost anything, that her logical choice was infinitely more significant than she first imagined. It had mattered to someone else, the same someone one who had broken her fall, caught her in His loving, forgiving arms, and set her down beside Reagan Cole to be escorted into His family. It was as if God had been waiting quietly in the backseat since 3 A.M. for the opportunity to respond to her decision. And His dramatic response not only gripped her mind but her whole being.

Beth caught her breath and whispered, "Thank *You*, God."

You're welcome. I am the Rock you seek. Build on Me.

The trembling began somewhere deep inside Beth and rippled out to her flesh in the form of a shudder, goose flesh, and tears. She was tempted to rationalize the phenomenon as the fallout from too little sleep after an emotionally taxing week. Perhaps she *was* physically and emotionally drained, ripe for a good cry. But she could not explain away the undeniable reality of the intimate bond forged in the last few moments at the deepest level of her existence. So she reached up to touch the unseen hand on her shoulder and let the unbidden tears of humility and joy flow.

Cole had meandered leisurely down Twelfth Avenue looking into store windows, while surreptitiously closing ground on the burgundy Town Car parked at the curb just beyond the University Motel. Barbosa was still at the wheel, so Cole, vulnerable to his gaze through the rearview mirror, tried to appear as unobtrusive a shopper as possible.

After ten minutes he stepped into the lobby of the motel where he could watch the Town Car without being seen. He pulled the phone out of his pocket and informed Beth quietly, "I'm in the lobby of the University Motel. Barbosa has been in the car since I turned the corner. I think he's awake, but I'm not sure about it. With all the traffic on the street, I can't tell who he's watching, if anyone. Maybe he's meeting someone here in the motel. I'll probably hang out here until he makes a move.

"Sorry you're not in on the fun. Hope you're not bored out of your skull. Talk to you in a few minutes. Over."

Sixty-two

Jakes and Margo's plan was very simple. Using the bank cards and PIN numbers hesitantly supplied by Evan and Shelby Rider and Libby Carroll, Margo accessed accounts by phone to determine account balances and credit limits. Then she recommended to Jakes specific cash amounts for each to withdraw, combinations from checking, savings, and credit lines. Each amount, she told him, was substantial while not depleting any account, which might attract the suspicion of vault tellers.

Jakes argued for a deeper hit on their hostages' accumulated wealth, but Margo's logic prevailed. Each was given a slip of paper with a total and a breakdown of the accounts from which it would be withdrawn. The total cash distribution from each would be: Libby Carroll—$90,000; Evan Rider—$110,000; Shelby Hornecker Rider—$130,000.

Jakes demanded that each contributor request bundles of bills in smaller denominations: fifties, twenties, and tens. The smaller denominations would offset the more-difficult-to pass $100 bills Jakes stole during the failed drug buy at Dodger Stadium. The Riders' money would be carried back to the coach in Evan's leather satchel, the contents of which had been emptied onto the sofa. Libby would use a large canvas shoulder bag Margo had found in the wardrobe.

Margo supplied each of their three victims with a plausible reason for their large cash withdrawals. They would not be required by the bank to supply such an explanation. Their cards and signatures were sufficient. But Margo asserted that a believable story, shared offhand, would reduce the risk of suspicion.

Evan and Shelby, who would go to the bank first with Margo while Libby waited in the coach, were to say that they were vacationing with relatives in the Seattle area and encountered a serious family emergency. If a nosy bank officer pried for more information, they would say only that it was a personal and private matter. Patrons who are able to withdraw a quarter-million dollars on their signatures could expect such confidentiality.

After Evan and Shelby succeeded, Jakes instructed, Margo would return to the bank with Libby. She was instructed to withdraw her money by saying something like, "I'm haggling with a guy over a yacht, and I've always wanted to march in with cash to back up my ridiculous offer." Libby said she didn't think she could pull off such an act. Jakes reminded her that she was in no position to refuse.

Before the Riders left with Margo, Jakes demanded that Evan gag and hogtie Malika with adhesive tape. Shelby started to protest, but Evan silenced her before Jakes could raise his gun against her again.

Malika lay on the bed, docile but with panic-filled eyes, as Evan closed her mouth and bound her hands and feet behind her with tape. Brett Carroll, similarly gagged and trussed, lay awake but unmoving on his stomach on the floor.

Shelby tried to assure the little girl that everything would be all right, that Daddy wasn't being mean to her. But the look of betrayal on Malika's face tore at both parents' hearts, provoking misty eyes and looks of despair. Jakes allowed them to leave the girl lying on her side, warning them again that he would hurt her if they failed in their mission to the bank.

As she walked across the hotel parking lot toward the bank between Margo and Evan, Shelby wondered about Libby Carroll. The strikingly beautiful black woman had emerged from Evan's past as someone he had been very close to: close enough to bury a serious crime together for two decades.

. What other secrets did they share? Evan had confessed to Shelby during their courtship that he had been promiscuous both before and after his brief marriage to Katrina Ewing. Though Evan had never named names—nor did Shelby want him to—his bride couldn't help but wonder if Libby Carroll had been among his conquests.

Fueling Shelby's tinge of jealousy had been Libby's eye contact with Evan as they all sat in the dinette together only minutes ago. Had a woman ever tried to communicate to a man without speaking, Libby had done so to Evan. What Libby's message was, Shelby could only guess. It certainly wasn't the look of a woman scorned. Nor was it a leer of desire or wantonness, at least not overtly. It wasn't even, "Remember the good, fast times we enjoyed?" But the message was potent, judging by Libby's articulate use of unspoken language.

Shelby wasn't convinced Evan had deciphered Libby's message. He seemed to read her eyes, brows, and unspeaking lips, as if trying to translate a manuscript in a language he hadn't spoken in years. He apparently recognized some of the words but had forgotten their meaning. And Shelby wasn't sure that if Evan *did* receive the message he would admit it to her or share it with her.

Shelby prayed as she walked casually to the bank in the bright sunshine and pleasant breeze. She prayed for the safety of little Malika, a prayer which had not been far from her mind the entire trip. She prayed for the successful withdrawal of funds and a safe return to the coach for her poor daughter's sake.

She prayed for Evan, the storehouse of so many secrets. What else did he have to tell her? What else was he hiding in the name of spiritual ignorance? How else would his dark past threaten the viability of their marriage?

And Shelby prayed for herself. She didn't belong in this scenario any more than she belonged on the dangerous end of a death threat on

Millennium's Eve. *God, give me strength, please,* she pleaded. *I can't make it without You.*

Shelby was relieved at how swiftly and courteously the vault officer processed their withdrawal. As Margo waited in a plush chair nearby, she and Evan completed the paperwork, submitted their cards for processing, cleared an electronic security check, and were admitted to a private office near the vault. The officer, a young man who seemed to regard his banking career as a divine calling, was almost too polite. He never so much as hinted an interest in the reason for such a large cash withdrawal. On the contrary, Shelby almost expected him to chip in with something like, "Are you sure this will be enough for you today? We're running a special on half-million-dollar cash withdrawals. All I have to do is change a few numbers on your form."

Shelby remained silent as Evan packed the bundles of bills into the satchel under the officer's watchful eye. Her husband apparently felt the need to fill the communication void. He muttered something about their vacation being interrupted by a family emergency and how glad he was to have a reserve of capital for such emergencies. The cheery officer nodded sympathetically without asking one meddlesome question. Instead he graciously offered the services of a security guard to walk the couple to their car. Evan thanked him just as graciously, but refused. The couple walked out of the bank with Margo less than fifteen minutes after they entered.

As they crossed Brooklyn Avenue and returned to the RV, Shelby thought about the money in the satchel. Two hundred forty thousand dollars was paltry compared to the huge sums which had passed through her hands thus far in her adult life. Having served as co-pastor and then pastor of a national television mega-ministry, she had managed the distribution of multiplied millions of dollars annually. And nearly a million a year, by order of a grateful and generous board of directors, had flowed into her personal account. Shelby Hornecker Rider was no stranger to wealth.

But neither was she possessed by it, especially since the dramatic events of Millennium's Eve prompted her to focus her life's work on a struggling mission to the poor, diseased, and downtrodden of inner-city Los Angeles. At that time she walked away from her lucrative ministry and funneled a substantial amount of her resources into King's House. She was now content with a simpler lifestyle and completely fulfilled in what she did for others.

The $130,000 in the satchel withdrawn from Shelby's accounts represented a significant segment of her liquid capital and signature borrowing-power. But it was a relatively small amount compared to her net worth. While Shelby had diverted much of her substance to the ministry in L.A., she had retained some key investments for their children's education and for their retirement. These accounts were beyond the immediate reach of Nolan Jakes and Margo Sharpe, though Shelby knew she would gladly give everything to assure Malika's safety.

They were getting off cheaply enough, Shelby acknowledged, as they approached the door to the RV. In the overall scheme of things, $240,000 was nothing in comparison to the safety of her family. She could hand the money over to Nolan Jakes without reservation. Her apprehension centered on her life with Evan *after* Jakes and Margo and the money were across the border. *I would also give everything to plumb the depths of Evan's secrets*, she concluded silently, *but would everything be enough?*

Libby's trip to the bank a few minutes later, with Margo as escort, was equally successful. Her withdrawal request was processed by the vault officer with the same dispatch and we-aim-to-please courtesy shown to the couple vacationing from California. Libby's comment about making an offer on a yacht sounded wooden and contrived to her. But Mr. Banking-Is-My-Life just smiled broadly and wished her good luck. After declining the services of a guard, Libby hurriedly packed the bundled $90,000 into the shoulder bag, pulled the strap over her shoulder, and left.

Libby and Margo were about to step off the curb to jaywalk across Brooklyn Avenue when a voice called out from the parking lot behind them, "Dr. Carroll." Margo quickly grabbed her elbow to hustle her across the street. But Libby knew that if she didn't respond, Brett's safety might be jeopardized further. So she turned around, and Margo reluctantly turned with her.

Reginald Burris was dressed for a summer day off: white tennis shorts revealing his tree-trunk legs, a size 3X purple polo—which he amply filled—with a Washington Husky embroidered above the left breast, well-worn canvas deck shoes, and a pair of sunglasses perched atop his gleaming bald head.

As Reginald approached them, Libby expected the big officer to play a role in front of the stranger, and he did not disappoint her. "How are you, Dr. Carroll?"

His question, asked as casually as any friend greeting another on the street, seemed innocuous enough. But Libby knew he was really asking, "Is everything going all right? Are you being hassled in any way? Do you need my help?"

Libby wished she had never called him in the first place. Margo was listening at her elbow, and Nolan Jakes was watching from the RV in the distance. If she screwed up this confrontation, Brett could pay the price. She would have to play her role to convince not only her captors but Reginald Burris.

"Just fine, Reginald," Libby answered with artificial cheer. Then without allowing him a moment to speak, she continued. "I'd like you to meet my old friend"—she grasped at a fake name with barely a pause—"Kathy Williams. Kathy is on vacation, and we're having a great time today. Kathy, this is a coworker of mine, Reginald Burris."

The platinum blonde joined in the act by offering her hand to Reginald, who shook it.

Reginald was obviously processing Libby's data and performance, but he didn't let on. "Weren't you meeting some other friends today?" he asked. Libby interpreted the root question, "Is this woman Kathy the business partner you mentioned, the one you were leery about, or were you talking about someone else?"

"No, that didn't work out," Libby said convincingly. "Kathy and I are spending the day together." She prayed that Reginald would not abandon the surface chatter to ask why she had requested him to come to the bank.

He eyed both women for a moment, then said, "Well, sounds like you two have a busy day ahead, and so do I. Good to meet you, Kathy."

Kathy Williams, the platinum blonde, flashed a plastic smile.

"Dr. Carroll, I'll probably see you on campus later this week." Libby again picked up Reginald's shrouded message, "I need to hear why you called me out here for nothing."

"Sure, see you on campus, Reginald," she said.

Reginald turned with a wave and retreated to his old gray Ford Taurus in the bank parking lot. Libby and Margo waited for a break in traffic, then jogged across the street. Libby breathed a prayer of thanks to God that she was able to evade Reginald, even though she wished she could have blurted out everything.

"Who was that big black guy?" Jakes snarled suspiciously as the two women stepped into the coach. Evan was already at the wheel with the motor running. Shelby had retreated to the bedroom, with Jakes' permission, to comfort Malika.

"He works at the university," Libby explained. Then she added a lie to divert suspicion, "He's a custodian in our building."

Jakes looked to Margo for her evaluation. "No problem, Nolan," she assured. "She did fine. Let's get out of here."

Satisfied, Jakes took the bag of money from Libby and checked its contents greedily. Then he stowed the bag with the satchel and the sports bag in the wardrobe.

"Give me the fastest way to I-5 north," he demanded of Libby.

"Eleventh Avenue to Fiftieth," she said. "There's an on-ramp at Fiftieth."

Jakes tapped Evan on the shoulder. "Go."

Evan hesitated. "Libby did her part, Nolan," he said in a respectful tone. "Can't we leave her and the boy here?"

"Not a chance," Jakes said with finality. "They go with us to the border so I know she stays quiet. Now go."

Evan complied. He guided the rig through the parking lot toward the driveway, waited for traffic, and turned south on Twelfth. After right turns on Forty-Fifth Street and then Eleventh Avenue, he accelerated gradually toward Fiftieth.

Handing the gun to Margo, Jakes said, "Keep them all in the bedroom."

"What about the kids, Nolan?" Libby asked over her shoulder as Margo herded her toward the rear of the coach. "May we please untie the kids?"

Jakes thought for a moment. "No, not until we reach the border," he announced.

"But the little girl won't cause any—"

"They both stay tied up!" he barked. "Now get back there and shut up!"

When Libby complied, Margo returned to Jakes for a moment of congratulating and kissing. They looked again at the three bags in the wardrobe and Margo allowed herself a little whoop of joy. Then she sat down in the dinette where she could keep an eye on the hostages in the bedroom. She set the Colt .44 beside her on the bench.

Shelby was curled up around the little black girl on the bed whispering words of consolation. Libby sat on the corner of the bed nearest Brett. Even with the pillow under his head he looked very uncomfortable. Libby choked back a sob.

"Are you doing all right?" she asked quietly, patting him on the leg.

Brett lifted his head about an inch off the pillow and uttered a muffled, "Um-hm." Libby knew he was holding himself together for her just as she was trying to do for him.

"Were you going to call Andie to pick you up at the bank?" she asked.

"Um-hm."

Libby put herself in the girl's place. "She's going to be worried when you don't call."

"Hm."

The coach rolled to the right as Evan turned left onto Fiftieth. Libby could hear the car carrier behind them creak through the maneuver. Moments later the action reversed as the RV turned right onto the on-ramp to I-5 north. Evan accelerated to freeway speed. In two hours they would arrive at the Canadian border.

Libby gazed the length of the coach to where Evan sat behind the wheel. Then she quickly looked away so as not to catch his eye in the rearview mirror. She had explained to Brett that Evan Rider was his father, and her son had responded remarkably well. But before she could fulfill the second part of her mission—explaining to Evan that Brett was his son—maniacal Nolan Jakes had butted in. At his order, Evan had bound and gagged his own son without knowing it.

How does Brett feel about being treated like a prisoner by his father? she wondered. She dare not ask him now with Shelby so near. *It wouldn't be right for Shelby to learn that she is Brett's stepmother before Evan knows he has a son.*

And how will Evan feel when I finally tell him about what else happened on that horrible night in Portland nearly twenty-two years ago? What will he think of me for keeping Brett a secret over all these years?

Libby again glanced forward. This time Evan happened to be looking back at her. Their eyes locked for two seconds over the length of the coach before Evan looked away.

Hang in there, Evan, she exhorted him silently. *You still have one more big surprise to deal with before this adventure is over.*

Sixty-three

Only a few minutes had passed since Beth's tearfully moving encounter, and she was already beginning to question what had happened to her. Thankfully, the answers came as readily as the questions.

Did I fall asleep? Was I dreaming?

No, I wasn't even resting my head. I was sitting right here, enjoying the pleasant breeze from outside, listening for Reagan to report on Barbosa from around the corner.

Did I imagine the sensation of a heavenly hand on my shoulder?

How could I? It felt so real that I jumped. There was the weight of a large hand on my shoulder. I could feel the separate fingers and thumb gripping me. There was the warmth of contact. The only thing missing was a visible hand and a person connected to it.

Did I actually hear someone speaking to me?

Not with my ears. I heard only cars passing and people chatting on the sidewalk. But sounds received by the ears must be processed by the brain to be understood. The words I heard behind me seemed to bypass the auditory canal and go straight to my brain. I heard nothing, but I understood every word!

So who—or what—was it? God? An angel? A departed saint? The devil himself playing tricks with my head?

It had to be from up above. I had just said, "Thank God." Actually, I didn't say it audibly any more than what I heard was audible. I just thought it, spoke it with my mind. I may not have been as sincere as I could be, but I was addressing God, not an angel or a saint, and certainly not the devil. And apparently He heard me and understood, because a voice—or should I call it an un-voice—said, "You're welcome." Then, "I am the Rock you seek. Build on Me." Who would say that except God?

But there was much more communicated at that moment than just those nine words, Beth reminded herself. *There was meaning beyond the words, the nonverbal dynamic you perceive in the inflection of a spoken message. The voice I heard in my mind was rich with compassion and authority. It was the voice of someone who knows all about me, knows what I'm thinking and feeling, knows just how to connect with me so I need no further proof. I know it was Him because I just know it was Him.*

At that moment, Cole's voice came through the speaker of Beth's phone on the console. He reported that Barbosa was still sitting in the Town Car, and that he would continue to watch him from the lobby of University Motel. Then he added, "Sorry you're not in on the fun. Hope you're not bored out of your skull. Talk to you in a few minutes. Over."

"Bored out of my skull? After what just happened to me?" Beth said aloud, aware that Cole could not hear her. "Wait till I tell you."

The idea of telling Cole what happened brought another question: *Will he believe me? Will anyone believe me? I've heard people talk about epiphanies before—that's what it was, wasn't it, an epiphany, a visitation from God?—and I didn't believe them. If a person as sane as I am alleges that God spoke to her, I immediately treat her as if Alzheimer's has suddenly set in. Who's to say that people won't regard me to be just as nuts.*

Beth recalled that Reagan Cole, the recently avowed follower of Christ, never mentioned anything about having a personal encounter with God. If he had experienced an epiphany during his conversion, he wasn't talking—at least not so far. Apparently even men of faith don't enjoy being viewed as wackos. Beth decided that she would keep her dramatic experience under wraps for the time being for the same reason. *Besides,* she mused, *if God wanted Reagan to know about what happened to me, He would have shown up when we were in the car together.*

Beth pondered other implications of her spiritual encounter for several minutes until Cole interrupted her again. This time his voice was more animated, "Beth, I turned my receiver back on. Are you there?"

Beth picked up her phone. "Right here where you left me." Intent on Cole's message, she didn't notice the thirty-foot Flair RV and its red Datsun wagon caboose slip by her on Fiftieth Street headed north.

"He's taking off again," Cole said. "Give him half a minute to get out of sight; then drive around and pick me up. I'll be at the curb in front of the University Motel. It looks like we're on the road again."

Beth leaned toward the Hawkeye on the floor for a better look. The blip had moved away from the position on the curb it had occupied for almost half an hour. "I see," she said over the phone. "He's turning right on Forty-Fifth Street. . . Now he's heading back this way on

Eleventh Avenue. I'm on my way." Then she tapped her phone off and tossed it on the seat.

Beth fired up the Buick and dropped into DRIVE, but the congestion on the street prevented her from pulling away from the curb. She glanced at the monitor again and gasped. "Barbosa is turning right on Fiftieth," she said as if Cole was still listening. "He's going to drive right by me."

Shoving the gearshift quickly into PARK, Beth threw her upper body across the console and onto the other seat to drop out of sight. She heard the stop-and-go traffic edge by. The Hawkeye warned that the Town Car was practically alongside her. She held her breath until the blip moved on to the next block.

Finding an opening in traffic, Beth pulled out and cut immediately down Twelfth Avenue to where Cole stood waiting for her. He jumped in quickly, and then they sat at the curb watching the blip while Beth described her close call with the passing Town Car. She said nothing about her brief but trenchant brush with the backseat visitor.

"He's headed back to the freeway," Cole said with a sigh, watching the blip move toward the northbound on-ramp to I-5. "Next stop, Canadian border—that's my guess."

"What about you?" Beth probed. "Do you want to follow him to the border?"

Cole pondered the question, then shook his head. "I don't need to go all the way to the Peace Arch, when I can watch the Town Car cross the border on the Hawkeye. But I would still like to know what this is all about." Cole gestured to the place on the street where Barbosa and the Town Car had been parked. "It's like that strange stop in Woodburn. He didn't talk to anyone here. He didn't buy gas or food. He just parked for half an hour and left. If he's going to Canada, why doesn't he just put the pedal to the metal and go to Canada? Why diddle around at 60 MPH and stop for no reason? That's the piece that doesn't seem to fit this puzzle. And I hate to leave a puzzle unfinished. I guess it's an occupational hazard for a detective."

"Journalists are similarly plagued," Beth said with a chuckle.

"So what shall we do with this brainteaser?"

Beth thought for a moment. "Let's stay with him as far as Mount Vernon—about another hour," she suggested. "If you're satisfied by then that he's headed out of the U.S., we can turn off to Whidbey Island. If you're not, we can keep going."

Cole wrestled with his thoughts while absently watching the blip streak northward on I-5. "Okay," he said at last, unconvinced that he could find the missing piece to the puzzle in the two hours before Barbosa entered Canada.

Back on the freeway, the Town Car resumed its maddeningly slow pace of 63 MPH. Beth pulled within two minutes of him again, punched the same speed, and settled in for the final leg of the journey, ending either at the Canadian border or at Beth's home outside Oak Harbor on Whidbey Island. The Seattle skyline, with its famous spaceneedle, slowly receded toward the horizon behind them.

The next twenty minutes in the Barego were silent as both passengers retreated into themselves. Beth's thoughts were dominated by what had just happened to her in Seattle—"The Miracle on Fiftieth Street," she termed it with an inner smile. She mentally retraced her steps along a curious path that had led her to a dramatic personal encounter with God: the crushing breakup with Colin Wendt in the Caribbean; the harebrained decision to divert to Los Angeles on the way home in order to attend Shelby Hornecker's wedding—for which she was late; the unexplainable attraction to Reagan Cole after more than a year of separation; another harebrained decision, insisting that Cole take her along on the pursuit of Rennie Barbosa; the arduous but personally rewarding I-5 marathon highlighted by a few minutes of heaven on Fiftieth Street.

It was all for a purpose, Beth assessed. *It's as if Barbosa's appetite was suddenly whetted for an all-night drive to Canada just so I could rediscover Reagan Cole and be confronted by the God I've been avoiding.* She couldn't wait to tell the whole story to Cole—when the time was right.

"Let's go back to the theory that Barbosa has been following someone," Cole said, breaking the silence. Beth wasn't surprised that he was still absorbed in the puzzle of Rennie Barbosa.

"All right," Beth said. "What are you thinking?"

"I'm thinking that he pulled off the freeway in Seattle for the same reason he pulled off in Woodburn, Oregon."

"Which reason?" Beth probed.

"We don't know, but it could be the same reason for each stop."

"Sounds reasonable."

"When he stopped in Woodburn, we guessed that he was either waiting for someone to catch up with him or pausing to stay behind someone."

"Uh-huh."

"So we passed him and several other vehicles to see if we noticed anything unusual in the slow lane ahead of him."

"Even though we didn't know what kind of 'unusual' we were looking for," Beth interjected.

"Right. But at that time we didn't find anything that looked unusual to us."

"I'm with you so far," Beth said encouragingly. She could almost hear the gears of suspicion and hypothesis turning in Cole's head. "What else are you thinking?"

"I'm thinking that we should pass him again."

"And look for something unusual again?"

"Yeah. Maybe something that looked *usual* to us before will look *unusual* if we see it again."

"But all we saw in the slow lane before were trucks and RVs," Beth said.

"And an old, restored Buick Riviera," Cole corrected.

"Oh, yeah. An old, restored Buick Riviera smoking up the highway," Beth added.

"That's the one."

"In other words," Beth continued, "if we pass Barbosa again and see the Riviera ahead of him again, that's unusual."

"Wouldn't you think it unusual if after 200 miles and a half-hour stop, Barbosa would still be following the Riviera at the same slow speed?"

"*If* we find the Riviera," Beth emphasized.

"Yes, or if we see anything else we saw when we passed him before."

"We saw trucks and RVs, lots of them," Beth said, enjoying her role as the devil's advocate. "Will we even recognize any we saw before?"

Cole shrugged. "I don't know."

"And by now any number of the rigs we saw could have stopped for a half hour to refuel or eat a quick lunch. How can we tell if Barbosa is following these rigs on purpose or by coincidence?"

"I don't know. But if we don't pass him and take a look . . . " Cole didn't feel a need to finish his argument.

"Got it," Beth said. Waiting until a minivan with British Columbia plates passed in the left lane, she accelerated, signaled, eased into the fast lane, and reset the cruise monitor to match the minivan.

"Won't Rennie think it unusual when we pass him again?" Beth said.

"Like you said, everybody traveling I-5 stops for gas or food. It's not unusual to be passed twice by the same car on a long trip. Besides, this is the last he will see us. At Mount Vernon, I'm turning this over to the FBI."

It took the Barego a little less than twenty minutes in the fast lane to crawl up on Rennie Barbosa's Town Car. As during their prior pass, Beth wore the UCLA cap and shades, while Cole reclined nearly out of sight in the passenger's seat.

With the Town Car slipping slowly behind them, Cole and Beth silently considered every vehicle they eased past in the right lane: a milk tanker bobbing along empty; unmarked triple trailers hitched to a leased tractor; an old Airstream vacation trailer plastered with decals and pulled by a white-haired couple in a one-ton Dodge pickup; a Kenworth tractor pulling two flatbed trailers stacked high with cut lumber; a white Flair motorhome with a car carrier bearing a bright red station wagon.

"We've passed that RV before," Beth said, as they came up behind the Flair.

Cole nodded. "Who could forget that cherry-looking Datsun wagon. But where did we see it before?"

"Somewhere after Eugene," Beth said, "but I don't remember if Rennie was ahead of it or behind it."

"California plates," Cole noted. "Number 86D4746. Thousand Oaks dealership on the frame."

"Smart Californians, escaping the southland for a Canadian vacation," Beth said.

Cole and Beth continued moving past the slower vehicles. A few of the trucks looked familiar but definitely not unusual or suspicious.

"No Riviera blowing smoke," Beth observed with a sigh, after a few more minutes of silent watching. She pulled off the UCLA cap and tossed it onto the back seat.

Cole hummed his agreement. "Nothing," he said, disappointment evident in his tone.

A freeway sign announced that exits for Mount Vernon, Washington were two miles ahead. Beth pressed the issue. "What do you want to do? Highway 536 to Whidbey Island is just ahead. Then it's an hour to my place."

"I'm tired and hungry, and I think the FBI will be happy to learn that their little project is on his way out of the country."

"Sounds like you're ready to bag it with Barbosa and head for the island."

"Yeah, I'm ready," Cole said with resignation.

"The guest room is ready for you, but my cupboards are bare, so we better stop for a sandwich in Mount Vernon."

"I'll call the FBI when we stop. And I'd better call mom again."

"After we get to the house and take a nap, we can go into town for some fresh salmon to barbecue tonight. How does that sound?"

"Great!" he said, starting to relax. "And tomorrow I'll drive the car back to SeaTac and drop it off for you. Then I'll get a flight to Reno."

Beth hoped Cole had more to say about going to Lake Tahoe. When he didn't, she said, "Aren't you going to invite me to go with you?"

"What? To Tahoe? You?" Cole exclaimed, both surprised and pleased.

"Well, thank you," Beth chirped, "I'd love to." Then she guided the Barego off I-5 at the Highway 536 exit.

The phone in the burgundy Town Car sounded.

"Are you in position, Mr. Barbosa?"

"Yes."

"Excellent. The time for action is at hand."

"I'm ready," the killer said, sounding very confident.

"When the motorhome leaves the freeway, keep it in sight. Move in only when I give you the word."

"I understand."

Sixty-four

In order to keep his heavy eyelids from sliding closed as he drove, Evan concentrated on the freeway mile markers—228, 229, 230, 231. According to his watch, another marker, representing another mile elapsed since crossing the Oregon–Washington border, drifted by every fifty-seven seconds. The fatigue was oppressive. Evan was nearly having to pinch his arm or bite the inside of his cheek to stay awake.

Mount Vernon was five miles behind them, Bellingham was twenty miles ahead, and the Canadian border was just twenty miles farther. This portion of I-5 rolled through quiet, spacious farmland, with Puget Sound less than ten miles to the west and the Cascade Range in the distance to the east. At 10,700 feet, snowcapped Mt. Baker unabashedly dominated the horizon to the northeast.

During the night Jakes had contacted someone in Vancouver by phone, a trusted ally who was eager to help an old friend disappear into the Canadian wilderness. Jakes had instructed the man to pick them up in Langley, B.C., eight miles north of the border. The RV would cross the border with a stream of other tourists, Jakes had informed Evan. A gun trained on Shelby and Malika would ensure Evan's full cooperation in getting the coach past Canadian customs.

Once they reached Langley, Jakes, Margo, and the money would disappear, and the hostages would be free to return to the States. Evan figured he could deliver his passengers to Langley and be back to Seattle before dark. Then he and Shelby, Libby, and Brett would need some time to talk.

Looking through the rearview mirror, Evan saw that Shelby and Malika had succumbed to exhaustion. They were asleep with Shelby curled around the trussed-up little girl. Libby was lying on the other side of the bed but was not asleep. She appeared to be talking quietly to her son, who was still on the floor beside her, bound with adhesive tape.

Margo had remained in the dinette facing the rear of the coach until a recent trip to the bathroom. Jakes had paced the center aisle for the last several miles, as if his nervous activity would get them to the border sooner. He would walk to the kitchen and pour a cup of coffee, then wear a path in the carpet between the kitchen and the cab as he drank it down. When the cup was empty, he returned to the kitchen again to refuel. Margo seemed unusually interested in Jakes' pacing.

It was during one of Jakes' brief stops behind the cab that the race for the border took an unexpected and terrifying turn, shaking Evan fully awake. Jakes stood just behind the step up into the cab staring at the road ahead. Evan happened to glance at him in the mirror just as a metallic gleam flashed through the air like lightning, followed by the sickening crunch of a skull cracking open. Jakes uttered barely a grunt, the murmur of someone turning in his sleep, as he dropped like a stone to the carpet in a contorted heap. Blood immediately began to pour from a gash on the crown of his head.

Behind him stood Margo Sharpe with the Colt .44 in both hands and her lips twisted into an expression of perverted vengeance. She had not delivered the tentative, glancing blow one might expect of a petite female or a novice to violence. Rather, with Jakes' back turned to her, Margo had stepped out of the bathroom, moved quickly and silently behind him, and wrenched the pistol down on the back of his head with calculated, two-handed force. The blow was clearly not intended to stun but to debilitate.

For an instant Evan feared that Shelby's moralizing had finally reached Margo, that Jakes' girlfriend had decided to end their flight and turn them all in. But in the next instant he realized Margo had no such intention.

"What was that for? Why did you hit him?" Evan demanded.

"That was for everything," Margo spat hatefully. Then for Jakes' unhearing ears, she vented, "That's for single-handedly blowing Billy's Los Angeles operation to kingdom come, Jakes. No wonder he assigned me to snuggle up close to you and keep an eye on you for him. You were an accident just waiting to happen. Lucky for me, your bumbling dropped over half a million in my lap, and your old friends here were good for another quarter million. I wasn't planning to retire this soon or this poorly. But at least you provided enough for me to duck out on Billy Fryman before he came to take me out to cover your mistake."

Margo turned her attention back to Evan. "Get off the freeway at the next exit," she ordered, lifting the gun for him to see. There was no hesitation in her voice and no compromise in the seriousness of her tone. Evan realized that whatever this small, pretty, unassuming young woman was about to do had been brewing in her brain for some time.

The commotion near the cab had attracted Libby's attention in the bedroom. Seeing Jakes motionless on the floor, she sprang from the bed and started forward. "Get back in there and stay there!" Margo shouted at her with a threatening wave of the gun. Libby stopped in her tracks, slowly backed into the bedroom, and sat down on the bed. Suddenly awake, Shelby sat up and gasped at the sight at the front of the coach. "Nobody steps out of that room!" Margo commanded. Libby and Shelby nodded obediently.

The next freeway exit was still two miles away. It was a two-lane road winding away into farmland. Evan feared the prospect of pulling off the freeway in an unpopulated area at the direction of unpredictable Margo Sharpe, but at the moment he had no options.

With her captives at bay, Margo retreated to the wardrobe behind the dinette and hastily began retrieving bags of money. First she pulled out the canvas bag containing $90,000 in bundled bills and dropped it by the door.

Next came Evan's leather satchel stuffed with $240,000. Finally she pulled out the large nylon sports bag containing over half a million dollars in cash. She dragged it forward by the strap and left it beside the satchel.

Evan glanced over his right shoulder at Jakes, who was folded awkwardly on the floor. Blood had turned most of his blond crew cut crimson, and it continued to ooze from the gash on his head and flow into the carpet. Evan's care-giving instincts leaped ahead of his dislike for Jakes and his fear of Margo. "Please let me treat that wound," he begged of the woman with the gun. "He could bleed to death."

"Don't stop until I tell you to," Margo hissed, gun in hand again. "Just get me off the freeway and do what I say. After I leave, you can do anything you want with him, although it won't do him or you any good."

Evan silently urged Jakes to hold on a few minutes longer as he accelerated toward the off-ramp.

Cole poked at the cubes in his iced tea while watching the blip continue northward on I-5. He and Beth sat in a booth awaiting their lunch orders—a ham stack with cole slaw and a patty melt with potato salad respectively—with the Hawkeye perched on the table. They had noticed through the window of their restaurant when the burgundy Town Car passed by moments earlier. The Flair RV with the red Datsun wagon preceded it by almost two minutes.

"Having a problem letting go?" Beth asked him after a couple minutes of silence. She reached across the table and patted his hand with understanding.

Cole's brow was wrinkled with concern. "I didn't think I would, but something really bothers me."

"*What* bothers you?"

Cole poked ice cubes and thought about it. "That RV pulling the station wagon, the only vehicle we recognized. It's the only scrap of a lead we have. It probably would have led nowhere, but I should have followed it up."

"Followed it up *how?*"

Beth's question was all the encouragement Cole needed. Without a word he pulled the Hawkeye closer and began tapping in keystrokes. Beth slid around the booth to sit beside him and watch.

The map on the monitor dropped into the background and a wireless communication window blinked open. Cole entered a long-distance phone number and in seconds the screen was filled with a colorful logo with this caption beneath it: STATE OF CALIFORNIA—DEPARTMENT OF MOTOR VEHICLES. Cole tapped in a series of access codes until a brief form appeared with the cursor flashing to the left of a blank line.

"What was the license number of that RV?" Cole asked himself as much as he asked Beth. "I think it started with 86D."

"Yes, 86D."

Cole entered 86D on the form.

Beth continued, "Then it was 4647 or 4645—forty-something, forty-something."

"In descending instead of ascending order," Cole remembered.

"Yeah, I think you're right, like 4645 or 4746 or 4847."

"Let's try 4645," he said, entering the digits and initiating the search.

In less than two seconds a detailed vehicle description for California license 86D4645 was on screen.

Cole read aloud, " '1998 Ford pickup,' no that's not it." He backed out of the document and returned to the blank form. "Let's go with 86D4746," he said as he tapped in the numbers. Another vehicle description filled the screen.

"There we go," Cole said. "1995 Fleetwood Flair, thirty-footer—"

"Geez, Reagan, look at this!" Beth tapped the screen excitedly.

Cole read the words, " 'Registered owner: Rider, Evan W.' "

"Isn't that the name of the guy Shelby married Saturday?" Beth asked.

Cole whistled his surprise. "Yes, Evan Rider. And that's his address: Foster road in Ventura. I can't believe this."

"I thought they were supposed to be on their honeymoon," Beth said. Her wrinkled brow reflected her confusion. "They were going to the Grand Canyon. What are they doing up here?"

Cole advanced a hasty theory. "Maybe we got wrong information about where they were going."

Beth shook her head. "I heard Shelby say they were driving the RV to the Grand Canyon. They were supposed to leave Sunday morning—that's yesterday."

"This is *very* unusual," Cole said, quickly closing the communication window and bringing the map forward again. The data line showed the Town Car to be 5.8 miles from the Hawkeye and proceeding north at 63 MPH. "In fact, this is *too* unusual," he added, tossing his napkin on the table. "Let's go."

"Go? After Barbosa again?"

"No, after the RV to see what they're doing up here. How could they be connected to Barbosa? This has to be one king-sized coincidence."

Cole lowered the lid on the Hawkeye and scooted out of the booth. "I think it's your turn to pay," he said to Beth.

Beth followed him out of the booth, dug $15 out of her wallet, and dropped it on the table. "Leaving before lunch again?" she said in mock complaint. "Is this one of the magic moments we will tell our grandchildren about?" She suddenly realized what she had said and blushed.

Cole turned to her long enough to say, "I hope so," and wink. Then he grabbed her hand and led her hastily out of the restaurant.

Cole peeled out of the parking lot like he was driving a police special V8 with competition suspension. The little Buick coupe bounced and swayed as Cole swerved it between cars through the intersection against the red light and raced up the on-ramp to I-5 North. Beth feared he would jam the accelerator through the floor as the Barego's speed climbed past 70 and then 80.

Pulling his phone out of his pocket, Cole tapped the memory code for Shelby Rider's personal phone. There was no answer, only the generic request to leave a message. He accessed Evan's number through directory assistance, with the same result. "Nobody's answering," he reported to Beth. "I should have known it couldn't be that easy."

Cole flashed back nearly fifteen hours to when he was tempted to bag the pursuit of Rennie Barbosa in Sacramento and take Beth to Lake Tahoe instead. And he remembered the strong impression—apparently from God—that prevented him from doing so. *Did that "check" have anything to do with Evan and Shelby Rider coming north instead of heading east to the Grand Canyon?* he wondered. *Am I supposed to be up here for some reason other than to wave good-bye to Rennie Barbosa when he crosses the border for his Canadian vacation? Is there some bizarre connection between the Riders and Rennie Barbosa?* The answers to Cole's questions seemed beyond his imagination. But he felt driven to the find them.

Sixty-five

Evan braked the RV down the off-ramp, then turned right at the stop sign according to Margo's direction. Jakes remained motionless and bleeding where her vicious blow had dropped him. Evan's repeated pleas that Margo allow him to stop and minister to Jakes' head wound had been rebuffed with curses.

In the few minutes since Jakes had been struck down, Evan had replayed everything he could remember Nolan Jakes and Margo Sharpe saying since they barged into his life. He was trying to understand Margo's violent act and suddenly barbarous demeanor. As he rehearsed the events of the past thirty hours, an explanation began to take shape.

Margo had apparently been an employee of Nolan Jakes' drug boss, whom she called Fryman. Margo had been assigned to spy on Jakes, a task she accomplished very effectively by giving herself to him. And Jakes had been thoroughly taken in by her beauty and charm—that much was obvious. That there had ever been any real romance on her part now seemed extremely unlikely to Evan.

Jakes had said that he had been arrested and forced into serving as a police informant. Evan deduced that Jakes had kept that information from Margo at first. When Jakes leaked to her about the police drug bust at Dodger Stadium, she dutifully and secretly informed Fryman, who had two of his goons ready to blow Jakes and the cop off the map and abscond with the drug money.

But something went wrong. A cop and Fryman's two goons died in a gun battle, and Jakes somehow got away with the money. Unaware that Margo was involved, he ran to her and proposed an escape plan. Margo read the handwriting on the wall: With Fryman's empire in jeopardy, she was expendable. At the same time she recognized her fantastic windfall and reacted quickly. This was her chance to lose Fryman and his organization and skip the country with over half a million dollars. Thanks to Jakes' blackmail plot, the stakes rose to nearly a million. All Margo had to do was play the role of the devoted girlfriend a little longer.

After leaving Seattle with all the money safely on board the RV, Jakes had become unnecessary baggage to Margo. With a carefully timed, savage blow to the head, she took control. Once across the border she could slip away to anywhere in the world in secret and live out her days in relative comfort, free from her former drug boss and a man she had only pretended to love.

Only one unanswered question, Evan thought uneasily. *Why would Margo turn off the freeway now? She could be across the border in less than an hour. Does this vicious female have another hidden trump card to play?*

The Flair drove east from the freeway between acres of young ornamental trees and shrubs being nurtured for commercial and residential landscaping. Another large field was filled with neat rows of Scotch pine seedlings which were destined to be cut, shipped, and sold as Christmas trees in the next seven to ten years.

About a mile from the freeway they approached a row of twelve-foot arborvitae on the left, running parallel to the freeway and stretched between two fields as a windbreak. A narrow dirt road ran along the far side of the tightly bunched line of trees.

As soon as she saw the road, Margo ordered, "Turn in here and stop." Evan braked hastily and turned, bringing the coach to a stop between the windbreak and a tulip field which had already yielded its spring harvest. "Now turn off the motor and give me your keys," Margo said. Evan obeyed.

Evan didn't like the location. The coach was effectively shielded from I-5 by the windbreak. There were no other cars on the two-lane road, which was flanked on both sides by irrigation ditches. None of the fields around them were being tended by workers. The five hostages—and the disabled Nolan Jakes—were alone and defenseless against a ruthless woman whose motives and propensity for violence were yet unknown.

"Carry those bags outside," Margo instructed, indicating the three large bags full of money. She opened the door and waited for Evan to move.

Evan looked carefully at Jakes as he stepped over him. "This man is dying," he said emphatically. "He needs trauma care immediately."

"Forget him!" Margo barked. "Get those bags outside! Do it now!" Then she turned to the rear of the coach, waving her gun for impact. "Do not come out of that room, any of you!"

Margo stepped out of the coach and motioned Evan to follow with the bags. It was warm and bright outside. The distant sounds of the freeway were thoroughly masked by the steady *whish* of the Puget Sound breeze playing the scalelike leaves of the tall arborvitae. Evan was disturbed at the realization that the noisy wind through the trees might also keep a cry for help from being heard.

Margo led Evan back to the car carrier. "Get the straps off the wheels and pull down the ramps," she demanded.

The final stroke of Margo's plan was now obvious to Evan. The RV and the hostages were no longer needed. She could more easily slip across the border in the Datsun wagon all alone. No one to keep quiet or out of sight. *No wonder she lobbied so strongly to bring the car along when Jakes wanted to leave it in Ventura,* he thought.

As Evan began to loosen the straps on the front tire, he felt guardedly relieved that the long ordeal was nearly over. *Malika and Libby's son, Brett, will soon be released from their bonds. We will be able get help for Nolan Jakes. And as long as Margo doesn't have another deadly trump card up her sleeve, we will all go home alive.*

Then a chilling reality quickly reduced Evan's tentative sense of relief to rubble. *Nolan Jakes and his secret are still alive,* he moaned inside. *If we take him to the hospital, he will be recognized and eventually taken into custody. Will he make good on his promise to take me down with him? Or will he be so grateful to be alive that he will bury our secret once again?* Evan was doubtful that if Jakes survived, he would return to health a more charitable person than he was before Margo clubbed him.

If *he survives,* Evan echoed darkly. *But if Jakes doesn't receive treatment soon, he will* not *survive. He will die from loss of blood or a more serious head injury yet to be diagnosed. All I have to do is delay getting him to a trauma center and the secret threatening Libby and me will die with him.*

Evan chastised himself for such an inhumane thought. He could not leave a wounded, dying person to die, even an enemy. It was barbaric. It was wrong. He must do what he could for Nolan Jakes and leave the secret in the hands of God.

"Barbosa's pulling off the freeway again," Beth announced, tracing the blip on the Hawkeye screen with her finger.

"Where?" Cole probed anxiously, edging the speed toward 90 in the wide open fast lane.

"Almost six miles ahead."

"Near some town?"

Beth shook her head. "Looks like he's out in the boonies. There are no symbols on the screen for gas stations or restaurants or anything."

"Which way is he going from the freeway?"

"Nowhere," Beth reported. "He just pulled off and stopped a few hundred feet from the exit."

"Like he did at Woodburn and Seattle?"

"Right. The big question is, where are the Riders?"

Cole gripped the wheel tighter. "That's what I intend to find out."

Evan released the wheel straps, pulled out the retractable ramps behind the two front tires, and detached the axle cable. Margo tossed him the keys. "Now load the bags into the back seat, on the floor," she said.

Evan was inserting the key into the Datsun's passenger side door lock when Nolan Jakes tumbled out the door of the RV and collapsed to a heap in the dirt. Margo whirled to face him and raised the .44. Evan stood frozen beside the red station wagon with its front wheels still perched on the car carrier.

Jakes struggled unsteadily to all fours. One side of his head and face were streaked red with blood. His eyes squinted against the glare and pain. His mouth was contorted into a grimace of rage, betrayal, and madness. "Margo!" he cried. Then he cursed her in garbled tones, adding almost unintelligibly, "I should have left you in Ventura."

He dragged one knee forward with great effort until he planted the bottom of his right foot on the dirt road. With one hand on his knee and another on the dirt, he tried to drag his left foot under him and push himself upright. But as soon as he lifted his hands from their stabilizing positions, his legs splayed out and he fell forward. Jakes' weakened arms were unable to prevent his face from hitting the ground full force.

"Get those bags inside, hurry!" Margo commanded Evan with her eyes and gun still trained on the prone, broken former athlete. Evan opened the front door of the Datsun to unlock the back door. He lifted the first bag into the backseat while watching Jakes writhe and battle to get up again. Blood continued to trickle from the gash in his head. Evan agonized for the man, but he resisted the urge to beg Margo for mercy again. The sooner she was on her way, the sooner he could care for Jakes. He quickly loaded the remaining two bags into the car.

Remarkably, Jakes fought his way to his hands and knees again and prepared to lift himself up. "Where's my money?" he growled with a slur. "You can't take my money," adding vile epithets.

"You're a loser, Jakes," Margo hurled at him without sympathy. "You were a loser working for Billy. And you were just plain stupid to think we would share paradise together. I was never going to let all that money rot with you in Canada."

With astounding effort fueled by Margo's bitter words, Jakes thrust himself upright, driving his shoulder into the side of the RV to keep himself on his feet. His eyes glowed with hatred and revenge.

"Back off, Jakes!" Margo warned. Then to Evan she said, "Give me the keys." As he passed the ring to her, Evan noticed that the gun was trembling slightly in Margo's hand.

Before Margo could step toward the car, Jakes charged, half stumbling, half lunging, shrieking her name in a flood of curses. Evan screamed, "No!" But the thundering report of the Colt .44 instantly drowned out the cries of both men. The slug penetrated Jakes' chest, lifted him off the ground for a fraction of a second, then threw him on his back where he lay motionless in a swirl of dust.

Margo stood frozen for several seconds, her face white with shock. Then she backed away from Evan, cursing under her breath, and circled behind the car. She unlocked the driver's door and stepped up on the metal ramp to enter.

The Datsun started on the first try. Margo ground into reverse and backed the car quickly down the ramp and onto the paved road, aimed toward the freeway. Then the red Datsun disappeared behind the windbreak. The sound of the accelerating four-cylinder engine was swallowed by the *whish* of the wind through the wall of arborvitae.

Evan ran to Jakes and knelt over him. A pool of fresh blood seeped from under the body. Evan pressed his fingertips to the carotid artery.

"Evan!" Shelby cried from the RV's doorway. "The gunshot . . . I thought . . ."

Evan stepped away from the fallen Jakes and hurried to his wife. Shelby fell out of the coach and into his arms. "I thought I'd lost you," she sobbed.

"It's all over, angel," he consoled. "Margo is gone."

Libby appeared in the doorway of the RV. She cradled Malika in her arms. Shreds of hastily cut adhesive tape dangled from the little girl's wrists and ankles. Behind Libby stood Brett, still peeling tape from his arms.

Shelby clung to Evan, her face buried in his chest. "What about Nolan?" she asked, afraid to look.

Evan looked at Libby as he spoke. "Nolan Jakes is dead."

As Margo sped toward the freeway, she opened the window and tossed the Colt .44 into the roadside irrigation ditch. It disappeared beneath a splash of muddy water. Smuggling two bags full of stolen money across the border was risky, although as an attractive, friendly tourist she would likely be waved into Canada without a blink of suspicion. But Margo was not about to be caught with a murder weapon in her possession—and she was sure it now indeed *was* a murder weapon. She had seen the results of the bullet hitting Nolan Jakes in the chest at near point blank range.

Margo had not intended on killing Jakes. As an undercover lieutenant and occasional lover to southland drug kingpin G. Billy Fryman, her crimes had been many. But they had never included murder. Margo was aware that people frequently died in the illegal drug business: users, dealers, enforcers, and even disloyal lieutenants. But she had determined early in her dark career that she would not kill—or be killed—if she could possibly avoid it.

It was not a moral issue to Margo, although she was repulsed at the thought of watching someone die. The shock of blowing away Nolan Jakes still had her shaking. Rather, it was a practical issue. With the likelihood of capture and incarceration always before her, Margo knew that she would be out of prison a lot sooner for felony trafficking than for murder one.

Killing was for professional killers, unconscionable men like Rennie Barbosa. It was fortuitous for Margo that a man of Barbosa's skill had been in Los Angeles when she needed him. And it was fortuitous that the boss had tapped Margo to eliminate Jakes and retrieve the minor fortune he had stolen from the police. Friday night, with Nolan Jakes and the money in her back pocket and Billy Fryman flying away to the Yucatan, Margo had seen her opening. She would lure Barbosa to the Canadian border, keeping secret contact with him by phone right under the nose of gullible Jakes, pay him to do the dirty work, then disappear into Canada and places beyond, saying good-bye to the equally gullible Billy Fryman forever.

Her plan had worked to perfection up until three minutes ago. Had Jakes remained unconscious a little longer, he would have been quickly and permanently silenced by Rennie Barbosa, along with the other hostages, as Margo streaked to the border in Evan Rider's Datsun wagon. But she had underestimated Jakes' determination, requiring her to do precisely what she was paying Barbosa to do.

I will still pay him, of course, Margo acknowledged as she raced toward the burgundy Town Car parked beside the road ahead. *Barbosa has followed me to the border as I asked. And besides, there are still five witnesses in the stranded RV who must be immediately silenced. Rennie Barbosa is worth every penny of the $90,000 I will hand to him. And I am still $800,000 to the good, a quarter million more than Jakes originally dropped in my lap, thanks to Evan Rider and Libby Carroll.* Margo felt the warm smile of Lady Luck upon her.

Barbosa stood outside the Town Car, hands stuffed into the pockets of his light jacket, as Margo slowed the Datsun to a stop across the road. She shifted into neutral and set the hand brake but left the motor running. "Mr. Barbosa, we meet in person at last," she said through the open window.

The man nodded and smiled his lady-killer smile. "Good afternoon, Ms. Bishop," he said, leaning casually against the burgundy luxury car.

Eager to get moving again, she reached into the backseat and pulled forward the bulging canvas shoulder bag. "You'll find everyone with the RV behind that row of trees back there," she said, nodding down the road. She decided not to mention that Jakes was already dead. She was paying Barbosa the full price anyway.

"Here's the amount we agreed on. I appreciate your patience." Margo lifted the bag to the window and held it out to him with both hands.

Barbosa strolled across the road. "Thank you for your generosity, Ms. Bishop," he said. But instead of reaching for the bag, lightning quick hands swathed in transparent surgical gloves flashed through the open window. He grasped the woman's neck and head and gave a sudden, powerful twist and chop. The accompanying *snap!* stifled a frantic cry in the woman's throat. The canvas bag dropped from limp hands to the pavement.

The killer switched off the ignition. When he shoved the lifeless torso down across both seats the platinum blonde wig fell to the floor.

Barbosa retrieved the dropped bag. Then he opened the back door, collected the two larger bags, and transported them all to the waiting trunk of the Town Car. "Thank you, Ms. Bishop," he said with a wave, as he closed the trunk. It was all for show to waylay any possible suspicions in the minds of casual observers streaking by on I-5.

Back behind the wheel, Barbosa opened his personal phone and tapped the redial key. "Good afternoon, sir."

"Rennie," came the reply. "Do you have good news for me?"

"Yes I do, sir. I am pleased to report that Ms. Bishop has been taken care of and all the money has been recovered."

"And the others?"

"I am almost in position now. The others will be eliminated within the quarter hour."

"Good, Rennie. How soon will you be able to join me here?"

"My flight leaves Vancouver for Mexico City this evening at 8."

"Excellent. I'll fly over from Mérida and pick you up."

"Thank you, sir. I look forward to spending some time with you."

"I knew I could depend on your loyalty, Rennie. I'm sure Ms. Bishop would agree now that disloyalty can be very unhealthy."

"Yes sir, Mr. Fryman. It's a pleasure to be of service. I'll see you later tonight."

Sixty-six

Cole held the Barego to the left edge of the fast lane at just under 90 MPH. Drivers in the right lane who saw the black coupe speeding up behind them eased closer to the shoulder to let him pass. As he moved within tailgate distance of traffic in the left lane, he flashed his lights and sounded his horn. Some vehicles would not move over, so Cole roared around them in the right lane or on the left shoulder.

"He's rolling again," Beth informed him, as she followed the blip on the Hawkeye monitor.

"Is he getting back on the freeway?" Cole asked anxiously.

"No, he's headed farther away from the freeway to the east," Beth reported. "The symbols show that there's nothing out that way but agriculture."

Cole swept around a red BMW whose obstinate driver would not yield the left lane in response to the flashing headlights behind him. Bits of gravel from the roadside peppered the gleaming red sedan, and the driver shook his fist angrily at Cole.

"How far are we from the exit?" he asked Beth.

"The computer says 3.2 miles."

"And how fast is Barbosa going?"

"Thirty-seven at the moment, but he's gaining speed slowly."

Cole's next questions were tinged with frustration and concern. "Where is he going now? Where is the RV? What do Evan and Shelby have to do with all this? What's happening here?"

Beth had no answer. Cole gripped the wheel and flashed his lights as he prepared to pass another dawdler in the fast lane.

Evan ushered Shelby back into the RV, away from Jakes' body lying in the dirt outside. Malika sought the security of her mother's arms. Libby and Brett embraced one another with relief. Before joining them, Evan pulled a large plastic tarp from the RV's outside luggage compartment, unfolded it, and draped it over the body. Then he stepped inside and closed the door behind him, isolating the occupants from the grisly death scene for the moment.

For several minutes the relieved former hostages stood inside the coach in stunned silence. Shelby was the first to speak. "What do we do now, Evan?" There was clearly more to her question than the logistics of getting the Carroll family back to Seattle and the Rider family back to Ventura. Not only had the threat of physical danger passed, but Jakes' stranglehold of blackmail had been permanently though tragically broken. Shelby's question reflected her continuing agony over Evan's moral dilemma regarding Neil McGruder.

Evan decided to deal with the most obvious element first. "Margo took our keys and phones, so I need to walk back to the freeway and find help."

"The police?" Shelby pressed.

Evan paused thoughtfully. "Yes, we have to report this to the police."

"And what do we report?"

Libby spoke before Evan could answer. "That's really an issue we all need to discuss, isn't it?"

Shelby yielded immediately. "Yes, of course. I'm sorry, Libby, I didn't mean to exclude you. You're right. The issue is much larger than just Evan and me."

Libby continued, "While we were in the bedroom and you were asleep, Shelby, I told Brett about Neil McGruder for the first time. Since his mouth was taped, he couldn't respond. Brett and I need some time to talk this over."

Shelby and Evan nodded. "We understand," Shelby said. "We all need time to process what has happened and decide what to do."

Libby hastened to continue. "But before we get into that, I have something very important to say. I'm sure it will come as a shock to both of you. I intended to bring this up much earlier, but we obviously didn't have the opportunity. It can't wait any longer."

Evan and Shelby returned questioning looks. Libby sat down at the dinette and motioned the others to sit also. Brett took his place opposite his mother in the dinette. Evan and Shelby, with Malika clinging to them, sat on the sofa.

"Shortly before you arrived at the bank, I told Brett something I have unfairly withheld from him his entire life. You see, I have never been married. Brett is the product of a brief romantic relationship I had as a college student. That man walked out of my life over twenty years ago. I have kept his identity a secret from Brett all these years. I thought my career might be jeopardized if I stirred up the issue that my son was born out of wedlock."

Libby continued. "Before today, Brett didn't even know his father's name. Sitting in the parking lot at the bank this morning, I apologized for my self-centeredness and finally told him about his father." She reached across the table and gripped Brett's hand.

Glancing at each other, Evan and Shelby's eyes telegraphed the same question: *What does this have to do with us or with our immediate situation?*

Libby spoke again before they could verbalize their thoughts. "But that's only half the story. When Brett's father and I parted company, I didn't know I was pregnant. And when I finally found out, I didn't tell him. Instead, I moved back to my parents' home, had the baby, and went on with my life.

"The man I told Brett about this morning doesn't even know he has a son. I used to think I had done Brett's father a favor by not telling him. But in talking with Brett over the last few days, I realize that I have been just as unfair to Brett's father as I have been to Brett. And I can't keep quiet any longer."

Libby's eyes were fastened on Evan, and he suddenly knew. The events of December 5, 1979 flashed through his mind in a moment of time. The Cal State Northridge football game against Portland State at Civic Stadium in downtown Portland. Post-game drinking and carousing with Nolan Jakes and Libby Carroll at River Jack's and other clubs until well past midnight. The backseat beating of obnoxious Neil McGruder which ended with the three friends dumping the unconscious body in dark Washington Park. And the surprising, unplanned sexual interlude with Libby in her room afterward, their first and only time together.

Libby and I produced a child that night, Evan gasped inside. *That's what she is about to say.*

Libby confirmed Evan's prediction. "Evan, I don't know how else to tell you this. That night I slept with you in the hotel in Portland, the awful night that Neil McGruder died, I conceived a child. I hadn't slept with anyone else for months, and I didn't again for years afterward. You're the father, Evan. Brett is your son."

Evan reached for Shelby's hand and gripped it tightly. Paralyzed with shock, he stared at Libby and Brett in silence. Brett averted his eyes, rubbing a spot of adhesive stuck to his wrist. He appeared as anxious as an orphan being introduced to prospective parents.

Wave after wave of emotion crashed over Evan like the pounding breakers along the Southern California shore. The initial shock gave way to disbelief. Evan had never considered that his night with Libby would result in a pregnancy. They had not discussed the possibility of it or taken preventive measures against it. The passions of the moment had carried them away.

In the morning, the horrifying news of McGruder's death buried the memory of their night of love under an avalanche of grief and panic. After he and Libby parted company, Evan never remotely considered that a child might have been conceived that night.

Yet Evan had no valid reason to doubt Libby's truthfulness. He *had* been with Libby that night, and Brett appeared to be the right age. And looking at the young man now, Evan thought he could see a slight resemblance—the shape of the jaw, the dark, heavy beard, more wave to the black hair than tight curl.

Evan's frail doubt was overpowered by a thundering wave of anger at Libby for not telling him about Brett sooner. Anger was submerged by a large swell of grief that twenty years of the boy's life had come and gone without Evan's knowledge or participation. Brett had progressed from an infant to a toddler to a schoolboy to a teenager to a college student, and those experiences had never been shared with the man who participated in his procreation.

Evan suspected that the woman at his side must be riding out her own storm of emotions. Less than twenty-four hours ago Shelby discovered that her new husband was partially responsible for the slaying of an innocent man. Now she learns that he is the father of a beautiful black woman's child. Evan's only assurance that Shelby was not drowning in a deluge of negative feelings was in the strength of her hand, which gripped his as tightly as he gripped hers.

Libby spoke again as if she had been reading Evan and Shelby's minds. Small tears formed in the corner of her eyes. "Evan, I am so ashamed at how thoughtless and selfish I have been about this. You have every reason to be angry with me for keeping this from you. I hope you will forgive me, but I understand if you cannot."

Evan acknowledged her apology with a slight nod. He was still bound by the silence of surprise.

"Shelby, this must be an awkward and painful moment for you also," Libby said. "But I want you to know that my relationship with Evan is strictly in the distant past. I make no emotional claims on him now, and I will stay completely out of your lives if you wish. But for Brett's sake, this had to come out. Ironically, if Nolan Jakes hadn't dragged us all into this, perhaps it never would have. I'm sorry for the grief I have caused you."

Shelby reached around Malika with her free hand to brush away her tears. Malika patted her mother's cheek gently in sympathy.

"I—I don't know what to say," Evan said at last to Libby, still processing the ocean of feelings washing over him. "I never imagined ...I had no idea..."

Then he turned to Brett. The young man had not looked at anyone in the circle since Libby began speaking. Evan's heart went out to him.

Brett had the look of a tough, independent collegian. But he seemed too obviously aloof at the moment not to be affected by it. Evan could almost feel the boy's trepidation of nonacceptance.

Pressing past his own feelings and a hundred questions he wanted to ask Libby, Evan released Shelby's hand and stood. He took one step to the dinette and said in a warm, friendly tone, "It looks like we have a lot to talk about, Brett." Then he stuck out his hand.

Brett turned toward the inviting words like a flower toward the light. The two men locked eyes and managed a smile for each other. Brett reached up and grasped his father's hand firmly.

"Isn't that Evan's car over there?" Beth gestured toward the bright red Datsun station wagon parked beside the road a few hundred feet from the freeway. From her vantage point, the car appeared to be unoccupied.

Cole had already moved into the right lane preparing to pull off the freeway where Rennie Barbosa had exited several minutes earlier. The Barego was still traveling at 80-plus when it left the right lane for the exit.

"It sure looks like his wagon," Cole said. "Where is Barbosa now?"

"About a mile and a half east," Beth reported. "There are a couple of jogs in this country road. He must be out there in the fields."

"What's the wagon doing off the car carrier? And where is the RV? Geez, Beth, I don't like the looks of this."

Beth read the concern in Cole's voice. She suddenly feared for the safety of Evan and Shelby Rider and lifted a silent prayer for them to the God whose warm hand seemed to rest on her yet.

Cole purposely hurtled the Barego down the off-ramp too fast to negotiate a safe turn at the stop sign. He braked hard at the last moment then cranked the wheel to the right, sending the car into a howling four-wheel slide past the sign, across the deserted intersection, and into the dirt shoulder. Beth held the Hawkeye securely on her lap with one hand while bracing herself against the dashboard with the other.

Before the car stopped sliding, Cole tromped on the accelerator and straightened the wheel in the direction of the red station wagon ahead. Gravel and dirt rattled loudly in the wheel wells as the spinning front tires sought traction at the edge of the pavement.

They reached the station wagon in seconds. Cole pulled alongside it and braked abruptly, leaving only a few feet between the driver's-side doors. He threw the gearshift into PARK, jumped out, and looked into the wagon's open window. Beth watched anxiously from her seat.

A second later, Cole jerked open the red car's door and leaned over something lying across both seats. Beth recognized the form as a human body. "Reagan, who is it?" she cried with alarm. "What happened?"

Cole leaped back into the Barego. "It's a woman—not Shelby, nobody I know," he said, jerking the car into gear and flooring the
accelerator. "She's dead. Broken neck—Rennie's specialty."

"Oh, dear God," Beth gasped. "What's going on? Shelby . . .
Evan . . . "

"I don't know," Cole muttered as he pulled the DAB gun out of the
compartment in the console, "but I'll bet Barbosa does."

Beth looked back at the monitor and gasped again. "He's stopped
now. He's less than two miles ahead."

As the car gained speed along the country road, Cole inspected the
pistol, then tucked it under his left leg. He began speaking again, but
Beth quickly understood that his comments were not directed toward
her.

"I don't know why You brought us up here, Jesus, but we could be in
big trouble right now. Please protect Shelby and Evan wherever they
are, and please stop Barbosa from hurting anyone else. And cover us,
Jesus . . . please."

Sixty-seven

Evan had scarcely released Brett's hand after their emotional introduction as father and son when he noticed a soft click at the door. The
sound alerted him that someone was trying to turn the outside knob
without being detected. Evan had locked the door when he closed it.
He always locked doors behind him at home and at the office. It was
one of many nitpicky safety and neatness measures that often bugged
his friends and coworkers.

Evan lifted a finger to his pursed lips to motion silence to the others.
Shelby, Libby, and Brett hadn't noticed the click, but they froze in their
places in response to Evan's signal. Malika, the perpetually quiet one,
clung to her mother, unaware of the suddenly imposed silence.

The nearly imperceptible click sounded again. This time all four
adults heard it. Evan took a quiet step to the top of the steps and leaned
toward the small, curtained window in the door. With the blinds still
drawn on all windows except the windshield, it was much darker
inside the coach than outside. Evan could peek through a tiny slit in
the curtain without being seen.

Evan was momentarily relieved not to see Margo Sharpe at the door
with gun in hand. The fact that she had killed Jakes but left alive
potential witnesses who could testify against her had puzzled him. He
would not have been surprised if Margo returned to silence those who

might later identify her as a thief and a killer.

Instead, the person trying the doorknob was a pleasant-looking man in stylish, casual clothes. In Evan's eye he appeared to be a vacationer or a traveling businessman who had lost his bearings on a country road and stopped to ask fellow travelers for directions. Judging from the lack of shock in the man's face, he apparently had not looked under the tarp on the road. Evan wondered if he might even be a cop who had trailed the kidnappers to this point.

But the harmless image was distorted in Evan's mind by two facts: He had heard neither a car drive up nor a car door slam, and the stranger was trying to open the RV's door before knocking on it. In light of the terrifying ordeal just completed, Evan, true to his nature, decided to exercise caution. He continued to watch through the curtain without making a sound.

Finding the door locked, the visitor looked left and right as if suspecting the occupants had left for a stroll. Then he stepped back to the door and rapped on it loudly. "Hello, is anyone inside?" he called.

Evan kept watching, wondering what to do. If the man happened to be a traveler or a local landowner, Evan would kick himself for remaining quiet and allowing the man to leave instead of using his phone to call for help. But again an inner warning directed his response. "Who is it?" Evan called back without touching the door.

Instead of identifying himself, the man quickly drew a yellow pistol from his jacket pocket and backed two steps away from the coach. Knifed with fear, Evan instantly realized that he had spoken too soon. Somebody *had* been sent to finish off the witnesses. Thanks to Evan's verbal response, the assassin now knew where they were.

As the man outside leveled his gun at the door, Evan cried out, "Get down!" The five occupants of the RV tumbled screaming onto the narrow floor of the dinette and kitchen. Evan dived on top of Shelby and Malika as the first bullet crashed through the metal door and blew out the window on the opposite side of the coach. The second shot produced a heavy metallic *whang! He's blowing away the lock!* Evan surmised in panic. *He's coming in! Dear Jesus, no, no!*

Cole and Beth heard the gunfire as their car squealed around a gentle turn in the country road at nearly 70. Emerging from behind a field of young Chinese elms, they saw the Town Car parked 100 yards ahead. It was nosed toward the ditch on the left side of the road. A line of tall arborvitae stretched away from the road just beyond the Town Car. Small spaces between the tree trunks provided a low view of the dirt road beyond.

"There's the RV, just on the other side of those trees," Cole announced tautly. "Hang on!" He slammed on the brakes, and the Barego skidded and swerved past the Town Car and the barrier of trees. With a final jerk on the wheel, Cole brought the car to a sliding stop in the middle of the road with its nose pointed toward a surprised Rennie Barbosa standing beside the RV about 100 feet away.

"Get down!" Cole commanded Beth, as he jumped out and crouched down, using the door and the front of the car as a shield. Beth instantly threw herself across the console and began praying hard.

Cole aimed his pistol between the open door and windshield. "Drop it, Barbosa!" he ordered. But Barbosa quickly dived and rolled behind the front end of the coach for cover. Cole squeezed off two rounds as the man moved, but he missed. The gel-cap slugs kicked up dust farther down the dirt road.

"Dial 911! Call in the State Patrol!" Cole instructed. But as Beth fumbled for her phone, Barbosa fired back. The windshield above her exploded, showering her with tiny nuggets of tempered glass. She screamed and instinctively covered her head. Peeking under her arm, Beth saw Cole still crouched behind the door, returning fire.

Barbosa fired twice more, his shots clanging into the Buick's grille, then he stopped. Cole returned shot for shot, aiming at the front of the RV even though his target was hidden behind it. Beth began digging through the glass fragments around her for the phone.

"Where are you, you snake?" Cole muttered as he looked for a sign of Barbosa. Beth found the phone and flipped it open to dial. Her hands were shaking and a trickle of blood ran down her dialing finger from a tiny cut on her hand.

Before she could enter 911, Cole shouted, "He's coming around behind the RV!" Beth elevated herself enough to see what Cole saw: Barbosa's feet as he took a position at the back corner of the coach next to the trees. The gunman now had a clear shot at the side of the Barego instead of the front.

Cole quickly moved inside the door as a shield and shifted to take aim at Barbosa's new position through the open window. As he did, a shot flew through the window and slammed into the headrest above Cole's seat. "Stay down!" he commanded. Beth dropped as low as she could on the glass-sprinkled seat, again covering her head. Another bullet ricocheted off the door jamb and blew out a back window of the car.

Barbosa's next shot pierced the door panel and hit Cole, knocking him off his haunches and throwing him backward against the car. The pistol dropped from his hand. He uttered a cry of pain and doubled over on the pavement, grabbing his chest. He writhed and noisily gasped for breath. Then he lapsed into unconsciousness.

"Reagan!" Beth screamed, trying to stay low as she reached for him. Cole was beyond her grasp. She knew she would have to rise up and crawl over the glass-strewn console and seat to get to him.

She ventured a quick look between the open door and the jamb.

Aware that his target was down, Barbosa had stepped out from behind the RV to take aim for a finishing shot. Beth realized with horror that Cole was seconds from death and that she would certainly be next.

In an instant, the events of the last forty-eight hours flashed through her mind. Her disillusioned retreat from the Caribbean. The surprisingly pleasant reunion with Reagan Cole at the wedding reception. The stakeout at the Hilton and her face-to-face meeting with the man who was now trying to kill her and Cole. The crazy, delightful, romantic all-night chase up I-5. The unexplainable, soul-warming encounter with God in the University District.

Everything in the sudden memory-burst of activities fit. Nothing seemed not to belong. It all appeared to her as one grand scheme orchestrated to reunite her with a loving policeman and a persistent, merciful God. *My life has just begun*, Beth thought, gathering her wits. *It's not supposed to end this way. It* can't *end this way. It* won't *end this way.*

Ignoring the glass fragments nicking at her exposed skin, Beth dug her elbows into the driver's seat and wriggled across the console until she was within reach of Cole's gun on the pavement. Cole was moving and moaning in a semiconscious state. She lifted the plastic weapon to the opening between car door and jamb, braced awkwardly with her left hand, and took quick aim.

Beth's first shot missed wildly, and the recoil of the small pistol snapped her wrist back painfully. The attempt successfully distracted Barbosa from the fallen Cole. But instead of ducking behind the RV, Barbosa charged Beth. Running in zigzag fashion with his gun down, he angled around the empty car carrier, disappearing from Beth's narrow line of vision. He would be upon her in seconds and it would all be over.

It can't end this way. It won't end this way. The impulse seemed like a drumbeat in her brain.

Realizing she would be giving Barbosa a clear target, Beth pushed herself up to the open car window. Raising the gun, she fired wildly and repeatedly at the figure juking toward her. After seven or eight errant rounds, she hit him once. He spun around from the glancing blow on the shoulder and fell to his knees about fifty feet from her. The exploding gel cap burned through his clothes and set his shoulder on fire with acid.

Beth kept firing in panic without aiming, hitting Barbosa once more in the thigh. He attempted to stand up but fell backward, gripping his burning leg. Stung with pain, he struggled to his feet and stumbled forward. The yellow plastic pistol was still in his hand.

This time Beth took careful aim at his midsection and squeezed the trigger. Nothing. She squeezed again and again. The clip was empty.

It can't end this way. It won't end this way. The drumbeat quickened to a dull roar in her head.

Barbosa's wounded leg gave way after a couple of steps, and he stumbled and fell. Hissing from the pain, he pushed himself up again. As he staggered nearer, he lifted the gun and sighted in on Beth. She ducked behind the door, fully aware that she could only delay the inevitable. *It can't end this way. It won't end this way.* The faint roar grew louder. Beth covered her head on the seat and began to pray her last prayer. "My Father, which art in heaven, hallowed be Thy name . . . " She could barely hear her own words above the relentless thunder bearing down on her.

Then a powerful voice pierced the thunder overhead. "Put down your weapon. Do it *now!*" The voice from the sky rang with the echo of a loudspeaker. Beth lifted her head to look. A white jet helicopter bearing the logo of the Washington State Patrol swept low and loud over the arborvitae and turned in a tight circle above the bullet-riddled Buick coupe. The propwash instantly filled the air around the car with dust. Beth covered her ears.

Barbosa stopped dead in his tracks, dropping his hand but still gripping the pistol. A marksman was poised in the open door of the chopper with an automatic rifle trained on the wounded assassin below. The pilot continued to issue the warning, "Put down your weapon *now!*"

Barbosa turned unsteadily in a circle, eyeing the hovering copter and cowering as if the death angel had come for him. A short burst from the marksman's rifle kicked up a furrow less than a foot behind Barbosa. He quickly tossed his gun aside and dropped to his knees.

"On your belly, hands and feet spread," commanded the voice from above. "Do it *now!*" The helicopter maintained its menacing, circular vigil. Barbosa prostrated himself obediently.

A white patrol car screeched to a halt beside the Buick. Two uniformed officers sprang from the car and converged on the suspect cautiously with weapons drawn. Seconds later another patrol car arrived and two more officers joined in the party. Barbosa was quickly handcuffed. With the ground troops in control, the helicopter peeled away to a wider, higher, quieter circle.

Beth pushed the door open and crawled out to Cole. He was squirming and gasping again. Blood oozed from a wound in his lower chest. Beth turned toward the small huddle of state patrolmen. "There's an officer down over here!" she yelled.

Two of the cops hurried to her side. "Medics are on the way, ma'am," they assured her.

"There may also be people hurt in the RV," she informed. One of the officers took the cue and left for the coach, stopping briefly to inspect the dead body underneath the plastic tarp.

Beth bent close to Cole's ear. "It's not going to end this way, Reagan," she whispered tearfully.

Cole turned his head slightly toward her. His eyes were squeezed tight from the pain. His words were weak but clear. "I know. I still owe you a dinner."

Beth laughed and cried all at once. "Two dinners," she reminded him as the officer took over. She stood on shaky legs to watch.

The cop radioed the helicopter to stand by to transport a wounded civilian. "I said he's a cop," Beth corrected. "Los Angeles Police Department."

The officer glanced at her. "Okay, ma'am, whatever you say. We'll take good care of him." Then he added, "You'd better sit down somewhere. You need the medic also."

Beth looked at herself. Her top and shorts were dotted with blood stains. Tiny rivulets of blood coursed from a number of minor glass cuts on her arms and legs. But she refused to leave Cole's side to sit down.

A third patrol car joined the convention. Beth noticed that the man hurriedly climbing out of the passenger's side was not a uniformed officer but a huge black man wearing a purple Husky T-shirt, tennis shorts, and a pair of sunglasses shoved atop his bald head. The big man ran past the other officers on a direct line to the RV.

Sixty-eight

Less than seven minutes had expired from the moment the gunman began shooting away the RV's lock until a state patrolman entered the coach to check for possible deaths or injuries. But to Evan and his fellow travelers, the terrifying firestorm outside the flimsy walls of the coach seemed to persist for an eternity.

The uniformed officer pulled open the broken door and shouted, "Police! Is anybody hurt in here?" The five occupants were still huddled on the narrow floor in a tangled heap like the victims of a mass murder.

Evan lifted himself off the top of the pile and turned to face a burly young man with close cropped russet hair and a thick brush mustache. The patrolman's name badge read D. MAYALL. "I think we're all right, officer," Evan answered. "Is it . . . over?"

Patrolman Mayall nodded. "Yes, sir, the man with the gun is in custody. It's all over."

Evan turned to help Shelby and Malika up. The small family hugged each other tearfully. "Thank God, thank God," Shelby said, weeping.

Malika, still nestled in her mother's embrace, surprised both her parents by mimicking, "Tank Gaw, tank Gaw."

Once Brett helped Libby to her feet, the group exchanged another round of emotional hugs while the patrolman inspected the damage to the window above the sofa.

Another figure entered, rocking the coach noticeably as he squeezed through the door frame and hurried up the steps. The big black man's bald head nearly grazed the ceiling and his hulking frame filled the center aisle.

"Reginald," Libby gasped with surprise. She slipped past Evan and Shelby in the kitchen and reached out her hands as if greeting a lifetime friend.

"Dr. Carroll, are you all right?" he said, engulfing her slender hands in his huge mitts.

"Yes, thank God, we're all fine." Then Libby quickly introduced Reginald to Evan and Shelby. The big man also shook hands with Brett. It was a more cordial meeting than their first in Libby's office Friday night. Regardless, Libby's son had difficulty looking the man in the eye.

"Reginald, what are you doing out here?" Libby questioned, with incredulity dominating her tone. "How did you know where we were?" Evan, Shelby, and Brett leaned in to listen also.

"I didn't buy your happy-go-lucky act back at the bank," he said. "I was pretty sure you were in some kind of trouble and couldn't tell me. I kept looking at that woman with you. I thought, 'I've seen that face before. I know this person from somewhere.' But I couldn't figure out when or where.

"After I left, I watched you get into the RV. I followed from a distance until you turned onto I-5 headed north. Then I went back to the office on a hunch to check mug shots faxed to us within the last week. There was your 'friend'—minus the blonde wig—on top of the pile next to a picture of Nolan Jakes: Margo Sharpe, wanted with Jakes for questioning in connection with the murder of a Los Angeles policeman and the theft of over half a million dollars in DEA drug money.

"I called in the State Patrol, and they found the RV from the air and followed you. It looks like the air unit got here just in time. I rode out in one of the patrol cars. Sorry I missed all the fun."

"The last few minutes have been anything but fun, Reginald," Libby said soberly.

Reginald dropped his head in embarrassment. "Yes, I'm sorry, Libby. I was thinking in terms of catching the bad guy. That's what we in the department call fun. I'm just happy that you're safe."

Shelby interjected a question. "Did the police catch Margo? She shot Nolan Jakes and ran off for Canada with all our money in Evan's car."

Reginald shook his head. "No, the police didn't catch her, but that maniac with the gun out there apparently did. The red station wagon is down the road by the freeway. When the State Patrol got there, Margo was still inside, dead—a broken neck—the work of a professional killer."

Shelby gasped in disbelief. "She was so young," she said more to herself than anyone else. "I tried to reach her, I tried to help her, but she wouldn't listen." Evan wrapped a comforting arm around her.

Reginald continued, "Apparently the guy who came gunning for you was also after her. I'll bet your money is still in the shooter's car out there by the road."

"Oh, thank God," Libby exclaimed with relief. Evan and Shelby echoed her expression of gratitude.

"The big question for me, Libby," Reginald continued, "is how in the world you people got involved with Nolan Jakes. From the data our department received, this former Canadian football player was a drug pusher in L.A. for one of the kingpins down there. How did you end up in a motorhome on Interstate 5 with Jakes?"

Libby turned toward Evan and they exchanged looks of mild despair. Reginald's question had quickly snapped them back to the dilemma they both wanted to forget.

Turning back to Reginald, Libby said, "It's a long and rather complicated story. I hope I can tell you about it sometime, but now is definitely not the time." Evan seconded her answer with a nod. Reginald didn't press the issue.

Shelby returned the conversation to the positive side. "Mr. Burris, we're indebted to you for your detective work. You and the State Patrol saved our lives."

Young Patrolman Mayall, who had been standing behind Reginald, interrupted. "The truth be known, ma'am, we weren't the first ones on the scene." The others turned toward him to hear more. "An off-duty policeman from California was engaged in a firefight with the suspect just before we rolled up. And he had a lady with him. Actually, the officer had been hit, and the lady was holding off the suspect with a DAB gun when the air unit arrived."

"Who are these people? Who told them we were here? How did they know we needed help?" Libby wondered aloud.

Mayall shrugged. "I don't know, ma'am. We haven't really talked about that yet. Our paramedic is getting the officer ready to be airlifted to the hospital in our helicopter."

"Is he seriously hurt?" Shelby asked with concern.

"I didn't get a very good look at him, so I—"

"They think Reagan is going to be fine." Mayall was interrupted by a tall, slender woman stepping up into the coach. Smears of blood on her limbs and clothes made it appear as though someone had sprinkled a paintbrush full of red paint all over her.

It took a moment for Shelby to recognize the woman. When she did, she emitted a small cry of consternation. Then her questions gushed out like an emotional dam break. "Beth! Dear Lord above, what are you doing here? You're all bloody; what happened to you? And what's this about Reagan being hurt?"

"Everything is all right, Shelby," Beth said, moving close enough to put a comforting hand on her shoulder and to pat little Malika's leg. "I just have a few cuts from broken glass; it looks worse than it really is. Reagan has been shot in the lower chest, but the bullet apparently missed his vital organs. They've stopped the bleeding, he's conscious, and his heartbeat is strong. The helicopter is taking him to Bellingham for surgery."

"Thank God," Shelby said, "but I don't understand what you're doing here. This is so bizarre."

Evan cut in for Libby, Reginald, and Brett's benefit. "Everybody, this is Beth . . . er . . . "

"Scibelli," Beth supplied.

"Yes, thank you, Beth," Evan said. "Sorry, but I'm a little rattled right now. And Beth this is Libby Carroll, a college friend, and Libby's friend, whom we just met and whose name, I'm sorry, has also left me."

"Reginald Burris," the big man said.

Turning to the young man, Evan said, "And this is Brett Carroll, Libby's son and . . . " he hesitated, grasping for the right words, "a new and very special part of my life."

Brett flashed a small but genuine smile at his father. Evan decided that, under the circumstances, the full explanation of their relationship could wait.

"I want to tell you how we got here," Beth said, "but Reagan would like to see you both before he leaves."

"Yes, and we must see him," Shelby agreed, passing Malika into Evan's arms.

The three of them eagerly followed Beth down the steps and out to the road. Libby and Brett trailed behind, anxious to meet the man who had put his life on the line to save them. Shelby and Evan purposely looked away from the tarp-draped body lying just beyond the rear wheels of the RV.

A mobile rescue unit had arrived and loaded Reagan onto a gurney. The helicopter was circling in to land on the road and receive the patient.

Shelby broke into tears at seeing Cole with his shirt cut away and a bloody compress taped just below and to the left of his heart. A portable IV and rack was mounted on the gurney. She knelt down on the pavement beside Cole and took his hand. Evan stood behind her, thankful that Malika was distracted from the wounded man by the approaching noisy helicopter. The others huddled nearby.

"Hello, Reagan," she said, trying to stifle her tears.

Cole managed a smile. "Shelby, it *was* you in the RV. Why aren't you at the Grand Canyon on your honeymoon?"

"It's an incredible story, one I can't even believe myself. The real question is, how did you get here? Why aren't you at Lake Tahoe on *your* vacation?"

"Incredible story, part two," Cole said with a weak smile. "Beth will have to fill you in."

The noise grew louder and the propwash stronger as the police copter descended to the road 100 yards away.

Reginald stepped up and put a large hand on Cole's shoulder. "Reginald Burris, University of Washington Police Department."

Cole acknowledged him with a nod. "Reagan Cole, LAPD," he said.

"Hey, man, thanks for being here for my friends," Reginald said, motioning toward Libby and Brett.

Cole's face contorted in pain. "I couldn't have done it without back-up," he said. "Thanks for bringing in the cavalry."

"No problem," Reginald answered, grinning.

The paramedics moved in to roll the patient into position for loading. Shelby begged thirty seconds more.

"You're an amazing person, Reagan," Shelby said, blinking away tears in the swirling, dusty breeze. "I might not have lived through Millennium's Eve, had it not been for you. And just when we're about to be gunned down by a stranger on a deserted road in Washington, you again show up out of nowhere to save my life. You must be my own personal guardian angel."

" 'To protect and to serve,' that's my motto," Cole said with difficulty. "Only next time this angel is going to wear his bullet-proof vest."

The paramedics abruptly ended the brief conversation by shoving the gurney away toward the waiting helicopter. "God bless you, Reagan," Shelby called after him. "We'll be at the hospital as soon as we can."

Beth caught up with the gurney and gave Cole a farewell kiss. The helicopter had room only for its crew, the patient, and one paramedic, so Beth would have to find her own transportation to the hospital. Evan offered her a ride in the RV, and she eagerly accepted.

Evan, Malika, Shelby, and Beth huddled closely as they watched the paramedics collapse the gurney and slide it into the helicopter beneath the whirling blades. Then the onlookers covered their ears as the jet engine accelerated and the craft lifted off for Bellingham.

After the helicopter was out of sight behind the arborvitae, Malika pointed a finger in its direction from her secure perch in Evan's arms. "Tank Gaw, tank Gaw," she said.

Malika's simple words touched an emotional chord in Beth, and her eyes moistened with tears. "Yes, sweet Malika," she said, pointing to the sky with the little girl, "thank God for Reagan Cole."

It took less than an hour for the Flair and its passengers—Evan, Shelby, Malika, Beth, Libby, Brett, and Reginald—to leave for Bellingham. Mercifully, the FBI, who arrived after Rennie Barbosa had been carted off to Bellingham to be booked, offered to delay the in-depth questioning of all parties for a day or two. And after the bodies of Nolan Jakes and Margo Sharpe were hastily removed by the coroner, the news media didn't hang around long. A police spokesperson issued a terse, just-the-facts statement, and the civilian participants retreated to the sanctuary of the RV to compose themselves after the ordeal.

Libby and Brett's phones were recovered from Margo's purse, as were Evan and Shelby's key rings. But the FBI took all the money as evidence, giving claim checks to Evan, Shelby, and Libby until after any proceedings on the case were completed. Tow trucks were summoned for the Town Car and the beat-up Buick Barego. Beth wondered if Galaxy Rent-a-Car would ever do business with her again. This was the second car she would return to them in less than two years that looked like she had run it through a destruction derby.

It took several minutes for Evan to cleanse Beth's many nicks and cuts and bandage the more serious ones. Two gashes, one on her right elbow and the other on her left knee, required a couple of stitches each. As Evan worked, Beth recounted how she teamed up with Cole to follow Rennie Barbosa, totally oblivious to the fact that the Peruvian hit man had been following the Riders' motorhome. The others listened in wonder to Beth's amazing tale. Shelby interjected her conviction that such an incredible turn of events was clearly the mark of divine intervention.

While Beth was being ministered to in the dinette, Libby and Reginald cleaned up the broken glass and duct-taped a plastic tablecloth over the open window above the sofa. Reginald secured the broken door with a bungee cord.

Brett called his girlfriend, Andie, who had been driving all over the University District in a panic looking for him, and related the details of the harrowing abduction and his introduction to his father. She scoffed at his outlandish story and pestered him for "the real reason" he left her stranded in Seattle without a clue. Brett told her to watch the 5 o'clock news, then call him and apologize. "I can't wait to hear her beg my forgiveness," he exulted after hanging up.

State patrolman Mayall and his partner followed the RV back to the freeway and helped Evan load the Datsun wagon onto the car carrier. Then Evan turned the big white Flair north toward Bellingham.

Sixty-nine

Surgeons successfully removed a nine-millimeter slug from Reagan Cole's chest and repaired two shattered ribs, a punctured lung, and minor tissue damage. The head of the surgical team was a swarthy, mustachioed Armenian with thick black and silver hair exploding from his scalp in Einstein-like disarray. He informed the small, anxious group in the waiting room that, had the bullet not penetrated the car door first, it could have wreaked even greater and possibly lethal damage to Cole's vital organs.

During the trip to the hospital, Evan, Shelby, and Libby had summarized the details of their abduction for Beth and Reginald. Evan and Libby explained that Jakes had been holding more than a gun to their heads in his demand for their help. They admitted that a long-buried, rather serious "situation" from their college days together effectively served as Jakes' lever to exert the cooperation of his friends. But the pair declined to fill in the critical details until they had talked privately with Shelby and Brett.

Beth and Reginald listened sympathetically and expressed their confidence that the situation would work out for the best for all concerned.

After Cole was moved to his room at just past 6 P.M., the RV entourage—minus Beth, who decided to spend the night at the hospital and meet the others at the FBI office tomorrow—left Bellingham for Seattle. Reginald volunteered to drive the coach as far as Mount Vernon, where he had left his gray Taurus to ride with the State Patrol. At his encouragement, Brett joined him in the cab as copilot.

Shelby parked Malika in the dinette while she served the hungry little girl a bowl of macaroni and cheese with fresh baby carrots and celery sticks from the refrigerator. Bone tired from lack of sleep and emotionally wrung out from their brush with death, Libby curled up under the afghan on the sofa, while Evan shut himself in the bedroom for a nap before taking the controls.

As much as he wanted to, Evan could not sleep. The relief he welcomed over the safety of his family and the end of two days of potentially deadly tribulation was offset by Mt. Everest-sized decisions looming before him. Nolan Jakes was dead, and with him died the threat connected to Neil McGruder. Evan had not wished or prayed for Jakes' death. To the contrary, the physician had even tried to minister to the man's head wound up until Margo shot him. Evan quietly acknowledged that if he was ever to face the consequences for what happened in Portland twenty-two years ago, it wouldn't be Nolan Jakes who precipitated it.

The secret was again buried—assuming that Libby was not motivated to come forward on her own and that Evan was able to convince Shelby to remain quiet. *Is that the tack I should take?* he pondered. *Do I want to return to living a lie and dealing with the persistent, low-grade guilt that accompanies it?*

Shelby had tearfully insisted to Evan during the night that God already forgave him for his part in the death of Neil McGruder. Then she had perplexed him by stating that he must come clean and deal with the legal consequences of his act. *Can she possibly be right? Is her evaluation a reflection of God's wisdom on the matter or a throwback to an irrelevant, more legalistic facet of her upbringing? Am I prepared to place my career and freedom in jeopardy on her word? Is full confession and its attending penalty the only way to clear my mind and soul of the blot from the past?*

Evan's turmoil was complicated by Libby Carroll's role in the drama. *If I decide to turn myself in, do I implicate her or lie during an investigation that will surely seek the identity of any co-conspirators? If I remain silent, will she experience a crisis of conscience and turn herself in, eventually implicating me? Or will she unwittingly take into her confidence that giant of a cop, only to have him blow the whistle on both of us?* Evan knew he and Libby must come to an understanding of each other's position before they spoke with the FBI. A botched cover-up would only make things worse for everyone.

Evan rolled to his belly and screwed his head into the pillow, hoping the new position would encourage a few minutes of sleep. But another mountainous obstacle in his mind stood between him and the tranquility he sought. *What am I supposed to do about Brett Carroll?* Evan pondered the irony of becoming, at age forty, the father of two children: a five-year-old black girl through marriage and adoption, and a twenty-year-old son of mixed heritage introduced to him by his former lover. Evan had had the opportunity to prepare for Malika, but the sudden appearance of Brett was a shock which still had him reeling.

Libby had intimated that she intended not to seek retroactive financial support from Evan for the twenty years of fatherhood he not only missed but knew nothing about. She seemed to be more in sympathy with Evan's plight as an instant father than greedy for what she might be able to squeeze out of him. *But she could have a change of heart and slap me with some kind of child support suit,* he acknowledged. *It happens in even the most enduring marriages that finally end up on the rocks. It could certainly happen between the principals of a one-night stand over their issue.*

But questions over legal and financial responsibility for Brett were the least troubling of those barraging Evan as tossed and turned on the bed. *What do I owe him emotionally, this child of mine who is already an adult? We're well past the play-catch-in-the-backyard stage. And he apparently already has a grasp on the facts of life and is on track with a college career. Does he need a father's wisdom, encouragement, or friendship? Does he want these? Considering the consequences under which we met, do I have anything of value to give him?*

Having adjusted to life without a father, does Brett have a valid need for a father-son bond with a white-skinned stranger who to date has been no more than a sperm donor to his existence? Should I take an active part in influencing his career? Should I plan to see him often? Will he want to live with us part of the year? Will we share any common interests? Will he want to learn anything from me or get involved in my life? Or will he go on his way satisfied that he knows my name?

The next wave of questions pushed Evan to a much deeper level of contemplation. He realized that had he met Brett only three years ago, these questions would have never entered his mind.

What is my spiritual responsibility to my son? Though imperfect and weak, I am a man of faith, a follower of Jesus Christ. Must I seek to convert Brett to personally accept my beliefs and adopt my way of life? Understanding what Nolan Jakes, his mother, and I did twenty-two years ago, will Brett even listen to anything I tell him about a life of faith and obedience? Will my beliefs about God and Jesus Christ and the Bible conflict with what Libby has taught him over the years? Will my attempts to influence Brett toward God provoke a rift between Libby and me, causing Brett greater unrest? Should I view Brett as a lost soul I am responsible to win at all costs? Or should I just butt out and let his mother be responsible for his eternal destiny?

Adrift in a turbulent sea of questions with no answers in easy reach, Evan began to pray. He quietly poured out his soul to God: his gratitude, his confession of weakness, his petition for wisdom, his commitment to obey. Had it not been for utter exhaustion and the hypnotizing drone of the tires on the freeway, he would have prayed all the way to Mount Vernon.

FRIDAY
October 12, 2001

Seventy

Portland, Oregon basked in the radiance of a 76-degree Indian summer day. Anticipating the good weather, many in the downtown work force had cashed in leftover vacation days and escaped the city for a three-day weekend lounging at the coast, hiking Mt. Hood, or raking red and gold leaves from the yard in preparation for the last barbecue of the fall.

The steps of the Multnomah County Courthouse in downtown Portland were bathed in afternoon sunshine and dotted with a small crowd of reporters and photographers waiting for the brief news conference which had been promised them. A small, portable lectern had been set in place at the base of the steps, equipped with the standard wireless audio feed for the cameras. The sentence had been pronounced, and courtroom footage had been recorded for the evening news. All that remained to be captured for public consumption was the human interest angle: the comments of the principals involved, their reactions to the county's justice system, and their plans for the future.

At 2:10 the courthouse doors swung open and a tightly packed cluster of about twenty people moved en masse down the steps to the lectern. At the core of the large group were men and women dressed in tailored business suits. On the periphery flitted members of the media whose attire looked good on camera but was clearly from the mall.

The man who stepped to the lectern, an attorney from Los Angeles, had earned the respect of the local media during his brief stay in Portland. Anson Fox was short, compact, and fiftyish, with a full head of neatly trimmed gray-blond hair. Fox had been straightforward and pleasant in all his dealings with the media, whose sometimes inane, redundant, or inappropriate questions regarding his client would have been scorned by less patient lawyers. In contrast, during his first week in town Fox had learned the names and affiliations of most of the reporters following his client's case. By using their names and treating them with patient dignity, the suave attorney had endeared himself to the press corps and thus gained the control he wanted during meetings such as this.

Anson Fox waited quietly for the flurry of premature questions to die down. When he was ready to begin the news conference, he smiled his characteristically warm smile for the reporters and their cameras and said, "Ladies and gentlemen, our visit to Portland concludes today. Dr. and Mrs. Rider and I wish to express our appreciation for your kindness and cooperation during this difficult time in their lives."

In truth, it had been the kindness and cooperation of Anson Fox that had kept the relationship workable in the face of the pushy, invasive press. But true to form, Fox gave credit where he hoped it would do the most good.

"Dr. Rider will be happy to entertain a last round of questions at this time," Fox continued. "As always, we prefer to operate in an orderly fashion. If you wish to be recognized, please lift a hand. I have encouraged Dr. Rider to be brief in his responses, so that we may answer as many of your questions as possible."

Anson Fox stepped aside to make room at the lectern for Dr. Evan Rider. Evan was smartly dressed in a dark suit, white shirt, and conservative tie. Shelby stood close behind him in a trim, stylish suit of navy and cream. Their heads were high and their expressions winsome.

Every reporter's hand shot high in their air before Anson Fox had concluded his statement. The crowd around the lectern looked like a class of kindergartners begging permission to be first in line for recess. Some of them momentarily forgot Fox's rules and squawked out a question or insisted on being recognized first. Fox waited for quiet, then pointed to an auburn-haired woman in a pale green suit standing to his left. "Ms. O'Neill, from the *Oregonian*, I believe."

"Yes, Mr. Fox, thank you. Dr. Rider, how do you feel about the judge's decision today?"

Evan offered a pleasant smile. "First, I'm just relieved that it's over. Second, I believe Judge Mangum's decision was fair—difficult to accept, but fair. Third, I'm gearing up mentally and emotionally for the next phase of my life." Evan glanced back to Fox for the next question. As soon as he did, hands flew up before them again.

Fox pointed to a man near the back. "Mr. Sandeberg, KATU."

"Dr. Rider, you were sentenced to eighteen months in the Oregon State Penitentiary followed by five years of probation. Are you disappointed that Judge Mangum didn't rule in favor of probation only?"

Evan glanced down at the lectern as he thought about the question. When he looked up his smile was not as full. "Yes, I'm disappointed. I'm not looking forward to being a prison inmate. On the other hand, even before Mr. Fox, my wife, and I decided that I should turn myself in, I was advised that incarceration was a likely consequence—even if I pleaded guilty to a lesser charge. My decision to confess my wrong was tantamount to accepting the legal consequences of that confession. So I was mentally prepared for whatever sentence the court judged to be fair."

"Let me remind you all," Anson Fox cut in as hands waved for recognition, "that Dr. Rider was indicted by the grand jury on one count of felony murder. When the district attorney agreed to drop the felony murder charge in exchange for a guilty plea for manslaughter, the severity of Dr. Rider's penalty was automatically reduced. We are grateful that the county was satisfied with the lesser charge. Although

Judge Mangum opted for a short prison term over straight probation, the greater charge would have resulted in a longer period of imprisonment."

Hands waved again, but Fox continued. "Let me also say that there is a good possibility Dr. Rider will spend no more than a year in the penitentiary in Salem and complete his term at the minimum security Columbia River facility here in Multnomah County."

Fox pointed to a man directly in front of him. "Mr. Grauman, KPTV."

"Dr. Rider, you have said that the foiled kidnapping and blackmail attempt by Nolan Jakes really brought the issue of your buried crime to a head. That ordeal was in June, but you didn't present yourself to county authorities until late July. Why did you wait so long to confess?"

Evan nodded his understanding of the question. "First, I had to be convinced to do so. I spent twenty-two years making myself believe that it would be a personal disaster for me to own up to what I did. With the help and encouragement of my wife over a period of a couple of weeks after the kidnapping, I came to realize that it would be a personal disaster for me *not* to confess my crime." Evan reached behind him for Shelby's hand and pulled her beside him.

Grauman tossed a follow-up question forward without receiving permission. "Isn't it true that your wife threatened to leave you if you didn't confess to the McGruder killing? Isn't that what you mean by a 'personal disaster'?" The question provoked a murmur among the crowd of reporters and onlookers, a subtle salute to Grauman for taking the first swipe at Evan Rider's jugular.

Evan dropped his head. Then after receiving an affirming glance from Shelby, he looked at the reporter. "Among the many things we discussed, Shelby and I talked about the impact of my continued silence on our marriage. She did not threaten to leave outright, but she did question the long-term health of a relationship which must cover up a grievous wrong to survive. I think she has a valid point. Whether she left me or not, I believe our relationship would have eventually been eaten away from within by the cancer of my unconfessed wrong. And that conviction did influence me toward my decision."

Evan spoke over the top of another unauthorized question to continue. "However, the 'personal disaster' I'm referring to involves much more than the impact on our marriage or my career. It involves being at cross-purposes with a God to whom I have committed my life and a faith I have chosen to embrace. The essence of Christian practice is integrity, striving to do what's right in every circumstance, even if no one but God knows you're doing it."

"Regardless of the consequences," Shelby interjected, her eyes misting with tears.

"Yes," Evan confirmed, "regardless of the consequences. Without integrity, I am without foundation as a person. And that is a personal disaster infinitely worse than a prison term, the loss of a marriage, or the loss of a career."

The crowd murmured again, like the spectators at a bullfight when the matador successfully evades the pass of the charging bull. Grauman seemed stunned by Evan's directness and conviction. He didn't even raise his hand for the next question.

"Ms. Khoi," Fox said, nodding to a petite Vietnamese-American, *The Eugene Register-Guard.*"

"Dr. Rider, didn't you in effect force Dr. Libby Carroll into confessing her part in the McGruder killing? After all, you have already admitted that you would have implicated her in your testimony." The bloodthirsty spectators hummed their approval again.

Evan turned to the tall, strikingly beautiful black woman standing behind his left shoulder next to her twenty-one-year-old son. "Would you like to answer the question?" Evan said to her with an amused smile.

Libby nodded and stepped forward. She was dressed in a three-piece olive suit with accents of gold and rust.

"Ms. Khoi, one reason Dr. Rider did not present himself in Portland sooner to confess was me. Contrary to your intimation that I was *forced* to join him in confessing our common secret, Evan delayed his confession, hoping he could *convince* me to come with him. He assured me that he would not lie about my involvement in the incident when questioned. But he also assured me that he would give me plenty of time to see his point of view before he came to Portland.

"In point of fact, Dr. Rider was unsuccessful at convincing me to confess. I have a growing admiration for Evan and Shelby and their religious convictions, but at the time I was more concerned about the negative impact my confession would have on my career at the University of Washington. I wasn't ready to imperil my future at the university to placate another's conscience.

"Lucky for Evan, he wasn't working alone. As fate would have it, a very gentle, wonderful man came into my life the same weekend Nolan Jakes threatened to uncover the dark side of my past. The threat was ended due in large part to the timely and heroic intervention of my new friend, Reginald Burris. In the tense weeks that followed, he convinced me that it would be difficult for him as a police officer to pursue a relationship with a possible felon in hiding. If anyone forced me to confess, it was Reginald. His loving encouragement and persistence convinced me that I had nothing to fear by telling the truth."

Libby turned and smiled to the bald, black behemoth towering over the knot of court officials behind her. Beads of sweat dotted Reginald's face and exposed pate. He looked uncomfortable in a beige suit that classed him more with the media than with the attorneys.

"For the uninformed in our midst," Anson Fox inserted, "last Tuesday Dr. Carroll was acquitted of the charge of aiding and abetting felony murder on the strength of an affirmative defense successfully presented by Dr. Carroll's attorneys. And she cannot be charged with wrongdoing for driving the car since the statute of limitations has expired on first degree kidnapping. Dr. Carroll is a free woman."

Fox pointed back into the crowd. "Just a few more questions. Mr. Salgado, KGW."

"What about the McGruder family? What sense of justice can they find in an acquittal and an eighteen-month prison sentence?"

Fox fielded the question as he and Evan had agreed he would if it came up. "Mr. Salgado, as you know, Mr. McGruder, Neil's father, died six years ago of liver cancer. Mrs. McGruder lives alone in a West Linn retirement home southwest of the city. Neil McGruder's two surviving siblings live out of state with their families. All have been present in Portland over the last six weeks for the two trials.

"Since the statute of limitations has also expired on possible civil suits in this case, the family has no further legal recourse. However, Dr. and Mrs. Rider have met privately with the McGruders and expressed their sorrow at what happened twenty-two years ago. Furthermore, of their own free will, Dr. and Mrs. Rider have committed to donate a monthly amount toward the care of Mrs. McGruder for the rest of her life, greatly relieving the financial burden to her family."

"And how did the McGruders respond?" Salgado probed.

"The family expressed to me that neither regret, apology, nor any amount of money can bring back the son and brother they lost. But they are satisfied with Dr. and Mrs. Rider's kind offer and have accepted it.

"Next question, please," Fox continued, moving quickly on. "Mr. Wygant, KEX radio."

"Dr. Rider and Dr. Carroll, what about your careers? What fallout do the two of you anticipate in your professional lives from the revelation of your past?"

Libby nodded to Evan, inviting him to speak first. "Regarding my license to practice medicine in California, it's too soon to tell. I appeared before an investigative committee from the State Board of Medical Examiners in September, while waiting for the trial here in Portland. The committee may recommend that the board revoke my license because I am a convicted felon. However, such action is not automatic. They may also recommend suspension, if they judge that I am a danger to the public. Or they may allow me to continue to practice under probation for up to ten years. It all depends on how they view the criminal evidence in light of my record of conduct in California which, if I may say so, is exemplary.

"Of course, the committee and board have eighteen months to come to a decision. However, I have been informed that the most likely scenario will involve a lengthy period of probation, so I am hopeful that I can return to my practice in Ventura after serving my term."

"Yeah, but will anybody want you for a doctor?" The questioner was not from the media corps but was an interested passerby. The snide inference to the physician being a murderer was present in the man's tone. Another murmur rippled through the crowd.

Evan didn't flinch. He had faced the question before and had asked it of himself countless times. "I'm sure some of my patients will be uncomfortable retaining me as their physician and will seek services from my associate or elsewhere. But I'm hopeful that I have developed a trust level in many of my patients and in the community as a whole. I am also considering a full-time appointment to the medical staff at King's House in Los Angeles. I'll be praying about my future for the next year and a half. It's all in God's hands."

Evan gave the floor to Libby, and she stepped closer to the lectern. "In late July, when the real story of my involvement in the motorhome 'death ride' came to light, the Seattle media had a field day. They predicted that I would be fired or demoted or at the very least placed on probation for my involvement in the Portland incident.

"Before the news broke, I met with the Board of Regents and explained everything to them. They were very understanding and supportive. Then last Friday, in light of the acquittal and my record with the university, the board gave me a wholehearted vote of confidence. I will be back to work on Monday."

The cluster of reporters hummed their amazement. Anson Fox quickly took control again. "We haven't heard from KOIN, yet. Ms. Cain, your question."

"Is it true that both of you have been offered substantial sums of money for the book and film rights to your story?"

Evan responded quickly. "Yes, we have. But we have both elected not to sensationalize or glorify our unfortunate experience for profit."

"But it's a natural," someone remarked. "It could be a runaway bestseller."

Another observer remarked, "A secret killing, a father and son finding each other as adults, an L.A. cop unwittingly chasing the man out to kill you, a UW policeman bringing in the State Patrol in the nick of time—wow, it has to be told!"

"If I could write fiction as exciting as what you've been through, I'd be off the news beat tomorrow," said another, provoking a chorus of laughs.

"The only book we have authorized," Evan responded, "is a nonfiction account being written by a certain journalist we all have grown very fond of. But it's her book, not ours." He winked in the direction of a talk, dark-haired woman standing a few feet beyond the throng of newspeople alongside an even taller man with thin, sandy hair. Beth and Cole winked back.

"Next question," Fox interrupted. "Ms. Lukens, Oregon Public Broadcasting."

"Dr. Carroll and Dr. Rider, we haven't heard from your son. May I ask how he feels about all this?"

Libby turned to Brett. He looked less than eager to address the somewhat cynical crowd. "It's up to you," she said.

Brett scanned the faces of the eager journalists nervously, then stepped to the lectern. "I only have one thing to say," he began. He sounded less confident than the other speakers, but his eyes blazed with conviction. "I'm proud of my mother and father for having the guts to do what's right. A lot of people run from their mistakes or bury them to get out of paying the consequences. I hate to see my dad go to prison just when I'm getting to know him. But I know we have a great future ahead. I have a lot to learn from him."

Evan reached in front of Libby to shake Brett's hand and mouth the words, "Thank you."

The OPB reporter pressed her luck to ask another question without raising her hand. "And Mrs. Rider, what are your plans while Dr. Rider is serving his prison term?"

Evan wrapped a supportive arm around his wife's waist. Over the past three months she had often become weepy when the topic of Evan going to prison came up. She paused a moment to collect her thoughts with a long sigh.

"While we hoped and prayed for a more lenient sentence, Evan and I prepared contingency plans in view of his possible incarceration. On Monday, after Evan returns to the courthouse to begin his sentence, these plans will be set in motion.

"Our daughter and I will move to Portland within the month so we can visit Evan in Salem regularly. While in Portland, I intend to stay busy. I will head up a small team from King's House, our mission to the disadvantaged in Los Angeles, seeking to establish a facility here, perhaps in the West Burnside area. I also intend to call on Mrs. McGruder regularly to see that she is being properly cared for."

The whispers in the crowd reflected pleased surprise at Shelby's revelation.

She continued, "Another plus about living in the Northwest is being closer to Libby and Brett in Seattle. In reality, we are kind of a family now. We have already discussed our hope to see each other often. And I will try to convince Libby to lend her organizational and administrative expertise to our King's House project." Shelby flashed a friendly smile at the University of Washington administrator, and Libby returned the expression.

"One last question," Anson Fox announced to the sea of waving hands. "Mr. Jacobs, KXL news, you're the lucky winner."

"Dr. Rider, how will you spend your last weekend of freedom before entering prison on Monday?"

Evan smiled broadly, but tears were not far from his eyes. "I plan to pour these last hours into my family: my wife, Shelby, our seven-year-old daughter, Malika, and my new son, Brett. We need to encourage each other to make the most of this time of separation.

"And tomorrow we will all be together on Whidbey Island for a very special event. You all know Reagan Cole and Beth Scibelli—our heroes and friends. Well, Reagan is fully recovered from the gunshot wound, so he's ready to take the plunge. The couple will be married tomorrow at Beth's home, and Shelby will perform the ceremony."

Spontaneous applause arose from the crowd of spectators, as Evan motioned a slightly embarrassed Cole and Beth to his side. The Portland media had come to appreciate the young couple for their heroics in the stranger-than-fiction account of the rescue along Interstate 5. The applause continued through a round of embraces behind the lectern.

"Where will you two settle down?" called out a spectator, who obviously knew the couple had homes in two different states.

After a moment of "You take it," "No, you take it," looks between Beth and Cole, Beth leaned into the mike. "Reagan has a career in Los Angeles, but I can work anywhere that is serviced by electricity and UPS. So we will live in L.A., but I—er, we—intend to keep the home on Whidbey Island and visit often."

Cole nodded, and the audience conveyed its approval with a collective smile.

"All right, friends, that's it for today," Anson Fox declared to the press corps. "Thank you again for your support. Good afternoon."

The reporters dispersed quickly, scurrying off to their respective offices to transform the raw ore of recently mined news into polished articles and gleaming sound bites for the next editions. Anson Fox and his associate embraced Evan and Shelby, then excused themselves. The Riders remained on the courthouse steps, surrounded by friends and well-wishers offering their encouragement. Soon the crowd had dwindled to a small knot—Evan and Shelby, Libby, Brett, and Reginald, Cole and Beth—discussing plans for leaving Portland shortly to caravan to Whidbey Island.

In the middle of the discussion, a skinny young man with a large head and a flowing mane of dishwater-blond hair approached the group. He had been one of the reporters who waved his hand frantically to ask a question without being recognized by Anson Fox. "Dr. Rider," he interrupted.

Evan turned toward him while the others in his group continued to debate the merits of stopping for dinner at the Falls Terrace in Tumwater, Washington on the journey to the Seattle area. "Yes, what can I do for you?" he said to the man as he stepped outside the circle to greet him.

"Elliot Rush, sir, with the *Statesman-Journal.* I apologize for breaking in, but I just can't leave without asking my question."

Evan searched the young man's eyes. There was a shadow of desperation lurking behind the youthful, ambitious gleam of this cub reporter. Evan perceived that the question gnawing at the man's insides was more personal than professional. "All right, Elliot. I have time for one more question."

Elliot Rush cleared his throat nervously. "Now that you have told the whole story of Neil McGruder, do you feel any different inside?"

Evan studied the young man, who gazed at him as if ready to pounce on the answer. He guessed that Elliot was probably a poor poker player, because his expression quickly gave away the meaning behind his question. Evan assessed that this young man was carrying a heavy, secret burden from which he longed to be free.

"Yes, Elliot," Evan said confidently. "I feel completely free. Even though I am on my way to prison, I have never felt more free in my life." After a brief pause, he added, "Is that what you hoped to hear?"

Elliot ignored the question. Wiping a trembling hand across his forehead, he pressed on. "So you would agree that confession is good for the soul?"

Evan grabbed the young man gently by the shoulder. "Elliot, I can't think of a better way to begin a new millennium."